# Vālmīki's Rāmāyaṇa

## *Abridged Edition*

Translated and with an Introduction by
Arshia Sattar

ROWMAN & LITTLEFIELD
*Lanham • Boulder • New York • London*

Executive Editor: Susan McEachern
Editorial Assistant: Katelyn Turner
Senior Marketing Manager: Kim Lyons

Credits and acknowledgments for material borrowed from other sources, and reproduced with permission, appear on the appropriate page within the text.

Published by Rowman & Littlefield
A wholly owned subsidiary of The Rowman & Littlefield Publishing Group, Inc.
4501 Forbes Boulevard, Suite 200, Lanham, Maryland 20706
www.rowman.com

Unit A, Whitacre Mews, 26-34 Stannary Street, London SE11 4AB, United Kingdom


First Rowman & Littlefield edition 2018
Originally published in 1996 by Penguin Books India.
Reprinted by permission.



British Library Cataloguing in Publication Information Available

**Library of Congress Cataloging-in-Publication Data Available**

ISBN 978-1-5381-1367-7 (cloth : alk. paper)
ISBN 978-1-5381-1368-4 (pbk. : alk. paper)
ISBN 978-1-5381-1369-1 (electronic)

∞™ The paper used in this publication meets the minimum requirements of American National Standard for Information Sciences—Permanence of Paper for Printed Library Materials, ANSI/NISO Z39.48-1992.

Printed in the United States of America

For my parents,
Hameed and Nazura Sattar,
with love

# *Contents*

# *Guide to Pronouncing Special Sanskrit Characters*

| | |
|---|---|
| a | like the 'a' in 'above' |
| ā | like the 'a' in 'father' |
| i | like the 'i' in 'bit' |
| ī | like the 'i' in 'liter' |
| u | like the 'u' in 'put' |
| ū | like the 'oo' in 'pool' |
| ṛ | like the 'ri' in 'rip' |
| e | like the 'e' in 'grey' |
| ai | like the 'ai' in aisle |
| o | like the 'o' in 'over' |
| au | like the 'ou' in 'loud' |
| c | like the 'ch' in 'chop' |
| ch | like the 'chh' in 'achhoo' in the sound of a sneeze |
| ṇ | like the 'n' in 'and' |
| ñ | like the 'n' in 'sing' |
| t | like the 'th' in 'thing' |
| th | like the 'th' in 'thump' (with an expulsion of breath) |
| ṭ | like the 't' in 'retroflex' |
| ṭh | like the 'th' in 'hothouse' |
| ḍ | like the 'd' in 'dart' |
| ḍh | like the 'dh' in roadhouse' |
| d | like the 'th' in 'the' |
| dh | like the 'th' in 'the' (with an expulsion of breath) |
| ś | like the 'sh' in 'shout' |
| ṣ | like the 'sh' in 'leash' |
| s | like the 's' in 'sin' |
| kṣa | like the 'ctio' in 'action' |

| | |
|---|---|
| tra | like the 'thr' in 'thrum' |
| jña | like the 'gn' in 'igneous' |
| h | like the 'h' in 'house' |
| ḥ | like the 'h' in 'house' (with an expulsion of breath) |

# *Translator's Note to the Updated Edition*

In the twenty years since this book was first published in India, Vālmīki translations and retellings have flourished. Most significant among these is the completion (in 2016), of *The Rāmāyaṇa of Vālmīki: An Epic of Ancient India*, what is commonly called the "Princeton Ramayana," edited by Robert P. Goldman and published by Princeton University Press. Goldman has brought together leading scholars of the Rāmāyaṇa who are also formidable Sanskritists and, with them, has translated verse of the Critical Edition of Vālmīki's text, which was compiled between 1961 and 1975 at MS University in Baroda. The Princeton Ramayana consists of seven independent volumes, each loaded with invaluable critical aids to reading the text as well as commentaries and essays. Further, the English translation conforms exactly to the Sanskrit in terms of verses. Late in 2017, Penguin Random House (India) published its own version of the Critical Edition of the Vālmīki Rāmāyaṇa. Translated by Bibek Debroy, it too is divided into seven volumes and packaged as a boxed set. During the same period, a number of retellings of Vālmīki have also made their presence felt. Ramesh Menon uses multiple English translations as well as a Sanskrit text as the basis of his Vālmīki Rāmāyaṇa (North Point Press, 2003). Ashok Banker's Rāmāyaṇa Series (Little Brown, 2003 onward) also uses many English translations (including this one) to tell the story of Rāma's adventures. In the last few years however, most of the retellings that have appeared in English are not translations. Instead, their authors gather together episodes and characters from various Indian-language versions of the Rāma epic to present their own versions of the story. This book remains the only one-volume abridged translation of the Rāmāyanā to bring Vālmīki's original narrative to English readers.

Thank you, Susan McEachern, for keeping the faith and being so calm and steady through this. Alden Perkins, your sharp eyes and infinite patience with difficult changes are very much appreciated. This new edition would not have been possible without the sustained enthusiasm and efforts of my agent, Priya Doraswamy. A thousand thanks, Priya, for your persistence.

# *Translator's Note*

In literal terms, to translate means to 'carry over', to cross boundaries and barriers without losing the material that you carry with you. In literary terms, to translate means to make another language read like your own, to preserve meanings and significances across grammars, syntaxes and vocabularies. And it is precisely at this point of grammars, syntaxes and vocabularies, i.e., at the very beginning, that it becomes apparent that there are certain problems unique to the translation of classics in general. Even if we translate a classic from within the same culture, we are never going to translate it from within the same time. The very notion of a classic implies that while it may be removed in time from the reader, it still speaks with relevance and meaning.*

Nonetheless translators of classics have a propensity to fall into forms of usage that are older, even, than the times in which they write. We have all encountered translations of the *Rāmāyaṇa* and the *Mahābhārata* as well as the *Iliad* and the *Odyssey* that are littered with 'thees', 'thous', 'wherefores' and 'it would behove you, sire' even though these translations were produced at a time long after such words and phrases fell out of common usage.

There seems to be something about ancient literature, particularly epics, that inspires translators to dig deep into their vocabulary of archaisms in an attempt to reflect the 'authentic' voice of the text. Perhaps they are led to the use of such language by the perception that epics are 'grand narratives' full of noble emotions, immense dilemmas, huge wars,

* The first part of this Note initially appeared as an essay on translation, 'A Classic Problem', in *The Indian Review of Books,* vol. 5, no. 1 (Sept.–Nov. 1995), pp. 17–18.

larger-than-life characters. Our common usage is considered inadequate to express this grandeur that has all but vanished from our mundane lives.

We must try and remember as we translate epics and traditional story literatures that even at their times of composition, these were not obscure texts meant for scholarly elites. They were living and vibrant and were composed in a language accessible to all kinds of people. Unlike highly refined poetry and drama, stories and epics had a common, ordinary audience. In the story literature and in the epics, it was the events and the characters that were more important than linguistic arabesques and curlicues. For us to cover these texts in a veil of language that obscures them is inaccurate as well as unfair.

There is a school of thought that believes that a classic should be retranslated every twenty-odd years so that it is always in a current idiom, always accessible and meaningful to the contemporary reader. The theory that classics always need to find a contemporary voice, that they should be re-presented every generation, is simple enough, but the practice does not follow quite as easily. The search for a current idiom that can simultaneously contain within it forms and patterns of speech as well as concepts, principles and values that are no longer real or viable presents the translator with a problem of many dimensions. These problems would, perhaps, not apply equally to translators of contemporary work primarily because they are responsible only for bridging space. The translator of a classic must also bridge time.

In translating Indian classics for Indian readers, I am not compelled to explain concepts like *dharma, karma, puruṣārtha,* etc in detail. However, I am still compelled to negotiate such terms as Rāma being described as a 'bull among men' and Sītā having 'the gait of a female elephant.' The ideas of bravery and beauty implied by such formulaic Sanskrit phrases are as foreign to the contemporary Indian as *dharma* may be to a Western reader.

The linguistic negotiation would normally involve flattening out formulae into more familiar constructions like 'Rāma was the best of men' and 'Sītā walked with a swaying grace'. While the literal images of the Sanskrit animal similes are being brushed over, their implied colours are being highlighted. The flattened phrases reflect the language we use today in our common speech as well as in literature even if they do not capture the original flavours and the subtle nuances of the language. They are, however, truer to our idioms and to the connotations of our current usage than images of bulls and elephants may be. At the same time, the task of the translator lies in making such phrases as 'Sītā walked with the gait of a female elephant' seem natural in their context. The translator must be able to carry the reader across both linguistic and cultural boundaries into a literary space where uncommon idioms, uncommon actions and uncommon events seem commonplace. In this translation, I have retained the 'exotic phrase' wherever it was unobtrusive. In other instances, I have flattened the Sanskrit usage into a more common English idiom.

What, then, of the grand and extended hyperbole that give epics their distinctive flavour? Warriors are as large as mountains, kings give away hundreds of thousands of millions of cows, gold and silver are as common as salt and pepper, people live for thousands of years. Everything is larger than life. Heroes are described by a string of superlatives that range from "righteous," "honourable," "steadfast," "splendid" and "effulgent" to "renowned." How does the translator maintain the grandeur of the emotions, the characters and the events without succumbing to a dull and formulaic litany of virtues? How do you carry the structures and restraints of a primarily oral tradition into a written one?

Once again, the theory is simple but the practice is not. A translation depends on evocations, echoes and resonances. These are generated by the translator and nurtured, in a sense, by the reader. Since the grandeur described and invoked by the epics and classical literatures no longer corresponds to reality (if it ever did, that is), it is the translator's task to suggest this meaningfully, to provoke the reader's imagination and to sustain her/his credulousness through an absolute engagement with the story and the characters. This can only be done through language that is transparent, that does not draw attention to itself (except very occasionally and very purposefully). The only language that will not draw attention to itself is one that seems natural, real and familiar.

Any contemporary idiom has the flexibility to evoke a response, to conjure up a universe, to create a sensibility. A translator can use this flexibility to create a delicate network of echoes and resonances that captures the moving spirit rather than the static letter of the original. Instead of allowing the source language to determine the flavour of the translation, we might be better off using our language to probe the nuances of the original, to seek out the significance of ideas, values and cultures that are available to us only as a view through a window. We cannot jump through the window and appropriate or participate in the world beyond ourselves, but we can appreciate it in our own terms and from our position in time and space.

Translating Vālmīki's *Rāmāyaṇa* is both an exhilarating and daunting task. Exhilarating because the story of Rāma is perhaps the best known and most enduring of all Indian tales and Vālmīki's telling of it is certainly the oldest version we have. And it is daunting for exactly the same reasons. Everyone I spoke to during the time I was translating this text stated categorically that they knew Vālmīki's *Rāmāyaṇa.* But when we talked further, it would become apparent that what most people knew was a regional, non-Sanskrit version of Rāma's adventures. Everyone knows that Vālmīki's is the oldest Rāma story and they assumed that what they knew of Rāma's adventures came from Vālmīki's poem. It was then that the magnitude of the task I had undertaken began to dawn on me: the presentation of Vālmīki's tale to an audience that already claimed to know it with a great deal of certainty and self-assurance.

My trepidation was compounded by the fact that I was contracted to produce an 'abridged translation' of Vālmīki's epic poem, an abridgement that carried the original, but that fitted snugly into a single volume. Abridging, i.e., deciding what would be left out rather than what would be left in, became the most critical question I faced during the translation.

The source for this translation is the Critical Edition of the Vālmīki *Rāmāyaṇa* prepared by the Oriental Institute at M.S. University, Baroda. As I began to work on the text, many of the issues that bothered me actually resolved themselves. Readers who are already familiar with the *Rāmāyaṇa* and other tellings of Rāma's story will notice that some of the incidents they know best are absent from this translation. For example, many of us know that when Lakṣmaṇa leaves Sītā alone in the forest and goes in search of Rāma, he draws a circle around her, telling her that she will be safe as long as she stays within it. This incident is so well known that the idea of Lakṣmaṇa's circle, the *lakṣmaṇrekha,* has passed into many Indian languages as a metaphor for a boundary that cannot be transgressed. But it does not appear in the Critical Edition of Vālmīki's text, not even in the appendies.

As it turns out, there are few incidents that have actually been left out in this translation. The major excisions have been story cycles, primarily from the *Bāla* and *Uttara Kāṇḍas.* The only incidents that have been completely left out are those that I firmly believe would have no bearing on the reader's understanding or appreciation of the text as a whole. Generally, passages have been shortened rather than excluded so that the story as well as the flavour of the text is retained.

Complete (and modern) translations of Vālmīki's text are readily available, most notably Hari Prasad Shastri's and N. Raghunathan's three-volume versions. An academically oriented *Rāmāyaṇa* translation is already in process. Robert Goldman heads a team of *Rāmāyaṇa* scholars, each translating one of Vālmīki's *kāṇḍas,* to produce a scholarly but readable version of the Baroda Critical Edition of the Sanskrit text. Parallel to these complete *Rāmāyaṇas,* there have always existed 'retellings' of the tale. As diverse a group as C. Rajagopalachari, R. K. Narayan, P. Lal, Kamala Subramaniam and William Buck have 'retold' or 'transcreated' the *Rāmāyaṇa* in English.

Given the fact that longer and shorter English *Rāmāyaṇas* abound, what then is the value and purpose of this translation? To begin with, it distinguishes itself from the shorter versions, the retellings of the *Rāmāyaṇa,* by being a *translation* of the Sanskrit text. While some material has been left out, nothing has been added to the story or to the nuances and tone of the original Sanskrit. In terms of the longer, complete *Rāmāyaṇa* translations that already exist, this particular one has the advantage of being contained within a single volume. It is also directed at the lay reader, someone with an active interest in ancient Indian texts and stories but who is not necessarily interested in scholarly details.

This translation would never have been completed without the support and cooperation of Prof. V. L. Manjul, Chief Librarian at the Bhandarkar Oriental Research Institute, Pune. I am deeply grateful to him and his staff, Satish, Megha and Gauri, for all their help. Since I have been involved with the *Rāmāyaṇa* and its accompanying materials for more than ten years, there are many people I must thank for helping me develop a familiarity with the text. Profs Alf Hiltebeitel, David Gitomer, Wendy Doniger and A. K. Ramanujan all shared their valuable insights with me and taught me newer and better ways to approach and understand the material. A. K. Ramanujan suggested that I translate the *Rāmāyaṇa* many years ago, at a time when it seemed unlikely that I would ever do so. I wish he could have been alive to see this published. Wendy Doniger has always been more to me than a teacher. Through this project, too, she provided long-distance support, advice and encouragement. I thank her for keeping the faith and bearing witness. Laurie Patton was instrumental in helping me clarify my thoughts about the Introduction as well as cheering me through the last few weeks of my work. Anmol and Sarita Vellani deserve sincere thanks for careful reading and helpful suggestions, for their patience with endless conversations about the *Rāmāyaṇa,* for food, drink and other kinds of sustenance. Ravinder Singh's timely interventions helped me fine-tune my thoughts on translation and I thank him for that. R. S. Iyer patiently read through early drafts and offered helpful suggestions. Ravi Singh, my editor, made my task infinitely easier with his careful readings and insightful queries. Thanks are also due to Sorab Mehta for silent but solid support and to Amrita Shodhan for always having something wise to say about anything that I do. Most of all, I thank Sanjay Iyer, who is a presence in all that I do and all that I write. He is in this book, too, and I can say with certainty that it would have been less without him.

This book is dedicated to my parents, Hameed and Nazura Sattar. Not only did they help me with the mechanics of books and libraries and the postal system, they fed, watered and sheltered me with unquestioning devotion for the last few months of this work. In many ways, this translation of the *Rāmāyaṇa* is the completion of a journey they allowed me to embark on many years ago. I can only hope that the book will bring them as much joy and satisfaction as the journey has brought me.

Arshia Sattar
December 1995

# *Introduction*

The story of Rāma spreads all over the cultures of the Indian Subcontinent and Southeast Asia. It appears in literatures, in music, dance and drama, in painting and sculpture, in classical and folk traditions, in hundreds of languages, in thousands of tellings and retellings from thousands of tellers. Each of these versions has its own special flavour, ambience and distinctive style. A. K. Ramanujan goes as far as to say that 'in India and South-east Asia, no one ever reads the *Rāmāyaṇa* or the *Mahābhārata* for the first time. The stories are there, "always already."'*

Vālmīki's *Rāmāyaṇa* is arguably the oldest surviving version we have of Rāma's tale, but in the multiplicity of Rāma stories received today, Vālmīki's Sanskrit poem is just one more version of Rāma's adventures.† Nonetheless, scholars hold that this telling is perhaps the most prestigious and influential of them all.‡

> Like any other monumental work of literature, the *Rāmāyaṇa* has always functioned on a variety of levels. Through the millennia of its popularity, it has attracted the interest of many kinds of people from different social, economic, educational, regional and religious backgrounds. It has, for example,

* A. K. Ramanujan, 'Three Hundred Rāmāyaṇas: Five Examples and Three Thoughts of Translation' in *Many Rāmāyaṇas: The Diversity of a Narrative Tradition in South Asia* edited by Paula Richman (Delhi: Oxford University Press, 1994), p. 46.

† For purposes of clarity in this Introduction, I will follow A. K. Ramanujan (see 'Three Hundred Rāmāyaṇas') and make a distinction, as does the tradition itself, between the story of Rāma *(Rām-kathā)* and the texts composed by specific people, like Vālmīki, Kamban, Krittibasa, etc. Thus, when it is Vālmīki's poem that is being referred to, I shall use *Rāmāyaṇa* and when the larger family or tellings and retellings is being referred to, I shall use the term 'Rāma story'.

‡ See Robert Goldman, 'General Introduction', *The Bālakāṇḍa of Vālmīki's Rāmāyaṇa: A National Epic of India* (Princeton University Press: 1985) and A. K. Ramanujan, 'Three Hundred Rāmāyaṇas'.

served as a bedtime story for countless generations of Indian children, while at the same time, learned śāstrins, steeped in the abstruse philosophical, grammatical and metaphysical subtleties of classical Indian thought, have found it a subject worthy of their intellectual energies.*

Vālmīki's *Rāmāyaṇa* tells the tragic story of a virtuous and dutiful prince, the man who should be king, who is exiled because of his stepmother's fit of jealousy. Rāma's real troubles begin when he enters the forest for fourteen years with his beautiful wife Sītā and his devoted younger brother Lakṣmaṇa. Sītā is abducted by the wicked *rākṣasa* king Rāvaṇa, who takes her away to his isolated kingdom on the far side of the southern ocean. Rāma and Lakṣmaṇa set out to rescue her and, along the way, they make an alliance with a dispossessed monkey king. The monkey king's advisor, Hanumān, becomes Rāma's invaluable ally and is instrumental in making the mission to rescue Sītā a success. At the end of a bloody war with the *rākṣasas,* Rāvaṇa is killed and Sītā is reunited with her husband. Rāma and his companions return to the city and Rāma reclaims the throne that is rightfully his.

Rāma's equanimity and grace in the face of all the terrible things that happen to him, Sītā's unflinching devotion to her husband, Lakṣmaṇa's and Hanumān's fierce loyalty to Rāma: these qualities have made the characters of the *Rāmāyaṇa* ideals in Indian culture, valued for their virtues and exemplary behaviour. Rāma is not just the perfect man, he is the ideal son, the ideal brother, and, most important, the ideal king. Likewise, Sītā, Lakṣmaṇa and Hanumān loom large in the cultural imagination as the perfect examples of their social roles.

Within this idealized and heroic tale of public honour and kingship is another intensely personal and intimate story. It is one of family relationships, of love between fathers and sons, brother and brother, friends and allies, husbands and wives. The *Rāmāyaṇa* is as much a tale of personal promises and private honour, of infatuation and betrayal, of harem intrigue, petty jealousies, destructive ambitions and enormous personal loss as it is a tale of rightful and righteous kings. Even as questions of kingly duty and nobility of character for the public realm are raised, the story revolves around fidelity, obligations and the integrity that refines individual relationships.

---

* Goldman, 'General Introduction' in *The Bālakāṇḍa of Vālmīki's Rāmāyaṇa,* p. 41.

## THE TWO REALMS OF THE *RĀMĀYAṆA*

The universe in which this tale occurs is expanded by gods and celestial beings, boons and curses, magical weapons, flying chariots, powerful sages, wondrous animals, heroic monkeys and terrifying *rākṣasas.* A crucial aspect of the expanded universe which includes the presence of the divine is the fact that Rāma himself is an incarnation, an *avatāra,* of the great god Viṣṇu. In Vālmīki's *Rāmāyaṇa,* Rāma does not know this about himself. While the gods are on his side in all that he does and often appear to help him or his allies, he goes through the story not knowing that he was born mortal for the express purpose of killing Rāvaṇa. The gods' divine plan becomes Rāma's personal destiny and must be played out to the bitter end. After the war is over, the gods appear and tell him who he is.

Vālmīki's *Rāmāyaṇa* is divided into seven books: *Bālakānda* (Childhood), *Ayodhyākāṇda* (Ayodhyā), *Araṇyakāṇda* (Wilderness), *Kiṣkindhakāṇda* (Kiṣkindha), *Sundarakāṇda* (Beauty), *Yuddhakāṇda* (War) and *Uttarakāṇda* (Epilogue). Of these, the first two and the last books ('Childhood,' 'Ayodhyā' and 'Epilogue') are situated firmly in the mundane world, in the kingdom of Ayodhyā, where Daśaratha and later Rāma rule wisely and well. The other books ('Wilderness', 'Kiṣkindha', 'Beauty' and 'War') are located in the forests south of Ayodhyā and in Lankā.

As with other Indian genres of literature, the magical and mundane, the natural and the supernatural encounter each other frequently in the *Rāmāyaṇa.* Usually, the supernatural and wondrous events occur outside the city, in the uncharted and dangerous regions through which the hero must pass. It is here, in the narrative freedom of the forests, deserts, islands and mountains, that Rāma meets monsters and magical beings. The magical and monstrous beings of the forests and wilderness are, most often, liminal creatures. They straddle the boundaries of more than one species, more than one category of being. Some of these liminal creatures test Rāma, others become his allies, as he goes further on his quest.

In the books located outside Ayodhyā, when the story enters the realm of magic and wonder, Rāma has to contend first with powerful sages and then with marauding *rākṣasas* before he meets the friendly animals who will help him get his wife back. While there are isolated instances of the magical breaking into the mundane world in the first and last books, the incidents either occur outside the kingdom (like the princes' encounter with Tāṭakā in 'Childhood') or under highly circumscribed situations (like Sītā's disappearance into the earth during the sacrifice in 'Epilogue').

Once Rāma leaves the city, the known world has been left behind and from this point on, there are few signposts. In 'Kiṣkindha', when Sugrīva is directing his monkey hordes to go out into the world and find Sītā, he provides a fascinating geography that begins with real kingdoms and real peoples and then opens up into a cosmology of wild and dangerous places where neither the sun nor the moon shine, where there are people with ears so long they can sleep inside them, and so on until you reach the regions where the gods and celestial beings live.

It is in the enchanted forests south of the kingdom that Rāma is truly tested for valour, patience and fortitude. Anything can happen here and it does. Rāma's initial encounters with the monstrous Virādha and Kabandha are only preludes to the larger and deadlier conflicts that await him in Janasthāna and Lankā. The forests, in a sense, represent the underbelly of the *Rāmāyaṇa*'s idealized human actors and the perfect city of Ayodhyā. There seem to be different rules of conduct in the forests and wilderness and certainly a different set of narrative parameters. Birds that speak, monkeys that fly, form-changing *rākṣasas* and headless torsos that run amok are not unnatural or bizarre. Rather, they seem to fall into the normal course of events.

It has been suggested that these forest creatures, particularly the monkeys and the *rākṣasas,* are the shadows of the *Rāmāyaṇa*'s ideal principal characters.* Because Rāma and Sītā cannot or will not act out their baser impulses, the monkeys and *rākṣasas,* who embody non-perfection, do it for them. For example, the monkey Vālī can banish his younger brother Sugrīva, who usurped the kingship of Kiṣkindha, but Rāma is bound by his *dharma* and his model nature to let Bharata, his younger brother, keep the kingdom. Likewise, Śūrpanakhā, the *rākṣasī,* can express her carnal desire for Rāma whereas Sītā can only express sublimated love and devotion.

These sets of contrastive figures provide the poets with a vehicle for portraying the ambivalence inherent in all real human beings while keeping the central characters largely free from inner struggle.†

---

* See Ramanujan, 'Three Hundred Rāmāyaṇas', Goldman, 'General Introduction' in *The Bālakāṇḍa* and Sheldon Pollock, *'Rākṣasas* and Others', in *Indologica Taurinensia,* vol. 13, 1985–86.

† Goldman, 'General Introduction' In *The Bālakāṇḍa,* p. 54.

It is also in the same southern lands that Rāma perpetrates the two acts that apparently mar his shining dharmic nature: the unlawful killing of the monkey Vālī and the rejection of his faithful wife Sītā.* By implication, it would seem that the strict moral and legal codes of Ayodhyā and the world of humans do not apply in the forests and the southern lands. Rāma operates here under a different code of ethics. In fact, in the early chapters of 'Wilderness', when Rāma, Lakṣmaṇa and Sītā have just entered the unpeopled forests, Sītā tells Rāma that here they must abide by separate rules for behaviour. She says that they must leave the codes of the city behind and learn to live by the rules of the forest dwellers. Ironically, though, Rāma's unlawful acts are the result of his imposing the rules and *dharma* of human city living upon events that occur outside the city.†

## REPLICATIONS IN THE *RĀMĀYAṆA*

While most of the animals and *rākṣasas* function as shadows of the main characters, Rāvaṇa, the wicked king of the *rākṣasas,* functions as a mirror image, an inversion, of Rāma. Even his city of Lankā is a replica of Ayodhyā: as magnificent, as prosperous and as well-defended. Rāvaṇa is brave, strong and powerful, he is handsome and majestic. He has the capacity to perform fierce austerities and was able to demand the boon of invulnerability from Brahmā. Motivated by the desire to avenge the insult to his sister Śūrpanakhā, Rāvaṇa decides to abduct Rāma's wife. Sītā refuses to submit to him and though he loves her to distraction, Rāvaṇa is honourable enough not to force himself upon her. Nonetheless, he also refuses to return her to Rāma and this stubborn refusal is, ultimately, the cause of his death.

We have seen that the magical beings of the forests can act as shadows for the *Rāmāyaṇa*'s principal human characters. This shadowing creates replications, i.e., the repetition of particular themes and structures in various ways in order to create and sustain a dominant mood, in this case, that of personal loss and tragedy.‡ The replications generated by these

* See the section on 'Rāma's Divinity' for a further discussion of this issue.
† See below for a longer discussion of this issue.
‡ See Goldman, 'Structure, Substance and Function in the Great Sanskrit Epics', p. 18. Paper delivered at the Festival of India Conference on Indian Literatures at the University of Chicago, April 1986. Goldman argues that the *Rāmāyaṇa* is dominated by *karūnarasa,* grief.

shadows, the way their stories invert and retell the stories of Rāma, Sītā, Bharata and Lakṣmaṇa, reveal other dimensions to the *Rāmāyaṇa,* enriching the text and opening up our understanding of it.

The dominant replication in the *Rāmāyaṇa* is that of brothers, their loyalty and disputed succession. It is through the loss of kingdoms and wives (who are often identified with royal power, *śrī*)* that the personal tragedies become publicly significant. The stories of Rāma and Bharata, Vālī and Sugrīva and Rāvaṇa and Vibhīṣaṇa all resemble each other. The issue of succession, duty and the rivalry between brothers is developed and explored in the juxtaposition of these three relationships.

Rāma is the rightful king of Ayodhyā. Not only is he the most virtuous and accomplished of all Daśaratha's sons, he is also the eldest and, therefore, should succeed his father. But, because of promises Daśaratha had made in the past, Bharata, his younger son, is crowned king. Bharata, however, motivated by *dharma* and his love for Rāma, tries to return the kingdom to Rāma and then swears that he will act as a regent and hold Kosalā in custody until Rāma returns from his fourteen-year exile. After Rāma has lost his kingdom, his wife is abducted, sealing, as it were, the loss of his royal power. But Sītā is stolen by Rāvaṇa and Bharata has not appropriated the kingdom for himself, leaving open the possibility that both wife and kingdom will be restored, unsullied, to Rāma.

In a direct parallel, Vālī, the older son of Ṛkṣarāja, becomes king of the monkeys. He disappears for a long time and his younger brother, Sugrīva, takes over the kingdom as well as his brother's wife, Tārā. But Vālī returns and accuses Sugrīva of having plotted to overthrow him and banishes his younger brother from Kiṣkindha. Sugrīva swears that he has been honourable and that he was forced to accept the kingship by the council of ministers. Unlike the love that persists between Bharata and Rāma, Vālī and Sugrīva become deadly enemies and the issue of who should rule the monkey kingdom is resolved only when Vālī is killed. Sugrīva inherits both the kingdom and Tārā, his elder brother's wife.

The third axis of brothers and rightful kings is explored in the story of Rāvaṇa and Vibhīṣaṇa. Rāvaṇa is the king of Lankā because he is older than Vibhīṣaṇa and because of his superior prowess. But Rāvaṇa is

---

* See, for example, Veena Das, 'Kāma in the scheme of *puruṣārthas:* the story of Rāma' in *Way of Life: King, Householder, Renouncer* edited by T. N. Madan (New Delhi, Vikas Publishing House: 1982).

governed by his addiction to sensual pleasures and by the arrogance he derives from his boon of invulnerability. His abduction of Sītā and his refusal to return her to Rāma makes him unrighteous and impels Vibhīṣaṇa to leave his brother and join forces with Rāma. Rāvaṇa's abduction of Sītā also symbolizes his usurpation of Rāma's position as lord of the worlds and it is for this that he must be punished. At one point in the battle, when Vibhīṣaṇa thinks Rāma might be dead, he is terribly upset because his only chance of securing the *rākṣasa* kingdom seems to have vanished. Thus, Vibhīṣaṇa's motives for deserting his brother have as much to do with his desire for the kingdom as with his desire to fight on the side of the right and the good. As a reward for Vibhīṣaṇa's loyalty to *dharma,* Rāma confers the *rākṣasa* kingdom on him after Rāvaṇa is killed in battle.

Among the three sets of brothers and their three different relationships to one another and to *dharma,* it is Rāma and Bharata who clearly display the ideal relationship. The other two sets of brothers represent variations on this ideal.

> Here again the relations we encounter are not expressed by the logic of simple binary oppositions but through a technique of strategic exaggeration and distortion. I can only express it analogically by saying that human relations are mirrored and echoed in the worlds of animals and demons, but the mirrors are the kind that not only invert but also exaggerate and distort.'*

## WOMEN IN THE *RĀMĀYAṆA*

Just as the monkey brothers, Vālī and Sugrīva, play out an alternate option to the problem of disputed kingship, so, too, does the *rākṣasī* Śūrpanakhā, Rāvaṇa's sister, provide a distorted mirror image of the chaste and virtuous Sītā.

> Sītā and Śūrpanakhā exemplify two types of women who appear almost universally in folklore and mythology: Sītā is good, pure, light, auspicious and subordinate, whereas Śūrpanakhā is evil, impure, dark, inauspicious and insubordinate. Although male characters also divide into good and bad,

* Veena Das, 'Kāma in the scheme of *puruṣārthas:* the story of Rāma,' pp. 194–95.

the split between women is far more pronounced and is always expressed in terms of sexuality.*

Śūrpanakhā comes upon Sītā, Rāma and Lakṣmaṇa in the forest. Rāma has just fought off the *rākṣasa* Virādha who had grabbed Sītā, a foreshadowing of the more serious abduction that will take place a little later. Śūrpanakhā desires Rāma for his good looks and suggests that he give up his ugly human female for her. The brothers proceed to tease and torment Śūrpanakhā, eventually cutting off her nose and ears, Śūrpanakhā's mutilation in the forest echoes the battle the princes had with Tāṭakā in which Rāma was reluctant to kill a woman until Viśvāmitra assured him it was all right. The assault on Śūrpanakhā also moves the story into top gear—she complains to her brother Rāvaṇa, at which point he decides to abduct Sītā in order to avenge the insult to his sister.

Both Katherine Erndl and Sally Sutherland† demonstrate that the major opposition between Sītā and Śūrpanakhā is in terms of sexuality. Sītā's is a domesticated, conjugal love while Śūrpanakhā represents untamed, aggressive and, therefore, potentially threatening desire. Sutherland suggests that the encounter between Sītā and Śūrpanakhā carries the potential of their becoming co-wives and therefore, they are set up as rivals for the same man's affections. She also interprets the mutilation of the *rākṣasī* as necessary to curb her dangerous sexuality because Rāma cannot make the same mistake as his father: he cannot be ensnared by a woman's charms. The *Rāmāyaṇa* implicitly argues that it is not wrong for Rāma and Lakṣmaṇa to assault and disfigure Śūrpanakhā, just as it was not wrong for them to have killed Tāṭakā the *yakṣinī,* because they are in the forest where different rules apply and because Rāma cannot afford to commit the same mistakes as his father.

The same sexual opposition between rival wives is played out between Kausalyā and Kaikeyī, the mothers of Rāma and Bharata.‡ While Kausalyā is the respected senior wife of Daśaratha, it is clearly Kaikeyī, the junior wife, who has the king enthralled by her beauty and charm. Kausalyā does everything right, including producing the perfect son, but

---

* Kathleen M. Erndl, 'The Mutilation of Śūrpanakhā' p. 83 in *Many Rāmāyaṇa* edited by Paula Richman.

† See Sally Sutherland, 'The Bad Seed: Senior Wives and Elder Sons' in *Bridging Worlds: Studies on Women in South Asia* edited by Sally J. M. Sutherland, Delhi: Oxford University Press, 1992.

‡ See Erndl 'The Mutilation of Śūrpanakhā ' and Sutherland 'The Bad Seed'.

she has little hold on the king's affections even though she is the ideal wife and mother. Kaikeyī, on the other hand, is wilful and stubborn and gets her way all the time. She conspires to obtain the kingdom for her son and earns the contempt of everyone, including Bharata.

Similarly, good and righteous wives recur in the multiple stories of kingship. Vālī, the monkey king, has a virtuous and wise wife named Tārā who first urges him not to destroy Sugrīva and then cautions him against fighting Rāma. Vālī does not heed her words and goes out to meet his fate. When Vālī dies, Sugrīva inherits Tārā along with the kingdom. As his senior wife, she remains the voice of righteousness and sanity in his court and Rūmā, Sugrīva's other wife, becomes the focus of his sexual attentions. The parallels with the Kausalyā-Kaikeyī situation are very clear: Kausalyā and Tārā are the wise, older wives who have the king's attention because of their virtues and Kaikeyī and Rūmā are the younger wives whose sexual charms have a hold on the king. Similarly, Rāvaṇa's chief queen, Mandodarī, tries her best to dissuade him from taking on the might of Rāma because she knows that Rāvaṇa is acting wrongly, but to no avail. While he holds Mandodarī in great respect, Rāvaṇa satisfies his sensual and sexual desires with the thousands of other women that fill his palace.

Along with dangerous, demonic women, female ascetics (like Svyamprabhā ) and the virtuous wives of sages (like Ahalyā and Anusūyā) also live in the forests. Their rigorous austerities have given them magical powers and a high spiritual status. But once again (as with Sītā), because their sexuality has been sublimated, they pose no threat to anyone. In Lankā, the good *rākṣasīs* Saramā and Trijaṭā, both of whom help Sītā during her imprisonment, mirror the female ascetics of the forest. The female ascetics and the good *rākṣasīs* are safe havens in the regions where dangerous, demonic women abound.

These variations on particular themes in the *Rāmāyaṇa* are expressed through replication, shadowing and mirror images. Within the text, they explore multiple possibilities in terms of relationships, characters and story lines. The tight normative roles prescribed for Rāma, Bharata, Sītā and Lakṣmaṇa are, in fact, heightened by the more realistic paths taken by the non-human and liminal characters in the text. Apart from presenting a contrast between the prescriptive behaviour of the human characters and the morally ambiguous actions of their non-human shadows, replications also serve to generate the narrative trope of foreshadowing. As in the case when Virādha snatches Sītā away, events, emotions and even behaviours are hinted at and suggested in smaller incidents and side tales well before the critical moment occurs. Foreshadowing acts as a powerful tool in the building and maintenance of a mood for the epic. It also provides a narrative rhythm as it lays out the primary concern of the text.

## THE MAGICAL BEINGS OF THE *RĀMĀYAṆA*

Traditional Indian literatures are filled with magical beings, some benign, others malevolent. While the benign beings (for example, the *siddhas* and *cāraṇas*) are very like each other, the malevolent ones are usually more ambivalent and, therefore, more interesting. Malevolent and dangerous beings occur in a hierarchy which places *asuras, daityas* and *dānavas* at the very top and *piśācas* and *yatudhānas* at the very bottom. *Rākṣasas, yakṣas, nāgas* and the like fall in between these two. The closer the beings are to the top of the hierarchy, the more they resemble the gods and, therefore, the more ambivalent they are likely to be.

*Asuras, dānavas* and *daityas* are 'not good' rather than being wicked or bad. They are classified as wicked mainly because they tend to oppose the gods. The *asuras,* especially, are defined only in opposition to the gods and spend much of their time and energy trying to conquer the kingdom of the gods and rulership of the worlds.* *Daityas* and *dānavas,* on the other hand, the sons of Diti and Danu respectively, are divine and are rivals of the gods.†

As we progress lower in the hierarchy, the wicked creatures become less ambiguously so. Most generally, *rākṣasas* appear in Indian stories as horrendous, vile, flesh-eating creatures. Prone to disrupting sacrifices and, therefore, to disrupting the universal order which is maintained by the careful performance of complex rituals, they are most powerful at night.

The *rākṣasas* of the *Rāmāyaṇa* are unlike any others in the vast corpus of Indian literatures. Rāvaṇa and most of his followers do not fit the general description of these creatures at all. On the contrary, they are

* In fact, the word *asura* literally means 'anti-god'.

† For a detailed discussion of this issue, see Wendy Doniger O'Flaherty, *The Origins of Evil in Hindu Mythology* (Berkeley: University of California Press, 1976).

magnificent and regal. Hanumān notices that Lankā even has *rākṣasas* who are virtuous about performing Vedic rituals. Rāvaṇa and his siblings are the children of the mighty sage Pulastya, who is a son of Brahmā. Rāvaṇa himself is so handsome and majestic that when Hanumān sees him for the first time, he is awed by his beauty and power and moved to remark that had Rāvaṇa not been so unrighteous, he was worthy of ruling over even the gods. Even though Rāvaṇa has ten heads, twenty arms and blazing red eyes, he clearly possesses compelling charisma. The women in his palace, each of them incomparably beautiful, have come to him of their own accord out of love. Rāvaṇa's chief queen is so beautiful that Hanumān thinks she might even be Sītā. Rāvaṇa's brother, Vibhīṣaṇa, is righteous and honourable like his grandfather Mālyavān. Rāvaṇa's sons are all excellent warriors and, except for Indrajit, fight ethically and honourably. There are also good and virtuous *rākṣasīs* like Mandodarī, Trijaṭā and Saramā.

At the same time, Rāvaṇa's sister Śūrpanakhā, whose lust for Rāma moves the story towards its climax, is ugly and crude. Likewise, Kumbhakarṇa, Rāvaṇa's gigantic brother, is terrifying and malformed. These two are more like *rākṣasas* are supposed to be—appetitive, gross and undesirable in every way. The lesser *rākṣasas,* like the ones who serve Rāvaṇa and the *rākṣasīs* who serve Sītā, fit the common description of *rākṣasas* far more closely. Almost without exception, they are greedy, ugly and deformed and eager to eat human flesh.

One of the defining features of the *Rāmāyaṇa*'s *rākṣasas* is that they are *kāmarūpī,* i.e., they can change their forms at will. This is amply borne out by Mārīca, who takes on the form of a jewelled deer to lure Rāma away from his forest settlement. During the war, Rāvaṇa's spies infiltrate Rāma's army by taking on the form of monkeys.

The counterparts of the *rākṣasas* are the monkeys of Kiṣkindha, who come to Rāma's aid and fight on his side during the war. Equally magical, they, too, can change their shapes at will, as Hanumān does when he searches for Sītā in Lankā. Like Rāvaṇa and his family, each of the important monkeys has a divine father. Even the lesser monkeys were fathered by celestial beings. In this lies the secret of all their magical powers.

The magical animals of the forest, Sugrīva and his monkeys, Hanumān, Jaṭāyu and Sampāti, have often been likened to the animals that appear in folk and fairy tales. They share the same characteristics of being able to speak human language as well as being able to do uncanny things. Hanumān's character and actions fit the mode of the animal helper in fairy tales who aids the hero in his enterprise, without whom, in fact, the enterprise could not succeed.

The *rākṣasas* and the monkeys are essential to the story that has to be told. Rāma needs an opponent worthy of himself, someone who will challenge him to the fullest and yet be unrighteous enough to warrant the harshest treatment. Just as Rāma has to be human in order to kill Rāvaṇa, so Rāvaṇa has to be exceedingly powerful in order to be a threat to the worlds. Thus, his semi-divine parentage and his enormous powers are crucial aspects of his position as the rival to the hero.

The narrative reason also applies to the fact that Rāma's allies are monkeys. Rāvaṇa's boon granted him immunity from all kinds of celestial and demonic beings, but in his self-assurance, he neglected to ask for invulnerability from mortals and the lower creatures. Thus, Rāma (or Viṣṇu) appears as a mortal aided by monkeys in order to vanquish Rāvaṇa. Over and above this, we have already discussed the possibility that these creatures function as shadows, counterparts and alternates for the human characters who are restricted by their mortality as well as by their morality from behaving in certain ways.

A great deal of *Rāmāyaṇa* scholarship has turned its attention to extranarrative explanations of who the monkeys and the *rākṣasas* really are. Several scholars have suggested that the monkeys and *rākṣasas* represent the non-Aryan tribes of India and that the defeat of the *rākṣasas* is, in fact, the story of Aryan expansion into India. This hypothesis, particularly the idea that the monkeys of the *Rāmāyaṇa* are the indigenous tribal peoples of the subcontinent, has had many supporters. Apart from the unpleasant racial overtones that such a notion elicits, the theory diminishes the power of the poetic imagination by insisting that meaning arises only from a reduction to mundane and identifiable reality.

Other scholars have suggested that the *rākṣasas* represent the 'other' of Hindu society upon which all its fears and terrors can be located.* This hypothesis, that the *rākṣasas* represent the innermost terrors of Hindu culture, is far more interesting because it attempts to analyse these creatures from within the mind of their creator(s). Besides that, it opens up

* See Sheldon Pollock, '*Rākṣasas* and Others'.

yet another dimension, another aspect to the text, further enriching it for its audience.

## RĀMA'S DIVINITY

The Indian Rāma stories that come after Vālmīki's *Rāmāyaṇa* all take Rāma's divinity as a starting point for their tale. However, in Vālmīki's *Rāmāyaṇa,* it is clear that for most of the story Rāma does not know that he is divine. It is precisely this fact that gives his trials and tribulations such poignancy—Rāma does not know why all these awful things are happening to him and why he has to suffer so much. It is at the very end of the war with the *rākṣasas,* after Rāvaṇa has been killed and Sītā has proved her chastity, that the gods appear and tell Rāma that he is Viṣṇu and not an ordinary mortal.

Scholars unanimously hold that the first and last books of Vālmīki's *Rāmāyaṇa* ('Childhood' and 'Epilogue') are later additions to the central five books.* In Vālmīki's text as it is constituted today, the only places where Rāma's divinity is unambiguously stated are the closing chapters of the sixth book ('War') and in the first and last books. In the first book, Daśaratha performs a sacrifice for the birth of a son. At the same time, the gods, who are being harassed by Rāvaṇa, plead with Viṣṇu to be born on earth as a mortal in order to kill the *rākṣasa.* A celestial being appears at Daśaratha's sacrifice with heavenly food that will cause the queens to become pregnant. Rāma and his brothers are born as a result of this. In the last book, Viṣṇu is recalled to heaven by Brahmā and so Rāma has to give up his earthly life. When Brahmā's messenger arrives, Rāma knows what is required of him and makes arrangements to leave his kingdom and ascend to heaven.

In the middle books, then, the only direct mention of Rāma's divinity is after the war. Nonetheless, arguing from within the narrative necessities of the text, Sheldon Pollock states firmly that Rāma has to be a god-man.† Pollock holds that Rāma's divinity is a 'higher order narrative feature,'

* See the following section of the Introduction for a longer and more systematic discussion of this issue.

† See Sheldon Pollock, 'The Divine King in the Indian Epic', in *Journal of the American Oriental Society* 104 (1984), pp. 505–28.

i.e., that it is constitutive of the text itself. His argument is as follows: since Rāvaṇa had been made invulnerable to all kinds of creatures by his boon, the only kind of being that could kill him could be a mortal. But since he is so powerful and magnificent an enemy, this mortal could not be ordinary. Therefore, a god-man is the only possibility, a man who has the powers of the gods without actually being one himself.

> The gods may never in such circumstances actually grant immortality itself. . . . Yet like so many others Rāvaṇa seeks to achieve the same result by a gambit widely familiar in folklore, by attempting to frame the perfect wish. The sheer impossibility of an exhaustive catalogue, however (in this case over-determined by Rāvaṇa's scornfully discounting man altogether), immediately implies that a solution is assured; the very provisions of the boon make it inevitable that some proxy will be found. Not a god, since the gods have become, so to speak, contractually impotent; nor yet a man, men being constitutionally impotent. . . . Instead, it must be some fusion of the two, a god-man.*

Despite these hypotheses and all the other extratextual reasons for Rāma being considered divine (like the suggestion that the Indian conception of kingship demanded that the king be divine), within the story Rāma must act as a human hero even though he is Viṣṇu. How else would the tale find its dramatic tension, its pathos, its tragedy? And perhaps most important, how could Rāma be seen as the ideal man, a model for human behaviour and a paragon of virtue?

Imagine if the story had, from the outset, two equally matched protagonists, Rāma and Rāvaṇa. Imagine if Rāma had known that his banishment served a larger and far more significant purpose than the petty ambitions of his step-mother. Imagine if he had known all along that the monkeys would help him rescue Sītā and that the throne of Kosalā would be restored to him. As it is, Rāma displays an almost unnatural equanimity in the face of all that happens to him. But because he functions as a human hero, he has his moments of torment. He regrets the fact that he was exiled because of his father's infatuation with a selfish and flighty woman. He is insane with grief when Sītā is abducted and vows to show the gods the extent of his wrath if she is not returned to him unharmed. He is pathetic

* Ibid., pp. 516–7.

and miserable without her and turns his anger on Sugrīva, who seems to have forgotten the terms of their alliance. It is moments like these that grasp the reader's imagination, for they make Rāma real, accessible and utterly human.

At the same time, Rāma must transcend his human limitations and restrictions if he is going to vanquish the king of the *rākṣasas,* the most powerful creature on earth. On an entirely mundane level, Rāma inverts the patterns of his father's life, rising above the temptations of anger, desire and greed to which Daśaratha was subject. Daśaratha unknowingly kills an ascetic in his youth, Rāma actively protects the ascetics, first on his journey with Viśvāmitra and then later when he is exiled into the forest. Daśaratha succumbed to desire *(kāma)* by agreeing to Kaikeyī's wishes, Rāma upholds *dharma* by publicly humiliating and then punishing his innocent and chaste wife. Both Rāma and Daśaratha as kings obtain their sons at sacrifices: Daśaratha's sons are born because of the efficacy of his sacrifice and Rāma is united with his unknown sons at his horse sacrifice.

As a human hero, Rāma does all he can to avoid repeating the mistakes of his father. As an *avatāra* of Viṣṇu (and as a human king), it is his job on earth to uphold *dharma* and protect the *brahmins* and the ascetics. As a human, Rāma sacrifices everything, his kingdom and his wife, to uphold *dharma.* As a god, he plays along with a cosmic plan. It is the tension between his mortal limitations and the conceivably unlimited powers he enjoys as Viṣṇu that makes his dilemmas and his resolution of them compelling.

> The *Rāmāyaṇa* is the portrait of a consciousness hidden from itself; or, one might say, of an identity obscured, and only occasionally, in brilliant and poignant flashes, revealed to its owner. The problem is one of forgetting and recovery, of anamnesis: the divine hero who fails to remember that he is god, comes to know himself, at least for brief moments, through hearing (always from others) his own story.*

If we hold that the core *Rāmāyaṇa* includes the first and last books, where Rāma knows and understands his own divinity, the situation becomes even more complex and Rāma's condition even more poignant.

---

* David Shulman, 'Fire and Flood: The Testing of Sītā in Kamban's *Irāmavatāram,*' p. 93 in *Many Rāmāyaṇas*, edited by Paula Richman.

Imagine if Rāma knew he was god and was still constrained to act as a man would and should. This is, in fact, the situation in the Rāma stories that come after Vālmīki's *Rāmāyaṇa.* Rāma has to continue to act as a man precisely because he is a god and not in spite of his divinity.

## KINGSHIP IN THE *RĀMĀYAṆA*

Since the dominant set of replications in the *Rāmāyaṇa* explores the theme of brothers and disputed thrones, one could argue that the central issue the *Rāmāyaṇa* tackles is that of rightful and the righteous kingship. Through the multiple variations on the theme of disputed kingship, we see that Rāma is clearly both the rightful and the righteous king while Rāvaṇa is not. Rāvaṇa is the rightful king of Lankā because he is the eldest of the brothers, but he is by no means the righteous king. After Rāvaṇa is killed, Vibhīṣaṇa becomes the righteous and rightful king of Lankā.

It is the relationship between the monkey brothers, Vālī and Sugrīva, and the throne of Kiṣkindha that is the most complicated. Vālī is the elder brother and, from all that we know about him, seems to be a good and righteous king. Sugrīva, on the other hand, takes over his brother's throne claiming that he is probably dead. He also takes over his brother's wife, a woman he should have treated as a mother. Sugrīva makes Rāma kill Vālī by saying that he was cruel and unrighteous. Once his older brother is dead, Sugrīva becomes the rightful king of Kiṣkindha. But once again, he takes Tārā, Vālī's wife, as his own. Ironically, taking another's wife is one of the unrighteous deeds for which Vālī is killed. Thus, Sugrīva's righteousness would appear to devolve from the fact that he makes an alliance with righteous Rāma and not from any of his own actions.

It is when he acts as the righteous king that Rāma commits the two deeds that appear incomprehensible for a man such as him—the killing of Vālī and the rejection of Sītā. Rāma forms an alliance with Sugrīva and takes his word that Vālī has wronged him and deserves to die. This expediency is compounded by the fact that Rāma kills Vālī while Vālī is fighting Sugrīva and Rāma himself is hidden behind a tree. As we learn more and more about Vālī, it would appear that he was a wise and just ruler, compassionate even towards his brother, whom he could have killed on several occasions.

As Vālī is dying, he excoriates Rāma for his unrighteous act and Rāma offers a series of arguments in his own defence. These include the fact that since Vālī was a low creature, a mere monkey, Rāma could kill him in any way he pleased because the ethics of battle did not apply. At the same time, Rāma says that Vālī deserves to die because he has violated *dharma* by taking his brother's wife. The sophistry in this argument is clear: if Vālī belongs to a lower order of being and the ethics of battle do not apply to him, why, then, should he be judged by the stringent rules of human *dharma* in his personal life?

The matter becomes somewhat clearer when Rāma states that he is acting on behalf of Bharata and the righteous Ikṣvāku kings who hold dominion over the earth. There can be no violations of *dharma* under their jurisdiction. The functions of a king include the meting out of punishments *(daṇḍa),* the nurturing of *dharma* and the righteous organization of society. Rāma is attempting to fulfil those functions in this case. He is compelled to act as a righteous king, no matter how specious his arguments may be for doing so.

Rāma's unjustified rejection of the chaste and virtuous Sītā, not once, but twice, is as problematic as the episode with Vālī. Through no fault of her own, Sītā is abducted and imprisoned by Rāvaṇa. When the war to reclaim her is over, Rāma humiliates Sītā, first by calling her out in public, and then by saying that he has no use for her any more, that the war was fought to salvage the honour of his clan. Sītā walks into the fire but is rescued by the fire god, who vouches for her innocence and chastity. At this point, all the gods appear and tell Rāma who he really is. Rāma takes Sītā back because the gods tell him to and also, he says, because he had always believed in her innocence but wanted to prove it to the common people. Later, after they have lived happily in Ayodhyā for many years, Rāma hears that the people still doubt Sītā. He decides that he must banish her from the kingdom because he cannot allow gossip and scandal to tarnish his reputation.

Once again, in both cases of rejection, Rāma plays the part of the righteous king who must always be above reproach. Anything or anyone connected with him must be equally so. Rāma has to sacrifice his personal feelings about Sītā in order to uphold *dharma,* as he had to do earlier when his father exiled him to the forest for fourteen years. It is here that the epic trope of the hero's personal destiny being inextricably linked with the plan of the gods is most clearly visible. But Rāma as a human hero proves equal to the task. Even though he is not always aware of his divinity, he acts in accordance with a higher law, *dharma,* which is divinely sanctioned and which it is his duty, as a king (albeit in waiting), to uphold.

## THE INTERNAL AND EXTERNAL AUDIENCES

Like the *Mahābhārata,* the *Rāmāyaṇa* is enclosed within a frame story. Besides that, it tells its own story several times within itself. There are, thus, at any given time, two audiences for the *Rāmāyaṇa,* the internal audience and the external audience.*

The opening frame of the *Rāmāyaṇa* involves the composer of the poem, Vālmīki, who is told Rāma's story by the celestial sage Nārada. Shortly thereafter, Vālmīki is moved to compassion when he sees the grief of a bird whose mate has just been killed by a hunter. His compassion expresses itself spontaneously in a new metre and Brahmā encourages him to sing Rāma's tale in this new metrical form. Vālmīki looks around for the students most likely to do justice to the tale and the metre and decides upon teaching it to the twins Kuśa and Lava. As Wendy Doniger O'Flaherty points out, the names Kuśa and Lava constitute the two parts of the noun *Kuśilava,* meaning 'wandering bard'.† Needless to say this has an added significance in the context of what is going to happen next.

Kuśa and Lava are also Rāma's estranged sons, born in Vālmīki's settlement when their mother, Sītā, was banished from Ayodhyā. Vālmīki encourages the boys to sing the story of Rāma's life at a huge sacrifice that Rāma himself is performing. The twin boys are handsome and charming, with melodious voices and fine musical talent. Their listeners are enthralled by the tale and are drawn to the young men. The audience notices that they are like mirror images of Rāma and even Rāma is fascinated by his own story.

As the boys sing the tale in the intervals between the rituals of the sacrifice, Rāma finally recognizes them as his own sons. He asks them to

---

* I borrow this phrase from David Shulman. See 'Fire and Flood: The Testing of Sītā in Kamban's *Irāmavataram,*' p. 95.

† Wendy Doniger O'Flaherty, *Other People's Myths* p. 150 (New York: Macmillan Publishing Company, 1988).

bring their mother to him. Vālmīki brings Sītā to the sacrificial enclosure and when she is asked to prove her chastity again, she disappears forever into the earth. Rāma is heartbroken, but Brahmā appears and encourages him to listen to the rest of his own story from his sons. The young princes continue with their tale, reciting, apparently, even the death of Rāma.

> The story is over. But the shocking and moving fact is that we experience these final chapters as Rāma does—not in the backward movement of the story, but rather with the past become present or future (and the future presented as past). There is no visible seam separating the text's statement that Kuśa and Lava sang the end of the poem from the actual content of this ending—the description of Rāma's depression, the golden image of Sītā, and so on. The frame has melted away, our sense of time is confused, past conflates with future—as it does already at the very beginning of the epic, in Vālmīki's proleptic vision of past and future combined—and we find ourselves once again listening with Rāma to the story of his own life, but at this point to that part of it that is still to unfold. We might ask ourselves if the 'actual' narrator, Vālmīki, is continuing his narration through the mouths of his pupils, or on his own, as it were—but does it matter?*

According to the outer frame of the *Rāmāyaṇa,* the first audience of the poem are the kings, *brahmins*, townspeople, monkeys and *rākṣasas* who are present at Rāma's sacrifice. The monkeys and the *rākṣasas* have participated in some parts of the story they are listening to and many of them have already heard about the events that they did not participate in. This was possible because the *Rāmāyaṇa* tells itself internally on several occasions.

When Rāma, Lakṣmaṇa and Sītā first meet the sage Agastya, Lakṣmaṇa introduces himself and his companions by telling Agastya's student how Rāma came to be exiled into the forest. After Sītā has been abducted and the princes reach Kiṣkindha, Lakṣmaṇa again tells Hanumān all that has happened up to that point. Once Hanumān enters the picture, he becomes the carrier of the story within the story, from one person to the next (from Rāma to Sītā and Rāma to Rāvaṇa, then back from Sītā to Rāma and finally, from Rāma to Bharata) as well as from one location to the next (from Kiṣkindha to Lankā, from Lankā to Kiṣkindha and then from

* David Shulman, cited in Wendy Doniger O'Flaherty, *Other People's Myths,* pp. 150–51.

Kiṣkindha to Ayodhyā). The tale precedes Rāma's presence in Lankā as well as his return to Ayodhyā.

Hanumān as the carrier of the tale assumes significance in terms of the boon Rāma grants him at the end of their adventures together. In the very last book ('Epilogue'), once Rāma has been crowned king of Ayodhyā, he lavishes gifts on the main monkeys and *rākṣasas.* On Hanumān, his special helper, he bestows the boon of conditional immortality: Hanumān will live as long as Rāma's story is told on earth. Thus, Hanumān has a vested interest in keeping the story alive, telling it again and again, in all the places that he can and to all the people that he can.

Scholars of oral epics will argue that the reason the *Rāmāyaṇa* tells itself within itself is to maintain the integrity of the text, i.e., to ensure that future tellers and scribes are reminded of the grid of major episodes upon which they can work. For example, the opening chapters of the first book ('Childhood') have Nārada telling Vālmīki the entire story of the *Rāmāyaṇa* which provides future tellers with an outline of the story. Further on, the frequent recapitulations of the story up to that point would, arguably, serve the same function.

However, if we keep in mind the fact that the *Rāmāyaṇa* always has more than one audience (i.e., there are multiple audiences inside the story itself) we can see how the repetitions are necessary and valid for narrative reasons as well as compositional ones. If we add Hanumān's boon to this, we see that for at least one of the storytellers within the tale, this is a matter of life and death. Besides, Shulman argues that Rāma himself has to keep hearing his own story told because the *Rāmāyaṇa* is 'the portrait of a consciousness hidden from itself' and that Rāma remembers his divine nature only through his story as told by someone else.

## THE *RĀMĀYAṆA* AS EPIC

The *Rāmāyaṇa* is considered by Western scholars to be one of the two Indian epics, the other being the *Mahābhārata.* The indigenous tradition, however, classifies these long poems differently. The *Rāmāyaṇa* is called *ādikāvya*, 'the first poem,' and the *Mahābhārata* is held to be *itihāsa,* 'legend' or 'history'. While scholars have yet to define 'epic' satisfactorily, there is a strong consensus that, as a genre, epic is circumscribed by certain compositional and formal features. Most simply, an epic is often oral, it is narrative and it is heroic.

Early scholars of Indian epics were confounded by the non-linear narrative style of the *Rāmāyaṇa* and the *Mahābhārata.* Their stories move forward episodically, in fits and starts. Where one might expect a grand elaboration, there is none. Action is often slowed down by a digression into another story or a long description of nature. While the central story does always come to a satisfactory conclusion, it winds and meanders through a 'chaotic' abundance of other tales and side tales, diversions into philosophies and moral discourses, genealogies and cosmologies, looping back on itself, framing one story after another, until finally it comes to rest.

Since epics are often oral in origin, they have a particular way of telling their stories. Each teller has the privilege, perhaps even the duty, to tell the tale in her/his own way, dwelling on well-loved parts, elucidating morality and ethics, adding comic relief.

> In a social milieu where the vast majority of the audience of traditional literatures are not literate, traditional texts must make heavy use of devices that maximize memorability. Among these devices are iteration, formulaic composition, simple metrical forms preferably subject to musical or quasi-musical recitation, copiousness, heavy use of epigrams and sententia, hyperbole and tales of wonder.*

Inside these formal constructs, epics basically tell the stories of legendary heroes, often kings, who must go through several hardships before they can 'live happily ever after'. The stories are complicated by disputed kingships, warring kingdoms, abducted or dishonoured wives, and journeys into dangerous unknown and uncharted territories. The hero of the tale must come through a series of adventures that test his valour as much as they test his virtue. He usually has a companion in his quest or on his journey who helps him come through the trials and tribulations that litter his path.

The epic hero has a special relationship with the gods. Sometimes he is fathered by a divine parent, sometimes he has the gods' particular favour and at other times he can be either a part of a god *(aṃśa)* or an incarnation

---

* Robert Goldman in 'Structure, Substance and Function in the Great Epics of India,' pp. 7–8.

of a god *(avatāra)*. An epic brings the human and cosmic realms together, often in the person of the hero. Epics posit a critical relationship between cosmic order and human destiny: the cosmic plan of the gods becomes the human hero's fate.* The gods take sides in the battle that must be fought and the battle is fought primarily to reestablish the dominion of the gods over the earth.

Apart from the gods *(daiva)* and fate *(vidhi)*, there are other significant forces that are active in the epic universe. In the Indian epics, *karma*, *dharma* and *kāla* (time) operate to determine what the hero can do, what he must do and what will happen to him. Curses and boons are further determining agents in these stories and elevate the stories to the level of mythic events.† The hero's actions are understood to be affected by any or all of these forces. Thus, the action in an epic, particularly in Indian epics, suffers from a certain degree of narrative hypercausality, where multiple causes are proffered for a single event.

Vālmīki's version of Rāma's adventures displays almost all these epic features: the hero's trials and tribulations, his intimate relationship with the gods and the operation of extrahuman forces such as boons and curses. But at the same time, the *Rāmāyaṇa* also shares several themes and motifs with stories that have come to be classified as fairy and folk tales: the beautiful princess who is abducted by the wicked, monstrous enemy and imprisoned in a faraway, inaccessible place, the talking, magical animal companions, the divine maiden who can stay with her husband only for a short time before she returns to her original state, the magical objects (in this case, weapons) that help the hero rescue the princess.

While the *Rāmāyaṇa* shares structural and thematic features with genres that have been defined primarily by Western scholars against Western texts, we must also take into consideration the fact that there is an indigenous category for the *Rāmāyaṇa*. The Indian tradition defines the *Rāmāyaṇa* as the *ādikāvya*, or *mahākāvya*, 'great poem', a category which appears to straddle the Western genres of drama and narrative lyric.

Perhaps the most characteristic feature of Sanskrit *kāvya* is *alamkāra*, or the adornment of verse with similes, metaphors and other figures of speech. The purpose of this is to create a distilled mood, a *rasa*. All *rasas*

* Alf Hiltebeitel, *The Ritual of Battle: Krishna in the Mahābhārata* (Ithaca: Cornell University Press, 1976).

† See Pollock, 'The Divine King in the Indian Epic,' p. 509.

are based on human emotions. But while emotions are fleeting and rarely encountered in their pure state, a mood can be cultivated and developed through the sustained use of language which can, then, generate the further distillation of an essence.

The most popular mood in *kāvya* remains *viraha,* i.e., love in separation. Through various techniques, the poet tries to create this mood of longing for the beloved among his audience which, ideally, consists of *sahṛdayas,* 'like-hearted' or 'sympathetic' people. As the hero or the heroine pines for the beloved who is far away, all of nature sympathizes—trees and flowers wilt, animals and birds weep, clouds gather and the world is covered in gloom.

The *Rāmāyaṇa* is completely self-conscious about its connection with *kāvya.* In the opening chapters of the text, we hear the story of how Vālmīki's compassion at the death of a mating bird was spontaneously expressed in metre. Vālmīki is then encouraged by Brahmā to recite the deeds of Rāma in this new metrical form and he teaches his poem, the *Rāmāyaṇa,* to his students Kuśa and Lava. They, in turn, recite the poem to Rāma. Rāma thus hears his own story for the first time as a poem. At the same time as the *Rāmāyaṇa* establishes itself as a poem, it is equally firm about its original oral status. The story is heard and retold many times before it reaches us, the last and outermost audience of the written text.

Even a cursory reading of the *Rāmāyaṇa* shows that its style is ornate, laden with similes and metaphors, metonymy and other features of classical Sanskrit poetry. Nature functions almost as another character. Descriptions of nature abound, especially in the sections where Rāma and Sītā have been separated. Easily the most beautiful parts of the poem are the ones where Rāma is waiting for Sugrīva to fulfil his promise and begin the search for Sītā. It is the rainy season, the conventional season for love in Sanskrit poetry, and Sītā is far away. Everything around him reminds Rāma of his gentle, sweet wife.

Further, the *Rāmāyaṇa* is a heroic poem, a heroic romance, in fact, and can be compared to classical Sanskrit *nāṭakas.* Under this set of parametres, the story is simple—the lovers meet, they fall in love, they are separated, and after a period of unhappiness and trial, they are reunited. As in the paradigmatic *nāṭaka,* Kālidāsa's *Abhijnānaśakuntalām,* Rāma, the hero from the city, falls in love with the woman of nature (Sītā is born from the earth and her name literally means 'furrow') and their union results in the birth of crucial male heirs.

Ramanujan believes that to classify the *Rāmāyaṇa* as an epic is to deprive it of the religious significance it holds in India and parts of Southeast Asia.* On the other hand, since the *Rāmāyaṇa* cannot obviously be contained by any single genre, the more genre considerations we apply to it, the more we open up the text for exploration. Each particular categorization highlights another aspect of the story and of the text and each of these deepens our understanding of the multiple layers the poem holds within itself. None of the genres, whether Eastern or Western, are mutually exclusive and it is entirely possible, perhaps even necessary, for a text as multivalent as the *Rāmāyaṇa* to straddle many boundaries. Seeing the *Rāmāyaṇa* as *kāvya* or a *nāṭaka* or as an epic or a fairy tale, or even as all of them, provides a rich and complex backdrop to the religious significance the text has acquired over the centuries.

## THE CRITICAL EDITION AND THE GREATER *RĀMĀYAṆA* TRADITION

It is very likely that the bulk of the *Rāmāyaṇa* was composed by a single author (or at least by like minds at a single period in time). Nonetheless, more and more scholars have come to believe over the years that Rāma's story was in circulation for a long time before Vālmīki composed it into his particular version.† The existence of the *Daśaratha Jātaka* and the *Rāmopakhyāna* in the *Mahābhārata* have been cited as evidence that Rāma's adventures were known before Vālmīki, that Vālmīki retold the story in his own unique way. Equally though, it has been argued that the Vālmīki version is the oldest Rāma story we have and that the *Daśaratha Jātaka* and the *Rāmopakhyāna* are derived from it.‡ Whichever camp scholars fall into, there is almost no one who suggests that Vālmīki's is an original tale.

* Lectures during a course on Indian Civilizations at the University of Chicago, 1986–87.

† Since the bulk of the *Rāmāyaṇa* was most probably composed by a single person and there is nothing that either proves or disproves the existence of a historical person called Vālmīki, scholars are willing to accept that Vālmīki was the primary author of the *Rāmāyaṇa*.

‡ Goldman, 'General Introduction' in *The Bālakāṇḍa of Vālmīki's Rāmāyaṇa*, pp. 32–33.

The *Rāmāyaṇa* has had a long history of transmission, from its presumably oral origins to written manuscripts and now to the printed text.* Even though Vālmīki probably composed his text sometime between 750 and 500 BCE, the earliest extant *Rāmāyaṇa* manuscript dates only to the eleventh century CE. *Rāmāyaṇa* manuscripts appear in different scripts from all over the Indian subcontinent. Because of the plethora of manuscripts and the multiplicity of manuscript traditions, scholars are compelled to sort through them and value them in terms of age and authenticity.

There is no longer any doubt about the fact that while books 2 through 6 were composed by a single person at a particular time, the first and the last books of the Vālmīki *Rāmāyaṇa,* the *Balā* and *Uttara Kāṇḍas,* were very likely to have been composed later than the rest of the text. From their style, content and linguistic features, they are also likely to have been composed by someone other than Vālmīki. Nonetheless, the Vālmīki *Rāmāyaṇa* as it is constituted today consists of all seven books, the first and the last serving as bookends, almost, to the central books where the main story is contained.

Since 1975, scholars of the Vālmīki *Rāmāyaṇa* have had at their disposal the Baroda Critical Edition of Vālmīki's poem. This presents a standard edition that can be cited easily and efficiently. The enterprise of critically editing an ancient text that has several recensions and manuscript traditions is primarily motivated by the scholarly desire to reconstruct the original text. On the basis of linguistic, cultural and historical evidence, experts attempt to reconstruct, as closely as is possible, the original text as it was composed by the author.

The critical edition is constructed by the meticulous and painstaking comparison of manuscripts and manuscript traditions. The passages that constitute the body of the critical text are those that appear in all (or at least most) of the manuscript traditions. These are considered to be indubitably a part of the original composition. Verses that are not substantiated by several manuscripts are judged to be late in composition and/or as the work of later redactors and editors of the text and these are placed outside the main body of the critical edition.

Such an enterprise involves, for example, the labeling and separation of verses and passages that were composed at a date later than the bulk of

---

* Most of the material in this section is taken from the introduction to my dissertation, 'Hanumān in the Vālmīki *Rāmāyaṇa:* A Study in Ambiguity', University of Chicago, 1990.

the text. These, then, are regarded as 'interpolations' or 'additions' to the main text. The material in these passages is marked off from the rest of the verses and placed either in appendixes or in multiple footnotes marked by asterisks and a separate set of numbers.

Opponents of the text critical method are accused of ascribing a non-rationality to the original producers of the text. Those who reject the critical edition and its findings are charged with romanticizing the oral tradition and crediting the composers with an entirely different method of text production, one that makes the criteria of critical apparatus irrelevant. On the other hand, complete reliance on and belief in the construction of such critical texts devalues the native traditions that produce them. This belief insists that the critically edited product is the legitimate text and ignores the cultural differences that inform the production and development of a text outside Western modes of authorship. Nonetheless, the idea that the critical edition defines the boundaries of the 'text' itself persists, despite the fact that all those familiar with Indian texts agree that a unique notion of tradition *(paramparā)* informs and circumscribes these texts.

The *Rāmāyaṇa* as we receive it today, whether it is Vālmīki's Sanskrit telling or the Rāma story as a cultural artefact (replete with all its multiforms in the performing and fine arts and different genres of literature), is more than a putative original or source text attributed to a legendary composer. The power of the *Rāmāyaṇa* lies in the stories it tells and it lives well beyond the confines of bound volumes. Each retelling is as integrally linked to the source as it is different from it. And it is the constant retellings and reformulations of the basic story that make the text both organic and dynamic—tied to its mythic origins as well as to its real multiforms.

In speaking of the *Mahābhārata,* Hiltebeitel declares that he prefers to think of the text as a

> narrative continuum, as a 'work in progress', rather than . . . a fixed or original text. By the same token, it strains matters to regard all the variants as synchronically equal in value. Some features must be older than others, and though indisputable rules for determining textual priorities will probably never be established, historical development through such processes as alteration, interpolation, and perhaps sometimes abridgement, must not be ignored.*

---

* Alf Hiltebeitel, *The Ritual of Battle: Krishna in the Mahābhārata,* pp. 14–15.

The same can be said about Vālmīki's *Rāmāyaṇa* as well as of the greater *Rāmāyaṇa* tradition which is, in fact, predicated on Vālmīki's text. While there are considerable differences of style, composition and perhaps even modes of production between the *Rāmāyaṇa* and the *Mahābhārata,* Hiltebeitel's observation applies equally to the former since he makes a point with regard to the way scholars should approach these 'reconstructed' texts, rather than a point about the possible way in which the texts come together.

## CONCLUSIONS

The Vālmīki *Rāmāyaṇa* and its critical edition eventually become layers within the greater tradition of Rāma stories that have proliferated over the centuries. Most Indian languages have their own tellings of Rāma's adventures and even cultures as far from India as Indonesia have made the tale of the exiled prince their own. But the question that remains is, what is it about this essentially simple tale that has compelled so many different kinds of people to hold it close to their hearts? The story is hardly unique, and some have argued that the idealized characters within it have little or no psychological complexities. Why then is it told and retold, by professional bards, by grandmothers, by teachers?

The answer to this question may well lie in the two unresolved issues that linger and haunt the reader/listener long after Vālmīki's story is over: Rāma's unlawful acts and his ignorance of his divine status. The killing of Vālī and his rejection of Sītā are so outrageously out of character that there is almost nothing within the premises and assumptions of Vālmīki's tale that can justify them. We can suggest that all the Rāma stories that follow Vālmīki's are attempts to resolve this issue narratively as well as structurally.

For example, Tulasidāsa's Hindi *Rāmcaritmānas* from the fifteenth century assumes Rāma's divinity as a starting point. Rāma kills Vālī so that the monkey will be liberated from his earthly life and body. This motif of salvation has already been established by the killings of Virādha and Kabandha, both of whom are liberated from their curses by their 'deaths' at the hands of Rāma. As in Vālmīki's story, Tulasi's Ahalyā, too, is freed from her petrified condition by Rāma's presence. Tulasi follows Vālmīki to justify Rāma's rejection of Sītā—he knew that she was innocent but had to prove it to the common people. But additionally in Tulasi, Sītā the goddess, was spirited away by the gods in the moment before Rāvaṇa grasped her hand in the abduction. The Sītā that suffered the separation and torment was but an illusion of the 'real' Sītā who returned only after the trial by fire. She is, therefore, utterly pure, untouched by the vile creature that Rāma must kill.

In Krittibasa's Bengali story, Rāma is filled with remorse after he has killed Vālī and after listening to Vālī's arguments Rāma apologizes profusely, saying that since he had already formed a pact of friendship with Sugrīva, he was bound to kill his ally's enemy. Instead of justifying Rāma's unrighteous killing of the righteous monkey king, Krittibasa has Tārā, Vālī's wife, curse Rāma: because he had killed Vālī and separated Tārā from her beloved husband, he, too, would not enjoy Sītā's company for long. He would regain her now but would end his days in loneliness and misery. If Rāma's acts cannot be justified, he can at least receive retribution for them.

Krittibasa again employs the curse to make sure that Rāma suffers. When the war is over and Rāvaṇa has been killed, Mandodarī, the *rākṣasa* king's virtuous wife, curses Sītā—because she has caused the death of Mandodarī's husband, her own husband will look upon her 'with poisoned eyes'. Rāma demands that Sītā prove her innocence in public and she walks into the fire. She was not to return, except that the gods are moved by Rāma's grief over the loss of his beloved and they restore Sītā to him.

These few examples show how the later tradition struggles with Rāma's odd behaviour and how various narrative devices are employed to exonerate him from censure. If he knows that he is god, as in Tulasi's story, all his 'wrong' actions are actually right ones from the correct perspective. In Krittibasa's case, curses are used to punish Rāma and to prevent him from acting freely.

As mentioned earlier, we can think of all the other Rāma stories as predicated on Vālmīki's for two reasons: they take Rāma's divinity for granted as a starting point for their stories, and they implicitly cite Vālmīki's text as they tell their own story.

To some extent, all later *Rāmāyaṇas* play on the knowledge of previous tellings: they are meta-*Rāmāyaṇas*. I cannot resist repeating my favourite ex-

> ample. In several of the later *Rāmāyaṇas* (such as the *Adhyātma Rāmāyaṇa,* 16th century), when Rāma is exiled, he does not want Sītā to go with him into the forest. Sītā argues with him. At first she uses the usual arguments: she is his wife, she should share his suffering, exile herself in his exile, and so on. When he still resists the idea, she is furious. She bursts out, 'Countless *Rāmāyaṇas* have been composed before this. Do you know of one in which Sītā does not go with Rāma to the forest?'*

Ramanujan's example demonstrates that Rāma stories absorb each other and nowhere, perhaps, is this more apparent than in the issue of Rāma's divinity. Each Rāma story that succeeds Vālmīki's version addresses this particular question head-on, usually in the opening chapters of the book. It is as if the later versions know how subtle Vālmīki's statement is and, therefore, they take it upon themselves to open out the issue, bring it into the foreground. It is almost possible to see the greater *Rāmāyaṇa* tradition as a commentary on this primary text.

In most of the Hindu Rāma stories that follow Vālmīki's in time, Rāma's unrighteous behaviour and his divinity are inextricably linked. Rāma killed Vālī to liberate him from his earthly body. Rāma rejected Sītā because he knew all along that she would be proved innocent in the trial by fire. Rāma could do and did these things precisely because he was god, not *despite* the fact that he was god. Because Rāma is aware of and participates in a higher order, his actions cannot be judged in earthly terms and by earthly conditions. Unlike in the Vālmīki *Rāmāyaṇa,* where he has to be reminded or told who he is, Rāma in the later stories acts in full awareness and full control of his divinity.

Shulman eloquently describes the narrative nexus of the *Rāmāyaṇa* as 'the portrait of a consciousness hidden from itself . . . an identity obscured and only occasionally, in brilliant and poignant flashes, revealed to its owner.' This formulation, of the hidden divinity, the obscured identity, can be extended into a heuristic device for a further understanding of the *Mahābhārata* as well. In the *Mahābhārata,* Kṛṣṇa's divinity is hidden from those around him. He reveals himself as the *mysterium tremendum* to Arjuna in the eleventh chapter of the *Bhagavad Gītā.* But he saves Arjuna from the memory of the epiphany which would have, in effect, made him utterly unable to act in the world. In the *Rāmāyaṇa,* Rāma must be

* A. K. Ramanujan, 'Three Hundred Rāmāyaṇas' in *Many Rāmāyaṇas.*

similarly protected from the knowledge of his own divinity so that he can act effectively as a mortal in the world, most especially to kill Rāvaṇa.

The hidden divinity at the centre of the narrative is a feature of both the Sanskrit epics. The progressive revelation of the true identity of the man-god is one of the drivers of the story. In many ways, the *Bhagavad Gītā* is the climax of the *Mahābhārata* and the war that follows is but a denouement, a fulfilling of individual and collective destinies that had been set in motion in the earlier parts of the story. Similarly, the *Rāmāyaṇa*'s narrative and spiritual climax occurs in the scene when, after Sītā's trial by fire, the gods tell Rāma who he really is. Once again, the events that follow this critical moment are but the tying up of loose ends as the story moves inevitably towards its conclusion. With the *Rāmāyaṇa* it is important to note that the revelation of Rāma's true identity occurs at the end of book 6, the last of the central books of the text. The seventh book, the *Uttara Kāṇḍa,* has always been considered an epilogue to Vālmīki's tale which rightly and powerfully ends in book 6.

The question that looms large over the *Rāmāyaṇa* is that of the relationship between myth and history, i.e., is the *Rāmāyaṇa* a 'true' story? When the early Orientalists were discovering Indian texts, they were struck by the absence of a formal and proper 'history', the kind they had found in ancient Greece and even in ancient China. Indians seemed to mix up their human heroes with their gods. Chronological lists of kings and dynasties were found in the Purāṇas, which were actually compendia of myths. This led them to think that Indians could not write history, that when they did attempt to chronicle the past, their fanciful minds came up with never-ending stories peopled with gods and monsters. Thus, to see the Indian epics simply as history is to fall into an Orientalist trap.

At the same time, most scholars of epic believe that an epic grows around a core legend or tale that probably did occur. Thus, it is possible some king (perhaps not named Rāma) did exist, that his wife was abducted and that he fought a war to get her back. Through many hands and many centuries, this set of events became the *Rāmāyaṇa,* a tale that no longer has any meaningful dependence on the 'reality' that spawned it. What we have now is a remarkable tale that captures the imagination of all kinds of people, not just because it is true, but because of the way it is told, because of the adventure and magic it contains, because of the way it takes a known and familiar reality and enlarges it to dimensions that are unknown and unfamiliar.

It has been argued that to trace Rāma's journey through the Subcontinent in literal terms, identifying each and every place in which he stopped and bathed, to insist that he was born in a particular spot and died at another, is a matter of faith and that it is critical to the religious sentiments of vast numbers of people. While this may well be true, literalizing a text of this magnitude does it a great injustice. The *Rāmāyaṇa* does not derive its meaning from a sacred geography or history: rather, it draws its significance from what it can tell us about ourselves, our decisions and the way we choose to live our lives.

# CHILDHOOD

# *Chapter One*

The great sage Vālmīki was a bull among men who practised austerities constantly. One day he said to the eloquent Nārada, 'Tell me, great one, who is the most virtuous man in the world of humans? Who is the most honourable, dutiful, gracious and resolute? Who is the most courteous, the most dedicated to the welfare of all beings, the most learned, the most patient and handsome? Who is the man with the greatest soul, the one who has conquered anger, who is intelligent and free of envy? Who is this man, whose anger frightens even the gods? I am sure you know of such a man and I am curious to hear about him from you.'

Nārada, who knows the past, the present and the future, was delighted with Vālmīki's question. 'There are few men with all the qualities that you have described,' he replied. 'But there is one man, O sage, who has all these virtues. Listen, and I will tell you about him.

'Born into the clan of Ikṣvāku, his name is Rāma. He is brave and illustrious, disciplined and renowned in all the three worlds. He is wise and well-versed in the science of polity. He is well-spoken and glorious. This man, a slayer of his enemies, has broad shoulders and strong upper arms, a graceful neck and a strong jaw. He is a skilled archer with a muscular body and long arms. He holds his head with pride and he walks with long strides. Splendid and prosperous, he has smooth skin and large eyes. His well-proportioned body is endowed with all the auspicious marks.

'Rāma is aware of his duties. He is truthful and dedicated to the welfare of his subjects. He is learned, virtuous and single-minded. He protects all

physical beauty in India is a marker of merit in past life - something you earn, so you can be judged for appearance the creatures of the world and he upholds *dharma.** He knows the four Vedas as well as the schools of thought that accompany each of them and he is equally knowledgeable about the finer points of archery. Well-versed in the sacred and philosophical texts, Rāma has a brilliant memory and a ready wit. This courteous, brave and wise man is loved by all who know him. As all rivers flow into the sea, so all good and noble people come to Rāma.

'This virtuous man is the son of Kausalyā. Viṣṇu's equal in valour, he is as deep as the ocean and as resolute as the mountains. As beautiful as the moon, he has the endurance of the earth, but he can be like the doomsday fire when he is roused to anger. As generous as Kubera, the god of wealth, Rāma is ready to sacrifice everything for the truth.

'Because of Rāma's many virtues, King Daśratha decided to declare him the heir apparent. Rāma is the oldest and most beloved son of King Daśaratha, who was devoted to the welfare of all creatures. But when Daśaratha's wife, Kaikeyī, saw the magnificent preparations for Rāma's coronation, she called up the promises Daśaratha had made to her in the distant past, promises that exiled Rāma to the forest and placed her son, Bharata, on the throne. Bound by *dharma* and his given word, Daśaratha had to banish his beloved heir. Rāma went to the forest to preserve his father's honour and to make Kaikeyī happy.

'Rāma's younger brother Lakṣmaṇa, the son of Sumitrā, followed him into exile because he loved him dearly and because it was the right thing to do. Rāma's virtuous wife Sītā, the most excellent of all women, also followed her husband into exile as the constellation Rohiṇī follows the moon.† When Rāma left the city, King Daśaratha and the townspeople went with him for a distance, but at the village of Śṛngavera, on the banks of the Gangā, Rāma dismissed his charioteer.

'The sage Bharadvāja told Rāma and his companions to go to Citrakūṭa and Rāma, Lakṣmaṇa and Sītā went from forest to forest crossing many deep rivers on their way. In the pleasant surroundings of Citrakūṭa, the three of them built a little hut and lived there as happily as the gods and

* *Dharma,* one of the central concepts in Hinduism, is impossible to translate into English with a single word. It encompasses ideas of the right, the good, truth, law (temporal and spiritual) as well as the 'ought.' Where possible in this translation, I have used the English words 'righteous' or 'honourable.' In sentences where these adjectives could not be used with felicity, I have retained the Sanskrit *dharma.*

† Rohiṇī is the ninth lunar asterism, personified as a daughter of Dakṣa and the favourite wife of the moon.

the *gandharvas*. Meanwhile, Daśaratha missed his son sorely and while Rāma was in Citrakūṭa, the old king died of grief.

'When Daśaratha died, the *brahmins* led by Vasiṣṭha offered the throne to the heroic Bharata. But Bharata refused the throne and went into the forest to meet Rāma. Rāma urged Bharata to return to the city to rule and finally he gave Bharata his sandals as a symbol of his regency. Bharata touched his older brother's feet and, acceding to his wishes, ruled the kingdom from Nandigrāma while he waited for Rāma's return.

'Rāma knew that if he stayed in Citrakūṭa the townspeople would visit him all the time. So he moved further into the Daṇḍaka forest. Rāma killed the *rākṣasa* Virādha there and then went onwards to visit the sage Agastya and his brother. Rāma took Indra's bow, a sword and two inexhaustible quivers of arrows from Agastya. While Rāma lived in the forest, he was approached by the sages who dwelt there. They asked him to kill the *rākṣasas* and *asuras* who harassed them and Rāma did so.

'An ugly and terrifying *rākṣasī* named Śūrpanakhā, who could change her form at will, lived in Janasthāna. On her instructions, Khara, Triśiras, Dūṣaṇa and all the other *rākṣasas* arrived in Janasthāna and made preparations to fight Rāma. But Rāma killed them and their companions, slaying fourteen thousand *rākṣasas* in all.

'Rāvaṇa was enraged when he heard about this massacre and enlisted the *rākṣasa* Mārīca to help him take revenge. Mārīca implored Rāvaṇa time and again not to oppose Rāma, whose strength was far greater, but impelled by destiny, Rāvaṇa ignored Mārīca's advice and took him to Rāma's forest dwelling.

'Mārīca drew the two princes away with his power to create illusions and Rāvaṇa abducted Rāma's wife Sītā, killing the vulture Jaṭāyu as he carried her away. Rāma met the dying vulture and when he heard about Sītā's abduction, he was overcome with sadness and began to weep. He performed funeral rites for Jaṭāyu and then wandered through the forest in search of his wife.

'In his wanderings, he came upon the deformed and fierce *rākṣasa* Kabandha. Mighty Rāma killed the *rākṣasa* and performed funeral rites for him so that Kabandha could go to heaven.

'By the shores of lake Pampā, Rāma met the monkey Hanumān. Following Hanumān's advice, Rāma went to meet Sugrīva and told him his entire story. In turn, Sugrīva related all that he had suffered as a result of his enmity with Vālī and he also warned Rāma about Vālī's strength. Rāma promised to kill Vālī but Sugrīva was not convinced of his prowess. To prove himself, Rāma kicked Dundhubi's immense carcass with his big toe and it landed ten *yojanās* away. Then he pierced seven *sāla* trees with a single well-chosen arrow. The arrow passed through a huge mountain and lodged itself in the bowels of the earth.

'Sugrīva's confidence in Rāma grew, as did his affection for him when he saw this. He returned to his cave in Kiṣkindha, taking Rāma with him. Yellow-eyed Sugrīva roared like thunder and Vālī, the king of the monkeys, came out to meet his challenge. Rāma kept his word to Sugrīva and killed Vālī in battle. Then he bestowed the monkey kingdom on Sugrīva.

'Sugrīva called together the respected monkey chiefs and despatched them in all directions to look for Sītā. Instructed by the vulture Sampāti, Hanumān leapt one hundred *yojanās* across the salty seas and entered the city of Lankā which was protected by Rāvaṇa. Hanumān found Sītā in a grove of *aśoka* trees, where she sat with her mind fixed on Rāma. He gave her Rāma's signet ring and told her all that had happened. After he had reassured and comforted Sītā, he tore down the city gate.

'Hanumān killed five of Rāvaṇa's generals and seven of his ministers' sons. He pulverized the mighty Akṣaya and ground him into the dust. Then he allowed himself to be captured. Even though Hanumān knew he could not be harmed by the weapon Brahmā had given Rāvaṇa, he submitted to the *rākṣasas* and suffered many indignities. He burned the city of Lankā, sparing only the place where Sītā was. Then he returned to give Rāma news of his beloved.

'He honoured Rāma and related all he had seen in great detail. Rāma went to the seashore with Sugrīva and pierced the ocean with his blazing arrows. The Lord of the Ocean himself appeared before Rāma and on his instructions, Nala built a bridge over the seas. Rāma used the bridge to reach the city of Lankā where he killed Rāvaṇa in battle. He crowned Vibhīṣaṇa king of the *rākṣasas*.

'Rāma took Sītā back but she was humiliated when he spoke to her harshly in front of all the people gathered there. Unable to bear the shame, that virtuous woman entered the fire. But as she entered the flames, flowers rained down from the sky and Agni declared her to be a chaste and honourable woman.

'The gods and the sages and all the animate and inanimate beings in the three worlds were delighted with Rāma's great deeds. The gods honoured Rāma and there was rejoicing among all the creatures. A boon from the gods brought all the slain monkeys back to life. Rāma climbed into Puṣpaka, the flying chariot, and set off for Nandigrāma. When he reached there, he cut off his matted locks. Now that he had regained his wife, Rāma, the sinless one, went back to his kingdom with his brothers.

'The townspeople were glad to have him back. Rāma's presence made them virtuous, free of sickness, famine, fear and danger. No one had to witness the death of their sons, no woman was widowed and they all lived lives of devotion to their husbands. There was no fear of storms, nor of death by water, nor fear of fire nor plague nor fever. With a great expenditure of riches and gold, Rāma performed all the necessary rituals and sacrifices, including the *aśvamedha* sacrifice.* He gave away many cows and large quantities of land. The prestige of his royal clan increased a hundredfold because of his deeds and all the four castes remained dedicated to their duties in this world. After ruling for eleven thousand years, Rāma went to Brahmaloka.

'The story of Rāma is edifying and bestows merit. Anyone who reads it is freed of all sins. The man who reads the Rāmayana will be honoured along with his sons, grandsons and companions when he dies and goes to heaven. The *brahmin* who reads this tale will become eloquent, the *kṣatriya* will become a king, the *vaiśya's* trade will prosper and even the *śūdra* will flourish in his own caste.'

* The horse sacrifice which dates back to the Vedic period. A perfect horse is allowed to wander freely through neighbouring kingdoms for one year. Anyone that stops the horse must fight the army that follows it. At the end of the year, the horse is ceremonially sacrificed. A hundred such sacrifices entitled the king who performed them to displace the king of the gods.

# *Chapter Two*

The great sage Vālmīki and his disciples honoured and praised Nārada when he had finished his story. Nārada bade them farewell, ascended into the skies and returned to the realm of the gods. Vālmīki went to the banks of the river Tamasā, not far from the Gangā. He gazed at the calm, clear waters of the river and said to his disciple who was standing behind him, 'Look at these clear waters, Bharadvāja! They are as calm and serene as the mind of a good man! I want to bathe here. Child, put down your pot and fetch me my clothes.'* Bharadvāja obeyed and brought his teacher's robe to him. Vālmīki who had controlled his senses, took the garment and walked around, enjoying the beauty of the verdant forests.

Vālmīki came upon two sweet-voiced *kraunca* birds making love. He saw a cruel hunter shoot the male, and the golden-crested bird fell to the ground. When his mate saw that he was dead, she cried out piteously. Compassion welled up in Vālmīki's heart when he saw the fallen bird, killed so unrighteously, and the grief of its mate. Deeply moved, he said, 'Hunter, because you killed this bird while he was making love, you shall never find a resting place!'

As soon as he had spoken, Vālmīki thought to himself, 'What are these words that I uttered in my grief for the bird?' Learned and wise, the sage said to his disciple, 'My words came forth in a metre of four feet with equal syllables that can be sung to the notes of the *vīṇā.* Since this metre arose from my grief, let it henceforth be known as the *śloka* metre.'†

---

* The Sanskrit word used here is *cīra,* literally, a long piece of bark. However, the meaning extends to rough or simple clothes. Ascetics, sages and hermits are often described as 'wearing *cīra,*' which I have chosen to translate throughout the book as 'simple clothes' or 'the clothes of an ascetic.

† There is a pun in Sanskrit here on the words *śoka,* i.e., 'grief' and *śloka,* the name of the new metre.

Bharadvāja committed the new metre uttered by his teacher to memory and Vālmīki was deeply satisfied.

Then Vālmīki took his ritual bath in the river and returned to his hermitage, lost in thought. His humble and courteous disciple followed after him, carrying the pot of water. The sage who knew *dharma* entered his hermitage with Bharadvāja and gave his customary discourse. Then he passed into a deep meditative trance.

Lord Brahmā himself, the glorious four-faced Creator of the worlds, appeared before Vālmīki. Speechless with wonder the sage rose hurriedly and bowed before Brahmā. He honoured the god with *arghya* water and asked after his welfare.

Brahmā seated himself on a beautiful throne and motioned to Vālmīki to sit on another seat. Even though he was in the physical presence of Brahmā, Vālmīki found that his mind was distracted and he remained immersed in his own thoughts. He kept thinking about the awful thing he had seen, the death of the sweet-voiced *kraunca* bird at the hands of the hunter who was clearly inclined towards cruelty. Vālmīki recalled the metre he had created in his grief for the bird. As he recited it again for Brahmā, he was filled with sadness.

Brahmā smiled gently and said, 'Your mind did not create this *śloka* metre. I produced this eloquence in you. O best of all sages, use this new metre to recite the tale of Rāma, the most righteous, the most virtuous and the wisest man in all the worlds, as you heard it told by Nārada. Recite the deeds of Rāma, deeds that are already known as well as those that are not, his adventures with Lakṣmaṇa and his battles with the *rākṣasas.* Recite the acts of Sītā, the known ones and the unknown ones. Whatever you do not know will become known to you. Never again will your words be inappropriate. Tell Rāma's story in this new metrical form! It will prevail on earth for as long as the mountains and the rivers exist! And as long as Rāma's story has currency, so long shall you live in my realm.' Brahmā disappeared after he had said this, but Vālmīki and his disciples remained struck with wonder.

The disciples repeated the new metre that had emerged from Vālmīki's sorrow over and over again and each time their delight and their wonder increased. Then the great-souled sage announced, 'I will recite the history of Rāma as a poem!'

And for the benefit of all creatures, this entertaining story of the glorious and renowned Rāma was composed as a poem in the new metre by Vālmīki.

The great sage went on to compose the tale of how Rāma had regained his kingdom, in the unique metre he had created. He composed twenty-four thousand verses and divided them into five hundred chapters in six books. Once he had finished this composition, including the *Uttara Kāṇḍa,* he began to wonder whom he would teach it to. As he was thinking about this, he was approached by two young bards wearing ascetics' clothes.* These two young boys were glorious princes who were well-versed in *dharma.* They were eloquent and had sweet voices and they lived, at that time, with Vālmīki in his hermitage.

When Vālmīki saw the two boys who had faith in the Vedas, he decided to teach them his new poem. The sage who had performed many sacrifices taught the boys the poem about Rāma's deeds, including the part about Sītā. The poem was also known as 'The Killing of Pulastya's Descendant'.† This sweet composition can be sung in either of three tempos, slow, medium or fast, and fits into the musical scale of the *vīṇā.* It contains all the aesthetic emotions like humour, romance, compassion, awe, fright and disgust.

The two brothers were skilled musicians and they had an excellent knowledge of melody and rhythm. They had sweet singing voices as well as good looks, which made them seem like *gandharvas.*‡ They were like twin images of Rāma himself. They committed the wonderful tale about *dharma* to memory and soon, they were able to recite it without a mistake. The two princes, who were learned and resolute, handsome and glorious, recited the poem before sages and *brahmins* as they had been instructed to do.

On one occasion, they sang the entire poem amidst a company of holy sages, The sages, who were devoted to *dharma,* were delighted and their eyes filled with tears of joy. 'Oh! What an exquisite poem!' they cried in wonder. 'The things it speaks of occurred a long time ago but it feels as

---

* The word for bard in Sanskrit is *kuśilava.* These two young men who approach Vālmīki are named Kuśa and Lava and thus, in the Sanskrit text, the word *kuśilavau* could mean either 'the two bards' or 'Kuśa and Lava.'

† Rāvaṇa was descended from the sage Pulastya and, therefore, carries the patronymic 'Poulastya.'

‡ *Gandharvas* are the celestial musicians who are known as much for their good looks as they are for their musical accomplishments.

though they are happening right before our eyes!' The boys continued to sing, their pleasing voices blending in sweet harmony. One of the sages affectionately gave them a water pot. Another sage, equally pleased, gave them a set of clothes. They exclaimed, 'What a wondrous tale! Its rules of composition shall be the foundation for all poets henceforth!'

Rāma happened to see the two young bards as he passed on the royal highway. He took the boys, Kuśa and Lava, with him to his palace. Rāma, the slayer of his enemies, honoured them there, for indeed, they were worthy of honour. The king, the scorcher of his foes, sat on his golden, celestial throne surrounded by his ministers and his brothers. Gazing at the handsome young boys holding their *vīṇās,* he said to Lakṣmaṇa, Bharata and Śatrughna, 'Listen to this tale set in this new metre as it is sung by these boys in their sweet, divine voices! This is a unique and wonderful story and it is exquisitely rendered by these ascetic bards who appear to carry all the marks of royalty!'

Encouraged by Rāma's words, the boys sang softly, displaying their musical talents. And as Rāma listened to them, he allowed himself to be drawn into the tale.

# *Chapter Three*

'Among all the victorious kings engendered by Prajāpati who ruled the earth in the days of old, one was named Sagara. He never went anywhere without his sixty thousand sons and he caused the entire ocean to be dug up. It was in his royal clan of Ikṣvāku that the ancient tale of the Rāmāyana was born and was told. This is the tale that I shall relate now from its beginning to its end. It is filled with *dharma, artha* and *kāma.** Listen to it with a pure heart.

'The great country of Kosalā lay on the banks of the river Sarayū. It was prosperous and beautiful and was inhabited by wealthy and contented people. Its capital was the city of Ayodhyā, famous in the three worlds, for it had been established by Manu, lord of all men.

Ayodhyā was a well-planned city. Its roads were wide, and as long as sixty *yojanās.* They were strewn with flowers and always sprinkled with water to keep the dust down. King Daśaratha ruled from there and protected his realm like Indra protected heaven. Ayodhyā's wooden gates were symmetrical, beautifully proportioned and were adorned with fine carvings. Its markets were well laid-out and the city's fortifications were carefully constructed by skilled artisans. Ayodhyā was filled with bards and musicians and its wealthy citizens hoisted colourful banners on their roofs.

Like a young bride adorned by a girdle of green, Ayodhyā was surrounded by gardens and groves. Its impenetrable fortifications were girt by a deep moat, making it impossible for enemies to enter the city. Horses,

* *Dharma* (righteous duty), *artha* (resources) and *kāma* (desire) are three of the four goals of Hindu life (*puruṣārthas*), the fourth being *mokṣa* (liberation).

elephants, camels and mules added to the city's wealth. Representatives from tributary states made their home in Ayodhyā and people from different lands traded there without obstacle or difficulty.

Ayodhyā was like Amarāvatī, Indra's celestial city. Its tall and stately mansions with their jewelled upper chambers shone like mountain peaks, adorning the city that was filled with gems and wealth. Groups of enchanting women wandered through the streets, enhancing the city's beauty. Even the houses of common people were carefully constructed so that they had no holes or leaks and they all stood on level ground. They were stocked with the finest rice and the water in Ayodhyā tasted like sugarcane juice. The music from drums, horns and stringed instruments filled the air. It was the best city on earth, equal to the celestial city in which the enlightened ones lived as a reward for their merit.

The best of men lived in Ayodhyā's beautiful homes. These men never shot an arrow at a retreating enemy nor at the unarmed. They were such skilled archers that they could locate and kill an enemy just by following the sounds that he made. They used their strong arms to kill roaring lions and tigers and maddened boars in the forests. Thousands of these great warriors lived in Daśaratha's city. There were also *brahmins* who performed sacrifices. They were learned in all the six branches of the Vedas and were so virtuous that they increased the value of the sacrificial offerings one thousand fold. In fact, they were like the great celestial sages and they strove for the welfare of all the citizens.

Ayodhyā was ruled by the great King Daśaratha who was learned in the Vedas. He was far-sighted and illustrious and he was loved by his people. The greatest of all the Ikṣvāku warriors, he had performed many sacrifices. Dedicated to *dharma,* Daśaratha was disciplined, equal to the best of seers and was known in the three worlds as a royal sage. The mighty Daśaratha was victorious over his enemies but he was loyal to his friends. He had complete control over his senses. His wealth and prosperity rivalled that of Indra and Kubera. Like the glorious Manu had protected his realm, so Daśaratha lived on earth and protected it.

Always associated with the truth, King Daśaratha supported the three upper castes and ruled his city the way Indra ruled Amarāvatī. The people who lived in Daśaratha's city were happy, learned and virtuous. There was no greed, for each was satisfied with what he had and spoke the truth. No one was poor in Ayodhyā. People lived happily with their cows, horses and families and with what wealth they had. Nowhere in Ayodhyā would you a see a man who was lustful, cruel or miserly, nor one who was illiterate nor an atheist. Men and women were righteous, disciplined and happy. They resembled the great sages in their conduct and behaviour. Everyone adorned themselves with earrings, coronets and necklaces. They bathed every day and anointed their bodies with sweet-smelling unguents. No one ate impure food nor did they let their neighbours go hungry. Just as no one was unadorned, so too, there was no one with a distracted mind.

Even though Ayodhyā had thousands of *brahmins*, people did not neglect the performance of household sacrifices and rituals. *Brahmins* were committed to the performance of public rituals and were allowed to accept gifts. They were learned and had conquered their senses because of their exalted characters. There were no unbelievers, nor were there any ignorant or unrighteous people in Ayodhyā. There were no libertines either. There was no sadness or poverty. Men and women were beautiful and wealthy and they were all devoted to their king.

A guest was honoured as a god in the homes of all four castes. People took refuge in the truth and lived well into old age. The *kṣatriyas* placed the *brahmins* first and the *vaiśyas* followed the *kṣatriyas*. And the *śūdras*, according to their duty, served the other three castes. Ayodhyā was full of warriors who were like the Fire, handsome and energetic. Skilled in the arts of warfare, they protected the city like fierce lions guarding their mountain lairs. They had the best of horses from Kāmboja and Bāhlika born of the celestial steed Vanāyu. The warriors also had elephants, as large and strong as the Vindhya mountains, whose temples ran with ichor. Protected by these mighty elephants of the Bhadra, Mandra and Mṛga breeds, Ayodhyā* was impossible to conquer. Thus, it was appropriately named and had gates with enormous padlocks. Ruled by a king equal to Indra, that city which was adorned with beautiful houses and thousands of worthy men, shone with a brilliance that could be seen for miles.

---

* 'Ayodhyā' means "should not be attacked."

# Chapter Four

Even though he had performed many austerities in order to have a son, Daśaratha, who was great-souled, glorious and righteous, remained without an heir. One day, the king considered the matter again and thought, 'Why don't I perform a sacrifice to ensure the birth of a son?' The wise monarch called together his ministers who were all intelligent men and said to his chief minister Sumantra, 'Bring the priests and teachers here immediately!'

But Sumantra took the king aside. 'Listen to the story that was told to me a long time ago by a priest who had performed many sacrifices!' he said. 'The blessed Sanatkumāra told this story among a gathering of sages about the matter of your having a son.

'It had been ordained that Vibhāṇḍaka, a descendent of Kaśyapa, would have a son named Ṛṣyaṣṛnga. This boy would live in the forest all alone with his father and would have no contact with other men and women. He would observe the double vows of *brahmacarya** that are well known in the three worlds and that are honoured by all the *brahmins*. Ṛṣyaṣṛnga would pass the time looking after his father and performing sacrifices.

'At this time, the brave and glorious king Romapāda ruled in the land of Anga. But his misdeeds resulted in a terrible drought that inflicted great suffering on all beings. This made the king very unhappy. He said to the elders and the *brahmins* that had gathered at his court, "You are all learned in the moral and social traditions of the world! Instruct me in a suitable method of expiation!" The *brahmins* who were well-versed in

* The double vows of *brahmacarya,* the student stage of a young man's life, are celibacy and austerity.

the Vedas replied, "Do whatever is necessary to bring the son of the sage Vibhāṇḍaka here with all the respect due to him! Then offer him the hand of your daughter, Śāntā, in marriage."

'The king began to think about the best way to bring Ṛṣyaṣṛnga to his court. He decided that he would send his ministers and priests to bring the young man to the city with all the appropriate honours. But the ministers were apprehensive when they heard the king's plans. They did not want to fetch Ṛṣyaṣṛnga because they feared his powers. At the same time, they did not want to incur the king's displeasure and so they began to think of ways to lure the young man into the city. They said to the king, "Let the sages's son be brought here by courtesans. The drought will end when you offer him your daughter in marriage!"

'And when Ṛṣyaṣṛnga becomes Romapāda's son-in-law, a son will be born to you, Daśaratha. This is what Sanatkumāra, surrounded by sages, said to me,' said Sumantra. Daśaratha was delighted to hear this and asked Sumantra to tell him in detail how Ṛṣyaṣṛnga was brought to Romapāda's kingdom.

In response to the king's request, Sumantra said, 'I will tell you how Ṛṣyaṣṛnga was brought to Romapāda's capital. Listen to this story with your ministers!

'Romapāda's priests and ministers announced that they had thought of a fool-proof plan. "Ṛṣyaṣṛnga is an ascetic, engrossed in the performance of austerities. He knows nothing about women or the pursuit of pleasure. We will bring him to the city by luring him here with sensual pleasures that agitate men's minds! Let the most beautiful courtesans adorned in all their finery go to him. They will seduce him with their wiles and bring him here." The king agreed to the plan and the priests and ministers went to tell the courtesans.

'The beautiful women went into the great forest and put their plan into action within sight of Ṛṣyaṣṛnga's hermitage. But the resolute son of the sage Vibhāṇḍaka, who had lived all his life with only his father for company, did not venture out of the hermitage. Never in his life had that ascetic young man seen a man or a woman or any creature that lived in a town or a city.

'One day, for some reason, Ṛṣyaṣṛnga came to the place where the courtesans were. He could not help but notice those lovely women who were wearing colourful clothes and singing in their sweet voices. They saw the ascetic and came up to him. "Who are you, *brahmin*?" they asked. "What are you doing here? We want to get to know you so tell us what you are doing all alone in this dense forest." Ṛṣyaṣṛnga had never seen such beauty and he was utterly entranced. He replied, "I am the son of Vibhāṇḍaka and my name is Ṛṣyaṣṛnga. Beautiful ones, our hermitage is very close by. Come there with me so that we can honour you appropriately!"

'The courtesans agreed to go with the ascetic. When they reached the hermitage, the sage's son honoured them with water to wash their feet and gave them fruits and roots to eat. The courtesans accepted his hospitality with enthusiasm but they were nervous about Vibhāṇḍaka's arrival and were in a hurry to leave the hermitage. "*Brahmin*, why don't you try our fruit? Here, eat it quickly!" they said to Ṛṣyaṣṛnga as they embraced him joyfully, offering him the various sweets they had brought with them from the city. Ṛṣyaṣṛnga accepted them thinking they were fruit, for he had never tasted anything like them before. As he ate them, he thought, "Ah! Such fruits are unknown to those who live in the forest!" Fearing Vibhāṇḍaka's return, the courtesans declined Ṛṣyaṣṛnga's offer of food, saying that they were fasting, and quickly left the hermitage.

'When they had left, that ascetic born in the line of Kaśyapa began to feel ill at ease and his heart was filled with sorrow. The very next day, he returned to the place where he had seen the beautiful, bejewelled women who had so charmed him. The courtesans were overjoyed to see the young *brahmin* walking towards them and they ran over to him and said, "Come with us to our hermitage where we will be able to entertain you better!"

'Their words struck a chord in Ṛṣyaṣṛnga's heart and he decided to go with them. As they led him into the city, it began to rain. The people rejoiced and the king knew that the sage had arrived in the city. He went to welcome Ṛṣyaṣṛnga himself. He honoured him with *arghya* water and led him in to the palace with great joy. He begged Ṛṣyaṣṛnga to grant him a boon which would protect him from Vibhāṇḍaka's anger and took him into the inner apartments. Greatly relieved, the king handed his daughter Śāntā to the sage in marriage with all due ceremony. Honoured by the people, all his desires fulfilled, Ṛṣyaṣṛnga lived happily in Romapāda's palace with his wife Śāntā.'

Sumantra continued, 'But listen further to my auspicious words, O Daśaratha. The wise sage Sanatkumāra told me what would happen next.

'In the clan of Ikṣvāku, he said, there will be born an illustrious king named Daśaratha. He will be a righteous man of his word. He will form an alliance with king Romapāda of Anga, the one who has the blessed daughter Śāntā. Daśaratha will approach Romapāda in order to beget a son. He will say, "I am childless. Unknown to you, Śāntā's husband can produce an heir for my clan. Let me take him away from here." Romapāda will consider the matter and allow his son-in-law to accompany Daśaratha. Daśaratha will joyfully take him away to perform a sacrifice. After he has got what he wants, he will gratefully honour Romapāda, the best among the twice-born. The purpose of Daśaratha's sacrifice will be to beget sons and ensure a place for himself in heaven. Daśaratha will ask Ṛṣyaṣṛnga to officiate at the sacrifice and as a result, he will have four heroic sons. They will increase the prestige of their clan and will be famous in all the worlds.

'This is what Sanatkumāra told me long ago in the age of the gods. Tiger among men, you must go to Anga and bring Ṛṣyaṣṛnga here yourself. Bring him in your mighty chariot with all the honour that is due to him.'

Daśaratha took Sumantra's advice. After taking permission from Vasiṣṭha, he went with his ministers to Anga. The entourage passed through forests and crossed many rivers. At long last, they arrived in the kingdom where Ṛṣyaṣṛnga lived. They saw the best of all the *brahmins*, the son of Vibhāṇḍaka, blazing like a fire, seated beside king Romapāda.

Romapāda honoured Daśaratha and Daśaratha was filled with joy at their friendship. When Romapāda told Ṛṣyaṣṛnga about his friendship with Daśaratha, the wise sage was pleased and blessed the alliance. Daśaratha said to Romapāda, 'I have undertaken a very important task, ruler of the earth! Please allow your daughter Śāntā and her husband to accompany me to my capital city.' Romapāda agreed and instructed Ṛṣyaṣṛnga to take his wife and go with Daśaratha. Ṛṣyaṣṛnga obeyed and Daśaratha embraced both him and his wife with deep affection as he praised the mighty king of Anga. Daśaratha bade his friend a fond farewell and then sent messengers ahead to Ayodhyā so that the citizens could decorate the city for his arrival.

The citizens of Ayodhyā were overjoyed when they heard of their king's return and immediately set about to do his bidding. Daśaratha entered the beautifully decorated city and Ṛṣyaṣṛnga was greeted with the sound of conch shells and drums when his arrival was announced. The people were delighted to see the *brahmin* entering their city, duly honoured by the terrestrial Indra as he would have been by the celestial Indra.

Ṛṣyaṣṛnga and Śāntā were taken into the inner apartments of the palace were they were honoured according to the prescriptions in the holy books. The ladies of the palace welcomed the large-eyed Śāntā and her husband with affection and happiness. Śāntā and Ṛṣyaṣṛnga, honoured even by the king himself, lived happily in Ayodhyā for some time.

The days passed easily and when Spring arrived, Daśaratha's mind turned to the sacrifice. He went to the god-like Ṛṣyaṣṛnga. He bowed before him and asked him to perform the sacrifice that would produce heirs for the Ikṣvāku clan. Ṛṣyaṣṛnga agreed and said, 'Have all the materials necessary for the sacrifice assembled and release the sacrificial horse!'

The king instructed Sumantra, the best among his ministers. 'Summon the most eloquent *brahmins* and priests!' Sumantra hurried off. With courtesy and respect, he invited all the priests who were well-versed in the Vedas and their accompanying schools of knowledge, including Vāmadeva, Jābāli, Kaśyapa, the royal priest Vasiṣṭha and other excellent *brahmins*.

The righteous King Daśaratha honoured them all and spoke to them humbly, concealing nothing. 'Despite my fervent wishes for an heir, I have no son. That is why I have decided to undertake the horse sacrifice. I want the sacrifice to be performed according to the prescriptions laid out in the sacred texts. I hope to fulfil my heart's desire with sage Ṛṣyaṣṛnga's assistance.' Led by Vasiṣṭha, the learned sages approved of the king's plan. As Ṛṣyaṣṛnga had done, they told Daśaratha to organize the collection of the sacrificial materials and release the horse. 'You have decided on a course that is in accordance with *dharma.* And you shall have four mighty sons!' they said.

The king was well-pleased with the words of the *brahmins* and he repeated them to his ministers. 'In keeping with my mentor's instructions, send out the horse accompanied by a battalion of soldiers and their commander! Prepare the sacrificial grounds on the northern bank of the river Sarayū and start performing the rites of protection as they are laid out in the sacred texts.' Daśaratha ordered his ministers to make sure that no impediments or obstacles arose during the period of the sacrifice. 'Sacrifices are often flawed by *brahmarākṣasas* who wander around and destroy the merits of the sacrifice. My sacrifice must be completed according to the prescribed rituals. You must see that all necessary precautions are taken to ensure its success.' The ministers paid their respects to the king before they departed to carry out his instructions. Dismissing the *brahmins* and the ministers, the king went into his private apartments.

When the year stipulated for the wandering of the sacrificial horse ended, the animal was brought back and the king proceeded with the latter part of the sacrifice on the Sarayū's northern banks. Led by Ṛṣyaṣṛnga, the learned priests performed the rituals prescribed in the holy books for the great-souled king. Well-pleased, the king completed this best of all sacrifices. Even for the greatest of kings, the horse sacrifice is not easy to complete, but it absolves the individual of all sin and ensures a place for him in heaven.

The king addressed Ṛṣyaṣṛnga. 'You who are true to your vows, only you can ensure the continuance of my clan!' The best of all *brahmins*, Ṛṣyaṣṛnga, said, 'It shall indeed be so! You shall have four sons who shall uplift your clan!'

After meditating for a little while, the wise *brahmin* who was learned in the Vedas said to the king, 'I will perform the rituals and recite the *mantras* prescribed in the Atharva Veda for the birth of a son. Your aim will be achieved by my recitation of these *mantras.*' The sage poured oblations into the fire as he recited the prescribed *mantras.*

The gods, *ṛṣis, gandharvas,* and *siddhas* gathered to receive their appointed portions of the sacrifice according to custom. They took their places according to hierarchy and then spoke to Brahmā, the Creator of the worlds. 'Lord, the *rākṣasa* Rāvaṇa obstructs us all because of the favours that he has received from you. He is strong and brave and none of us can subdue him. Long ago, when you were pleased with him, you gave him a boon and now we have to suffer this constant oppression. Wicked Rāvaṇa is our enemy and he has already defeated the guardians of the three worlds. Now he wants to humble Indra himself! Intoxicated with the boon from you, that awful creature crushes divine *ṛṣis*, *yakṣas, gandharvas,* gods and *brahmins*. The sun does not shine and the wind does not blow in his presence and even the mighty ocean, garlanded with waves, is stilled. We live in constant fear of that *rākṣasa* who has a terrifying face. You must think of a way to kill Rāvaṇa!'

Brahmā thought for a while and then he said, 'There is a way to kill this dissolute creature. "May I be invulnerable to gods, *gandharvas, yakṣas and dānavas*!" were the words Rāvaṇa spoke and I replied that it would be so. He was contemptuous of humans in general and so he did not ask for protection from them. Therefore, he can be killed only by a human being.'

Brahmā's words delighted and reassured the gods, the divine *ṛṣis* and all the others. At that very moment, the effulgent Viṣṇu arrived at the gathering and after he had honoured Brahmā, he took his accustomed place. The gods praised him with hymns and songs and then they said to him, 'O Viṣṇu, we plead with you for the welfare of the three worlds! The king of Ayodhyā, Daśaratha, is a righteous and truthful man, effulgent like a great sage. He has three wives and they are all chaste, beautiful and illustrious. Viṣṇu, divide yourself into four parts and go to earth as their offspring. Become a human being and destroy Rāvaṇa, the enemy of the three worlds, for he cannot be killed by gods or divine beings in battle! The *rākṣasa* Rāvaṇa, encouraged by his own strength, obstructs the gods, *gandharvas, siddhas* and divine *ṛṣis.* Destroy this creature who is the enemy of the gods, whose arrogance increases every day, whose roaring disrupts the meditation of ascetics. Release the holy ones from their fear!'

Praised by all the gods, Viṣṇu humbly asked them a question, although he already knew the answer. 'How can this king of the *rākṣasas* be killed? Tell me and I will use that very method to kill this creature who torments the *ṛṣis*!'

The gods cried out together, 'Be born as the son of a mortal woman and kill him in battle! O Scorcher of your foes, Rāvaṇa practised severe austerities for years and gratified Brahmā, the Creator of the worlds, the most revered. Brahmā was so pleased that he gave Rāvaṇa a boon by which he was invulnerable to all beings except humans. In the old days, Rāvaṇa scorned humans and so he did not include them in his boon of invulnerability. O Enemy-burner, Rāvaṇa can only be killed by a human.' Viṣṇu considered the words of the gods and decided to choose King Daśaratha as his father.

At that time, the effulgent king, the slayer of his enemies, was conducting a great sacrifice for the birth of a son. A huge being of immense strength rose out of Daśaratha's sacrificial fire, heralded by a roll of drums. His dark skin gleamed with a red glow, his hair was the colour of a lion's mane and he wore crimson robes. His voice was deep and resonant and he was adorned with all the auspicious marks. Tall and straight as a mountain peak, as mighty as a striding tiger, he wore celestial ornaments that were studded with jewels. Bright as the sun, glowing like a flame from a blazing fire, he carried a golden bowl that was decorated with silver and filled with *pāyasa.* He held the bowl out to the king, offering it to him as would a beloved wife.

'King, know that I have been sent here by Prajāpati!' he announced. Daśaratha bowed to him and said, 'You are welcome, blessed one! What can I do for you?' The man sent by Prajāpati replied, 'Today you will receive your reward for worshipping the gods. Accept this divine *pāyasa.* It will produce sons for you and make you healthy and wealthy! Ask your wives to eat this one after the other and you shall beget the sons for whom you performed this sacrifice.'

The king was delighted, and humbly he took the golden bowl that contained the gift from the gods. He honoured the marvellous being by touching his feet reverentially and his joy knew no bounds as he circumambulated the divine man. When Daśaratha accepted the celestial food, he was as happy as a man who gets a meal after not eating for days. The wondrous being gave the king the bowl and vanished.

Daśaratha's queens were overjoyed with the events and their faces glowed with a radiance like that of the late autumn moon in the night sky. Daśaratha entered the inner apartments and said to Kausalyā, 'Eat this *pāyasa* so that you can bear a son!' and he gave half of it to Kausalyā and a third of it to Sumitrā. Then he gave Kaikeyī an eighth portion and after some thought, he gave the remainder to Sumitrā. In this way, he divided the *pāyasa* among his wives. His wives were filled with joy and they felt themselves truly honoured when they received the *pāyasa.*

When Viṣṇu had become the offspring of the great-souled Daśaratha, Brahmā addressed the other gods. 'Heroic Viṣṇu, the ocean of truth, desires what is best for us all. You should create mighty beings who can change their shape at will in order to help him. They should know the arts of magic, they must be brave, as swift as the wind, resourceful, wise and equal to Viṣṇu in valour. Create invincible beings who are as handsome as divine creatures, skilled in the use of all kinds of weapons and like unto the gods themselves!

'Beget sons upon the *apsarases* and *gandharvīs,* upon the daughters of the *yakṣas* and the *pannagas,* the *ṛkṣas* and the *vidyādharas,* upon *kinnaris* and *vānarīs.* Let them have the form of monkeys and let them be equal to yourselves in valour! Long ago, I created Jāmbavān, the best among the *ṛkṣas,* in the same way. He emerged from my mouth as I was yawning!'

The gods followed Brahmā's instructions and created sons in the form of monkeys. The great-souled *ṛṣis,* the *siddhas* and the *uragas* also ensured that mighty sons were born to creatures that lived in the forest. Indra created Vālī, the king of the monkeys, equal to the king of the gods himself. Sūrya, the best among the shining ones, created Sugrīva. Bṛhaspati created the great monkey Tāra who was incomparably wise. Kubera's son was the excellent monkey Gandhamādana and Viśvakarmā created Nala. Agni created the illustrious Nīla, who blazed like the fire and was the most accomplished and bravest of all the monkeys. The two *aśvins,* resplendent in wealth and beauty, created Mainda and Dvivida. Varuṇa created Suṣeṇa and Parjanya the mighty Śarabha. Vāyu's son was the excellent monkey Hanumān, whose body was as hard as a diamond and whose speed equalled Garuḍa's. He was the mightiest and most intelligent of all the monkeys.

These heroic warriors, who could change form at will, were created in the thousands for the purpose of killing Rāvaṇa and they were unmatched in strength, courage and valour. Strong as elephants and as mighty as mountains, the *ṛkṣas, gopucchas* and *vānaras* were like their divine fathers in demeanour and courage. They could fight on foot with stones, using their nails and teeth, and they were also skilled in the use of all kinds of weapons. They could pulverize mountains and uproot huge trees, moving as swiftly as flowing water. They could tear up the earth with their feet and cause the ocean to overflow. They could even reach into the sky and take hold of the clouds.

As they wandered through the forests, they would capture rutting elephants and their roars would cause birds to fall out of the air in mid-flight. These mighty monkey leaders gave birth to other heroic monkeys. Some of them lived in the mountains while thousands of them dwelt in the forests. The leaders of the monkeys lived with the brothers Vālī and Sugrīva, the sons of Indra and Sūrya. Countless monkeys of immense strength, like banks of clouds on mountain peaks, came together to help Rāma.

When King Daśaratha's sacrifice ended, the gods took their appointed shares and returned to their own realm. The king, too, having distributed gifts at the end of the sacrifice, prepared to return to his city along with his queens, courtiers and attendants. The other kings who had come to attend the sacrifice were honoured by Daśaratha and they returned happily to their cities after paying their respects to the presiding priest, Vasiṣṭha.

Daśaratha entered Ayodhyā preceded by the priests and the *brahmins*. Then, the worthy sage Ṛṣyaṣṛnga returned to his home with his wife Śāntā and Daśaratha accompanied them for part of the journey.

Kausalyā gave birth to the fortunate Rāma, who was endowed with all the auspicious marks. This son was a part of Viṣṇu and was the joy of the Ikṣvāku clan. Just as Aditi's glory was enhanced by Indra, so, too, Kausalyā's glory was enhanced by the glory of her son. Kaikeyī gave birth to Bharata who was a quarter part of Viṣṇu. He was the essence of valour and was endowed with all the virtues. Sumitrā gave birth to Lakṣmaṇa and Śatrughna, who were heroic and skilled in the use of all kinds of weapons. They represented the remaining parts of Viṣṇu. The four princes were born one after the other and they were all virtuous, handsome and effulgent.

*Gandharvas* played celestial music and the *apsarases* danced with joy. Celestial drums sounded and flowers rained from the skies. The citizens of Ayodhyā celebrated the births with a grand festival, and the streets were filled with joyous people. Dancers, poets, singers and musicians performed everywhere and the king gave them gifts of jewels. He also distributed silver and cattle to thousands of *brahmins*.

The princes were named on the eleventh day after they were born. The oldest, the great-souled one, was named Rāma and Kaikeyī's son was named Bharata. Sumitrā's first son was named Lakṣmaṇa and the second one Śatrughna. Vasiṣṭha performed the naming ceremony with great joy and all the rituals were properly completed.

Rāma, the eldest, was the best among the princes and he was his father's beloved. He became the greatest of all beings and was equal to Brahmā himself. The illustrious and heroic Rāma was first among those who were noble and learned in the Vedas, among all those who rejoiced in virtue and derived pleasure from the welfare of others.

From their childhood, Lakṣmaṇa was most attached to his eldest brother. He was devoted to Rāma's success and did everything to please him. The fortunate Lakṣmaṇa loved Rāma more than he loved his own life. He would not sleep without his brother and even if he were given plain rice, he would not eat without Rāma. If Rāma went hunting on his horse, Lakṣmaṇa would be behind him protecting him with his bow. Śatrughna, Lakṣmaṇa's younger brother, loved Bharata in the same way, and Bharata was dearer to Śatrughna than life.

Such were the four illustrious sons of the fortunate Daśaratha. They loved their father as the gods love Brahmā, the Grandfather. The princes were learned and endowed with all the virtues. They were all-knowing, far-sighted and prudent, but even though they were renowned, they were modest.

# *Chapter Five*

Soon, King Daśaratha began to think about getting his sons married and the wise monarch consulted his teachers and elders. As he was holding discussions with his ministers, the great and illustrious sage Viśvāmitra arrived. He was eager for an audience with the king and so he said to the chief guard, 'Go at once and tell the king that I, Viśvāmitra, the son of Gādhi, born in the line of Kauśika, am here!' The guards ran into the king's audience chamber in confusion. Daśaratha and Vasiṣṭha went in person to escort Viśvāmitra into the palace. Daśaratha welcomed the sage with happiness, as Indra would have welcomed Brahmā. With great joy, Daśaratha gazed at Viśvāmitra who shone with the power of his austerities and welcomed him with the *arghya* water.

Viśvāmitra accepted the honour and asked after the welfare of the king and his family. Then he asked about Vasiṣṭha and the other sages and about all other beings, as was customary. The king happily answered the questions and they entered the palace together. Daśaratha said, 'Your visit here has made as happy as if I had obtained the nectar of immortality. Your presence is like rain in a drought, like the birth of a son to a childless man, like the recovery of wealth for a man who has lost everything. I welcome you from the bottom of my heart.

'Your glance bestows merit and deems me fortunate. My life has been fulfilled by your arrival. Tell me what I can do to please you. Long ago, you were a warrior. You have become a *brahmin* by dint of your ascetic practices. You are worthy of my undying worship and honour. Your presence has purified my kingdom. Tell me the purpose of your visit and what I can do to help you in your enterprise.'

Viśvāmitra, who was the repository of all virtue, was pleased with the king's words which were humble and sincere and gladdened the heart.

'None on earth except one from such a great clan and one schooled by Vasiṣṭha could have spoken thus,' he replied. 'I shall certainly tell you what you can do for me. And then you must do it and prove the truth of your words!

'I am conducting a ritual which will ensure that I reach my spiritual goal. But there are two *rākṣasas,* able to change form at will, who obstruct it. Just as the ritual is drawing to a close, these two *rākṣasas,* Mārīca and Subāhu, who are learned as well as mighty, throw flesh and blood on the sacrificial altar. My hard work and all my efforts are in vain because of these two creatures. Totally discouraged, I have left the area where I was performing the ritual. I cannot release my anger while I am meditating for the ritual and so I have not been able to curse them.

'Give me your oldest son Rāma, that hero with hair as dark as a crow's wing! He will be able to kill these wicked *rākṣasas* with his own divine energy and with help from me. Have no fear. I will bless him so that he becomes famous in the three worlds. The two *rākṣasas* will attack Rāma, but with no success because he is the only human capable of killing them. Though they are strong, they will be caught in the web of their own destinies.

'You did not obtain Rāma as a son by your own efforts. You cannot regard him as your son alone. I can say with certainty that the two *rākṣasas* will be killed.

'I am well aware of Rāma's virtues and his heroism, as is Vasiṣṭha and the other sages who sit here in meditation. If you want righteousness to flourish and if you desire fame on earth, then give Rāma to me! Your ministers, led by Vasiṣṭha, will advise you to do this, so send Rāma with me! Let your oldest son, the lotus-eyed Rāma, stay with me for the ten nights of the sacrifice. Do not let the auspicious time for the ritual pass. Make me happy by doing what I want and do not grieve for your son!'

Viśvāmitra fell silent after he had made this righteous speech. But his words pierced Daśaratha's heart, filling the great king with fear and grief as he trembled on his throne.

Daśaratha lost consciousness for a moment and when he had recovered himself, he said, 'My lotus-eyed Rāma is only fifteen years old. I don't think he can face the *rākṣasas* in battle! Take my entire army with me as the commander. My men are brave and heroic and skilled with their weapons. I will go with my warriors to fight the *rākṣasas.* We are capable of facing them. But do not ask for Rāma!

'With my bow and my arrows I will lead the army myself and I will fight the *rākṣasas* until my last breath. We shall protect you and you can complete your ritual without any further obstructions. I will come with you, but do not take Rāma!

'He is only a child and his education is not yet complete. He does not know strength from weakness. He does not have the required skill with weapons nor is he seasoned in battle. He cannot face the *rākṣasas* who fight unfairly!

'I cannot bear the thought of living without Rāma for even a day. Do not take him away! *Brahmin* of great vows, if you must take Rāma, then take me and my army with four divisions as well. I am sixty thousand years old and I obtained my son with great difficulty. Do not take Rāma away! He is the dearest of all my four sons. He is the eldest and he is the support of *dharma.* Do not take him away!

'How strong are these *rākṣasas*? How big are they? Whose sons are they? Who protects them? Why did you decide that Rāma could face them? *Rākṣasas* are proud of their strength and it is well known that they are wicked, that they fight by unfair means. Tell me how I can face them on the battlefield.'

Viśvāmitra said, 'The great *rākṣasa* Rāvaṇa is born in the line of Pulastya. He torments the three worlds because of a boon from Brahmā. He is strong and brave and has many *rākṣasas* around him. This Rāvaṇa, king of the *rākṣasas,* is Kubera's brother and the son of the sage Viśravas. He does not obstruct my sacrifice himself, but the mighty Mārīca and Subāhu do it on his behalf.'

After hearing what Viśvāmitra had said, Daśaratha replied, 'I cannot face these wicked creatures in battle. O knower of *dharma,* take pity on my little boy and on me, unfortunate as I am. You are my spiritual teacher, blessed one, and you are like a god to me. If the gods and the *dānavas,* the *gandharvas* and *yakṣas,* the divine birds and serpents cannot stand up to Rāvaṇa, how then can a mere mortal do so? He can defeat the best of warriors in battle. I cannot face him and his army in battle, even with all my forces and my sons.

'How can I send my young son, god-like and so inexperienced in battle, with you, O *brahmin*? The two *rākṣasas* who obstruct your sacrifice are the sons of Sunda and Upasunda. They are like Death itself on the battle-field. I cannot give you my son! Mārīca and Subāhu are experienced and skilled warriors. I might be able to fight one of them at a time. Since that is not the case, please excuse me and my family from this task.'

When Viśvāmitra heard Daśaratha's plea which was filled with affection for his son, he grew angry. 'You gave me your word that you would give me anything that I asked for. Now you go back on it! This change of heart is not worthy of the Ikṣvāku clan! If this is what you wish, then I shall return to my home. With your false promises, Daśaratha, live in happiness with your family!'

The earth trembled at Viśvāmitra's anger and even the gods became fearful. The great sage Vasiṣṭha, resolute and true to his vows, saw the earth's agitation and said to the king, 'Born in the Ikṣvāku clan, you are *dharma* incarnate on earth. You are true to your vows and duties, you are wise and illustrious. You cannot go against *dharma.* Your clan is renowned in the three worlds for its righteousness. Perform your duty and do what is right. You have said, "I will do what you want." You cannot go back on your word, Daśaratha, for you will lose the rewards of the sacrifice. Let Rāma go!

'It matters little whether Rāma is skilled in the use of weapons. The *rākṣasas* cannot harm him for he is protected by Viśvāmitra, the way the nectar of immortality is protected by fire! Viśvāmitra is *dharma* itself, he is the best among the brave, the wisest man in the world and the abode of austerities. Of all the animate and inanimate beings, of all the gods and the *ṛṣis,* the *asuras* and the *rākṣasas,* the *gandharvas* and the *yakṣas,* the *kinnaras* and the *uragas*, he knows the most about weapons.

'Long ago, the righteous sons of Kṛṣāśva gave Viśvāmitra all the weapons so that he could establish his kingdom. The sons of Kṛṣāśva are the grandsons of Prajāpati. They take many forms and they are extremely strong. Blazing with their own splendour, they are the agents of victory. The lovely Jayā and Suprabhā were the daughters of Prajāpati and they gave birth to hundreds of shining weapons.* Long ago, Jayā gave birth to

* It should be noted that special weapons in the Hindu classical texts are not physical, like bows and arrows, swords and maces. Activated by the recitation of the *mantras,* these 'weapons' can cause the opponent to be tied up in knots, for example, or fall to the ground stunned, or have his head burst into a hundred pieces. Learning to use a weapon involves learning the *mantra* that controls it. Quite often, weapons belong to the gods and so there is the weapon of Vāyu, the wind god, the weapon of Varuṇa, the sea god and so on. Weapons like these can only be used in a state of ritual purity, and the bestowing of the weapons has a spiritual dimension.

five hundred sons, all of them unmatched, able to take on any form and born for the destruction of the *asura* hordes. Soon after that, Suprabhā also gave birth to five hundred sons called the *Samhāras*. They were so mighty that they could not be overcome, nor could anyone withstand them.

'Viśvāmitra has knowledge of these weapons and this righteous sage can create other new weapons as well. This splendid ascetic is also a mighty warrior. Have no fear for Rāma, let him go with Viśvāmitra!' Reassured by Vasiṣṭha's words, Daśaratha felt better and agreed to send Rāma with the sage.

Daśaratha's relief showed on his face as he sent for Rāma and Lakṣmaṇa. When the time for their departure arrived, Rāma took the blessings of his parents and Vasiṣṭha conducted auspicious rituals. Daśaratha kissed his beloved son on the forehead, his heart overflowing with affection, and handed him over to Viśvāmitra.

# Chapter Six

As the lotus-eyed Rāma left with Viśvāmitra, Vāyu sent forth a pleasant breeze that was free of dust. Showers of blossoms rained down from the sky. Conches blew and drums sounded as the great-souled Rāma left the city.

Viśvāmitra led the way with Rāma behind him, carrying his bow, his hair dark as a crow's wing, and Lakṣmaṇa followed Rāma. Holding their bows and arrows and appearing like three-headed serpents, the two boys lit up the cardinal directions as they followed Viśvāmitra like the *aśvins* follow Brahmā.

When the three had gone one and a half *yojanās* along the southern bank of the Sarayū, Viśvāmitra spoke gently to Rāma. 'Child, let us not waste any time. Purify yourself with water and receive the *balā* and *atibalā mantras* from me. Neither fatigue, nor sickness nor age will affect you. *Rākṣasas* will not be able to harm you even when you are asleep or off guard. None on earth will have the strength of your arms and you will be unmatched in the three worlds in knowledge, skill and eloquence.

'*Balā* and *atibalā* are the mothers of all martial knowledge and when you have acquired them, you will be unrivalled as a warrior. O best of men, neither hunger nor thirst will afflict you when you recite these *mantras*. Learn them well and you shall achieve success on earth. These brilliant sciences are the progeny of Brahmā. I shall bestow them on you for none is as righteous as you are. Indeed, many of the qualities these weapons bring already belong to you. But these multi-faceted skills, nurtured by asceticism, shall also be yours.'

Happily Rāma performed his ablutions and received the *mantras* from the sage who had realized himself. Rāma shone with renewed energy after he had accepted the weapons. The boys performed the prescribed duties for their teacher and the three spent a pleasant night on the banks of the Sarayū.

When dawn broke, the great sage affectionately roused the two princes who were sleeping on a bed of grass. 'Rāma, worthy son of Kausalyā, the dawn is breaking. Rise and perform the morning worship!' The princes bathed and recited the *gāyatri,* the best of all *mantras.* Then they honoured Viśvāmitra, rich in austerities, and made preparations to go onwards.

As they went on, they came to the point where the Gangā, the divine river that flows in all three realms, meets the Sarayū. There, they saw a hermitage inhabited by mighty and glorious sages who had been practicing severe penances for thousands of years. The princes were filled with joy and said to Viśvāmitra, 'We are very curious about whose hermitage this is and who the people are who live here. Tell us about this!'

Viśvāmitra smiled and said, 'Listen then, Rāma, and I will tell you who lived here in the old days. Kandarpa, whom the wise call Kāma, once took on a corporeal body. He performed austerities here and meditated on Śiva. Meanwhile, Śiva had just been married and he passed this way with his celestial attendants. A wicked thought entered Kāma's mind and he tried to harm Śiva. Śiva snorted and Kāma was burned to ashes by Śiva's fiery eye. All Kāma's limbs fell from his body and now, because of Śiva's wrath, he has become bodiless. Since then he has been known as Ananga, 'the bodiless one,' and the place where his limbs fell to earth is known as Anga.

'This is Śiva's hermitage and the holy sages who live here have been meditating on him for a long time. These flawless men are extremely righteous. Rāma, let us stay the night here, and tomorrow we can cross the sacred rivers.'

As they were talking, the holy sages from the hermitage saw them and were delighted when they recognized Viśvāmitra. They performed the *arghya* ritual for him and welcomed Rāma and Lakṣmaṇa as honoured guests. Viśvāmitra and the princes stayed happily in the hermitage, entertained by wonderful tales.

The next day, after performing the morning worship and honouring Viśvāmitra, the princes made preparations to cross the river. Viśvāmitra thanked the sages in the hermitage and stepped into a boat along with the two princes. When they reached the other side, the princes paid their respects to the river and started along its northern bank with long strides. Soon, they saw before them a dense and impenetrable forest. Rāma asked Viśvāmitra, 'What is this terrible forest? The air is filled with the sound of crickets and over that rises the roar of lions and tigers and the screeching of birds of prey. What is the name of this awful forest?'

The glorious sage replied, 'Listen, child, and I will tell you whom this terrible forest belongs to. Long ago, two flourishing cities, Malada and Karuśa, were created by the gods. In the old days, when Indra slew Vṛtra, he was guilty of killing a *brahmin*. He was overcome by hunger and impurity so the gods and the *ṛṣis* bathed him with pots of water. The dirt and impurities fell from his body onto this place. The gods were very happy when they had purified Indra's body of the terrible sin and so was Indra. In his joy, Indra blessed this place with a great boon. "This area shall prosper and be famous all over the world. It shall be known as Malada and Karuśa for taking the dirt from my body!"* The gods were pleased with the way Indra had honoured the area.

'The two cities prospered for many years, Rāma, and they were filled with grain and wealth. Some time later, a *yakṣī* appeared here. She can change her form at will and has the strength of a thousand elephants. Her name is Tāṭakā and she is Sunda's wife. The *rākṣasa* Mārīca is her son and he is equal to Indra in valour.

That wicked Tāṭakā constantly destroys the cities of Malada and Karuśa. She lives half a *yojanā* from here, right across our path. Rāma, no one can pass through this region because of her. Use your strength to kill this wicked creature—make this region free of danger again! Now I have told you everything about this terrible forest and how, to this day, Tāṭakā has made it impassable!'

Rāma asked another question in his sweet voice. 'I have heard that *yakṣas* have very little power. How can it be that Tāṭakā has the strength of a thousand elephants?'

Viśvāmitra replied, 'Listen and I will tell you. She was given a boon that bestowed this incredible strength upon her. Long ago, there lived a mighty *yakṣa* named Suketu. Although he was very virtuous, he had no children and so he performed many great austerities. Brahmā was pleased with Suketu and, as is well known, gave him a jewel of a daughter named

---

* Malada means dirty and Karuśa means famine-striken.

Tāṭakā who had the strength of a thousand elephants, but he did not bless Suketu with a son.

'Tāṭakā grew up into a beautiful young woman and was given to Sunda, the son of Jambha, in marriage. Soon, she gave birth to a son, Mārīca the invincible, and he became a *rākṣasa* because of a curse. When Sunda was killed, Rāma, Tāṭakā decided to attack Agastya, the best of sages, along with her son. Agastya flew into a mighty rage when he saw Tāṭakā rushing towards him and he cursed Mārīca to become a *rākṣasa.* He cursed Tāṭakā as well. "You shall lose this beautiful body and become an enormous *yakṣī,* ugly and deformed, an eater of men." Enraged at being cursed like this, Tāṭakā now haunts the region where Agastya used to live.

'Rāma, for the welfare of the *brahmins* and the cows, you must kill this wicked *yakṣī,* this doer of evil deeds! No one in the three worlds but you can kill this accursed creature. Have no hesitation about killing a woman, for you must do what is best for the four castes. A king must do what will benefit his subjects, even if it is unrighteous, for such is his duty. Don't you know how Indra killed Mantharā, the daughter of Virocana, because she wanted to destroy the earth? Viṣṇu himself killed Bhṛgu's wife, the mother of the resolute Kāvya, because she wanted to rid the world of Indra! Prince, other great beings have also killed unrighteous women, so suppress your pity and kill Tāṭakā!'

Listening to Viśvāmitra's words, young Rāma, son of the best of kings and firm in his vows, felt his heart swell with courage. He said, 'My father told me to follow your instructions. I shall do whatever you ask without hesitation to honour my father's word and to bring him glory. He gave me these instructions in Ayodhyā, in the presence of the elders and the teachers. I cannot disregard what he said. My father is an honourable man and his words bind me. Therefore, I will slay villainous Tāṭakā. For the sake of the *brahmins* and the cows and for the welfare of this region, I am eager to carry out your command!'

Rāma grasped his bow and drew back the string with such force that the four directions resounded. Tāṭakā and the other forest creatures grew agitated and Tāṭakā, overcome with confusion and rage, charged in the direction from which the sound had emanated.

When Rāma saw her ugly face distorted with anger, he noticed that she was very old. He said to Lakṣmaṇa, 'Watch how I cut off the nose and ears of this creature who has mastered the art of illusion and who is practically invincible! I will not kill her because she is a woman. But I will destroy her strength and her ability to move.' Even as he was speaking, the enraged Tāṭakā charged towards him, roaring, her arms raised above her head.

Viśvāmitra ran towards Tāṭakā as he urged the princes on with shouts of encouragement. Tāṭakā raised a huge cloud of dust and for a few moments the princes could see nothing at all. Resorting to her magic powers, she let loose a rain of stones and rocks upon the two brothers. Rāma returned a shower of arrows in anger and he ran towards her and cut off her hands. Then Lakṣmaṇa attacked the creature and cut off her nose and ears.

Tāṭakā tried to confuse the princes by taking various forms, even by vanishing. All the while, she threw stones and rocks at them.

Viśvāmitra had been watching this ferocious battle and now he cried out, 'Show this wicked creature no mercy, Rāma! If you let her live, she will regain her strength through her magic powers and go back to obstructing our sacred rituals! The day is ending and such beings are practically invincible at night.' Even as he said this, there was another shower of boulders.

Viśvāmitra showed Rāma where Tāṭakā was hiding. The *yakṣinī* hurtled towards Rāma with the speed of a thunderbolt, raising a thick cloud of dust. Rāma hit her in the chest with an arrow and she fell to the ground, dead.

Led by Indra, the gods praised Rāma and honoured him when they saw that huge creature dead on the ground. With great delight, thousand-eyed Indra, the destroyer of cities, and the other gods addressed Viśvāmitra. 'Great sage, we are all very pleased that this task has been accomplished. We wish to show our appreciation to Rāma. We ask you to bestow the powerful and mighty progeny of Prajāpati on him, the ones you acquired through your austerities. He is worthy of them and he is your devoted follower. Moreover, this prince has an important task to accomplish for the gods!' As evening fell, the gods returned to their realm.

The sage was deeply satisfied with the killing of Tāṭakā and he kissed Rāma on the forehead. 'Rāma, we shall stay the night here and tomorrow we can go onwards to my hermitage.'

# *Chapter Seven*

When the night was over, Viśvāmitra smiled and spoke to Rāma sweetly. 'Illustrious prince, I am pleased with you. I shall happily bestow on you all the mighty weapons that will make you victorious over your enemies, be they gods or *asuras,* even if they are aided by the *gandharvas* and *nāgas.* These weapons are extremely powerful and can take any form at will. Mighty prince, these are the best of weapons. Prepare yourself to receive them!'

The sage purified himself and stood facing east. Then, with great pleasure, he bestowed the *mantras* on Rāma. As Viśvāmitra recited the sacred verses, the weapons appeared before Rāma in human form. They joined their palms in respect and, full of joy, they said, 'We are your attendants, Rāma!' Rāma took them by the hand and caressed them and instructed them to come to him when he called them to mind. Rāma bowed to Viśvāmitra and they continued on their journey.

As they walked along, Rāma said to Viśvāmitra, 'I have acquired the weapons that make me invincible even to the gods. Now, I want to know how to call them back.' The resolute sage taught Rāma how to recall the weapons once they had been unleashed. Once Rāma had learnt the *mantras,* the weapons appeared again in human form. Palms joined in respect, they spoke to Rāma in gentle voices. 'We are at your service. What can we do for you?' Rāma replied, 'You can go wherever you like. Help me when I call on you at the appropriate time.' The weapons bowed to Rāma and went back to where they had come from.

'What is that grove of trees over there, near the mountain? It looks like a bank of clouds,' asked Rāma as they walked further. 'It seems to be a pleasant place, filled with deer and the sweet sounds of birds. We have left the region that was so awful, it made our hair stand on end. Now we are in a place that calms the mind. Blessed one, whose hermitage is this? Tell me, have we reached the place where wicked creatures who kill *brahmins* obstruct the sacrifice?'

'Long ago, this was the hermitage of the great-souled Vāmana,*' explained Viśvāmitra. 'It is called Siddhāśrama because the austerities that were performed here bore fruit.

'At that time, Bali, the son of Virocana, had defeated all the gods, including Indra, and he ruled over the three worlds. When Bali began the performance of a huge sacrifice, the gods, led by Agni, came to this hermitage to speak to Viṣṇu. "O Viṣṇu," they said, "Bali, the son of Virocana has begun a magnificent sacrifice. You must accomplish your task before the sacrifice is completed. Brahmā grants favours to all who ask, wherever they may come from. Resort to your powers of illusion for the sake of the gods! Become a dwarf and do whatever is necessary for the welfare of all beings. Accomplish the work of the gods, Viṣṇu! Then this place will be called Siddhāśrama because of your grace!"

'Glorious Viṣṇu was born from Aditi and took the form of a dwarf to approach Bali. He asked Bali for all the ground he could cover in three strides. When his request was granted, he stepped over the three worlds, determined to do the best for all beings. Once he had subdued Bali with his strength, he handed the three worlds back to Indra.

'This hermitage which banishes fatigue belonged to Vāmana in the old days. It belongs to me now because I was his devotee. The *rākṣasas* who impede the sacrifice come to this very hermitage. It is here that you will have to kill them. We shall reach my hermitage today, which is as much yours as it is mine!'

The sages who lived there saw Viśvāmitra approaching and they greeted him with enthusiasm. They honoured him and welcomed the princes. The princes rested for a little while. Then they went to Viśvāmitra and suggested that he begin his initiation for the sacrifice without any further delay. The sage calmed his mind and began the preparatory meditation. The princes also spent the night in meditation.

The next morning, the two princes, who knew what was appropriate, said to Viśvāmitra, 'Blessed one, tell us at what point in the ritual the

* Viṣṇu's incarnation as a dwarf through which he reconquered the three worlds for the gods.

*rākṣasas* attack. We must be prepared for that moment so that we can protect the sacrifice.' The sages were delighted when they saw that the young men were eager to do battle. 'Viśvāmitra has taken a vow of silence as the first step in the ritual,' they said. 'From now on, you will have to keep watch for six nights.'

The princes kept watch over the forest hermitage for the next six nights. They sat guarding the sage resolutely, armed with their bows. The days went by and on the sixth day, Rāma said to Lakṣmaṇa, 'Today, you must be alert!'

As he was speaking, eager for battle, the sacrificial fire tended by Viśvāmitra and the other sages, blazed up. The sacrifice continued with the recitation of *mantras* and within moments, a terrifying sound came out of the sky. As clouds cover the sky in the monsoon, so the two *rākṣasas* bore down on the sacrifice with the aid of their magical powers. Mārīca, Subāhu and their terrifying attendants poured forth a shower of blood.

Rāma saw the *rākṣasas* descending from the sky and turned to Lakṣmaṇa. 'Watch me get rid of these evil flesh-eating creatures with the Mānava weapon, the way the wind dispels the monsoon clouds!' he cried. Rāma hurled the shining weapon in anger, straight onto Mārīca's chest. The *rākṣasa* was thrown one hundred *yojanās* and landed in the ocean. Felled by the arrow, Mārīca whirled around in confusion before he lost consciousness. Looking over at the senseless heap, Rāma said to Lakṣmaṇa, 'Look, Lakṣmaṇa, how this weapon powered by Manu's righteousness has knocked Mārīca unconscious without killing him! But I will kill these other blood-drinking, disgusting, wicked *rākṣasas* whose mischief disrupts the sacrifice!'

Rāma grabbed Agni's weapon and threw it towards Subāhu, who fell to the ground as soon as he was hit. Rāma killed the other *rākṣasas* with Vāyu's weapon, much to the delight of the sages. They honoured Rāma as they had honoured Indra long ago. When the sacrifice had been completed, Viśvāmitra noticed that all the four directions had been cleared of trouble. 'I have accomplished my aim, Rāma,' he said. 'And you have fulfilled your teacher's request. You have made the Siddhāśrama live up to its name!'

Rāma and Lakṣmaṇa passed the night pleasantly, thrilled that they had accomplished their mission. At dawn, they performed their ablutions and the morning worship before they approached Viśvāmitra. They bowed to the sage who blazed like the fire and said to him in their gentle voices, 'We present ourselves as your servants! What are your commands? Tell us what you want done.'

'The king of Mithilā, Janaka, is performing a magnificent and righteous sacrifice which we are all going to attend,' said Viśvāmitra. 'You must come with us. You shall see a truly marvellous jewelled bow there. This shining bow of immeasurable strength was given to Janaka by the gods at another sacrifice, a long time ago. Since none of the gods nor the *gandharvas,* neither the *asuras* nor the *rākṣasas* are able to string the bow, how can a mere man possibly do so? Many great rulers have tested their strength against this bow, Rāma, but none have been able to string it. If you come with us, you will see Janaka's golden bow, and be able to attend the wonderful sacrifice.' Will win Sita if he succeeds

The sages and the two princes left for Mithilā after honouring the forest deities. 'May good fortune attend you! Now that my purpose has been achieved, I am leaving Siddhāśrama and going to the northern banks of the Gaṅgā, to Mount Himavat, the best of mountains,' said Viśvāmitra as he circumambulated the hermitage and set off towards the north. Viśvāmitra was accompanied by one hundred carts filled with his disciples who were all learned sages. Even the birds and the beasts of the forest followed him for part of the way.

After travelling a long distance, the group stopped on the banks of the river Śoṇā at sundown. They bathed and performed the evening rituals and those sages of limitless power sat around Viśvāmitra. Rāma and Lakṣmaṇa honoured all the sages and then took their places beside Viśvāmitra.

# *Chapter Eight*

The next morning, Viśvāmitra woke the princes. 'Rāma, may good fortune attend you. Dawn is breaking and the morning twilight shall soon pass. Rise, for we must continue our journey.' Rāma performed the morning worship and made preparations to depart. 'The river Śoṇā is sandy and shallow,' he said. 'Where shall we cross it?' Viśvāmitra replied that the *ṛṣis* had told him where to ford the river and went further along the bank.

At midday, they saw the great river Gangā, beloved of the sages. The sacred waters were filled with swans and cranes and all kinds of waterbirds and the sight filled the travellers with joy. They stopped at her banks and after they had bathed, they honoured the gods and the ancestors. Then they lit the sacred fires and ate the sanctified offerings that were as delicious as the nectar of immortality. They sat around the great sage, their minds at peace and their hearts filled with joy.

'I want to hear all about the Gangā, blessed one,' said Rāma. 'The Gangā flows in all three worlds. How does she reach the ocean, the lord of all rivers?'

Viśvāmitra began the story of Gangā's birth. 'The king of mountains is named Himavat. He is the repository of all precious metals. He had two daughters whose beauty was unmatched on earth. Their mother, Himavat's beloved wife, was the slim-waisted Menā, daughter of Meru. The older daughter was named Gangā and the second one was named Umā.

'The gods had chosen Himavat's older daughter for the fulfilment of their aims. They begged Himavat to give them Gangā, the river that flows through the three worlds. Himavat was bound to righteousness and desired the welfare of the world, so he gave Gangā, the one who chooses her own path and purifies the world, to the gods. They accepted her gratefully and went away.

'Himavat's other daughter remained unmarried but she grew rich in austerities as she undertook difficult vows and performed great penances. The king of mountains gave this daughter, Umā, so intent on penance and revered by the world, to Śiva.

'Both Himavat's daughters, the river Gangā and the goddess Umā, are honoured by the worlds. I have told you everything about how Gangā reached the heavens.'

Rāma and Lakṣmaṇa praised Viśvāmitra's story and then asked, 'You have told us a tale that is full of good things, *brahmin*! But tell us more about Himavat's elder daughter. You know the complete story. Tell us in detail how she came to be connected with celestial beings as well as with mortals. How did Gangā, the purifier of the worlds, come to flow through the three realms?'

Viśvāmitra continued his story. 'Long ago, Rāma, the great ascetic Śiva was married to the goddess Umā. He was overcome with desire when he saw her and soon they began to make love. One hundred celestial years went by in their lovemaking, but despite that no child was born to them.

'The gods grew increasingly agitated and thought, "Who will be able to contend with a being born of this union?" They approached Śiva and bowed before him. "Best of gods, you have the world's welfare at heart, we bow to you. There is no one in the world who can bear your effulgence and might. Great ascetic, why don't you remain absorbed in austerities prescribed in the holy books along with the goddess? Retain your seed for the welfare of the worlds! Protect the worlds from destruction!"

'Śiva agreed to contain his seed within himself. "Umā and I will hold back our reproductive fluids so that the worlds can live in peace. But who will bear the semen that has already been released from my body?" The gods replied that the earth would bear the seed that had been released. Śiva let his semen fall and it covered all the mountains and the forests of the earth.

'The gods urged Agni, the eater of oblations, and Vāyu: "Quickly, enter Śiva's semen!" They did so and a huge mountain of semen was formed. It was covered with a forest of reeds which shone with the splendour of the sun. The effulgent Kārtikeya was later born from this blazing splendour. The gods and celestial *ṛṣis* were filled with happiness and they worshipped Śiva and the goddess.

'But Umā was outraged. Her eyes blazing with anger, she cursed the gods. "Since my desire for a son ended in this sterile union, the same thing shall happen to all your wives. From this day onwards, your wives shall be barren!" Then she cursed the earth. "You shall take many forms and be a wife to many men. You shall never know the pleasure of having a son and you shall endure my wrath because you prevented me from having a child!"

'Śiva saw that the gods were terribly disappointed but he prepared to depart for the north. He settled on a peak named Himāvatprabhava with the goddess and they continued their austerities there.

'I have told you the story of Umā in great detail, Rāma. Listen now, along with Lakṣmaṇa, to the story of Gangā.

'While Śiva was absorbed in his mighty penance, the gods and *ṛṣis* needed a commander for their army. Led by Agni, they went to Brahmā. They bowed to him and said, "The god you appointed long ago as the commander of our forces is practising austerities with the goddess. You know what the right course of action is. Act for the welfare of the worlds—you are our only refuge!"

'Brahmā, the grandfather of the universe, reassured the gods with sweet words. "The goddess' curse, that your wives shall be barren, cannot be repudiated. It will hold true in all circumstances. But Agni shall create a son on the celestial Gangā and he, a scorcher of his foes, shall be the military commander of the gods. Gangā will treat him like her own son and Umā will accept this solution." The gods were pleased that their mission had been accomplished and they bowed to Brahmā and left.

'The gods then went to Mount Kailāsa, the repository of all metals, and urged Agni to produce a son. 'Eater of oblations, consider what must be done for the benefit of the gods. Release your semen into Gangā!' Agni agreed and so the gods went to Gangā. 'Goddess, do what is dear to the gods and accept this seed into your womb!'

'Gangā assumed the form of a divinely beautiful woman. Agni spilled his seed all over her the moment he saw her. She was drenched with Agni's semen, even her veins seemed filled with it. Gangā cried out to Agni, who was the priest of the gods, 'I cannot bear the intensity of your ejaculation! My body burns like a fire and my mind is completely confused!'

Agni told her to place the foetus at the foot of the Himālayas. Gangā released the effulgent foetus that glowed with the splendour of the finest gold. As it was discharged, it covered the earth in pure, shining gold. Its acidity produced silver, copper and iron while its residue gave rise to zinc and lead. The earth received all these metals into herself but the place where the foetus had fallen glowed brightest of all. The mountains and the forests turned into an especially lustrous gold called jātarūpa.

'Indra and the other gods gave the child thus born to the six Kṛttikās to nurse. They all produced milk for him as soon as he was born and decided among themselves that they would be his mothers together. The gods told them that the child would be called Kārtikeya and that he would be famous in the three worlds.

'The Kṛttikās bathed the shining child and called him Skanda because he had slipped out of the womb. When the Kṛttikās' breasts filled with milk, the child developed six faces so that he could suckle from all six at the same time. He grew into a young man in a single day by drinking their milk and was able to rout *daitya* armies with his own power. Led by Agni, the gods anointed him the commander-in-chief of their forces.

'Now I have told you the story of Gangā in detail and about the birth of Kārtikeya, a tale that bestows great merit,' said Viśvāmitra and went on to tell another tale.

'Long ago, the king of Ayodhyā was a brave man named Sagara and his subjects loved him dearly. But he had no children. His senior wife, Keśinī, the princess of Vidarbhā, was truthful, righteous and virtuous. His second wife was Sumatī, the daughter of Ariṣṭanemi and her beauty was unmatched on earth.

'The king went with his wives to a mountain named Bhṛguprasravaṇa in the Himālayas to perform austerities. After one hundred years had passed, the sage Bhṛgu, best among the truth seekers, was gratified and gave Sagara a boon. "You shall have many sons, and you shall achieve fame and renown on earth! Child, one of your queens shall give birth to sixty thousand sons and the other to a single son who shall continue your lineage."

'The queens were thrilled and bowed to the sage, "Which one of us will have the single son and which one many? Your words will come true and we would like to know." Bhṛgu said that it was for them to decide. "One valiant and renowned son who will perpetuate the dynasty or many—which will you choose?" he asked. In the presence of the king, Keśinī chose to have the single son who would carry on the family. Sumatī, who was Garuḍa's sister, chose to have the sixty thousand brave sons. The king honoured the sage and returned to his city with the queens.

'Time passed and Keśinī gave birth to a son who was named Asamanja. And Sumatī gave birth to a pumpkin. Sixty thousand sons emerged from it when it was split open. Their wet nurses placed them in a pot of butter and cared for them there. After a number of years, they grew into young boys. It took a long time for Sagara's sons to grow into handsome, brave, young adults.

Sagara's oldest son, Asamanja, would grab the little boys and toss them into the waters of the Sarayū, laughing as he watched them flail around. He enjoyed harassing the citizens of Ayodhyā and so his father banished him from the city. But Asamanja's son Anśuman was a brave and well-spoken young man and he was loved by everybody.

'After a number of years, Sagara decided to perform a great sacrifice. He began the sacrifice without delay, along with priests who were learned in the Vedas.'

'I want to hear more about this. How did my ancestors perform the sacrifice?' asked Rāma.

'Listen and I will tell you about the great-souled Sagara's sacrifice,' said Viśvāmitra smiling.

'Himavat, the best of mountains, was Śiva's father-in-law. There is a place on the earth where Himavat and the Vindhya mountain stand close, looking at each other. The area between them is uncommonly good for sacrifices and it was here that Sagara began his rituals. Anśuman, the mighty warrior and skilled charioteer, was appointed to protect the sacrificial horse as it wandered.

'Indra assumed the form of a *rākṣasa* and stole the horse on the day it was to be sacrificed. The priests saw the horse being carried off and they ran to Sagara, crying, "Today is the day of the sacrifice and the horse has been stolen! Kill the horse thief! It will be very inauspicious if the sacrifice remains incomplete! You must do whatever is necessary to ensure that the ritual is not interrupted!"

'The king addressed his sixty thousand sons in the midst of the huge assembly. "This sacrifice was being performed with all the *mantras* required to protect it. I cannot understand how the horse has been stolen. My sons, may good fortune attend you! Go at once and scour the entire earth, garlanded with oceans. Search every inch of the earth until you find the horse and the thief. I have been initiated into the sacrifice so I shall stay here with Anśuman and the priests until you return with the horse. May all go well with you!"

'The valiant princes were filled with happiness and went off to search the earth as their father had instructed. They looked carefully over every inch of its surface and then they began to dig into the earth with their fingernails, which were as hard as diamonds.

'The earth cried out in pain when she was pierced with those diamond-hard nails and cruel ploughs. *Nāgas, asuras, rākṣasas* and other earth creatures screamed as they were killed during the digging of the earth. The heroic princes dug the earth sixty thousand *yojanās* deep, as if they were trying to penetrate the underworld. They dug up the whole of Jambudvīpa with all its mountains in search of the horse.

'Then the gods, *gandharvas, asuras* and *uragas* grew worried and went to see Brahmā. Greatly agitated, they bowed to him and said, "Blessed one, the entire earth is being torn up by Sagara's sons. They are killing all kinds of creatures in their search for the horse thief!"

'Brahmā calmed the gods who were terrified at this impending disaster. "The earth belongs to Viṣṇu. He upholds it in the form of the sage Kapila. He knows the eternal earth is being violated by the sons of Sagara. This destruction will not last much longer." The gods were reassured and went back to their homes.

'Meanwhile, Sagara's sons continued to dig enthusiastically. When they had dug up the entire earth, they went back to their father. They bowed to him and said, "We have searched every corner of earth and in the process, we have killed gods, *dānavas, rākṣasas, piśācas* and *kinnaras.* But we have found neither the horse nor the thief. We don't know what to do next. Consider the matter and give us further instructions."

'Sagara was angry. "Go and dig up the earth again and find the thief. Do no return until your mission has been accomplished! May good fortune go with you!"

'And so the sixty thousand sons of Sagara went back to dig up the earth. They dug and dug until they reached the underworld. As they were digging, they saw the mighty elephant Virūpākṣa, who bears the earth, with its mountains and forests, on his head. When Virūpākṣa grows weary and moves his head, there is an earthquake. Sagara's sons honoured the elephant, the guardian of the quarter, and dug further into the underworld.

'Since they had already dug up the east, they now dug up the south. In that quarter, they saw another great elephant, Mahāpadma, and they were filled with wonder for he was the size of a huge mountain. He, too, carried the earth on his head. They honoured him and continued to dig towards the west. There, they saw Saumanasa, the elephant guardian of that region. They bowed to him and asked after his welfare. They dug further towards the north where they saw the elephant Himapaṇḍara, supporting the earth on his massive body. They honoured him as they had done the others and they proceeded to dig into the underworld.

'They dug in a north-easterly direction, tearing up the earth with fury. They came upon the eternal Viṣṇu in the form of the sage Kapila. The stolen horse grazed close by him. They thought he was the one who had destroyed their father's sacrifice and they charged towards him in anger, shouting, "Stop! You are the wicked thief who stole our sacrificial horse! Know that the sons of Sagara have come to get you!" Kapila grew angry and snorted and all the sixty thousand sons of Sagara turned to ashes in an instant.

'Sagara grew anxious about his sons' long absence and said to Anśuman, his grandson, who shone with his own splendour, "You are brave and learned and share the lustre of your forefathers. Go and search for your uncles and the horse thief! Take your bow and arrows with you for you will have to fight the many powerful creatures who live in the earth. Honour those who are worthy of honour and kill those who obstruct the sacrifice. Accomplish your task so that my sacrifice can be completed."

'Given such clear instructions by the great-souled Sagara, Anśuman took his bow and set off with long strides. He followed the path dug by his mighty uncles into the earth. He saw the elephant guardian of the quarter being honoured by *dānavas, rākṣasas, daityas, piśācas,* birds and serpents. He bowed to the elephant and asked after his welfare and then he inquired about his uncles and the horse thief.

'The elephant replied affectionately, "Anśuman, you will fulfil your promise and return with the horse in a short time!" Anśuman honoured the other elephant guardians appropriately in a similar fashion and asked the same questions of them. All the elephants, who were eloquent and knew the truth, said that he would return with the horse. Anśuman followed their instructions and went quickly to the spot where his uncles had been burned to ashes. He was filled with sorrow when he saw the heap of ashes and wept for those that had died. Overcome with grief, Anśuman saw the sacrificial horse grazing nearby.

'He wanted to perform the funeral rites for the dead princes and looked around for a body of water. But he could see no water there. He scanned the area with his sharp eyes and suddenly noticed Garuḍa, the king of the birds, swift as the wind, who was the brother of his uncles' mother.

'"Do not grieve," said Garuḍa. "The princes were killed for the welfare of the worlds. You cannot perform their funeral rites with terrestrial water because they were killed by the incomparable Kapila. You must immerse your uncles' ashes in the Gangā. She is the older daughter of the mountain and the purifier of the worlds. Sagara's sons will go to heaven when their ashes are scattered in the water of that river, so dear to all the worlds. Take the horse and help your grandfather complete his sacrifice."

'Anśuman took the horse and went away. He returned to Sagara and told him everything Garuḍa had said. Sagara completed the sacrifice but his mind dwelt on Garuḍa's words. He went back to his city after the sacrifice was over but he could not think of a way to bring the Gangā to earth. Pondering the problem, he ruled for thirty thousand years and then went to heaven.

'When Sagara died, Rāma, his subjects made Anśuman king. Anśuman was a good king and he had an equally great son known as Dilīpa. Anśuman handed over the kingdom to Dilīpa and went into the mountains to practice austerities. After thirty-two thousand years of penance, Anśuman grew rich in austerities and went to heaven.

'Dilīpa knew about the death of his great-uncles and it filled him with sorrow, but he could think of no solution to the problem. He worried about how he could bring the Gangā to earth and perform the funeral rites which would help them to cross over into heaven. Even as he worried about how he could possibly fulfil his duty, a righteous son named Bhagīratha was born to him. Dilīpa performed many sacrifices and ruled for thirty thousand years. Unable to find a solution to the problem of his forefathers, he grew ill and finally died. He anointed Bhagīratha king and went to Indra's realm by virtue of his own merit.

'Bhagīratha was a royal sage and beloved of his people. Though he wished for a son, he had no children. So he went to Gokarṇa to practice austerities. He stood in a circle of five fires, his arms stretched above his head. He ate only once a month and controlled his senses. He stood in this awesome position for one thousand years and finally, Brahmā, the lord of all creatures, was pleased with him.

'Brahmā came with the other gods to Bhagīratha who was still practising austerities and said to him, "Bhagīratha, lord of all peoples, I am pleased with you. Choose a boon!" Bhagīratha joined his palms in respect and bowed to Brahmā. "If I have pleased you, if my austerities have borne fruit, then let me complete the funeral rites for the sons of Sagara. My forefathers will go to heaven only if their ashes are scattered in the waters of the Gangā. As my second boon, I ask that I have an heir so that my family is not extinguished."

'"Bhagīratha, mighty warrior, your wishes are honourable. It shall be so! May good fortune attend you!" said Brahmā sweetly. "Gangā is the older daughter of the mountain. You must get Śiva to bear the impact of her descent from heaven. The earth will not be able to endure the force with which she will descend. I see no one other than Śiva, the trident bearer, capable of withstanding this." Then Brahmā and all the gods returned to their realm.

'After Brahmā had left, Bhagīratha stood on his big toe, pressing its tip into the earth, for one hundred years. Finally, Śiva spoke to him. "Best of men, I am pleased with you and will do what you ask. I will bear Gangā on my head."

'Then Gangā, honoured in all the worlds, took the form of a mighty river and descended from the sky with tremendous force onto Śiva's auspicious head. The mighty Gangā thought, "I will carry Śiva into the underworld with the force of my streams!" But Śiva knew her thoughts and grew angry. He decided to make her disappear.

'Gangā fell onto Śiva's head and got entangled in his matted locks which seemed like the Himālayas. She could not find her way out and reach the ground. Confused by the abundance of Śiva's locks, Gangā wandered around in his hair for a countless number of years. When Bhagīratha did not see Gangā on earth, he propitiated Śiva for another long period. Śiva was gratified and let Gangā fall into the Bindusaras lake.

'The roaring waters made a tremendous noise as they fell from Śiva's head onto the earth. Gods, *ṛṣis, gandharvas* and *siddhas* gathered to watch the descent of the Gangā from the sky. Shining with their own splendour, they came with their horses and elephants to attend this marvellous event in their chariots that were as large as cities. The effulgence of the gods and the brilliance of their jewels lit up the sky with the brightness of a hundred suns.

'Flashing fish and restless water creatures were thrown up by the descending torrent and shot through the sky like lightning. Foam and spray filled the air like flocks of swans or autumn clouds. In some places, the waters flowed straight and swift, in others, they wound and meandered. They rose into the sky, they broadened as they flowed swiftly and quietly. The torrent crashed against rocks and against itself and rose before sinking to the earth. The waters that fell from Śiva's hair were clear as crystal and sanctified everything they touched.

'The *ṛṣis* and *gandharvas* and earth dwellers sprinkled the waters of the Gangā on their bodies and were purified by their touch. Even those who had been thrown out of heaven by a curse were made free of impurities when they poured the water onto themselves. Cleansed of their wicked deeds and restored to a state of purity, they went into the sky and re-entered heaven. Wherever the Gangā flowed, living beings sprinkled themselves with her waters and were restored to purity.

'As Gangā fell, she split into seven streams. Hlādinī, Pavanī and Nalinī flowed east, Sucakṣu, Sītā and Sindhu flowed west and the seventh stream followed Bhagīratha's chariot. The royal sage went forward in his chariot and the Gangā followed him. Gods and *ṛṣis*, all the *daityas, dānavas, rākṣasas, gandharvas, yakṣas, kinnaras, apsarases* and mighty *uragas* affectionately accompanied Gangā as she followed Bhagīratha's chariot. Wherever the king went, Gangā, the destroyer of bad deeds and the greatest of all rivers, went, too.

'Followed by the Gangā, Bhagīratha reached the ocean and entered the region where his ancestors had been reduced to ashes. He threw the ashes into the river. Then, Brahmā said to him, "Best of men, the sixty thousand sons of Sagara have crossed over into heaven and have been saved. As long as the waters of the ocean remain on earth, so long will Sagara's sons remain in heaven with the gods. Gangā will now be your daughter and she shall be known on earth by your name. This celestial river that flows in all the three worlds shall be called Bhāgīrathī. She will be known as Tripathagā because her three streams flow in the three worlds.

'"Complete the funeral rites for your ancestors and fulfil the promises you made. Your illustrious forefathers, who were so righteous, could not accomplish this goal. Even Anśuman, the most effulgent of all the people on earth, could not achieve this, though he pleaded with Gangā. Dilīpa, your father, a virtuous royal sage, equal to the divine *ṛṣis* in effulgence and equal to me in austerities, firm in his duties as a warrior, could not bring Gangā here even though he wanted to.

"'You have accomplished this magnificent task. You shall achieve fame in all the worlds. You have attained the highest *dharma* by bringing Gangā to earth. It will always be appropriate to bathe in her waters. Do so now, tiger among men, and receive the fruits of your merit. Perform the rites for your ancestors and return to your city. I, too, shall return to my realm!"

'Brahmā and the gods vanished and Bhagīratha performed the prescribed rites for the souls of Sagara's sons after he had purified himself with the waters of the Gangā. He went back to rule his kingdom since he had achieved his purpose. His subjects were delighted because his presence made them feel fulfilled and made them free of sorrow and disease.

'This is the story of Gangā in detail, Rāma, and it is a tale that bestows merit, success, long life, heirs and the attainment of heaven. May good fortune attend you!'

Rāma and Lakṣmaṇa were filled with wonder after they heard the story. They said to Viśvāmitra, 'Your story about the descent of the Gangā and the filling of the ocean is truly marvellous.' As they dwelt on Viśvāmitra's story in their minds, the evening ended.

When the new day dawned, Rāma completed his ablutions and said to the great sage, 'The night passed so quickly while we were listening to your tale and thinking about it. Let us now cross the Gangā, the greatest of all rivers. The sages have heard about your arrival and they have sent a well-equipped boat to make your journey more pleasant.'

Viśvāmitra crossed the river with a group of sages and the two princes. They disembarked on the northern shore where they saw the city of Viśālā which was as beautiful as a celestial city. Viśvāmitra approached Viśālā with the princes and along the way Rāma joined his palms in respect and asked Viśvāmitra about the city.

'Great sage, I am curious about the royal clan to whom this city belongs. Tell me all about it.'

Viśvāmitra began the history of Viśālā from ancient times.

'Listen, Rāma, and I will tell you a story about Indra.

And you shall also hear what happened in this region.

'In the old days, Rāma, in the *kṛtayuga,* the sons of Diti were powerful and the sons of Aditi* were fortunate, heroic and righteous. They began to think of ways to make themselves immortal, free of sickness and old age. They decided to churn the ocean of milk and extract the nectar of immortality from it. They used the serpent Vāsuki as the rope and Mount Mandara as the churning pole.

'After one thousand years of churning, Vāsuki crushed rocks and stones between his teeth in agony and vomited up the terrible *halāhala* poison. It rose from the sea like a flame and scorched the entire universe with its gods, *asuras* and humans. The gods sought refuge with Śiva. They appeased him with songs of praise and cried, "Save us, save us!" At that very moment, Viṣṇu arrived, bearing his discus and conch. "Whatever arose first from the churning of the ocean belongs to you because you are the foremost of the gods," he said to Śiva and smiled. "Accept the *halāhala* poison as your due for being the first born!" And then Viṣṇu disappeared. Śiva noticed that the gods were truly terrified and so he obeyed Viṣṇu's words and swallowed the poison.

'Śiva dismissed the gods who went back to churning the ocean with the *asuras.* But the mountain that they were using as a churning pole sank into the underworld. This time, the gods and the *gandharvas* praised Viṣṇu, the destroyer of Madhu. 'You are the refuge of all beings including the gods,' they pleaded. 'Help us by raising the mountain!' Viṣṇu took the form of a tortoise and plunged deep into the waters. He placed the mountain on his back and stood between the gods and the *asuras* as they continued to churn the ocean.

'The resplendent *apsarases,* the very essence of womanhood, arose from the churning waters. Sixty thousand of these beautiful women were produced and their attendants were countless in number. But none of the gods or the *gandharvas* would take them as wives and so they are known as *sādhāraṇās,* 'common to all.'

'After this came Vāruṇī, the daughter of Varuṇa and she sought a husband. The sons of Diti would not accept her so the sons of Aditi took her

* The sons of Diti are the *asuras,* the anti-gods, and the sons of Aditi are the *suras,* the gods. Hindu mythology has complex and often varied genealogies for the gods and their enemies. This story in this text declares that Aditi and Diti were their mothers.

as a wife. Diti's sons are called the *asuras* and Aditi's sons are the *suras*. The *suras* were delighted at having obtained Vāruṇī for a wife.

'The best of all horses, Ucchaiḥśravas, and the best of all gems, the Kaustubha, also appeared along with the nectar of immortality. Because of this, Rāma, there was a split in the family. Diti's and Aditi's sons began to fight with each other. In the terrible war that ensued, the heroic sons of Aditi defeated the *asuras* and Indra happily became king. He ruled over the worlds of the *ṛṣis* and the *cāraṇas*.

'Alambuṣa was a righteous son of the Ikṣvāku clan and he was known in the world as Viśāla. He founded a city named after himself at this very spot. His son was the mighty Hemacandra. After him came Sucandra, renowned in the world. Sucandra's son was Dhūmrāśva and his son was Sṛnjaya. Sṛnjaya's son was the illustrious Sahadeva and his son was the righteous Kuśa. Kuśa's son was the valiant Somadatta and his son was known as Kākutstha. Kākutstha's son Sumati, like unto a god and invincible, lives in the city of Viśālā. By Kākutstha's grace, Viśālā's kings are great-souled, brave, righteous and long-lived.

'We can spend the night here in comfort and go onwards to Mithilā in the morning.'

When King Sumati heard that Viśvāmitra had arrived in his kingdom, he went out to welcome him with his priests and his attendants. He joined his palms in respect and honoured the great sage, saying, 'Your presence in my kingdom makes me fortunate!'

# Chapter Nine

Viśvāmitra and the princes spent the night in Viśālā and were treated hospitably by the king. The next morning, they continued their journey to Mithilā. The sages that had accompanied Viśvāmitra praised beautiful Mithilā when the city came into view.

Rāma saw a hermitage outside the city that was old and deserted but still very pleasant. 'Blessed one, how come there is no sage in this hermitage?' he asked Viśvāmitra. 'Whose hermitage was this in the old days?'

The eloquent sage replied, 'Listen, Rāma, and I will tell you whom this hermitage belonged to and how it was cursed by a great soul.

'This hermitage belonged to the sage Gautama, whom even the gods honoured, and it was like a celestial place. Long ago, Gautama practised austerities here along with his wife Ahalyā. Once, knowing that Gautama was away, Indra, the thousand-eyed god and the husband of Saci, disguised himself as a sage and approached Ahalyā.

'"Slim-waisted lady, the passionate man does not wait for the right season. I want to make love to you now!" Ahalyā recognized Indra in his disguise but she was curious about the king of the gods and agreed to sleep with him. When her desire had been satisfied, she said to the best of the gods, "I am completely fulfilled, Indra! Now go from here quickly and protect yourself and me from my husband!" Indra laughed at Ahalyā's words. "You have gratified me, O lady with the lovely hips! I shall return to my own realm!"

'He left the hut after he had slept with her and went away quickly, for he feared her husband. As he was leaving, he saw Gautama enter the hermitage. The sage was so rich in austerities that he was invulnerable to the gods and the *dānavas*. Purified by the sacred waters, Gautama shone like a fire and he was carrying fuel for the ritual altar. Indra saw him and grew pale with fear.

'Gautama recognized Indra, who had done a terrible thing in his disguise as a sage. The virtuous Gautama was enraged and cried, "You have assumed my form and done a wicked thing! You will lose your testicles for what you have done!" At that very moment, the thousand-eyed Indra's testicles fell to the ground. Then Gautama cursed his wife. "You shall live on air, without food, and you shall sleep on ashes. You shall be invisible to all creatures as you do penance in this hermitage! You shall be purified only when Rāma, the invincible son of Daśaratha, comes to this forest. Wicked woman, when you offer hospitality to Rāma, you shall be freed of your lust and passion. You shall regain your earlier form in my presence!" Gautama left the hermitage and went to a beautiful peak in the Himālayas to practise austerities.

'Indra, now without his testicles, went to the gods, the *ṛṣis* and the *cāraṇas.* In anguish, he cried, "I have destroyed Gautama's penance by provoking him to anger and this benefits the gods. I caused him to curse me, but I have lost my testicles as a result and his wife has been made formless. You must help me regain my testicles because I acted in your best interest!"

'Led by Agni and accompanied by the *māruts,* the gods went to the ancestors. "Here is a ram with testicles and here is Indra without any. Take the ram's testicles and attach them to Indra's body. The gelded ram will still please you and so will the humans who desire infinite happiness and will offer such rams for your satisfation!" The ancestors got together and plucked off the ram's testicles and offered them to Indra.

'And from that day onwards, Rāma, the ancestors have accepted a gelded ram as an offering. Those who present it to them get a suitable reward. And from that day onwards, Indra has had the testicles of a ram because of the power of Gautama's austerities.

'Enter this hermitage, Rāma, and do the right thing by liberating Ahalyā who is as beautiful as a goddess!'

Rāma and Lakṣmaṇa followed Viśvāmitra into the hermitage. Even though Ahalyā was invisible to the gods and the *asuras* and the people of the world, Rāma and Lakṣmaṇa were able to see the fortunate woman who shone with the power of her austerities. Her celestial beauty was the result of a special effort by the Creator. She appeared like a flame veiled in smoke, like the light of the full moon covered by a delicate mist, like the sun's rays reflected by water, so beautiful that she was almost an illusion.

Gautama's curse had made her invisible to all beings until the moment she saw Rāma. The princes touched her feet, and recalling Gautama's words Ahalyā welcomed them. With a serene mind, she honoured them with the *arghya* ritual. Flowers rained from the sky and the sound of celestial drums was heard as the *gandharvas* and *apsarases* gathered. The gods honoured Ahalyā who had been reunited with her husband because of her austerities. Gautama and a joyous Ahalyā honoured Rāma and then Gautama returned to his ascetic practices. Rāma accepted the ritual honours from Gautama and went onwards to Mithilā.

# *Chapter Ten*

Rāma and Lakṣmaṇa followed Viśvāmitra in a north-easterly direction until they reached Janaka's sacrificial grounds. 'The preparations for Janaka's sacrifice are truly magnificent,' they said. 'Thousands of *brahmins*, learned in the Vedas, have come here from different countries. And look at the camps of the holy men and the cartloads of materials for the sacrifice! Choose a place where we can stay.' Viśvāmitra picked a spot that was secluded and supplied with water.

Janaka heard that the great Viśvāmitra had arrived and came there to greet him along with his illustrious family priest Śatānanda. Sacrificial priests carried the *arghya* for Viśvāmitra and honoured him with the appropriate *mantras.* Viśvāmitra accepted the honours graciously and inquired about Janaka's welfare and the progress of the sacrifice. Then he enquired about the priests and sages according to their status, delighted to be in their company.

Janaka joined his palms in respect and said to Viśvāmitra, 'Blessed one, take your place among the best of sages!' The sage seated himself and the king, his ministers and the priests sat around him. Janaka said, 'The gods have made my preparations bear fruit. Your presence here today bestows the benefits of the sacrifice upon me. I am deeply grateful you have come to my sacrifice along with these other sages. There are twelve days left for the completion of the rituals. Then you will see the gods when they arrive to claim their shares.'

Then Janaka asked Viśvāmitra about the two young men that were with him. 'May good fortune attend you! Who are these two young men? They seem to have the valour of the gods and are as strong as lions and elephants, tigers and bulls! Armed with swords, bows and quivers, they are as handsome as the *aśvins* with their eyes shaped like lotus petals. Are they immortals who have come to earth? Why have they come here on foot and what is their purpose? Whose sons are these well-armed warriors? They light up this area as the sun and the moon light up the sky. They resemble each other in looks and deportment and their hair is as dark as the crow's wing. Tell me all about them!'

Viśvāmitra introduced the valiant sons of Daśaratha. He told Janaka about the incident at Siddhāśrama, the killing of the *rākṣasas* and their safe arrival at Viśālā, about the liberation of Ahalyā and the meeting with Gautama and about their desire to see the great bow which had brought them to Mithilā.

The next day, the king performed his ritual worship in the pure light of the dawn and sent for Viśvāmitra and the princes.

Righteous Janaka honoured them as was the custom and then addressed the great-souled sage. 'Blessed one, you are indeed welcome. I am here to follow your commands. Tell me, what can I do for you?' The eloquent sage replied, 'These two *kṣatriya* princes are the sons of King Daśaratha and they are renowned in the world. They want to see the mighty bow which is in your keeping. Be kind enough to show it to them and let their wish be fulfilled. They will have accomplished their purpose when they see the bow.'

'Listen and I will tell you how the bow came to me!' said Janaka. 'There was a great king named Devarāta, sixth in the line of Nimi. This bow was given to him as a sacred trust. Long ago, at the time of Dakṣa's[*] sacrifice, the great god Śiva grabbed this bow in anger and teased the other gods saying, 'You did not keep my share of the sacrifice even though I wanted it! Now I shall cut off your limbs with this weapon!' Terrified, the gods appeased Śiva and gratified him. He gave his mighty bow to the gods who then gave it to my ancestor, Devarāta, in trust.

'Once, when I was ploughing the sacrificial grounds in order to clean them up, the blade of my plough turned up a little girl. This child who was born from the earth has grown up as my daughter and she is known in the world as Sītā. I announced that since this child was not born from a human womb, she would be won in marriage only after a test of strength.

Rām's future wife

* Dakṣa was Śiva's father-in-law. Once he performed a huge sacrifice to which he invited all the gods except Śiva. Śiva was enraged at the insult and went to destroy Dakṣa's ritual.

'When she grew up, kings from all over the world wanted to marry this daughter of mine who had been produced by the earth. They were all keen to take her as a bride, but I said that I would give her away only for the price of valour. The kings came here together to test their strength but they could not even lift this great bow, let alone draw its string! I refused to give my daughter to any of them when I saw how little strength they had.

'The kings felt that I had cast aspersions on their ability and they grew angry at the insult. They laid seige to the city of Mithilā and made life difficult for us. After a whole year had passed and my resources had been depleted, I began to worry. I appeased the gods with a series of penances. When they were gratified, they gave me a four-divisioned army.* I attacked those cowardly and wicked princes and, terrified, they fled in all directions with their advisors.

'Now I will show this splendid bow to Rāma and Lakṣmaṇa. If Rāma can string the bow, I will give this mighty son of Daśaratha my daughter Sītā in marriage!'

Viśvāmitra said, 'Send for the bow!' and Janaka instructed his attendants to fetch the divine bow which was decorated with garlands of flowers and anointed with sweet perfumes. Janaka's attendants went into the city to bring the bow and came back bearing it before them. Five hundred tall and hefty men struggled with the eight-wheeled iron cart that held the bow. They dragged the cart into the king's presence and then Janaka's ministers said, 'Here is the best of all bows that you wished to display, the one that is revered by all beings, O king!'

Joining his palms respectfully, Janaka addressed Viśvāmitra and the princes. 'This magnificent bow has been honoured by my clan for generations. Not even the bravest of all men has been able to bend it. Neither the gods nor the *asuras,* neither the *rākṣasas* nor the foremost of the *gandharvas* and *yakṣas,* not even the *kinnaras* and *uragas* have been able to draw this mighty bow! What chance does a mere mortal have of lifting it, stringing it, placing an arrow in it and then drawing it? Let the two princes see the bow!'

'Child, examine the bow,' said Viśvāmitra to Rāma. Rāma walked over and opened the iron casket that contained the bow. 'May I touch this splendid bow? May I try and lift it and take a measure of it in my hands?'

---

* An army traditionally consisted of four divisions: elephants, chariots, infantry and cavalry.

he asked courteously. The king and the sage gave him their permission and Rāma casually grasped the bow in the middle. Watched by thousands of people, righteous Rāma lifted the celestial bow with ease. He strung the bow and drew it to its fullest extent and fitted an arrow into it. Then, Rāma snapped the bow in half. It broke with a huge sound like a thunder-clap and the earth shook as if all the mountains had collapsed. Stunned by the sound, all the spectators, except Janaka, Viśvāmitra and the two princes, fell to the ground.

The king was relieved when the people recovered consciousness. 'Blessed one, I have now witnessed Rāma's strength!' he said to Viśvāmitra. 'I never thought that such a thing was possible! My daughter Sītā will bring honour to my family when she becomes the wife of Rāma, son of Daśaratha! And my promise that she would be won only by a man of valour will also be redeemed when I bestow my beloved daughter on Rāma! With your permission and blessings, let me send my ministers to Ayodhyā at once! Let them tell King Daśaratha how I vowed to give my daughter in marriage to a man of valour. Let them tell him what happened here and bring him to Mithilā. Let them tell him that his sons are here with you and then they will bring him here with all speed, rejoicing.'

Viśvāmitra agreed and messengers were dispatched to Ayodhyā to give Daśaratha the good news and escort him to Mithilā.

The messengers wore out their horses as they travelled without stopping for three days and nights until they entered the city of Ayodhyā. On the strength of their master's message, they were able to gain entry into the royal chambers, where they saw the venerable old King Daśaratha, who was like a god. Respectfully joining their palms, they spoke to the king in sweet voices. 'Janaka, the king of Mithilā, along with his teachers and elders, asks after your welfare. With deep affection and solicitude, he asks about everyone in your family. The king of the Videhas sends you this message with Viśvāmitra's permission.

'"As you already know, long ago, I made a vow that I would give my daughter away for valour. Because of this, I drove away many cowardly kings. My daughter has now been won by your brave son who came here by chance in the entourage of Viśvāmitra. Rāma snapped the divine bow in half in the midst of a huge assembly. I will give my daughter Sītā, who was to be won by valour alone, to Rāma and fulfil my promise. I seek your agreement in this matter. Great king, may good fortune attend you!

Come to Mithilā as soon as possible along with your elders and your family priest. You will give me great pleasure and you will be delighted to see your sons again."

'This is the message that Janaka sends you with Viśvāmitra's permission and his family priest's support,' said the messengers.

Daśaratha was delighted with the news. He summoned Vasiṣṭha, Vāmadeva and his other ministers. 'Rāma, Kausalyā's beloved son, has been in Videha with his brother Lakṣmaṇa and the sage Viśvāmitra. King Janaka has seen Rāma's strength and courage and wishes to bestow his daughter Sītā on Rāma in marriage. If this news pleases you, let us go to Videha quickly without wasting another moment!' The ministers and sages agreed with the king's plan and Daśaratha announced that they would leave the next day. Janaka's messengers spent the night in Ayodhyā in great comfort, supplied with all that they could desire.

# *Chapter Eleven*

When the night had passed, Daśaratha joyfully gave his minister Sumantra instructions in the presence of his teachers and elders. 'Let the officers of the treasury go ahead of us, well-guarded. Let them carry vast quantities of wealth and all kinds of jewels. Call in the four-divisioned army from all its stations at once and ready the best of our chariots when I give the order. Let Vasiṣṭha, Vāmadeva, Jābāli, Kaśyapa, Mārkaṇḍeya Kātyāyana and all the *brahmins* leave before us. Prepare my chariot immediately so that there is no delay. The king's messengers are in a hurry!'

The four-divisioned army accompanied the king as he set out with the great sages. After travelling for four days, the entourage reached the land of the Videhas. As soon as Janaka heard about Daśaratha's arrival, he prepared to meet the great king himself with full honours. Janaka's joy knew no bounds as he approached the old King Daśaratha. His heart filled with delight, he addressed the best of kings. 'Welcome, great king! Your presence here makes us fortunate. Rejoice in the valour of your sons. It is also a great honour to have the blessed Vasiṣṭha here with all the other *brahmins*.

'Fortunately, I have been able to overcome all obstacles with the sacrifice that I have undertaken. It is a privilege for my clan to make an alliance with the mighty Ikṣvākus! We must perform the wedding ceremony tomorrow morning since the great sages have said that it must be done at the end of the sacrifice.'

The eloquent and wise Daśaratha replied, 'I have been told before that the manner in which gifts are received depends upon the giver and so we shall do as you wish!' This humble speech from Daśaratha, who was illustrious, righteous and honourable, filled Janaka's heart with wonder.

The groups of sages were happy to be in each other's company and they passed the night in easy companionship. King Daśaratha was overjoyed to see his sons again and, suitably honoured by Janaka, he spent the night in comfort and happiness. Janaka knew all that needed to be done and he spent the night performing all the rituals connected with the sacrifice and those necessary for the wedding of his daughter.

The next morning, Janaka completed his ablutions and instructed his family priest Śatānanda in the presence of all the sages. 'My illustrious brother Kuśadhvaja is exceedingly righteous. He lives in the city of Sāmkāśyā whose walls are washed by the waters of the river Ikṣavatī. It is as beautiful as the flying chariot Puṣpaka* and as auspicious as a store of meritorious acts. I wish to see my brother now so that he can help me with the rituals and share in my happiness.'

Janaka's messengers went quickly to Kuśadhvaja's city to summon him as Viṣṇu had been summoned to Indra's court. Kuśadhvaja arrived and honoured his brother, the great-souled king, and the priest Śatānanda before he seated himself on a splendid throne. The two brothers of limitless effulgence summoned Sudamana, the chief minister, and ordered him to escort Daśaratha, his sons and his ministers into the city.

Sudamana went to Daśaratha's camp and bowed to him. 'Great king of Ayodhyā, the king of the Videhas wishes to see you along with your teachers and family priest!' Daśaratha went to Janaka's court with his entourage and addressed the king. 'I am sure you know that our family sees the blessed Vasiṣṭha as a god and that he speaks for us in all matters. With Viśvāmitra's permission and in the presence of all these great sages, he will now announce my ancestry.'

The eloquent Vasiṣṭha began to speak directly to Janaka and Śatānanda. 'Brahmā, the eternal and imperishable, arose from the unmanifest. From him came Marīci whose son was Kaśyapa. Vivasvān was born to Kaśyapa and his son was the progenitor Manu. Manu's first son was Ikṣvāku. Ikṣvāku was the first king of Ayodhyā and his son was the prosperous king Kukṣi. Kukṣi's son was the effulgent Vikukṣi and his son was the mighty Bāṇa and his son was the valiant Anaraṇya.

---

* Puṣpaka was a legendary chariot that fell into the hands of Rāvaṇa. After Rāma defeated him in battle, he rode home in it to Ayodhyā. Cities are often likened to the chariots that belonged to the gods and we can assume, therefore, that these celestial cars were extremely large.

'Anaraṇya's son was Pṛthu and Pṛthu's son was Triśanku and his son was the illustrious Dhundhumāra. Dhundhumāra's son was the famous chariot-warrior Yuvanaśva and his son was the prosperous Māndhātā, ruler of the earth. Māndhātā's son was the fortunate Susandhi and he had two sons named Dhruvasandhi and Prasenajit. Prasenajit's son was Bharata and the effulgent Asita was Bharata's son.

'Asita's son was Sagara whose son was Asamanja whose son was Anśuman. Anśumān's son was Dilīpa and his son was Bhagīratha and his son was Kākutstha whose son was Raghu. Raghu's son was the effulgent Pravṛddha who became Kalmāṣapāda, the eater of men, and his son was Śankhana. Sudarśana was born to Śankhana and Agnivarṇa was born to Sudarśana. Agnivarma's son was Maru.

'Maru's son was Praśuśruka and his son was Ambarīṣa and his son was Nahuṣa, ruler of the earth. Nahuṣa's son was Yayāti and his son was Nabhaga and his son was Ajā whose son is Daśaratha. Daśaratha's sons are the brothers Rāma and Lakṣmaṇa. These two boys are born in a pure line of kings who are known for their righteousness, their courage and their devotion to truth. Give your daughters to Rāma and Lakṣmaṇa and you will be giving them to those who are worthy of them!'

'May good fortune attend you! Now I will recite my ancestry!' said Janaka. 'Great sage, a man must provide the complete history of his family when he gives away a child in marriage, so listen!

'There was once a king who was famous in the three worlds on the strength of his own deeds. His name was Nimi and he was the very soul of *dharma,* the best of all honourable men. He had a son named Mithi whose son was the first Janaka. That Janaka's son was Udāvasu. The virtuous Udāvasu had a son named Nandivardhana and his son was the renowned Suketu. The righteous Suketu's son was the mighty Devarāta and his son became the royal sage Bṛhadratha.

'Bṛhadratha's son was the mighty Mahāvīra and his son was the valiant Sudhṛti. His son was the righteous Dhṛṣṭaketu and his son became famous as the royal sage Haryaśva. Haryaśva's son was Maru and Maru's son was Pratindhaka and his son was the honourable king Kīrtiratha. His son was Devamīḍha whose son was Vibudha whose son was Mahīdhraka. Mahīdhraka's son was the great king Kīrtirāta and his son was the royal sage Mahāroma. Mahāroma's son was Suvarṇaroma and his son was

Hṛaṣvaroma. Hṛaṣvaroma had two sons. I am the older son and my younger brother here is the valiant Kuśadhvaja.

'My father made me king because I was older. He entrusted my brother to my care and went into the forest to meditate and perform austerities. When my father died, I bore the weight of this kingdom and looked after my younger brother, handsome as a god, with great affection. Some years later, the mighty king Sudhanva of Sāmkāśyā laid siege to Mithilā. He ordered me to hand Śiva's splendid bow as well as my daughter, the lotus-eyed Sītā, over to him. When I refused, he declared war on me. I killed him in single combat and then I appointed my younger brother, Kuśadhvaja, king of Sāmkāśyā.

'May good fortune attend you! Today, I give you my two daughters as brides with the deepest of affection—Sītā, my daughter who is as beautiful as a divine being, who was won by valour, for Rāma and Urmilā, my second daughter, for Lakṣmaṇa. I confirm three times that I give you my daughters with joyous heart, O king!

'Let Rāma and Lakṣmaṇa begin the distribution of cows that will make the ancestors happy and let us get on with the preparations for the wedding. Today, the Maghā constellation prevails. In three days, Phalguni will be in the ascendant. That will be the best day for the ceremony. Meanwhile, let Rāma and Lakṣmaṇa start distributing the gifts that will ensure their happiness!'

'Best of men, the clans of Janaka and Daśaratha are matched beyond all expectation. None other can equal them,' said Viśvāmitra. 'Rāma and Sītā, Lakṣmaṇa and Urmilā, are matched in virtue and in beauty. There is one more thing that I would like to add. Kuśadhvaja, your younger brother, is a righteous king and he has two daughters who are unrivalled on earth for their beauty. Let them marry prince Bharata and the wise Śatrughna. The other two sons of Daśaratha are like the guardians of the worlds in their looks and they are equal to the gods in valour. Let the two families be united through this alliance as well, best of kings!'

Janaka saw that Vasiṣṭha agréed with Viśvāmitra's proposal and so he joined his palms in respect and said to the two sages, 'May good fortune attend you! I am delighted that this suggestion has come from you. Let Kuśadhvaja's daughters be given as wives to Bharata and Śatrughna, for then the alliance between our clans will be strengthened! All four couples shall be married on the same day, the one determined by the wise as best for marriages.'

Bowing to the two great sages, Janaka spoke further. 'You have made it possible for me to fulfil my highest duty and for that I shall be your disciple forever. Take these seats of honour. Like Daśaratha's Ayodhyā, my city is also open to you. You can do as you please here!'

Daśaratha was also very pleased with the new alliances. 'Both you brothers, lords of Mithilā, have innumerable virtues and you have honoured all the sages and royal attendants appropriately. May good fortune and prosperity attend you always! I will now return to my camp and begin the necessary ceremonies.'

Led by the sages, Daśaratha left Janaka's court and returned to his camp where he embarked on the various rituals that preceded the wedding ceremony. He rose at dawn the following day and, according to prescription, he distributed one hundred thousand cows for each of his four sons. The cows had gilded horns and each of them had a calf and produced huge quantities of milk. Because he loved his sons so dearly, he also gave all kinds of other gifts to the *brahmins*. Surrounded by his four sons, Daśaratha was as resplendent as Prajāpati surrounded by the guardians of the quarters.

On the day of the gift giving, the valiant Yudhājit arrived to see Daśaratha. Yudhājit was the son of the king of the Kekayas and he was Bharata's maternal uncle. 'The king of the Kekayas asks after your health with great affection,' he said to Daśaratha. 'All is well with those whose welfare you desire. The king wished to see my sister's son and so I went to Ayodhyā. When I got there, I heard that you were here in Mithilā for the weddings of your sons. I came here as soon as I could to see my nephew.' Daśaratha welcomed his beloved guest and honoured him appropriately and then he spent the night with his sons.

The next morning, at the appointed hour, Daśaratha was led by the sages to the sacred area. Rāma and his brothers, adorned with jewels, came there at the auspicious moment and took their wives by the hand and walked around the sacred fires. They circumambulated the kings and sages as they went through the prescribed rituals for marriage. Bright flowers rained down from the heavens and the air was filled with the sound of celestial drums, music and song. The wedding was particularly wonderful because all the *gandharvas* sang and the *apsarases* danced as the princes walked around the fire with their wives under the gaze of the sages and their loving families.

# *Chapter Twelve*

The next morning, Viśvāmitra bade the kings farewell and left for the northern mountains. Soon after that, Daśaratha made preparations to leave for Ayodhyā. Janaka sent his daughters away along with a great deal of wealth, one hundred thousand cows, fabulous carpets, textiles and fabrics as well as an army of horses, elephants and chariots, adorned with jewels and shining with celestial splendour. He also gave them the best of his male and female attendants and heaps of gold, silver, pearls and coral. His heart filled with joy, Janaka said goodbye to Daśaratha and returned to his royal apartments.

Daśaratha, his four sons and their huge army went onwards, led by a group of sages. Huge birds screeched as they travelled and forest animals ran around them before fleeing. Daśaratha was deeply disturbed when he saw this and asked Vasiṣṭha, 'Why are these birds screeching and these animals running away from us? Why is my heart pounding and my mind oppressed by a nameless fear?'

In a calm and soothing voice, Vasiṣṭha reassured the king. 'Listen and I will explain this to you. The screeching of the birds foretells great danger but the movement of the animals is a good omen, so do not be overly anxious.' Even as Vasiṣṭha was speaking, a mighty gale arose and the earth trembled so that all the leaves fell from their trees. The sun was enveloped in darkness and nothing could be seen in any direction. Everything was covered with a fine layer of dust and ashes.

Daśaratha, his sons, Vasiṣṭha and the other sages grew agitated. Their army, covered with ash, was in visible confusion and the other members of their entourage had fainted. And then, out of that terrible darkness,

Paraśurāma appeared,* awesome in his vengeful aspect. As immense and immovable as Mount Kailāsa, the killer of kings blazed with his own splendour and was as difficult to look upon as the doomsday fire. His matted locks were coiled on top of his head and he carried his axe on his shoulder. With his mighty bow, which was like a bolt of lightning, and his arrows, he appeared like Śiva out to destroy Tripura.†

Vasiṣṭha and the other sages began to recite sacred *mantras* when they saw this terrifying sight and they whispered amongst themselves. 'Could it be that Paraśurāma's anger at his father's murder has not cooled?

'But he has already destroyed the entire race of *kṣatriyas* in the past to calm his passion and bring peace to his mind! Surely he does not want to annihilate the *kṣatriyas* all over again!' Cautiously, they offered Paraśurāma the *arghya* and spoke to him in gentle tones, calling him 'Rāma'.

Paraśurāma, son of Jamadāgni, acknowledged their greeting. He turned to Rāma, son of Daśaratha, and said, 'Rāma, I have heard much about your uncommon valour! And I have also heard that you broke the jewelled bow, a truly wondrous and unthinkable feat. Now I have brought you another fabulous bow, awesome to behold, that belongs to Jamadāgni, my father. I have tested your might, now I will engage you in single combat so that I can see your courage!'

Daśaratha turned pale when he heard Paraśurāma's challenge. He joined his palms in respect and pleaded with Paraśurāma. 'You have already wreaked revenge on the *kṣatriyas*. You are an illustrious *brahmin* and should be offering my young sons protection! Born in the line of the famous sage Bhṛgu, you have studied the Vedas and have undertaken a great many terrible vows. You renounced the use of all weapons because of a promise that you made to Indra. You yoked yourself to the highest *dharma* when you gave the earth away to Kaśyapa and made your home in the wilds of Mount Mahendra. Great sage, why do you wish to destroy my clan? None of us will survive, even if only Rāma is killed!'

---

* Paraśurāma, or 'Rāma with the axe,' was one of Viṣṇu's incarnations, sent to rid the earth of the *kṣatriyas*. Born of a *brahmin* father and a *kṣatriya* mother, Paraśurāma was incensed at the unlawful murder of his father, Jamadāgni, by a king. He vowed to annihilate all the *kṣatriyas* for several generations. When he had accomplished his task, he retired to the mountains to meditate and perform austerities.

† Śiva destroyed the city of Tripura, which was a stronghold of the *asuras*, with a single arrow.

The mighty Paraśurāma ignored Daśaratha's plea and spoke to Rāma again. 'There are two celestial bows that are famous in all the worlds. Superior to all others, they are tough and strong and were crafted specially by Viśvakarmā. The bow you broke was given to Śiva by the gods and he used it to destroy Tripura. The one I have is the second of these indestructible bows and the gods gave it to Viṣṇu. It is the equal of Śiva's bow in every respect.

'The gods asked Brahmā who was stronger, Viṣṇu or Śiva. Brahmā, the best of all those who are devoted to truth, understood the intentions of the gods and so he created hostility between Viṣṇu and Śiva. The conflict that arose between the two was terrifying as both Viṣṇu and Śiva were determined to humble the other. An enormous war-cry from Viṣṇu unstrung Śiva's bow and the great god was stopped in his tracks, stunned. Then the gods, the *ṛṣis* and the *cāraṇas* begged Viṣṇu and Śiva to stop their fight and the hostility between them ended. The gods deemed Viṣṇu the superior of the two because he had destroyed Śiva's bow. In a fit of anger, Śiva gave his bow and arrows to the illustrious royal sage Devarāta, king of the Videhas.

'Rāma, this is Viṣṇu's bow and it is known for destroying enemy cities. He gave it to Ṛcika of the Bhṛgus as a sacred trust. The mighty Ṛcika gave it to his matchless son, my father, the great celestial *ṛṣi* Jamadāgni. When my father renounced the use of all weapons and took refuge in the power of his austerities, he was killed by the wicked king Arjuna.* I heard about the dastardly killing of my father and in anger I exterminated the *kṣatriyas* again and again, as they were born. I won over the whole of the earth but I gave it away to the meritorious Kaśyapa as a fee for the performance of a sacrifice. Then I went to Mount Mahendra to engage in austerities. But when I heard that you had snapped Śiva's bow, I came here as soon as I could.

'Viṣṇu's fabulous bow has come to me from my ancestors. Take it and fulfil your duty as a *kṣatriya!* Fit it with this arrow that destroys hostile cities. If you can accomplish that, I will challenge you to single combat!'

Rāma had remained silent all this time out of respect for his father. But now he spoke to Paraśurāma. 'I have heard all about your deeds, Paraśurāma, and I applaud what you did to avenge your father's murder.

* Arjuna Kārtavīrya, who is not connected in any way with the more famous Arjuna of the *Mahābhārata*.

But you think of me as a weakling and a coward, unable to fulfil my duties as a *kṣatriya*. You obviously do not know my power. I will demonstrate it for you today!'

Rāma grabbed the magnificent bow from Paraśurāma and fitted the arrow into it. Angrily, he said, 'I must honour you because you are a *brahmin*. Out of respect for Viśvakarmā, I cannot release this arrow which will definitely kill you. But I shall destroy either your ability to move or the incomparable worlds that you have won through the power of your austerities, whichever you wish. For Viṣṇu's arrow crushes arrogance and never misses its mark. It cannot be loosed in vain!'

The gods and the groups of *ṛṣis* with Brahmā at their head, the *gandharvas, apsarases, siddhas, cāraṇas* and *kinnaras* gathered to marvel at the sight of Rāma holding the celestial bow and they were struck with wonder. Even Paraśurāma stood there, rooted to the spot, deprived of all his strength by Rāma's valour, gazing at Rāma holding the magnificent weapon. Finally, he spoke to the lotus-eyed Rāma in a gentle voice. 'Long ago, when I gave the earth to Kaśyapa, he told me that I could no longer inhabit this region. In keeping with my teacher's instructions, I have not spent a single night on earth since then because of the promise that I made to Kaśyapa. Rāma, you must not destroy my ability to move as quickly as thought. Let me return to Mount Mahendra, the best of all mountains. Without any further delay, use the magical arrow to destroy the worlds that I have won on the strength of my austerities.

'I knew that you were Viṣṇu, best of all gods, the one who scorches his enemies, the invincible killer of the demon Madhu, from the moment that you touched the bow! Even the gods have gathered to witness your unparalleled deeds and your invincibility in single combat! It is not a matter of shame for me to have been defeated by you, the lord of the three worlds. Rāma, you are true to your vows. Release the arrow and I shall return to my home in Mount Mahendra!'

Rāma released the arrow and immediately the darkness lifted from all around. The gods and the groups of *ṛṣis* broke into praise for Rāma, who was still holding the fabulous bow. Paraśurāma honoured Rāma, the son of Daśaratha, and then left for his home.

After Paraśurāma left, Rāma handed the bow and its wondrous arrows over to Varuṇa and honoured the sages led by Vasiṣṭha. Then he noticed that his father was still uneasy. 'Paraśurāma has gone,' he reassured

Daśaratha. 'Let the four-divisioned army that is protected by you, our leader, go onwards to Ayodhyā!' Daśaratha was filled with relief when he heard the words 'Paraśurāma has gone!' and joyfully he embraced his son and kissed him on the forehead. He instructed his army to proceed towards the city.

Soon, Daśaratha entered Ayodhyā, which was gaily decorated, filled with music and fluttering banners, its clean streets sprinkled with water and strewn with flowers. He was welcomed by his rejoicing subjects. Kausalyā, Sumitrā, the slim-waisted Kaikeyī and the other ladies of the royal household came forward to receive the new brides. The fortunate Sītā, the illustrious Urmilā and Kuśadhvaja's two daughters were dressed in the most exquisite silks and were wearing the loveliest jewellery. They were welcomed with auspicious music and led away to the temple. The young brides greeted all those who welcomed them and then they retired to private apartments with their new husbands.

Now that they were married, the four princes lived happily with their wealth and jewels, their possessions and their friends. They treated their father with respect and honoured his wishes. Of all the people in the world, Rāma was the most illustrious and the most valiant, just as Brahmā is the most virtuous of all beings. Rāma spent many happy seasons with his wife Sītā. She was always in his thoughts and he was always in her heart. He loved her dearly because she had been given to him as a wife by his father but his love for her deepened because of her beauty and her many virtues. Sītā loved Rāma twice as much as he loved her. She was able to tell him all her thoughts and whatever was in her heart. Besides that, this woman who was equal to the gods in her powers of perception and like Lakṣmī in beauty, was able to read Rāma's innermost thoughts. The marriage between Rāma and Sītā, which united the son of a royal sage with the noblest of princesses, was like the union of Viṣṇu, the lord of all men, with the illustrious Lakṣmī.

# AYODHYĀ

# *Chapter Thirteen*

After a while, King Daśaratha, the joy of the Ikṣvāku clan, sent for Bharata, his son from Kaikeyī, and said, 'Son, your uncle Yudhājit from the kingdom of the Kekeyas is here and wants to take you back with him.' With the king's permission, Bharata made immediate preparations to depart along with his brother Śatrughna. Delighted to have the two young princes with him, Yudhājit took them back to his father's kingdom. Bharata stayed there for some time with Śatrughna, pampered by his uncle who loved him as if he were his own son. But while they had every desire of theirs fulfilled, Bharata and Śatrughna thought constantly about their ageing father, King Daśaratha.

Daśaratha, too, missed his two absent sons who were like Indra and Varuṇa. He loved all his four mighty sons who had been born from his flesh and were as important to him as his arms. But of them all, Rāma was his father's favourite because he was distinguished by his many virtues.

While Bharata was away, Rāma and Lakṣmaṇa honoured and served their father well. Rāma placed his father's wishes before everything else and worked for the welfare of his people. He was also devoted to his mothers and honoured his teachers and elders at the appropriate times. Rāma's conduct endeared him to Daśaratha, the *brahmins* and to the citizens of Ayodhyā.

Rāma always spoke calmly and gently, never allowing a harsh word to pass his lips. A learned man, he was a patron of the arts and the sciences and a good judge of character. Rāma knew when and how to give and receive gifts. He was skilled at collecting taxes and he redistributed them judiciously. Rāma was not lazy and performed all his duties happily and well.

He was the best archer in the world and was also held in high esteem by chariot warriors. He rode a horse and an elephant with equal ease and was a skilled commander of troops. Even if the gods and the *asuras* had united against him in anger, Rāma would have remained undefeated in battle.

Rāma never grumbled and he had conquered anger. He was neither proud nor envious and insulted no one. He was the master of his own destiny. Like Bṛhaspati in wisdom and like Indra in valour, Rāma was greatly respected by the three worlds because of his virtues which shone from him like the rays of the sun. His father and all the citizens loved him dearly.

Daśaratha saw that his son was unrivalled in virtue. 'When shall I see my beloved son crowned king?' he wondered. 'He is devoted to the welfare of all creatures and he is dearer to the people than I am. To them, he is like Parjanya, the rain god, is to an arid land. He is as brave and wise as the best of the gods, he is as steadfast as the earth itself and he is more virtuous than I. After I have established my son as the ruler of the earth, there will be nothing more for me to do at this age other than ascend to heaven!'

Daśaratha and his advisors decided to proclaim Rāma the heir. The king summoned people from different towns, the leading citizens of Ayodhyā and all the mighty monarchs of the earth.

When the other kings and their retinues had gathered in Ayodhyā, Daśaratha addressed the huge assembly, his voice as deep as thunder, as resonant as a bell. 'The earth has been protected by my family, the Ikṣvākus, for many generations. I want the benefits of this rule to continue uninterrupted. I have walked in the footsteps of my forefathers and protected the earth to the best of my abilities. Working for the welfare of all beings, my body has grown old and feeble in the shadow of the royal canopy. I have been granted a life of many thousands of years but now I want to give my tired body a rest.

'I have resolutely borne the burden of kingship and of *dharma,* but I am tired now. With the approval of the good *brahmins* around me, I wish to turn over the welfare of my people to my son. My eldest son Rāma is virtuous and brave and the foremost among all righteous men. I wish to consecrate Rāma my heir. He is truly worthy and the three worlds will have the best of rulers when he becomes king. I shall be free of all worries when I entrust the earth to this illustrious man.'

The kings were delighted to hear Daśaratha's words and they broke into cries of joy, like peacocks do when they see long-awaited rain clouds. The learned men gathered there knew that Daśaratha wanted the best for them and they agreed that the king had grown old after ruling for many thousands of years. They endorsed his plan to make Rāma his heir. But Daśaratha wanted to know what they really felt and so he asked the gathering, 'Why are you so eager to see my son rule in my place? Have I not ruled the earth righteously?'

The people replied, 'Sir, your son has many virtues and admirable qualities which make him like Indra, king of the gods. He is the most outstanding of all the Ikṣvākus. Honourable Rāma is the refuge of all the righteous people in the world. He is devoted to *dharma* and to the truth. He is the epitome of virtue. He is even-tempered and has a calm mind. He speaks gently and with respect to the *brahmins*, the learned and the aged. He is a great warrior and has never been defeated in battle. When he returns to the city after being away, he asks after the citizens as if they were members of his own family. He shares in their joys and sorrows as if he were their father.

'Your son will bring you glory in the same way that Mārīca brought glory to his father Kaśyapa. All the people in the kingdom wish Rāma a long and healthy life when they remember him in their daily prayers. You will be fulfilling their wishes by installing Rāma, your beloved son, as your heir, great king. Crown him without further delay for the benefit of all creatures!'

'How proud and pleased I am that you wish my oldest and most beloved son to be installed as my successor!' exclaimed Daśaratha. He addressed Vasiṣṭha and Vāmadeva in the presence of the assembly. 'We are in the auspicious month of Caitra and the trees are in full bloom. Begin the preparations for Rāma's coronation!' The *brahmins* left at once to carry out the king's instructions with joyful hearts. Then Daśaratha summoned his bard and charioteer, the wise Sumantra, and told him to bring Rāma into the assembly.

Daśaratha sat with the great kings of the earth who had come from the north and the south, the east and the west. They were Mlecchas and Aryans, kings from the wooded regions and from the mountains, and they surrounded Daśaratha the way the *māruts* surround Indra. Daśaratha saw his son's chariot approaching the palace. Rāma, the most famous of all men on earth, rivalled the *gandharvas* in his good looks and he walked with the majesty of a rutting elephant. His moon-like face was beautiful to behold and he seemed to draw people's eyes to himself. Their hearts filled with joy, the citizens gazed at him as the thirsty, parched earth looks at the monsoon clouds with longing.

Accompanied by Sumantra, Rāma climbed the stairs of the palace that glittered like the peaks of Mount Kailāsa. He bowed to his father and touched his feet as he announced himself. Daśaratha drew his son up and embraced him and pointed him to a magnificent golden throne that was studded with gems. Rāma took his seat, his splendour enhancing the lustre of the assembly as the moonlight enhances the beauty of the star-studded autumn sky. Daśaratha's heart overflowed with joy as he gazed at his beloved son, for Rāma was a mirror image of himself. Smiling, he said, 'Rāma, you are the child of my eldest queen, a noble son of a noble mother. You are my favourite son because of your many virtues. Your good qualities have endeared you to the people and now, under the auspicious Puṣya constellation, take over as regent of the kingdom!

'I know that you are naturally virtuous and noble but I say this to you out of affection and for your own good. Always be courteous and keep a tight rein on your passions. Renounce desire and anger. Pay heed to your counsellors in public and in private. He who rules with the affection and consent of his people brings joy to his friends. My son, always conduct yourself with restraint!'

Rāma's friends heard the news of his consecration and rushed off to inform his mother, Kausalyā, of his good fortune. Overjoyed, Kausalyā bestowed gems and cows and gold on the messengers. Meanwhile, Rāma honoured his father and left the assembly to return to his own palace, cheered by the crowds that had gathered. And the citizens returned happily to their homes to thank the gods for fulfilling their wishes.

Daśaratha consulted his advisors and after taking all the factors into consideration, came to the following decision. 'Since the Puṣya constellation will prevail tomorrow as well, let my lotus-eyed Rāma be anointed heir in the morning!' He retired to his private apartments and summoned Rāma again. Rāma was concerned when he received the second summons and rushed to his father's palace somewhat agitated. He bowed to the king, who raised him up and embraced him and seated him on a throne.

'My son, I am old now,' began Daśaratha. 'I have had a long life and have fulfilled all my desires. I have performed one hundred sacrifices, complete with the offerings of food and the payment of the *brahmins*' fees. I have given the appropriate gifts and studied the great books. And in you, best of men, I have a son who is unrivalled on earth today. Great hero, I have experienced all the joys and pleasures that I wanted and I have paid my dues to the *ṛṣis,* the gods, the ancestors and the *brahmins*. I have no duties left to perform except to anoint you my heir.

'But Rāma, I have had strange and terrifying dreams. Blazing meteors thunder from a cloudless sky and fall to the ground. The astrologers have told me that my birth star is in the grip of malignant forces. This configuration of the planets usually means that the king will either die or experience terrible misfortune. Rāma, make sure that I anoint you before I change my mind, for the human heart cannot be trusted! I have been told that you must be installed under the Puṣya constellation and so I am determined to anoint you tomorrow. Go now and undertake the prescribed rituals. Steady your mind and fast tonight along with your wife and sleep on a mat of *kuśa* grass. Surround yourself with your friends. Let them watch over you. Such rituals often fall prey to all kinds of disruptions!

'I have a strong feeling that I should install you as my heir while your brother Bharata is away from the city. He is an honourable and righteous man, devoted to his elders and slow to anger, but I know that the human mind is fickle. However, even he will have to honour an act that has been accomplished.'

Rāma left his father and went to call on his mother and tell her about his imminent consecration as Daśaratha's heir. He found his mother dressed in white, praying for his welfare. Lakṣmaṇa and his mother Sumitrā had heard the good news and were already there with Sītā. They waited silently as Kausalyā prayed and meditated. Kausalyā was roused when she heard Rāma's voice and her heart filled with joy. 'Mother, my father has appointed me to care for our people,' said Rāma. 'Tomorrow, I shall be anointed heir and shall join my father in ruling the land. I have been told to fast all night together with Sītā. Sītā and you must do all that is necessary and perform the auspicious rituals for my coronation.'

Tears of joy rolled down Kausalyā's face when she heard the words she had waited so long to hear. 'May you live long, my son, and may all who wish you ill perish! May your success bring your mothers continued joy! You were born to me under a lucky star! Your father respects you for your many virtues and the majesty of the Ikṣvākus now rests with you!'

Rāma turned with a smile to his brother Lakṣmaṇa, who sat quietly, his palms joined in respect. 'Lakṣmaṇa, you must help me rule the earth, for you are my other half. You share my royalty and now you must also share the pleasures and fruits of kingship with me. They have meaning for me only because of you!' And then Rāma honoured his mothers and left for his own palace with Sītā.

The news of Rāma's consecration spread through Ayodhyā and as soon as it was morning, the joyous citizens began to decorate the city. Banners and buntings danced in the breeze from temple spires that gleamed like white clouds, from the homes and terraces of rich and prominent citizens, from roads and city squares, from private homes and public buildings. Even the tallest trees were decorated with brightly coloured flags. Actors, dancers and musicians filled the air with songs that delighted the hearts of all those who heard them.

All over the city, people talked of nothing but Rāma's imminent consecration. Even children playing on their doorsteps spoke of nothing else. Flowers were scattered in the streets, sweet incense filled the air and wooden torches as large as trees lined the main roads. Townspeople gathered in groups, talking among themselves. 'The Ikṣvāku king is a wise man indeed. Because he was growing old, he has entrusted his kingdom to Rāma.'

'We are fortunate that Rāma is to be our king for he knows good from evil,' they said to each other. The tumult of the crowds gathering for Rāma's installation swelled and thundered, like the roar of the ocean when sea monsters are at play.

# *Chapter Fourteen*

Queen Kaikeyī had an old servant whose origins and birth were completely unknown. She had brought this woman, Mantharā, with her when she came to Ayodhyā from her father's house. That night, Mantharā happened to climb to the palace terrace. She looked down upon the city and saw that the roads had been cleaned and decorated with garlands of lotuses. Banners hung everywhere, temples had been washed down with sandal-scented water and crowds milled in the streets. She noticed Rāma's wet-nurse standing nearby, obviously celebrating something. Mantharā said to her, 'Why is Rāma's mother distributing this great wealth among the people? What are the people celebrating with such abandon? What is the king up to, that he is so pleased?'

Rāma's wet-nurse was beside herself with joy and she told the hunchbacked Mantharā about the honour that had been bestowed upon Rāma. 'Tomorrow, under the Puṣya constellation, King Daśaratha will anoint the flawless Rāma his heir!' Mantharā seethed with anger and she quickly climbed down from the terrace that was as beautiful as the peaks of Mount Kailāsa. She went directly to Kaikeyī's apartments.

'Get up, you clueless woman!' she cried, bent on making trouble. 'How can you sleep? Have you no idea of the terrible disaster that is about to befall you? You boast of your good fortune from your marriage—well, that is about to end. It will dry up as quickly as a river in summer!'

Kaikeyī was disturbed by the hunchback's outburst. 'Mantharā, you seem so agitated! Is there something wrong? she asked gently. Kaikeyī's concern did nothing to abate Mantharā's anger. She pretended to be woebegone and downcast. Keeping Kaikeyī's welfare in mind as she plotted against Rāma, she chose her words carefully. 'My dear lady, a great disaster looms that will be the very end of you! King Daśaratha has chosen Rāma as his heir! My fear is like a bottomless pit and my grief burns me like fire! I have come here to help you! Your sadness makes me even sadder, Kaikeyī, for there is no doubt that my welfare is linked to your success!

'You were born in a royal family and you have been married to a mighty monarch,' continued Mantharā. 'How can you be so ignorant about the ruthless business of statecraft? Your husband appears righteous but he is a devious man! He speaks sweet words to you, but in reality, he is harsh and cruel. You cannot see his deceit because you are so trusting. Your husband pampers you with caresses and sweet nothings, but today he has proved that his real concern is for Kausalyā! The wicked king sent your son Bharata away to his relatives and now he uses this time to place Rāma securely on the throne. Daśaratha has revealed his true colours today, like a snake that has gone unnoticed. He has destroyed you and your family even while he kept you happy with his lies and deceits! Kaikeyī, seize the moment and act for your own benefit! Don't look so surprised—do whatever you must to save yourself, your son and me!'

Beautiful Kaikeyī rose from her bed and with great joy she gave the hunchback an exquisite jewel. 'Mantharā, you have made me very happy,' she said. 'You have brought me such good news. What else can I do for you? I see no difference between Rāma and Bharata. I am delighted that the king has chosen Rāma as his heir. You could not have brought me better news. Let me do something for you that will make you as happy as you have made me. Ask for anything and I shall give it to you!'

Mantharā flung the jewel away and cried out in rage and frustration. 'Silly woman! How can you be so happy? Don't you see that you are sinking into an ocean of suffering? Kausalyā is the lucky one. It is her son who shall be installed as the heir tomorrow. She will attain the greatest happiness and her rivals will be destroyed. You shall be her slave, bowing to her every whim! Rāma's women will reign supreme while your daughters-in-law will lament Bharata's downfall.'

Alarmed at Mantharā's distress, Kaikeyī began to enumerate Rāma's many virtues. 'Rāma is the oldest son and deserves to be the king. Besides that, he is well-versed in *dharma,* courteous, honourable and respectful to his elders. He will protect his brothers and his retainers like a father all through his long reign. Why does the news of his consecration distress you so? Bharata will succeed Rāma after one hundred years and occupy the throne that belongs to his forefathers. Mantharā, this is a time of celebration for us all since our future welfare is guaranteed. Why do you grieve? Rāma treats me with even greater respect than he treats Kausalyā!'

Mantharā grew more and more agitated as Kaikeyī spoke. 'Your simplicity does not allow you to see your own downfall or the fact that there is only sadness and oppression ahead for you,' she sighed. 'Rāma will be king and his sons shall succeed him. Then, Kaikeyī, his descendants will scorn Bharata. It is true that all princes cannot become kings since that would lead to chaos. That is why kings place their oldest sons on the throne, irrespective of the virtues of their other sons. Your defenceless son shall be excluded from all of the pleasures of kingship.

'I have come here to help you but you misunderstand me. You give me a jewel to celebrate the good fortune of your rival! I have no doubt that once Rāma is firmly established on the throne he will either banish Bharata or have him killed. Even inanimate beings develop closeness and sympathy as a result of physical proximity, but you sent Bharata away to your brother's family while he was still a child. Lakṣmaṇa, the son of Sumitrā, has been able to attach himself to Rāma. Those two brothers are like the *aśvins* and are known all over the world as a pair. Rāma will never harm Lakṣmaṇa and it is clear that he will be hostile towards Bharata. Let Rāma be sent into the forest! I am sure this will benefit you and Bharata. If Bharata gains the throne legitimately, it will ensure the prosperity of your clan. Your child deserves the best and Rāma is his natural enemy. How can you expect Bharata to live in deprivation in the house of a man who has everything? Protect Bharata from Rāma! He is in trouble, like an elephant attacked by a lion in a forest! Rāma's mother's pride was crushed in the past by your good fortune. You must expect her hostility!

'When Rāma inherits the earth, it will mean the end of Bharata. Think! How can your son gain the kingdom and his rival be exiled?'

Kaikeyī was blazing with anger by the time Mantharā had finished speaking. She took a deep breath and said, 'I shall see to it that Rāma is exiled into the forest this very day and that Bharata is anointed heir to the throne at once! Mantharā, think of a plan by which Bharata will inherit the kingdom in such a way that Rāma can never challenge him!'

Mantharā was bent on Rāma's destruction and on making trouble, so she said, 'Listen, Kaikeyī, and I will tell you how to secure kingship for Bharata alone!' Kaikeyī half rose from her couch, her diaphanous veil slipping, and urged Mantharā to explain her scheme. The malicious hunchback continued, 'During the war between the gods and the *asuras,* your husband took you with him when he went to Indra's aid. Daśaratha was wounded in battle and fell unconscious. You carried him to safety and took care of him and protected him. He was pleased with you and granted you two boons. You told the king to hold the boons until you asked for something and he agreed. Even I did not know this until you told me about it long ago. Ask your husband for those two boons now! Make Bharata heir to the throne and banish Rāma into the forest for fourteen years!

'Kaikeyī, pretend to be angry and go into a darkened room. Put on soiled clothes and throw yourself on the ground. Refuse to speak to the king or even to look at him! I have no doubt that the king loves you dearly and that he would even jump into the fire to please you. He would never make you angry, nor can he bear your anger. He would give up his life for your sake. He cannot refuse you anything. Gentle lady, understand the power of your charms!

'Daśaratha will offer you pearls and shining jewels of all kinds but do not be satisfied with any of them. Keep your purpose in mind and remind him of the two boons that he gave you during the war between the gods and the *asuras*. He will promise to fulfil the boons and will raise you from the floor. Make him swear that he will give you anything you ask for. Then tell him that he must banish Rāma into the forest for fourteen years and make mighty Bharata king of the earth!

'When Rāma is banished, he will lose his place in the hearts of his subjects and Bharata, rid of his rival, will establish himself firmly as king. By the time Rāma returns from the forest, your son will have won allies and collected his friends around himself. The time has come to act! Do not be afraid. Make the king stop the preparations for Rāma's consecration!'

Thus, Mantharā managed to turn their misfortune into good and Kaikeyī became happier. 'I had no idea, dear hunchback, that you were such a good advisor! You are the most intelligent and determined of all the hunchbacks on earth!' she cried. 'You have always been devoted to me and I would never have understood the king's intention had it not been for you. Some hunchbacks are wicked and twisted, the cause of grief, but you, you are as beautiful as a lotus that bends in the breeze! Your breasts rise up to your shoulders as if to rival them. Your waist, adorned by a lovely navel, is small, as if shrunk by modesty. Your wide hips are decorated with this girdle that tinkles as you walk. Your thighs and calves, even your feet, are well shaped. O Mantharā, when you are clothed in the finest silks and walk before me, you shall be as elegant as a swan!

'That hump of yours, which rises high and proud as a chariot wheel, is the repository of all your wisdom and cunning. When Bharata has been consecrated and Rāma sent into the forest, I shall adorn your hump with a necklace of gold! When I have accomplished my aims, I will anoint your hump with sandal paste and cover it with beaten gold, I will place a gilded crown upon your head and load you with the finest ornaments. You shall wear the best of clothes and walk like a goddess. Your face will rival the moon and you can throw scorn at your enemies! And other hunchbacks shall wait on you and serve you as you have served me.'

Mantharā was greatly flattered. She looked at Kaikeyī lying on her couch, blazing like a flame on a sacrificial altar, and said, 'There is no point in building a dam after the river has flooded. Get up and put the plan into action. Let the king see you!' Large-eyed Kaikeyī, proud of her position as the king's favourite, went with Mantharā into a darkened room. She took off her necklace made of hundreds of thousands of pearls and threw off her other ornaments and her fine clothes. Swayed by Mantharā's words, golden-skinned Kaikeyī flung herself on the ground. 'Mantharā, go and tell the king that I lie here dying. Unless Rāma is sent into the forest and Bharata anointed in his place, I shall kill myself!' Lying on the ground, her face dark with anger, her flowers and jewellery scattered, Kaikeyī looked like the night sky after the stars have set.

# *Chapter Fifteen*

After ordering the preparations for Rāma's consecration, Daśaratha entered the inner apartments to share the news with all those that deserved to hear it. The aged king, completely unaware of all that had happened, saw his beloved wife lying on the hard ground which should never have been her bed, burning with grief, her heart set on a terrible deed. He caressed her gently with deep humility, as a tusker might stroke his mate who has been injured by a hunter's arrow.

The lovelorn king spoke anxiously. 'Has someone been rude to you or spoken to you harshly? It hurts me to see you lying in the dust like this, like a woman possessed by an evil spirit. Could I have displeased you in any way? I have many competent physicians who can make you feel better, if only you would tell me what is wrong! Is there anything I can do to make you happy? Would you like an innocent man punished? Or a guilty man set free? I will do anything you ask, even give up my life!'

Kaikeyī listened to the besotted king and felt reassured. She set about to do what would cause her husband boundless grief. 'No one has hurt me or been rude to me,' she said. 'But there is something I want you to do for me. Promise me that you will do as I wish or I shall not tell you what I want.'

Daśaratha, who was held completely in thrall by his favourite wife, smiled at her and said, 'You know that there is no one except Rāma who is dearer to me than you. You know how much I love you. Ask me for anything and lift my heart from the depths of despair. I swear by all the merit I have earned for my good deeds that I shall do whatever you ask!'

Delighted by his promise, Kaikeyī revealed her intentions to Daśaratha, intentions that were like a fatal blow. 'Since you have sworn to grant me a boon, let the thirty-three gods led by Indra hear this! The moon and the sun, the stars, the planets and the sky, day, night and the four directions, the earth, all divine and living beings, let them all hear what you said! Let all the gods hear that this man, devoted to *dharma,* truthful, and totally in control of himself, has given me a boon!' Thus did Kaikeyī praise the mighty warrior who had given her two boons while he was overcome with desire and she bent him to her will.

'Great king, you had offered me two boons a long time ago. Today I ask that they be redeemed. Listen to my words! Let the preparations being made for Rāma's consecration be used to anoint my Bharata as your successor! His hair matted, wearing the rough clothes of an ascetic, let Rāma live in the Daṇḍaka forest for fourteen years! Proclaim Bharata your heir today! I want to see Rāma leave for the forest without further delay.'

The king reeled in confusion when he heard Kaikeyī's words. He looked at her as a deer would look at a tigress. He heaved a great sigh and fell to the floor, like a great serpent made powerless by a spell. 'Damn you!' he screamed in anger and lost consciousness. After a few minutes, the distraught king regained his senses but his anger remained unabated. 'Heartless, wicked creature!' he cried, his eyes blazing. 'Destroyer of my clan! Vile woman! What have Rāma or I done to deserve this ? Rāma has always treated you like a mother. How could you be bent on his destruction? I let you into my house thinking that you were from a royal and noble family. I had no idea that you were a poisonous snake, determined to destroy me!

'The whole world sings of Rāma's virtues. How can I reject my most beloved son? I can renounce Kausalyā or Sumitrā or my kingship, even my life, but how can I renounce Rāma, who loves me so dearly? The sight of Rāma makes me happy. If I do not see him, my spirits sag. The world may survive without the sun and crops without water, but I cannot live without Rāma. Wretched woman, don't go through with this terrible plan. Have mercy on me! I shall even place my head at your feet!'

The great king, protector of the earth, wept like a man who has lost everything. He was so enslaved by this woman that he fell at her feet. But she moved away so that he could not touch them.

The mighty king lay on the floor, a place wholly unsuited to him, like Yayāti who fell from heaven when his merit ran out. But wicked Kaikeyī, the very incarnation of terror, was unmoved. 'Great king, you say that you are a man of your word, that you are firm in your resolve,' she persisted fearlessly, for she had not yet been granted her boon. 'Why are you trying to cancel the boons you gave me?'

As the king sat there in stunned silence, the day ended. The night was made bright by the moonlight but the king did not see its beauty. The aged Daśaratha looked up at the moon and sighed. 'Let the morning arrive quickly! Or maybe, bright moon, you should fade away so that I do not have to look upon this cruel woman, this despicable creature who has brought this terrible calamity upon my family!' He turned to Kaikeyī again and joined his palms in supplication. 'Dear lady, be kind to an old man who is powerless under your spell, a man who has lived a virtuous life and is, moreover, a king! I have publicly announced my intention to consecrate Rāma! Behave in a way that will make me and my sons and all our loved ones happy!' pleaded the noble king, his eyes brimming with tears.

Cruel Kaikeyī ignored her husband's plea. When Daśaratha saw that his wife, who had never displeased him before, was determined to exile Rāma, he swooned with grief.

Kaikeyī looked at the scion of the Ikṣvākus lying on the ground, overcome with grief. She paced restlessly and said, 'You have heard my words. Why do you persist with doing wrong? Lying on the floor like this does not become you! Learned men say that *dharma* is the highest truth. I resorted to the same truth when I asked you to do what is appropriate. King Śibi was prepared to sacrifice his own body for the dove and he was suitably rewarded for that. Alarka plucked out his eyes when a *brahmin* asked for them. The ocean submits to the cosmic order and maintains his bounds even though it would be simple for him to transgress them. If you do not do what I ask, I shall kill myself right here in front of you!'

The king was trapped by his oath as Bali was trapped by Indra's bonds. His mind was in a whirl and his face was drained of all colour. Blind with grief, he could see nothing at all. With a great effort of will, he collected himself but Kaikeyī, still intent upon her wicked course of action, spoke harshly to him, choosing her words with care. 'You will have done the right thing when you place my son on the throne. Banish Rāma into the forest and rid me of my rivals!'

Daśaratha was stung by Kaikeyī's words the way a thoroughbred horse is lashed by a whip. 'I may have lost my senses but I know that I am bound by the dictates of *dharma,*' he said. 'I want to see my beloved

Rāma!' Kaikeyī herself ordered Sumantra to bring Rāma into the king's presence. Sumantra hurried away, sure that the summons indicated more good news for Rāma.

Sumantra stepped out of the place and saw the great kings and the wealthy citizens who were beginning to gather for Rāma's consecration. The sun rose into the bright sky and the Puṣya constellation was in the ascendant. All the ritual materials for the ceremony had been collected and the *brahmins* were waiting to begin. The main streets of the city were decorated with flags and flowers and everywhere Sumantra heard people discussing the consecration.

Wise Sumantra left the crowds behind and approached Rāma's palace. He entered the central courtyard and was greeted by young men adorned with bright ear rings and armed with spears and bows. They were all keen and alert and devoted to their duties. Close by were the elders, the palace chamberlains who wore clothes of ochre and many fine jewels, standing guard at the doors of various rooms. They rose from their seats when they saw Sumantra and rushed inside to tell Rāma that he had arrived. Rāma immediately ordered that he be allowed in.

Sumantra saw Rāma seated on a golden couch covered with the finest linen, adorned with jewels like Kubera himself. His body was smeared with rare and sweet-smelling red sandal paste, the colour of a boar's blood. Sītā sat beside him and Rāma appeared as beautiful as the moon in conjunction with the Caitra constellation. He blazed with his own effulgence like the sun and the humble Sumantra, who was held in the highest regard by King Daśaratha, bowed before Rāma.

'Noble son of Kausalyā, your father and queen Kaikeyī wish to see you. You must go to them at once!' Rāma was pleased and, giving the summons the respect they deserved, he said to Sītā, 'Obviously my father and the queen are discussing something related to the consecration. The queen knows my father's innermost thoughts. She probably wants to make him happy, which is why she has asked him to call me there. I am sure the king will crown me today. I must go there at once. Amuse yourself here with your attendants!' Dark-eyed Sītā, who flourished in the respect that her husband gave her, accompanied him to the door of the palace and invoked the blessings of the gods upon him.

Rāma saw his well-wishers gathered outside and they cheered loudly when he appeared. Then he climbed into his magnificent chariot which blazed like a fire. It was covered with gold so bright that it dazzled the eyes and was drawn by the best of horses the size of young elephants. Like the thousand-eyed Indra, Rāma shone with his own splendour as he sat in the chariot which thundered through the streets of Ayodhyā like a rain cloud. Rāma left his palace like the moon emerging from behind a cloud. Lakṣmaṇa stood behind him, holding the ceremonial umbrella and plume. The massing crowds cheered with joy as he went by and Rāma could hear snatches of their conversations.

'Rāma will receive a vast kingdom today because the king has shown him favour!'

'We are fortunate to have Rāma as our ruler. He shall fulfil all our wishes!'

'It will be to our great advantage if he rules for a long time!'

Rāma drove through Ayodhyā which was filled with the joyous sounds of horses neighing, elephants trumpeting and bards and musicians singing songs of praise. He looked upon his prosperous city, its squares and highways crowded with horses and elephants and chariots and its people who displayed their abundant wealth, lined with shops overflowing with goods for sale, and he felt proud and happy.

Rāma reached his father's magnificent palace that shone like the peaks of Mount Kailāsa. He entered the king's private apartments and saw his father sitting on his splendid throne along with Kaikeyī. But the king seemed unhappy, his face dark with grief. Rāma humbly touched his father's feet and then, his mind calm and serene, he bowed at the feet of Kaikeyī. The grief-stricken king could barely speak and he dared not look Rāma in the face. His eyes filled with tears, he whispered his son's name and fell silent.

When he saw how upset his father was, Rāma felt fear clutch at his heart, as if he had stepped unawares on a snake. He had never seen him like that before. Daśaratha's deep sorrow was evident on his face and in his long sighs which were like the uneven sound of the ocean during a solar eclipse. Rāma sensed his unhappiness and his mind, too, resembled the ocean tormented by the full moon. Rāma was always concerned about Daśaratha's well-being and wondered why his father did not greet him joyfully as usual. 'Normally, he is very glad to see me, even if he has been angry before my arrival. But today, the sight of me does not appear to lift his spirits. He seems miserable and depressed.'

After he had greeted Kaikeyī, Rāma said to her, 'Is my father angry with me today? Have I unknowingly offended him in some way? Tell me if this is so and then intercede on my behalf! He seems so unhappy, as if he were suffering some mental anguish or physical pain. I know one cannot be happy all the time, but what is the cause of his pain today? Has something happened to Bharata or Śatrughna or to any of my mothers? If he is angry with me, tell me what I can do to appease him. I cannot live for a moment with his anger. A man can do nothing other than to place himself at the mercy of the one he considers his master. Did you speak harshly to him, arrogant in the love that he has for you? Or did you say something to hurt him? I ask in all sincerity, why is the king so unhappy?'

'The king is neither angry nor is he upset about anything,' replied the selfish Kaikeyī without batting an eyelid. 'But there is something on his mind that he is reluctant to talk about. He cannot bear to say anything unpleasant to you because he loves you so much. But you must fulfill what he has promised me.

'Long ago, he honoured me by giving me a boon. And now, even though he is a king, he regrets his promise like a common man. He is trying to build a dam after the river has flooded. Rāma, good people know that *dharma* is the root of all action. You must ensure that the king's anger does not allow him to ignore *dharma.* If you promise to abide by the king's wishes, whether they be right or wrong, I shall tell you what he wants. He cannot bear to speak them himself!'

Rāma was disturbed by Kaikeyī's words and, in front of the king, he said, 'Madam, how can you speak to me like this? I would jump into fire or into the ocean, even take poison, if that is what the king commands! The king is my father as well as my teacher and he wishes the best for me. Tell me what the king wants and I swear that I will do it. Rāma does not speak with a forked tongue!'

'In the distant past, during the war between the gods and the *asuras,* your father was wounded in battle,' began ignoble Kaikeyī. 'I took care of him and he gave me two boons. I have asked the king to install Bharata as his heir and to send you into the Daṇḍaka forest, Rāma!' she continued cruelly. 'Best of men, if you want to fulfil your oath and allow your father to keep his word, obey his command and go into the forest for fourteen years! Renounce the consecration and live as an ascetic in the forest with matted hair and rough clothes! Bharata shall rule the land from this city which is filled with jewels, elephants, horses and chariots!'

Her cruel and unkind words were like death, but they did not perturb Rāma in the least. 'It shall be as you say. I shall live in the forest as an ascetic to fulfil the king's promise. But I still want to know why the king does not greet me with joy as he normally does. Do not be angry with me. I say again to reassure you that I will gladly live the life of an ascetic in the forest. How can I refuse to do this when it is my father who asks? But one thing still rankles in my heart—why did the king not tell me himself about the consecration? I would gladly have given my brother Bharata everything myself—my kingdom, my wealth, my wife, all that I hold dear, including my life.

'You must convince my father that I will do this without sadness. Why does he stare at the floor and weep silent tears? Let messengers be sent at once to bring Bharata back from his uncle's home. And I shall leave for the Daṇḍaka forest to respect my father's word.' Kaikeyī was beside herself with joy and she urged Rāma to leave for the forest. 'There is no need to delay things. The king was too ashamed to speak to you himself. But think nothing of it and do not hold it against him. Now go quickly, for your father can neither eat nor bathe until you have left.'

The king muttered 'Damn you! Damn you!' before he fell onto the gilded couch in a faint. Rāma lifted him up but urged by Kaikeyī, he made haste to leave for the forest, like a horse that has been whipped. 'You know I do not crave wealth nor material things, that I am like a *ṛṣi* in my devotion to *dharma.* I would do anything to please my father. There is no greater *dharma* than service to one's father and obedience to his whishes. Kaikeyī, did you think that I was lacking in virtue that you spoke to the king about this? You could have commanded me yourself!

'I shall leave for the forest after saying goodbye to my mother and after telling Sītā that she has to stay here. Let Bharata rule the kingdom and serve my father, for that is his highest duty.' Rāma bowed at the feet of his unconscious father and wicked Kaikeyī and left the room. He came out of the inner apartments and did not even glance at all the materials that had been collected for his consecration. The loss of a kingdom did not dim his royal lustre just as the darkness of the night cannot destroy the cool moonlight that soothes the world. Though Rāma had renounced the kingdom and decided to live in the forest, his mind was calm, as though he had transcended the world.

Collecting himself, he suppressed his grief as he went into his own apartments to tell his mother the unhappy news. He entered his palace where everyone was celebrating, but he disguised his emotions so that the ones that he loved most would suspect nothing.

# *Chapter Sixteen*

Rāma sighed as he entered the inner courtyards and saw his aged chamberlain and the learned *brahmins* whom the king held in special esteem. He greeted them with his usual courtesy and respect and went in to the next courtyard where he encountered the young women who guarded the entrance to his mother's apartments. They invoked the blessings of the gods on him and ran inside eagerly to tell Kausalyā that Rāma had arrived.

Kausalyā had fasted all night and now that it was morning, she was praying to Viṣṇu for her son's welfare. This devout woman, who always kept the prescribed fasts, was dressed in pure white and was pouring oblations into the fire as she recited the auspicious *mantras.* When she saw Rāma, she rose and ran towards him joyfully, as if she had not seen him for a long time, as a mare would run to her foal. Overflowing with love, she spoke sweetly to her resolute son. 'May you be blessed with a long life and all success, like the other wise rulers of our clan! Your father has kept his word, Rāma. Today he shall anoint you his heir.'

Rāma, whose nature it was to be humble, joined his palms in respect and bowed to his mother. Dear lady,' he said, 'you do not know what has happened. It is a terrible thing and it will bring great sorrow to you, Sītā and Lakṣmaṇa. I must go and live in the forest for fourteen years as an ascetic, eating honey, roots and fruit and renouncing meat. The king has chosen Bharata as his heir and has asked me to live in the Daṇḍaka forest.'

Kausalyā, who was as delicate as a banana plant, fainted when she heard these words. Rāma lifted her and gently wiped the dust that covered her when she had fallen like a mare who rolls on the earth after dropping her heavy load. Kausalyā deserved all happiness but now she spoke sorrowfully to her son who was attending to her with concern. 'Had I never given birth to you, Rāma, I would have known the grief of a childless woman. But the sorrow I feel now is far greater. Earlier, too, I had neither the good fortune nor the happiness of being my husband's favourite. But I waited for the joy that would arise from having a son!'

'Though I am superior to all the king's other wives, I have had to tolerate many remarks from them that have wounded me deeply. Whose sorrow could be greater than mine? I have been insulted while you were still here. Imagine what will happen when you are gone! Life for me shall be worse than death! Even my loyal retainers shall turn away from me because they fear Kaikeyī's son Bharata!

'From the moment you were born seventeen years ago, I have waited anxiously for an end to my sorrows. I have raised you with prayers and fasts and all kinds of austerities but these have brought me nothing but unhappiness. Ah! my heart must be hard indeed that it does not crumble like a riverbank assaulted by fast-flowing waters! I cannot even die, for Yama has not approached me the way a lion approaches a deer. Yes, my heart is hard! It should have broken to pieces and fallen to the ground under this terrible load of grief. Death cannot come before its time! My fasts and penances for the birth of a son have been in vain, like a seed sown in the sand! There can be no greater sorrow than this! If only death would come when one wanted! Then, without you, I would die of grief today, like a cow without her calf!' wailed Kausalyā as she thought of the unhappiness that lay in store for her.

As Kausalyā wept, Lakṣmaṇa spoke, his words appropriate to the situation. 'Mother, I, too, do not like the fact that Rāma has to give up the kingdom and go into the forest because of a woman's whim! The king is old and senile and succumbs to his lust. Who knows what he might say in the throes of passion! I cannot think of any crime that Rāma has committed, nor can I think of a flaw in his character. How can he be banished into the forest? There is no man on earth, even if he is Rāma's enemy or someone that Rāma has insulted, who would speak badly of him.

'How can someone who treads the path of *dharma* reject a son without reason, that, too, a son who is so god-like, so upright and so restrained? Which son would honour the word of a father who is so patently in his second childhood? Rāma, seize the kingdom with my help before the news of the king's change of heart spreads! When I am by your side, protecting you with my bow, there is no one, not even death, who can get the better of you!

'Best of men, if there is any opposition to you in Ayodhyā, I shall kill every single man with my sharp arrows! I will kill all Bharata's supporters, for the cowardly are scorned in this world! If our father antagonizes you and me, what power can he possibly have to bestow the kingdom on Bharata?

'Though I love my own mother dearly, I swear to you, lady Kausalyā, that if Rāma enters the forest or jumps into the fire to kill himself, I shall have gone ahead of him! I shall dispel your sorrow as the sun dispels the darkness. You and Rāma shall see my courage! I shall kill my father who is impotent and infatuated with Kaikeyī! His dotage beckons, but he frolics like a youth!' Lakshman offers to fight for Ram

'Son, you have heard what your brother has to say,' said the weeping Kausalyā to Rāma. 'Follow his advice if the plan appeals to you. Ignore the unrighteous words of my husband's wife. You cannot go away and leave me here tormented by grief! You know *dharma* and you are devoted to righteousness. Stay here and look after me—that would be the highest *dharma* of all! Even the great sage Kaśyapa stayed to care for his mother. He went to heaven because his service was equal to the most severe austerities!

'Just as you honour the king and respect his majesty, so, too, should you honour me. I forbid you to go into the forest! I would eat grass with you and be happy but I have no use for a life without you. If you go without me, I shall starve myself to death. And then, my son, you shall go to hell and the whole world shall hear about it, just as they heard about how the Ocean was punished for the unjust killing of a *brahmin*!'

Devoted to righteousness, Rāma spoke gently to his weeping mother. 'I cannot ignore my father's wishes, but I bow my head before you and ask for deliverance. I want to go and live in the forest. The *ṛṣi* Kāṇḍu killed a cow at his father's behest even though he knew it was wrong to do so. In our own family, long ago, the sons of Sagara died a terrible death digging up the earth because their father had commanded them to do so. Rāma, the son of Jamadāgni, killed his mother with his own axe in the forest because his father told him to. I am not the only one to obey my father's order. All the men I have just named did exactly that and I must follow their example. I am doing the right thing by fulfilling my father's wishes. Besides that, no one would ever come to harm by following his father's command.'

Rāma then turned to his brother. 'Lakṣmaṇa, I know you have the greatest affection for me. I also know you are upright and restrained. *Dharma* is the most important thing in the world, truth is established because of it. And obeying a father's command is the highest *dharma* of all, as is conforming to the wishes of a mother and *brahmin*. I cannot disobey my father simply because Kaikeyī, our mother, asked him to command me thus. Give up your ignoble ideas inspired by the duties of a *kṣatriya!* Follow my example. Take refuge in *dharma* and not in violence.'

'Allow me to go into the forest,' said Rāma to Kausalyā, bowing his head. 'I beg you on my life to let me go! When I have fulfilled this unpleasant promise, I shall return to the city. I cannot turn my back on the greatest good just for the sake of a kingdom. Life is too short for me to enjoy the pleasures of royalty unjustly!'

Lakṣmaṇa's sorrow was mixed with anger and his eyes blazed as he listened to Rāma speak. But Rāma remained calm and composed as he went on. 'Lakṣmaṇa, make sure that the preparations for my consecration are dismantled with the same speed and efficiency with which they were assembled. Do this in such a way that the fears of our mother Kaikeyī are allayed, since the thought of my installation makes her anxious. I cannot bear the fact that she should be unhappy on this account.

'I have never knowingly or unknowingly caused the slightest pain to our father or to any of our mothers. My father is an honourable man and now he worries about his afterlife. Let him be relieved of this fear. If the ceremonies for me are not cancelled, his mind will not be at ease and that would make me uncomfortable. So, Lakṣmaṇa, cancel the preparations for my consecration. I want to leave for the forest as soon as possible. My departure will fulfil the wishes of the queen and she can begin the arrangements for her son's coronation without further anxiety. Her mind will be at ease when I have left. And so will my father's.

'Lakṣmaṇa, you have to see destiny at work in my exile and in the reversal of the kingship that was entrusted to me. How could Kaikeyī have worked against me unless it was destiny that directed her to do so? Especially since I have never made any difference between her own son and me. It can only be destiny that has made her act like this. Why else would a noble princess, rich in virtues, speak like a common woman in her husband's presence?

'That which is unthinkable and which cannot be countered by any creature is an act of destiny. This is what I have learned from what has just transpired between Kaikeyī and me. Where is the man who can fight against fate which is manifest only in its workings? Joy and sorrow, fear and anger, gain and loss, existence and non-existence—destiny reveals itself in all these things. I have no regrets about the cancelled consecration and neither should you. Lakṣmaṇa, do not think badly of our mother who has taken the kingdom away from me. Understand that she was fated to do this and recognize the power of fate!'

Lakṣmaṇa looked away, his eyes on the floor, as his mind seemed to swing between grief and happiness. His frowning face was as hard to look upon as that of a fierce and angry lion. He wrung his hands and shook his head, watching his brother out of the corner of his eye. 'You seem perturbed about the violation of *dharma* and the doubts that may arise in the minds of others. This is most unlike you, Rāma. Such confusion does not become you.

'How can a man like you, who stands so strong and proud in the *dharma* of the *kṣatriya*, sing praises of this thing called destiny? Fate is the refuge of the weak and the impotent. How can you grant the benefit of the doubt to those two wicked people? They pretend to follow the dictates of *dharma* when, in fact, they know nothing about it! The citizens will never accept anyone other than you being installed as the king's heir! I feel only contempt for a *dharma* that makes even someone as resolute as you vacillate like this! It is your attachment to *dharma* that confuses you!

'I cannot accept that all this happened because of fate. An explanation like that is for cowards, not for the brave! No capable man would ever be oppressed by the workings of destiny. And a real man would never allow fate to frustrate his aims. I will show you which is stronger, fate or manliness. The people will see that fate, which reversed your consecration, has been defeated by my courage.

'My courage will turn back this fate which comes rushing headlong at us, like a rogue elephant that has broken his bonds and ignores its goad. Not the guardians of the three worlds nor all the gods together can prevent Rāma being crowned today, let alone our father! Those who plotted to banish you shall live in the very same forest for fourteen years. I shall destroy all the hopes that my father and Kaikeyī had of placing Bharata on the throne and depriving you of the kingdom. I am stronger than any fate and anyone who opposes me shall suffer the consequences!

'When you retire to the forest after ruling for one thousand years, your sons shall be kings. The great sages have decreed the forest life for a king only after he has enjoined his sons to rule over the people as if they were their children. Rāma, if you feel anxious about losing the throne after you have gained it because the king may change his mind, have no fear. I will secure your position for you. I promise you this and may I never reach the world of the brave after my death if I prove untrue!

'Have yourself consecrated with due ceremony. I shall hold off the mighty kings with my strength. Tell me which ones oppose you and this very day I shall see to it that they are deprived of their wealth, their families and their lives. Order me to bring the kingdom under your control! I am your servant!'

Rāma wiped Lakṣmaṇa's tears of rage and calmed him. 'I am determined to follow my father's orders. That would be walking on the right path,' he said.

By now, Kausalyā had realized that Rāma was not to be swayed. 'How can a cow not go with her calf,' she said, her voice thick with tears. 'I will follow you wherever you go, my son!'

But Rāma explained gently, 'The king is being controlled by Kaikeyī. When I have gone, he will not survive if you, too, were to desert him. A woman cannot abandon her husband. It would be a cruel thing to do and is, therefore, impossible. Put that thought out of your mind. As long as my father, the ruler of the earth, is alive, so long shall you attend and care for him. That is the eternal *dharma.*'

Kausalyā was somewhat comforted and agreed to stay with her husband. But her heart overflowed with sorrow as she blessed Rāma. 'Go, my son, you have made up your mind. May good fortune attend you always!' She tried to suppress her grief as she purified herself with water and invoked the blessings of the gods upon him. 'May the *sadhyas,* the *viśvadevas,* the *māruts* and the great *ṛṣis* protect you. May you be protected by the Creator, by Bhaga, Pūṣa and Aryamā. May the seasons, the fortnights, the months, the years, nights, days and the minutes work for your benefit. May your learning and meditation and your adherence to *dharma* stand you in good stead always,' chanted Kausalyā as she called upon each of the gods to look after her son during his time in the forest. She kissed him on the forehead, held him close to her breast and said, 'Go in happiness, my son, and may you achieve your goals! I shall see you again when you return to Ayodhyā in good health, your aims accomplished, happy and firmly established in the royal palace.'

She completed her blessings and her rituals but she could not bear to let him go and hugged him again and again, her eyes streaming with tears. Rāma touched her feet and then went to see Sītā, blazing with his own splendour.

# *Chapter Seventeen*

Rāma had to return along the main thoroughfare of Ayodhyā. It was still full of people whose hearts' overflowed with love when they saw him. Meanwhile, the virtuous Sītā had heard nothing at all of what had happened and she thought constantly about her husband's consecration. Being familiar with royal ceremonies and rituals, she had worshipped the gods and offered them thanks and now she waited for Rāma's return.

Rāma's apartments were filled with joyous people but he entered quietly, his head down. Sītā rose at once when she saw her husband, growing anxious when she noticed that he seemed sad and careworn, his face beaded with sweat. 'You seem so unhappy,' she cried. 'What could possibly have happened? Today is the auspicious day determined by the *brahmins*. Why do you appear so disheartened? Your face, normally as radiant as the moon, does not shine from below the royal canopy. Nor can I see eloquent bards and musicians singing your praises. The learned *brahmins* have not anointed your forehead with curds and honey as prescribed by the rituals. No one follows you in procession and the royal horses and ceremonial elephant, dark as a rain cloud, did not precede your chariot. Where is your throne that should be carried by a retainer? Everything is ready for the formal installation. How is it that your face is unusually pale and shadowed with sorrow?'

'Sītā, my respected father has banished me into the forest,' said Rāma in answer to her anxious questions. 'You were born into a noble family so you are familiar with *dharma* and live by its rules. Listen, Sītā, and I will tell you how all this happened.

'My father Daśaratha is a man of his word and long ago, he gave Kaikeyī two boons because he was pleased with her. Today, when everything was ready for the consecration and the king's commands were being carried out, Kaikeyī recalled the boons. Even at a time like this, the king had to fulfil them because of *dharma*. Kaikeyī wants me to live in the Daṇḍaka forest for fourteen years and she wants my father to appoint Bharata heir in my place. I have come to see you before I leave for the forest.

'Do not speak of me or of my virtues in Bharata's presence because successful men do not like others being praised. Do not expect anything special from him because I am your husband. Be sure to stay within his circle of well-wishers. I must leave today to honour the promises of my elders, but you, dear one, must remain calm.

'When I am in the forest, the home of sages, busy yourself with fasts and vows. Worship the gods at the appropriate times as prescribed and honour my father Daśaratha who is the king of all men. Place *dharma* before all else and take care of my mother Kausalyā who is now old and burdened with sorrow. And always show respect to my other mothers for they have loved me as much as my own. Treat my brothers like your sons, especially Lakṣmaṇa and Śatrughna, for they are dearer to me than my own life. Never displease Bharata for he is the head of our family and of the kingdom. Kings show favour to those who honour them and strive to serve them. They are not well-disposed to those that work against them. They even renounce their own sons who act against their wishes. But kings always welcome capable men, even if they are commoners.

'Dearest wife, I am going to the forest. But you, my queen, must stay here and live in such a way that no one can criticize you. This is what I want you to do!'

Sītā was a soft-spoken person who was worthy of affection and respect. But now she spoke to her husband with an anger that arose from her love for him. 'Prince, a father, a mother, a brother, a son and a daughter-in-law face the consequences of their own actions and of what their fate has in store for them. Only a wife shares the fate of her husband. It is clear to me that I, too, must go into the forest. In this life, Rāma, a woman follows neither her father nor her son, not her mother nor her friends, not even her own inclinations. She follows only her husband.

'When you leave for the forest today, I shall walk ahead of you, crushing the prickly thorns on your path under my feet. Rid yourself of any anger or envy that you may have, as one throws away the water that is left after one has drunk from a cup. Take me with you, for I have never done anything wrong. A woman must be like the shadow of her husband's feet, whether he lives in a palace or walks through the air.

'My mother and father taught me how to behave in various situations. I need no advice on what I should do now. I shall live in the forest as happily as I lived in my father's house, with not a care in the world, concerned only with my loyalty to my husband. I shall find joy in the fragrant, flowering forest as I care for you and live the life of an ascetic.

'Rāma, you manage to protect all kinds of other people, why can't you protect me? I can live on roots and fruits. I shall cause you no trouble at all. I long to see all the different kinds of trees, the rivers and the mountains and the lakes where the lotuses bloom and the swans and the waterbirds play. I have nothing to fear because you shall be by my side. I am happy just to be with you. I can enjoy these simple pleasures even for one hundred thousand years!

'Rāma, my dearest, I could not bear to live in heaven without you. How can I possibly stay here when you have gone? I, too, shall go to the dense forest, filled with deer and monkeys and elephants, and live there as if it were my father's house, close by you, my mind calm and serene. My thoughts are with you constantly and my heart overflows with love for you. I would die without you. Listen to what I am saying and let me go with you!'

But even though Sītā begged and pleaded, Rāma, the best of men, who was devoted to *dharma,* had made up his mind to go without her. He began to enumerate the trials of life in the forest in an attempt to dissuade her.

'Sītā, gentle one, you come from a noble family and you are familiar with the dictates of *dharma.* If you stay here and do your duty, you will set my mind at ease. Do as I say, for the forest is full of trials and tribulations. Listen, and I will tell you about them.

'Give up the thought of coming with me. The forest is known for its hardships. I say this for your own good. I know that the forest offers no happiness and that difficulties abound there. It is not a pleasant place:

mountain waterfalls roar like thunder and their noise is exaggerated by the roar of lions from their caves. When you are tired and have to sleep at night, it shall be on a bed of fallen leaves. You shall have to fast as much as possible, your hair shall be matted and you shall wear ragged clothes. The wind blows fiercely and the nights are dark. One is always hungry in the forest! Snakes of all shapes and sizes slide uncaring through the bushes. Even water snakes slither across forest paths, curving and winding like the rivers in which they make their homes. Gentle lady, moths, scorpions, insects and mosquitoes shall hover around you all the time. Thorny bushes will rustle their branches in your face and reeds and grasses shall toss in the great winds. See how unpleasant the forest is!

'But enough of this! The more I talk about it the more I realize how many difficulties and dangers there are. The forest is not the place for you.'

Sītā realized that Rāma was determined to go without her. Her face wet with tears, she said, 'The horrors of living in the forest that you have just described seem like virtues to me. You will understand that only if you know how much I love you. Besides, I should go with you to respect the wishes of the elders. Rāma, if I am separated from you, I will die! No one can harm me, not even Indra, the king of the gods, if I am with you. You yourself have told me that a woman's place is with her husband.

'Apart from all this, there is something you should know. While I lived in my father's house, I was told by *brahmin* seers that I would have to live in the forest. Ever since I heard this from those men who could read signs, I have been eager to go to the forest. That prophecy has to come true and its time has arrived. So, my dear, I can do nothing else but come with you.

'I know that people who have not restrained their passions have a hard time in the forest. But, when I was a young girl, I heard a lot about life in the forest from a female ascetic. Since then, even though I have been living here in the palace, I have been curious to experience life in the forest. I am eager to leave now and the idea of looking after you in the forest appeals to me.

'When we were married, the sacred texts recited by the *brahmins* declared that when a woman is given away by her father, she stays with her husband even in the lives to come. That is her *dharma.* I am yours now and I am devoted to you. I shall be with you even in death, so why can't you take me to the forest with you? I shall be miserable without you. Take me with you to share your joys and sorrows. Otherwise, I shall kill myself by jumping into the fire, by drowning or by taking poison!'

Despite Sītā's many pleas, Rāma refused to change his mind. She wept hot tears that bathed the earth. Rāma tried hard to console her, but she was lost in her grief.

Slowly, though, Sītā grew angry and said indignantly to Rāma, 'How did my father, the king of Mithilā and the lord of the Videhas, get you, a woman disguised as a man, for a son-in-law! The world is wrong when they say that there is no one greater than Rāma, who blazes like the sun! What could possibly have made you so depressed and frightened that you wish to leave me here, I, who have no other refuge! I shall cling to you like Sāvitrī clung to Satyavān.

'I have never even thought about another man, unlike other women who bring shame on their families. Under no pressure at all, Rāma, you have decided to leave your wife with others, the wife you married as a young virgin girl and who has lived with you for so long! You are like an actor playing a role. You cannot go to the forest without me. I will go with you wherever you go, whether to the forest, to perform austerities or to heaven!

'I shall feel no fatigue as I walk behind you on the forest paths, no more than if we were playing in our bed. Coarse grasses, reeds and thorny plants along the way shall feel as soft as the finest cotton if I am with you. When I am covered by the dust raised by the mighty winds, I shall think of it as the rarest sandal paste. And could the leaves that we lie upon in the forest be any softer than our finest rugs and exquisite bed linen? The roots and fruits that you gather for me, however few, shall taste sweeter than ambrosia.

'I shall not give a thought to my father, my mother or my home, for I shall be enjoying the fruits and flowers. I will never cause you unhappiness nor place you in any danger. You must take me with you. My love for you makes it heaven for me to be with you and hell to be separated from you. If you leave me here, I shall drink poison because I do not want to fall into the hands of my enemies. I swear I will kill myself if you abandon me! If I cannot bear to be without you even for an hour, how will I survive ten years and then three more and then one after that!'

Sītā wept long and piteously until she wore herself out. She clung to her husband and kissed him again and again. His many excuses to leave her behind had stung her the way a female elephant is stung by a hunter's darts. Sītā let flow the tears she had held back for so long, like a tinder emitting sparks. Her bright tears fell from her eyes like water draining off the petals of a lotus. Rāma took her in his arms and comforted her.

'Darling, I would not want heaven itself if it were to make you sad!' he whispered, reassuring her. 'And I fear nothing except the Creator! I know I can protect you, but I would never have taken you into the forest without knowing what you really felt. Since you are destined to live in the forest, I can no more be separated from you than a famous man from his celebrity! Dear lady, I shall walk on the path of *dharma* that has been established by the good men who have gone before. And you shall follow me as Suvarcalā follows the sun!

'*Dharma* demands that we obey our father and our mother. I could not bear to live for a moment ignoring my mother Kaikeyī's wishes. I want to live in accordance with my father's decree, for he stands firm in *dharma* and that *dharma* is eternal. Come with me and be my partner in the life I must lead! Go quickly and distribute your wealth to the *brahmins* and food to the hungry mendicants!'

When Sītā realized that she was to go with her husband, she was overcome with happiness and began to distribute her wealth and personal belongings. Her mind was filled with her husband's words and her heart was light as she gave away her jewels and her fine clothes.

# *Chapter Eighteen*

Rāma turned to heroic Lakṣmaṇa, who stood beside him. 'If you come with me to the forest,' he said, 'then who will take care of Kausalyā and Sumitrā? The mighty king, who showers the earth with his munificence like a monsoon cloud, has been caught in a web of lust. Kaikeyī will not treat the other queens well, now that she has gained the kingdom.'

Lakṣmaṇa chose his words carefully as he replied. 'Rāma, you will definitely be able to persuade Bharata to act honourably towards Kausalyā and Sumitrā. And Kaikeyī's noble family has been granted a thousand villages for its maintenance. They can support scores of people. Let me walk before you with my bow and arrow, hewing a path for you with a basket and spade. Everyday I shall pick roots and fruits for you, the kind of food that is appropriate for ascetics. I shall stay awake while you sleep and you can enjoy yourself on the hills with Sītā while I do all that is necessary!'

Rāma was thrilled with Lakṣmaṇa's determination. 'Come, let us go quickly and say goodbye to all our friends,' he said. 'The two divine bows that strike terror into the hearts of all that see them, those that Varuṇa himself gave to Janaka at the time of the sacrifice, as well as the two impenetrable coats of mail, the inexhaustible quiver of arrows and the two gold-hilted swords that shine like the sun—fetch them all from our teacher's house where they are stored and worshipped.' Lakṣmaṇa did as he was instructed and brought the divine weapons, adorned with flowers, back to Rāma. 'You have arrived just when I needed you,' said Rāma. 'Together we must give away all our wealth and our possessions to the best of *brahmins* who live in the city and honour their teachers as well as all our retainers. Call for Vasiṣṭha's son, the noble Sujanya. I will honour him and the other *brahmins* and then leave for the forest.'

When the two princes and Sītā had given away all their possessions, they went together to see the king. Sītā had decorated the weapons with flowers and they blazed with splendour as the princes carried them through the main streets of the town. All the wealthy citizens climbed to their terraces to watch, their hearts heavy with despair. The streets were filled with people who had come to see Rāma and Lakṣmaṇa. When they saw Rāma walking through the streets, no royal canopy above his head, they were saddened and spoke among themselves.

'Ah! This man who used to lead the four-divisioned army now walks alone with only Sītā and Lakṣmaṇa behind him!'

'This man has enjoyed all material comforts and has fulfilled the wishes of other men. But he is so rooted in *dharma* that he cannot make a liar of his father!'

'It used to be that even the birds could not see Sītā! Now she walks in the streets stared at by all the common people!'

'Sītā is used to rare unguents and the finest sandal paste. She will grow pale in the rain and the cold!'

'Daśaratha is behaving like a man possessed! Otherwise he would never have banished his favourite son! Even a worthless son is not exiled. How could he do this to a son who has conquered the world through his conduct alone?'

'We, too, shall follow Rāma, with our wives and our families, like Lakṣmaṇa has done! We shall abandon our homes and our gardens and our fields and follow Rāma to share in his joys and sorrows!'

'Let Kaikeyī have our empty homes which have been stripped of their wealth and grains and material stocks, whose desolate courtyards have been covered with dust and abandoned by the gods!'

'The forest will be the city for us because Rāma will be there. This abandoned city shall turn into a desolate wasteland!'

Rāma heard these and many other similar remarks but his mind remained calm. He saw the woebegone faces of his retainers but he smiled and walked on, eager to see his father and carry out his command. Though he was anxious to depart for the forest, Rāma did not enter his father's palace immediately. 'Tell the king that I am here!' he said to Sumantra.

Sadly, Sumantra went to announce Rāma's arrival. He saw the grieving king sighing heavily. 'Sire, your son has given away all his wealth to *brahmins* and to his courtiers. Rāma has said goodbye to all his friends.

Now he waits at the door to see you,' said Sumantra with his palms joined and his head bowed. 'Be pleased to grant him audience! Shining with his royal virtues like the blazing sun, he is ready to go to the forest.'

The righteous and honourable king, whose heart was as deep as the ocean and as vast as space, said, 'Sumantra, summon all my wives who live in this palace. I wish to see Rāma with all of them here!' Sumantra went into the inner apartments and announced to the women there that the king had sent for them. There were three hundred and fifty virtuous women in Kausalyā's attendance and all of them, their eyes red from crying, went into Daśaratha's chambers. 'Sumantra! Bring in my son!' said the king as he saw them approaching.

Sumantra led Rāma, Lakṣmaṇa and Sītā into the king's presence. Daśaratha rose when he saw his son and moved quickly towards him. But before he could reach Rāma, he sank to the floor in a faint. The palace was filled with the wailing of hundreds of women mixed with the jingling of their ornaments. Rāma and Lakṣmaṇa ran towards the fallen king and lifted him in their arms. Weeping, they laid him on the couch with Sītā's help. After a few moments, the king recovered consciousness.

Rāma spoke gently to his grieving father. 'Great king, you are the lord of us all. Put an end to your grief. I ask for your permission to leave for the Daṇḍaka forest. Look kindly upon me! Sītā and Lakṣmaṇa insist on accompanying me though I have tried hard to dissuade them. Give all three of us your permission to leave.' Ram waited with his palms joined, for the king's response.

'Rāma, I have been trapped by Kaikeyī's boons. Take over as king of Ayodhyā today and have me arrested!' cried the king. Rāma, the best among all righteous men, replied calmly. 'Sir, you shall rule the earth a thousand years and I shall live in the forest. I cannot be the cause of your dishonour!'

'Go in peace my child! Free from fear, may you always walk along paths that are pleasant! Return home when you have won fame and glory!' said Daśaratha. 'But look, it is already evening. Do not leave today. Stay here this one night so that your mother and I can gaze at you to our heart's content and fulfil your every desire. Leave in the morning!'

'Tomorrow, who will offer me the things that I can get today,' said Rāma sadly. 'It is best if I leave immediately. Let Bharata have all that I leave behind—the earth, this kingdom with all its citizens, its abundant wealth and grain. Hold back your tears and calm yourself, like the ocean which does not allow itself to be agitated.

'I desire neither the kingdom nor happiness, not even Sītā. I wish only that your honour be maintained. Give this city and all that I have renounced to Bharata and I shall live in the forest. Let Bharata rule this earth covered with mountains and valleys, cities and forests and well-guarded frontiers. I am not interested in worldly pleasures or in desire, or even in those that are dear to me. Do not grieve on my account. I cannot have the kingdom, with all this wealth and happiness, at the cost of your honour. I shall be happy in the forest, living on roots and fruits and enjoying the rivers and streams and the different kinds of flowers. Do not be agitated.

'I consent to everything being given to Bharata. Bring me simple clothes and two baskets and two spades, for I must live in the forest for fourteen years'

Kaikeyī went herself to fetch the clothes and she said boldly to Rāma in front of everyone, 'Here! Put these on!' Rāma took the clothes from her and taking off his fine garments, dressed himself in the ascetic's robes. Lakṣmaṇa did the same but Sītā, who was used to the most delicate fabrics, looked at the robes in terror, the way a doe looks at a tiger. She took the clothes from the wicked Kaikeyī and turned to her husband who stood there, handsome as a *gandharva,* and asked timidly, 'How do the ascetics wear these?' Holding the clothes up to her throat, the princess stood there in utter confusion. Rāma quickly fastened the clothes over her silken garments. All the people who had gathered there were incensed when they saw how helpless and vulnerable Sītā was and they murmured against the king.

'Kaikeyī, Sītā does not deserve to wear these clothes,' sighed the king. 'Wretched woman! Is it not enough that Rāma has been banished? Why do you add to your crimes with more and more vile behaviour?' and he hung his head in shame.

'My mother, the righteous Kausalyā, is known for her virtues and she is free of petty jealousies,' said Rāma to his father. 'She is old now and she has never criticized you. She will drown in an ocean of sorrow when I have gone. Please treat her better than you have before. Be good to my mother who shall be pining for me, so that she does not die of grief while I am in the forest!'

Righteous Rāma joined his palms and honoured his mother. 'Mother,' he said, 'do not be unhappy. Look after my father. My exile into the forest shall end very soon. These fourteen years shall pass like a single night that you have slept through. Soon, you shall see me here again, surrounded by my friends, having done my duty.'

Then Rāma turned to his three hundred and fifty other mothers. 'Forgive me if I have ever spoken harshly to you or unintentionally hurt you in the course of our living together so closely. I now ask your permission to leave.' Daśaratha's distressed wives began to wail like *krauna* birds and the house that used be filled with the thunder of celebratory drums was now filled with wailing and crying because of the terrible tragedy that had descended upon it.

Rāma, Lakṣmaṇa and Sītā joined their palms and honoured the king sadly. Dulled by grief, they bid their mothers goodbye and touched their feet. Sumantra, who was courteous by nature and familiar with court ritual, spoke to Rāma as Mātali would to Indra. 'May good fortune go with you, prince!' he said humbly. 'Climb into the chariot and I will take you wherever you want to go! Today is the first day of your fourteen-year exile as decreed by the queen!'

Sītā, adorned by the many jewels that Daśaratha had given her, climbed into the shining chariot with a happy heart. The two brothers loaded the chariot with their divine weapons and the coats of mail which had been wrapped in animal skins. Sumantra made sure that all three of them were in the chariot and then, steeling himself against the grief which threatened to overwhelm him, goaded the horses which were as swift as the wind.

# *Chapter Nineteen*

As Rāma drove out of Ayodhyā for his long stay in the forest, the city was filled with the sounds of horses' trappings jingling, of elephants trumpeting, of agitated people. The sounds swelled and reverberated as the entire city, old and young, ran behind Rāma's chariot as they would run towards water in the parched months of the summer. They clung to the chariot's back and sides, their faces turned to Rāma as their tears streaked the earth. 'Charioteer, rein in the horses,' they cried. 'Drive slowly so that we can gaze at Rāma for a little longer. We will not see him again for many years!'

The king stepped out of his palace surrounded by sorrowing women. 'Let me see my beloved son!' he cried. The wailing of the king's women filled the air like that of female elephants when their mate has been captured. And the mighty Ikṣvāku Daśaratha, both father and king, his face was clouded like the moon during an eclipse.

A huge tumult arose behind Rāma as the people saw the king fall to the ground in his grief. Some of the people called out to Rāma, others wept aloud for his mother as they joined in the lamentations of the palace women. Rāma turned around and saw his grieving parents following him down the road on foot. Bound by the noose of *dharma,* Rāma dared not look at his mother's face. Rāma could not bear to see his aged parents' grief and he urged Sumantra to go faster. Weeping, Kausalyā ran behind the chariot, stumbling and falling, calling out to Rāma, Sītā and Lakṣmaṇa.

'Stop!' cried the king, 'Faster! Faster!' cried Rāma, and Sumantra felt as if he were trapped between the two giant wheels of the chariot. 'If the king should censure you for not stopping,' said Rāma, 'tell him that you did not prolong the agony of this moment of parting.' Sumantra announced Rāma's farewell to the citizens and though the horses were already flying like the wind, he spurred them on even faster. The king's retainers fell back but the townspeople did not consider that option for a moment. The ministers told the king that it was inauspicious to follow the one whose return was eagerly awaited. Daśaratha heard their wise words and stopped, bathed in sweat, as he looked longingly after his disappearing son.

Daśaratha gazed at the road as long as the dust from Rāma's chariot was visible, unable to tear his eyes away. He seemed to grow taller as he stood on his toes and strained to catch a last glimpse of his son. When even the dust from Rāma's receding chariot had disappeared, the mighty Ikṣvāku fell to the earth in his grief.

Kausalyā came and took his right arm to lead him away and Kaikeyī, who loved Bharata best, took his left arm. Even though the king was engulfed by sorrow, he was rich in *dharma* and retained his natural courtesies. 'Do not touch me, you wicked creature!' he cried to Kaikeyī. 'I never wish to set eyes on you again! Henceforth, you are neither my wife nor even a member of my family! You and your circle of friends and dependents are nothing to me and I am nothing to them. You have renounced *dharma* and seek only material prosperity and so I renounce you! Now and for all the lives to come, I reject that hand of yours that I took in marriage. And if Bharata is pleased that he has received an undivided kingdom, then let no offering that he makes for my welfare be efficacious!'

Grieving Kausalyā lifted the king, who was covered with dust from the road, and turned back towards the palace. When Daśaratha thought of his son, headed for the forest to live the life of an ascetic, his grief scorched him as if he had touched fire or raised his hand against an innocent *brahmin*. Again and again, he turned to look at the chariot's tracks and his face clouded over like the sun during an eclipse. He wailed aloud as his thoughts turned to his beloved Rāma.

When he felt that Rāma had probably crossed the city limits, he sighed. 'I can see the tracks of the chariot that carried my son away but I can no longer see my son! Who knows where he will sleep tonight, sheltering by the roots of some tree or other, a log or a stone for his pillow. And when he awakes, his body covered with dust, he will sigh like a great tusker. And the forest animals will see Rāma going forth, alone and unprotected, even though he is the lord of the earth. Ah Kaikeyī! Your desires shall be fulfilled. Live in this kingdom as a widow, for I cannot bear to live without my son!'

The king wept in front of all the people that had gathered and as he re-entered the city, he saw that all of Ayodhyā mourned for Rāma. The streets were deserted, the houses were empty and the shops and temples were silent. The distraught king went into his palace like the sun sinking into the ocean. But his home was empty without Rāma, Lakṣmaṇa and Sītā. 'Take me quickly to the apartments of Kausalyā, Rāma's mother,' he said to his attendants. When he reached there, he lay down on the bed but his mind was restless and tortured. 'Oh Rāma!' he cried. 'You have abandoned me! Lucky are those who shall live until Rāma returns. They shall embrace each other when they see him! Kausalyā, touch me. I cannot see you. My eyes which followed Rāma have not yet returned to me!' Kausalyā sat beside the grieving king and wept softly.

As the mighty Rāma proceeded towards the forest, he was followed by the people of Ayodhyā. Even though the king had been persuaded to return by his well-wishers, the people continued to follow the chariot, since they loved virtuous Rāma. He was as dear to them as the full moon. They begged Rāma to come back but he was determined to fulfil his father's promise and maintain his resolve to go to the forest.

Rāma spoke to his people with deep affection, as a father would to his children. 'All the love that the people of Ayodhyā have for me, let them give that and more to Bharata. That would make me very happy. Kaikeyī's Bharata is a generous man and he shall do all that is necessary for your happiness and prosperity. Though he is young in years, he is old in wisdom. He is gentle but firm and he is amply endowed with all the virtues. He will make a good ruler and keep all your fears at bay. He has been chosen as the crown prince and all of us must respect the king's decision. If you want to make me happy, you must behave such that the king has nothing to worry about while I am in the forest.' But the more Rāma argued in favour of *dharma,* the more the people urged him to be king.

Rāma and Lakṣmaṇa seemed to draw the wretched, weeping people of Ayodhyā with them, keeping them bound by the strength of their virtues. Even the old *brahmins*, rich in age and wisdom, called out from afar, their heads trembling with the weight of years. 'O thoroughbred horses that carry Rāma away, turn back! Go no further! Do what is right for your master and bring him back into the city instead of carrying him into the dense forest.'

Rāma dismounted at once when he saw the old *brahmins*. His compassionate heart could not bear to see the old men on foot as he rode in his chariot. He began to walk to the forest with small strides, Sītā and Lakṣmaṇa by his side. Seeing that Rāma was continuing his journey, the *brahmins* called out, 'Rāma, with our hair white as a swan's wing, our ancient bodies covered with dust, we beg you to turn back! Even inanimate beings are devoted to you. Show your love for those that love you! These trees would follow you if they were not prevented from doing so by their roots. They cry out to you as the winds blow through their branches. Birds sit silent without eating a single thing and plead with you, who have compassion for all creatures.'

As the *brahmins* called to Rāma in their anguish, the river Tamasā appeared, as if to prevent Rāma from going any further. When they reached the pleasant banks of the river, Rāma looked over at Sītā and said to Lakṣmaṇa, 'This is the first night of our lives in the forest. Both of you must have no regrets about your decision. These silent woods are now filled with the cries of birds and animals as they return to their homes for the night. In Ayodhyā tonight, I have no doubt that the citizens will be mourning our departure. I am also sure that noble Bharata will be consoling my mother and father with kind words that are filled with *artha, dharma* and *kāma.* I remind myself of Bharata's gentleness and so I do not grieve for my mother and father. Neither must you, Lakṣmaṇa! You did the right thing by coming with me for otherwise I would have had to seek help for Sītā's protection.

'Tonight I shall drink only water,' continued Rāma. 'I prefer to abstain from all the food the forest has to offer.' Then Rāma told Sumantra to look after the horses. Since the sun was setting, Sumantra tethered the horses and after making sure that they had enough to eat, returned to the group. As night fell, Sumantra performed the evening rituals and helped Lakṣmaṇa make a bed for Rāma in a grove of trees. Rāma lay down with Sītā and when Lakṣmaṇa saw that they were asleep, he began to recount Rāma's many virtues to Sumantra, who was keeping watch.

As he was doing so, the sun rose. Rāma had spent his first night on the banks of the Tamasā with his subjects sleeping nearby. Rāma woke and saw the people. 'Ah Lakṣmaṇa! Look at those people asleep under the trees!' he said. 'They love us so much that they show little concern for their own homes. They are so determined to take us back that they would rather die than give up their mission! Let us climb into our chariot and slip away quietly while they are still asleep. Then the citizens of Ayodhyā will no longer have to sleep under trees for my sake. It is the duty of a prince to protect his people from hardship that he has created. They cannot be made to suffer on account of the prince!'

'I like the plan,' said Lakṣmaṇa as Rāma stood there like *dharma* incarnate. 'Climb into the chariot quickly!' Sumantra had harnessed the horses and stood waiting for Rāma's instructions. 'Turn the chariot around. Drive us far away and then return here, so that the people will not know where we have gone,' said Rāma. Sumantra did as he was told and quickly came back to where Rāma was. The princes and Sītā mounted the chariot and drove down the road that had no obvious dangers but was still frightening to behold.

The citizens awoke to find Rāma gone. They were terribly disheartened and fell to grieving. They looked everywhere but they could not see him and soon, they were exhausted by their tears. They followed the chariot tracks for a while but they soon disappeared and the people were plunged into a deeper grief. They turned back saying, 'What can we do now that even fate is against us?' Utterly distraught, they went home along the road on which they had come.

The people who had accompanied Rāma went back to their homes and surrounded by their wives and children they wept bitterly. There were no signs of joy anywhere. Shops looked bare and empty as merchants did not lay out their wares. Even food was not cooked in homes that night. Mothers did not celebrate the births of their first sons nor was there rejoicing among people who had recovered long-lost wealth. In every home, weeping women berated their returning husbands with words as sharp as a goad on an elephant.

'What use is a home, work, family, wealth, sons and happiness to someone who cannot see Rāma?'

'There is only one heroic man in the world and that is Lakṣmaṇa. He has followed Rāma and Sītā into the forest!'

'The rivers and the lotus pools are fortunate indeed, for Rāma shall plunge into their clear waters to bathe!'

'The mountains and forests shall welcome Rāma like a beloved guest when he arrives!'

'Trees laden with flowers and haunted by bees shall burst into unseasonal fruits when they see Rāma! Mountains and flowing streams shall proudly display their rushing waterfalls for Rāma!'

'There can be no fear or suffering where Rāma is, for he is a great hero and Daśaratha's son!'

'Let us go after him quickly before he gets too far away. The shadow cast by so great a man is a blessing in itself! He is our protector and our refuge!'

'We shall serve Sītā and you can serve Rāma,' said the grieving women to their husbands. 'Rāma will see to your welfare in the forest and Sītā will look after us women. Why should we stay in this city with its unhappy memories and its despairing citizens?'

'If Kaikeyī's reign turns out to be unrighteous and we are all made vulnerable, what will the be the use of our sons and our wealth, of even our lives?'

'Kaikeyī has already betrayed her husband and his son for the sake of power. How can we expect this woman who has dishonoured her family to take care of us?'

'With Rāma gone, the king will not live very long. Everything will be destroyed when he dies.'

Thus did the women of Ayodhyā lament, tormented by their grief. They suffered Rāma's exile as if it were the banishment of their own son or brother, for he meant more to them than their families.

# *Chapter Twenty*

Meanwhile, in what remained of the night, Rāma travelled as far as he could, keeping his father's command in mind. When the sun rose, Rāma performed the morning rituals and found that they had reached the borders of the kingdom. He looked around and saw the well-ploughed fields and further, in the distance, the flowering trees of the forest. He sped the horses on faster and as he drove along, he could hear the villagers criticizing his father for being a slave to his lust.

'O that cruel and wicked Kaikeyī, so bent on making mischief! She has transgressed all the bounds of decency!'

'She made the king banish his wise and righteous son, a son so self-restrained and calm, into the forest!'

Listening to these and other similar sentiments, Rāma, the ruler of Kosalā, passed beyond the frontiers of his kingdom. He crossed the river Vedaśruti with its cool and pleasant waters and turned the chariot in the direction of Agastya's hermitage. Crossing the rivers Gomatī and Syandikā, Rāma showed Sītā all the lands that Manu himself had bestowed upon the Ikṣvāku kings in the distant past. 'When shall I return to the flowering groves of the Sarayū and hunt the deer in the company of my parents?' he said sadly to Sumantra, his voice as sweet as a bird's. 'Not that I wish to hunt all the time in these woods, but it is a prescribed recreation for kings!' And so they travelled further, Rāma speaking sweetly to the charioteer about all the things that entered his mind.

Rāma turned towards Śṛngaverapura and soon they came upon the Gangā, the magnificent river that flows in all three realms. Her waters are so clear and pure that they are constantly frequented by *ṛṣis*. The air was filled with the sound of swans and cranes and *cakravāka* birds and the waters were full of porpoises, crocodiles and all kinds of water creatures. Rāma looked at the dancing waters with delight and decided that they would spend the night there. He dismounted from the chariot under the shade of a tree with Sītā and Lakṣmaṇa while Sumantra freed the horses from their harness.

The king of this region was a man named Guha. He was a Niṣāda and famed for his strength and courage. He was a good friend of Rāma's. As soon as he heard that Rāma had arrived in his kingdom, Guha hurried to meet him, accompanied by the elders, his ministers and his family. Knowing that the Niṣāda king had come a long distance, Rāma and Lakṣmaṇa went to greet him. Guha embraced Rāma sadly and said, 'Treat this place as you would treat your own city. Tell me, Rāma, what can I do for you?'

Guha sent for all kinds of food and drink and performed the *arghya* ritual for his honoured guest. 'Welcome, great hero! The whole earth belongs to you. We are your servants. Treat this kingdom as yours. Accept all that we offer you, this food and drink that we have brought and this fodder for your fine horses.'

'You have honoured us and made us very happy with all these things,' said Rāma affectionately as he embraced Guha tightly in his strong arms. 'You came all the way here on foot! I am delighted to see you, Guha, in good health and surrounded by your family. I trust that all is well in your kingdom, with your family and with your finances.

'I thank you for all the gifts you have brought with so much affection, but I cannot accept them. You know that I have taken the vows of an ascetic. I must live in the forest, wear simple clothes and eat only fruits and roots according to the ascetic's code of conduct. I can accept nothing other than the fodder for the horses. You will have honoured me adequately by giving me that. These horses are very dear to my father Daśaratha and if they are cared for then I, too, am satisfied.'

Guha told his men to feed and water the horses. Rāma performed the evening rituals and drank only water that Lakṣmaṇa had brought for him. Lakṣmaṇa washed Rāma's feet and when Rāma and his wife lay down for the night, he went and sat under a nearby tree. Guha, armed with his bow, sat and talked with Lakṣmaṇa and Sumantra as they kept watch through the night. As that mighty son of Daśaratha, who was made for happiness and was unused to sorrow, slept, even the night seemed to linger in vigil.

At dawn, the broad-chested Rāma woke and spoke to Lakṣmaṇa. 'The sun has risen, Lakṣmaṇa! The black *koel* sings and you can hear the cries of the peacocks from the forest. Let us make preparations to cross the Gangā as she hastens towards the sea.' Lakṣmaṇa alerted Guha and Sumantra and returned to his brother. The princes strapped on their armour, picked up their weapons and went down to the river with Sītā. Sumantra, the humble charioteer, came up to Rāma and with his palms joined in respect, he said quietly, 'What shall I do now?'

'You must return,' replied Rāma. 'You have done all that you were supposed to do for me. We must release the chariot here and go onwards to the forest on foot.'

Sumantra was filled with sorrow when he learned that he was to go no further. 'There is no one who approves of your going to live in the forest with your wife and brother like a common person,' said Sumantra. 'If you are faced with hardships, I cannot believe that there is any merit in abstinence and fasting, in goodness or in honesty. By living in the forest with Sītā and Lakṣmaṇa you will gain as much fame as you would have if you had conquered the three worlds. But we who come to you for refuge shall surely die, left under the power of wicked Kaikeyī!' Gazing at Rāma, whom he loved more than his own life and who was going so far away, Sumantra began to weep.

When he stopped crying, Rāma consoled him gently. 'The Ikṣvāku clan has no greater friend than you. Make sure King Daśaratha does not grieve for me. I say this to you because the king is very upset and he is also swayed by his lust. Whatever the king orders for Kaikeyī's pleasure must be executed without any delay. Kings rule for the sole purpose that their wishes never be denied. Behave such that the king never knows a moment of sorrow or displeasure. Give that aged and sorrowing man who has conquered his senses my regards. Tell him of my words and my intentions.

'Say to him, "Neither Sītā nor I nor Lakṣmaṇa have any regrets about leaving Ayodhyā for the forest. These fourteen years shall pass quickly and when we return, you shall see us again!" And when you have said this to the king, Sumantra, then tell my mother and all the royal noble ladies with her, including Kaikeyī, that Sītā and I and the noble Lakṣmaṇa touch their feet and inquire about their welfare. Tell the king to send for Bharata immediately and to install him as heir as soon as he arrives. Tell him that once he has anointed Bharata his heir, he has no further need to grieve for me. And tell Bharata that he should behave towards all our mothers the way he behaves towards the king. He should treat my mother Kausalyā exactly the way he would Sumitrā and Kaikeyī.'

Sumantra heard Rāma through and spoke to him affectionately. 'What I am going to say now may seem inappropriate but my words come from my love and devotion to you, so you should pardon me. How can I return to the city without you? It has been plunged into grief as if for a lost son. The citizens will be overcome with despair when they see the empty chariot, like an army that sees the empty chariot of its commander who has been killed. The noise they made when you left will be nothing in comparison to the sound of wailing that will rise when they realize that you have really left them and gone.

'What will I say to your poor mother to prevent her from grieving further—that I have taken her son to his uncle's house? I cannot tell a lie, but I cannot speak the painful truth either. If you leave me here despite my pleas, I shall drive the chariot into a raging fire. Rāma, I can use my chariot to drive away any animals that disturb the practise of your austerities. You let me be your charioteer. Show the same kindness and let me stay happily with you in the forest.' Sumantra pleaded over and over and proffered many reasons.

But Rāma was compassionate towards his retainers and so he replied, 'Faithful servant, I know how devoted you are to me. Listen and I will tell you why I am sending you back into the city. Kaikeyī, my youngest mother, will be convinced that I have gone to the forest when she sees you return. That will make her happy and then she will no longer suspect my righteous father of speaking an untruth. I fully intend to give my youngest mother the joy of seeing her son Bharata rule this prosperous kingdom. You must take the chariot back to Ayodhyā and give everyone my messages. That will please me and my father most!'

Then Rāma turned to Guha and choosing his words with care, he said, 'I must mat my hair. Bring me the sap of the *nyāgrodha* tree.' Guha fetched the sap and Rāma matted his own hair as well as Lakṣmaṇa's with it. But even with their matted hair and their simple clothes, the two brothers shone like *ṛṣis*. Rāma took the required vows and thus it was that Rāma and Lakṣmaṇa took their first steps along the ascetics' path.

Before going further, Rāma gave Guha good advice on how to administer his kingdom, the army, the treasury, the fort and all the citizens, since the ruling of a kingdom is a difficult task. He bade Guha farewell and went quickly onwards with Sītā and Lakṣmaṇa, his mind serene.

They came to the swiftly flowing Gangā and found a boat tied to the shore. Lakṣmaṇa helped Rāma and Sītā into the boat and after a last farewell to Guha and Sumantra, the boat was pushed off into the river. Sītā honoured the mighty river, and soon, they reached its southern shore.

'Walk ahead, Lakṣmaṇa,' said Rāma. 'Sītā and I will follow you. I shall bring up the rear, walking behind you and Sītā so that I can protect you both. Today Sītā will be acquainted with the hardships of forest life!'

Sumantra had kept his eyes on Rāma until he reached the far shore. Now that he could no longer see him, he wiped away his tears. Meanwhile, the two brothers had killed a boar, two antelopes and a deer to appease their hunger as they made their way into the forest.

# *Chapter Twenty-One*

They found a large tree and Rāma performed the evening worship. 'This is our first night away from human habitation and without Sumantra. You must not give in to despair,' said Rāma to Lakṣmaṇa. 'You must stay awake and watch all night because Sītā's safety depends on us. Let us make some sort of bed with all the materials we have collected. We shall get through this night somehow!'

Rāma, who deserved the best of beds, lay down on the bare earth and continued talking sadly. 'Lakṣmaṇa, I am sure that the king will have trouble sleeping tonight! But Kaikeyī's wish has been fulfilled so she should be happy. But, when she sees Bharata, she may want to kill the king for the sake of the kingdom. And what will that poor helpless old man do, now that he has succumbed to lust and placed himself in Kaikeyī's power? Especially since I am not with him!

'When I think of the disaster that has befallen me as a result of the king's infatuation I feel the pursuit of pleasure must be even more compelling than the pursuit of wealth or *dharma*. Even an ignorant man would not renounce his son for the sake of a beautiful woman. But our father has abandoned me, his most obedient son! Ram recognizes his father's weakness

'Ah! Bharata is so fortunate! He is happy with his wife by his side, enjoying the pleasures of ruling over Kosalā. He alone enjoys the pleasures, since my father is too old and I am stuck in the forest! He who abandons wealth and *dharma* and chases after pleasure shall soon destroy himself, like Daśaratha did! Kaikeyī must have come to our family with the sole intention of destroying Daśaratha, banishing me and securing the kingdom for Bharata! complaining a lot for the most virtuous men ever

'Suppose Kaikeyī, intoxicated by her good fortune, starts to torment Kausalyā and Sumitrā because of me? Lakṣmaṇa, I do not want Sumitrā to suffer on my account. You must return to Ayodhyā as soon as it is morning. You can protect Kausalyā as well. She is so vulnerable. I shall go into the Daṇḍaka forest alone with Sītā!

'Kaikeyī is base and mean and may treat Kausalyā badly. Place my mother under Bharata's care, for he is a righteous man! My mother must have caused the separation of mothers and sons in her past life for her to be in this situation now! She looked after me for so many years and bore a number of burdens for my sake. Now I have been snatched away from her just as it was time for her to bear the fruits of her efforts! Damn me! May no woman ever have a son like me, one that causes her so much sorrow!

'I could easily conquer Ayodhyā and the entire earth in anger with just my arrows. But one should never use one's strength without reason. If I do not crown myself today, Lakṣmaṇa, it is only because I fear the consequences of violating *dharma* in my next life!'

Rāma wept in his sorrow and then spent the rest of the night in silence in that lonely forest. When his tears had spent themselves as a forest fire dies down or the ocean calms itself after a storm, Lakṣmaṇa consoled his brother. 'Rāma, best of all warriors, I know the city of Ayodhyā has lost all its lustre today, like the night without a moon! But there is no use in your being miserable. You will only make Sītā and me feel worse. Neither of us can live without you for a single hour, like fish cannot live without water. I have no desire to see our father or my mother Sumitrā or Śatrughna or even heaven if I am not with you!'

Fortified by Lakṣmaṇa's wise and sensitive words, Rāma resolved to stay in the forest with Lakṣmaṇa for the stipulated period.

After they had spent the night under the huge tree, Rāma, Sītā and Lakṣmaṇa waited for daylight and then proceeded towards Prayāga, the confluence of the Gangā and the Yamunā. They travelled through regions that were more beautiful than anything they had ever seen before. They walked at an easy pace, looking at the trees and plants around them.

Around noon, Rāma said, 'Look, Lakṣmaṇa, the smoke around Prayāga rises up like the banner of the fire god! We must be close to the great sage's hermitage. We must have reached the confluence of the rivers. I can hear their waters crashing against each other!' By sunset, they had reached the sage Bharadvāja's settlement.

Though they were eager to see the sage, the three of them stopped at some distance from the hermitage. 'We are Rāma and Lakṣmaṇa, the sons of Daśaratha,' announced Rāma. 'And this is my virtuous wife Sītā, the daughter of Janaka. She has followed me into the deserted forest where sages practice austerities. When my father banished me, my beloved younger brother, who is a man of firm resolve, decided to come with me. We shall enter the mighty forest as my father decreed and we shall live on roots and fruits as prescribed by the *dharma* of the ascetics!'

Surrounded by birds and animals and other sages, Bharadvāja welcomed Rāma as an honoured guest. 'It has been a long time, Rāma, since I saw you here,' he said. 'I have heard about your unjust banishment. There is a quiet and deserted spot between the two rivers. It is a pleasant place, conducive to gaining spiritual merit. You can live there simply and easily.'

'I am afraid that if we live there, the citizens of Ayodhyā will keep coming to see Sītā and me,' replied Rāma. 'Can you tell us of a lonely, uninhabited place where we could establish a small settlement and live in peace?' Bharadvāja saw that Rāma's words were wise and he told him about a place that would meet his requirements.

'Child, there is a mountain about ten *yojanās* from here. It is very beautiful and has a pleasant view from all sides. *Ṛṣis* often visit it since it is a holy place. The mountain is called Citrakūṭa and like Mount Gandhamādana it teems with bears and monkeys. A man who sees Citrakūṭa is filled with goodness and is disinclined to act inappropriately. A great many sages have practised austerities there for hundreds of years and have ascended to heaven with ease, their heads as bare as skulls. It is extremely isolated. You could live there in peace and comfort. Or you can stay here with us and live the life of an ascetic.'

Night fell as the sage and Rāma talked of many things. Rāma, Lakṣmaṇa, and Sītā spent the night at Bharadvāja's hermitage and at dawn, Rāma went to the sage, who shone with his own splendour. 'We have passed a pleasant night with you. Now we ask for permission to leave for the place where we must live.' 'Go to Citrakūṭa which abounds in roots and fruits and honey,' said the sage. 'Go to that blessed place which is filled with the songs of birds and made beautiful by herds of elephants and deer that wander there. Go, Rāma, and make your home there.'

Bharadvāja blessed the departing travellers as he would his own children. They walked in the direction of the mountain, crossing the

Yamunā as they went. 'Take Sītā with you and walk in front,' said Rāma to Lakṣmaṇa. 'Give her fruits and flowers that might please her.' Walking between the brothers, Sītā appeared like a female elephant between two tuskers. The gentle woman asked Rāma about every single flower and creeper that she had never seen before. Fired by her enthusiasm, Lakṣmaṇa brought Sītā all kinds of plants and flowering stems. Sītā was filled with delight when she saw the dark sands of the Yamunā frequented by swans and cranes and waterbirds.

After they had gone some distance, the brothers killed a few animals and ate them on the banks of the Yamunā. They amused themselves with the sights and sounds of the forest until they found a suitable resting place for the night.

The next day, they reached Citrakūṭa and found that it was indeed a pleasant region, inhabited by different kinds of birds and animals. 'We shall be happy here,' said Rāma as he asked Lakṣmaṇa to fetch leaves and logs to make a small thatched hut. Lakṣmaṇa killed a black antelope as an offering to the spirits of the area. They roasted it over a blazing fire. When it was fully cooked and all its blood had been absorbed, Lakṣmaṇa said, 'Rāma, this animal is suitable as an offering. It has been roasted to a dark brown colour and all its limbs are intact so it looks as if it is alive. You can worship the gods with it.'

Rāma bathed, recited *mantras* to ward off evil and offered the antelope as a sacrifice to the gods. Then all three of them entered the hut which had different areas within it, designated for various activities.

Now that they had settled on the mountain with their minds calm and serene, Rāma's heart was filled with joy and he no longer felt any sadness at leaving the city.

# *Chapter Twenty-Two*

Once Rāma had left for the forest, Guha and Sumantra spent a long time talking sadly before Sumantra harnessed the horses and set off for Ayodhyā. He drove quickly through towns and villages and fragrant forests until on the third day he arrived on the outskirts of the city.

Sumantra saw that Ayodhyā was completely joyless, silent and deserted and was filled with despair. 'Can it be that the entire city with its horses and elephants, commoners and noble people has been consumed in a fire of grief for Rāma?' he thought as he entered the gates.

Thousands of people ran after Sumantra when they saw that he had returned. 'Where is Rāma?' they asked. 'I left the great-souled Rāma on the banks of the Gangā when he asked me to return,' replied Sumantra. The people sighed and cursed and called out to Rāma as the tears streamed down their faces. They gathered in small groups and Sumantra could hear them talking among themselves. 'Our lives are truly over,' they said. 'We shall never see Rāma again.'

Sumantra's face was pale as he drove through the main streets to the king's palace. He entered the inner courtyards and saw Daśaratha's women talking sadly about Rāma's absence. Deep inside the palace, in the white chamber, Sumantra saw the king still distraught with grief for his son. He bowed to the king and repeated Rāma's message.

The king listened in silence and then fell to the floor in a faint. The women began to wail as Kausalyā lifted the king with Sumantra's help. 'Speak to Sumantra. He has returned from the forest with a message from Rāma, who has undertaken such a difficult task,' she said. 'You have treated him unjustly and now you are ashamed of your actions, great king! But no one can help you in your sorrow! Get up. May your health be restored! The woman who incites fear, Kaikeyī, is not here, so you can speak freely!' she wept.

The men and women in the city heard the wailing from the palace and young and old wept anew as the city was plunged into turmoil.

Kausalyā continued her lament. 'Did you think, lord of all men, how your sons and the gentle Sītā, who is used to the best of things, would bear the hardships of the forest? How will that delicate woman survive the heat and the cold? All her life, that gentle creature has eaten the best of foods, flavoured with subtle spices. How will she eat the crude foods of the forest?

'Rāma is accustomed to hearing the finest music. Now he must listen to the harsh sounds of the beasts of the jungle. Rāma's mighty arms are as strong as Indra's flagstaff. Now he must use them to pillow his head! Ah! my heart must be as hard as a diamond that it does not break into a thousand pieces!

'Even if Rāma returns after fourteen years, there is no guarantee that Bharata will give up the kingdom and all its wealth. An elder brother can only feel contempt when he is offered a kingdom that has already been enjoyed by his younger brother! A tiger will not eat what another animal has killed and Rāma, that tiger among men, will not accept what has been enjoyed by another. If you were truly devoted to *dharma* you would never have exiled your virtuous son! You have destroyed the kingdom and the state, yourself and your ministers. You have destroyed me and my son! You have destroyed everything! And your other wife and her son rejoice!'

Daśaratha was deeply pained by Kausalyā's harsh words. Suddenly, he remembered the terrible thing he had done out of ignorance in his past and his sorrow increased.

'Have pity on me, Kausalyā!' he begged. 'You are kind and loving even towards strangers. I beseech you! You are righteous and know the best and the worst that a human being is capable of! You also know that to a wife, a husband is like a god, whether he is good or bad. Do not speak to me so cruelly, even though you are overcome with your own grief!'

Kausalyā's tears flowed afresh when she heard the king's piteous words. 'Forgive me!' she wept as she placed the king's hands upon her head. 'You do me a great wrong by pleading with me! A husband who is known through all the world for his goodness cannot debase himself at his wife's feet in this manner! I know that you are an honourable and righteous man and I am familiar with the dictates of *dharma.* I do not know what terrible things I said in my grief for my son!

'Grief is the greatest enemy because it destroys fortitude, knowledge and everything. The five nights that have passed since Rāma left have seemed like five years to me. When I think of him, my hearts swells with grief like the ocean when it fills with water from the rivers!'

As she was speaking, the light grew gentle and soon night fell. Soothed by Kausalyā, the grieving king fell asleep.

After a while, Daśaratha awoke and still depressed, he began to brood. He kept thinking about the terrible thing that he had done in the past and finally, he spoke about it to Kausalyā.

'A man reaps the fruit of all he does, be it good or bad, my dear. A man who acts without knowing the consequences of his action is called a fool.

'When I was a young man, Kausalyā, I was known for being the archer who could find a target just by hearing its sound. It was this skill that led me to commit a terrible crime. This sorrow that has befallen me is of my own making. I am reaping the consequences of shooting an arrow in ignorance after hearing a sound.

'This happened before I married you, when I was the heir-apparent. It was the middle of summer, when passions run high. The sun had sucked all the moisture from the earth, and leaving her dry and spent, had moved into a lower orbit. The heat diminished, and soon, soothing clouds were visible. Peacocks and frogs rejoiced in the forests.

'During that pleasant season, I had not yet learned to control my passions. I was restless and so, armed with my bow, I climbed into my chariot and went to the banks of the river Sarayū. I was hoping to kill either a boar or an elephant or some other large animal. In the darkness, I heard the sound of a pot being filled with water. It sounded like an elephant to me. I carefully chose an arrow that was as deadly as a poisonous snake and shot it from my bow.

'I heard a human voice call out from the direction in which it flew. "Why would anyone shoot an arrow at a hermit? I came here to these deserted banks at night to draw water. Why would anyone loose an arrow at me? What harm have I ever done that person? I live like a *ṛṣi,* eating only what the forest produces. How can anyone use a weapon against me when I have renounced violence? This is an unrighteous act, without cause or purpose. It is as terrible as sleeping with a teacher's wife!

'"I have no sadness at the prospect of my own death. I grieve only for my father and mother who will be inconsolable when I die. I have supported them for so long. They are old, how will they live without me? Who is this immature person who has destroyed everything for me with a single arrow, simply because he could not control himself?"

'The bow and arrow fell from my hands when I heard these heart-rending words. I had always wanted to walk the path of righteousness. In terrible agitation, I followed the voice and on the banks of the river I found a young hermit, his genitals pierced by my arrow. He scorched me with his glance and said, "What harm could I, a forest dweller, have ever done to you, great king? All I wanted was to collect water for my parents. When you killed me with that single arrow, you also killed two old people, my blind mother and father! They are waiting anxiously for my return. How long can they endure their thirst, sustained only by hope?

'"Ah! the fruits of austerities and penance and learning are useless since my father has no idea that I lie here like this! And even if he knew, what could he do, helpless as a tusker that cannot go to the aid of another wounded elephant! Go quickly and tell my father what has happened lest he consume you with his wrath, as the fire consumes the forest.

'"This path leads to my father's hermitage. Appease him before he curses you in anger. But before that, have mercy on me and pull out this arrow. The pain washes over me as the river water swell over its banks! I am not a *brahmin*, so you need have no fear on that account.* I was born of a *śūdra* mother and a *vaiśya* father."

'As he lay there curled up in his pain, I pulled the arrow from his body. I looked at him, half in the river, soaked by its waters, and I felt fear clutch at my heart. I realized I had done a terrible thing in my ignorance and I began to think how I could make amends for it.

'I filled his pot with water and went down the path he had indicated until I reached his hermitage. I saw his blind parents with no one to lead them around, like birds with clipped wings. They sat there, unable to move, utterly vulnerable, talking about their hopes which I had shattered.

'"What took you so long, my son?" said the old man when he heard my footsteps. "Give me the water! Have you been playing in the river? Your mother's throat is parched. Bring me the water quickly! Have we offended

---

* Killing a *brahmin* was the worst of all possible crimes. The young ascetic is trying to reassure Daśaratha that he is not guilty of that.

you in any way? You should not hold anything against us, you are an ascetic. We cannot walk and you are our feet. We cannot see and you are our eyes. Our lives depend on you. Why are you so quiet?"

'I was so overcome with fear and panic that I could not speak. With a great effort, I controlled myself. I found my voice and began to tell the old couple about the terrible thing that had happened to their son.

'"I am not your son, great sage. I am the warrior Daśaratha. I have earned the contempt of good men and this grief through my actions. Blessed one, I came to the banks of the Sarayū armed with my bow, eager to kill an elephant or any other animal that came there to drink. I heard the sound of a pot being filled with water and mistaking it for an elephant, I loosed an arrow in the direction of the sound.

'"When I got to the riverbank, I saw a young ascetic lying on the ground, an arrow through his heart, taking his last breath. I wanted to kill an elephant and so I shot my arrow guided by the sound. In doing so, I killed your son! He died the moment I pulled the arrow from his body, crying for you and lamenting your blindness. I killed your son accidentally in my ignorance. What happens next depends on you and your capacity for mercy!"

'The sage was overwhelmed with grief when he heard my story. I stood before him with my palms joined and he said, "If you had not confessed this to me, your head would have shattered into a thousand pieces. A *kṣatriya* who wilfully kills an ascetic falls from his position in society. You are alive only because you committed this act in ignorance. In fact, your entire clan could have been wiped out today. Where would you be then? Take us to where our son lies," he said to me. "We wish to look upon him for the very last time, even if his body lies on the ground covered with blood, his clothes in disarray!"

'Alone, I led the devastated old couple to where their son lay and helped them to find his body. They touched it and threw themselves upon it weeping. "Even if you do not love me, my son, think of your mother," cried the old man. "Sweet child, embrace me, say something! Who shall I hear reciting the sacred verses in the morning in a voice so pure and clear that it rises straight to the heavens? Who shall speak to me the way you used to after you had bathed and performed the evening rituals? I cannot beg and have no one to protect me. Who shall gather roots and fruits for me? Who shall treat me like an honoured guest? How shall I take care of your mother, this virtuous woman who is old and blind and yearns for her son?

"Stop here, my son! Don't leave for the world of the dead just yet! Tomorrow your mother and I shall come with you! In any case, overcome with sorrow, alone in this forest, we shall soon follow you! When I meet the god of death I shall ask him to spare you so that you can support your aged parents. Ah! my son, even though you were blameless in this, you were killed by a wicked act. But the power of my austerities will ensure that you attain the world of heroic warriors."

'The old man wept as he performed the last rites for his son along with his wife. Then he turned to me and said, "With a single arrow, you made me childless. Now kill me, too. Death shall not cause me any pain. But because you killed my innocent son in your ignorance, I shall place a brutal curse upon you that shall cause you great pain. You too shall grieve for a lost son as I have. And you shall die grieving for your son!"

'The words of that powerful sage have come true today, dear Kausalyā. I shall indeed die grieving for my son. If only Rāma could embrace me now and come back to the kingdom! But I could not have acted otherwise and neither could he!

'Ah! Kausalyā, my eyes dim, I cannot see you any more. My memory fades. Death's messengers hurry me along! What greater sorrow could I have than not being able to see noble and honourable Rāma at the moment of my death! Those who shall see Rāma again after fourteen years shall be as blessed as the gods!'

King Daśaratha died around midnight in a paroxysm of grief for his beloved son.

The king died like a fire that has been extinguished, like the ocean without its waters, like the sun without its light. Kausalyā wept as she placed the king's head on her lap. 'You can have your heart's desire, Kaikeyī!' she said. 'You renounced the king so that you could have your own way, you cruel and wicked woman! Now enjoy the kingdom without rivals!

'Rāma has left me and gone and now my husband is dead. Alone and abandoned on this unpleasant path, I have no wish to continue my life. What woman, other than one like Kaikeyī who has renounced both her husband and *dharma,* would have any wish to live now? Kaikeyī destroyed this entire clan because of the hunchback!' Distraught, Kausalyā fell upon her husband's body and clung to it until the attendants led her away. The king's advisors did not want to perform the funeral in the absence of his sons and so they ordered that the body be preserved. The palace retainers placed the king's body in a huge trough of oil and began the preparations for his last rites.

# *Chapter Twenty-Three*

Vasiṣṭha gathered the king's advisors and ministers and the learned *brahmins*. 'Bharata and his brother Śatrughna are staying happily with Bharata's mother's family in Rājagṛha,' he said to them. 'Let messengers be dispatched at once on our fastest horses to bring the brothers here.' The assembly agreed and Vasiṣṭha summoned the special messengers. 'Go to Rājagṛha without delay. Follow my instructions carefully. Hide your grief and speak to Bharata thus. "The ministers and priests ask after your welfare. You must come to Ayodhyā with us immediately, for there is some urgent work for you there." Do not tell him about Rāma's exile or his father's death or the terrible calamity that has befallen the royal family. Take these silken garments and jewels for Bharata and the king and go quickly!'

The messengers left immediately. Because of their love for their king and their desire to protect his family, they rode quickly and reached Rājagṛha by nightfall.

Bharata had a most unpleasant dream on the night that Ayodhyā's messengers arrived in Rājagṛha. Since the dream occurred in the early hours of the morning, the prince was greatly disturbed. His friends and well-wishers gathered around him when they saw how agitated he was. They began to talk of this and that in order to distract him. They sang and danced and told jokes and presented pieces of theatre. But though they tried hard to make him laugh, Bharata remained downcast. 'Why are you so depressed when all your friends are with you?' asked his best friend. Bharata replied by telling him about his dream.

'In my dream I saw my father, dirty and with his hair dishevelled, falling from a mountaintop into a pit of cow dung. I saw him jumping up and down in the dung, drinking oil from his cupped hands and laughing desperately. He ate some rice and then, his head hanging low, he dived into a trough of oil over and over again until his body was covered with it. In the same dream, I saw the ocean dry up and the moon crash to the earth like a huge fire dying down. Trees withered and I saw the mountains tremble and smoke as the earth fell into a chasm. Black and yellow women laughed at my father who sat on an iron throne in clothes of black. Then, smeared with red sandal paste and wearing a garland of red flowers, my father hurried off towards the south in a chariot pulled by donkeys. My dream was so terrible that I feel that either Rāma or Lakṣmaṇa or I will surely die! If you see a man in a chariot pulled by donkeys in a dream then you shall surely see the smoke from his funeral pyre before long!

'This dream is the reason I am so depressed and you cannot amuse me. My throat is dry and my mind is uneasy. I see no cause for fear but I am frightened despite myself. I worry about the king whom I saw in a such an unimaginable situation in my dream.'

Even as Bharata was recounting his dream to his friends, the messengers from Ayodhyā entered the beautiful and well-fortified city of Rājagṛha on their exhausted horses. They went directly to the king and were courteously received. They bowed and said to Bharata, 'The ministers and priests send you their good wishes. You must return with us at once, for there is urgent work for you to attend to in Ayodhyā.' Bharata received the gifts that had been sent for him and his uncles and then, because he loved his own people, he showered the messengers with all that they could possibly desire.

'Is everything all right with my father King Daśaratha?' asked Bharata. 'Are Rāma and Lakṣmaṇa well? And what about Kausalyā, wise Rāma's mother, who is devoted to *dharma* and sets an example for others? And the righteous Sumitrā, mother of Lakṣmaṇa and Śatrughna, is she well? And what of my mother Kaikeyī who is so self-willed, quick to anger and sure of her own opinions? Has she sent a message for me?' The messengers assured him that all the people he had asked about were well.

Bharata turned to his grandfather. 'I must go at once to my father, for these are the messengers' instructions. I shall visit you again whenever you call for me.' His grandfather kissed him on the forehead and said, 'Go, my child, go with my blessings. Give my regards to your father and mothers and my greetings to the priests and the learned *brahmins* and to your mighty brothers Rāma and Lakṣmaṇa.'

The king ordered that Bharata be given elephants, money and many fine gifts, horses and gold. Bharata's uncle instructed his most trusted men to accompany the prince. Bharata bade his family farewell and along with Śatrughna, mounted his chariot. Protected by his grandfather's army and accompanied by men as brave as himself, Bharata left the palace like Indra himself.

After travelling for seven days, Bharata came within sight of Ayodhyā. 'This city is ruled by mighty kings,' said Bharata to his charioteer. 'It is inhabited by learned *brahmins* and virtuous people. It is filled with pleasant parks and with stately shining buildings. But even from this distance, it appears to be plunged in sorrow. Earlier, one could hear the buzz of people and the gardens were full of men and women coming and going. It all looks different now! The gardens seem to weep, deserted as they are by young lovers. The whole city seems like a wilderness—there are no people on the streets, nor elephants or horses. These unusual and unpleasant sights disturb me!'

Bharata drove his tired horses into Ayodhyā through the Vaijayanti gateway where the guards greeted him with shouts of joy. He dismissed them courteously and then, turning to his charioteer, he said, 'I see all the signs associated with the death of a king. People are walking around with their clothes soiled, looking careworn and depressed.'

As Bharata looked around, he saw that the city's buildings which normally shone like Indra's palaces were covered with dust and had their doors locked. He grew more and more agitated. With a sense of terrible foreboding, he entered his father's palace.

Bharata did not find his father in his usual chambers so he went to his mother's apartments. Kaikeyī was delighted to see her son who had been away for so long and she jumped up from her couch to greet him. Bharata noticed that the atmosphere was subdued but the first thing he did was touch his mother's feet. Kaikeyī kissed him and hugged him and drew him close to her as she questioned him eagerly.

'When did you leave my father's house? Are you tired from this long chariot journey that you made with such speed? Is my family well? Were you happy during your stay with them? Tell me everything!' she cried.

'I left Rājagṛha seven days ago,' said Bharata. 'Your family is well. The king gave me so many gifts that the porters grew weary and so I left them and came on ahead. The message from Ayodhyā made me hurry along. Now, mother, you must tell me all I need to know!

'Your golden couch is empty and all the retainers seem to be upset about something. The king was always in your chambers and though I have come here specifically to meet him, I do not see him anywhere. Tell me where he is, for I must go and touch his feet. Is he with his elder wife Kausalyā?'

Kaikeyī who was obsessed with royal power, replied harshly to innocent Bharata who knew nothing of what had happened. 'Your father has gone the way of all flesh!' Overwhelmed with grief, Bharata fell to the floor when he heard these words. He wept aloud, his eyes clouded with confusion. 'In the old days, this very couch was adorned by my father's presence. Today its lustre is dulled by his absence!'

Kaikeyī raised the grieving Bharata. 'Get up, prince! Why are you lying on the ground like this?' she said. 'Great kings like you are lauded by huge gatherings. How can you wail like this?!' Rolling on the floor with grief, Bharata cried for a long time. 'I came here joyfully, expecting that the king was either ready to perform a sacrifice or was going to crown Rāma his heir,' wailed Bharata. 'Everything has turned out so different! I cannot even see my father who always wished the best for me! Mother, what disease did my father have that he died before I could get here? How fortunate are Rāma and the others who were able to perform his funeral rites!

'Tell the wise Rāma, who is my brother and like a father to me, that I have arrived. For the man who knows *dharma* an elder brother is like a father! Let me fall at Rāma's feet. He is my only refuge now! Ah! my father was so noble and honourable! What were his last words to me?'

Kaikeyī told him exactly what had happened. 'He cried, "Oh Rāma, Lakṣmaṇa, Sītā!" and passed into the world where the best of men go. And as your father was being enveloped by Time, like a mighty tusker caught in a noose, his last words were, "Those who shall see the return of Rāma, Lakṣmaṇa and Sītā are fortunate indeed!"'

Bharata grew even more agitated when he heard this. His face pale, he asked, 'But where has virtuous Rāma, Kausalyā's joy, gone with Lakṣmaṇa and Sītā?'

Thinking that it would please her son, Kaikeyī told him about the terrible calamity. 'My son, prince Rāma has gone to the Daṇḍaka forest along with Sītā wearing the clothes of an ascetic and Lakṣmaṇa has followed him!' When Bharata heard this, he began to question the propriety of his brother's actions, given the high standards of his family.

'Did Rāma appropriate a *brahmin*'s wealth? Did he mistreat an innocent person? Did he lust after another man's wife or insult another prince? Why has he been exiled to the Daṇḍaka forest like a man who has killed a *brahmin*?'

Then his flighty mother, true to the nature of all women, began to tell him what she had done. 'Rāma did not steal a *brahmin*'s wealth or oppress an innocent man or even raise his eyes to look at another man's wife. My son, when I heard that Rāma was to be crowned, I begged your father to send him into exile and give the kingdom to you. Your father stuck to his principles and did as I asked. Rāma was sent away along with Lakṣmaṇa and Sītā. Once Daśaratha was separated from his beloved son, he sank into a depression and died slowly. You know *dharma.* You should take over the kingdom without any delay. I did all this for your sake! Perform the king's funeral with the help of those who know the rituals and then anoint yourself king!'

'What use is the kingdom to a wretched creature like myself who has been deprived of his father and of his brother who was like a father to him,' said Bharata consumed with grief. 'By making Rāma into an ascetic and causing my father's death you have piled unhappiness upon unhappiness, like rubbing salt into a wound! You entered this family like Death! And my poor father unknowingly embraced glowing embers! It will be a miracle if the grieving Kausalyā and Sumitrā survive, now that they are in your hands, mother!

'Didn't the noble Rāma, so well behaved and devoted to *dharma,* always treat you well, as he would his own mother? My elder mother Kausalyā, who is so virtuous, has always treated you like a sister! How can you not be sorry that you have exiled the son of such a virtuous woman into the forest in the clothes of an ascetic? How could you have exiled a man who is so self-controlled and so noble? You obviously have no idea how I feel towards Rāma. You have created a terrible disaster out of your greed for the kingdom!

'What strength do I have to protect this kingdom unless I am with Rāma and Lakṣmaṇa, those tigers among men? Even King Daśaratha depended on Rāma's strength, the way Mount Meru depends on its forests. How can I carry this great burden? Can a calf carry the burden of a mighty ox? Even if I were able to do this because of my inherent qualities, I refuse to help you achieve your ends because you favour your own son! I shall go to the forest and bring my brother back!'

Thus did Bharata rage in his grief, like a mighty lion roaring from its mountain lair.

'Kaikeyī, you are a wicked and cruel woman!' he cried. 'Leave the kingdom at once! You have renounced all righteousness, so you can stop weeping for the dead! What did Rāma or Daśaratha ever do to you that you caused the banishment of one and the death of the other? By destroying this family, you have sinned as much as a man who kills a *brahmin*! Go to hell, Kaikeyī! The worlds of your husband are closed to you forever!

'You have implicated me in this terrible thing by exiling the man whom the entire world loves! You have brought me ill fame in all the worlds! Cruel creature who coveted the kingdom! You are my enemy in the guise of a mother! You have murdered your husband and your behaviour is completely unacceptable! Never speak to me again! You cannot be the daughter of the wise and righteous Aśvapati! You are a *rākṣasī* born to destroy my father's family!

'I shall do what I can to honour my father and brother and act in such a way that I add to their glory. I shall bring wise Rāma back from the forest by going there myself!' Bharata fell to the ground. Lying there with his eyes bloodshot, his clothes dishevelled and his ornaments awry, he appeared like Indra's flagpole at the end of a celebration.

Then Vasiṣṭha, the most eloquent of all sages, came to Bharata who lay burning in his grief. 'May good fortune attend you, prince!' he said. 'Control your grief for the time has come for you to perform the funeral rites for your father so that he can go on to the best of all worlds.'

Bharata knew *dharma*. He understood what he had to do and performed all the prescribed rites. Daśaratha's pyre was lit on the banks of the Sarayū and the royal family entered ten days of mourning.

On the tenth day, Bharata was free of pollution and on the twelfth day he began the *śrāddha* ceremonies. He gave away money and jewels and herds of cows and goats to *brahmins* and chariots and houses to his retainers to ensure his father's happiness in the worlds beyond. On the morning of the thirteenth day, Bharata wept openly as he collected his father's bones from the cremation grounds with Śatrughna. The princes spoke to each other in quiet tired voices, their eyes red with weeping, as their father's ministers urged them to continue with the prescribed rituals.

'Rāma is the most powerful man on earth and he is the refuge of all sorrowing creatures,' said Śatrughna to Bharata. 'Why did he allow himself to be exiled by a woman? And Lakṣmaṇa is so strong and brave. Why didn't he release Rāma from his dilemma by arresting the king? After duly considering right and wrong, Lakṣmaṇa could have arrested the king earlier, for he was obviously under the spell of a woman and could not think clearly!'

As Śatrughna was speaking, Mantharā, the hunchback, appeared in the eastern doorway, adorned with jewels and ornaments. She had anointed her body with sandal paste and dressed herself in expensive clothes. She looked like a monkey on a leash with her many girdles and necklaces. The doorkeepers grabbed hold of her and brought her to Śatrughna.

'This is the cruel creature who caused Rāma's exile and your father's death!' they cried. 'Do with her as you will!'

'This wretched woman has caused immeasurable grief to my father and brothers,' said Śatrughna. 'Let her now eat the fruit of her actions!' He caught hold of the hunchback who was surrounded by her friends. Mantharā screamed loudly but when her friends saw Śatrughna's rage, they scattered in all directions. 'Look how angry he is,' they cried. 'He will surely kill us all! Let us go to the gentle Kausalyā. She is our only refuge!'

Śatrughna's eyes blazed in anger as he dragged the screaming hunchback across the floor. Her scattered jewels added to the palace's lustre, making it seem like the star-studded autumn sky. Śatrughna gripped Mantharā more and more tightly and yelled at Kaikeyī.

Terrified of the raging Śatrughna and hurt by his cruel words, Kaikeyī ran to her son for protection. 'Control yourself!' admonished Bharata when he saw how angry Śatrughna was. 'Women should be protected from assault from all creatures! I would have killed vile Kaikeyī myself had I not known that righteous Rāma would condemn me for killing my mother! If Rāma hears that we have killed this miserable hunchback, he will never speak to us again!'

Śatrughna calmed himself and released Mantharā, who fell at his feet, weeping and sighing. Kaikeyī comforted the terrified creature, who looked around herself in fear, like a bird caught in a net.

# *Chapter Twenty-Four*

On the morning of the fourteenth day, Daśaratha's ministers gathered and addressed Bharata. 'Our King Daśaratha was the greatest of all teachers. He has gone to heaven after exiling his eldest son Rāma and the mighty Lakṣmaṇa. Now you must become our king, O prince! Fortunately, our kingdom is united and has not fallen prey to chaos and anarchy. The materials for the coronation have been gathered and your own people are waiting for you! Receive the kingdom of your ancestors Bharata! Crown yourself and protect us all, bull among men!'

Bharata bowed respectfully to the coronation materials, but he had made up his mind. He addressed the assembly. 'In our family, only the eldest son becomes king. You should know better than to ask me to do this! Our elder brother Rāma shall rule and I shall live in the forest for fourteen years! Prepare a mighty army with all the four divisions and I shall bring my brother back from the forest!

'Since all the materials for the coronation have been organized, I shall take them with me to the forest and present them to Rāma. And when he has been crowned there, I shall bring him back here with all the honour due to him. I shall not let this woman who claims to be my mother have her way. I shall live in the dense forest and Rāma shall be king!'

The assembly saw how concerned Bharata was for Rāma's welfare and they showered blessings upon him. His selfless words brought tears to the eyes of the noble people gathered there and they said, 'May the goddess of fortune protect you always for it is clear that you want the king's eldest son to rule!'

When the night was over, the bards and minstrels who sang to wake the king sang for Bharata, praising him and wishing him well. Ceremonial drums beaten with golden sticks rang out, conch shells were blown and many different kinds of instruments played in harmony. The music filled the skies but it only depressed Bharata further. He had the music silenced as soon as he awoke. 'I am not the king!' he said to Śatrughna. 'Kaikeyī's actions have had terrible consequences. Daśaratha is dead and there is only sadness for me! The sovereignty of the mighty king which was rooted in *dharma* now wanders like a rudderless ship!'

Meanwhile, Vasiṣṭha entered the assembly hall of the Ikṣvāku kings. Surrounded by his attendants, he inspected the area which was beautifully decorated with gold and jewels. He sat down on a golden couch that was covered by a priceless fabric and called for his messengers. 'Go quickly and summon the *brahmins*, the warriors, the generals, ministers and merchants. We have urgent business to conduct!'

There was a huge tumult as the people gathered on their horses, chariots and elephants. When Bharata arrived, they greeted him the way they used to greet Daśaratha, as the immortals in heaven greeted Indra. The assembly shone for Daśaratha's son like a pool filled with bright fish and precious jewels, the way it had shone for Daśaratha himself.

Bharata gazed upon the assembly that seemed as bright as the night of the full moon when the clouds part. When Vasiṣṭha saw that all the regions of the kingdom were duly represented, he spoke softly to Bharata. 'Child, Daśaratha has fulfilled his duties and gone to heaven. He has left you a prosperous kingdom abundant in grain and wealth. Honourable Rāma is dedicated to truth and being mindful of his duties, could not ignore his father's words any more than the moon can give up its light. Your father and brother have left you an unencumbered kingdom. Crown yourself without further delay and enjoy its pleasures with your ministers!'

Bharata was eager to do the right thing but his mind travelled to Rāma and he was plunged into grief. In a voice thick with tears, he rebuked the royal priest in front of everyone. 'How can someone like me take the kingdom away from Rāma? He has entered the second phase of his life* and he is dedicated to *dharma*. How can a son of Daśaratha usurp the throne? The kingdom and I both belong to Rāma. You should be telling me how I should behave in this situation.

* The stage of the householder.

'Rāma is the oldest and the best amongst us. He is the most worthy to rule, equal to Daśaratha himself! If I did the wrong thing now I would definitely go to hell! I would also defame my clan in the entire world! My mother has done an abominable thing and though I stand here, my thoughts are with Rāma, who braves the dangers of the forest!

'My brother Rāma is the one who deserves to be king. If I cannot persuade him to return from the forest, I shall live with him there, like Lakṣmaṇa does. I will use all the means at my disposal to bring him back!'

'Go quickly, Sumantra, and carry out my instructions. Get the army ready to move and prepare for the journey at once!' said Bharata.

Sumantra was delighted with Bharata's plans, as were the common people and the army commanders. The prospect of a journey to bring Rāma back filled them with excitement and happiness. Sumantra yoked the best of horses to Bharata's chariot as each family of Ayodhyā, whether *brahmin*, *kṣatriya*, *vaiśya* or *śūdra*, prepared themselves for the journey, harnessing their camels, mules, horses and elephants.

Bharata started on his journey preceded by his ministers and priests who rode in chariots that shone like the chariot of the sun. He was followed by ninety thousand elephants, sixty thousand chariots carrying archers and one hundred thousand cavalrymen. Rich people, leaders of trade guilds and commoners also went along, their conversations revolving around Rāma and Lakṣmaṇa, their hearts filled with joy. Bharata decided to camp and rest on the banks of the Gangā and after the army had settled down, he began to think of ways to persuade Rāma to return.

The king of the Niṣādas, Guha, came to meet Bharata, bearing gifts of fish, meat and honey. Sumantra, who knew about matters of protocol, said to Bharata, 'Here comes the mighty chief of this region surrounded by thousands of his people. He is an elderly man and a good friend of your brother's. He is familiar with the Daṇḍaka forest and is bound to know where Rāma and Lakṣmaṇa are. You must go and receive him!'

'Here are some roots and fruits gathered by my people as well as fresh and dried meats and other forest produce,' said Guha bowing low. 'Let your army stay here for the night and we shall look after them. You can leave here in the morning.'

Bharata questioned Guha eagerly, 'Tell me, Gūha, where did Rāma, Lakṣmaṇa and Sītā spend the night? What did Rāma eat? Where did he sleep?' And Guha gladly told Bharata how he had welcomed Rāma as a friend and as an honoured guest.

'I brought Rāma many different kinds of food as refreshment. He was gracious, but in keeping with the *kṣatriya* code, he refused to accept any gifts from me. "It is our duty to give and not to accept gifts" is what he said to us with great courtesy as he turned down our offerings. He drank only the water that Lakṣmaṇa brought him and then he and Sītā fasted for the night. Lakṣmaṇa drank what was left over before he, too, began his fast. Then they said their evening prayers.

'Lakṣmaṇa gathered wild grasses and quickly made a bed for Rāma and when Rāma and Sītā had settled down for the night, Lakṣmaṇa stood at a distance keeping vigil. That is the *ungudi* tree under which they slept as Lakṣmaṇa kept watch with his bow strung and his quivers full of arrows. And I stood beside Lakṣmaṇa, armed with my bow and arrow, surrounded by my alert and watchful people.'

Bharata walked over to the tree under which Rāma had slept. He turned to his mothers who had accompanied him on his journey and spoke sadly. 'This is where Rāma spent the night. Look, you can still see the imprint of his body on the ground! It is not right that someone as noble as Rāma, born into the family of Daśaratha, should sleep like this. He has slept under the finest quilts, blankets and sheets, how can that tiger among men now sleep on the ground?

'From today onwards, I, too, shall sleep on the bare ground. I shall eat only roots and fruits. I shall mat my hair and wear simple clothes. I shall live happily in the forest for Rāma's sake and take on the fulfilment of his pledge. Śatrughna will live with me while I carry out Rāma's promise and he can protect Ayodhyā with Lakṣmaṇa. May the gods grant me my wish!

'If I cannot persuade Rāma to return, even by laying my head at his feet, then I shall live with him in the forest for fourteen years. He cannot deny me that!'

Bharata rose early the next morning. He woke Śatrughna and told him to instruct Guha to make arrangements to ferry the army across the river. Boats carried the army over the Gangā and they entered the forests of Prayāga at an auspicious time. Bharata halted the army and went ahead with his ministers to meet the sage Bharadvāja.

Bharata knew how he should approach the sage so he left his weapons behind and went on foot. He wore only clothes of silk and was preceded by the royal priest.

When Bharadvāja saw Vasiṣṭha coming towards him, he rose from his seat and instructed his disciples to bring the *arghya* water. Then he saw

Bharata and recognized him as Daśaratha's son. He honoured his visitors appropriately and asked if all was well in Ayodhyā. He had learned about Daśaratha's death and so he did not refer to him. Prompted by his affection for Rāma, he asked Bharata, 'Why have you come here when it is your job to rule the kingdom? My mind is uneasy about this. Tell me everything!

'Isn't it true that Kausalyā's son has been exiled into the forest for fourteen years with his wife and brother because his father fell under the spell of a woman? I assume you have not come here to harm that innocent man so that you can rule the kingdom unhindered, a kingdom that should belong to your brother!'

'I am utterly destroyed if even a holy man like you thinks this of me!' replied Bharata with tears in his eyes, his voice choking. 'I know that I have never had an ignoble thought or wicked intentions! What my mother did in my absence did not make me happy and I never asked her to do it. You should not accuse me thus! I am going to meet Rāma so that I can throw myself at his feet and beg him to return to Ayodha with me. Be kind to me and tell me where I can find Rāma, the lord of the earth!'

Bharadvāja was reassured by Bharata's words. 'You are truly worthy of your clan, tiger among men! I know you are obedient to your elders and self-restrained and that you walk in the ways of good men. I knew your innermost thoughts but I wanted to be absolutely sure.

'Your brother is living on the mighty Citrakūṭa mountain. Go there tomorrow but stay here tonight with your ministers. You know how to make others happy, so grant me this favour!'

Bharata agreed and his retinue spent the night in comfort, their every wish fulfilled by Bharadvāja.

# *Chapter Twenty-Five*

The next morning, Bharata made preparations to depart after profusely thanking the sage for his hospitality. 'Tell me, great sage, how I can find my brother's settlement? I am anxious to see him,' he asked.

'The Citrakūṭa mountain lies in the midst of the uninhabited forests not far from here, Bharata! The river Mandākinī flows along its northern side and is almost hidden by groves of flowering trees. I am sure you will find your brother's thatched hut between the mountain and the river,' said Bharadvāja. 'Take your army along the southern road and turn east. That road will lead you to your brother!'

The royal party gathered around the sage before mounting their chariots. Thin, wan and trembling, Kausalyā and Sumitrā clung to Bharadvāja's feet. Even Kaikeyī, whose wish had not been fulfilled and who was despised by the whole world, fell at his feet. She honoured the sage and then went and stood by Bharata, her eyes cast down. 'Tell me all about your mothers,' said the sage to Bharata.

'This woman that you see here, so emaciated and wretched with grief is my father's chief queen, Kausalyā. She is like a goddess and gave birth to the wide-striding Rāma like Aditi gave birth to Dhatṛ. This one standing here so woebegone, wilting like a flowering tree is Sumitrā, the mother of the heroic Lakṣmaṇa and Śatrughna. This one here is Kaikeyī. She appears to be a noble woman but she is utterly deceitful. She is greedy and cruel, this mother of mine! I see only disaster ahead for myself because of what she has done!' Bharata broke down and began to weep.

Bharadvāja comforted him. 'Do not censure Kaikeyī, Bharata, for Rāma's exile will have happy consequences!'

Bharata took the sage's permission to leave and ordered the army to march onwards. People rushed to their gilded chariots, yoked their horses and climbed in, eager to depart. Slowly, the elephants decorated with golden harnesses and bells began to move. With their bells tinkling and their banners fluttering, they looked like the dark clouds at the end of summer. Large and small vehicles started up and the foot soldiers kept pace with them. Eager to see Rāma, Kausalyā and Sumitrā climbed into a separate chariot.

Bharata was surrounded by his retainers and rode in a chariot that was as bright as the rising sun and as beautiful as the moon. The mighty army with its horses, elephants and chariots rumbled through the forest, which was filled with birds and animals, sounding like distant thunder clouds.

The forest animals grew agitated when they saw the huge army. Rutting tuskers fled away followed by their herds. Bear, antelope and deer stood petrified in the forest clearings on the mountain slopes. And Daśaratha's honourable son marched onwards with his thundering army, complete with all four divisions. The army was as vast as the ocean and covered the earth as completely as rain clouds cover the sky in the monsoon.

When they had gone about halfway, Bharata's horses grew tired. 'This looks like the area Bharadvāja described to us,' he said to Vasiṣṭha. 'This must be the river Mandākinī and so this has to be Mount Citrakūṭa. I can see the dense forests in the distance, dark as rain clouds.

'Already the beautiful ridges of the mountain slopes are being flattened by my elephants who are as large as mountains themselves. The trees here rain flowers on the ground the way clouds rain water! Look Śatrughna! look at this mountain teeming with deer like the ocean teems with water creatures! This forest was terrifying in its silence just a little while ago. Now it is so full of people, it is like Ayodhyā!

'The dust from the horses' hooves darkens the sky but there is a gentle breeze that blows it away, as if for my pleasure! Our chariots descend upon the mountain and the peacocks display their plumage as they rush to their homes. This region is the home of ascetics and hermits. It is so beautiful, it is like heaven! Let the army move carefully through the forest, keeping a sharp lookout for Rāma and Lakṣmaṇa!'

The army penetrated deeper into the forest and soon they saw smoke rising into the air. They ran to tell Bharata. 'There cannot be fire in a place uninhabited by men. Rāma and Lakṣmaṇa must be here! And if not them, then there must be other ascetics just like them.' Bharata told the massive army to stop where it was. 'I shall go ahead with Sumantra and Vasiṣṭha,' he declared.

Rāma, meanwhile, had lived in the forest for some time now. He loved the mountains and the trees and he was showing Sītā the beauty of Citrakūṭa, as Indra might show his wife. 'I am not upset about the loss of the kingdom nor do I miss the company of my friends when I see the natural beauty of the mountain slopes,' he said to her.

As they sat chatting pleasantly with each other, the noise and the dust from Bharata's army rose into the sky. The animals were disturbed and herds fled in all directions in fright. Rāma heard the tumult and saw the animals fleeing. 'Listen, Lakṣmaṇa!' he said. 'What could that terrifying sound be? Could it be a royal hunting party? Or some huge beast of prey? Go and find out what it is, quickly!'

Lakṣmaṇa immediately climbed up a tall tree and looked in all directions. In the north, he saw the army with its horses and elephants, chariots and foot soldiers. He told Rāma what he had seen. 'Put out the fire, Rāma, and send Sītā into the hut! Put on your armour and prepare your bow and arrows!'

'Look again, Lakṣmaṇa,' cautioned Rāma. 'Whose army do you think it is?' Lakṣmaṇa turned to him with a look of such anger that he could have consumed the entire army. 'It is obvious that Kaikeyī's son is here to kill us. He has been crowned and wants to enjoy the kingdom without any hindrances! The *kovidāra* banner flutters from the chariot in which he rides. The men mounted on horses and elephants seem eager and happy.

'Let us move further up the mountain with our bows and arrows. Or we can make a stand here. Bharata's banner shall surely fall to us in battle! I want to see Bharata who has brought this terrible calamity upon us! Rāma, he has deprived you of the kingdom and kingship. Now that your enemy has arrived here, I shall kill him!

'There is nothing wrong with killing Bharata, Rāma! To kill someone who has harmed you is not a violation of *dharma.* And when he is dead, you shall rule the entire earth. Today Kaikeyī shall drown in sorrow when she sees me kill her son in battle, as easily as a tree is snapped in half by an elephant. Then I will kill Kaikeyī and her entire family. The earth deserves to be rid of such a creature! Lakshman is ready to kill them

'I shall no longer hold back the fire of my wrath which I have controlled for so long. The slopes of Citrakūṭa will be drenched with the blood of our enemies as it pours forth from the wounds my arrows shall inflict! Beasts of prey will drag away the corpses of men and elephants that I have killed. I have repaid the debt to my weapons in many a great battle and I shall do so again today by destroying Bharata and his entire army!'

'What use are all our weapons when Bharata the mighty archer has come here himself?' said Rāma, trying to calm Lakṣmaṇa. 'He has come to see us. The thought of harming us would never cross his mind! He has never harmed you in the past so you should not suspect him like this. Do not speak harshly to him for an unkindness to him would be an unkindness to me. Under no circumstances can a son kill his father or a brother kill his brother.

'If you are saying all this on account of the kingdom then listen. When Bharata comes here I will ask him to give me the kingdom. And I have no doubt that Bharata will give it to me even before I ask for it.' Lakṣmaṇa was ashamed when he heard Rāma's words, for he was devoted to his brother.

Meanwhile, the mighty Ikṣvāku army with its horses and elephants and chariots surrounded the mountain and settled on its slopes. It had been ordered to do so by Bharata who placed *dharma* above all else and who had suppressed his own pride. The army had come there to take Rāma back and so it behaved with deference and humility.

Once the army had settled down, Bharata spoke to Śatrughna. 'Dear brother, go and search every inch of the forest with a group of men. I shall have no peace until I have seen Rāma, Lakṣmaṇa and Sītā!'

Bharata himself entered the forest on foot. The best of men walked through the flowering groves that covered the mountain slopes. When he reached the *sāla* tree at the top of the mountain, he saw the smoke from Rāma's fire rising into the air like a banner. Bharata was filled with joy and shouted to his companions 'Rāma is here!' like a man who has reached the far shores of the ocean. He went ahead quickly with Guha, asking the others to stay back.

He instructed Vasiṣṭha to fetch his mothers. Sumantra followed closely behind Śatrughna for his longing to see Rāma was as great as Bharata's. As he walked on, Bharata saw his brothers' thatched hut.

In front of the hut there were split logs of wood, heaps of flowers and piles of deer and buffalo dung which had been collected to make a fire to ward off the cold. The hut was thatched with many different kinds of leaves and its floor was covered with *kuśa* grass, like a sacrificial altar. Inside the hut, Bharata could see his brothers' mighty bows and arrows, equal to the weapons of Indra himself. They were adorned with gold and blazed with such splendour that they would make their enemies tremble. Even the arrows with their gleaming tips in their quivers shone like the rays of the sun. Swords glistened in their golden scabbards and shields were decorated with gold designs.

A sacrificial fire burned in the northern corner of Rāma's hut. Bharata had to look hard before he saw Rāma sitting in a corner, his matted locks piled on top of his head. The lord of the earth, who had always walked the path of the righteous, was seated on the skin of a black antelope, his arms and shoulders like that of a lion, his eyes as beautiful as a lotus. Rāma sat on the *darbha* grass like the eternal Brahmā, with Lakṣmaṇa and Sītā next to him.

Kaikeyī's honourable son ran forward, overcome with grief. For a moment he could not speak but then he collected himself and cried out in a voice thick with tears. 'My older brother who should be honoured by his people in the halls of state sits here surrounded by forest animals! He used to wear the finest clothes and now he covers himself with deerskin, as *dharma* dictates! Rāma used to have flowers in his hair. How can his locks be matted? He who should have earned merit from the performance of sacrifices now earns merit through mortifying his body! This noble man's body used to be anointed with sandal paste and now it is covered with dust! Rāma deserves all happiness but he suffers these hardships because of me. Damn this life that I must live!'

Weeping, Bharata fell to the ground before he could touch Rāma's feet. Śatrughna also wept and fell at Rāma's feet and Rāma raised his brothers and embraced them, his face wet with his own tears. Then Rāma and Lakṣmaṇa embraced Guha and Sumantra and even the forest dwellers were moved to tears when they saw this reunion.

Rāma kissed Bharata on the forehead and drew him to sit beside him as he questioned him calmly. 'What has happened to our father, child, that you have come to the forest? You should not have come here while he is alive. Ah Bharata! It has been so long since I saw you. And now, when I see you in the forest after you have come so far, I find you greatly changed in appearance. Is everything all right with the righteous and truthful King Daśaratha?'

'And the wise and learned *brahmin*, ever devoted to *dharma,* the royal priest of the Ikṣvāku clan, is he honoured appropriately? My child, how are our mothers Kausalyā and Sumitrā? Is the noble Kaikeyī happy?

'Have you appointed ministers who are self-restrained and brave, who are well-born, trustworthy and skilled in the arts of diplomacy? Decisions taken after due consideration by ministers who are learned in polity as well as reliable are very important for the success of the kings. I trust that you do not sleep too much, that you wake at the appropriate time and spend the early hours of the morning thinking about how you can achieve your ends.

'Do not take advice from only one man, nor either from too many and make sure that your innermost thoughts are not spread all over the kingdom. Do you act quickly and without delay so that you can achieve your ends by simple means? Do your tributary kings know about your plans only after they have been implemented or do they hear about them while they are in process? No one should know about the process of your deliberations unless you have taken that person into confidence.

'Choose one learned and intelligent man as your advisor instead of a thousand foolish men, for the learned can do a great deal of good and achieve all your goals. A thousand foolish men can do nothing for a king, but one advisor who is skilled, observant, brave and intelligent can bring a king great glory.

'Give the best of your retainers the most important tasks to perform, the less important work to the middling retainers and the least important work to those who rank the lowest. Trust the significant affairs of state to men who are pure in thought, to those who have been tested and found true and to those who are hereditary holders of office. Do not let your subjects think badly of you. You must quickly get rid of a brave and skilled man who has conspired against you and aspires to power, or you will be killed by him.

'Have you appointed a brave, resolute, wise, skilled and nobly born man as the commander of your army? The men who lead your army are strong and skilled in the arts of war. Do you honour and praise them appropriately? Do you supply your army with proper food and pay each man his due? You must do this without any delay at the appointed time. For if food and wages are delayed, the army will rise against its master in anger.

Rām is asking him about his actions as king

'Are all the princes and your retainers devoted to you? Will they calmly give up their lives for your sake? Have you chosen a man who is eloquent, wise, skilled and learned as your personal messenger? Do you keep the important men in other kingdoms and in your own under constant watch by three spies each, unknown to each other and to the world? Do you keep a special watch over your exiled enemies who have returned? Never think of them as weak or ineffectual.

'Do not honour the *brahmins* who are materialist philosophers, for they are not worthy. Even though there are prescriptive sacred texts for all aspects of life, these men of twisted intellect reject the Vedas and depend on pure rationality.

'Child, the city ruled by our forefathers that is filled with horses, elephants and chariots, inhabited by thousands of noble people and *brahmins*, *kṣatriyas* and *vaiśyas* who are all enthusiastic, disciplined and devoted to their duty, do you protect that city of Ayodhyā such that its name which means "should not be attacked" stands true? It is a king's duty to protect his people with *dharma*. Do you reassure the women and make sure that they are safe? Do you ensure that you do not confide in them nor trust what they say?

'Do you wake up early in the morning and show yourself to the people, fully adorned, in the assembly hall and in the main street? Are all your forts well supplied with grain and water, with weapons and machines, workmen and archers? Is your income greater than your expenditure? Do not waste your money on inconsequential things. Spend your money on worshipping the gods and the ancestors and in honouring *brahmins*, *kṣatriyas* and your allies.

'If a noble man who is pure in spirit and deed is accused of theft by conspirators, he must be questioned by experts before his wealth is attached out of greed. If a thief is caught and questioned and evidence is found against him, he should not be set free for reasons of greed. And when a man is in trouble, be he rich or poor, do your learned ministers inquire into the matter? The tears of a man unjustly accused can destroy the progeny and wealth of a king who rules for selfish pleasures.

'Do you keep the elders happy by giving them what they want? And children happy by giving them affection and scholars happy by speaking with gratitude? Do you honour the elders and the teachers, ascetics, gods and guests, *brahmins* and those who have accomplished their ends?

'Do not pursue *dharma* at the expense of material gain or power at the cost of *dharma* or neglect them both out of a desire for pleasure. Bharata, you know the appropriate time for all these things and, therefore, pursue each at the right time. Do the *brahmins* and the common people pray together for your welfare? Avoid the flaws that mar the personality of a great king, including atheism, untruth, anger, licentiousness and procrastination. Do not taste your food yourself and give generously to your friends and those who need help,' said Rāma.

'What will I do with this advice on the duties of a king when I have renounced kingship?' replied Bharata. 'The eternally established *dharma* states that while an older son lives, a younger son cannot be king. Come back with me to prosperous Ayodhyā and crown yourself king for the glory of our clan! They say that kings are mortal men. But I think of you as a god because your life has been devoted to *dharma.*

'When I was away in the kingdom of the Kekayas and you had left for the forest, the great king who was loved and respected by all, went to heaven,' said Bharata sadly. 'Rise, Rāma, and perform the last rites for your father. Śatrughna and I have already done so, but there is no doubt that you were our father's favourite. That which is offered by a beloved son is of great value in the world beyond.'

Bharata's news hit Rāma like a thunderbolt and, swooning with grief, he fell to the ground like a tree felled by an axe. His brothers and Sītā sprinkled water on his face and when he had recovered consciousness, he broke into tears. 'What use am I, this ill-born son, to that great king! He died of grief for me and I was not even able to perform his last rites!' sighed Rāma. 'Ah Bharata! You were able to achieve your life's goal when you and Śatrughna performed the funeral rites for the king!

'I have no desire to return to Ayodhyā after my exile. Now that my father has gone, who will guide me when I rule the kingdom? Who will speak those gentle words of reassurance and praise?' Rāma completed the necessary rituals and returned to his hut. The brothers and Sītā mourned together and the sound of their weeping echoed across the mountains.

Bharata's army heard the sound and knew at once that Bharata was with Rāma and that they were weeping for their dead father. They left their camp and hurried in the direction of the sound, making a great din themselves. Some went on their horses, others on elephants, others in their splendid chariots and some even went on foot, all of them eager to see

Rāma again. Even though it had been only a short while since Rāma had left them, it already seemed like an eternity.

Struck by hooves and chariot wheels, the earth groaned like a thunder cloud. Wild elephants grew extremely agitated and ran from the area. Boar, deer, lions, buffalo, bears, monkeys, tigers and antelope fled in panic. Birds scattered in all directions and covered the sky so that it looked like the earth teeming with people.

When Rāma saw those eager people with tears rolling down their faces, he ran forward to embrace them as would a mother or a father. Some he embraced, others fell at his feet, but each friend and family member was greeted appropriately. The sound of weeping filled the earth and the sky and the caves and the mountains. It resounded in all directions like the throbbing of drums.

Daśaratha's wives, thirsting for a glimpse of Rāma, had been escorted to the hut by Vasiṣṭha. As they approached, they saw Rāma, as beautiful as an immortal fallen from heaven, but the mothers wept when they saw the privations that Rāma endured. Honourable Rāma rose and fell at their feet and they wiped the dust from his back with their soft hands, soothing him with their gentleness. When Lakṣmaṇa touched their feet, they treated him as affectionately as they had Rāma. Sītā honoured her mothers-in-law and now stood before them, her head bowed.

Kausalyā embraced her daughter-in-law who had become thin and pale from her forest life. 'Ah Sītā! You are the daughter of Janaka, the daughter-in-law of Daśaratha and the wife of Rāma! How is it that you have to suffer the hardships of a life in the forest? My heart goes out to you, Sītā. Your face is like a lotus that has been scorched by the sun, like a lily crushed underfoot, like gold covered with dust, like the moon hidden by clouds!'

Rāma touched the feet of Vasiṣṭha, his teacher, who blazed with his own effulgence, as Indra would touch the feet of Bṛhaspati, and then sat down beside him. Bharata collected his ministers, prominent citizens, army commanders and men learned in *dharma* and seated them around Rāma and Vasiṣṭha. Before he himself sat down, Bharata joined his palms in respect before Rāma, who shone with splendour even in his ascetic's clothes. 'What will Bharata say now?' whispered the people who had gathered there. 'But whatever he says, it will certainly be right and just!'

# *Chapter Twenty-Six*

Rāma saw the affection that Bharata had for him and he began to question him gently along with Lakṣmaṇa. 'Tell me, Bharata, why have you come here wearing ascetic's clothes and with your hair matted? Why are you here wearing the skin of a black antelope? Why have you abandoned the kingdom?'

'Noble one, our father went to heaven grieving for his son after he had made the mistake of banishing you. He was led to that by a woman. My mother Kaikeyī and the king did a terrible thing which destroyed the king's glory. Kaikeyī failed to gain the kingdom, which was supposed to be the consequence of her actions. Now she is a grieving widow. She will definitely fall into the worst of all possible hells.

'Consider me your servant and crown yourself king today! All our people and even our mothers have come here to ask this of you. Grant them their wish. You will be acquiring the kingdom through the ordinances of *dharma,* by lawful succession and by the strength of your virtues. Let the earth be united with you, her rightful husband, as the autumn night is with the moonlight!

'I beg you with head bowed as do these ministers. I am your brother, your disciple and your servant. Look kindly upon me! Do not delay listening to this council of ministers who have served our father and who are worthy of respect.' Bharata laid his head at Rāma's feet and waited for his response.

'Bharata, you are so noble, so honourable, so effulgent and so resolute by nature. How could anyone believe that you would act dishonourably for the sake of a kingdom? I see no faults in you, but you should not behave immaturely and despise your mother for her actions. Because you know *dharma,* you should know that a mother deserves as much respect as a father. How could I have refused when my honoured parents told me to go into the forest?

'Rule the kingdom from Ayodhyā and I shall live in the forest wearing these simple clothes. Daśaratha made this division in front of the whole world before he died. That righteous king should serve as an authority for you. Enjoy the share that our father has given you! By living in the forest for fourteen years, I, too, shall be enjoying the share allotted to me! My father was honoured by the entire world and he was an equal of the gods. I take what he has said to me to be a higher good than the sovereignty of the earth!'

The company sat in silence, waiting to hear what Bharata would say. Finally, he spoke in the presence of his family and friends. 'This kingdom was given to me to satisfy my mother. Now, I give it to you. Accept it, for it has no encumbrances! The kingdom has become like a bridge breached by a flood. Only you can make it secure again. I cannot compare myself with you, ruler of the earth, any more than a donkey can equal a horse, or an ordinary bird match Garuḍa.

'Rāma, life is difficult enough when others depend on a man. But it must be harder still when a man is dependent on others. Suppose a man plants a sapling and nurtures it until it grows into a mighty tree, a tree so tall that no small man can climb it. If the tree bears flowers and does not fruit, it offers no benefits to those for whose sake it was planted. The significance of this metaphor cannot be lost on you. This is what would happen to us if we were ruled by anyone other than you. Let the prominent citizens see you firmly established as king. Elephants will trumpet with joy when you enter the city and there will be much rejoicing by the women in the inner apartments!'

All the people gathered there felt that Bharata's request was appropriate. Rāma saw Bharata's despair and comforted him. 'Bharata, no man can do exactly as he pleases, for he is not his own master. His fate drags him hither and thither. All wealth is spent, men rise only to fall, all unions lead to separations and death is the end of life. As a ripe fruit has nothing to fear but falling, so a man has nothing to fear but death. As a house supported by huge pillars must decay and collapse, so a man must fall prey to disease and old age. Days and nights move on, diminishing the lives of all beings, just as surely as the heat of the sun dries up the moisture in the earth.

'Do not mourn for yourself or for others. Life moves on, regardless of whether you stay still or are active. Death is always by your side. It walks with you and sits down with you. If you go on a journey to a far away place, death will return with you. Wrinkles appear, hair whitens. Men are worn down with age. How can we control these things? We rejoice when we see the sun rise every morning and set every evening without realizing that with it our lives are passing too.

'Our father has gone to heaven because he did good deeds and was respected by people. He also performed many sacrifices with ample gifts and fees to the *brahmins*. He has renounced his aged human body and attained divinity which he now enjoys in the world of Brahmā. How can someone as intelligent as you grieve for him? A wise man would not succumb to grief and mourn like this under any circumstances. Calm yourself. Put an end to your sorrow. Go back and live in the city as our father had asked you to do, for he was an honourable man. And I shall live here as he asked me to. I cannot ignore his wishes and neither should you, for he was our father and our mentor.'

'I was born of the noble and righteous Daśaratha,' said Bharata. 'How can I, knowing what is right and just, do what is wrong and despicable? The virtuous king was our father and our teacher. He was like a god to us. He is dead now, so I should not speak ill of him in this company. But who would do such an unjust and cowardly thing, so against his own interests, simply to please a woman? There is an old saying, that living beings lose their minds at the time of their death. That has certainly been borne out by the king's actions.

'Rāma, you should make good the wrong committed by our father in his rage and his infatuation. The son that rights his father's wrongs is considered worthy in the eyes of the world. Prove yourself worthy by repudiating our father's actions that are condemned by all righteous people. Redeem us all, me, Kaikeyī, our father, our family, our friends, our people, by doing the right thing!

'How can a *kṣatriya* live in the forest? How can a king have matted hair? You should not be acting like this. If you truly want to walk on the path of *dharma* that is littered with hardships and difficulties, you should be ruling the four castes justly. Wise men say that of all the four stages of life, the stage of the householder is the greatest. You know *dharma,* how can you renounce this stage? I am younger than you in age and inferior to you in rank and learning. How can I possibly rule while you are still alive?

'Do your duty and rule this land! Let Vasiṣṭha crown you right here by Vedic rites in the presence of all the citizens. Then leave for Ayodhyā and rule from there. Bull among men, lift this stigma from my mother and save our father from public condemnation! But if you decide to ignore my pleas and stay in the forest, then I shall stay with you!'

Though Bharata begged and pleaded, resolute Rāma had made up his mind and was determined to abide by his father's wishes. The people admired Rāma's determination and it made them both happy and sad, sad that he was not going to return to Ayodhyā but happy with the firmness he displayed.

'What you have just said is worthy of someone born to Daśaratha, the best of kings, and the noble Kaikeyī,' said Rāma. 'Dear brother, long ago, when our father married your mother, he promised your grandfather that she should have the kingdom as a price worthy of her. And then, during the war between the gods and the *asuras,* he gave her two boons because he was pleased with her. That promise had to be honoured. Your noble mother took all that into consideration when she asked him to redeem the boons. Bound by his promise, the king granted her two wishes. One gave you the kingdom and the other exiled me to the forest. I have come here with Sītā and Lakṣmaṇa to honour my father's word. You should do the same by crowning yourself without further delay.

'Bharata, make good our father's debt and please your mother! You must be the king of men and I shall rule over the forest animals. Return to the city today and I, too, shall leave for the Daṇḍaka forest. The royal canopy shall shade you from the rays of the sun and I shall be shaded by the great trees of the forest. The world knows that Lakṣmaṇa is my best friend and companion and Śatrughna will help you in your task. Daśaratha's four sons shall prove the king's devotion to truth! Grieve no more, Bharata!'

As Rāma was consoling Bharata, Jābāli, the greatest of all the *brahmins*, spoke these unrighteous words. 'Rāma, a noble and intelligent man like you should not think like a common person! Every man is born alone and dies alone. Who is related to whom? What is the meaning of family? A man who clings to a mother or a father must be considered deluded. No one is anything to anyone! Just as a man arrives in the village and stays somewhere for the night and leaves the next morning, so mothers and fathers are mere stops along the way in life. A wise man does not cling to these.

'Do not renounce your father's kingdom and take the difficult path which will cause you much hardship. Crown yourself in the prosperous city of Ayodhyā which waits for you like a virgin bride, her hair in a single braid! Enjoy the royal pleasure of your city as Indra enjoys heaven. Daśaratha is nothing to you and you are no one to him. You and the king are entirely unrelated to each other. The king has gone where he had to go, for that is the destiny of all mortals. You should concern yourself with irrelevant matters!

'I feel sorry for those people who pursue wealth and those that pursue *dharma.* They suffer in this life and the next. See how men waste food by performing rituals for the dead! Can a dead man eat? The books that tell you to perform sacrifices, do penance and give gifts are written by wily men who want to help others spend their money! You are wise enough to know that there is no world other than this one. Believe in what you can see and turn your back on the unseen! Take the kingdom, as Bharata has asked you to!'

'What you have just said is totally unacceptable though it seems appropriate, completely improper even though it seems reasonable,' replied Rāma passionately. 'The man who lives without restraints walks an unrighteous path. He does not live in accordance with our sacred teachings and he shall never have the respect of good men. It is a man's character and his deeds that determine whether he is high or low born, pure or impure, brave or simply a hoax.

'The timeless rules of kingship are bound by truth and compassion. Truth is the mainstay of kingship and the world is established in truth. The gods and sages declare truth to be the highest goal. It is supreme in the world and exalts one to heaven. Men despise a liar as they despise snakes. Truth controls the world and is the only refuge. It is the basis of everything. Nothing is greater than truth. Gift giving, sacrifices, penances, good deeds, even the Vedas, are established in truth and, therefore, it is the highest good.

'How can I fail to carry out my father's promise when I am committed to it by an oath of truth? I cannot violate my father's bond with truth out of greed, delusion or even out of ignorance! Gods and ancestors reject the offerings of men who are fickle and do not keep their word. It is clear to me that every man must hold to the truth, that it is his *dharma.* It is for this reason alone that ascetics command so much respect. I renounce the *dharma* of a *kṣatriya* because it is fundamentally unrighteous even though it has some good things about it. It attracts the base, the cruel, the greedy and those inclined to be wicked.

'What you have just asked me to do is wrong, even though you have supported it with a great many arguments. I promised my father in the presence of elders and teachers that I would live in the forest. How can I do what Bharata wants without breaking that promise? By living in the forest, I shall be able to pursue purity by eating simple foods and making offerings to the gods and the ancestors. I shall nourish my body but go through life without deceit, depending on my powers of discrimination!'

'Every man born into this world has three mentors, Rāma, his father, his mother and his teacher,' said Vasiṣṭha, the royal priest. 'His father gives him birth. A teacher gives a man knowledge and wisdom and so he, too, is called a mentor. I was your father's teacher and I am yours too. If you do as I say, you shall not be acting unrighteously.

'All the leaders of the people are gathered here. If you do your duty by them you shall not be acting unrighteously. You cannot ignore the wishes of your virtuous mother. If you do as she says, you will not be acting unrighteously. You who are devoted to truth and *dharma* shall not be untrue to yourself if you do as Bharata asks!' said Vasiṣṭha gently.

'My father Daśaratha brought me into this world,' replied Rāma. 'I cannot ignore what he ordered me to do. Neither Bharata nor I can invalidate what my father said and did while he was alive. Nor can I appoint a substitute to live in the forest. That would be worthy of contempt. What Kaikeyī asked for was right and what my father did was appropriate.

'I know Bharata to be self-restrained and respectful to his elders. He is a virtuous and honourable man and with him as the king everything will be all right. When I return from the forest, I shall rule the kingdom along with my honourable brother!'

'Place your sandals adorned with gold upon your feet,' said Bharata to Rāma, who was as beautiful as the moon and shone like the sun. 'They shall guarantee the welfare of the worlds in your absence!'

Rāma placed the sandals on his feet and then took them off and gave them to Bharata. Bharata bowed to the sandals and said, 'I too shall mat my hair and wear simple clothes for fourteen years. I shall live on roots and fruits outside the city and wait for your return even as your sandals inspire me in the affairs of state.' Bharata received the sandals humbly, bowed to Rāma and placed them on the head of the royal elephant.

Then Rāma, steadfast as the mountains and firm in the pursuit of his own *dharma,* said goodbye to his brothers, his ministers and his elders with all the respect that was due to them. His mothers, choked by their tears, could say nothing to him as he bowed to them and went into his hut, weeping quietly.

# *Chapter Twenty-Seven*

Bharata and his mighty army with its horses and elephants and chariots departed for the city. Soon after they had left the pleasant surroundings of Śṛngaverapura, Bharata saw Ayodhyā in the distance. 'Look how dark and silent Ayodhyā lies!' said Bharata sadly to his charioteer. 'All joy and brightness have deserted the city!'

Travelling quickly in his chariot that rumbled like thunder, Bharata entered Ayodhyā. Cats and owls prowled the streets but there were no men or women to be seen anywhere. The city was shrouded in a darkness deeper than the black nights during the dark fortnight of the moon. 'How sad that the city stands silent today,' sighed Bharata. 'It used to be filled with music and song! The sweet smells of unguents and flower garlands and liquor no longer fill the air. Now that Rāma is gone, there are no sounds of elephants trumpeting, horses neighing and chariot wheels rumbling.' Deeply depressed, Bharata entered his father's apartments that were now like a mountain cave without a lion.

Though he was still very upset, Bharata said to his ministers and advisors, 'I ask your permission to leave. I am going to Nandigrāma. Bereft without Rāma, I shall live there with my grief! The king has died and my older brother is in the forest. I shall wait for his return for he is the rightful king.' Bharata honoured his mothers and with a lighter heart, climbed into his chariot with Śatrughna.

As Bharata left, he was followed by his priests and ministers and the entire army with its horses and elephants and chariots as well as by all the citizens who came along unbidden. Holding Rāma's sandals on his head and filled with love for his brother, honourable Bharata soon reached Nandigrāma.

'This kingdom has been entrusted to me by my brother,' said Bharata to the elders after he had dismounted. 'His sandals, adorned with gold, shall guarantee the welfare of the kingdom until he returns! I shall place them on his feet myself when he comes back.

'I shall lay down the burden of kingship when I am reunited with Rāma and serve him as an elder brother should be served. Only when I have returned the sandals as well as the kingship that has been entrusted to me shall I be free of this terrible shame. When Rāma has been crowned in front of his rejoicing people I shall be four times as happy as I could ever have been as king!'

Bharata matted his hair and put on the clothes of an ascetic. He lived in Nandigrāma with his army and his ministers and ruled from there with the authority bestowed upon him, waiting for his beloved brother's return so that his pledge could be fulfilled.

After Bharata returned to the city, Rāma continued to live in Citrakūṭa. Soon, however, he noticed signs of discomfort among the ascetics who lived there under his protection. They would raise their eyebrows, give him sidelong glances and whisper amongst themselves with great agitation. Rāma wondered if he had offended them in some way and so he went to their master and bowed before him.

'Have the ascetics noticed some change in my behaviour which makes them act differently towards me?' he asked deferentially. 'I trust that Lakṣmaṇa has not acted indifferently through carelessness. Has Sītā, in her devotion to me, slighted you all in a way that is not appropriate for women?'

The master was an old man who had aged further by the practise of severe austerities. Trembling, he replied, 'Not at all! How could virtuous Sītā ever fail in her duties towards ascetics? The ascetics whisper among themselves because your presence here makes them fear an attack by *rākṣasas*. Khara, Rāvaṇa's younger brother, lives close by and he wants to throw all the ascetics out of Janasthāna. He is cruel and crude, and impossible to defeat in battle. Arrogant and wicked, he is a man-eater and he does not like you at all, my child!

'Ever since you came to live here, the *rākṣasas* have been tormenting the ascetics. They appear in unnatural shapes and in disgusting and terrifying forms. They turn their malicious gaze on us. They throw impure things at the ascetics who are performing sacred rituals and frighten others by suddenly appearing before them. They hide all over the place and take great pleasure in harassing us. When it is time for us to perform our rituals, they throw our sacrificial vessels around. They pour water on our sacred fires and break our pots.

'The ascetics want to leave the area these vile creatures have desecrated and move to another place. We must leave here before the *rākṣasas* inflict bodily harm on us. There is a pleasant wooded area not far from here, full of roots and fruits. I plan to live there with my followers. You can come with us if you like, before Khara begins to torment you. You have to be doubly alert at all times because your wife is with you. Even though you are capable of looking after yourself, it will not be easy for you to live here.'

The ascetics were so disturbed by the *rākṣasas'* behaviour that Rāma could not persuade them to stay. They honoured Rāma and left with their master to form a new settlement.

After the ascetics had left, Rāma was disinclined to continue living there for a number of reasons. 'This is the place where I last saw Bharata, my mother and all the people of Ayodhyā. I am constantly reminded of them and this makes me sad,' he thought. 'It has also been spoiled by pitched tents, trampled grasses and horse and elephant droppings. We should go on to another place.'

Rāma, Sītā and Lakṣmaṇa set off for the hermitage of the sage Atri, who welcomed them as if they were his own children. He presented them to his wife, Anusūyā, who was so virtuous that she was honoured by all people.

'For ten long years,' said Atri, 'the world was scorched by a terrible drought. Anusūyā, known for her awesome austerities and rigid discipline, forced the Gangā to flow and made roots and fruits appear. She practised severe penances for ten thousand years and by the strength of her vows, she was able to remove all obstacles to the sacred practices of the sages. Intent on helping the gods, she compressed ten days into a single night.

'She will be like a mother to you, Rāma. Let Sītā serve this virtuous woman who has controlled her anger and is worshipped by all creatures!' Rāma instructed Sītā to do as the sage had said, for Anusūyā was renowned in the world for her deeds.

Anusūyā was old and wrinkled. Her hair was white and she was so enfeebled by age that she shook like a slender banana tree in a high wind. Sītā touched her feet and stood before her with her head bowed and her palms joined in respect.

'You are truly virtuous, Sītā,' said Anusūyā kindly. 'You have given up your family and friends, splendour, wealth and adoration, to follow your husband into the forest. Women who love their husbands no matter whether they live in the city or the forest, whether they be wicked or virtuous, are the ones that go to heaven. Even if a husband be immoral, or lustful or a pauper, he is the supreme divinity to a noble woman. A husband is the best companion in any situation, like the imperishable fruits of penance.

'There are some women whose hearts are filled with a lust for power. They dominate their husbands and choose between right and wrong for themselves. They are ruled by vice and they fall from propriety, becoming notorious because of that. But you are not like that, Sītā. You are virtuous and there is a place for you in heaven.

'Here is a flower garland worthy of the gods and clothes and jewels and rare unguents and ointments for your body! Take these and adorn yourself for they shall never fade or wither. You shall add to your husband's glory by using these, as Śrī enhances the glory of Viṣṇu!' Sītā accepted the affectionate gift with due respect.

'Now the sun has set,' continued Anusūyā, 'ushering in the lovely night. Birds that have flown all over in search of food chatter as they settle down to sleep in their nests. Ascetics walk back together from their evening baths with their pots of water, their clothes still wet. Smoke, grey as pigeon feathers, rises from the sacred fires of the sages and is scattered by the gentle wind. The trees around us appear like clumps of darkness and nothing is visible in any direction. Look how the deer lies down beside the sacrificial altar. It is time for the creatures of the night.

'Sītā, the night has arrived adorned with stars and the moon fills the sky with a veil of light. Go to Rāma and take care of him. I have derived much happiness from your company. I have been waiting for you to adorn yourself with these ornaments. Let me have the pleasure of seeing you wear them all!'

Sītā adorned herself with the jewels and garlands and was as beautiful as a daughter of the gods. She bowed to Anusūyā and went to Rāma. Rāma was delighted with the affection that the old woman had shown Sītā and both Rāma and Lakṣmaṇa were gratified with the honour done to Sītā, an honour rare in the world of men.

Rāma spent a pleasant night at the hermitage, honoured and entertained by the ascetics. The next morning, after the rituals had been completed, the mighty warriors prepared to depart. The ascetics told them how the *rākṣasas* created obstacles to their movements in the forest. 'This is the path that the sages take when they go into the forest to collect fruit,' they said. 'Take the same path, Rāma!'

The ascetics called blessings upon Rāma as he entered the forest with his wife and Lakṣmaṇa as the sun enters a circle of clouds.

# WILDERNESS

# *Chapter Twenty-Eight*

When Rāma entered the mighty Daṇḍaka forest, he saw that it was inhabited by deer and various other animals, including bears and tigers. The trees in the forest had been enveloped by enormous creepers and vines and none of its ponds and lakes had been looked after. The birds were silent and the only sound that filled the air was the chirping of crickets.

In that forest which was the home of all kinds of fierce animals, Rāma came upon a huge *rākṣasa* who fed on human flesh. The *rākṣasa,* with his sunken eyes and huge maw, roared like thunder. His limbs were twisted and deformed, his huge belly quivered and shook when he moved and he was terrifying to look at. This awful creature, who wore a tiger skin dripping with blood and fat, tormented all the forest animals. He had three lions, four tigers, two wolves, ten deer and an elephant's head, its tusk still smeared with gore, impaled upon the point of his spear as he came rushing towards Rāma, Lakṣmaṇa and Sītā.

Looking like Death, the *rākṣasa* charged at them and his roar made the earth tremble. He grabbed Sītā and tucked her under his arm. 'You are in the forest with the matted hair of an ascetic. But you have brought your wife with you!' he shouted. 'Consider your life at an end! You have entered the Daṇḍaka forest armed with bows and arrows! How can you live an ascetic's life when you have a woman with you? Who are you, unrighteous men, who malign the life led by the great sages?

'I am the *rākṣasa* Virādha. Every day, I wander through this dense forest preying on sages and eating their flesh. This beautiful woman shall be my wife! And I shall drink the blood of both you wretched creatures on the battlefield!' Sītā trembled like a slender banana plant in a high wind when she heard the *rākṣasa's* terrible words.

'Look, Lakṣmaṇa,' said Rāma, his face pale as he saw his wife under the *rākṣasa's* arm. 'This beautiful princess, the delicate daughter of Janaka and my lovely wife, who has been reared with every comfort imaginable, is being forced to sit on Virādha's hip. What Kaikeyī wished for when she asked for her boons has come to pass all too soon! Not satisfied with the kingdom for her own son, she sent me, whom everybody loves, into the forest. That mother of mine has been granted her wish today! I cannot bear the thought of Sītā being touched by another man. It upsets me more than the death of my father and the loss of my kingdom!'

Rāma broke into tears as he said this but Lakṣmaṇa was enraged and burst out, hissing in his anger, 'Rāma! You are Indra's equal and the lord of all creatures! How can you act so helpless! You have nothing to fear when I am at your service. I shall kill this *rākṣasa* with my arrows and the earth shall drink his blood. I shall direct the anger that I feel for Bharata over the loss of the kingdom towards this creature, just as Indra turned his anger upon the mountains. My mighty arms shall release an arrow with great force. May it drive the breath from his body and leave him lifeless upon the ground!'

'Who are you and where are you going?' asked Virādha in a voice that filled the entire forest. 'Tell me, I must know!' Rāma replied that they were from the Ikṣvāku clan. 'We are virtuous *kṣatriyas* who have come to spend some time in the forest. Who are you and why do you wander through this forest?' he asked the *rākṣasa* who blazed like a fire.

'Is that what you want to know?' said Virādha. 'Listen, then, and I will tell you! I am the son of Jaya and my mother is Śatahṛdā. I am known to all the *rākṣasas* on earth as Virādha. Brahmā gave me a boon because of all the austerities I performed. There is no weapon on earth that can maim, cut or pierce me! Leave this woman with me and go from this place with no further expectations. Return to where you came from. I shall not kill you!'

Rāma's eyes blazed with anger as he shouted back at the *rākṣasa* who had bloodshot eyes and wicked intentions. 'Shame on you for your base motives! You are obviously seeking death. Stand and fight me and you shall certainly find it!' Rāma fitted his straightest and sharpest arrows into his bow. Seven gold-tipped arrows blazed like tongues of flame as they flew with the speed of the wind, resounding through the air. They pierced the *rākṣasa's* body and he fell to the earth. Virādha let out a deafening roar. He seemed like Death with his mouth wide open and his spear that was as huge as Indra's flagstaff. Rāma, the best among all those who fight with weapons, split Virādha's spear with two arrows as it came through the air like a thunderbolt. Then, Lakṣmaṇa quickly cut off his right arm and Rāma his left one.

The *rākṣasa,* who was as dark as a cloud, fell to the earth with his arms hacked off, like a mountain felled by a thunderbolt. 'I knew that you were Rāma, the illustrious son of Kausalyā, and that this was the virtuous Sītā and that the famous Lakṣmaṇa,' said Virādha to the brothers. 'I am actually the *gandharva* Tumburu. I have this hideous *rākṣasa* body because I was cursed by Kubera. When I begged his forgiveness, he generously said I would be liberated when Rāma, son of Daśaratha, killed me in combat, and I would recover my natural state and return to heaven.

'Now I have been freed from this awful curse by you. I shall return to my own home. May all go well with you! The great sage Śarabhanga lives close by, less than one and a half *yojanās* from here. He is as effulgent as the sun. Go to him quickly, for he shall ensure your welfare. As for me, throw me into a pit. That is the primordial ritual for a dying *rākṣasa.* Those who are buried in pits shall attain worlds of everlasting happiness.' Virādha was overcome with pain from his wounds as he spoke. He was ready to go to heaven, waiting only to be released from his body. Rāma and Lakṣmaṇa hurled him into a deep pit and the *rākṣasa* with ears like conch shells howled as he fell.

Now that they had recovered Sītā and the incident with the *rākṣasa* was behind them, Rāma and Lakṣmaṇa went deeper into the forest with their golden arrows, shining like the sun and the moon in the sky.

Rāma, Lakṣmaṇa and Sītā visited the settlements of many sages in the forest, including the hermitages of Śarabhanga and Sutīkśṇa. Wherever he went, the sages pleaded with Rāma to protect them from the harassment of the *rākṣasas.* Rāma promised that he would kill any and all the *rākṣasas* who bothered the sages.

When Rāma had said farewell to Sutīkṣṇa and they were proceeding on their way, Sītā spoke gently to her husband. 'You are a man of great deeds and when you consider the matter carefully, I am sure you will see that *dharma* is very subtle.

'There are three major weaknesses that arise from desire. One is telling lies. The other two are much worse: one is lusting after another man's wife and the other is cruelty without a justified cause for hostility. You have never lied, Rāma, nor will you ever do so. You do not covet the wives of others and you have not acted in violation of *dharma.* These things would only be done by a man who has no control over his senses. I know you are perfectly disciplined.

'But the third weakness which men succumb to because of their passions, the inflicting of violence and cruelty upon other beings without reason or enmity, that weakness appears to be present in you now. You have promised to kill the *rākṣasas* in combat in order to protect the sages who live in the Daṇḍaka forest. This has brought you and your brother to this forest, armed with your bows and arrows.

'It disturbs me a great deal when I see you like this. I know you well and I am concerned about your welfare now and in the future. Our journey into the Daṇḍaka forest makes me anxious and I am not comfortable. Listen and I will tell you why.

'Now that you are here with your brother and both of you are armed, you shall see many forest creatures. Inevitably, you will be tempted to use your arrows. Like dry fuel bursts into flame when it is near a fire, so too, a *kṣatriya*'s passions are ignited when he has a bow at hand.

'Long ago, there was an ascetic who lived somewhere in a forest which was filled with birds and animals who dwelt together in peace. But Indra wanted to place obstacles in the path of the ascetic's practise of austerities. So one day he took the form of a soldier and carrying a sword, he went to see the ascetic. He left the sword with the ascetic for safe-keeping and went away. Once he had the weapon, the ascetic guarded it zealously. He even took it with him when he wandered through the forest searching for roots and fruits, determined to guard what had been entrusted to him. That man who had been known for his ascetic merit renounced his ascetic vows and his mind turned to cruelty. He began to relish brutality and he fell into unrighteous ways. Eventually, that holy man went to hell, all because of his proximity to a weapon.

'I am reminding you of this tale not because I presume to instruct you but because I love and respect you. May it never happen that you attack the *rākṣasas* of the forest without reason, simply because you carry a weapon. I cannot bear the thought of innocents being killed, O hero! A *kṣatriya* should use his bow in the forest only to protect the oppressed. What a difference there is between the life of weapons and that of the forest, between the vows of a *kṣatriya* and those of an ascetic! We must learn to respect the code of behaviour of the world we now inhabit. Here, the mind is perverted by extreme proximity to weapons. You can return to the code of the *kṣatriyas* when we go back to Ayodhyā!

'But if you were to give up the kingdom entirely and embrace the life of an ascetic, I am sure that my parents-in-law would be very happy. Everything in this world, including wealth and happiness, come from *dharma.* There is nothing greater than *dharma.* Great men strive for *dharma* by subjecting themselves to severe physical mortifications, since true happiness cannot come from the pursuit of pleasure.

'Enjoy the beauties of the forest with a pure mind, my love. You already know all there is to be known in the three worlds about these things. I have spoken from the foolishness of being a woman. Who is capable of teaching you anything about *dharma*? Discuss what I have said with your brother and then do whatever you think best.'

'My dear, you have spoken sweetly for my benefit because you love me,' said Rāma, who always stood firm in *dharma.* 'Your words show that you are truly worthy of your noble family. But I must remind you of what you yourself said, that *kṣatriyas* are armed so that the cries of the oppressed may never be heard. Those resolute sages who live in the forest are being tormented. They are the refuge of other beings, and yet they are the ones who approached me for protection. They live quietly in the forest, eating only roots and fruits, intent on practising their *dharma.* But they can no longer live in peace because of the *rākṣasas'* wicked deeds.

'The sages live in the forest all through the year, practising austerities, but they are preyed upon by man-eating *rākṣasas.* The sages approached me of their own accord. The best among them spoke to me and I was deeply embarrassed. "Forgive me," I said. "I am truly ashamed that people like yourselves, whom I should be serving, have had to come to me." I asked them what they wanted me to do. In one voice they replied, "Rāma, we are being horribly harassed by the *rākṣasas* who live in the Daṇḍaka forest and who can change their shapes at will. You must protect us from their attacks. They descend upon us when we are performing sacrifices. These wretched carrion-eaters assault us during the time of the new moon and the full moon. You are the only refuge for these tormented sages! Of course, we could easily destroy them with the power of our austerities. But we would be nullifying our long years of penance by doing so. Austerities are so difficult and there are so many obstacles in our way in any case! So even though the *rākṣasas* harass us, we do not curse them. You and your brother must help us. We have no other protector in the forest!"

'I promised the sages of the Daṇḍaka forest that I would protect them, Sītā. And now that I have given them my word, I cannot go back on it as long as there is a single breath left in my body. You know that truth is dear to me! I could more easily give up my life or renounce you or Lakṣmaṇa than break a promise, especially one that I have made to *brahmins*! It is my duty to protect holy men under any circumstances. Now it is even more so because they have asked for my protection.

'I am glad you said what you did, for you spoke out of love. We never give advice to those we do not care for. Dear girl, your words were typical of your noble character and your family background!'

Rāma, Lakṣmaṇa and Sītā wandered through the forest pleasantly, spending time with the many sages there, and finally arrived at the settlement of the great *ṛṣi* Agastya. Lakṣmaṇa went up to one of Agastya's students. 'The eldest son of King Daśaratha, mighty Rāma, has arrived here with his wife Sītā and wishes to meet the great sage. I am his younger brother Lakṣmaṇa. You may have heard about us. I am devoted to Rāma and committed to doing what will make him happy. We are here in this terrible forest because of our father's wishes. Tell the sage we would like to see him.'

The student went into the ritual chamber to announce Rāma's arrival to the sage, whose power from austerities was truly awesome. 'The sons of Daśaratha, Rāma and Lakṣmaṇa, have come here along with Rāma's wife Sītā,' said the student, repeating Lakṣmaṇa's words. 'They wish to see you and serve you. What shall I tell them?'

'How wonderful that Rāma has come to see me!' exclaimed the resplendent sage. 'I have waited a long time for him to come here. Why did you not let them enter immediately? Go quickly and bring him in! Show all due respect to him, his brother and his wife.' The student bowed and went out to do the sage's bidding. 'Where is Rāma?' he asked Lakṣmaṇa eagerly. 'He must go in at once and meet the sage!'

Lakṣmaṇa led the student to the settlement gates and pointed Rāma and Sītā out to him. With great respect, the student repeated Agastya's words to Rāma and escorted him and Sītā in with full honours. Rāma walked through the settlement and saw that it was filled with tame deer. He also noticed that there were shrines dedicated to the worship of Brahmā, Viṣṇu, Indra, the Sun, the Moon, Bhaga, Kubera, Dhatṛ, Vidhatṛ and Vāyu.

Rāma looked up and saw the great sage, blazing with splendour, surrounded by his students and disciples, coming forward to greet him. 'Look, Lakṣmaṇa! That must be Agastya coming towards us. I assume that it is he because of the shining aura that surrounds him.' Filled with joy, Rāma prostrated himself at the feet of the sage who shone like the sun, and honoured him. Then, he stood to one side with Lakṣmaṇa and Sītā, his palms joined in reverence. Agastya accepted Rāma's homage and welcomed him with the traditional *arghya* ritual. He asked after his welfare and offered him a seat. The sage made offerings to the fire and treated Rāma, Lakṣmaṇa and Sītā as honoured guests, plying them with food that was appropriate for ascetics.

'Rāma, this bow decorated with gold and jewels belonged to Viṣṇu and was made for him by Viśvakarmā. This arrow, best of all arrows, was given to me by Brahmā. It shines like the sun and never misses its mark. And these inexhaustible quivers were given to me by Indra, along with this mighty gold-hilted sword in this exquisite sheath. Long ago, Viṣṇu used this bow to kill the *asuras* and recapture power for the gods. Take these weapons from me and use them to vanquish your enemies, as Indra uses the thunderbolt!' said Agastya as he handed the weapons to Rāma.

'May good fortune attend you always, Rāma,' continued the sage. 'I am very pleased that you came to see me with Lakṣmaṇa and Sītā. You must be tired from your long, arduous journey. I can see that Sītā is completely exhausted. This poor woman has never experienced hardships like those of the forest. She has come to this troubled place out of love for her husband. Make sure that she has a pleasant life here, Rāma, for she has braved a great deal to follow you. It is in the nature of women to stay with a husband while he is prosperous and comfortable and to leave him in times of adversity. Women have the impetuosity of lightning, the sharpness of a weapon and the whimsy of the wind. But your wife, Rāma, is free from all these faults. She is praiseworthy and as fine an example as the steadfast Arundhatī herself. Her presence will adorn any place you choose to live in with Lakṣmaṇa.'

'It is our good fortune, blessed one and giver of boons, that you are pleased with us because of our virtues,' replied Rāma humbly. 'Tell me of a place where we can settle down and live in peace, a place that is gently wooded and has abundant water.'

Agastya thought for a while and then spoke with deliberation. 'About two *yojanās* from here, there is a place abundant in roots and fruits and water, filled with different kinds of animals. It is called Pañcavaṭī. Go and establish a settlement there with Lakṣmaṇa so that you can fulfil your father's wishes with relative ease. I know all that happened to you and Daśaratha, blameless Rāma, through the power of my austerities and because of my affection for you. When you said you wanted to live here in the forest, I thought about your motives and now I understand what you have in mind. That is why I have asked you to live in Pañcavaṭī. It is a pleasant place and it is close to the river Godāvarī. Sītā will like it there. It is quiet and deserted and is a place of great sanctity.

'Rāma, your wife is with you and I know you are capable of looking after her. But, by living there, you will also be able to protect the sages. Do you see that grove of *mahua* trees? Walk left from there and you will come to another grove of banyans. Go up the mountain and you will see Pañcavaṭī with its perennially flowering trees.'

Rāma, Lakṣmaṇa and Sītā said their farewells to the sage who was devoted to truth and prostrated themselves at his feet. He blessed them and the three set off. Armed with their bows and arrows, the two princes who were so courageous in battle went along the path the sage had indicated, heading for Pañcavaṭī.

Soon, they came to an area that was full of terrifying serpents and many kinds of deer. 'This must be the place to which Agastya meant to send us,' said Rāma to his brother Lakṣmaṇa, who blazed like the fire. 'This must be Pañcavaṭī, since it is so pleasant with its flowering trees. You know so much about forests. Look around and find a spot that will please us, where we can build our settlement. Find a place with water close by, from where we can enjoy the beautiful view, where sacrificial materials and flowers will be close at hand.'

'Rāma, I am your servant, even if you live for a hundred years!' said Lakṣmaṇa with his palms joined. 'You pick the spot and show it to me.' Rāma was pleased with Lakṣmaṇa's words and soon found a spot that met all his requirements. Taking Lakṣmaṇa's hands in his own, he said, 'This is the perfect spot, surrounded as it is by flowering trees. Build the hut here, dear brother! Look, there is a pond close by that shines like the sun and is filled with fragrant lotuses! And there is the river Godāvarī, just as the sage described it, lined with trees, visited by swans and all kinds of songbirds. The mountains dotted with caves are neither too close nor too far. Deer wander there amidst the trees laden with flowers and we can hear the cries of the peacocks! This spot has great spiritual merit—we shall live here, Lakṣmaṇa!'

Mighty Lakṣmaṇa, destroyer of his enemies, quickly built a hut for his brother. The hut was spacious, with a thatched roof supported by pillars, rafters of bamboo and a level floor. Lakṣmaṇa went down to the Godāvarī to bathe and came back with lotuses and fruit. He offered the flowers to the gods and after completing the prescribed rituals, he brought Rāma to show him the finished hut.

Sītā and Rāma were thrilled with their pleasant little dwelling. Rāma hugged Lakṣmaṇa and said, 'I am delighted with your wonderful work. All I can give you in return is this loving embrace. You are compassionate, gracious and righteous and so I feel that my father is not dead, he lives on in you!'

Rāma settled down happily in that bounteous region. Served by Lakṣmaṇa and Sītā, he lived there for some time, like a god in heaven.

# *Chapter Twenty-Nine*

One day, Rāma, Sītā and Lakṣmaṇa returned to their hut as usual after bathing in the Godāvarī. Rāma and Lakṣmaṇa completed the morning worship and sat down under the thatched area in front of the hut. With Sītā by his side, Rāma looked as beautiful as the moon in the Caitra constellation. The brothers chatted about this and that, telling each other stories and tales. As Rāma sat there, absorbed in conversation, a *rākṣasī* happened to pass by. She was Śūrpanakhā, the sister of the *rākṣasa* Rāvaṇa. When she saw Rāma sitting there, glorious as a heavenly being, she fell in love with him.

Rāma was young and handsome and radiant. His chest was as broad as a lion's, his arms were mighty and strong and his eyes were shaped like the petals of a lotus. He was dark as a blue lotus, as handsome as the god of love, equal to Indra in strength. The *rākṣasī* gazed at this man in wonder and was overcome with desire. Rāma presented a contrast to her in every possible way. He was handsome, she was ugly. He was slim-waisted, she was potbellied. His eyes were large and set wide in his face, she was cross-eyed. His hair was smooth and dark, hers was coppery and dried out. His voice was sweet and gentle, hers was raucous and harsh. He was young, handsome and honourable, she was old, cruel and deceitful. He walked the path of virtue, she was wicked. He was charming and refined, she was crude.

'Your hair is matted like an ascetic's but you carry a bow and arrow and you are in the company of a woman,' she said to him, brimming with lust. 'What are you doing in this region filled with *rākṣasas*?'

Rāma replied by telling her all about himself. 'There was a king named Daśaratha, as mighty as the gods themselves. I am his oldest son and I am known in the world as Rāma. This is my brother Lakṣmaṇa, who is deeply devoted to me. This is my wife Sītā, the princess of Videha. I have come to live in the forest and reap the fruits of my actions because I am bound by the wishes of my father, the king, and my mother. Now I want to know about you. Tell me, who are you? Where do you come from? Why are you here?'

The *rākṣasī* was entranced. 'Listen, Rāma, and I will tell you all about myself,' she said. 'I am the *rākṣasī* Śūrpanakhā and I can change my form at will. I do as I please. I wander through this forest by myself and I strike terror into the hearts of all creatures. My brother is Rāvaṇa, the king of the *rākṣasas,* and I have another brother, the mighty Kumbhakarṇa, who sleeps all the time. My third brother is the honourable Vibhīṣaṇa and he is not like a *rākṣasa* at all. My other two brothers are Khara and Dūṣaṇa, famed for their prowess in battle. But none of them have any control over me.

'I am in love with your good looks, Rāma. I think you must be the best of men. Be my husband and stay with me for a long time! What use is this Sītā? She is ugly and deformed and simply no match for you. But I am your equal, consider me for a wife! I will devour this ugly mortal woman whose belly hangs so low. I shall eat your brother as well! And then, my love, you and I can roam through Daṇḍaka forest and enjoy the mountains and grasslands!'

Rāma laughed when he heard this speech from Śūrpanakhā, whose eyes were drunk with lust. He spoke sincerely and gently to that poor creature who was a prisoner of passion. 'I am a married man and Sītā is my dearly beloved wife! I know women like you do not want to share your man with another. But, there is my younger brother Lakṣmaṇa. He is strong and brave and handsome and he is single. He needs a wife, for he has not yet experienced the joys of marriage. He will suit you as a husband, for you, too, are so beautiful! Take my brother as your husband, lovely lady, and enjoy him exclusively, as the sun enjoys the peaks of Mount Meru.'

Utterly confused and still overwhelmed by passion, Śūrpanakhā let go of Rāma and turned to Lakṣmaṇa. 'You are as beautiful as I am and so you are a worthy match for me. Come with me and roam happily through the Daṇḍakas!'

Lakṣmaṇa also had a way with words. He smiled and replied in the same light vein. 'I am the servant of my noble brother. Why do you want to marry a slave like me, lady as lovely as a lotus, and become a slave yourself? You, with your glowing complexion, should become the second wife of my older brother who has everything. Then all your wishes will be fulfilled! He will grow attached to you and renounce this ugly mortal wife of his. She is deformed and old and her belly hangs so low! Who would remain attached to a mortal woman when he could have you with your lovely skin and dazzling beauty?'

Potbellied Śūrpanakhā took Lakṣmaṇa seriously as she had no sense of humour. Even more bewildered, she addressed Rāma, who was sitting under the thatch with Sītā. 'You think nothing of me because you are so devoted to this ugly, old mortal with a hanging belly! I shall eat her up right now, in front of you! Then you and I can be together happily, without any interference.'

Her eyes blazing like fire, Śūrpanakhā charged towards the gentle-eyed Sītā, like malignant planets circling the Rohiṇī constellation. But Rāma stopped her headlong rush. 'Lakṣmaṇa, you should never joke with cruel and base creatures! Look how frightened Sītā is!' he cried. Angrily, Lakṣmaṇa pulled out his dagger and cut off Śūrpanakhā's ears and nose.

Śūrpanakhā screamed in pain and bolted back into the forest from which she had come. Her cries were like thunder during the rains and with blood streaming from her face she looked even more terrifying than usual. She went straight to her brother Khara who lived in Janasthāna, surrounded by his *rākṣasa* forces. She threw herself in front of him, as a bolt of lightning would fall from the sky.

Khara grew angry when he saw his sister lying on the ground, mutilated and dripping blood. 'Who did this to you?' he asked. 'You are so strong, capable of going wherever you please, able to change your shape at will, like unto Death itself! Tell me who it was that mutilated you. Was it a god, a *gandharva*, a great-souled *ṛśi*, a *bhūta* or some mighty human hero? I cannot think of anyone in this world other than the thousand-eyed Indra who would dare incur my wrath. Whoever it was, I shall take his life this very day with my deadly arrows! Who is this, whose blood shall be drunk by the earth as it surges, frothing, from his breast which has been pierced by my arrow? Who is this, whose flesh shall be pecked at by birds when he lies dead after I have killed him in battle? Not the gods nor the *gandharvas*, not the *rākṣasas* nor the *piśacas* shall be able to save him once I have laid my hands on him! Calm yourself, gather your wits about you and tell me who did this to you in the forest.'

Drenched in blood and almost fainting from fear and confusion, Śūrpanakhā told Khara all about Rāma and Lakṣmaṇa and her mutilation. 'There were these two handsome young men, brave and strong, with eyes shaped like lotus petals,' wept Śūrpanakhā is response to her brother's angry words. 'They were wearing the skin of the black antelope but they looked like kings or *gandharvas* since they bore all the marks of royalty. I could not tell if they were gods or mortals. There was also this beautiful woman with them, slim-waisted and adorned with jewels. They used her as an excuse and did this to me, as if I were a loose woman without anyone to protect me! I want to drink their blood, fresh and frothing, when they have been killed in battle. Help me do this and you will have fulfilled my dearest wish!'

Khara summoned fourteen mighty *rākṣasas* who were like Death incarnate when his sister had finished her tale. 'Two men wearing the skin of the black antelope, fully armed and accompanied by a woman, have entered the Daṇḍaka forests. Kill the men and the woman, for my sister wishes to drink their blood! Then come back here. Go quickly, *rākṣasas*! Crush them with your might and grant my sister her wish!' The fourteen *rākṣasas* left immediately, like clouds driven by the storm winds.

Fierce Śūrpanakhā led the fourteen *rākṣasas* to Rāma's settlement and pointed the two brothers and Sītā out to them as they sat under the leafy thatch in front of the hut. Rāma noticed that Śūrpanakhā had come back along with the *rākṣasas*. 'Stay here with Sītā for a bit,' he said to his valiant brother, 'while I kill the *rākṣasas* who have come here with that woman!' Rāma was aware of his own strength and so Lakṣmaṇa agreed.

Rāma strung his mighty bow which was decorated with gold and addressed the *rākṣasas*. 'We are the sons of Daśaratha, the brothers Rāma and Lakṣmaṇa, and we have come into the dense and impenetrable Daṇḍaka forest with my wife Sītā! We live here quietly in the forest, eating only roots and fruits and following the code of righteous ascetics. Why do you wish to harm us?

'I am ready to fight you, with my bow and arrow. I have been instructed to do so by the sages living in the forest whom you harass! Stand where you are! Do not turn back! But if you value your lives, rangers of the night, then you had better run!'

The fourteen *rākṣasas* had all killed *brahmins*. Armed with their spears, their eyes red with anger, they replied, 'You have incurred the wrath of our master, the mighty Khara. And for this, it is you who shall lose your life in battle today! How can you face us in battle when you are alone and we are so many? You couldn't possibly stand up to us in any circumstances! Your bow and arrows shall fall from your hands when we attack you and then you shall die!'

The fourteen *rākṣasas* fell upon Rāma eagerly with all their weapons. They hurled their spears at him but the invincible Rāma shattered the spears with fourteen arrows decorated with gold. Then he fitted another fourteen arrows into his bow. They had been sharpened against the hardest stone and had iron tips that glittered like the sun. He released them as Indra looses his thunderbolt and they blazed through the air like lightning in the sky. In a flash, they had pierced the *rākṣasas'* breasts. Drenched in blood, the *rākṣasas* sank to the ground, like snakes plunging into an anthill. Their hearts split open, their bodies bathed in blood, the ugly creatures hit the ground like trees felled by an axe.

Śūrpanakhā screamed with fright and nearly swooned when she saw them fall. Bellowing with rage, she ran back to Khara and threw herself before him. The blood from her own wounds had dried up, except for a little trickle, like sap oozing from a cut vine.

'It was only a little while ago that I asked those bloodthirsty *rākṣasas* to do what you asked,' said Khara to that ill-omened creature when he saw her lying on the ground in a fit of temper. 'What are you crying for now? They are loyal and devoted to me and will do whatever I ask. They cannot possibly be dead, for they are the ones that do the killing. Tell me, why are you writhing on the ground like a snake and wailing "Alas, my lord!" over and over again? Why are you weeping as if you had no one to protect you? I am here to take care of you! Don't be frightened! Get up! There is no need to panic while I am around!'

Somewhat reassured by her brother's words, the wretched Śūrpanakhā wiped her tears. 'It is true that you sent out fourteen heroic and fierce *rākṣasas* to kill Rāma and Lakṣmaṇa in order to please me. But Rāma killed all those mighty *rākṣasas* armed with all their great weapons with arrows that pierced their vitals! I was terribly frightened when I saw Rāma's prowess and those mighty warriors dead on the ground. I have come to you for refuge again, great *rākṣasa,* for I am terrified and very disturbed. I feel threatened from all sides! I am plunged into an ocean of terror with waves of fright and sea monsters of despair. Help me!

'Those mighty eaters of human flesh that you sent with me now lie dead, slain by Rāma's arrows! If you have any compassion for me or those dead *rākṣasas,* if you have the strength and courage to face Rāma, then get rid of him. He is a thorn in the side of the *rākṣasas* now that he has come to live in the Daṇḍaka forest! If you do not kill Rāma, my enemy, this very day, then I shall kill myself right now, right here in front of you!

'I know you cannot challenge Rāma in battle, even if you stood at the head of a huge army!' she taunted. 'You are known for your valour but it must be a lie! You have no courage! You cannot even kill these two mortals, Rāma and Lakṣmaṇa! How can you live here without courage and strength? Take your followers and leave Janasthāna immediately! You will soon be destroyed by Rāma's might. Daśaratha's son is very powerful and his brother, who mutilated me, is also very strong!'

'I am outraged by this insult to you,' said heroic Khara in front of all the *rākṣasas.* 'My anger cannot be contained, it rises like the ocean at high tide! I have no respect for Rāma! He is a mere mortal and is doomed to die. He will forfeit his life today for the terrible thing he has done! Stop this weeping and fretting. I shall send Rāma and his brother to meet the god of death! You shall drink Rāma's warm blood on the battlefield today as it wells from his body which has been struck by my battle axe.'

Śūrpanakhā was delighted to hear this and foolishly she began to praise her brother again. Alternately insulted and praised by his sister, Khara called for the commander of his forces, Dūṣaṇa. 'There are fourteen thousand *rākṣasas* at my command,' he said to Dūṣaṇa. 'They are incredibly swift, but they never turn and flee in battle. Dark as rain clouds, frightening and cruel, these immensely strong and powerful *rākṣasas* delight in hurting others. Make sure these courageous fellows with the pride of tigers and huge mouths are prepared for battle. Bring me my battle chariot at once and also my bows and arrows, my beautifully decorated swords and my spears of all kinds! I want to be in the forefront of the descendants of Pulastya! I shall slay Rāma in battle!'

# *Chapter Thirty*

When Khara's army went forth, an enormous donkey-coloured cloud thundered and rained dirty water, the colour of blood, upon the troops. As Khara's chariot proceeded along the main road, which was strewn with flowers, his swift horses stumbled without reason. Even the sun was dark, circled by a blood-red aureole that was like the arc described by a fire-brand. A huge, vicious vulture flew over the battle banner which fluttered on its golden staff and hovered there for a little while.

As the army approached Janasthāna, birds and beasts of prey cried out in their harsh voices. Jackals howled hideously at the sun, their open mouths blazing, presaging ill for the *rākṣasa* army. Khara stood in his chariot and let out his great battle cry, but his voice quavered and his right arm trembled and twitched. When he looked around him, his vision blurred and his head throbbed, but in his immense foolishness, he would not turn back. He laughed as he observed these ill omens that were enough to make the hair stand on end.

'These omens do not worry me even though they are really frightening,' he said to his army. 'Unlike these weak mortals, I rely on my own strength and courage! I can bring the stars down from the sky with my arrows! When I am angry, I can kill Death himself! Rāma is arrogant in his prowess but I shall not return without killing him and his brother Lakṣmaṇa! I shall slay them with my sharp arrows for treating my sister so badly. She shall have her wish and drink their blood! I have never been defeated in battle. You have seen that for yourselves so you know that I am not lying. I can even kill Indra, the king of the gods, when he rides into battle on his rutting elephant Airāvata, flourishing his thunderbolt! What then of these ridiculous mortals!' The army cheered with delight when they heard these mighty boasts even though they were firmly within the noose of death.

Meanwhile, the gods, the *ṛṣis,* the *gandharvas, siddhas* and the *cāraṇas* gathered, eager to witness the great battle. As those meritorious and virtuous beings came together, they whispered among themselves, 'May all go well with the cows and the *brahmins* and those who wish for the welfare of the worlds. May Rāma defeat the *rākṣasas* who are descended from Pulastya as Viṣṇu defeated the *asuras*!'

Rāma and Lakṣmaṇa saw the same inauspicious signs as the *rākṣasa* army approached their settlement. The portents of evil, which boded ill for all creatures, made their hair stand on end. 'Look at these signs, mighty Lakṣmaṇa, that spell disaster for all beings,' said Rāma. 'They rise today for the destruction of the *rākṣasas*! Donkey-coloured clouds scud across the sky, thundering and raining bloody water! But my arrows are smoking, so eager are they to do battle. And my gold-encrusted bows quiver with anticipation, Lakṣmaṇa! The cries of the birds and animals indicate to me that something truly terrifying is close by, something that puts all lives in danger. My left arm twitches all the time. I have no doubt that there is going to be a great battle, but these signs indicate that we are going to defeat our enemies.

'Take your bow and arrows and go into that cave with Sītā. It is hidden by trees and hard to access. Take refuge there. Please don't argue with me, just promise me that you will go!' When Lakṣmaṇa started towards the cave, Rāma sighed with relief that his brother had obeyed his instructions.

Rāma put on his armour that blazed like the fire and appeared like a smokeless flame shining in the dark. The great warrior lifted his bow, chose his arrows and filled the sky with the sound of his twanging bowstring. Soon, the *rākṣasa* army could be seen. It approached from all directions, flying its battle banners and raising a tremendous din as it struck terror into the hearts of all beings. The *rākṣasas* roared and yelled, each one louder than the other. They twanged their bowstrings and stamped their feet and beat their huge drums and the forest reverberated with the noise they made. Animals and birds ran from their shelters in panic without looking back as they made for a quieter place. The huge army with all its weapons moved inexorably towards Rāma like the surging ocean.

Rāma watched the eager army approaching. He drew his bow and readied his arrows, determined, in his anger, to kill all the *rākṣasas.* He blazed like the doomsday fire and his face was terrible to behold. He resembled Śiva, the wielder of the Pinaka bow, at the time when he destroyed Dakṣa's sacrifice.

Khara drew near the settlement and saw Rāma, the destroyer of his enemies, standing there with his bow. Khara armed himself and told his charioteer to go forward. The charioteer urged the horses on towards Rāma and when Khara's ministers saw that he was ready to do battle, they gathered around, roaring out their battle cries.

With shouts of anger, the *rākṣasas* assailed Rāma with all kinds of weapons. The troops rained arrows on Rāma like clouds rain water upon a mountain, but Rāma countered their weapons with his own arrows like the sea engulfs a river. Though he was attacked from all sides, Rāma was no more perturbed than a mighty mountain that is assailed by thunder and lightning. Pierced by arrows and bleeding from all over his body, Rāma was as red as the setting sun.

Rāma pulled his bow back as far as it would go, turning it into a circle. He loosed hundreds of thousands of crescent-headed arrows which created havoc among the *rākṣasas,* placing them firmly within death's noose. Some of the especially powerful and brave *rākṣasas* confronted Rāma and attacked him with their swords, maces and spears. Rāma warded off their weapons with his arrows and cut off their heads.

The *rākṣasas* that survived ran to Khara in terror, seeking protection from Rāma's arrows. Dūṣaṇa reassured and rallied them, sending them back to face Rāma. They attacked with renewed vigour, picking up trees and rocks and stones, raising a din that was absolutely terrifying.

Rāma grew angrier and blazing like fire, he turned his arrows upon Dūṣaṇa. The army commander grabbed his mace that was as big as a mountain peak and terrifying enough to make the hair stand on end. Brandishing that huge club, he rushed headlong towards Rāma. Rāma loosed two arrows that severed the charging Dūṣaṇa's bracelet-covered arms. Dūṣaṇa's enormous body hit the ground and his mighty club, which was like Indra's flagstaff, fell from his hand.

Rāma continued his attack on Dūṣaṇa's followers, and the *rākṣasas* fell to the earth bleeding, their armour, weapons and ornaments scattered, their heads and bodies split wide open. Bloodied, and with their hair streaming back from their faces, they covered the battlefield the way a sacrificial altar is strewn with *kuśa* grass. In no time at all the entire forest, now littered with dead *rākṣasas,* was transformed into a gory hell strewn with flesh and blood. Fourteen thousand *rakṣasas* who were capable of terrible things were slain by a lone man who fought on foot. The only survivors from that army were the great chariot-warrior Khara, the *rākṣasa* Triśiras* and Rāma himself.

Triśiras saw that Khara was preparing to attack Rāma himself. 'Let me go and fight him, O mighty warrior,' he said to his commander. 'You can watch the great Rāma fall in this fight! I swear to you, I will kill this man who deserves to die!' Eager to embrace death, Triśiras pleaded insistently and finally, Khara allowed him to advance upon Rāma.

Triśiras climbed into his horse-drawn chariot and surged towards Rāma, looking like a three-crested mountain. With a single arrow, Rāma toppled the battle banner that fluttered above his chariot. Dazed and bewildered, the *rākṣasa* dismounted, but Rāma pierced him through the heart as he stood there. Then, with three peerless arrows that were sharp and swift, Rāma severed Triśiras' heads. Drenched in blood, the *rākṣasa's* body followed his heads and fell to the ground.

Khara watched Dūṣaṇa and Triśiras being slain in battle and was somewhat disturbed by Rāma's strength and skills. The fact that the mighty *rākṣasa* army had been routed and its generals killed by Rāma single-handed frightened Khara, but he attacked Rāma fiercely. He drew his powerful bow and loosed blood-seeking arrows at Rāma which flew through the air like venomous snakes. He displayed his archer's skills with great flourish and standing in his chariot, performed many impressive battle manouevres. Khara filled the sky with arrows but Rāma countered them with his own that were like flames, bringing down a rain of sparks as they flew.

Then Rāma picked up Viṣṇu's mighty bow that had been given to him by Agastya. He loosed golden-feathered arrows from it and brought down Khara's battle banner. The golden banner, so beautiful to behold, now lay on the ground in tatters like the sun fallen to the earth. Khara knew which were the vulnerable spots on a mortal's body and sent four arrows into the region of Rāma's heart. Blood dripping from his body, Rāma grew angrier still and he was truly an awesome sight.

---

* Triśiras obviously had three heads, as indicated by his name.

With three well-chosen arrows, he pierced Khara's head and arms. With another thirteen, he brought down Khara's bow, his chariot, his horses and his charioteer. He used his thirteenth arrow to wound Khara in the heart. Khara grabbed his mace and leapt to the ground, ready to confront Rāma. He hurled his gold-decorated mace at Rāma and it came flying through the air like thunder accompanied by lightning. It burned trees and bushes, but Rāma cut it to bits with his arrows even before it reached the ground.

Khara frowned and looked around for something to throw at Rāma. He saw an enormous *sāla* tree and wrenched it from the ground with his huge arms. He hurled it at Rāma, roaring, 'Now you shall die!' But Rāma slashed it to pieces with a veritable flood of arrows. He was now determined to kill Khara. His eyes blazed with anger and his body was bathed in sweat as he unleashed a shower of arrows which pierced the *rākṣasa's* body. Blood poured from Khara's wounds, frothing like the waterfalls on Mount Prasravaṇa.

Bewildered by arrows and maddened by the smell of blood, Khara charged at Rāma, but Rāma was an experienced warrior and took a quick step aside. Then he chose a fiery arrow which rivalled Brahmā's weapon and fitted it into the bow that had been given to him by Indra. He pulled the bow back as far as it would go and released the arrow which thundered through the air and felled the *rākṣasa.* The fiery arrow consumed Khara in the same way that Death is consumed by Śiva's fires at the end of time.

The gods and other wondrous beings who had come to witness the battle rejoiced and praised Rāma with joy in their hearts. Lakṣmaṇa and Sītā came out of the cave where they had been hiding and entered the settlement. Victorious Rāma, lauded by all the sages, returned to his hut, where he was greeted with delight and respect by the heroic Lakṣmaṇa. Sītā embraced her husband, overjoyed that he was unharmed as well as victorious.

# *Chapter Thirty-One*

Śūrpanakhā had watched while Rāma performed the impossible task of slaying fourteen thousand *rākṣasas* as well as Dūṣaṇa, Triśiras and Khara single handed. Roaring like a thunder cloud, she went to Lankā, the city ruled by Rāvaṇa.

She saw Rāvaṇa in his wondrous chariot Puṣpaka, blazing with splendour and surrounded by his ministers like Indra is surrounded by the *māruts.* Sitting on a golden throne as bright as the sun, Rāvaṇa was as magnificent as the fire on a sacrificial altar. Undefeated and heroic in battle, he was like death itself, no matter who faced him, gods, *gandharvas, bhūtas* or the great *ṛṣis.* Rāvaṇa had been wounded many times in the battles between the gods and the *asuras* and he still carried the scars from when Airāvata had gored him on the chest with his tusks. Broad-chested, with ten heads and twenty arms, Rāvaṇa bore all the marks of royalty and looked like a king. He was as large as a mountain, had smooth dark skin and sparkling white teeth as bright as his gold earrings.

Rāvaṇa could stir up placid oceans, he could play with mountains and he could defeat the gods in battle. He did whatever he liked whenever he liked. He constantly violated *dharma.* He lusted after the wives of others, he was capable of using every celestial weapon and he was always disrupting sacrifices. He had gone to the city of Bhogavatī, defeated Vāsuki and then abducted Takṣaka's lovely wife after he had defeated him as well. In Kailāsa, he conquered Kubera and took the flying chariot Puṣpaka from him, a chariot that could go anywhere at any time. He was so strong that in his anger he could destroy the forests of Caitraratha, Nandana and other celestial gardens and pleasure groves.

With his enormous size and prodigious strength, Rāvaṇa could stop the sun and moon from rising. Long ago, he had performed austerities for ten thousand years in the forest and had offered his heads as a sacrifice to Brahmā. For this, he had been granted invulnerability in battle with the gods, *dānavas, gandharvas, ṛṣis* and *uragas,* every kind of being, in fact, except mortals. Mighty Rāvaṇa had even defiled the *soma* juice as it was being pressed inside the sacred enclosure by *brahmins*. This cruel and wicked *brahmin*-killer would ruin sacrifices just as they were about to be completed. Ruthless and harsh, Rāvaṇa wished ill for all beings and the entire universe was terrified of him.

Śūrpanakhā gazed at her mighty brother, dressed in celestial clothes and ornaments, who was descended from Pulastya and who was the king of the *rākṣasas.* That poor mutilated creature, terrified and confused, showed Rāvaṇa her wounds. Pathetic and angry, Śūrpanakhā spoke harshly to Rāvaṇa, who made the worlds weep, in front of all his ministers. 'Intoxicated with lust, indulging all your desires, living entirely by your whims and totally without any restraint, you have no idea of the danger you are in! You should know this but you don't!

'Subjects have no more regard for a wayward and wilful ruler who seeks vulgar pleasures than they have for the flames of a funeral pyre. A king who gives no attention to the affairs of state will be destroyed along with his kingdom because of this neglect. Now that you have angered the gods, *gandharvas* and the *dānavas*, how can you go on without the services of spies and informers? The king who has no control over his spies, his finances and his administration is no better than a commoner, great hero!

'You don't even know that your people have been massacred in Janasthāna. I can only conclude from this that you have no informants and that you are surrounded by incompetent ministers. Fourteen thousand fierce *rākṣasas* as well as Khara and Dūṣaṇa were killed by Rāma alone! Janasthāna has been destroyed and the Daṇḍaka forests have been cleansed. The sages no longer live in fear because of Rāma, who always does the right thing. Rāvaṇa, you are greedy, lustful and utterly dependent upon others! How could you not know about this catastrophe which occurred within your own kingdom?'

Rāvaṇa, the king of the *rākṣasas,* with all his power and wealth and pride, thought long and hard about Śūrpanakhā's insulting remarks.

'Who is this Rāma? What does he look like?' asked Rāvaṇa when his sister had finished her invective. 'How brave is he? Is he strong and skilled? Why has he come to the inhospitable Daṇḍaka forest? What weapons did he use in battle to kill Khara, Triśiras and Dūṣaṇa?'

Śūrpanakhā began to describe Rāma as he really was, her anger rising. 'Rāma is the son of Daśaratha. He has strong and powerful arms and his eyes are large and beautiful. He wears the skin of the black antelope and he is as handsome as the god of love. He uses a bow decorated with gold that is so beautiful it equals Indra's. He showers blazing arrows that fall like poisonous snakes. I never saw mighty Rāma drawing his bow or releasing a single arrow when he was fighting. All I saw was the huge army felled by a rain of arrows, as the ripened crop is laid low by Indra's storms.

'Fourteen thousand *rākṣasas,* each capable of terrible things, as well as Khara and Dūṣaṇa, were killed by the sharp arrows of a man who fought alone and on foot! In one and a half hours, the sages were relieved of their fear and the Daṇḍaka region was made safe. I was the only one who escaped, disgraced by Rāma, who obviously hesitated to kill a woman.

'Rāma has a brother, brave, strong and his equal in virtue, quick to anger and invincible against all beings. His name is Lakṣmaṇa and he is devoted to Rāma. He is Rāma's right arm, the breath outside his body. Rāma also has a beautiful wife named Sītā. Large-eyed and delicate, she is the princess of Videha and she is the best of all women. Not even among the gods, the *gandharvīs,* the *yakṣīs* or the *kinnaris* have I seen a woman as lovely as this one. Whoever has her as a wife and shares her embraces will be the happiest person in the world. She would be an ideal match for you. I tried to carry that peerless creature, with the ample hips and high full breasts, away as a wife for you. When you see her face, which is as beautiful as the full moon, you shall be a victim of love's arrows. If you want her as your wife then put your best foot forward without any further delay!

'Take revenge for your people, king of the *rākṣasas,* and kill cruel Rāma, who lives like a hermit. Once you have killed Rāma and the great warrior Lakṣmaṇa, Sītā will be vulnerable and helpless and you can have your way with her. If you like my plan then set forth immediately with no second thoughts!'

Rāvaṇa dismissed his ministers and began to think about what he should do. He considered the matter from all angles and after weighing its virtues and shortcomings, he decided to go ahead with Śūrpanakhā's idea. He ordered his charioteer to prepare his chariot which was decorated with gold and studded with jewels. It was drawn by asses with the faces of *piśācas* and could go absolutely anywhere.

The king of the *rākṣasas,* the younger brother of Kubera, rumbled like thunder in his chariot and went towards the ocean. On the far shore, he saw a solitary hut deep inside a forest in a quiet, sacred spot. And there, Rāvaṇa came upon the *rākṣasa* Mārīca. Mārīca wore the skin of a black antelope, his hair was matted into locks and he hardly ate anything at all.

Mārīca greeted Rāvaṇa with all the rituals appropriate for a guest. 'Listen to me, Mārīca,' said Rāvaṇa. 'I am in trouble and you are the only one who can help me. You know that my brothers Khara and Dūṣaṇa, my sister Śūrpanakhā, Triśiras who feeds on human flesh, and several other mighty *rākṣasas* live in Janasthāna. They live there under my instructions and they torment the sages who practice *dharma* in the forest. There were fourteen thousand *rākṣasas* capable of terrible things, brave and eager to do battle, under Khara's command. They got into a fight with Rāma.

'Even though Rāma was in a rage, he was totally silent on the battlefield. But he used his bow so effectively that all the fourteen thousand *rākṣasas* were killed. Killed by the arrows of a man fighting alone and on foot! Triśiras, Dūṣaṇa and Khara were also killed, and the Daṇḍaka forests are now free of danger.

'This Rāma shall have a short life! His angry father exiled him and his wife to the forest. Now that he has slain the entire *rākṣasa* army, he is a disgrace to the *kṣatriyas*. His conduct is improper, he is dull-witted and controlled entirely by his senses. He violates *dharma* and wishes ill for all living creatures. Taking refuge in his superior strength, he mutilated my sister in the forest by cutting off her nose and ears. He did all this without reason, without enmity.

'I am going to abduct his wife Sītā from Janasthāna. She is as beautiful as a daughter of the gods. And I want you to help me with this. With my brothers and someone as mighty as you by my side, I would not worry even if I had to meet the gods in battle! You are unrivalled for your courage and pride on the battlefield. Give me all the help you can, *rākṣasa*!

'I came to you for this reason alone. Listen and I will tell you what I need you to do. Turn yourself into a wondrous golden deer with silver spots and graze in front of Rāma's settlement, within sight of Rāma and Sītā. I have no doubt that when Sītā sees you as the deer, she will ask Rāma and Lakṣmaṇa to get it for her. That place is absolutely deserted, so I can carry Sītā away in their absence, just as the eclipse grasps the moon, without anything to hinder me. After that, when I have fulfilled my dearest wish and Rāma is grief-stricken because of his wife's abduction, I shall attack him without any problems.'

Mārīca turned pale as he listened. His mouth was dry with fear and he licked his lips, agitated because he had had an earlier encounter with Rāma. He decided to give Rāvaṇa some advice that would stand them both in good stead.

'It is easy to find someone who will speak to you pleasantly, king!' said the wise and eloquent Mārīca. 'It is much harder to find people who will tell you unpleasant truths, or people who will listen to them. You obviously have not made use of competent spies or you would know that Rāma is a man of great courage and virtue, like unto Indra and Varuṇa. I wish all was well with the *rākṣasas* and that Rāma did not want to wipe them off the face of the earth in his anger.

'A foolish king, like you, who is a slave to his passions, acts improperly and is advised by wicked ministers can only lead himself, his kingdom and his people to total ruin. Rāma has not renounced his father nor has he transgressed the bounds of decency. He is neither greedy nor badly behaved and he is certainly not a disgrace to the *kṣatriyas*. He is virtuous and desires the best for all beings.

'When he realized that his honourable father was besotted with Kaikeyī, he agreed to go to the forest on the basis of *dharma.* He renounced the kingdom and all its royal pleasures to make Daśaratha and Kaikeyī happy. He is not cruel or dull-witted or unrestrained. It is not appropriate for you to utter such slanderous lies! Rāma never transgresses *dharma.* He is good and true and is as justifiably the king of the world as Indra is the king of the gods.

'How could you even think of abducting Sītā? She is protected by her own power. It would be like trying to rob the sun of its glory. Why do you want to do this absurd and unnecessary thing? The moment Rāma sees you on the battlefield will be your last! If you value your life, your kingdom and your happiness, all of which are not easy to obtain, then take the advice of your righteous ministers led by Vibhīṣaṇa.

'I think it is folly for you to face Rāma in combat. But more than this, king of the *rākṣasas,* let me tell you something that will indicate to you what is possible and what is not!

'Long ago, when Rāma was just a boy, the sage Viśvāmitra brought him to his hermitage to prevent me from interrupting and destroying his sacrifice. I entered the hermitage with my weapon held high, not giving Rāma a second look. He saw me and calmly strung his bow. I was stupid to have ignored him simply because he was a boy. I charged towards Viśvāmitra's sacrificial altar. Rāma loosed a single arrow that was sure and true and when it struck me, I was lifted and thrown into the ocean, hundreds of *yojanās* away.

'If you make an enemy of Rāma despite my warnings, you will be bringing a terrible calamity upon yourself. You will cause the destruction of the *rākṣasas* who love to play and celebrate and enjoy all kinds of pleasures. You will see your fabulous city of Lankā, adorned with gems and glorious buildings, laid low because of Sītā. You will see Lankā consumed, its mansions pierced by arrows going up in flames.

'You have thousands of beautiful women as your wives and concubines. Amuse yourself with them and protect your race! Don't do anything that would displease Rāma if you want to preserve your power, prestige, your kingdom and your life. I am your friend and I wish you well. If you ignore my advice and persist with your plan to abduct Sītā, Rāma's arrows will take your life. Your army will be destroyed and your people shall die!

'Rāma's arrows spared me and when I escaped with my life, I came to live here, to meditate and practise austerities. I see Rāma in every tree! Clad in his antelope skin, he carries his immense bow like the god of death carries his noose! In my terror, Rāvaṇa, I see thousands of Rāmas, the entire forest seems to have turned into Rāma! I see Rāma where he isn't. He enters my dreams and I scream in terror! Even words that start with 'R' frighten me! I tremble when people use words like *'radha'* or *'ratha*!"

'I know Rāma's strength, Rāvaṇa! You cannot stand up to him in battle! Fight with him openly if you insist or keep the peace. But never mention Rāma again if you wish to see me!'

Even though Mārīca's advice was simple, Rāvaṇa would not listen to him. He dismissed his words the way a man who wishes to die refuses all medication.

'My dear Mārīca, your words are as useless as seeds sown in the sand,' retorted Rāvaṇa rudely, impelled by his fate. 'Your words will not stop me from facing Rāma in combat. He is stupid and wicked and, above all, he is a mere mortal! He gave up his kingdom, his friends and his family and fled into the forest to honour the words of a low and vulgar woman.

'I swear before you that I will abduct Sītā, the wife of the man who killed Khara in battle! I have made up my mind and even the gods, led by Indra, cannot persuade me otherwise!

'Had I asked you about the merits of my plans, you might have had the right to speak like this. But I never asked you that. All I asked is that you help me carry them out! Turn yourself into a wondrous golden deer with silver spots and Sītā will definitely want to possess you. She will be enthralled by the deer and will ask Rāma to capture it for her. And when Rāma and Lakṣmaṇa are out of the way, I shall carry her off swiftly, the way Indra carried off Saci.

'You can do exactly as you please after you have done what I ask. I shall give you half my kingdom, resolute *rākṣasa*! I shall take you to Lankā with me once my task has been accomplished. You must do this for me, even if I have to force you! The man who opposes his king never comes to a good end. You may have survived Rāma but you will not survive me if you oppose my wishes! Consider this and then do what you think best!'

'Ah Rāvaṇa! Who is the wicked person who has advised you to do this foolish thing? It will lead to the destruction of you, your sons, your kingdom and all your people!' cried Mārīca. 'Who does not wish to see you happy? Who wants you at death's door? Rāma will kill you shortly after he has killed me! I am going to die in either case. But if you abduct Sītā, you can be sure that you, too, shall soon be dead!'

Marica warns Rāvaṇa of the dangers of his plan

# *Chapter Thirty-Two*

Despite his better judgment, Mārīca decided to go with Rāvaṇa because he feared the king of the *rākṣasas.* Feeling terrible, he sighed, 'Let us go, then! The weapon that Rāma raises when he sees me will be the instrument of my death! Now that you are so determined to go through with your plans, there is nothing more I can do. Let us go, my child, and may good luck go with you!'

Rāvaṇa was delighted with Mārīca's decision. 'These brave words could just as easily have been spoken by me!' he said as he embraced Mārīca warmly. 'Now you sound like Mārīca! You must have been someone else when you were speaking earlier! Come with me! Climb into my flying chariot which is made of gold and is drawn by *piśācā*-faced donkeys!'

Rāvaṇa and Mārīca flew over towns and forests, mountains and rivers, kingdoms and cities. When they reached the Daṇḍaka forest, Rāvaṇa spotted Rāma's settlement and they dismounted. Taking Mārīca by the hand, Rāvaṇa said, 'Look, you can see Rāma's hut circled by banana trees. Go quickly, my friend, and put our plan into action!'

Mārīca transformed himself into a magnificent deer in an instant and began to graze at the entrance to Rāma's settlement. His horns were tipped with emerald and his face had black and white streaks. One side of his face was as beautiful as the red lotus, the other was like the blue lily. One of his ears was blue, the other a rich green. His neck was gracefully arched and his belly gleamed softly like the moon. His body was the colour of the *mahua* flower and his hooves were lapis lazuli. Slim and strong, the deer's tail shone with the colours of the rainbow and his entire body seemed to be studded with jewels. The *rākṣasa* lit up the woods at the entrance to the settlement with the splendour of the magical form that he had taken on.

The many-coloured deer wandered around so that Sītā would see him. His shining spots caught the eye as he grazed on the new shoots and grasses. He went over to the banana trees and browsed among the house flowers, lingering in the places where Sītā would see him. The magnificent deer, shining with his lotus hues, wandered lazily in the vicinity of the hut. Sometimes, he would walk away and then come back, or rush off as if he were in a great hurry and return yet again. He joined a herd of deer at the entrance to the settlement and after frolicking there awhile, he returned and lay on the ground, trying to attract Sītā's attention.

The deer leapt into the air, twirled and landed back on the ground. All the other forest animals came to see him, but when they got close, they fled in all directions. The *rākṣasa,* who normally enjoyed killing these animals, did not attack them in order to preserve his disguise. He contented himself with merely touching them.

At that very moment, the large-eyed Sītā appeared and strolled among the flowering trees and bushes. That beautiful woman who did not deserve to live in the forest suddenly noticed the magnificent, jewelled deer. Her eyes wide with wonder, she gazed at the exquisite creature with the shimmering body and sparkling pearly teeth. When the deer saw Rāma's beloved, he strutted up and down, lighting up the forest with his brilliance. Sītā was totally wonderstruck by the deer, the likes of which she had never seen before.

Beautiful Sītā, her own skin glowing like gold, watched the glittering deer as she gathered her flowers. He seemed to be golden on one side and silver on the other. She called out delightedly to her husband and to mighty Lakṣmaṇa. They looked over in her direction and they, too, saw the deer.

Lakṣmaṇa was immediately suspicious. 'I am sure that deer is the *rākṣasa* Mārīca!' he said to Rāma. 'Vile Mārīca can take any form he chooses. He has killed many kings while they were hunting in the forest. A jewelled deer like this simply cannot exist anywhere in the world. This has to be some trick!'

But the sweetly smiling Sītā would not allow Lakṣmaṇa to speak any further. She had been completely deceived. 'Noble one, this deer has captivated my mind,' she said to Rāma happily. 'Bring him to me, great hero! He can be our pet! All kinds of animals come to our hut but I have never seen a deer like this! He lights up the whole area with his splendour!

'If you can capture this deer alive, he will be the source of great wonder and amazement. When our exile is over and we return again to Ayodhyā, this wondrous deer can adorn our private apartments. He will delight Bharata and my mothers-in-law as well as you and me! I will be happy even with his skin if you can't get him alive. I would love to sit with you on the golden skin of this deer when he is dead.

'I know it is inappropriate for a woman to speak cruelly like this out of greed, but the deer's magnificent body has me completely enthralled!'

Rāma, too, was captivated by the golden creature with the jewelled horns that seemed to shine like the sun or like a galaxy of stars. He listened to Sītā's words and watched the deer with delight. 'Look Lakṣmaṇa,' he said, 'this deer has captured Sītā's imagination. It is so beautiful that it may not actually be a deer. Nowhere in this forest or on earth, nor even in Nandana or Caitraratha, can there be a deer to match this one! Look at his exquisite fur with those shining spots! His tongue is like the flame from a fire. He yawns like lightning from a cloud! Who could resist an animal like this with its emerald face and pearly belly?

'Beautiful Sītā shall sit with me on the jewelled skin of this incredible deer! I cannot imagine that the fur of any other animal could be as soft as this one's!

'And if, as you suggest Lakṣmaṇa, this deer is the creation of sorcery and magic, that it is really a *rākṣasa,* then it is my duty to kill it! Wicked, ruthless Mārīca has killed many sages in the past in this very forest. He has killed kings, too, by appearing suddenly during the hunt. For that, too, the deer deserves to die!

'I am always self-controlled and I cleave to *dharma.* This *rākṣasa* will die because he has challenged me. Look after Sītā, Lakṣmaṇa, and be prepared for any emergency! Protecting Sītā is our most important duty. I shall return after I have either captured this deer or killed it. Sītā longs for this deerskin, but look after her while I am gone! This deer shall die today because of its skin! Stay here in the settlement and be on your guard!

'I shall kill the deer with a single arrow and return as soon as I can. Be careful until then!'

Mighty Rāma girt his gold-hilted sword, picked up his bow, strapped on his quivers and left quickly. The deer hid in fright when he saw Rāma

has Lakṣmana stay w/ Sītā, anticipating a trick

coming and then showed himself again. Rāma ran to where he thought he had seen the deer. Visible one moment and invisible the next, the deer ran deep into the forest, seeming to look back every now and then at the man armed with the bow.

The deer leapt into the air in apparent confusion, appeared for a little while, and then disappeared into the trees as the autumn moon disappears behind the clouds. For one instant, he seemed to be close but the very next moment, he seemed far away. Darting in and out of view, the deer made Rāma angry. But he stayed focused and did not give up the chase.

Rāma grew tired and sat under a tree to rest. He saw the deer close by, surrounded by a group of forest animals. Rāma decided to kill him at that very moment and he fitted an arrow into his bow. He loosed the flaming arrow which hissed through the air like a serpent, as would Brahmā's special weapon. The arrow tore through the deer's body and pierced Mārīca's heart. Mārīca let out an awful scream and leapt into the air. He fell to the ground with barely a breath in his body. At the moment of his death, Mārīca gave up his artificial form. *kills Mārīca*

Mārīca knew that the moment had arrived and in a voice exactly like Rāma's, he cried out, 'Oh Sītā! Oh Lakṣmaṇa!' He renounced the deer's body and appeared as he really was. His body was as large as a mountain and he had enormous teeth. Wearing all his ornaments and jewels, Mārīca breathed his last. *uses dying breath to trick them*

Rāma looked at the fierce *rākṣasa* lying on the ground and remembered what Lakṣmaṇa had said. His thoughts went immediately to Sītā. 'The *rākṣasa* cried "Oh Sītā! Oh Lakṣmaṇa" as he was dying. What will Sītā think when she hears that? And what kind of state will mighty Lakṣmaṇa be in?' thought Rāma and shuddered. He felt sure that something terrible was about to happen and fear clutched at his heart. He killed another deer and hurried back to Janasthāna with its meat. *why is he wasting time?*

Sītā heard the piteous cry which sounded just like her husband. 'That sounded like someone in trouble! My mind and heart are uneasy! Go quickly into the forest! Your brother is in trouble! He has fallen into the hands of the *rākṣasas* like a bull among lions!'

'I will not go,' said Lakṣmaṇa, who was bound by his brother's instructions. *Sītā pushing him*

'You pretend to be your brother's friend, Lakṣmaṇa,' cried Sītā angrily, 'but you are really his enemy! You do not go to help him when he is in trouble! You wish him dead because of me! You rejoice in his misfortune! You have no love for your brother. That is why you stand around here without a care in the world, even though Rāma is nowhere to be seen! What are you doing here, when the one for whose sake you came here is in danger?' Sītā burst into tears like a frightened doe.

Lakṣmaṇa tried to reassure her. 'Dear lady, there is not a single creature who can defeat Rāma in combat. Everyone knows that, for he is Indra's equal. You should not speak to me like this. I cannot leave you alone in the forest without Rāma! Even if the kings of the three worlds and all the gods and all their armies were to attack Rāma, they could not defeat him.

'Don't panic. Be calm. Your husband will be back very soon after he has killed the deer. It was not his voice we heard. It was something else. That *rākṣasa* can do anything with his magical powers. Rāma left you in my care, so I cannot leave you here and go away. The *rākṣasas* are hostile to us after the death of Khara and the massacre at Janasthāna. Those violent creatures can make all kinds of sounds in this forest. Do not be worried!'

Sītā grew angrier and her eyes blazed. 'Ignoble creature! Heartless wretch!' she said harshly to honourable Lakṣmaṇa. 'Disgrace to your family! I can only think that you talk to me like this because you are delighted that Rāma is in trouble. But I am not surprised at this kind of behaviour from a wicked kinsman! You hide your real feelings and act like a hypocrite!

'You followed Rāma, who is vulnerable and without protection, into the forest only so that you could have me! But this plan, whether yours or Bharata's, will never work! I have been loved by the golden-skinned, lotus-eyed Rāma! How can I ever settle for an ordinary man? I shall kill myself in front of you right now! I cannot bear to live on earth for a single moment without Rāma!'

Lakṣmaṇa's hair stood on end when he heard Sītā's cruel words. But he controlled himself, joined his palms respectfully and said, 'I cannot argue with you because you are like a goddess to me. But I am not surprised to hear such words from a woman, Sītā! Women are like this everywhere in the world. They are unrighteous and fickle and they breed mischief. May the gods of the forest bear witness to the fact that everything I said was just and true and that your words were harsh and unfair. Shame on you for doubting me, when I am bound by my elder brother's instructions! But then, you have acted from the essentially corrupt nature that all women have.) I am going to find Rāma. May all be well with you and may the deities of the forest protect you, large-eyed lady!'

'Lakṣmaṇa, without Rāma I shall plunge into the Godāvarī or get rid of this body by hurling it upon sharp rocks! Or drink poison! Or walk into fire! But I will not touch any man other than Rāma, not even with my foot!' wept Sītā. Upset by her tears, Lakṣmaṇa tried to console her, but Sītā would not say a word to her husband's brother. Lakṣmaṇa joined his palms, made a slight bow and left to search for Rāma, turning back anxiously every now and then to look at Sītā. *he suspects that they're being set up*

# *Chapter Thirty-Three*

Lakṣmaṇa was angry at having been spoken to like that, but he was also concerned about Rāma and so he left the settlement hurriedly.

Rāvaṇa pounced upon the moment that he had been waiting for. He appeared in front of Sītā in the form of a renunciant. He was wearing clean saffron robes, his hair was in a knot on top of his head, and he wore sandals on his feet. He carried an umbrella and a water pot and the traditional staff on his left shoulder.

Mighty Rāvaṇa approached that woman who was alone in the forest without Rāma and Lakṣmaṇa, like the oncoming darkness at twilight when neither the sun nor the moon shines. Cruel Rāvaṇa came closer to the beautiful princess, like a malignant planet moves towards the constellation Rohiṇī in the absence of the moon.

Even the trees in Janasthāna dared not move when they saw that awful creature, and the wind died down. The fast-flowing Godāvarī slowed in fear when she saw Rāvaṇa watching Sītā with his blood-red eyes. Nearer and nearer came the *rākṣasa* to that lovely woman whose lips were red, whose face was like the full moon, whose eyes were like lotus petals, as she sat there in her yellow silks, weeping, under the thatch in front of her hut.

The king of the *rākṣasas* was struck by the arrows of love. Muttering the Vedas, he spoke to Sītā in that lonely and deserted place. She seemed to him the most exquisite woman in the three worlds, like Śrī herself, without the lotus.

'Who are you, lovely creature, with your golden skin, your yellow silk garments and your garland of lotuses as beautiful as the lotus pond itself? Your teeth are small and pearly white, your large eyes are tinged a delicate pink in the corners and your pupils are a deep black. Your hips are wide and your thighs are as strong as an elephant's trunk. Your breasts are round and full, tilted upwards and their nipples quiver. They are firm and rest close together like the fruit of the palm tree. They are adorned with jewels and catch the eye.

'You have overwhelmed me with your charming smile, your lovely teeth and your beautiful eyes, as the river in spate floods its banks. Your tiny waist can be circled with a single hand! Your breasts rise high and your hair is gorgeous. You are not a *gandharvī* or a *kinnari* or a *yakṣī,* for I have never seen anyone as beautiful as you on this earth.

'May good fortune protect you! You should not be living here. This is the region in which fierce and cruel *rākṣasas* abound! You should be living within a city, in a stately home with a perfumed garden! Dark-eyed lady, you should have the best of flowers and foods and clothes, even the very best of husbands! This place is the home of *rākṣasas.* What are you doing living here? There are monkeys and lions and elephants and tigers and bears and leopards and all kinds of other animals here. Aren't you afraid of them? How can you be here alone and not be frightened?

'Who are you? Who do you belong to? Where did you come from? What are you doing alone in these terrible Daṇḍaka forests which are filled with *rākṣasas*?'

Thus did the black-hearted Rāvaṇa praise Sītā and she honoured him with all the respect due to a guest, for he had come to her in the form of a *brahmin.* 'Seat yourself comfortably,' she said, handing him a grass mat. 'Here is water to wash your feet and forest produce for you to eat. I hope you enjoy it!' Rāvaṇa gazed at the princess who treated him so respectfully, and the moment he decided that he had to carry her off, he sealed his fate.

Meanwhile, Sītā waited anxiously for her husband who had gone off after the deer and for his brother. But though she scanned the forest, all she could see was the green of the trees and no sign of Rāma or Lakṣmaṇa.

Sītā told Rāvaṇa all about herself in response to his questions and related the circumstances that had brought her to the forest with her husband. 'But who are you?' she asked. 'What is your name and what is your clan? Tell me, *brahmin*, why do you wander alone in the Daṇḍaka forest?'

'I am Rāvaṇa, the king of the *rākṣasas*!' he said quickly to Rāma's beautiful wife. 'I am the one that all the worlds, the gods, the *asuras* and the *pannagas* dread! I am Rāvaṇa, Sītā, the king of the *rākṣasa* hordes! When I set eyes on you with your golden skin and your yellow garments, I lost all interest in my own women, even though they are the finest in all the worlds. Become my chief queen!

'My capital city, Lankā, is on a mountaintop in the middle of the ocean. Give up this awful life! We can wander in the lovely groves there! If you become my wife, five thousand women adorned with every kind of jewel will be your slaves!'

Sitā was outraged. 'I am devoted to Rāma, who is as steadfast as Mount Mahendra and as deep as the ocean,' she retorted scornfully. 'He has mighty arms and a broad chest and the gait and valour of a lion. I follow that lion among men like a shadow. How can a jackal like you covet a lioness like me? I am as far from you as the shining, golden sun! Trying to abduct me would be like carrying off Mount Mahendra with your bare hands, or drinking the deadly *kālakūṭa* poison and hoping to stay alive and well! If you think you can carry off Rāma's beloved wife, you might as well pluck out your eyes with a needle, or lick the edge of a knife with your tongue!

'The difference between you and Rāma is like that between a lion and a jackal, between a tiny stream and the mighty ocean, between the drink of the gods and coarse rice gruel, like that between gold and iron, sandal paste and mud, a house cat and a magnificent tusker!' But even though the chaste woman spoke so fearlessly to the wicked *rākṣasa,* she was trembling like a slender banana plant in a high wind.

'I am the brother of Kubera, the god of wealth!' said Rāvaṇa, frowning. 'Lovely lady, I am Rāvaṇa, the mighty ten-headed *rākṣasa.* The gods and *gandharvas,* the *piśācas,* the birds and the serpents run in fear of me! All creatures see me as death!

'For a number of reasons, I developed an enmity with my brother Kubera and I challenged him to combat. I defeated him with my superior strength. Terrified, he surrendered his realm and now lives on Mount Kailāsa. I took his flying chariot, the magical Puṣpaka, from him. It can go anywhere. Even the gods led by Indra flee when they see my wrathful face. The wind does not blow where I go and the sun becomes as cool as the moon for fear of me. Leaves do not dance on their trees and rivers stop flowing in the places I visit.

'Lankā, my exquisite city, lies on the far side of the ocean. It is filled with *rākṣasas* but it rivals Indra's Amarāvatī. Surrounded by sparkling white walls, it has gates of lapis, inside which are mansions decorated with gold. It is filled with the noise of elephants and horses and the sweet music of pipes. It abounds in beautiful gardens which have trees that bear flowers and fruit all through the year.

'Princess Sītā, when you live there with me, you shall have so much fun that you will forget all about mortals. You shall enjoy human and celestial pleasures and soon forget about that mortal Rāma, who is as good as dead! King Daśaratha placed his favourite son on the throne and exiled the eldest, Rāma, because he was weak! You should not reject me, I am the king of the *rākṣasas*! Struck by the arrows of love and driven by passion, I came to you because I wanted to!'

'If you so much as touch me,' blazed Sītā, her eyes red with anger, 'you might as well have drunk poison!'

Rāvaṇa rubbed his hands together and reverted to his natural form. 'Crazy woman!' he said harshly. 'You were obviously not listening when I told you about my power and strength. I can stand in the sky and lift the earth in my hands! I can kill Death in battle!' confident of his power

Rāvaṇa's eyes blazed red like the setting sun and were as bright as fire. He had thrown off the disguise of the gentle ascetic and appeared in his true form which was as terrifying as Death, and stood there with his ten heads and his bright jewels. 'Lovely lady, if you want a husband who is known in the three worlds, then come to me! I am worthy of you! Give yourself to me and I shall be worthy of your love. I will never do anything that makes you unhappy. Give up your attachment to this wretched mortal and turn your affections to me. You think of yourself as wise, but you are very foolish. How can you remain attached to a man who has given up his kingdom, who cannot accomplish his goals and whose days are numbered?'

Speaking brutally to gentle Sītā, who deserved only kindness, Rāvaṇa grabbed her roughly. With his right hand, he caught her by the hair, and he placed his left arm under her knees. The forest deities fled in terror when they saw Rāvaṇa with his great arms and huge teeth. Rāvaṇa's golden chariot appeared, drawn by braying donkeys. Rāvaṇa lifted Sītā by the waist and ranted on as he placed her in the chariot.

Virtuous Sītā cried out to Rāma, who was far away in the forest. She screamed like a madwoman in her anguish, as Rāvaṇa flew into the sky with her. 'Oh mighty Lakṣmaṇa! You who live to please your older brother! You have no idea that I am being carried off by this *rākṣasa* who can change his shape at will!

'Oh Rāma! You would sacrifice life and happiness for *dharma,* but you cannot see that I am being abducted by this unrighteous creature! You are the chastiser of the wicked and the destroyer of your enemies! Why can't you punish wicked Rāvaṇa?

'Flowering trees of Janasthāna! I beg you, tell Rāma as soon as you can that Sītā was carried off by Rāvaṇa! Mighty mountain Prasravaṇa, covered with flowers, I beg you, tell Rāma that Sītā has been carried away by Rāvaṇa! Creatures of the forest, tell my husband, who loves me more than his own life, that Sītā was beside herself with grief as Rāvaṇa carried her off! When mighty Rāma hears what has happened, he will come to reclaim me, no matter where I am!'

The enormous bird Jaṭāyu was dozing gently nearby, but he woke when he heard the screams and saw Rāvaṇa and Sītā. Best of all birds, Jaṭāyu was the size of a mountain and had a sharp beak. He spoke sweetly to Rāvaṇa from his perch on the tree.

'Ten-headed Rāvaṇa, I am Jaṭāyu, the king of the vultures. I am strong and mighty and honourable and I cleave to the eternal *dharma.* Rāma, the son of Daśaratha, is the lord of all the worlds. Equal to Varuṇa and Indra, he is devoted to the welfare of all beings. This woman you are abducting is his wife, she is the best of all women.

'How can a righteous king carry off another man's wife? The wives of kings should be especially protected, mighty one! Rid yourself of this base desire! Rāma has not harmed you, or your city or your kingdom. Why do you want to harm him? If Rāma killed Khara in battle in Janasthāna, it was because the *rākṣasa* transgressed the bounds of his duty for Śūrpanakhā's sake. Rāma never does anything wrong. What was Rāma's crime, that you feel compelled to abduct Sītā? Release this large-eyed woman at once, or Rāma will consume you with the fire of his eyes.

'I am sixty thousand years old now, Rāvaṇa. You are young. You are mounted on a chariot, clad in a coat of mail and armed with a bow and arrows. Despite that, you cannot carry Sītā off so easily! If you are truly brave, step out for a moment! You, too, shall lie dead on the ground like

Khara! You shall not succeed in abducting this lotus-eyed lady, Rāma's beloved wife, as long as I am alive! Wait and watch, Rāvaṇa! I shall pluck you from your chariot like a fruit from a tree!'

Rāvaṇa's golden earrings glittered and his twenty eyes turned red with rage. The king of the *rākṣasas* pounced on the great bird and a huge battle ensued in the sky between the two mighty beings, like the clash of winged clouds.

Rāvaṇa rained iron-tipped arrows upon Jaṭāyu, but the king of the birds caught them all. He wounded the *rākṣasa* several times with his talons and sharp beak. He shattered Rāvaṇa's bow and destroyed his chariot, biting off the head of his charioteer and also the heads of the donkeys that were yoked to it. Rāvaṇa fell to the ground, still holding Sītā on his lap.

Rāvaṇa noticed that the aged bird was tiring and gleefully he rose into the air again, taking Sītā with him. But Jaṭāyu pursued him and threw himself on Rāvaṇa's back. He dug his talons into the *rākṣasa* and mauled him all over, riding him as if he were a rogue elephant. He bit off Rāvaṇa's ten right arms with his beak. Rāvaṇa attacked the bird with his fists and feet. But even though Jaṭāyu fought harder and harder for Rāma's sake, Rāvaṇa cut off his wings and his feet with his sword. The wingless bird fell to the earth, scarcely a breath left in his body. Sītā ran to him and wept as she would for a member of her own family.

Rāvaṇa, king of the *rākṣasas,* pounced on Sītā as she wept, her clothes crumpled and her ornaments in disarray. 'Let go! Let go!' he shouted as she clung to the trees like a climbing vine and rolled on the ground. 'Rāma! Rāma!' she wailed in that empty forest as the *rākṣasa* who looked like Death pulled her by the hair and called his own death upon his head.

Rāvaṇa dragged her into the sky as she cried out to Rāma and Lakṣmaṇa. With her glowing, golden skin and her clothes of yellow silk, the princess looked like a bolt of lightning from Mount Sudāma. As her yellow garments fluttered in the wind and the red lotuses from her garland scattered over him, Rāvaṇa's face blazed like a mountain on fire. Golden Sītā held tight against Rāvaṇa's black body was like a golden belt around an enormous black elephant.

Sītā's flowers fell from her body as she was being dragged away and they showered upon the earth like rain. They seemed to follow Rāvaṇa like a train, pulled along by the speed of his flight. The flowers followed him like the garland of stars which follows Mount Meru. As Rāvaṇa carried her further into the sky, Sītā shone with her own splendour like a comet. Her necklace of sparkling pearls slipped between her breasts and fell to the earth, like Gangā descending from the sky.

The speed of their flight disturbed the treetops. The birds nesting there seemed to call out to Sītā not to be afraid. The lotus pools, filled with drooping flowers and agitated fish, seemed to mourn as if for a lost friend. Lions and tigers and other forest animals gathered from all over and ran behind Sītā, following her shadow on the ground. Even the mountains seemed to weep, their waterfalls like tears, their peaks like outstretched arms. The sun turned pale and dimmed his lustre as Sītā was being carried off.

Sītā looked around desperately for someone to help her but she could see no one. As they flew over a mountain, she noticed five gigantic monkeys sitting on its peak. Sītā tossed her yellow shawl and her jewels among them, hoping that they would tell Rāma. In his excitement, Rāvaṇa did not notice this. But the huge monkeys, with their yellow unblinking eyes, watched as the weeping Sītā was carried off.

Rāvaṇa crossed Pampā and went towards Lankā. His heart full of joy, he held on to the woman who was to be his death as one might carry a sharp-fanged poisonous snake. He sped like an arrow over forests and rivers, mountains and lakes, until he reached the ocean, the home of Varuṇa, the refuge of all rivers and the abode of fish and crocodiles. The ocean was frightened when it saw Sītā and it stilled its waves, freezing the fish and the other water creatures into immobility. In the sky, the *siddhas* and *cāraṇas* whispered to each other, 'This will be the death of Rāvaṇa!'

Meanwhile, Rāvaṇa reached the beautiful city of Lankā with Sītā in his arms and entered his own apartments. 'Let no man or woman see Sītā without my permission!' he ordered the *piśacīs.* 'And whatever she wants—pearls, gold, jewels, clothes—let her have them at once, as if I myself were asking for them! Anyone who says anything to upset her, consciously or accidentally, can consider themselves as good as dead!'

Rāvaṇa, king of the *rākṣasas,* left his apartments and wondered what he should do next. As he was thinking about this, he happened to notice eight valiant *rākṣasas* who lived on human flesh. Arrogant because of the boons that he had been given, Rāvaṇa began to praise them. 'Arm yourselves and go to Janasthāna, where Khara lived before it was destroyed. That area has now been cleansed of *rākṣasas.* You can stay there without fear, relying on your strength. My army which was stationed there was slain in battle by Rāma's arrows and so were Khara and Dūṣaṇa.

'I am angrier than I have ever been and my wrath is greater, even, than my courage! The massacre has also led to the bitter enmity with Rāma. I have to kill my enemy. I shall not sleep a wink until I have slain him in battle! Go and stay in Janasthāna. Keep an eye on Rāma and tell me all that he does!'

The eight *rākṣasas* were pleased with the praises showered upon them and were eager to perform the task ahead of them. They left Lanka together immediately, without being seen.

And Rāvaṇa, now that he had captured Sītā and purchased Rāma's enmity along with that, was full of joy, delighting in his folly.

Rāvaṇa believed that he had achieved his life's goal. Helpless with love, his mind turned again to Sītā and he went back to his apartments eagerly, to see her. The king of the *rākṣasas* entered the palace and there, surrounded by *rākṣasīs,* he saw the grieving Sītā. Her face was stained with tears and the weight of her sorrows made her pathetic. Utterly helpless, she was like a tiny boat on the open seas, tossed about by storm winds. She hung her head, like a doe that has strayed from the herd and is surrounded by hunting hounds.

Rāvaṇa forced her, vulnerable and unwilling, to see his palace, which was like the abode of the gods. Its huge buildings were studded with gems of all kinds and inhabited by thousands of women and many types of beautiful birds. It had pillars of gold and silver and crystal which were inlaid with diamonds and lapis and dazzled the eye. Rāvaṇa climbed a flight of stairs made of beaten gold with Sītā, and they resounded with each footstep like celestial drums. Its arches were decorated with exquisite silver and ivory lattices. Rāvaṇa pointed out the floors inset with pearls and showed Sītā the lotus pools surrounded by flowering trees.

'There are thirty-two million *rākṣasas* here, not including the sick, the old and children,' he boasted, after he had shown Sītā the entire palace. 'Each and every one of them is fierce and terrible. Sītā, I am the lord and master of all these forbidding creatures. I have one thousand of them just to wait on me personally! I give you my kingdom and all this, large-eyed lady, because you are dearer to me than my life! You can do what you want with it.

'Ah beloved! Become my wife and mistress of the thousands of women in my harem. Listen to me, for I mean well. What will you gain by doing otherwise? I burn with desire for you, submit to me! Lankā is one hundred *yojanās* long and is surrounded on all sides by the ocean. Not even the gods led by Indra can beseige it or capture it!

'There is no one in the three worlds who is my equal in strength and courage. What are you doing with that mortal Rāma? He has little power and no kingdom. He lives the life of an ascetic and will soon die! Give yourself to me, Sītā, I am a worthy husband for you! The days of our youth are short, enjoy them with me while you can!

'Do not be ashamed, thinking that this is a violation of *dharma.* Our union is destined and it has the sanction of the *ṛṣis.* Look, I lay my ten heads at your delicate feet. I am your slave. Be gracious to me! Rāvaṇa has never ever placed his heads at the feet of a woman! I have never debased myself like this before, these humble words arise from my anguish.' As he spoke and placed his heads within the noose of death, Rāvaṇa thought triumphantly to himself, 'She is mine!'

Vulnerable and anguished, Sītā placed a blade of grass between herself and Rāvaṇa. 'King Daśaratha upheld *dharma* and everyone knew him as an honourable man. Rāma is his righteous son and his glory has spread throughout the three worlds,' she said to Rāvaṇa. 'That powerful man with large eyes is my husband, he is like a god to me. Born in the line of the Ikṣvākus, he is brave and has shoulders as mighty as a lion's. He and his brother Lakṣmaṇa will surely kill you!

'If you had tried to abduct me in his presence, you would now be lying dead in Janasthāna, just like Khara! You may be invulnerable to the gods and the *asuras,* Rāvaṇa, but now that you have sought Rāma's enmity, you will not escape alive. Rāma will take what remains of your life. You have as much chance of survival as a sacrificial animal tied to a stake!

'Just as a *caṇḍāla* cannot touch the sanctified pots and ladles and the fire-altar for the sacrifice, so, too, you cannot touch me, you base *rākṣasa*! I am Rāma's lawful and virtuous wife! You can imprison and injure this corporeal body of mine. I have no desire to protect my body or my life. What I cannot bear is the shame that has been heaped upon me!' she said angrily.

'Listen to me, Sītā!' said Rāvaṇa, trying to intimidate her. 'If you do not submit to me in the next twelve months, my cooks will chop you up for my breakfast!'

Rāvaṇa turned to the *rākṣasīs*. 'You fierce and deformed creatures who live on flesh and blood must crush her pride!' he said. The *rākṣasīs* joined their palms and gathered around Sītā. Stamping his feet as if he would smash the earth to pieces, Rāvaṇa said, 'Take Sītā to the *aśoka* grove and guard her zealously, safe from prying eyes. Threaten her and cajole her alternately, the way wild elephants are tamed. Convince her that she must accede to my wishes!'

The *rākṣasīs* surrounded Sītā and took her to the *aśoka* grove. The grove was filled with trees which bore every kind of fruit and flower and were visited by birds all the year round. But in the hands of the rākṣasīs, Sītā was like a doe surrounded by tigers. Overwhelmed with grief and terrified by those ugly creatures, she found no peace in the *aśoka* grove. Her mind was constantly on her god-like husband.

# *Chapter Thirty-Four*

Meanwhile, Rāma, had killed the form-changing *rākṣasa* Mārīca who had been wandering around as a deer, and was hurrying back to his settlement. As he was returning, anxious to see Sītā, a jackal howled behind him. Rāma recognized that hair-raising sound and grew worried. 'This is terrible! The cry of a jackal is a bad omen! I hope all is well with Sītā and that the *rākṣasas* have not been harassing her. If Lakṣmaṇa heard Mārīca cry out in my voice while he was disguised as a deer, he will have left Sītā alone, on her insistence, and come after me. I just hope they are both all right without me. I have earned the enmity of the *rākṣasas* after the incident at Janasthāna. Oh dear! I see more and more bad omens!'

Worrying about the omens and the fact that he had been drawn away, Rāma reached Janasthāna, full of anxiety. Birds and animals saw the agitated Rāma coming and they ran around him, calling out in harsh voices. Rāma considered that a bad omen too. Before long, he saw Lakṣmaṇa, downcast and miserable. Soon, they were face-to-face, both of them anxious and upset.

The older brother berated the younger one for leaving Sītā alone in a forest overrun with *rākṣasas*. 'Ah Lakṣmaṇa! You should not have left Sītā alone and come here!' said Rāma as he took Lakṣmaṇa by the right hand. But his strong words were softened by the gentleness with which they were uttered. 'Will we find everything all right when we reach home? I feel certain that Sītā has been either devoured or abducted by the *rākṣasas* that wander through this forest. I see evil omens all around me. I can only hope that Sītā is safe and sound!

'That deer which led me far away was actually a *rākṣasa* that deceived me. It was only when I killed him that he revealed his true form. My left eye twitches, my mind is uneasy. Lakṣmaṇa, I fear that we shall find Sītā either missing or dead!

'If I go back to our settlement and Sītā is not there to welcome me with her sweet smile and her gentle words, I shall kill myself,' continued Rāma. 'Tell me, Lakṣmaṇa, is she alive? Or has she been eaten by *rākṣasas* because of your carelessness? She is young and not used to these hardships. She must have been frightened and lonely while I was gone. Even you must have been frightened when that wicked *rākṣasa* called your name in my voice!

'I have a feeling Sītā was frightened when she heard that voice, so like mine, and she sent you out to look for me. But whatever it was, you should not have left her alone, giving the *rākṣasas* a chance to take revenge on me! The *rākṣasas* are incensed over the killing of Khara. I am sure that they have eaten Sītā.'

Hurrying on with his brother, Rāma was pale and out of breath, tired, hungry and thirsty. He reached the settlement and found no one there. He went straight to the hut and then to all the places in which he and Sītā had enjoyed themselves and been so happy. He grew more and more agitated as he saw that they were all empty.

'I did not leave Sītā alone because I wanted to,' said Lakṣmaṇa miserably. 'I came to look for you because she goaded me with her sharp words. When that voice that sounded like yours called out to us, I told her not to panic, as weak-minded women are wont to do. "There is no creature in the three worlds, born or unborn, who can defeat Rāma in combat," I said to her. 'But she became angry and began to cry and, in her confusion, she said to me, "You have improper feelings towards me. You want to have me when your brother is dead, but that will never happen! Since you do not go after him it means that you are hatching a plot with Bharata. You followed Rāma into the forest because of me and you are delighting in his misfortunes!"

'I was very angry when she spoke to me thus. My lips trembled and I stalked out of the settlement.'

'You did wrong, dear brother,' insisted Rāma. 'You knew that I was capable of defeating the *rākṣasas* and still you left her, just because of her angry words. It does not please me that you came way just because an angry woman spoke to you harshly!'

Rāma looked all over the settlement. Without Sītā, the trees there seemed to weep, the birds and animals appeared downcast. It was as if the forest deities had abandoned the area. Deerskins and reed mats had been scattered and *kuśa* grass lay everywhere. Rāma called out to Sītā again and again. 'She has been abducted! She is dead! She has been eaten! Or, perhaps, the poor, frightened thing went and hid in the forest! Maybe she went out to collect roots and fruits! Or to the lotus pond, or to the river!'

But though he searched high and low, Rāma could not find his beloved in the forest. His eyes red from weeping, he seemed like a madman as he ran from tree to tree, from the mountains to the river, weeping more and more as he plunged deeper and deeper into an ocean of grief.

'O *kadamba* tree, have you seen my beloved who loved your fruit so? Tell me if you know where that lovely woman is! Bilva tree, where is she, the woman whose breasts are like your fruits, who is as delicate as your new shoots in her yellow silks? O palm tree, take pity on me and tell me if you have seen that beautiful woman! Rose-apple tree, my beloved's complexion has the hues of your fruit. You must have seen her. Tell me where she is!

'Little deer, you must know where the doe-eyed Sītā is! Is she with you in the forest? O best of elephants, Sītā had thighs like your trunk, you must know where she is! O Lakṣmaṇa, have you seen my beloved anywhere? Oh Sītā! My darling Sītā, where have you gone?' he cried over and over again.

Rāma called out as he ran hither and thither in the forest. He leapt and jumped and spun around as if he were crazy. He could not stand still for a moment, so he ran through the forest, over the mountains and down to the streams and rivers. But though he searched every corner of that forest, he found no trace of his beloved. Still, he would not give up and renewed his efforts to find her.

Utterly miserable, Rāma said wretchedly to Lakṣmaṇa, 'Go to the river Godāvarī quickly and see if Sītā went there to gather lotuses.' When Lakṣmaṇa did not find her, Rāma went there himself.

Equally upset, the two brothers walked along. Suddenly, they saw a trail of flowers on the ground. 'I recognize these flowers, Lakṣmaṇa,' said Rāma when he saw them. 'I gave them to Sītā in the forest and she braided them into her hair!' Looking further, Rāma found the huge footprint of a *rākṣasa*. His heart hammering in his chest, Rāma called out to his brother. 'Look, Lakṣmaṇa, there are all kinds of flowers scattered here and little bits of gold from Sītā's broken ornaments! The ground is covered with drops of blood that gleam like gold. Sītā must have been torn to pieces by form-changing *rākṣasas,* or she must have been eaten by them!'

'These signs suggest that there was a great battle here between two mighty *rākṣasas* over Sītā. Look at this broken bow, this shattered armour and royal umbrella, these dead donkeys with *piśāca* faces, this wrecked chariot and scattered arrows!

'My hostility towards the *rākṣasas* has now multiplied a hundred times. I shall kill all these form-changing *rākṣasas*! If Sītā has been devoured or abducted, Lakṣmaṇa, there is no one in all the worlds who would dare challenge me! Perhaps the gods think I am a weakling because I am gentle and compassionate and devoted to the well-being of all creatures! Even this virtue has become a flaw in my character! But today I will show the *rākṣasas* and all the other creatures my true powers!

'The *yakṣas,* the *gandharvas,* the *piśācas* or *rākṣasas,* the *kinnaras* and mortals shall not have a moment's happiness, Lakṣmaṇa! I shall fill the sky with my arrows and missiles, making it impassable for all those who travel through the three worlds. I shall stop the planets in their orbits, obstruct the course of the moon, destroy the fire and the wind, eclipse the radiance of the sun. I shall smash the mountain peaks, dry up the lakes, uproot trees and creepers and bushes and stir up the waters of the ocean!

'If the gods do not deliver Sītā to me unharmed, they will see the kind of destruction I can wreak in a single hour! There will not be a single god, *dānava, daitya, piśāca* or *rākṣasa* left when I have finished destroying the three worlds in my anger. Even as old age, sickness, death and fate cannot be escaped, so, too, I cannot be diverted from my purpose! If the gods do not return Sītā to me, sweet and smiling as she was before, I will destroy the universe along with the gods, *gandharvas,* mortals and serpents!'

Lakṣmaṇa had never seen Rāma so angry before. His mouth dry with fear, he joined his palms and said, 'Rāma, you have always been gentle and compassionate and devoted to the welfare of all creatures. Do not let your anger control you and make you act against your natural disposition.

'I do not know whose chariot this is that lies here, smashed to bits. I have no idea who used it and for what purpose. The earth has been gouged by chariot wheels and hooves and the ground is splattered with blood. Clearly, a battle was fought here. But I think there was only one chariot and not two.

'You cannot destroy the worlds because of the crimes of a single person. Great kings mete out punishments judiciously and dispassionately. Armed with your bow and arrow and with me by your side, we can find out what happened to Sītā with the help of the *ṛṣis*. We shall scour the oceans, the mountains and the forests, the caves, the rivers and the woods. We shall search through the worlds of the gods and the *gandharvas* without rest until we find your wife's abductor!

'And after all that, if the gods do not restore your wife to you, then, O king of Kosalā, it will be time for you to take action! If you cannot get Sītā back through diplomacy and conciliation, then you can achieve your ends through a rain of gold-tipped arrows that fall like Indra's thunderbolt!'

Even though he was the older brother, Rāma took Lakṣmaṇa's wise and judicious advice seriously. He controlled his anger and leaning on his great bow, he said, 'What shall we do now, Lakṣmaṇa? Where shall we go next? Think about how we can find Sītā.'

'We should first look carefully here in Janasthāna which is full of trees and teeming with *rākṣasas*. There are many mountainous places here that are hard to reach, as well as clefts and hollows in the rocks and caves that are homes of fierce wild animals,' said Lakṣmaṇa. Rāma and Lakṣmaṇa searched the entire forest. Rāma was still angry and he carried his great bow fitted with a sharp and deadly arrow.

Suddenly, they came upon the bird Jaṭāyu, huge as a mountain, lying on the ground, drenched in blood. 'I am sure Sītā has been devoured by this thing here!' said Rāma when he saw that enormous creature. 'This is a *rākṣasa* who has taken the form of a vulture to wander through these forests. He has eaten large-eyed Sītā and now he lies here resting! I shall kill him with my fiery arrows!'

Rāma fitted the arrows into his bow and approached the bird with a tread that would have stirred up the ocean. But the bird addressed the sorrowing Rāma, vomiting frothy blood as he spoke. 'The woman you search for like a rare herb in the forest has been carried away by Rāvaṇa, who has taken my life as well! I saw her being abducted against her will while you and Lakṣmaṇa were gone. I rushed to her rescue and fought with Rāvaṇa. I destroyed his chariot which lies there on the ground. Rāvaṇa cut off my wings with his sword when I grew tired and flew into the sky with Sītā. You don't have to shoot me, the *rākṣasa* has already killed me!'

When Rāma heard this news about his wife, he embraced the bird along with Lakṣmaṇa and began to weep. He was deeply distressed to see Jaṭāyu lying on a narrow path, having difficulty breathing. Rāma and Lakṣmaṇa caressed the dying, wingless, bloodied bird with affection, as if he were their child. 'Where shall I find Sītā?' cried Rāma and threw himself upon the ground.

Then he turned and spoke to Lakṣmaṇa. 'This bird made such a tremendous effort for my sake and was struck down in battle. Now he has to give up his life, which most creatures cling to. His voice quavers and he sees but dimly. There is still some life in his body but he is weak and feeble. Jaṭāyu, if you can still speak, tell me about Sītā and how you were wounded.

'Why did Rāvaṇa take Sītā away? What harm have I ever done him that he should abduct my beloved? What does he look like? How strong is he? What can he do? Where does he live? Answer these questions if you can, dear bird!'

Jaṭāyu told Rāma in great detail how he had been struck down. 'Do not grieve for Sītā!' he continued. 'It won't be long before you kill this *rākṣasa* in battle and enjoy the pleasures of Sītā's company once again,' said the dying bird whose mind was still lucid. Then he vomited more blood and bits of flesh. 'The son of Viśravas and the brother of Kubera,' began the bird, but his breath left him and he died.

'Tell me, tell me!' begged Rāma with his palms joined but the bird's soul had left his body and gone to heaven. His head fell to the ground, his legs sprawled forward and his body jerked violently.

'This mighty bird died for my sake!' said Rāma to Lakṣmaṇa. 'Even among the lower orders of beings there are those who are virtuous, honourable and brave, who are the refuge of the weak and helpless. Even the sadness of Sītā's abduction does not match the grief I feel at the death of this bird who died for me!

'He is as worthy of honour and respect as my father Daśaratha. Collect some wood, Lakṣmaṇa, and I shall start a fire. We must cremate the king of the vultures. Mighty bird, you shall enjoy worlds of incomparable bliss with the last rites that I perform for you!' Rāma placed the bird's body on a blazing pyre and cremated him, mourning as he would for a member of his family.

The two brothers went further south through the forest, looking for Sītā. Secure in their prowess, they scoured the forest when, suddenly, there was a huge sound that seemed to tear the forest apart. The trees were agitated as if by storm winds and the huge sound filled the sky.

Armed with their bows and arrows, Rāma and Lakṣmaṇa tried to find out where the sound had come from and came upon an immense *rākṣasa* with a huge chest. As they came closer, they saw what appeared to be a headless torso. Its mouth was on its belly and it was covered with short spiky hair. The size of a mountain and dark as a rain cloud, the torso rumbled like thunder. There was one huge yellow eye with a red eyelid in the middle of its forehead which was stuck on its chest.

The *rākṣasa,* Kabandha, had enormous arms, each of them one *yojanā* long, and he swept the air with them, gathering bears and flocks of birds and herds of deer into his mouth. The *rākṣasa* stretched his arms to their fullest extent and grabbed Rāma and Lakṣmaṇa. Even though they were strong and brave and armed with swords and bows, the brothers were utterly helpless against this powerful force.

Kabandha saw that the brothers were trapped in his arms as if they were in the noose of death and said, 'Why are you standing there, mighty *kṣatriyas*? Can't you see that I am ravenous? Fate has sent you to me. Consider yourselves dead!'

The two brothers knew what was appropriate for time and place and they hacked off his arms at the shoulder, experiencing great delight as they did so. Rāma faced no resistance as he swiftly cut off Kabandha's left arm. Lakṣmaṇa took off his right arm with his sword.

The *rākṣasa* fell to the ground and his howls filled the earth, the sky and the four quarters. Looking at his bloodied, severed arms, the *rākṣasa* asked humbly, 'Who are you?'

'This is the famous Rāma, born in the line of the Ikṣvākus,' said auspicious Lakṣmaṇa, 'and I am his younger brother Lakṣmaṇa. While this god-like man was living in the deserted forest, his wife was abducted by a *rākṣasa.* We have come here in search of her. But who are you and what are you doing in the forest, a headless torso, struggling on the ground?'

'Welcome, best of men!' the *rākṣasa* responded with joy, and proceeded to tell Lakṣmaṇa all that Indra had told him. 'It is my great good fortune that you came here. These arms were my bonds and you have severed them. Listen and I will tell you how I came to have this terrifying form because of my arrogance and pride.

'Long ago, Rāma, I was handsome and strong and famous in all the three worlds. I was as beautiful as the sun and the moon, as beautiful as Indra, even! But I would take on this hideous shape and harass the world, especially the *ṛṣis* of the forest. One day, when I was in this form, I angered the sage Sthūlaśiras while he was collecting food in the forest. He looked straight at me and uttered this terrible curse: "This cruel and wicked form shall stay with you!" I pleaded with him to pronounce an end to the curse which I had brought upon myself and he said, "When Rāma cuts off your arms and cremates you in the deserted forest, then your original beauty will be restored to you."

'And so I would eat all that I could in the hope that one day I would find you. I will help you in any way that I can. When you have cremated me, I shall tell you where to find an ally!'

'When my brother and I were away from Janasthāna, the *rākṣasa* Rāvaṇa carried off my lovely wife with facile ease,' said Rāma. 'I only know the *rākṣasa's* name. I do not know what he looks like, where he lives or how powerful he is. It would be wonderful if you would sympathize and help us. We have no allies and we have been wandering from place to place in search of Sītā, overwhelmed with grief.

'We will return the favour. We shall gather dry wood which has been brushed off trees by passing elephants and cremate you in a big pit that we shall dig. Tell us who abducted Sītā. It will be a great favour if you tell us where she has been taken.'

'I have no divine knowledge now and I know nothing about Sītā,' said Kabandha. 'But when you cremate me and I regain my original form, I will be able to tell you about someone who has all this information.'

The brothers carried Kabandha to a hollow and there, with flaming torches, Lakṣmaṇa lit the pyre. It soon broke into a roaring blaze. Kabandha's enormous body was like a mound of fat and the fire consumed it slowly. Scattering the pyre, Kabandha rose like a flame, wearing shining white clothes and a garland of celestial flowers, adorned with jewels all over his body. He leapt off the pyre joyfully, blazing with splendour.

'Listen, Rāma, and I will tell you how to get Sītā back!' he said. 'You and Lakṣmaṇa are vulnerable and have fallen into adverse circumstances.

That is why it was easy for your wife to be abducted. You must acquire a friend and ally. I can see no way for you to achieve your ends without one.

'There is a monkey named Sugrīva who was displaced by his brother Vālī, the son of Indra, in a fit of anger. With his four monkey companions, he lives on the Ṛṣyamūka mountain whose beauty is enhanced by Lake Pampā. Sugrīva is strong and brave.

'Leave here immediately, Rāma, and make friends with Sugrīva, with fire as a witness to your mutual loyalty. That mighty king of the monkeys is brave and he can change his shape at will. Do not slight him, Rāma. He needs your help and he will be ever grateful for it. Together, you can achieve his ends, but he will help you even if his task is not accomplished. He knows all there is to know about any place over which the sun shines. He will search the rivers, the mountains and the deep caves with his monkeys and he will find your wife. He will send his mighty monkeys in all directions to find Sītā, who is pining in her separation from you!'

'Go west from here, through the forest and over the hills, until you reach Pampā, the lake which teems with fish and is surrounded by flowering trees. Mount Ṛṣyamūka lies to the east of the lake,' continued Kabandha. 'There is a cave in that mountain which is impossible to enter, for its mouth is closed by a rock. On the eastern side of the cave is a large pool of cool water. The area abounds in roots and fruits and all kinds of animals gather there. That is where Sugrīva lives with his monkey companions. Sometimes, he can be found on the summit of the mountain.'

These were the directions that splendid Kabandha gave Rāma and Lakṣmaṇa as he stood in the sky with his celestial garland. 'Go forward,' he said, 'and may your mission be successful!' Shining like the sun in his rightful form, Kabandha called out again from the sky, 'Make an alliance with Sugrīva!' and went on his way.

# KIṢKINDHA

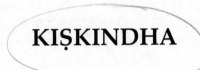

# *Chapter Thirty-Five*

Finally, Rāma and Lakṣmaṇa arrived at lotus-covered Pampā, but Rāma was still depressed. Even though a tremor of delight ran through his body when he saw Pampā, he found that his thoughts turned to his beloved.

'Ah, Lakṣmaṇa! How beautiful these trees are that surround Pampā,' he said. 'They are as tall as the mountains, their heights as dazzling as mountain peaks! I am already grieving over Bharata's sadness and Sītā's abduction and I find that this lovely place makes me even more unhappy. This gentle breeze! This season! The mind turns to thoughts of love, Lakṣmaṇa! The spring air is fragrant and all the trees burst forth in fruits and flowers. Look at how the woods bloom! The wind scatters flowers all over the ground and the trees shower blossoms like clouds shower rain! But this same breeze can be gentle and soothe us with its touch, cool and fragrant as sandalpaste!

'The springtime air, filled as it is with the songs of birds, sharpens my sorrow at the separation from Sītā. My body is consumed by passion and the *koel* mocks me with its happy song! And that bird that calls from near the waterfall! It fills me with sadness, for I am caught in the grip of passion! I am already so oppressed by my grief, yet doe-eyed Sītā torments me further with her absence, like this cruel breeze. The peahen who walks with her mate on the hillside overwhelms me with emotion.

'Ah! my sweet-voiced beloved must be suffering as much as I am! The cool, gentle breezes burn me like a fire, they make me think of my beloved Sītā. These birds that brought me the news of Sītā's abduction should lead me to her now. When I look at the petals on the blossoming lotus buds, I think of Sītā's eyes. The breeze that has brushed against flowers as it comes through the trees reminds me of Sītā's sweet breath!'

Thus did Rāma lament as he and Lakṣmaṇa looked everywhere for Sītā, even inside caves and behind waterfalls, and his heart grew heavier with sorrow and despair.

Sugrīva saw those two mighty heroes as they approached the vicinity of the Ṛṣyamūka mountain and his mind was filled with dread. He noticed that the brothers were well-armed and that made him very suspicious. Deeply disturbed, he looked around him but could not find a place to hide. Keeping an eye on the heroes, he found that he was restless, unable to sit in one place or decide what to do, and fear gripped his heart. Agitated and confused, Sugrīva discussed the matter with his companions and explained to them why he was so frightened.

'Those two men have definitely been sent here by Vālī to spy on us! They are wearing these rough clothes and wandering in the forests just to hide their identity!'

Sugrīva's companions looked at Rāma and Lakṣmaṇa armed with their bows and arrows and fled to another peak. There, they gathered around their leader, the best of monkeys, and together, they leapt from peak to peak, shaking the earth with the force and speed of their movements. The powerful monkeys toppled flowering trees on the slopes as they raced all over the mountain, disturbing deer, wild cats and tigers. They reassembled on the very top of the mountain and stood before their leader with their palms joined in respect.

Sugrīva was quaking with fear at the thought of what Vālī might have planned, but the eloquent Hanumān spoke to him reasonably. 'Bull among monkeys, I cannot see cruel and fierce Vālī anywhere here! And yet, you have been running all over the place in fear of him! Your wicked brother, whom you fear so much, is nowhere to be seen, my friend, and I see no cause for alarm! Unfortunately, you have just displayed your essential monkey nature! Your mind is so flighty and distracted that you cannot even sit in one place and consider the situation calmly. You are wise and intelligent and should be able to read the motives of other people and act accordingly. A king who does not use his intelligence cannot rule his people properly.'

Sugrīva listened to Hanumān's sensible words and his response was equally well-reasoned. 'Those god-like men with their mighty arms, their lotus-petal eyes and their bows and arrows and swords would make anyone apprehensive! I feel sure that Vālī has sent out these mighty men.

Kings have many friends and we should not become complacent! One must be able to detect disguised enemies. Men such as these are always alert, they strike the complacent when the right moment presents itself.

'Mighty Hanumān! Disguise yourself as an ordinary man and go and meet them! Find out all you can through their mode of dress and speech, their manners and their conduct. Examine their feelings and attitudes. If they seem friendly, gain their confidence by flattering them with praises and pleasant words! Position yourself such that I can see you and then ask them why they have come to this forest armed with bows and arrows.'

Hanumān leapt off the Ṛṣyamūka mountain, fully understanding what Sugrīva wanted, and landed close to Rāma and Lakṣmaṇa. He threw off his own form and approached them in the guise of a mendicant. He addressed them in a sweet voice, praising them, as had been planned. 'Your glowing skin makes you look like kings, or royal sages, or resolute ascetics! What brings you to this region? You disturb the deer and other forest animals as you wander along the wooded shores of Pampā. You enhance the brilliance of these sparkling waters with your shining skin! But who are you, dressed like this in the clothes of ascetics? You seem to have the valour of lions. You are armed with bows that rival Indra's, you are as handsome and powerful as bulls, your arms are as mighty as elephants' trunks, and you radiate energy!

'Your splendour lights up the mountain. But you, who are comparable to the gods, should be ruling a kingdom. What are you doing here? You are clearly warriors, but your eyes are like lotus petals and you have the matted locks of ascetics! You bear a close resemblance to each other and seem to have come from the realm of the gods, like the sun and the moon come to earth by chance! Why is it that your massive arms are not adorned with jewelled ornaments as they should be? You seem capable of ruling the entire earth with the oceans and forests and mountains like Meru and Vindhya that adorn it! Why are you so silent despite my many questions?

'There is a righteous monkey here named Sugrīva and he is the lord of the monkey clans. He was unfairly treated by his brother and now wanders the earth in sorrow. My name is Hanumān and I have been sent here by Sugrīva who is regarded as king by many of the important monkeys. I am the son of the Wind, and I am Sugrīva's advisor. Honourable Sugrīva wishes to make friends with you! I can take any form that I choose and I can go anywhere I want! I have come here from the Ṛṣyamūka mountain in the form of a mendicant to carry out Sugrīva's instructions!' Knowing that Rāma and Lakṣmaṇa were perceptive enough to understand his meaning, the eloquent Hanumān fell silent.

'This is Sugrīva's minister!' said Rāma in delight to his brother who stood beside him. 'I have been looking for that great king of the monkeys and he has found me instead!. This advisor has been friendly and eloquent. He is well-spoken and knows what to say and when to say it. Speak to him, Lakṣmaṇa!'

Hanumān was thrilled when he heard what Rāma said and his thoughts flew immediately to Sugrīva. 'Sugrīva is bound to regain his kingdom soon since Rāma has obviously come to him with a purpose!' he thought.

'What has brought you and your younger brother to these dense forests that surround Pampā, that are filled with wild animals and beasts of prey?' he asked Rāma. Lakṣmaṇa told Hanumān all about the great-souled Rāma, son of Daśaratha.

'There was a great and celebrated king named Daśaratha who loved *dharma.* This is his renowned eldest son, Rāma. This hero is the best of all Daśaratha's sons because of his many virtues. He is the refuge of all beings and he is devoted to carrying out his father's wishes. Having been deprived of his kingdom, he came to live here with me and his wife Sītā, who accompanied him like rays follow the sun at the end of the day. I am Rāma's younger brother and my name is Lakṣmaṇa. I am devoted to Rāma because of his many virtues, his graciousness and his immense learning. Rāma, who deserves glory and every kind of happiness and is intent on the welfare of all creatures, has been deprived of his royal majesty and has come to take refuge in the forest.

'A form-changing *rākṣasa* abducted Rāma's wife in our absence. We have no idea who that *raksasa* was. Kabandha, who had become a *rākṣasa* because of a curse, told us that Sugrīva, the king of the monkeys, was capable of helping us. "Sugrīva is mighty and strong and he will know how to find the *rākṣasa* who abducted your wife" is what he said to us as he went to heaven, radiant and shining.

'I have now answered your questions and told you everything. Rāma and I have come here to seek Sugrīva's help. In the past, Rāma distributed huge amounts of wealth, won great fame and was the lord of the earth. Now he comes to Sugrīva for refuge. He is overwhelmed with grief and utterly distraught. Sugrīva and his monkey hordes should be gracious to him!' said Lakṣmaṇa sadly, with tears in his eyes.

'It is Sugrīva's good fortune that such wise and disciplined men as you, whom he should have sought out, have come to him!' replied Hanumān. 'He, too, has been deprived of his kingdom and Vālī has become his sworn enemy. Separated from his wife, Sugrīva wanders sadly through the forests, all because his brother treated him so unfairly. Sugrīva, son of the Sun, and all of us monkeys will definitely help you in the search for Sītā! Let us go and meet Sugrīva!' Hanumān said in his sweet and mellifluous voice.

Lakṣmaṇa honoured Hanumān and then turned to Rāma. 'This monkey, son of the Wind, is obviously very pleased with what he has heard. His happy face shines brightly and he seems to be telling the truth. Sugrīva also needs help to achieve his ends and so you can consider your mission as good as accomplished!'

Hanumān took the two princes to meet the king of the monkeys. Shining with his own splendour, the famous Hanumān was delighted with his success and reached the top of the mountain on the strength of his powerful thighs. From Ṛṣyamūka, Hanumān went to Mount Malaya and introduced Sugrīva to Rāma and Lakṣmaṇa.

'This is the wise and resolute Rāma, exceedingly brave and honourable. He has come here with his brother Lakṣmaṇa. Born into the family of the Ikṣvākus, Rāma is the son of Daśaratha. He is known for his righteousness and for his devotion to his father's wishes. While Rāma was living a life of discipline and restraint in the forest, a *rākṣasa* abducted his wife. Now Rāma has come to you for help. Son of the king who performed all the important sacrifices correctly, who paid generous fees and distributed cows by the hundreds of thousands, a king who ruled the earth wisely and well, such a man had to come into the forest because of a woman! Rāma and Lakṣmaṇa are here to make an alliance of friendship. Treat them well, for they are the best among those who should be honoured!'

Sugrīva was pleased with what Hanumān said, and his fear of Rāma left him as a fever leaves the body. He took on the form of a charming and handsome young man and spoke warmly to Rāma. 'Hanumān has rightly described all your virtues to me. Indeed, you are disciplined and firm in the practice of *dharma,* you are strong and brave and your love embraces all creatures. It is a great honour as well as a great advantage for me that you seek my friendship and that of the monkeys. Take my hand and let us enter into a firm alliance!'

Rāma took Sugrīva's outstretched hand and gripped it firmly. Pleased that he had made the alliance he wanted, Rāma embraced Sugrīva with affection. Hanumān, meanwhile, relinquished the mendicant form that he had taken on and, in his own form, gathered some wood and made a fire. He worshipped it with an offering of flowers and then, with a glad heart, he placed the blazing fire between Sugrīva and Rāma. The two of them walked around the fire to cement their new friendship, gazing at each other fondly, as if they would never tire of the sight of the other.

'My advisor Hanumān has told me how you came to live in this uninhabited forest,' said Sugrīva to Rāma, 'and also that while you were living there with your brother Lakṣmaṇa, a *rākṣasa* abducted your wife Sītā, the daughter of Janaka. The *rākṣasa* waited for the right moment and did this in your absence. He killed the vulture Jaṭāyu as he carried your wailing wife away. But you shall not suffer this separation from your wife for long! I shall bring her back, just as the sacred scriptures were recovered! Whether she be in the highest heaven or the lowest hell, I shall bring your wife back to you! I promise you this and you can count on my word, Rāma!

'I feel sure, from logical deductions, that it was Sītā I saw being carried off by a cruel *rākṣasa.* She was crying out "Oh Rāma! Oh Lakṣmaṇa!" piteously as she writhed in Rāvaṇa's arms like a serpent. Then she saw me and four other monkeys sitting on the top of a mountain and she threw down her shawl as well as some jewelled ornaments. We caught them and have kept them safely. I shall bring them here so that you can identify them.'

'What is the delay, my friend?' urged Rāma. 'Have them brought here as soon as possible!' Eager to please Rāma, Sugrīva ran to his inaccessible cave and fetched the jewels. Rāma's eyes blurred with tears, as the moon is covered by mist, when he saw the jewels and the shawl. Overcome by his love for Sītā, he burst into tears. Crying, 'Ah! my beloved!' he threw himself on the ground. He clutched the jewels to his chest and sighed heavily, like an angry serpent hissing in its hole. His tears flowed thick and heavy and he turned to Lakṣmaṇa, who stood by his side.

'Look, Lakṣmaṇa! These are the jewels and the cloth that Sītā threw from her body onto the ground as she was being carried off!' he said pathetically. 'She must have thrown them onto the grassy slopes, for the ornaments are not in the least damaged!'

'I cannot recognize her ear and hair ornaments,' said Lakṣmaṇa. 'I only know her anklets because I would touch her feet every morning.'

'Tell me, Sugrīva,' said Rāma, 'where was this wicked *rākṣasa* taking my beloved wife, dearer to me than my own life, when you saw them? Where does that *rākṣasa* live? He has caused me so much grief that because of him, I am determined to exterminate the entire race of *rākṣasas*! Who is this creature who has opened the door of death for himself by abducting Sītā and incurring my terrible wrath? Tell me, great monkey, who was this who abducted my beloved from the forest? I shall send him to meet the god of death this very day!'

Sugrīva's eyes filled with tears and in a voice thick with emotion, he replied, 'I have no idea where that wicked creature lives. Nor do I know anything about his family or his strength and prowess. But do not grieve, I promise you that I shall make every effort to get Sītā back! I shall use all my capacities, that you will find worthy of praise, and kill Rāvaṇa and his *rākṣasa* hordes. I shall do all that it takes to please you for as long as you want! Do not succumb to this weakness. Resort to your natural fortitude and forbearance! Such behaviour is for lesser men. It does not become you!

'I, too, have suffered the terrible grief of separation from my wife. But I do not weep and lament and I have not lost heart. Even though I am only an ordinary monkey, I do not go on and on grieving. You are great-souled and self-restrained, you should be even stronger! Dry your tears! Do not lose the fortitude that governs the conduct of resolute men!

'I speak like this out of concern for the welfare of a friend, Rāma. I do not presume to teach you! Respect my friendship and renounce your sorrow!'

Somewhat comforted, Rāma wiped the tears from his face with his upper garment. Regaining his natural composure because of Sugrīva's words, Rāma embraced the monkey. 'You have fulfilled the duty of a friend who loves and wishes the best for someone,' he said. 'You have done what is right and worthy. My natural equanimity has been restored thanks to your persuasive words. It is hard to find friends as good as you, especially at a time like this!

'What do we need to do now in order to find Sītā and the vicious *rākṣasa* Rāvana? And you must also tell me, without any hesitation, what I have to do to help you. Our efforts will bear fruit like seeds sown just before the rains! You can count on my word, Sugrīva! I have never spoken an untruth nor shall I ever do so! I swear this by all that is true and I shall keep my promise!'

Sugrīva and his advisors were delighted to hear Rāma's words, reinforced by his solemn oath. The man and the monkey sat and chatted intimately about all that was important to them. And the king of the monkeys knew in his heart that his ends were as good as achieved.

# *Chapter Thirty-Six*

In a voice that trembled with happiness, Sugrīva began to tell Rāma his story. 'I have been treated unfairly by my brother and because of that I have to wander around this Ṛṣyamūka mountain, bereft of my wife and stricken with fear and sorrow. I live in constant terror, distracted and disoriented by this fear of my brother Vālī who has taken all that I had and become my mortal enemy. You are the one who rids the world of fear. Take pity on me! I am terrorized by Vālī and I have no protection!'

'To help is the sign of a friend, just as to harm is the sign of an enemy!' said Rāma, who knew and loved *dharma* and was a man of great power. 'Today I shall kill the monkey who took your wife away from you! You shall watch as your brother, who has done you wrong and is your enemy, is slain by my arrows as a mountain is split!'

'Good! Good!' said Sugrīva, reassured by Rāma's words. 'Rāma, I am tormented by my troubles and you are the last resort for creatures like me! I come to you with my sorrows because of our mutual alliance. I can tell you about the troubles that consume me like a fire because we are friends!' Sugrīva's eyes filled with tears and he could barely speak as they threatened to choke him. His tears flowed like a river in spate but with a great effort he managed to stanch them. He wiped his beautiful eyes, sighed deeply and continued.

'Long ago, I was driven out of the kingdom by Vālī who was stronger and very critical of me. He stole my wife who was dearer to me than my own life and he imprisoned all my friends and well wishers. That blackguard tried many times to destroy me and I have killed several monkeys that he sent here with that express purpose. That is why I was so suspicious when I saw you and did not move from this place! Everything is terrifying when there is a cause for fear!

'Hanumān and the others are my only companions. And though I am in a bad way, I have survived only because of them. They protect me from all sides and look after me because they love me. They go where I go and stay where I stay. This, in short, is my story, Rāma. Why go into any details? The gist of it is that my own older brother, who is known for his strength, is my deadly enemy. My sorrows will end when he is destroyed. My life and my happiness depend on his death!'

'But what is the reason for this hostility?' asked Rāma. 'I would like to hear about that! Then I will consider the matter carefully and decide upon the best way to restore you to happiness. The tale of your humiliation makes me very angry. You shall see your enemy destroyed the moment I release my arrow!'

The monkeys and Sugrīva were thrilled when they heard what Rāma said and with a lighter heart Sugrīva began to tell Rāma the whole story.

'My brother, the slayer of his enemies, is named Vālī. In the old days, my father thought very highly of him and so did I. When my father died, Vālī was placed on the throne by the ministers because he was older and because they held him in high regard. He ruled the kingdom that has come down to us from our forefathers and I obeyed him at all times.

'Long before that, Vālī had a famous fight over a woman with Māyāvī, the oldest son of Dundubhi. One night, when everyone was asleep, Māyāvī came to the gates of Kiṣkindha and created a mighty din, challenging Vālī to a fight. My brother was also asleep but he woke when he heard that great shout and, unable to tolerate the insult, came out quickly. Determined to kill that mighty *asura,* Vālī left Kiṣkindha immediately. Even though his wives and I pleaded with him in all humility, he brushed us aside. But I followed him out of affection.

'When the *asura* saw my brother and me coming after him from a distance, he fled in terror. We both ran after him and the moon lit up our path. The *asura* ran into a crevice that was covered with grass and seemed hard to access but we followed him to the mouth of the cave. Vālī was enraged when he saw his enemy disappearing into the hole and in a frenzy he said to me, "Stand here, Sugrīva, and guard the entrance to the cave. I will go and kill this hostile creature!" I begged him to let me go with him but he made me swear that I would stay there and plunged into the cave.

'An entire year went by after he entered there and all that time I stood guard at the entrance. I saw no sign of Vālī and I assumed the worst. I presumed that he was dead and because of my affection for him, I was very upset. I heard the shouts of the *asura* but I heard nothing from my brother who was engrossed in the fight. That made me think that my brother was dead. I covered the entrance to the cave with a rock that was as big as a mountain and after performing the funeral rites for my brother, I returned to Kiṣkindha with a heavy heart.

'Though I made every effort to hide the truth, the ministers heard what had happened and after consulting each other they crowned me king. While I was ruling the kingdom justly and well, Vālī returned, having killed the hostile *asura.* His eyes blazed with anger when he saw that I had become king. He imprisoned my councillors and berated me harshly. I could have had him thrown into prison but, out of respect for the fact that he was my older brother, I did not want to treat that wicked creature so badly. I honoured him and treated him with respect but Vālī did not invoke blessings upon me.

'I tried to placate my brother who was in a towering rage. "Thank goodness you are well and that the enemy has been destroyed! I am vulnerable and you are my only protector! Accept this fly whisk and this royal umbrella, that shines like the moon, which I shall hold over your head. You are the rightful king now, as you were before. I return to you the kingdom that I held in trust. Do not be angry with me, dear brother! I beg you with my palms joined and my head at your feet! The councillors and the citizens felt that a kingless country would be vulnerable to conquest and so they conferred and forced me to be king!"

'And though I spoke from deep and sincere affection, that monkey was not moved. "Damn you!" he shouted and began to berate me and say all kinds of terrible things about me in front of the citizens and the ministers whom he had called together. "You know how the *asura* Māyāvī came here one night. That cruel and wicked fool, eager for battle, challenged me to a fight" he said. 'I came out of Kiṣkindha when I heard his call and this ill-intentioned brother of mine followed me quickly. When the great *asura* saw us coming after him, he ran away in fright and entered a huge hole in the earth. I saw that and told this wicked brother of mine to wait for me at the entrance because I could not return to the city without killing Māyāvī. I thought my brother would do as I asked. When I entered the cave, it took me a whole year to find the *asura.* I saw that creature who strikes terror into the hearts of his opponents and I killed him and his entire family. Blood poured out of the *asura's* mouth when I killed him and it filled the cave. I wanted to get out but I found that the entrance was blocked. I called out to Sugrīva again and again and was very angry when there was no response. I began to kick at the blocked entrance until, finally, I got out and returned to the city. This ruthless creature forgot all about filial love and trapped me in there because of his desire for the throne!"

'Then Vālī threw me out with only the single piece of clothing that I was wearing. He threw me out and took my wife. Since then, I have wandered all over the earth with its forests and oceans, living in fear of him. Grieving for my lost wife, I came to live here on the Ṛṣyamūka mountain because the area is forbidden to Vālī for a certain reason.

'Now that I have told you everything about this terrible enmity, you will see, Rāma, that I have been made to suffer even though I am utterly innocent. You rid the world of fear. Be gracious to me and destroy this creature that I fear so much!'

Righteous Rāma smiled. 'My arrows are sharp and as bright as the sun. They never miss their mark. They shall be sped on their way by my anger and shall fall upon the wicked Vālī!' said Rāma, his words filled with *dharma.* 'Immoral Vālī, the abductor of your wife, shall not live a single moment after I have set eyes on him! From my own experience, I know that you must be plunged in an ocean of sorrow. But I shall help you across it and you shall have what your heart desires.'

Sugrīva listened to Rāma's words which were intended to make him take heart and feel better and he honoured Rāma and praised him. 'I have no doubt you can consume the world with your flaming arrows, like the fire at the end of time!' he said. 'Listen carefully and I will describe Vālī's courage and strength and his skills. Then you can decide what you should do.

'Vālī can travel from the eastern ocean to the western and from the northern ocean to the southern before the sun has risen and not feel any fatigue. He climbs to the tops of the highest mountains and, breaking off their peaks, he tosses them into the air and catches them before they fall. Vālī breaks sap-filled trees in the forest just to prove his strength to himself.

'There was an enormous buffalo named Dundubhi, white as the peaks of Mount Kailāsa, and he had the strength of a thousand elephants. He was wicked at heart, proud of his strength and courage, and he had become arrogant because of the boons he had received. Himāvat, the lord of the mountains, sent Dundubhi to challenge Vālī to a fight, for Vālī was invincible. Dundubhi arrived at Kiṣkindha in a rage. He had taken on the form of a terrifying buffalo with sharp horns, dark as the rain-filled clouds in the monsoon sky.

'Mighty Dundubhi roared like the rumble of war drums and it was a sound that made the earth tremble. Nearby trees split open and the buffalo dug up the earth with his hooves. In his arrogance, he gouged at the city gates with his horns, like an elephant in rut. Vālī was in the inner apartments at the time but he came out in a temper when he heard that sound, like the moon surrounded by stars.

'Vālī, lord of the monkeys and of all the forest creatures, spoke clearly and distinctly to Dundubhi. "Why are you blocking the gates of my city and roaring like this? I know that you are Dundubhi. Protect yourself, mighty one!" Dundubhi's eyes blazed with anger as he replied. "You should not speak like this in front of women, hero! Come and fight with me so that I can assess your strength! Or if you like, I shall contain my anger for the night. Indulge your pleasures until the morning, monkey!"

'Vālī dismissed Tārā and the other women and smiled slowly. "Do not assume that I am drunk!" he shouted in his rage. "Unless, of course, you are scared to fight me! Assume that I have drunk what heroes drink before they go into battle!" Vālī threw off the golden necklace that had been given to him by his father Indra and prepared himself for combat.

'He grabbed the mountainous Dundubhi by his horns and with a mighty roar, flung him to the ground. Blood poured from Dundubhi's ears when he hit the ground and he lay there, dead. Vālī lifted that heavy and inert body in his arms and hurled it away with great force. It landed one full *yojanā* away but a few drops of blood fell from the body and were carried by the wind to the sage Matanga's hermitage. Matanga saw the enormous carcass of the buffalo lying nearby and, inflamed with anger, he cursed Vālī, who had thrown it. "Whoever threw this thing can never enter this area. He will die if he does so!" Vālī begged the sage to release him from the curse but to no avail. Since then, Vālī has not set foot on the Ṛṣyamūka mountain, nor even looked at it, for fear of the sage's curse.

'And I wander through these forests with my companions, free from fear, because I know that Vālī cannot set foot here. Look, you can see Dundubhi's skeleton over there, large as a mountain. He was so proud of his strength that he brought about his own death.

'See those seven *sāla* trees over there with their thick branches? Vālī could shake the trees and make the branches fall to the ground. I am giving you examples of Vālī's strength. How will you kill him in battle, Rāma? If you can pierce even one of those *sāla* trees with a single arrow then I shall believe that you have the capacity to kill Vālī.'

Rāma playfully lifted Dundubhi's skeleton with his big toe and kicked it a distance of ten *yojanās*. Sugrīva watched and then, in front of Lakṣmaṇa, he said significantly, 'The body was covered with flesh and blood when it was kicked away before, my friend! Now, Rāma, it is all bones and is as light as straw. Under these circumstances, I cannot judge who is stronger, you or Vālī!'

Sugrīva's pointed words made Rāma lift his mighty bow. He fitted it with a single arrow, aimed at the *sāla* trees and let it go with all his strength. The arrow resounded through the air and pierced all the seven trees as well as the mountain behind them before entering the earth. A little while later, the wondrous arrow came back and lodged itself in its quiver. The monkey was astounded and fell on the ground before Rāma, his head bowed, his ornaments dangling. Filled with delight, he honoured Rāma with his palms joined.

Thrilled with Rāma's feat, Sugrīva said to the man who knew *dharma,* who was the foremost among skilled warriors and who stood before him like a hero, 'Bull among men, you are capable of destroying all the gods in battle, even Indra, with your arrows! What then, of Vālī! Who can face you in combat when you have pierced seven trees and a mountain and the earth with a single arrow? Today my sorrows end and happiness returns, for I have the equal of Indra and Varuṇa as a friend! Gratify me by killing Vālī today, this enemy in the guise of a brother! I beg you, Rāma, with folded hands!'

Rāma embraced the happy Sugrīva and spoke words that Lakṣmaṇa also agreed with. 'Let us go to Kiṣkindha! Go ahead of us, Sugrīva, and challenge Vālī, who is your brother in name only, to a fight.'

# *Chapter Thirty-Seven*

Swiftly, they all went to Kiṣkindha, Vālī's city, and stationed themselves in the forest, hiding behind trees. Sugrīva girded his loins and, outside the gates of Kiṣkindha, he let out a mighty roar that pierced the sky, challenging Vālī to fight. Vālī heard his brother and charged out in a rage, red as the sun over the western mountains. A huge and noisy fight ensued between Vālī and Sugrīva, like the clash of Mercury and Mars in the sky. In their fury, both the brothers attacked each other with their fists and feet, hitting one another with the force of thunderbolts.

His bow at the ready, Rāma watched the two monkeys fighting. They looked exactly like each other, like the *aśvins*. Rāma could not tell which was Vālī and which Sugrīva, so he held back the arrow that was bound to kill one of them. Worsted in combat, his spirit broken, Sugrīva ran back to the Ṛṣyamūka mountain because he could not see his protector, Rāma, anywhere. Vālī followed him, wounded, tired and covered with blood. But when he saw Sugrīva enter the area where he could not go because of the curse, he shouted, 'You have escaped this time!' and went back to Kiṣkindha.

Rāma, Lakṣmaṇa and Hanumān returned to find Sugrīva, his head hanging low, feeling utterly disgraced. 'Rāma, you showed me your skills and urged me to challenge Vālī. Then you let me be injured by my enemy! Why did you do this?' said Sugrīva plaintively, wretched and miserable. 'If you had made it clear before that you were not going to kill Vālī, I would never have left his place!'

'Listen to me, dear Sugrīva, and do not be angry,' said Rāma. 'Listen to why I held back my arrows. You and Vālī are exactly alike. You look like each other, your movements are the same, even your clothes and ornaments do not distinguish you from one another! Monkey, I could not even tell you apart by voice and complexion, nor by your skills, your speech or your personalities. I was thoroughly confused by these resemblances and so I did not release my deadly arrow which would have taken a life. But within the next hour, you shall see Vālī laid low by my arrow, writhing on the ground. Put on something that will distinguish you from him so that I can recognize you when you are fighting. Lakṣmaṇa, take this flowering creeper and place it around Sugrīva's neck as a garland!'

Lakṣmaṇa picked up the creeper, abundant with flowers that grew on the hillside, and arranged it around Sugrīva's neck. With that garland, the monkey shone like a cloud in the evening sky. Then he made for Kiṣkindha, reassured by Rāma's words.

Once again, they all hid themselves in the trees of the forest. Sugrīva looked around the forest that he loved and worked himself up into a rage. Again he let out a great roar that seemed to pierce the sky and challenged Vālī to fight. Sugrīva blazed like the morning sun and his gait was like a lion's. He turned to Rāma, who was skilled at his task, and said, 'We have arrived at Vālī's city with its golden arches and flying banners, filled with powerful monkeys. Fulfil the promise that you made earlier, as the season brings the vine to fruit, and kill Vālī!'

'You are wearing the flower garland as a sign. I shall recognize you by that!' replied Rāma. 'It makes you shine brightly like the moon with a necklace of stars in the sky! I shall release a single arrow, monkey, that will free you from the fear of your enemy Vālī! As soon as that enemy in the guise of a brother appears, I shall strike him down and he will roll in the dust. If he is still alive after I set eyes on him, Sugrīva, then the fault will be mine and you can criticize me and berate me all you want. I have never told a lie, not even in an adversity, and I never shall, for I cannot bear to violate *dharma.* Have no doubt, I shall make good my promise, as Indra ripens the crops with timely rains! Challenge Vālī, the wearer of the golden necklace! Raise the cry that will bring out that monkey who is so eager to fight!'

Golden-yellow Sugrīva let out a harsh cry that seemed to split the sky. It troubled the placid cows, who turned pale like high-born women would at the prospect of violence and anarchy. Deer fled like war horses that have been turned loose on the battlefield. Birds fell out of the sky like heavenly bodies that have exhausted their merit. Sugrīva, son of the Sun, his confidence and strength swelling like the ocean agitated by the winds, yelled with all his might, sounding like thunder from gathering clouds.

Vālī was in the women's apartments and he was terribly annoyed with his brother's yells. The sound which had made all the creatures tremble jogged Vālī out of his intoxication and roused him to anger. His anger distorted him so much that Vālī, who was normally the colour of the evening sun, dimmed like the sun in eclipse. He rushed out of the palace, tearing up the earth with his powerful feet.

Tārā was very upset and she clung to him and spoke to him affectionately, displaying her concern for his welfare. 'Throw away this anger, hero, that has come upon you like a river in spate, as one who wakes throws away flowers from the night before! Your rushing off like this makes me uneasy. Listen and I will tell you why I want you to hold back!

'Sugrīva came here once before and challenged you to a fight. You went out in a rage and defeated him and he ran away. The fact that he comes to challenge you again after being wounded in body and spirit makes me suspicious. The arrogance and pride with which he shouts now cannot have a trivial cause. I am sure Sugrīva has come here this time with allies and help. He must have an ally who gives him the confidence to shout like this!

'Sugrīva is intelligent and cunning. He would not have come here without making sure of his ally's strength. I should also tell you what I heard earlier from Prince Angada, hero! I shall repeat it now for your benefit. Your brother's ally is none other than Rāma, who is ruthless in battle and all-consuming like the doomsday fire! But he is also like the shady tree under which the virtuous can gather. He is the refuge of the oppressed and a worthy heir of fame. You should not seek enmity with him, for he is invincible and unrivalled in battle.

'Listen to me, mighty one, I have to say this to you and you must not be angry. I speak for your benefit. Take my advice. Make Sugrīva your heir apparent without any further delay. You should not have enmity with your brother, great king! Put an end to these hostilities. Earn Sugrīva's affection and make friends with Rāma! Your brother is younger than you and deserves your love and affection. Even if he is not with you now, he remains your brother wherever he is! If you believe that I have your best interests at heart and if you want to make me happy, then do as I ask!'

When Tārā with her star-bright face had finished speaking, Vālī brushed aside her advice contemptuously. 'Why should I listen quietly to my brother shouting like this, especially when he is an enemy!' he said. 'For brave men who are undefeated in battle and who never turn and flee from the battlefield, to have to listen to threats like this is worse than death! I cannot tolerate this from Sugrīva! He is eager to fight but soon his neck will be lopped off in battle!'

'Don't worry about Rāma injuring me. He knows and loves *dharma* and he is gracious. He would never do anything unethical! Why are you still following me, Tārā? Go back inside with your women. You have amply demonstrated your love and devotion to me! I must go forward and confront Sugrīva. Don't worry, I will crush his pride but I will spare his life. Promise me that you will go back inside. Wish me well and I shall return, having defeated my brother in combat!' Tārā embraced Vālī, weeping softly. She wished him well and invoked blessings upon him with the appropriate *mantras*. Then, full of sorrow, she went back into the inner apartments with her women.

Vālī rushed out of the city, hissing like an angry serpent. Breathing heavily, he looked around for his enemy. Then he saw Sugrīva, shining yellow and golden, blazing like the fire, ready to do battle. Vālī, the mighty one, girded his loins and clenched his fists and advanced towards Sugrīva, eager to fight. Sugrīva raised his fists and came towards Vālī who was wearing his golden necklace. Vālī pounced upon Sugrīva and began to pummel him. Blood poured from Sugrīva's body like cascades from a mountain but he was undaunted. Enraged, Sugrīva uprooted an enormous *sāla* tree with all his strength and assaulted Vālī with it, like a thunderbolt striking a mountain. Stunned by the blow, Vālī reeled, as a small boat carrying merchants and their goods is rocked upon the ocean.

Those mighty monkeys, who had powerful bodies and the speed and strength of Garuḍa, fought each other like the sun and the moon in the sky. Sugrīva began to slow down, his pride crushed by Vālī, and he tried to point Vālī out to Rāma. Rāma picked an arrow that was like a poisonous snake and released it from his bow. It struck Vālī in the chest and he fell to the ground. Drenched with blood and sweat, Indra's mighty son collapsed, unconscious, on the battlefield, like an *aśoka* tree felled by the wind or Indra's toppled flagstaff.

# *Chapter Thirty-Eight*

Vālī lay sprawled on the ground with his golden ornaments like Indra's fallen banner when the ropes that hold it are severed. And when Vālī, the lord of the monkeys and the bears, lay like that on the ground, the earth's lustre was dimmed like a moonless sky. But still, Vālī's personal lustre and majesty did not leave his body, held there by the golden gem-studded necklace that had been given him by Indra. The necklace made him seem like a rain cloud tinged with the light of the setting sun.

Rāma and Lakṣmaṇa came over and saw that great monkey lying there with his massive arms, his chest as broad as a lion's and his yellow shining eyes. Vālī looked at Rāma and began to speak righteous words that were harsh and critical, but he spoke them gently.

'What did you gain by shooting me in the back and killing me in this fashion? I was facing away from you and was absorbed in battle with another! You are renowned in the world. All creatures say that you are noble and honourable, that your conduct is impeccable, that you are radiant and compassionate, devoted to the welfare of all beings, resolute in your vows, circumspect, and that you always do the right thing. I knew you had all these great qualities and so, despite Tārā's advice, I confronted Sugrīva in battle.

'Because I could not see you anywhere, I assumed that you would not attack me when I was fighting Sugrīva. I did not know then that you are, in fact, wicked and unethical, though you pretend to be honourable, like a deep well that is hidden by grass. I could not see the wicked man behind the noble creature, the fire under the ashes. I have never harmed your kingdom or your city. Nor have I ever insulted you. Then why did you do me such grievous harm?

'Why did you do this to me, a harmless monkey who lives in the forest and eats roots and fruits, who had no quarrel with you but was concentrating on fighting with someone else? You are a prince, handsome and distinguished. You carry all the outward signs of *dharma*. How could someone like you, born a noble *kṣatriya*, who has all his ethical doubts resolved by the wise, how could you do something so cruel, hidden under the trappings of *dharma*?

'Truth, patience, courage, the ability to pursue conciliation, generosity and the meting out of punishment are the duties of a king, Rāma! We are but creatures of the forest. We live on roots and fruits, for that is our natural state. But you are human and you are a king. The usual reasons for conquest are land and wealth. What do I have in the forest apart from fruit that you could want so badly? Kings should not live by their whims and do as they please. But you are wilful, quick to anger, and seem to have no fixed views. You do not live by the code of kings and you seem eager to expend your arrows.

'You have killed an innocent creature like me! How will you justify this disgraceful act to good men? My skin cannot be used by men of virtue, my hair and bones are forbidden to them and my flesh cannot be eaten by those who practise *dharma*. Of all the five-toed animals, the *brahmin* and the *kṣatriya* can only eat the rhino, the porcupine, the alligator, the rabbit and the turtle. You have killed me, a five-toed animal, whose skin and bones no virtuous man will touch and whose flesh is forbidden.

'Rāma, if the earth has you as a master, she is as vulnerable as a virtuous woman whose husband is a rake. How could you, so base, mean, deceitful and lying, be a son of Daśaratha's? If you had fought me face-to-face you would have met the god of death today! You would never have challenged me in battle and yet today I lie dying because of your deceitful arrows, like a sleeping man who has been bitten by a serpent. You killed me to make Sugrīva happy. But if you had come to me first with the same alliance, I would have brought that wicked *rākṣasa* to you in an instant! If only you had asked me, I would have recovered Sītā from the depths of the ocean or from the bottom of the earth and brought her back to you. It is right that Sugrīva should inherit the kingdom after my death, but it is not right for you to have killed me in this way!'

His face pale from the pain of his wound, Vālī, the son of Indra, fell silent, looking up at Rāma, who shone like the sun. He had spoken harsh words to Rāma which seemed righteous, and were intended for his benefit. Rāma looked at the monkey who was like a dimming sun, a cloud emptied of its rain, a dying fire, and said things that really were filled with *dharma* and were intended to educate the monkey king.

'Your criticisms of me are childish and immature for you have not truly understood the meaning of *dharma, artha, kāma* or worldly living. You have never been exposed to the teachings or the wisdom of learned men and yet, you, with your monkey nature, presume to teach me!

'This earth with its mountains and forests belongs to the Iṣkvākus. They have the right to praise or condemn all the birds, beasts and men who inhabit it! It is ruled by the righteous and honourable Bharata. He is learned in the principles of *dharma, artha* and *kāma* and he is devoted to justice. We and other kings execute his orders which are rooted in *dharma,* here and all over the earth so that the eternal *dharma* may flourish. When the earth is ruled by the righteous and honourable Bharata it is not possible for anyone anywhere to violate *dharma* and not be punished for it.

'You have transgressed the bounds of *dharma.* Your conduct is inappropriate because you are ruled entirely by pleasure. You are not fit to be a king! The elder brother and the teacher who imparts knowledge are all regarded as equal to a father by the man who pursues the path of righteousness. A younger brother and a virtuous student are regarded as equal to a son, according to the dictates of *dharma.*

'Monkey, the *dharma* followed by truly good men is subtle and hard to understand. How can a fickle creature like you, who learns from other equally fickle monkeys, know anything? Blind men learn nothing from confronting each other! Let me explain things to you. Control yourself and listen to me!

'Here is the first reason for my killing you. You have rejected the eternal *dharma* and slept with your brother's wife. You lust for Rūmā and sleep with her even though Sugrīva is still alive. This is unacceptable because you should treat her as a daughter-in-law. I killed you for sleeping with your brother's wife and because you were motivated by lust! There can be no other punishment for this violation of *dharma* and of the worldly code. The man who sleeps with his sister, his daughter or his brother's wife is punished by death according to the traditional texts.

'My friendship with Sugrīva is equal to my love for Lakṣmaṇa. Our pact is that I will restore to him his wife and his kingdom and in return for that, he will devote himself to my interests. I gave him my word on this in front of the other monkeys. How could I then not fulfil my promise? It is the duty of a righteous man to help his friend. All the reasons I have given you are rooted in *dharma.* You have to agree that you have been justly punished! Stop your laments! You were killed because *dharma* demanded it. We cannot act as we please!

'Traps and ropes and snares of all kinds are used to capture animals. Animals are caught and killed when they are running away, or when they are agitated, even when they have no idea of the danger they are in. Men kill animals for their flesh even when their faces are turned away. There is nothing wrong with that! Royal sages, learned in *dharma,* go hunting. I killed you with an arrow, monkey. Whether you were in a position to fight back or not is irrelevant, for you are nothing but an animal!

'*Dharma* is certainly hard to understand. Kings are the source of it, as they are the source of all good things. One should not harm kings, or attack them or criticize them or displease them, for they are gods on earth in the form of men. You are ignorant of these things and that is why you condemn me for following a code that has come down from the time of my forefathers!'

Vālī began to regret his outburst. 'What you have said is absolutely true,' he said with his palms joined. 'An inferior cannot refute what his superior says. I was careless and wrong when I spoke to you so harshly before. But do not hold it against me, Rāma! You know all there is to know about the goals of life and you are devoted to the well-being of your subjects. You have a clear understanding of cause and effect. I failed in my duties and I violated *dharma*!'

Vālī's eyes filled with tears and he continued, slowly and sincerely, looking at Rāma like an elephant caught in quicksand. 'I have no sorrow for Tārā or any of my other relations, only for my virtuous son, my golden boy, Angada. I have loved him and cared for him since he was a child. He will be miserable without me. Treat Angada and Sugrīva as you would Bharata and Lakṣmaṇa. Correct them when they do wrong and support them when they are right. Make sure that Sugrīva is not harsh with virtuous Tārā. She has done nothing wrong, unless my mistakes are judged to be hers as well.'

Seeing that Vālī was now thinking righteously, Rāma reassured him. 'Do not worry about these things or about the future of your soul, king of the monkeys! I acted on the basis of *dharma.* The wrongdoer who suffers punishment and the one who metes out the punishment have both done their duty and the score has been settled!'

'I was critical of you because the pain from this arrow had clouded my mind!' said Vālī. 'You are Indra's equal! Be gracious to me!'

Meanwhile, Tārā had heard that her husband had been fatally wounded by Rāma in battle. She ran out of her mountain cave with her son, greatly agitated. She saw Angada's mighty retainers fleeing in terror, as fast as if they had been seated on Rāma's arrows, for they had seen Rāma armed with his bow. Tārā stopped and asked the terrified monkeys, 'How can you run like this in fear when you are supposed to be in the vanguard of the forces? How can you run when Vālī is lying there bloodied, killed by Rāma at the insistence of Sugrīva who only wants the kingdom?'

Those monkeys who could change their forms at will had understood the situation well. 'Death has arrived in the form of Rāma and claimed Vālī!' they said to beautiful Tārā. 'Your son is still alive. Turn back and watch over him, lovely lady! When Vālī, who was Indra's equal, was killed, all the monkeys fled in different directions. Protect the city gates and place your son on the throne immediately. The monkeys will rally round Vālī's son if he takes his place!'

Tārā, the one with the lovely smile, cut them short. 'What do I care for the kingdom or my son or myself,' she retorted, 'when my husband, that auspicious lion among monkeys, lies dead! I am going to throw myself at his feet!' and she ran from there weeping, beating her head and breast.

She arrived at the spot where her husband lay, the monkey who had killed *dānavas,* who never fled from battle, who hurled mountains on the battlefield as Indra hurled thunderbolts, whose battle cry was like the rumbling of thunder. She saw Rāma leaning on his bow and she saw Lakṣmaṇa and her husband's younger brother. She ran past them all to where her husband lay on the battlefield and when she saw him, she swooned in grief and fell to the ground. Recovering consciousness, she rose like one who wakes from a deep sleep and seeing Vālī bound by death's noose, she wailed, 'Oh my noble husband!' Sugrīva saw her weeping and noticed that Angada had also arrived and he felt a consuming sadness.

Tārā, with her star-bright face, embraced her husband's body. 'Oh great hero, so ruthless in battle, why do you not speak to me? I stand here before you, utterly wretched! Stand up, tiger among monkeys, and come back to your soft bed. The ground is not an appropriate place for a king like you! Ah! my heart must be hard indeed that it does not shatter into a thousand pieces when I see you dead on the ground! You exiled Sugrīva and took his wife. Now you are paying the price for that!

'But Rāma, who did this terrible thing, killing Vālī while he was fighting another, feels no remorse! And I, who have never known any sorrow, shall burn in the fires of my grief as a widow with no one to protect me. What about my son Angada? He has been raised in the lap of luxury and has known only happiness! How will he live with an uncle who is a slave to anger?

'My son, take a good look at your father, who loved *dharma,* for you shall not see him again. Reassure your son and give him some final advice. Kiss him on the forehead, for you have embarked on your final journey! Rāma did a great thing by killing you and paying off his debt to Sugrīva. You have got what you wanted, Sugrīva, you have Rūmā back. Enjoy your kingship, for your brother who was your enemy is now dead! Why do you not speak to me even as I babble on with love as I weep? Look at all your lovely wives, king of the monkeys!'

Seeing Tārā's distress, all the other female monkeys clung to Angada and began to wail.

Vālī was now breathing with difficulty and his life was ebbing fast. He looked around him and saw Sugrīva standing in front of Angada. 'Sugrīva, do not hold a grudge against me for what I have done!' he said affectionately to the victorious king of the monkeys. 'I did it because my mind was confounded by fate and there is no resisting that! I can only think that we were not destined to enjoy kingship and brotherly love at the same time! Today, you shall take over as the king of the monkeys and I shall go to the abode of death.

'Look at Angada, lying on the ground and weeping! He is still a boy but he is no fool! He has grown up without any hardships and he deserves all happiness. He is dearer to me than life, this son of mine. Look after him as your own and protect his interests at all times. Be his protector and benefactor in times of trouble, as I have been. Tārā's son is equal to you in strength and courage and he will be in he forefront of the battle with the *rākṣasas.* He is young but his performance in battle will be worthy of him in every way.

'Tārā, the daughter of Suṣeṇa, is intelligent and understands the subtleties and nuances of every situation. She can see danger and prepares for it.

You should follow her advice without hesitation. Her judgement is flawless and she is never wrong. Do Rāma's work without thinking twice. To not do so would be unrighteous. But do not slight him for he will punish you! Take this celestial golden necklace, Sugrīva. I will not need its glory when I am dead!'

Sugrīva's elation vanished before Vālī's affection like a moon under an eclipse, and he began to feel wretched and sad. His resentment disappeared and eager to follow Vālī's instructions, he stepped forward to receive the necklace. Vālī was ready to give up his life, but then his eye fell on his son.

'Receive the good and the bad with equanimity,' he said lovingly. 'Learn to understand what is appropriate for time and place and always listen to Sugrīva. Do not ally yourself with his enemies or those that oppose him. Be restrained. Devote yourself to your king and obey his orders at all times!'

Vālī's eyes rolled upwards, and baring his teeth in a grimace of pain, he fell back, dead. His subjects were distracted and confused like cows in a forest frequented by lions, when the leader of the herd dies. Tārā was plunged into an ocean of grief as she gazed at her husband's lifeless face. She threw herself on the ground beside Vālī like a creeper entwined around a tree that has been cut down.

'You would not listen to me and now you lie here on this hard, bare ground, covered with stones!' wept Tārā as she kissed Vālī's dead face. 'The earth must be dearer to you than I am for you lie here in her embrace and you do not even speak to me! You lie on a hero's bed on this battlefield, where you yourself killed so many enemies in the past!

'Ah! my hero, so eager to fight! Your bloodlines were pure and noble! You looked after me so well, and now you have left me unprotected! No thinking man should ever marry his daughter to a valiant warrior. Look at me, widowed and destroyed in an instant! A woman without a husband is considered vulnerable, no matter how many children she has, or how much wealth or how much grain!

'You lie in a pool of your own blood, as you used to lie in your bed with its blood-red quilt! Your body is covered with dust and blood but I cannot hold it in my arms. Sugrīva gained his objectives with a single arrow. Rāma liberated him from this deadly enmity as well as from the fear that shadowed him. I can only look at your dead face. I cannot even hold you because of the arrow that sticks out of your heart!'

Nīla pulled the arrow out of Vālī's body and it emerged like a poisonous snake that had hidden in a rocky crevice. It shone like the sun as it sets behind the mountains and blood poured forth from Vālī's many wounds like mountain waterfalls carrying coppery ore. Tārā wiped the dust from the battlefield off her husband's body and bathed him with her tears.

'Excess grief is of no help to the dead,' said Rāma practically to Sugrīva when he noticed that all life had left Vālī's body. 'You must now get on with the task at hand. You have shed enough tears, now do what is required for worldly life. Everything has its proper time and place.'

Lakṣmaṇa organised Vālī's cremation and helped Sugrīva perform the last rites for the king of the monkeys. Then Hanumān, the son of the Wind, his face shining like the rising sun, joined his palms and said to Rāma, 'Thanks to you, Sugrīva has gained the lordship of the monkeys, which is hard to obtain and which has come down from his forefathers. With your permission, he would like to enter the city and begin the tasks of administration in consultation with his supporters. Come with us to our beautiful city set in a hollow of the hills! Accept our loyalty and make us all happy!'

'Hanumān, by the orders of my father, I am pledged not to enter a city or a village for fourteen years. But let Sugrīva enter his city and be crowned king of the monkeys without any further delay,' said Rāma. Then he turned to Sugrīva. 'Anoint Angada your heir!

'This is the first month of the rainy season which will last for four months. The rains are heavy and this is not the right time for us to start on our expedition. Go into your city and Lakṣmaṇa and I will live here on this mountain. The cave is large and pleasant and the area abounds in water and lotus ponds. We shall start on our journey to kill Rāvaṇa in the month of Kārtik. Now that we have agreed on this, go back and crown yourself among your friends and well-wishers and give them cause to celebrate.'

Sugrīva returned to the city of Kiṣkindha which had been under Vālī's protection and thousands of monkeys surrounded him and greeted him joyfully. All kinds of monkeys, from the common and ordinary to the noble and high-born, bowed low and prostrated themselves at his feet. Valiant Sugrīva spoke to them all kindly and raised them up from the ground and then he entered his brother's beautiful palace. When he emerged, his friends and supporters crowned him the way Indra had been crowned by the gods.

# *Chapter Thirty-Nine*

Meanwhile, Rāma went with Lakṣmaṇa to Mount Prasravaṇa, which was full of deer and tigers and fierce, roaring lions. It was heavily wooded and thick creepers covered the trees and bushes. Bears, different kinds of monkeys and wild cats also lived on this mountain where fresh, clear water was plentiful, and which was as huge as a bank of clouds.

Rāma and Lakṣmaṇa settled in a long, wide cave at the top of the mountain. But though they lived on such a pleasant and bounteous mountain, Rāma was not happy. He thought constantly about his abducted wife who was dearer to him than life. He would lie down every night, but the beauty of his surroundings made it impossible for him to sleep. Never really free from sadness, Rāma would find his eyes brimming with tears at times like this. But his brother, who was equally unhappy, would plead with him.

'You must stop grieving like this! It does not become you. You know all is lost when you succumb to grief! You believe in destiny, in the value of human effort, and you also believe in the gods. You are righteous and enterprising. You cannot overcome your enemy if you do not pull yourself together. Especially since he is a *rākṣasa* who uses unfair tactics in battle. Pull out your sorrow from its roots and then you will be able to destroy the roots and the branches of the *rākṣasa's* tree with a sincere effort! You can turn the world with its forests and oceans and mountains upside down! What of Rāvaṇa? I am only trying to rouse the valour that sleeps inside you with my words, like a fire is raised from smouldering ashes when oblations are added at the right time!'

Rāma considered Lakṣmaṇa's sound advice which was intended for his benefit. 'Ah, Lakṣmaṇa! You have spoken sweetly to me, brave words that are imbued with love and intended for my welfare,' he said affectionately. 'I shall cast off my grief and revive the spirit that makes me triumph against all odds. We are in the middle of the rains now so I shall wait for the autumn. Then I shall destroy the *rākṣasa* along with his forces and his kingdom!'

One day, Rāma said, 'The rainy season has begun. Look at the sky covered with mountainous clouds! It is as if the sky drank the ocean's essence through the rays of the sun and after holding it in her womb for nine months, now puts it forth! You feel as if you could climb to the sky on this ladder of clouds and place a garland of flowers around the sun. The sky is like a pining lover, the gentle breeze his sighs, the evening clouds the sandalpaste upon his chest, the white clouds the pallor of his face.

'The earth parched by the summer heat and now flooded with water reminds me of Sītā shedding tears after being scorched by her grief. The mountain covered with flowers is drenched by the rains as Sugrīva was drenched in auspicious liquids when he was anointed king. The sky, struck with lightning's golden whip, cries out in pain in a rumble of thunder. And the lightning flashing across the dark clouds makes me think of Sītā writhing in Rāvana's dark arms!

'Look at the flowers on the hillside, Lakṣmaṇa! They rejoice in the fresh rainwater and make me think of love, even though I am so depressed. The dust has settled, the breezes have cooled and the discomforts of summer have passed. Kings have stopped their expeditions and all the travellers have returned home. Streams flow swift and sure, tinted red with the ores in the mountain soils. They carry flowers with them and peacocks call from their banks.

'Clouds as big as mountains, which have lightning as their banners and flocks of cranes as their garlands, rumble like rutting elephants on a battlefield. Cranes are drawn to the clouds by desire and fly around them in formation, like a garland of white lotuses that streams in the wind across the sky. Sleep comes as slowly as a river moving to the ocean, but the crane rushes to the cloud and the woman runs to her lover.

'Elephants enjoy themselves inhaling the fresh fragrance of flowers. Excited by the sounds of waterfalls, they trumpet in time with the peacocks' calls. An elephant walks along familiar paths in the hills and hearing the rumble of distant thunder he thinks it is a rival elephant trumpeting and turns back, eager to fight. Birds of many colours, anxious to quench their parched throats, drink the drops of water that hang like crystals on the leaves and have been sent to them by the lord of the forests.

'This is the month in which the *brahmins* of the Sāma Veda begin their studies in the correct modes of chanting. Bharata, king of Kosalā, must have finished with his administrative activities and should be starting on the vows and rituals for the month of Aṣādha. The river Sarayū must be swelling with water the way the noise will swell when I return to Ayodhyā.

'Sugrīva has defeated his enemy and regained his kingdom and his wife. He must be enjoying these torrential rains. But I have lost my wife and my kingdom, Lakṣmaṇa, and I suffer like the banks of a river which are being slowly eroded. My grief is boundless, the rains seem endless and Rāvaṇa is a deadly enemy! How will I ever overcome all this, Lakṣmaṇa?

'I did not suggest that we start on our enterprise, even though Sugrīva would have been amenable, because I knew that the roads would be impassable and that travelling would be dangerous. Besides that, Sugrīva has suffered and been separated from his women for a long time. My mission is very important, but I did not want to start on it then. When he has rested and recovered, I am sure Sugrīva himself will remember that the time has come to start. I have no doubt that he will remember his debt to me.

'So I wait for that time, the time when Sugrīva and the rivers will be gracious to me! A good man always returns the favour done to him!'

'The king of the monkeys will soon do as he promised,' said Lakṣmaṇa. 'Wait patiently for the rains to end and autumn to begin. Stay firm in your resolve to destroy the enemy!'

After four months, the sky was clear of clouds and lightning. It was filled, instead, with the sounds of cranes and was bathed in a gentle moonlight. Sugrīva had achieved his ends and seemed disinclined towards the path of righteousness. He was obsessed with the gratification of his senses. He turned away from all his official duties and spent his time indulging all his pleasures. Not only had his own wife been restored to him, he now had Tārā as well and he had always desired her. He spent all day and all night enjoying himself with them, with not a care in the world. Sugrīva played all day like the gods with the *apsarases* in Nandana. He had handed over all the affairs of the state to his ministers and did not even bother to supervise them.

Hanumān knew what was appropriate for time and place, he knew *dharma* and he understood the need of the hour. He approached Sugrīva with sweet words and gentle talk to put him in a good mood. Then he spoke to him about his duties, about conciliation and the return of favours.

'You have regained your kingdom and with that you have acquired fame and fortune. Gaining friendships is all that is left and you should attend to that now. He who stands by his friends at the appropriate time augments his own fame, his kingdom and his strength. You have always held to the traditional code of conduct. You should see to the fulfilment of your friend's goals as you had promised. He who fails to help his friend at the right time will never gain his specific goal, however hard he tries and whatever else he gains.

'Let us start on Rāma's venture and begin the search for Sītā. It is long overdue! Rāma knows the appropriate time for action and he knows that the moment for beginning the search is passing. But he will not remind you of this because he expects you to remember it yourself. Mighty Rāma is your well-wisher and he supports your entire clan. His skills and strength are immeasurable and his virtues unrivalled. He did what you wanted. Now you should do what he wants. Get the best of the monkeys started on his task.

'King of the monkeys, you help even those who do nothing for you. You must help the one who has helped you regain your kingdom and your wealth. You are strong and powerful and can do what will please Rāma. Why do you delay? Rāma can subdue the gods, the *asuras* and the *uragas* with his arrows, but he looks to you and your promise to help him with his task. He helped you at the risk of his life. Let us begin searching the earth and the heavens for Sītā. Not the gods nor the *gandharvas,* the *asuras, yakṣas* or the troops of *māruts* hold any fear for Rāma, what then is a mere *rākṣasa*? King of the monkeys, we would go anywhere, to the forests, waters or the sky, at your command! There are hundreds of thousands of monkeys, strong and powerful, who will do anything you ask!'

Now that he had been reminded of his duty at the appropriate time, the virtuous Sugrīva made a decision. He summoned Nīla and instructed him to call in all the monkeys from all directions. 'Tell the army commanders and their forces to assemble here immediately. Call in even the swift and brave monkeys who guard the borders of the kingdom. See to it personally that my orders are carried out. Any monkey who is not here within fifteen days shall be punished with death, let there be no doubt about this!' Once he had given these instructions, Sugrīva retired to the inner apartments again.

Meanwhile, Rāma had lived through the rainy season and was now tormented with grief. He gazed in anguish at the clear sky and the white orb of the moon. On those autumn nights bathed in moonlight, he thought about Sugrīva who had attained his ends and about Sītā's absence. He saw that the time he and Sugrīva had agreed upon had passed. But he controlled his anger and, sitting on top of that mountain streaked with metallic ores, his thoughts turned to Sītā.

'Ah! My beloved! Her voice was as sweet as a bird's! How can she rejoice in birdsong now as she used to in our forest hut? How can she enjoy these golden flowering bushes like she used to when I was by her side? How must she feel now when she hears birds calling to their mates? I feel no joy in wandering through the woods with their streams and pools without doe-eyed Sītā by my side!' cried Rāma, lord of all men, lamenting like the *cātaka* bird begging the gods for water.

Lakṣmaṇa came home from a pleasant walk on the hillside to collect fruit and found Rāma in this state. Seeing that his brother was consumed by grief and was sitting despondent in a lonely place, valiant Lakṣmaṇa said, 'Why have you succumbed to the pain of separation and longing and allowed your manly spirit to be sapped? You must be firm and resolute and not fritter away your energies. If you are going to achieve your purpose, you must be active, you must concentrate your mind. Display your courage and utilize the strengths of your allies. Sītā cannot be so easily snatched away when she has you as a protector. How can one touch a flame and not be burned?'

Rāma listened carefully to Lakṣmaṇa's sympathetic words that were just, filled with *dharma* and intended for his benefit. 'Certainly, we must get on with our mission in such a way that we ensure its success,' he said. 'But should we also not think about the reward that awaits us at the end?' And Rāma's thoughts turned back to the lotus-eyed Sītā. Scorched by grief, he continued, 'The god of the rains has gratified the earth with water and now that his task is done, he is at rest. The clouds have shed their load of water with pleasant rumblings and, exhausted, they sail lightly over the mountaintops. The storm winds, which were filled with rain and, laden with the scent of flowers, pushed the clouds along, have died down, their task complete.

'All of a sudden, thunder clouds, waterfalls, elephants and peacocks have fallen silent. Mountain peaks have been washed clean by the great clouds and now they seem painted in bright colours and shine like rays of moonlight. The autumn streams slowly reveal their sandbanks like a modest woman revealing her breasts during her first experience of love.

'This is the time, Lakṣmaṇa, when kings set out on expeditions against their enemies and those they want to conquer. This is the time when journeys begin. But I see no sign of Sugrīva or of our expedition! The four months of the rainy season have gone by but for me, tormented by grief, they have seemed like a hundred years! I live here, deprived of my wife and kingdom, but Sugrīva has no sympathy for me, Lakṣmaṇa! "Without his kingdom, with no protection, harassed by Rāvaṇa, pathetic, lovelorn and far from home, he has come to me for refuge!" That is what the wicked king of the monkeys thinks of me. He regards me with contempt.

'Sugrīva knows the time has come to begin the search for Sītā. But now that he has what he wants, he behaves irresponsibly! Go to Kiṣkindha and find that idiot king of the monkeys! Give him this message from me— "The lowest of all creatures is he who raises the hopes of those who come to him for help, those who have helped in the past and who are quite capable of enforcing what is due to them! The best of men stick to their word, whether it is given rightly or wrongly. Obviously, you want to see me draw my bow, decorated with gold, that flashes like lightning on the battlefield! You wish to hear again the thunderous resonance of my bowstring as I draw it back in anger!" threatens Sugrīva

'It is quite amazing that even though Sugrīva knows my skills and my power and knows that I have you by my side, he still does not seem to care. Absorbed in his pleasures, the king of the monkeys does not seem to have noticed that the season of the rains is over. Drunk all the time, he enjoys himself with his ministers and spares not a single thought for us here, tormented and miserable.

'Go to Sugrīva and tell him how angry I am! Tell him, also, "The road that Vālī took is not yet closed! Stick to your commitment, Sugrīva, and do not follow Vālī down that path! I killed Vālī with a single arrow. I can also kill you and your entire family!" You know what is appropriate, Lakṣmaṇa! Tell him whatever else you like after you have assessed the situation, keeping in mind that the moment is passing!'

# Chapter Forty

Lakṣmaṇa understood that his brother was depressed and miserable as well as angry. 'The king of the monkeys is unrighteous! He does not realize that today he is reaping the fruits of his past actions. He will not enjoy this royal splendour for much longer and so he chooses to ignore our task. Like a fool, he immerses himself in pleasure and does not think about repaying your kindness. Such immoral creatures should not be given kingdoms! I cannot control my anger! I shall kill him and he can join his brother Vālī! Vālī's son can go out with the best of monkeys and recover Sītā!' said Lakṣmaṇa and he leapt up and grabbed his bow.

'The best of men is the one who can control his anger,' said Rāma calmly, choosing his words carefully. 'Behaving like this is not worthy of you. Act in the spirit of our alliance. Do not be harsh. Speak sweetly and only remind Sugrīva that the time for beginning our enterprise is slipping away.'

Lakṣmaṇa took his brother's words to heart and entered the city. Wise Lakṣmaṇa, devoted to his brother's well-being, controlled his anger and went towards the monkey's palace. Tall as Mount Mahendra and looking like Death, Lakṣmaṇa carried his mighty bow that rivalled Indra's and gleamed like a mountain peak. As he walked along, he rehearsed in his mind what he would say to Sugrīva, what Sugrīva's answer might be and what he would say in return.

Filled with the fire of his brother's anger, Lakṣmaṇa was not in a good mood as he strode towards the city like an approaching hurricane. His lips trembled with rage and soon, he saw immense monkeys outside Kiṣkindha. The monkeys noticed Lakṣmaṇa coming towards them and at once, those monkeys who were the size of elephants, armed themselves with boulders and trees. Lakṣmaṇa's fury doubled, like a fire replenished with fuel, when the monkeys armed themselves. The monkeys saw that he was incensed, that he blazed like the doomsday fire, so they fled in their hundreds in all directions.

They ran to Sugrīva's palace and told him about the arrival of the enraged Lakṣmaṇa. But Sugrīva, totally absorbed in making love to Tārā, did not hear them. His ministers ordered a band of monkeys, as dark and immense as mountains, to go forth from the city to confront Lakṣmaṇa. Fierce and cruel-looking, the monkeys had the valour of lions and they used their teeth and nails as weapons. But Lakṣmaṇa grew angrier still when he saw the monkeys guarding Kiṣkindha and when he thought of his brother's frustrations and Sugrīva's addiction to pleasure.

Angada approached Lakṣmaṇa with some trepidation. 'Tell Sugrīva that I have come, my child,' roared Lakṣmaṇa, his eyes blazing. 'Tell Sugrīva, "Rāma's younger brother Lakṣmaṇa stands at your door, burning with grief at his brother's suffering. Lakṣmaṇa, the subduer of his foes, has come to see you!"' Angada ran to tell his uncle that Lakṣmaṇa had arrived.

Meanwhile, the monkeys watched Lakṣmaṇa bearing down upon them like an angry flood. They raised a hue and cry in their terror which sounded like the rumbling of thunder. Their noise woke Sugrīva and he rose, his eyes red and rolling back in his head with drunkenness, his garlands dishevelled, his ornaments awry. Two of his ministers, who had heard Angada's news, came with him, for they were intimate with Sugrīva and were allowed into the presence of his women.

Plakṣa and Prabhava, Sugrīva's advisors on *artha* and *dharma,* told him about Lakṣmaṇa. 'Rāma and Lakṣmaṇa are righteous and honourable and they made an alliance with you. They are worthy of kingship themselves and they gave you a kingdom. One of them, Lakṣmaṇa, stands at your door, armed with his bow. The monkeys tremble and weep for fear of him. He has come here at Rāma's command. Go with your son and your family and prostrate yourself at his feet. Calm his anger. Honour your promise and fulfil your commitment, O king!'

Eloquent Sugrīva rose from his seat and presented the proposition to be considered before his wise and experienced ministers.

'I have neither said nor done anything wrong. Why is Lakṣmaṇa so angry? My enemies are always looking to harm me and they must have carried tales of my imagined lapses to Lakṣmaṇa! Use all your wisdom and experience to try and understand what his behaviour indicates. I have nothing to fear from Rāma or Lakṣmaṇa, but when a friend is angry for no apparent reason, one tends to get confused and bewildered. Making friends at any time is easy, but maintaining a friendship is difficult. The heart is so fickle that even a trivial thing can ruin a friendship. That is what worries me, for I can never hope to repay Rāma for all that he has done for me!' he seems to forget what he owes him

After deliberating privately, Hanumān offered his conclusions in front of all the ministers. 'No one is surprised that you recall Rāma's affectionate favour to you, king of the monkeys! Heroic Rāma set aside all fear and killed Vālī, who was Indra's equal, in order to make you happy. I am sure Rāma has sent his brother here in anger because of your agreement.

'Though you are the foremost among those who know the right time to act, you have been otherwise engaged and seem not to have noticed that autumn has come. The time to begin our mission has arrived. It is clear that you have been rather careless. That is why Lakṣmaṇa has come here. Do not resent the harshness of Rāma's message. He is in terrible pain because of the separation from his wife. You have made a mistake, and I see no course of action other than appeasing Lakṣmaṇa with joined palms.

'Ministers are appointed to give kings advice that will benefit them. So I have given you my opinion without fear of reprisal. Go to Lakṣmaṇa with your son and your family and bow your head before him. Honour your promise and fulfil your commitment, O king!'

Following Rāma's orders, Lakṣmaṇa, the destroyer of enemy heroes, entered the huge city of Kiṣkindha that was built into the side of a mountain. The enormous monkeys standing at the gates bowed to him respectfully, but when they saw that he was angry and breathing heavily, they were apprehensive and stayed away from him.

Lakṣmaṇa looked around the city nestling in the valley with its jewel-studded buildings and flower-filled gardens. Full of elegant mansions and shops, Kiṣkindha overflowed with trees which flowered and fruited all through the year. The monkey citizens were the children of gods and *gandharvas* and they could change their forms at will. They were beautiful to behold in their fine clothes and celestial garlands. Kiṣkindha's roads were perfumed with flowers and sandal paste and the fragrance of natural liquors like mead and toddy wafted through the air. Lakṣmaṇa saw the homes of the great monkey chiefs and the wide thoroughfares that gleamed like white clouds. They were decorated with celestial flowers, filled with wealth and grain and adorned by women who shone like jewels.

The king's palace rivalled Indra's. It was surrounded by sparkling white walls which were hard to breach. It had several white towers like the peaks of Mount Kailāsa. Its garden had trees gifted by Indra that gave any kind of fruit that you could wish for. They were covered with flowers and provided generous, soothing shade.

Mighty Lakṣmaṇa entered Sugrīva's palace uninvited, as the sun enters a huge cloud. He passed through seven courtyards before he came to the heavily guarded inner apartments which were filled with couches of gold and silver and seats covered with rich and beautiful brocades. Lakṣmaṇa could hear soft and melodious music as he walked in and he saw scores of women, all of them revelling in their youth and beauty. They sat there, adorned with rare flowers and exquisite jewels, weaving garlands. Lakṣmaṇa could not see a single retainer who was lazy, discontented or not fully adorned.

Finally, he saw Sugrīva sitting on a golden couch covered by a priceless brocade, shining like the sun. Around him sat beautiful women adorned with flowers and jewels. In his fine clothes and celestial jewels and garlands of flowers, Sugrīva appeared like Indra himself as he sat with Rūmā in his arms. The golden monkey stared at indomitable Lakṣmaṇa with his large eyes.

Sugrīva was terribly agitated when he realized that Lakṣmaṇa had entered the palace unhindered. He saw that Lakṣmaṇa was breathing heavily and was blazing with splendour, that he was clearly angry about his brother's suffering. Sugrīva leapt up from his seat and his women rose with him, making him seem like the moon surrounded by stars in the sky. He stood trembling before Lakṣmaṇa, his eyes red and his palms joined.

'A king gains renown in the world by being honourable, truthful, noble, self-controlled, compassionate and grateful to those who have helped him,' said Lakṣmaṇa angrily. 'There is no one more cruel and heartless than an unrighteous king who makes false promises to those who have helped him. He who does not fulfil his commitments after making use of his friends deserves to be killed by all creatures!

'You are a base and ungrateful liar, monkey! You made use of Rāma's skills and you have not repaid him! If you have any memory of what

Rāma did for you, you should now be making efforts to find Sītā! You have indulged in all these vulgar pleasures and you have broken your promise. Rāma did not recognize you for what you are, a snake imitating a frog! Moved by pity, the great-souled Rāma secured the monkey kingdom for you, you wretched creature! If you can't remember what blameless Rāma did, then, slain by these arrows, you shall soon meet Vālī! The road that Vālī took is not yet closed. Keep your promise, Sugrīva, and do not go the way of Vālī! You have obviously not seen the arrows which fly like thunderbolts from the bows of the Ikṣvāku heroes! That is why you indulge yourself and pay no attention to Rāma's affairs!'

'You should not say such things, Lakṣmaṇa,' cautioned Tārā with her star-bright face. 'The king of the monkeys does not deserve these harsh words, especially from you! Sugrīva is not deceitful. Nor is he cruel or ungrateful. He is neither dishonest nor a liar. He has not forgotten what Rāma did for him, which was something others would have found hard to accomplish on the battlefield.

'It is thanks to Rāma that Sugrīva regained the ancient kingdom of the monkeys as well as Rūmā and me! Sugrīva has found himself amidst these pleasures after so many nights of deprivation and he has lost track of time, just as the sage Viśvāmitra did! When Viśvāmitra was infatuated with Ghṛtāci, didn't he find that ten years had passed like a single day? If even a sage like Viśvāmitra, who understands and knows everything about time, could lose track of its passing, what then of ordinary creatures like us? Rāma should forgive this obsession with sensual pleasures in someone who has been deprived for so long and who, despite these gratifications, is still not satisfied.

'And you, my child, should not get angry like this, like a common man, without really knowing Sugrīva's intentions. Resolute men like you should not succumb to such bursts of passion! You know *dharma.* I plead with you on Sugrīva's behalf not to hold on to your indignation. Calm yourself. I know Sugrīva would give up everything, the kingdom, Rūmā and me, just to make Rāma happy!

'Sugrīva will kill Rāvaṇa in battle and restore Sītā to Rāma. You know that there are thousands of *rākṣasas* in Lankā. Without killing those fearsome creatures who can change form at will, you cannot hope to kill Rāvaṇa. They cannot be killed without allies, Lakṣmaṇa. Especially Rāvaṇa, he cannot be killed without assistance.

'Mighty monkeys have already been despatched to summon hundreds of monkey chiefs to fight in this war for your sake, Lakṣmaṇa. Sugrīva has not set forth himself because he is waiting for the arrival of these powerful and magnificent monkeys who will support Rāma's cause. Sugrīva sent out these instructions long before you came and the monkeys should arrive here today. Get rid of your anger, subduer of enemies. Hundreds of thousands of monkeys and bears will join you today!'

Lakṣmaṇa was gentle by nature and he accepted Tārā's conciliatory words. When Sugrīva saw that he had been placated, he cast off his fear of Lakṣmaṇa as one would cast off wet clothes. He tore off his garland made of rare and beautiful flowers and ripped it apart as he shrugged off his intoxication.

'Lakṣmaṇa, it was thanks to Rāma that I regained the ancient kingdom of the monkeys and this royal splendour,' said Sugrīva humbly, his palms joined. 'How can I ever hope to repay that god-like man for the great deed he performed? Rāma will kill Rāvaṇa and get Sītā back with his own powers, I shall only be a helper! How can anyone help the man who can pierce seven *sāla* trees with a single arrow? If I have transgressed the bounds of our friendship by presuming too much, then you must forgive me. Who is there that has never offended a friend?'

'My brother has all the support he needs with you as an ally, especially since you are so affectionate!' said Lakṣmaṇa, pleased with Sugrīva's words. 'You deserve the kingdom and all its pleasures, Sugrīva, because of your pure heart and your openness. I have no doubt that with your help, Rāma will soon slay all his foes in battle!

'What you have just said, Sugrīva, shows that you know *dharma,* that you are grateful and that you are not likely to turn and flee in battle. Where would my brother and I find another like you, best of monkeys, one who admits to a fault even when he has the capacity to cover it up? You are Rāma's equal in strength and courage and you were sent by the gods to be his ally!

'But come quickly with me now, and console your friend who grieves so desperately for his lost wife! You must pardon the harsh words that I spoke after hearing Rāma's lamentations!'

# *Chapter Forty-One*

Sugrīva turned to Hanumān, who stood at his side, and said, 'Summon all the monkeys who live in all corners of the world by donations, conciliation and diplomacy! I know we have already sent messengers to them, but send more monkeys out after them to hurry them up. Bring all the monkeys here at once, even the ones engaged in making love and those that are inclined to be slow. If they are not here within ten days, they shall be killed for disobeying their king!

'There are thousands of millions of monkeys under my command. Let them all be brought into my presence. Send out the immense monkeys that are the size of clouds and who blot out the sky to make my commands known to all! Send out the monkeys who know where all the other monkeys live on the earth!'

Hanumān did as he was instructed and sent the powerful monkeys out in all directions. Wherever they found other monkeys, in the forests, in the mountains, in the seas and lakes, they urged them to come forward and help Rāma. And the monkeys came because they feared Sugrīva who was their king of kings and who was as formidable as death.

Three hundred million monkeys, black as kohl, came from the Añjana mountain, one hundred million dazzling golden monkeys came from the sunset mountains, hundreds of millions, tawny as a lion's mane, came from Mount Kailāsa, a thousand million who live on roots and fruits came from the Himālayas. Hundreds of millions came from the Vindhyas and they were as fierce as Mars and capable of terrible things. Countless numbers came from the shores of the ocean of milk where they dwelt in palm groves and lived on coconuts. The monkey forces came over the hills and the valleys and the rivers, drinking up the sun, as it were.

The swift-footed monkeys who had gone out as messengers returned first. Within an hour, they had come back to Sugrīva. They gave him the roots and fruits and rare medicinal herbs they had gathered on the way and said, 'We have been everywhere, to the mountains and the oceans and the forests, and all the monkeys are coming here in obedience to your commands!' Sugrīva was delighted and gladly accepted all the gifts they had brought him.

He dismissed the monkeys who had accomplished the task assigned to them, feeling sure that he and Rāma were well on their way to achieving their goal. 'Let us leave Kiṣkindha, if you are ready!' said Lakṣmaṇa politely. Sugrīva agreed and sent Tārā and the other women away.

He called for his retainers in a loud voice, and those that were allowed into the presence of the royal women came quickly and stood with their palms joined. Their king, who shone like the sun, told them to prepare his palanquin. Lakṣmaṇa and Sugrīva climbed into that golden vehicle which shone like the sun. It was a joy to behold and was carried by a group of exceptionally strong monkeys. Surrounded by hundreds of fierce monkeys who were armed with all kinds of weapons, Sugrīva went to see Rāma.

He dismounted and approached Rāma with his palms joined and the other monkeys did the same. Rāma saw the huge army of monkeys which looked like a pool of lotuses and was very pleased with Sugrīva. He raised the king of the monkeys who had prostrated himself at his feet and embraced him with affection and regard.

He asked Sugrīva to sit down and then he said, 'A true king is one who divides his time proportionately between the affairs of the state and pleasure. He who pursues only pleasure and neglects *dharma* and material gain is like a man who goes to sleep in a tree and wakes only when he has fallen out of it. A king who destroys his enemies and is devoted to the welfare of his friends enjoys the fruits of all three goals of life. He lives in accordance with *dharma.* The time to begin our enterprise has arrived, destroyer of enemies! Now confer with your ministers and advisors!'

'It is thanks to you that I have been restored to fame and glory and have regained the ancient kingdom of the monkeys!' said Sugrīva. 'You and your mighty brother helped me achieve this. And he who does not repay a kindness is the worst of men.

'Here are hundreds of monkeys who have brought thousands of other monkeys with them from the ends of the earth. There are bears and fierce cow-tailed monkeys who know their way through the most impenetrable forests. Monkeys who are the sons of gods and *gandharvas* and who can change their shapes at will are coming with their huge armies. Monkeys whose valour compares with Indra's, monkeys who live in the Vindhyas and are the size of the mountains Meru and Mandara, hundreds of thousands of millions of monkeys are on their way here! They will kill Rāvaṇa and his family and bring Sītā back to you!'

Rāma's eyes grew wide in astonishment, like a blooming lotus, when he saw the size of the expeditionary force that Sugrīva had gathered and he was very pleased.

At that very moment, a huge cloud of dust arose which blotted out the sharp, hot rays of the sun. It covered the sky and obscured the directions. The ground began to shake. The entire surface of the earth was covered with countless numbers of immensely strong monkeys, large as mountains, with sharp teeth and nails. In a matter of minutes, the area was overrun with monkey chiefs and their millions of followers, all of whom could change form at will. There were powerful, mighty monkeys from the rivers, seas and mountains as well as those who lived in forests and had voices that rumbled like thunder. The monkeys from all over the earth came there, shouting and roaring, leaping and jumping, and they surrounded Sugrīva the way clouds surround the sun. In their excitement, the monkeys made a terrible din. They bowed their heads to Sugrīva and introduced themselves. Other monkey chiefs were more restrained and they came up to Sugrīva and stood quietly with their palms joined. And Sugrīva, who knew *dharma*, introduced them all to Rāma.

# *Chapter Forty-Two*

Sugrīva, the king of the monkeys, had a great many resources at his disposal. He said to Rāma, the tormentor of his enemies, 'All these powerful monkeys live under my jurisdiction and they can all change their shapes at will. Fierce monkey chiefs have come here with their troops whose courageous exploits have made them feared for their valour. Famous for their strength, they never tire. They can move through mountains and forests and waters with equal facility. Countless in number, they are all at your service. They are loyal and enthusiastic and devoted to the well-being of their master. They will do anything you ask, Rāma! The time has come for us to set out on our expedition. This army is under your command, instruct it as you wish. I know well what has to be done now, but it is for you to issue orders!'

Rāma embraced Sugrīva and said, 'My dear friend, let them find out if Sītā is alive and let them locate the place where Rāvaṇa lives. When they have done that, I will confer with you and decide what should be done next. But it is not for either Lakṣmaṇa or me to direct this enterprise, you should be the one to do it, king of the monkeys! You know what needs to be done, you are my well-wisher and friend. You are devoted to our cause, you are brave and wise and know the appropriate time to act.'

Sugrīva summoned the monkey chief named Vinata and in the presence of Rāma and Lakṣmaṇa addressed him in a voice like thunder. 'Take with you the monkeys that resemble the sun and the moon in their splendour, the ones who know what is suitable for time and place and those who are expedient at completing a task. Take hundreds of thousands of these swift monkeys and go to the hills, forests and rivers of the eastern regions and look for Sītā and for Rāvaṇa's home there.

'Go to the lovely rivers Bhāgīrathī, Sarayū and Kauśikī, to the Yamunā and the mountains in which it rises, to the Sarasvatī, the Sindhu, the Soṇā with its water that sparkles like jewels, to the Mahī and the Kālamahī with their hilly and wooded banks. Search in the kingdoms of Brahmamālā, Mālava, Kosalā, Kāśi, in Magadha's great villages, and in Puṇḍra and Anga. Look in the regions where the silk worm is bred and where silver is mined.

'Look in the hills of Mandara, where there are people with ears that cover their bodies, and people with ears that hang below their lips, and people whose faces seem to be made of iron, people who move quickly on one leg and people who eat the flesh of men. Look where the beautiful golden-skinned hunters with ornaments in their ears live, and where the island people who hunt and eat raw fish live. And among those who live under water and are known as human tigers. Search the hills and the forests there.

'Go to the places that can only be reached by jumping over hills and seas, until you come to the island of Yavadvīpa with its seven kingdoms, where gold and silver is mined. Go beyond Yavadvīpa until you come to the winter mountain Śiśira, whose peaks touch the heavens. Gods and *dānavas* live there. Look among its inaccessible peaks and forests.

'Look for Rāvaṇa and Sītā among the terrifying islands of the ocean. There are enormous *asuras* there who have been hungry for centuries. They catch creatures by their shadows and eat them, for Brahmā has allowed them to do so. Then you will come to the shores of a mighty ocean whose waters are dark as clouds and which rumble like thunder. It is filled with sea serpents. After that, you will see the blood-red waters of the ocean called Lohita. There, you will find Garuḍa's home, studded with jewels, large as Mount Kailāsa, that was built by Viśvakarmā.

'You will see the fierce *rākṣasas* called Mandehas who are as huge as boulders and have many frightening forms, hanging upside down from mountain peaks. Burned by the heat of the sun, every day they fall into the ocean and then they hang upside down again. Then you will see an uncrossable ocean, white as a cloud, known as the Ocean of Milk, its waves like a garland of pearls. In the middle of it, you will find the mountain Ṛṣabha surrounded by trees that flower with a celestial fragrance. After that, you will see Lake Sudarśana, covered with gleaming lotuses which have gold filaments, where swans come to play. *Cāraṇas, yakṣas, kinnaras* and hosts of *apsarases* come to that lotus lake to enjoy themselves.

'And when you have passed beyond the Ocean of Milk, you will come to the greatest ocean of them all, the ocean of pure water, that inspires dread in the hearts of all beings. It is there that the fiery creature, the horse-faced child of anger, was placed. It is said that those swift waters and all moving and unmoving things will be consumed by that fire at the end of time. The sound you hear there is the wailing of the creatures of the deep, for they cannot bear to look upon that horse-faced being.

'On the far side of the ocean, at a distance of thirty *yojanās,* there is a golden mountain called Jātarūpa. Sitting on its summit is a serpent with a thousand heads. The god Ananta, honoured by all beings, sits on it. A golden, triple-headed palm tree, the flagstaff of the deity, rests on the crest of the mountain. Beyond that is the mountain of the rising sun. Its summit ridge touches the heavens and is more than a hundred *yojanās* long. Made of pure gold, it dazzles the eyes. There are all kinds of trees on it, golden and as bright as the sun itself.

'There is a golden peak on that ridge, one *yojanā* high and ten *yojanās* long, called Saumanasa. It was there that Viṣṇu took his first step in his dwarf incarnation, before he took his second step by placing his foot on the top of Mount Meru. The sun travels along the northern edge of Jambūdvīpa and is visible to the people who live there in all its glory. The great *ṛṣis,* the Vālakhilyas and the Vaikhānasas live here, blazing like the sun and practising their austerities.

'Look carefully for Rāvaṇa and Sītā among those peaks and forests. Look there and in all the places I have not mentioned. Nobody can go further east than that, because beyond is the region where the gods live. Because there is no sun and moon there, the region is covered in darkness. Monkeys can go no further than this because there is neither the sun nor anything familiar, and we do not know what lies ahead.

'Go and find Sītā, and Rāvaṇa's home, and having reached the mountain of the rising sun, return here within a month!'

Sugrīva prepared a band of monkeys to go south. Nīla, the son of Agni, Hanumān, the mighty Jāmbavān, son of Brahmā, and several others were placed under the command of valiant Angada.

'Go to the thousand-peaked Vindhya mountain, covered with different kinds of trees, and search in the river Narmadā which is hard to cross and is filled with water serpents, and in the beautiful Godāvarī and the long and winding Kṛṣṇaveṇī. Look through Mekhalā and Utkalā and the cities of Darśana, Aśvavantī and Avantī. Search Vidarbhā, Ṛṣika and the pleasant Māhiṣaka and Banga, Kalinga and Kauśika thoroughly.

'Then scour the Daṇḍaka forest with its hills and rivers and caves. And then the regions of Andhra, Puṇḍra, Chola and Kerala until you come to the Ayomukha mountain that abounds in ore. It is a glorious mountain with its flowering trees and sandalwood groves. Search it thoroughly. Then you shall come upon the celestial stream, the beautiful, clear Kāverī, where the *apsarases* love to play. On top of the Malaya mountain, you will find the *ṛṣi* Agastya, blazing like the morning sun. With his blessings and permission, you can go further and cross the river Tāmraparṇī, filled with crocodiles. The river is hidden by a belt of sandalwood trees and is dotted with islands. It makes its way to the sea like a young girl rushing to her lover.

'Then you will come to the golden walls that guard the Pāṇḍya kingdom, decorated with pearls and other gems. When you reach the ocean, you shall have to decide what to do next. Mount Mahendra, golden and made beautiful by its trees and forests, is on those shores, placed there by Agastya. It has every kind of tree and creeper and the gods, *ṛṣis, yakṣas,* and *apsarases* like to spend time there. Indra comes there at every new moon and the *siddhas* and *cāraṇas* also enjoy it immensely.

'On the far shore of the ocean there is a bright and shining island that is closed to mortals. You must search there very carefully for Sītā. That is where the wicked *rākṣasa* Rāvaṇa, who deserves to die, lives, equal to Indra in his splendour. And in the middle of that southern ocean lives a *rākṣasī* named Angārakā who grabs the shadows of her prey and then eats them.

'One hundred *yojanās* beyond that, further out into the ocean, lies the mountain Puṣpitaka where the *siddhas* and *cāraṇas* come. Bright as the sun and the moon, surrounded by the ocean on all sides, its lofty peaks seem to touch the sky. The sun shines on one of its peaks turning it gold and the moon shines on the other, turning it silver. The cruel, the ungrateful and the non-believers cannot see it, but you should honour it by bowing before it, monkeys!

'Fourteen *yojanās* beyond that, on a path that is rough and inaccessible, is the Suryavān mountain. And when you have crossed that, you will find Mount Vaidyuta, where the trees flower in all seasons and you can find any fruit that you could wish for. Eat your fill there of those excellent roots and fruits and drink that honey before you go on your way.

'Then you will come to Mount Kunjara, which delights the mind and the eye. Viśvakarmā built a home there for Agastya, which is one *yojanā* wide and ten *yojanās* long, made of gold and adorned with celestial jewels. Go to the city of Bhogavatī, home of the mighty serpents. It is surrounded on all sides by fierce and poisonous snakes with sharp fangs and so it is hard to reach. Search carefully in that city which is ruled by the king of the serpents, Vāsuki.

'When you pass beyond Bhogavatī, you will come to a huge mountain shaped like a bull called Mount Ṛṣabha, studded with jewels. Sandal trees that provide pastes of all colours, yellow, red and dark brown, grow there. If you see them, do not touch them, for those forests are guarded by the fierce *gandharva* Rohita. Five *gandharva* kings live there and each of them is as bright as the sun.

'Beyond that lies an inaccessible path that leads to the realm of those enlightened beings who have won a life in heaven. And beyond that, still further, is the realm of the ancestors, the capital city of Yama, the god of death, shrouded in impenetrable darkness. You can go no further than that, monkeys. Explore all the places I have mentioned and any others that you see. Bring back information about Sītā. Whichever one of you returns within a month and says, "I have seen Sītā!" shall get riches equal to my own and will be able to live in comfort. He will be my dearest friend, dearer even than my own life, even if he has harmed me in the past.

'You are all immeasurably strong and brave. You are nobly born and virtuous. Spare no effort in your search for Sītā!'

Sugrīva summoned Suṣeṇa, the mighty monkey chief who was Tārā's father. He joined his palms and bowed to him and addressed him with respect.

'With two hundred thousand monkeys, my dear, go and search the western regions.

'Go to Surāṣṭra, Bāhlika, Sura and Bhīma. Search in the delightful countryside and in the big cities, in all the forests and the groves, in the cool and swiftly flowing streams, in the forests where the ascetics live and in the wooded hills. When you have searched the western region that is circled by mountains, you will come to the western ocean which is filled with fish and other water creatures. The monkeys will be happy when they find themselves in groves of coconut and date palms.

'Look for Sītā and for Rāvaṇa's home in Marīcipaṭṭanam and in the pleasant Jātipura, in Avantī and Angalopā in the dense forests, the kingdoms and the coastal cities. At the point where the river Sindhu flows into the sea, there is an enormous mountain with a hundred peaks, covered with trees. It is called Hemagiri. There are winged lions that live on its slopes and they carry off fish and other water creatures and elephants to their nests. The monkeys who can take any form at will should search this sky-touching mountain with its varied trees carefully.

'The monkeys will see the peaks of the golden mountain Pāriyātra, which is not normally visible, standing out from the ocean. Hundreds of thousands of *gandharvas* live there. They are fierce and as bright as the fire, and they can take any form they choose. The monkeys, even though they are strong and brave, should not go too close to them, nor should they take any fruit from this region. The *gandharvas* are very powerful and courageous and they guard their roots and fruits zealously. Make every effort to find Sītā there and you will have nothing to fear from the *gandharvas* if you behave like monkeys.

'Mount Cakravān occupies about a quarter of that ocean and that is where Viśvakarmā made the disc with a thousand spokes. Viṣṇu killed Pancajana and the *dānava* Hayagrīva there and took the disc and the conch shell from them. Look for Sītā and Rāvaṇa on the broad slopes and deep caves of that mountain.

'In that immeasurably deep ocean stands Mount Varāha, sixty-four *yojanās* high with golden peaks. There is a golden city there called Prāgjyotiśa and the wicked *dānava* Naraka lives there. Look for Sītā and Rāvaṇa on the broad slopes and deep caves of that mountain.

'When you have passed that, you will see a mountain made entirely of gold. Even the insides of its caves and the water that flows from them are gold. Lions and tigers and elephants and boar roar and bellow all the time, taking pride in their own voices. Indra, whose horses are black, was crowned king by the gods on that mountain and it is called Meghavān.

'When you have passed that mountain which is protected by Indra, go to the sixty thousand golden hills that shine like the rising sun and are covered with flowering trees that glow golden. In the middle of them is the king, the best of all mountains, Mount Meru. Long ago, the sun god was pleased with the mountain and gave it a boon. "Whoever comes to you, by day or night, shall be turned into gold by my grace. The gods and the *gandharvas* and *dānavas* that live here shall glow golden and shall be devoted to me!" The gods go to Mount Meru every evening to worship the sun and the sun, after he has received their worship, goes to the mountain behind which he sets and becomes invisible to all creatures. The sun travels ten thousand *yojanās* in half an hour and reaches the top of the mountain.

'There is a huge, shining mansion on its peak that was built by Viśvakarmā. It is surrounded by trees and birds of all kinds gather there. That is the home of the great-souled Varuṇa, who carries the noose. Look for Sītā and Rāvaṇa in those lakes and rivers that are hard to access. The great sage Merusavarṇi lives there. This righteous sage is Brahmā's equal and he glows with his own splendour. Prostrate yourselves before him and ask him where Sītā is.

'When the night is over, the sun lights up the world of living beings by passing from the mountain of the rising sun to the mountain where it sets. Beyond this, it is not possible to go, best of monkeys. Beyond this there is no sun and nothing familiar. Go up to the mountain of the setting sun to look for Sītā and for Rāvaṇa's home and return here within a month. If you do not, I will have to punish you.

'My valiant father-in-law, Suṣeṇa, is going with you. Listen to what he says and obey him at all times. This mighty one is my teacher and mentor. I know that you are all brave and strong and capable of acting by yourselves. But you must search the western region under his direction. When you have found Rāma's wife, we shall have repaid our debt for the favour that he did us.' Sugrīva then summoned the powerful chief Śatabali.

'Take hundreds of thousands of monkeys who are your equals in valour and your ministers and explore the northern region which has Mount Himavān as its crest. Look there for Rāma's blameless wife. When we have accomplished this task, we shall have done what Rāma wants and in doing so, we will have freed ourselves from debt and will have achieved our dearest goal.

'Search the regions of the Mlecchas, of the Pulindas and Sūrasena, the countries of the Prasthalas, the Bharatas, the Kurus, the Madras, the Kambhojas and the Yavanas. Search the coastal lands of the Śākas, the kingdoms of the Bāhlikas, Ṛṣikas, Pauravas and the Ṭankaṇas. Look in China and the regions beyond China, in Nihāra, Daradā and in the Himālayas, among the forests and groves.

'Go to Somāśrama, where the gods and *gandharvas* play, and then on to the golden-peaked Mount Kāla. Look for Sītā in the caves and crevices of that mountain. Crossing over that, you will come to Mount Sudarśana whose insides consist entirely of gold. Look in those forests and streams and caves for Sītā and Rāvaṇa. One hundred *yojanās* from there is a barren waste, with no mountains, trees or rivers and no form of life. Pass through that awful place quickly and make for the white Mount Kailāsa which will bring you great happiness. Kubera's home, white as a cloud and decorated with gold, is situated there. Viśvakarmā built it for him. There is a beautiful pool in his gardens, filled with lotuses and lilies, where hordes of lovely *apsarases* come to play. Kubera, the god of wealth and the king of the *yakṣas*, lives there happily with his *guhyakas,* honoured by all beings. Look for Rāvaṇa and Sītā in those moonlit hills, forests and caves.

'Go carefully into the caves of Mount Kraunca, for they are hard to access and entry into them is not easy. Great celestial sages who shine like the sun live there and even the gods worship them. Search through the peaks and valleys and slopes and caves of this mountain. Look especially carefully on the main peak of the Kraunca mountain as well as on the next mountain which is treeless and on Mount Mānasa, the home of the birds. No beings, not even the gods, *dānavas* and *rākṣasas*, can go there, but you should explore the area carefully.

'After you have crossed Mount Kraunca, you will come to the mountain named Mainaka where the *asura* Maya lives, in a home that he built himself. Search on the slopes of the mountain and in its caves and in the homes of the horse-faced women who live there, wherever those homes may be. Beyond that lies the region in which the *siddhas* and the Vālakhilyas and the Vaikhānasas live in their hermitages, practising austerities. Honour them, for their austerities have made them pure and given them magical powers. Ask them for news of Sītā. Lake Vaikhānasas is covered with lotuses and sun-bright swans play in its waters. The elephant Sarvabhauma, Kubera's mount, wanders in that region with his mates.

'Beyond that lies a region that has neither sun nor moon nor stars, that has neither beginning nor end. But it is illuminated by the god-like people who live there. They have won magical powers and the ability to illuminate themselves by the practise of austerities and they enjoy their leisure in that place. Then you will come to the river Śailoda with its banks of bamboo. These bamboos carry the *siddhas* to the other side of the river and back. Thousands of streams run there, fed by pools with golden lotuses which have petals the colour of lapis. There are huge bodies of water there, covered with lotuses, some the colour of blood, some gold, and some bright as the rising sun. All over the area, there are fields of bright lilies the colour of sapphire with filaments of shining gold. The riverbanks spill the roundest pearls and the rarest gems of every kind. The mountains there blaze like fire. Made primarily of gold, they are filled with gems and jewels.

'The divinely scented trees have fruits and flowers all year round. They fulfil all your wishes and even to touch them is to experience heaven. There are other trees there that produce clothes adorned with pearls and lapis for men and women. There are others that produce golden couches, exquisitely worked and beyond price. Still others produce flowers that have never been seen before and the finest food and drink, even young and lovely women whose charms are irresistible. *Gandharvas, kinnaras, siddhas, nāgas* and *vidyādharas,* bright as the sun, seek their pleasures there with their women. The air is always filled with music and song and laughter that delights the hearts of all creatures. There is no one there who is unhappy, nor anyone who is without his beloved and each day their pleasures and happiness increases.

'Beyond this region lies the northern ocean in the middle of which stands the great golden mountain Somagiri. Those who go to the realms of Indra and Brahmā and the world of the gods can see that king of mountains. Even though the region is sunless, it is lit up by the glow of the mountain. Brahmā, the soul of the universe, lives here, waited on by *ṛṣis.*

'You must not go beyond the Kurus for any reason whatsoever for the regions beyond are closed to all creatures. Even the gods cannot go beyond Somagiri. Take a look at it and return as quickly as you can. The monkeys can go no farther than this. Beyond this there is no sun and nothing familiar. Search in all the places that I have mentioned and also in the places that I have not, as you think best.

'You are like the wind and the fire. When you have accomplished your goal and found Sītā, you will have pleased Rāma, the son of Daśaratha, and gratified me even more! And when you have done that, you will be free to go wherever you want with your families and loved ones. You can seek your pleasure, for I will have honoured you and placed infinite resources at your disposal!'

Sugrīva had a special message for Hanumān because he felt sure that of all the monkeys, he was the one most likely to be successful. 'Not on earth or in the sky, not in the heavens or the abode of the gods, nor in the waters is there anyone to rival your skills, bull among monkeys! You know all the worlds with their oceans and mountains. You know all the gods, the *gandharvas, asuras* and *nāgas* who inhabit them. Mighty monkey, your speed, power, energy and splendour can be compared only to the your father's, the wind god's! There is no creature on earth who is your equal and so I look to you to find Sītā. I find strength and wisdom, courage, knowledge of place and time, as well as familiarity with modes of diplomacy and negotiation in you alone!'

Rāma understood Hanumān's unique gifts and realized that he was particularly well-equipped to make the mission a success. He thought to himself, 'The king of the monkeys clearly feels that Hanumān is the most likely to succeed and so I, too, must assume that he is the most capable of all. He must have proved his capacities by his past achievements for his master to have singled him out like this!'

Rāma gazed at the enterprising monkey with deep satisfaction and felt as if his ends had already been achieved. He gave Hanumān his signet ring with his name engraved upon it so that Sītā would recognize him as a messenger from Rāma. 'By this sign, best of monkeys, Sītā will know that you have come from me and will receive you without fear. Your visible energy, spirit and valour, as well as Sugrīva's words, indicate to me that you shall be successful!'

The great monkey took the ring and honoured it by placing it upon his head. Then he touched Rāma's feet and joined his palms and set off on his journey. At the head of the monkey army, Hanumān, son of the Wind, looked like the moon surrounded by stars in a cloudless sky. 'Son of the Wind, with your strength and courage that rivals a lion's, I depend on you to find Sītā!' said Rāma.

# *Chapter Forty-Three*

The great monkeys, knowing how ruthless and harsh Sugrīva could be, started on their journey, covering the earth like moths. And Rāma continued to live on the Prasravaṇa mountain with Lakṣmaṇa, waiting for the end of the one month that Sugrīva had stipulated for finding Sītā.

Heroic Śatabali set off for the beautiful northern regions ringed by the king of mountains, Himālaya. Vinata went west with his followers. Hanumān, the son of the Wind, went south with Angada to the region where Agastya lived. And Suṣeṇa went to the dreaded west, to the regions guarded by Varuṇa. Now that he had despatched the monkeys, Sugrīva, their king, went back to his happy life.

The monkeys went forth eagerly in their appointed directions. They roared and shouted and yelled in their excitement. 'I shall bring Sītā back!' 'I shall kill Rāvaṇa!' they boasted. 'I will kill Rāvaṇa and pulverize all the other *rākṣasas* that I see! I will be the one who brings Sītā back!' 'Even if I am weak with exhaustion, I shall bring Sītā back, no matter if she is in the underworld!' 'I will uproot trees, tear down mountains, dig up the earth and agitate the ocean!' 'I can leap over the distance of one hundred *yojanās*!' 'I can leap more than that!' 'Nothing can stop me from searching the earth, the ocean, the mountains and the forests, even the underworld!' And so the monkeys, proud of their strength and abilities, bragged and boasted to each other in the presence of their king.

The monkeys did not have too much trouble following Sugrīva's directions as they searched all over for Sītā. They looked everywhere, in lakes and rivers, in wide-open spaces and in thickets, in cities and areas in the mountains that were difficult to get to. They looked in the hills and forests of the regions Sugrīva had mentioned and they divided themselves into smaller groups to scour the area, determined to find Sītā. They would search all day and gather under fruit trees at night to sleep.

When a month had passed, they returned to their king, dejected and forlorn. Mighty Vinata, who had searched the east with his followers as he had been instructed, returned without seeing Sītā. Śatabali, who had searched the north with his forces, returned at the same time. Suṣeṇa, who had searched the west with his monkeys, came back at the end of the month.

They all went to Sugrīva, who was living on the slopes of Prasravaṇa with Rāma, and said, 'We have looked in all the oceans, the mountains, the forests, the rivers, the cities and all the uninhabited places. We have looked in the caves that you mentioned and in the dense jungles overgrown with vines and creepers. We have looked in inaccessible places, in rough and impenetrable regions over and over again. We have seen impossibly huge creatures and we have killed them. But the great-souled Hanumān has gone to where Sītā has been taken and he is bound to find her!'

Meanwhile, Hanumān had gone with Angada to search the region assigned to them and they had started on their task. He went deep into the south with his monkeys and scoured the caves and the thickets of the Vindhyas. The monkeys looked everywhere, on the peaks, in places that were hard to access because of rivers, in lakes, in the huge trees and on other mountains dense with undergrowth, but nowhere did they see Sītā, the daughter of Janaka.

They moved from place to place in their search, living on different kinds of roots and fruits. They crossed over the Vindhyas into the neighbouring region that was barren and frightening. The bare trees bore neither fruit nor flowers. The rivers there ran dry and even roots were hard to find. There were no buffalo, no deer or elephants, no tigers, birds or any other kind of forest animals. There were no pools filled with fragrant lotuses and there were no bees.

The sage Kāṇḍu had once lived there. He was rich in austerities, but he was quick to anger and his solitary life had made him stern. His ten-year-old son had been killed in that forest and so the angry sage had cursed the entire forest, making it inhospitable to birds and animals. But the monkeys searched calmly even through that wilderness with its hills and hollows and thickets. Though they were eager to please Sugrīva, they saw no sign of Sītā or her abductor.

They went further into another frightful forest, thick with bushes and creepers, where they came upon a fearsome *asura* who was not afraid even of the gods. The monkeys saw him standing in front of them, as large as a mountain, and they girded their loins in preparation to attack. The mighty *asura* charged towards them, his clenched fists raised, shouting, 'You are dead!' Angada, the son of Vālī, mistook him for Rāvaṇa and struck him with his open palm. Blood poured from the *asura's* mouth and he fell to the ground like a toppled mountain. Once he was dead, the victorious monkeys resumed their search of the caves. But they found nothing. Exhausted and utterly dejected, they assembled under a tree.

Though he was tired and miserable, Angada spoke gently to the monkeys and comforted them. 'We have looked everywhere, in mountains, forests, rivers and deep caves but we have not find the goddess-like Sītā or the *rākṣasa* who carried her away. A great deal of time has passed. But Sugrīva is a hard taskmaster so we must continue to search. We must ignore our fatigue and disappointment and the drowsiness that steals over us and keep looking until we find Sītā. Enthusiasm, enterprise and a mind that does not give in to defeat are all necessary ingredients for success. That is why I am saying this to you.

'Let us scour this dense and impenetrable jungle today. Raise your spirits and begin the search again! A sincere effort always produces results. Let us not sit around here and wallow in our depression! Sugrīva can mete out terrible punishments when he is angry. We must protect ourselves from his wrath as well as Rāma's! I speak for your benefit. If you agree with me, do as I suggest, otherwise, you had better come up with another plan!'

Gandhamādana spoke up, his voice faint with fatigue and thirst. 'Angada has made a good plan. You should accept his suggestion, monkeys, because it will be for your own good. Let us search through these hills and forests and caves and groves and these desolate mountains again!'

So the mighty monkeys rose and went back into the dense forests of the Vindhyas. They climbed the silver mountain, white as an autumn cloud, and searched among its peaks and valleys, its forests and groves, eager to find Sītā. But even when they reached the top of the mountain, utterly exhausted, they had found no sign of Rāma's beloved. They examined every inch of the mountain and finally, they climbed down, looking around them as they came. They reached the bottom, tired and miserable, and rested for a moment before they reassembled under a tree. Somewhat revived, they began their search of the south all over again. Led by Hanumān, they searched every single inch of the Vindhyas.

They searched among the rocks and the hilly tracts of the mountains that were haunted by lions and tigers and they searched among the fast-flowing streams and waterfalls. And as they searched, the stipulated period of one month approached its end. The caves and crevices were hard to explore, but Hanumān searched them all. They went all over the southern region which was ringed by mountains on one side and the ocean on the other.

Exhausted and tormented by thirst, they finally came upon a cave which was almost entirely hidden by trees and creepers. They saw all kinds of birds flying out of its mouth, their bodies wet and smeared with the pollen from red lotuses. The monkeys were amazed for as they came closer, a delightful fragrance wafted from the cave. But the cave appeared hard to enter and they drew closer, suspicious and on their guard.

Hanumān, large as a mountain and familiar with forested areas, said, 'We are tired and thirsty and though we have looked all over this area ringed by mountains, we have seen no sign of Sītā. But we have seen birds drenched with water coming out of this cave. There must be a stream or a well deep inside it. That would also explain these lush trees at the entrance.'

Following Hanumān, all the monkeys entered the enveloping darkness where no sun or moon was visible, a darkness so frightening, it made their hair stand on end. Inside the cave, there were all kinds of trees and, holding on to each other, the monkeys walked for a distance of about a *yojanā.* Fainting with hunger, thirst and fatigue, the monkeys went still deeper. Depressed and miserable, the monkeys had given up all hopes of survival when they suddenly came upon a wide-open space that was brightly lit.

They found themselves in a pleasant forest where trees of gold blazed like fire and dazzled their eyes. There were all kinds of trees, some of them flowering, all of them as bright as the rising sun. They were surrounded by lapis and by blue lotuses and they were filled by birds. Pools the colour of the young sun teemed with gleaming golden fish and turtles. The monkeys saw huge mansions made of gold and silver by the waters. Their bright windows were decorated with strings of pearls, their gold and silver floors were studded with lapis and rubies. All around them were fruits and flowers that shone like coral and pearls, golden bees and lots of honey. There were couches and seats made of gold and studded with gems, huge vehicles, piles of gold and silver and bronze, heaps of priceless sandal and other unguents, the best and purest food and fruit, excellent drinks of honey and other juices as well as piles of exquisite clothes, carpets and fabrics.

The monkeys looked around the cave in wonder and suddenly, not far from them, they saw a woman ascetic. The monkeys were quite terrified when they saw her: she wore the skin of the black antelope, she obviously ate very little and she blazed with the power of her austerities. Hanumān joined his palms and honoured the old woman. 'Who are you?' he asked. 'Tell us whom this cave, these mansions and these jewels belong to!'

'We came into the impenetrable darkness of this cave by chance,' he continued. 'We were tired and thirsty and wretched. But now that we have seen all the wonderful things inside the cave, we are thoroughly confused and a little frightened. Whom do these trees belong to, that shine like the sun? And these perfect foods and fruits? And these magnificent mansions made of gold and silver with windows decorated with strings of pearls? Whose power created these fruits and flowers with this divine fragrance, and the lotuses in crystal clear water? Are the fish and turtles that swim here really of gold? Is all this your doing? Or has it been created by the power of someone else's austerities? Explain all this to us!'

'There is an immensely powerful *dānava* named Māya,' replied the virtuous woman, who was devoted to the welfare of all beings. 'He created this golden forest with his magical powers. Long ago, he was the architect of the *dānavas* and that was when he built these golden mansions. He practised austerities in the forest for thousands of years and Brahmā gave him the boon of immense wealth. Māya made this forest and lived here happily for many years. But then, he fell in love with the *apsaras* Hemā and Indra killed him with his thunderbolt. Brahmā gave this wondrous forest, this golden house and these resources for unending pleasure to Hemā.

'I am Svyamprabhā, the daughter of Merusavarṇi. I am the caretaker of this forest. My friend Hemā is an excellent dancer and musician and she allows me to take care of her home. What are you doing here? What are you doing in these dense forests and how did you find this magical place?

Eat these wondrous foods, these roots and fruits, and enjoy these marvellous drinks. Then you can tell me everything!'

When the monkeys had refreshed themselves, Hanumān told the ascetic all about the abduction of Sītā, Rāma's alliance with Sugrīva, their own fruitless search in the south and how they had chanced upon the cave. 'You have fulfilled your duties towards your guests by giving us this food. But you have also saved our lives, for we were starving. Tell us what we can do to repay your kindness,' said Hanumān as he finished his tale.

'There is nothing to repay. I only did my duty and I am very pleased with you all,' replied the omniscient ascetic.

Her righteous words moved Hanumān to say to that woman whose conduct was above reproach, 'We beg you to help us, virtuous lady! While we have been in this cave, the time stipulated by Sugrīva has passed. You must help us get out of here and save us from Sugrīva's wrath! We have been entrusted with an immensely important task and we have been unable to pursue it while we have been here.'

'It is impossible to leave this cave alive once you have entered it!' said the ascetic. 'But I shall get the monkeys out with the powers I have earned from my disciplined life and from the practise of austerities. The monkeys will have to close their eyes tightly. No one gets out of here with his eyes open!'

The monkeys covered their eyes with their hands and in an instant the ascetic got them out of the cave. 'This is the auspicious Vindhya mountain covered with trees and creepers,' she said reassuringly. 'That one there is Mount Prasravaṇa and there lies the ocean Mahodadhi. May all go well with you! I must now return to my home!' she said and disappeared into the cave.

The monkeys gazed in horror at the massive ocean with its huge waves that roared and thundered. They realized that the month stipulated by Sugrīva had elapsed while they had been in the magic cave and now, sitting at the foot of the densely wooded Vindhya mountain, the mighty monkeys fell to worrying.

Crown Prince Angada, with shoulders as strong as a lion's and mighty arms, spoke. 'We all left Kiṣkindha under strict instructions from the king. But the month has passed without our knowing. We have no option now but to fast until we die!

'Sugrīva is our king and he is ruthless. He will definitely kill us if we return unsuccessful. He will never forgive us if we return without any news of Sītā. It is better to die here, fasting, than to die at his hands. It was not Sugrīva who made me the heir, it was Rāma! Sugrīva was our sworn enemy before this and now he is our master! I am sure he will not hesitate to inflict a terrible punishment upon me! Why should my friends and family suffer by watching me die? It is far better that I starve to death here by the shores of the sacred ocean!'

The monkeys agreed with what Angada had said. 'Indeed, Sugrīva is cruel by nature and Rāma is madly in love! The month has passed without us getting even a glimpse of Sītā! If we return without success, Sugrīva will definitely kill us to make Rāma happy!' they said.

Tāra heard the frightened monkeys chattering and he said, 'Enough of this sadness! We can go and live in that cave and enjoy ourselves! It is a magical cave and it is difficult to enter. It is filled with trees and water and roots and fruits. We have nothing to fear in there, even from Indra, let alone from Rāma or Sugrīva!' The monkeys heard Tāra's speech that seemed to agree with Angada's plan and they were reassured. 'Do whatever it takes to ensure that we are not punished!' they begged.

At this point, Hanumān realized that Angada had all but won the kingship of the monkeys. He saw Angada growing in power, strength and majesty, like the waxing moon at the beginning of the bright lunar fortnight. Angada, who was as wise as Bṛhaspati and as brave as his father, seemed willing to fall in with Tāra's plan.

Hanumān was devoted to his master and skilled in the arts of politics. He began to create dissension among the monkeys. Once he got the monkeys away from Angada, he started to intimidate Angada with angry threats. 'You are a greater warrior than your uncle and as capable of ruling the monkeys as your father, Angada! But you know that monkeys are fickle by nature. Without their wives and children here, they will soon stop obeying your commands. And let me also tell you, that none of us, not me, not Jāmbavān, Nīla or Suhotra, will join you! You cannot win us over from our allegiance to Sugrīva by offering us bribes or with threats.

'The mighty can fight with the weak and establish themselves, but the weak should never take on the strong if they want to survive. You think this cave is an impregnable defence, but I tell you that Lakṣmaṇa can destroy it with his arrows as if it were nothing! If you decide to stay where you are, the monkeys will desert you in no time. Pining for their wives and children, living in fear and starvation, regretting the hard beds on which they must lie, they will soon turn their backs on you!

'Without your family and friends and your well-wishers, you shall live in terror, frightened even of a trembling blade of grass! And Lakṣmaṇa's arrows, swift, sure and deadly as they are, will haunt you all the time! But if you return with us humbly, Sugrīva will make you king in the course of time. Your uncle loves *dharma.* He is determined to do the right thing and win your affection. His heart is pure and he keeps his promises. He will never kill you! He wants to win your mother's love. In fact, that's what he lives for! Besides that, he has no son of his own. Come back with us, Angada!'

Angada listened to Hanumān's speech which was filled with devotion to his master. 'Steadiness, purity of mind, compassion, resolution and courage are all virtues that Sugrīva lacks!' he replied. 'How can he know and love *dharma* when he takes his elder brother's chief queen as his own, even while his brother is alive? He should regard her as a mother! How can he know *dharma* when he blocked the entrance to the cave while his brother was engaged in combat? How can he be honourable when he made a pact with Rāma and after gaining his own ends, forgot about his part of the bargain?

'He ordered the search for Sītā because he was terrified of Lakṣmaṇa, not because he was reluctant to violate *dharma*! How can it be said that he loves *dharma*? How can a noble and well-born kinsman trust this creature who is fickle and ungrateful, conveniently forgetting the favours that he receives? A son is installed as a successor, whether he is good or bad. How will Sugrīva tolerate the continued presence of his enemy's son? Why should I go and live in Kiṣkindha, weak, vulnerable, powerless and without a friend, especially when I have failed in the task assigned to me?

'Sugrīva is ruthless, deceitful and cruel. He will at least have me imprisoned as a lesser punishment in order to keep the kingdom! Death by fasting brings me greater glory than imprisonment! Let the monkeys give me permission to do this and they can return home! I swear before all of you that I shall not enter that city! I shall fast to death right here. This death shall be more glorious.

'Pay my respects to Sugrīva, the king of the monkeys, and give him my best wishes for his welfare. Ask with sincerity about the health of my aunt

Rūmā and console my mother Tārā. She has been a loving mother and she has suffered a lot. When she hears that I have died here, I am sure that she will kill herself!' Angada honoured his elders and fell weeping onto the ground that was covered with *darbha* grass.

All the other monkeys also began to weep when they saw Angada so distressed. They condemned Sugrīva and sang Vālī's praises as they gathered around Angada, determined to die with him. They felt sure that his decision was good for them, too. They purified themselves with ritual ablutions and lay down on the *darbha* grass that lined the northern shore of the ocean. The mountain echoed the wailing of the monkeys who were as large as mountains themselves, as if it were echoing the thundering of rain clouds.

# Chapter Forty-Four

The king of the vultures, a wise old bird named Sampāti, happened to come by the place where the monkeys lay, determined to starve themselves to death. He was Jaṭāyu's brother and was famous for his strength and courage. He came out of a hollow in the Vindhya mountains and was delighted to see the monkeys lying there.

'Truly, destiny looks after all the creatures in the world and provides for their needs,' he said happily as he watched them. 'The food I have waited for so long has finally come to me! I shall eat each generation of monkeys as they die one after the other!'

Angada heard what the hungry bird said and, terrified, he turned to Hanumān. 'The god of death has arrived in this form to finish off the monkeys! And it is all because of Sītā! Rāma's mission is incomplete, the king's orders have not been fulfilled and now this calamity has come upon us from who knows where! We have all heard what Jaṭāyu, the king of the vultures, did for Sītā's sake. Even the lower orders of beings will do anything for Rāma. They are even prepared to sacrifice their lives for him as we are doing now!

'Jaṭāyu was lucky to have been killed by Rāvaṇa in battle. He does not have to live in fear of Sugrīva and he has gone straight to heaven! The deaths of Daśaratha and Jaṭāyu as well as the abduction of Sītā have brought the monkeys to this terrible pass! Rāma and Lakṣmaṇa living in the forest with Sītā, Rāma's killing of Vālī by a single arrow, the massacre of the *rākṣasas* because they earned Rāma's wrath, these are the unhappy consequences of the boons given to Kaikeyī!'

Sampāti heard what Angada was saying and that sharp-beaked bird spoke in an enormous voice. 'Who is this that speaks of the death of my brother Jaṭāyu? He was dearer to me than my own life! My mind is disturbed when I hear this! I have heard my brother's name mentioned after many long years! How come there was a fight in Janasthāna between my brother, who is a vulture, and a *rākṣasa*? My younger brother was virtuous and brave and worthy of praise for his many exploits. I want to know how he died, best of monkeys! My brother lived in Janasthāna. How did he become friends with Daśaratha whose eldest son is Rāma, loved by all? My wings were burnt off by the sun so I am unable to move. But I want to get off this mountain, great monkey!'

Though Sampāti seemed feeble and his voice quavered with emotion, the monkeys were still very suspicious because they had heard his earlier words. Despite the fact that the monkeys had decided to die by starvation, they came to the grim conclusion that Sampāti wanted to eat them. 'If he eats us we will die quickly and go to heaven!' they thought and that seemed a better prospect.

Angada helped Sampāti down from the mountain and told him how the monkeys had come to be on the shores of the ocean. 'While we were in the magical cave, the stipulated time period elapsed. We are all subservient to the king of the monkeys and since the time has passed, we fear his anger and are resolved to fast to death. We would not live even if we were to return!'

Sampāti listened sympathetically to the pitiful tale from the monkeys who were ready to die. 'Jaṭāyu was my younger brother and now you tell me that he was killed by a *rākṣasa* who was stronger than him,' he said, choking on his tears. 'I am old and wingless now, so I must bear this insult. I no longer have the strength to avenge the death of my brother!

'In the old days, when Vṛtra had been killed,* my brother and I were racing each other and we flew up to the sun. Higher and higher we flew, faster and faster, in spirals. When the sun had reached the middle of the sky, Jaṭāyu grew tired. I saw that he was almost fainting from the heat, so I spread my wings over him and shielded him. My wings were burnt off and I fell here, on top of the Vindhya mountain. I have lived here since then but I have had no news of my brother.'

'If you are Jaṭāyu's brother,' said young Angada, 'and if you have been listening to what I was saying, then you must tell us where that *rākṣasa*

---

* Vṛtra controlled the drought and as god of the rains, Indra was always in conflict with him. They had a series of battles, and Indra was finally able to kill him.

lives! Tell us, does that foolish, shortsighted Rāvaṇa live close by or far away? You must tell us if you know!'

The mighty old bird's words gave the monkeys hope. 'I am old and wingless now and I have lost all my strength,' he said, 'but I shall do my best to help Rāma with my words!

'I know the worlds ruled by Varuṇa. I know which ones belong to the striding Viṣṇu. I have witnessed the war between the gods and the *asuras* and I have seen the churning of the ocean of milk for nectar. Helping Rāma should be my first priority, but age has sapped my powers and I am worn out!

'I saw a beautiful young woman, adorned with jewels, being carried away by the wicked *rākṣasa* Rāvaṇa. She cried "Rāma! Rāma! Lakṣmaṇa!" as she writhed in his arms and tore the jewels from her body. Her fine silken garments shone like a sunbeam on a mountain or lightning against a dark cloud as she was held in the *rākṣasa's* dark arms. I assumed she was Sītā because she cried out to Rāma over and over again. Listen and I will tell you where that wicked *rākṣasa* lives!

'Rāvaṇa is the son of Viśravas and the brother of Kubera. He rules over the city of Lankā. The city was built by Viśvakarmā and it is situated on an island in the middle of the ocean, one hundred *yojanās* from here. That is where the distraught Sītā in her fine silken garments has been taken. She lives in his inner apartments, guarded by *rākṣasīs,* pathetic and weeping.

'You will find the princess in that city which is surrounded on all sides by the sea. Use your strength and go there. I am certain that you will find her in Lankā. I can see Rāvaṇa and Sītā very clearly from here with the divine eyes that all vultures have. This natural gift allows us to see things that are far away, even one hundred *yojanās* away!

'Think of some way to get across the salty seas. You are bound to find Sītā and you can return, your mission accomplished. Now take me to the shores of the ocean so that I can perform the last rites for my brother who has already gone to heaven!'

The powerful monkeys carried the wingless Sampāti to the shore and then brought him back, delighted at having received some news of Sītā.

The monkeys assembled and shouted with joy as they returned to the seashore in great spirits, eager to see Sītā. They camped on the northern shore and gazed at the ocean which seemed to mirror the entire world. The sight of the immense ocean with its huge and fantastic creatures frolicking in its rolling waves disturbed them. In some places, the ocean seemed to be asleep, in others, it seemed playful, and in still others, its waves rose up as high as a mountain. It seemed filled with fierce *dānavas* from the underworld, frightful enough to make the hair stand on end, and it filled the monkeys with despair. They stared miserably at the ocean which was as vast as the sky and they said to one another, 'What shall we do now?'

Angada saw that the vast monkey army was stricken with terror. 'Don't be afraid,' he said. 'Despair is your worst enemy and can kill a man as easily as a snake can kill a sleeping child. He who is despondent when the situation calls for courage will never achieve his ends!'

When the night had passed, Angada consulted the elders and veterans. Surrounded by his army of monkeys, he looked like Indra surrounded by the *māruts*. There was no one there apart from Angada and Hanumān who could keep that mighty force in order. Angada took the permission of his elders and addressed the monkeys.

'Who has the power to leap over the ocean and keep Sugrīva's promise? Which of you heroic monkeys can leap one hundred *yojanās* and relieve the others of their fear? Whose prowess will enable us to return in happiness and see our wives and our children and our homes again? Whose strength will allow us to return joyfully to Rāma and Lakṣmaṇa and Sugrīva? If there is anyone here who can do this, then let him speak up quickly and release us from our fear!'

Angada's words were greeted with total silence as the monkey army stood there petrified. Angada spoke again. 'You are all strong and brave and extremely powerful. You are well born and have been honoured for your exploits. None of you has ever been stopped by an obstacle. Come forward now and declare how strong you really are, best of monkeys!'

The monkeys responded enthusiastically. Gaja said 'I can leap ten *yojanās*!' and Gavākṣa said he could leap twenty. Gavaya told the others that he could leap thirty, Śarabha announced that he could definitely cover forty. And then the mighty Gandhamādana said that he could leap fifty *yojanās.* Mainda said that he could leap at least sixty and Dvivida declared that he could reach seventy. Suṣeṇa said that he could almost certainly leap eighty *yojanās.*

Then the oldest of them all, Jāmbavān spoke up. 'In the old days, I, too, was swift and strong. But now I am almost at the end of my life. But given the situation, I cannot be indifferent to the task at hand which means so much to Rāma and the king of the monkeys. Despite the changes that time has wrought, let me tell you that I can still leap ninety *yojanās*.

'This was not all that I could do in the past,' he continued. 'When Viṣṇu took his three strides to cover the earth, I was able to circumambulate him! Now I am old and my capacities to leap are greatly reduced. But in my younger days, I was unrivalled! I think all I can do now is ninety *yojanās*. But our task is not going to be accomplished by speed and power alone!'

'I can cover this huge distance of one hundred *yojanās* but I am not sure if I will be able to come back,' said Angada, displaying his magnanimity.

'We know your speed and power, best of all monkeys!' said Jāmbavān, who knew the right words for every situation. 'You could probably leap one hundred or even one thousand *yojanās* and return with ease. But my child, as the leader of our expedition, you should not go yourself. Send others out for we are all here to do your bidding. You have been appointed leader of this force and we must ensure your safety. We must look after you as we would our own wives. You are the primary force behind the successful completion of this mission with your skills, intelligence, courage and energy. Besides that, you are the son of our master and we can only follow your lead!'

'If I must not go and no one else can go, then we have no choice but to fast till we die!' replied Angada. 'I do not know how we will save our lives if we do not fulfil Sugrīva's wishes, even if we do go back! He is our master and he can do whatever he wants, in anger and in joy. If we go back unsuccessful, our destruction is guaranteed!. You are wise. Consider the matter carefully and tell us how we can achieve our ends!'

'This task which is so important to you will not fail! Let me persuade the only one who is capable of making it succeed!' said Jāmbavān. He set about trying to urge the heroic Hanumān, the very best of all the monkeys, who was sitting happily by himself.

Jāmbavān called upon Hanumān because he saw that the monkey troops, which consisted of many thousands, were very depressed. 'Hero among monkeys, so learned in all the traditional texts, you sit alone and in silence. Why do you not speak, Hanumān?

'You are Sugrīva's equal and you are like Rāma and Lakṣmaṇa in splendour and strength. Garuḍa is the foremost of all the winged creatures and I have often seen that mighty one carrying off snakes from the ocean. The strength of your arms is like the strength of his wings. Neither his strength nor his speed surpass yours. Best of monkeys, strength, intelligence, splendour and a commitment to truth make you special among all beings. Awake to yourself!

'Punjikasthalā was the best of the *apsarases* but she was better known as Añjanā, the wife of the monkey Kesarī. She became a monkey because of a curse and was born as the daughter of Kunjara, king of the monkeys. But she was able to change her shape at will. Even in her monkey form she was exquisitely beautiful with well-formed limbs, and sometimes she took on the form of a young and lovely young woman.

'One day, adorned with garlands and dressed in fine silks, she wandered alone on top of a mountain. As the large-eyed woman stood there, her yellow cloth edged with red was gently pulled away by Vāyu, the wind god. He saw her well-rounded thighs, her slim waist, her large breasts and her lovely face. Vāyu embraced that blameless woman in his strong arms and lost himself, desire overpowering his limbs.

'"Who is this who wants to destroy my vows of fidelity to my husband?" she cried in agitation. "Do not be afraid," replied Vāyu. "I will not harm you, lady with the lovely hips! My heart went out to you when I embraced you. You shall have a son who is brave and endowed with wisdom!"

'When you were a child, Hanumān, you saw the sun rising over a large forest. You thought it was a fruit and you leapt towards it to grab it. You leapt a distance of three hundred *yojanās* and though the sun's rays were strong, you did not falter. Indra hurled his thunderbolt at you as you flew through the air. You fell onto the peak of a mountain and your jaw broke. And from that you were given the name Hanumān by which you are now famous.*

'Vāyu, the bearer of soft fragrances, saw you fall and was very angry. He ceased to blow in the three worlds and all creatures suffered terribly. The gods were confused and decided to appease Vāyu. So Brahmā gave you a boon, my child, by which you cannot be slain by any weapons in battle. When Indra saw that you were relatively unharmed after your fall, he was pleased and gave you the best boon of all. Your death will be of your own choosing!

* 'Hanu' in Sanskrit means 'jaw.'

'Son of the Wind, you are Vāyu's equal in splendour and you rival his capacity to get from one place to another. We are dispirited today and you sit among us, endowed with strength and power, like the king of the birds. I am old and have lost my strength but you have all the skills and powers necessary for the occasion.

'Expand yourself, Hanumān! You are the foremost of all those who can leap. The entire monkey army waits to see your valour! Stand up, tiger among monkeys, and leap over the ocean! You are the swiftest of all beings! How can you ignore the anguish of the monkeys?' exhorted Jāmbavān.

Mighty Hanumān, worthy of all the praise showered upon him, began to increase in size. Waving his tail with joy, he attained his full strength. He swelled with energy and his form became unparalleled and the monkeys sang his praises. As a lion stretches at the mouth of a cave, so Hanumān stretched and expanded. His open mouth resembled a smokeless fire as he yawned.

He stood among the monkeys, his hair standing on end with joy. He honoured the elders and said, 'I am the son of Vāyu, the wind that shatters the mountain peaks, the friend of the sacrificial fire, the mighty immeasurable wind who roams the skies! No one is my equal! I can circle Mount Meru one thousand times even though it is enormous and seems to touch the sky. I can churn the sea by thrashing my arms and inundate the earth with its mountains, rivers and lakes!

'I can go to where the sun rises with its garland of shining rays and return here without touching the ground! I can stride further than all those who travel in the sky. I can agitate the ocean and split the earth! I shall make the mountains tremble when I leap and repel the ocean! Flowers from plants and trees will follow in my wake as I leap across the sky. My path shall be like that of the stars and all creatures will see me as I fly! I shall pierce the clouds, I shall shake the mountains. Nobody except Vāyu and Garuḍa can rival me for speed!

'I know I shall see Sītā, so rejoice, monkeys! I can leap over ten thousand *yojanās* and after turning Lankā upside down, I shall return!' roared Hanumān.

'Ah, dear boy!' said Jāmbavān joyfully to the splendid Hanumān. 'You have dispelled the profound grief of your companions. We wish you well and will perform the auspicious rites necessary for your success. Our best thoughts will be with you as you leap over the ocean. We shall all stand on one foot until you return. Remember, our lives depend on you!'

'The earth will not withstand the power of my leap,' said Hanumān. 'But the rocky peaks will bear the thrust of my feet as I take off.' Hanumān, the scourge of his foes, climbed up Mount Mahendra which was covered with flowering trees and creepers and grassy meadows where deer roamed. Lions and tigers and elephants wandered among its waterfalls.

Hanumān went to the very top, and crushed under the feet of that mighty monkey the mountain roared like a rutting elephant attacked by a lion. Water was squeezed from the mountain and gushed out from the scattered stones and rocks. Deer and elephants were frightened away and the trees shook and trembled. The slopes of the mountain were deserted by the *gandharvas* who were busy making love as well as by the *vidyādharas* and all the birds. Huge serpents that lurked in rocky crevices were thrown up and as they emerged, hissing, from their holes, the great mountain shone as if it were decorated with flags. The sages fled from the peaks in agitation and the mountain was like a traveller, deserted by his companions, sitting alone in a forest.

# BEAUTY

# *Chapter Forty-Five*

Mighty Hanumān quickly crossed over the grassy slopes, the green forests and the emerald meadows that led to the top of the mountain which was adorned with dark and light metallic ores and blue and red lotuses. It was the home of *uragas, yakṣas, kinnaras* and various gods. Hanumān stood on the summit of the mountain and gazed at the vast, deep ocean, the home of Varuṇa. Full of water serpents, it thundered mightily and seemed endless. The monkey faced the east and honoured the gods as he prepared to depart. He had decided to make his leap for Rāma's sake, and so he enlarged his body, like the ocean swells during the fortnight of the waxing moon. The other monkeys watched him in wonder.

He pressed down upon the ground with his arms and legs. The mountain shook so hard that all the flowers fell from the trees and bushes, covering it so that it appeared as if it were made entirely of flowers. It oozed water like a rutting elephant oozing ichor and released rivers of gold and silver and black collyrium and disgorged huge stones of red arsenic. Birds and animals shrieked in pain as they were being crushed and their discordant cries filled the air. Serpents spread their hoods, displaying their markings and spewed fire as they chewed rocks with their fangs. Rocks blazed and burst into flames. Even the medicinal herbs on the mountain slopes could not neutralize the venom spewed by the serpents. The ascetics and sages and *vidyādharas* fled from the mountain and joined the *siddhas* and *cāraṇas* who stood, watching, in the sky.

Resembling a mountain himself, Hanumān shook his body and roared like thunder. He hurled his coiled, furry tail, which looked like a huge snake, onto the ground. He spread his stout arms which were as tough as iron bars. He crouched on his haunches and drew his feet inwards. Tensing his neck and shoulders, Hanumān summoned up all his energy and vitality. He raised his eyes and stared at the aerial path that he would take and inhaled deeply. He steadied his feet and drew back his ears. 'I shall go to Lankā, Rāvaṇa's city, as swiftly as exhaled breath, like an arrow shot by Rāma! And if I do not find Sītā there, I shall go just as swiftly to the three heavens. And if Sītā is not there either, I shall uproot Lankā and bring it back here along with the king of the *rākṣasas,* bound hand and foot!' he yelled.

Hanumān leapt forward without a moment's hesitation. He flew upwards into the clear sky, taking plants and creepers and birds nesting in the flowering trees with him. He was a truly wondrous sight. The trees fell into the salty seas, the way the mountains had plunged into the ocean from fear of Indra. Followed by a train of multi-coloured flowers, Hanumān seemed like a cloud adorned with lightning. His arms, spread out into the sky, looked like five-headed serpents sticking their heads out of their mountain holes. His eyes blazed bright as lightning, like twin fires upon a mountain slope, like the sun and the moon frozen in place. His curved tail flew like Indra's banner and circled the flying monkey like a halo. The wind under his arms rumbled and he shot forward like a blazing comet.

The disturbance he caused in the skies agitated the ocean but Hanumān flew above the water, counting the waves. His shadow, which was ten *yojanās* long and thirty *yojanās* wide, became even more magnificent over the waters and it followed him like a streak of shining white cloud. The gods, *gandharvas* and the *dānavas* rained flowers upon the monkey as he flashed by. The sun did not burn him and the wind served him for Rāma's sake.

'I must do something to help this great monkey,' thought the ocean. 'Otherwise, I shall be condemned by all beings! I was raised by Sagara, the lord of the Ikṣvākus. I must do something so that this monkey can rest for a while and then cover the remaining distance with ease.'

The ocean called upon gold-naveled Mainaka, the hidden mountain. 'You have been placed here by Indra as an obstacle to the *asura* hordes that live in the underworld,' he said to the mountain. 'You can grow in any direction, upwards, downwards and sideways. I urge you now to rise up! Look! There is Hanumān, flying through the sky in order to help Rāma. Help me be of service to the Ikṣvākus. Rise up above the waters and let the monkey stand upon you. He is our guest and he must be honoured!'

Mainaka rose from the ocean, covered with great trees and creepers. He pierced the surface of the waters as the sun pierces the clouds with his rays, and grew extremely large. Hanumān saw the mountain and assumed that it was an obstacle in his path. He thrust his chest forward and knocked the mountain over as the wind might knock over a cloud. Mainaka was pleased with the monkey's strength and so, he took the form of a man and stood upon his own summit.

'I am the golden mountain,' he said. 'Rest on me! I have risen to help you! The ocean told me all about you, that you are going to Lankā for Rāma's sake and that you would definitely find Sītā there! Alight on my summit. Eat the fragrant roots and fruits that grow here and continue with your journey after you have rested.'

'Why do you live in the waters of the ocean infested with sea monsters?' asked Hanumān.

'Listen and I will tell you,' replied Mainaka. 'Long ago, in the *kṛtayuga,* all the mountains had wings and they flew everywhere with the speed of the wind. But the gods and the sages and all the creatures were terrified that the mountains would fall down. So Indra clipped the wings of all the mountains with his thunderbolt. Indra came to me, too, his weapon raised. But suddenly, I was hurled away by the wind and thrown into these salty waters with my wings intact. Your father, the Wind, protected me and so there is a bond between us that I must honour, monkey! Rest upon me and relieve your fatigue!'

'The time for the completion of my task is fast expiring and I had said that I would not stop along the way,' said Hanumān. 'I cannot alight on you, but I shall touch you with my finger!' Hanumān touched the mountain with reverence and flew onwards and upwards, leaving the mountain and the ocean far behind. He flew higher and higher into the sky, taking the path of his father, the wind.

The gods, the *gandharvas,* the *siddhas* and the *ṛṣis* called upon Surasā, the mother of serpents. 'Hanumān, the splendid son of the Wind, is flying over the ocean. Present yourself to him as an obstacle. Take on the form of a fierce and mountainous *rākṣasī* with a coppery face and a gaping maw filled with teeth. We want to know if Hanumān has the necessary strength and fortitude. Will he overcome you or will he be disheartened?'

Surasā took the form of a hideous and terrifying *rākṣasī* and rose from the depths of the ocean. She stopped the flying Hanumān and said, 'You have been sent to me as food by the gods. I want to eat you. Enter my mouth!'

Hanumān joined his palms respectfully. 'I am on a mission from Rāma to find his wife Sītā, who was abducted by Rāvaṇa. You should help with Rāma's enterprise! Once I have seen Sītā and gone back to Rāma, I promise I shall return to enter your mouth.'

'No one gets past me. This is the boon that I was given!' said Surasā, curious about Hanumān's strength. 'Enter my mouth now and then go on!'

'Open this mouth of yours by which you hope to subdue me!' cried Hanumān in anger. Equally angry, Surasā expanded by ten *yojanās*. Hanumān did the same. Surasā grew to twenty *yojanās* and Hanumān expanded to thirty. Surasā opened her mouth as wide as forty *yojanās* but Hanumān increased in size to fifty. They went on like this until Hanumān had reached a size of one hundred *yojanās*. He looked into Surasā's mouth that was like a fiery hell and suddenly he contracted his body to the size of a thumb and flew in and out of her mouth in an instant. 'I have entered your mouth and fulfilled your boon,' said Hanumān, standing in the air. 'Now I will go onwards to the place where Sītā is!'

Surasā reverted to her natural form and blessed the monkey. 'Go forward and accomplish your goal with ease! Unite Sītā and the mighty Rāma!' she said. And Hanumān went onwards.

Meanwhile, an immense *rākṣasī* named Simhikā, who could take any form that she pleased, saw Hanumān. 'Today I shall have a huge meal! Such an enormous creature has come my way after a long time!' she thought to herself and seized his shadow.

Suddenly, Hanumān felt himself being caught. 'What is this? I have been gripped by something, crippled as I fly, like a boat upon the ocean seized by a contrary wind!' He looked around and saw a huge creature rising out of the waters. 'This must be the enormous shadow-snatcher who was described to us by Sugrīva!' he thought and expanded his body like a cloud in the rains.

Simhikā saw his body growing larger and she stretched her mouth wider so that it resembled the sky and the nether worlds. Hanumān stared into her deformed mouth and noted the proportions of her body and her vulnerable spots. Hard as a diamond, the monkey threw himself into her mouth and flew out again. The *siddhas* and the *cāraṇas* saw him disappear into her mouth like the moon engulfed by Rahu during an eclipse.

But the monkey had ripped apart her entrails with his sharp nails and flown out again, as quick as thought. Simhikā fell dead and the sky-dwellers rejoiced.

'You have done a great deed by killing this terrible creature today!' they said to Hanumān. 'May you attain your goals safely! Creatures like you, who have the four qualities of intelligence, determination, vision and competence, never fail in their tasks!'

Hanumān accepted their blessings and went onwards to Lankā. But as he approached the city, he noticed that he was as large as a cloud that covered the sky. 'When the *rākṣasas* see my huge body and my immense speed, they will be very curious,' he thought quickly. He contracted his mountainous body and reverted to his natural shape, like one who has been unconscious regains his senses.

Now that he had crossed the ocean, which was garlanded with waves and filled with strange creatures, and reached its far shore by his own strength, Hanumān gazed at Lankā which was as lovely as Amarāvatī, the city of the gods.

As Hanumān stood on top of Mount Trikūṭa and looked upon the city, a rain of flowers fell upon him from the trees. Even though he had just leapt over one hundred *yojanās,* the valiant monkey was not breathing heavily and showed no signs of fatigue. He approached the city slowly, walking through meadows of fresh new grass, wooded hills, fragrant groves and flatlands strewn with rocks and boulders. The city of Lankā lay beyond these, on the summit of a mountain.

Hanumān saw trees of all kinds, laden with beautiful flowers, their swaying tops filled with nesting birds. The trees which stood in the parks and groves and pleasure gardens provided fruit and flowers all year round. Lotus pools were haunted by swans and other waterbirds. As he came closer, Hanumān noticed that even the moats which surrounded the city were filled with lotuses and lilies. But they were also guarded by well-armed *rākṣasas* since the time Rāvaṇa had abducted Sītā.

Hanumān gazed in wonder at the city of Lankā which seemed like the city of the gods. It had beautiful golden gateways and ramparts, with climbing vines carved on them, that surrounded hundreds of mansions festooned with flags and banners. Situated on top of a mountain, the city with its dazzling white buildings looked like it was hanging in the air. Ruled by Rāvaṇa, it had been created by Viśvakarmā and seemed to float in the sky. It teemed with fierce *rākṣasas* as Bhogavatī teems with serpents. This city of unimaginable perfection had once belonged to Kubera. It was now guarded by terrifying *rākṣasas* with sharp nails and teeth who were armed with every kind of weapon.

Hanumān reached the northern gates and saw the city spread before him like a woman, the walls and ramparts her body, the vast ocean her clothes, the fortifications her hair and the upper stories of the mansions her earrings. Lankā was as high and lofty as the peaks of Kailāsa and seemed to touch the sky. Her tall buildings seemed poised to take off into the air.

Hanumān considered Lankā's formidable defences, the fact that it was surrounded by the ocean and that it contained an opponent as mighty as Rāvaṇa. 'Even if the monkeys manage to get here, it will be no use, for Lankā cannot be conquered even by the gods! What will Rāma do when he reaches this impregnable fortress protected by Rāvaṇa? But first let me find out if Sītā is here or not. I shall think about this problem after I have seen her!'

'But I cannot enter the city of the *rākṣasas,* guarded on all sides by fierce and cruel creatures, in this form!' he thought. 'I will have to outwit these brave and terrible creatures in order to find Sītā! I should enter the city at night in a form that is barely visible. This important task must be performed at the right time!'

Gazing at the city which was unassailable even by the gods, Hanumān sighed in despair. 'How will I manage to see Sītā and remain unnoticed by Rāvaṇa? I want to see Sītā alone and in secret. Intentions and plans can be brought to naught by circumstances of time and place as well as by a careless emissary. Sometimes, even a firm intelligence cannot illuminate the difference between advantage and disadvantage. Messengers who consider themselves wise can often ruin what they are sent to do!

'How can I make sure that our mission is not ruined, that my leap over the ocean has not been in vain? If the *rākṣasas* see me, Rāma's intentions to destroy Rāvaṇa will be fruitless. The *rākṣasas* will recognize an outsider even if he were to take the form of a *rākṣasa.* There is no hope for me if I stay like this. No one, not even my father the Wind, could get past these creatures undetected! If I remain here in my natural form I will be destroyed and my master's plans will be foiled. I will make myself tiny and enter the city at night and look into every single house until I find

Sītā!' Having made this decision, Hanumān waited anxiously for the sun to set.

When night fell, he rose and entered the magnificent city which was divided into quarters by huge, wide roads. Its multi-storied mansions had floors of crystal set in gold and the mansions themselves were studded with pearls and gems. Their golden doorways were beautifully decorated and the entire city was brightly lit at night. Hanumān was delighted with the loveliness of the city, but he was also filled with despair when he saw how impossible it would be to conquer Lankā.

At that very moment, a full moon with its many thousand rays rose up into the night sky, accompanied by a cluster of stars. It flooded the earth with light as if to help Hanumān. And as the monkey watched the moon rise in all its glory, white as a conch shell, white as milk, white as lotus stalks, it reminded him of a swan gliding on a lake.

# *Chapter Forty-Six*

Hanumān entered the city filled with lofty mansions that were like autumn clouds. It was served by the wind and the seas, and from a distance the tumult within the city sounded like the rumbling of the swelling ocean. Hanumān climbed onto Lankā's ramparts which were made of precious metals, and stared in astonishment at the golden gates adorned with pearls and lapis and diamonds, decorated with beaten gold and silver.

Hanumān saw the moon, brilliant and shining in the middle of the sky, strutting like a restless bull as it poured its light over the earth. It purified all beings and made the ocean swell as it lit up everything. Like a white bird in a silver cage, like a lion in its den on Mount Mandara, like a heroic warrior on the back of a proud tusker, the moon shone in the sky. It dispelled the darkness and seemed to leave the gates of the heavens wide open as it shone down upon the flesh-eating *rākṣasas.*

Sweet music filled the air and fell gently on the ears as virtuous women slept by their husbands' sides. Other night-stalking *rākṣasas,* who were capable of terrible things, were all at play. The wise monkey saw hundreds of houses filled with drunken *rākṣasas* who seemed unaware of their surroundings. Their houses had chariots and horses and magnificent furniture and everywhere Hanumān could sense the pride the *rākṣasas* had in their strength and heroism. All around him, *rākṣasas* got into drunken brawls, they insulted each other and gesticulated with their sturdy, powerful arms. They ranted and raved in their intoxication. They threw out their chests with pride and clasped their beloved women in their arms, pressing them against their bodies. Hanumān saw beautiful women anointing themselves and others who were asleep.

Lankā had its share of good men who deserved to be honoured and respected, as well as heroes spoiling for a fight. Hanumān saw *rākṣasas* who were among the most intelligent of all beings, others who were devout and pious and those who were eloquent and learned. He was delighted to see that some of them were handsome and virtuous and followed the rules of good conduct. But he also saw *rākṣasas* who were ugly and deformed and seemed to have wicked ways.

Hanumān saw exquisite women who appeared to be high-minded, virtuous and pure. They shone like stars, absorbed in their lovers and in drinking. He saw other women who were illuminated by their own beauty, but they were shy and hid in their lovers' arms, like birds clinging to their mates, enjoying a night of bliss. He saw still others on the terraces of their mansions, sitting in their lovers' laps in the throes of passion. He saw women with smooth complexions, bare-breasted, with skin the colour of molten gold, others with skin like moonlight. Some were alone, without lovers. Some went out to meet their lovers, anticipating a night of ecstasy, and others were satisfied with the lovers who came to their homes.

Everywhere he looked, Hanumān saw rows upon rows of moon-bright faces, eyes with long, curling lashes and ornaments that glittered like garlands of lightning. But nowhere did he see the supremely beautiful Sītā, born into a family that adhered to *dharma,* Sītā who clung to the eternal vows of marital fidelity, whose eyes rested only on Rāma whom she loved so dearly, who was firmly lodged in her husband's heart and who was better, even, than the best of women. This same woman, who had worn beautiful necklaces, whose voice had been sweet, whose eyelashes were curved and long, who had wandered lovely as a peacock in the forest, was now tormented by separation from her love and her throat was choked with tears. She was like a barely visible streak of moonlight, like a flash of gold hidden in the dust, an arrow-wound covered with blood, a scrap of cloud scattered by the wind.

Terribly disheartened that he had not found Sītā in the city, Hanumān took on a form that seemed appropriate and searched through the tall mansions again. As he wandered through Lankā, he came to Rāvaṇa's palace complex which was surrounded by walls as bright as the sun. It was guarded by fierce *rākṣasas* like a forest is by lions, but the monkey took a good look around it. Its decorated, arched doorways led into pleasant courtyards and enclosures that teemed with warriors on elephant back who never knew fatigue and highly bred horses that were well trained. There were chariots covered with lion and tiger skins, adorned with ivory, silver and gold that hummed musically when they moved. The enclosures were filled with enchanting birds and animals of all kinds.

The king's palace, guarded by deferential *rākṣasas,* overflowed with lovely women who were like jewels, and it murmured like the ocean with the tinkling of their ornaments. The air was fragrant with sandal and other rare unguents and filled with the music of drums and conch shells. Worship and sacred rituals were performed there regularly and the entire place was as vast and as noisy as the ocean. The monkey looked around the palace complex which was studded with gems and filled with good people and rightly decided that this, indeed, was the jewel of Lankā.

Fearlessly, Hanumān went from house to house and garden to garden, systematically examining each one, and everywhere he saw evidence of wealth and opulence. When he had explored all the houses in the area, he returned to the main palace. He saw the deformed *rākṣasīs* who guarded Rāvaṇa as he slept and noticed that those cross-eyed creatures were armed with spears and other weapons. Inside, there were groups of armed soldiers and the best of horses, red and white, as well as magnificent pedigreed elephants who were capable of crushing enemy elephants in battle. Highly disciplined and equal to Airāvata in the arts of war, they dripped ichor as clouds drip water, as mountains drip cascades, and they trumpeted like thunder.

There were thousands of golden vehicles and heavily carved palanquins that shone like the sun. There were vine-covered arbours, opulent rooms, picture galleries, recreation areas with hills fashioned out of wood, pleasant sitting rooms and lavish bedrooms. The palace shone like the sun because of its jewels and because of Rāvaṇa's own splendour. Flowing with honey and all kinds of liquor in jewelled vessels, it was like the palace of the god of wealth.

In the middle of the vast residential area, Hanumān saw Rāvaṇa's own magnificent mansion. It had many floors and was one *yojanā* long and half a *yojanā* wide. Hanumān began to search every inch of it, looking for the large-eyed Sītā. Inside, he saw elephants with four tusks, some with two and some with even three tusks, and mighty armed warriors ready to attack. The mansion teemed with Rāvaṇa's wives and with other princesses he had carried away by force. It was like an ocean tossed by storm winds, teeming with fish and whales and crocodiles and other aquatic creatures. Hanumān saw that the opulence and wealth of Kubera were firmly established in Rāvaṇa's mansion and that it equalled the splendours of Indra's and Kubera's homes together.

In the middle of it all, Hanumān saw an exquisitely fashioned structure, carved all over with elephants. This jewelled vehicle was the fabulous Puṣpaka, created by divine Viśvakarmā for Brahmā to use in heaven. Kubera had won the Puṣpaka from Brahmā because of the austerities he had performed but Rāvaṇa had taken it away from him on the strength of his superior powers.

Its dazzling pillars of gold and silver were covered with carved animals. Puṣpaka was so large that it even had rooms within it for rest and recreation, as vast and lofty as the mountains Mandara and Meru. The great monkey climbed into the magnificent, celestial Puṣpaka and saw stairways of gold inlaid with lapis and emerald and sapphire, and golden windows with delicate lattices. Hanumān inhaled deeply and the air was redolent with the fragrance of food and drink, so thick that it seemed to have taken corporeal form. Like an old friend, it invited him in to where Rāvaṇa was.

Going further in, Hanumān came upon large and pleasant rooms which were as dear to Rāvaṇa as his beloved wife. There was golden lattice work over the windows, the stairs were studded with jewels and the crystal floors were inlaid with pearls, ivory and coral. The decorated pillars were uniform and well-proportioned and seemed to soar into the sky as if they had wings. A magnificent embroidered carpet covered the floor and the design on it represented the entire earth with all its various regions and rows of houses. The rooms in Puṣpaka were filled with the songs of birds and divine fragrances and priceless fabrics. Rāvaṇa, king of the *rākṣasas,* used them as his personal apartments.

'This must be heaven or the realm of the gods!' thought Hanumān in utter amazement. 'Or Indra's city! Or the reward for all efforts!' To Hanumān, it seemed as if the entire place was on fire, blazing as it was with Rāvaṇa's splendour, with glittering ornaments and bright lights.

He saw thousands of lovely women wearing all kinds of different clothes and jewels and garlands lying on the priceless carpet. They lay there, sleeping, after they had finished with their pleasures for the evening. The gentle tinkling of their ornaments had been stilled, like a pool where the birds and the bees have fallen silent. Hanumān stared at them as they lay there with their eyes shut, lips closed over pearly teeth. Their faces seemed like fragrant lotuses that had closed their petals for the night. Those lovely women lit up Rāvaṇa's apartments like the autumn sky adorned with stars. 'These must be stars that have fallen to earth when they still had some merit left,' thought the monkey.

Their thick garlands and lovely ornaments had fallen into disarray as the women had played their games of love drunkenly before falling asleep. The vermillion on the foreheads of some of these women had smeared and spread, others had lost an anklet, yet others had their pearls over to one side where they had slipped. The necklaces of some women had broken, the girdles of others had snapped, some even lay there totally naked like mares who, with their burdens removed, were free to roll in the grass. Pearl necklaces gleaming like soft moonlight lay between their breasts like sleeping swans. Even the marks left by their ornaments on their bodies were as lovely as the ornaments themselves.

Stirred by their soft breathing, their upper garments fluttered over their mouths and their earrings quivered gently. Their naturally sweet breath mingled with the fragrance of wine and liquor and fanned Rāvaṇa gently. Some of his wives kissed their companions again and again, imagining that they were kissing Rāvaṇa. One slept with her arm thrown over another's breasts. Overcome with love and alcohol, they slept happily, their limbs entwined, breasts, hips and thighs pressed to each others'. Even when their ornaments, garlands and limbs were in the right places, it was not possible to tell which belonged to whom.

With Rāvaṇa peacefully asleep, it seemed as if the golden lamps watched over those splendid women with fixed, unblinking eyes. There were women from the families of royal sages, *daityas, gandharvas* and *rākṣasas* and they had all come to Rāvaṇa out of love. None had been carried away against her will, they had all been won over by Rāvaṇa's personality. None had ever loved another or been the wife of another, none except Sītā, the daughter of Janaka. Each of Rāvaṇa's wives was nobly born, beautiful, skilled in the arts of pleasure and extremely desirable. And the monkey, who had only worthy thoughts, said to himself, 'How lucky Rāma would be if his wife was like the wives of the *rākṣasa* king!' Then he grew very agitated and reminded himself that Sītā was far better than these other women and that the king of Lankā had done a terrible and ignoble thing.

Then, Hanumān saw a magnificent crystal bed, studded with jewels. A white canopy which shone like the moon hung over it, decorated with garlands. Young women stood around it waving fly whisks and perfumes filled the air. The bed was covered with luxurious sheepskin and had rare flowers strewn all over it.

Rāvaṇa lay upon it, dark as a mighty rain cloud, with red eyes and huge, powerful arms. He wore a cloth of gold and glittering earrings. Anointed with rare red sandal paste, he was like a cloud in the red evening sky with lightning playing upon it.

Rāvaṇa, joy of the *rākṣasas,* was loved by all his women. He had fallen asleep after a night filled with drink and sensual pleasures, adorned with all his jewels. Hanumān came upon him suddenly, and saw him asleep upon that dazzling bed with his breath hissing like angry snakes. The monkey was startled and leapt back in fright. He fled up a flight of stairs onto a raised platform and settled down there to get a better look at the sleeping *rākṣasa.*

He saw Rāvaṇa's mighty arms adorned with bracelets, sturdy as Indra's flagstaff. They were scarred with battle wounds from Airāvata's tusks and Viṣṇu's discus and his shoulders bore the marks of Indra's thunderbolt. Rāvaṇa's shoulders were strong and powerful, his arms mighty, and his fingers were finely shaped, right down to their nails. Sturdy as rounded iron clubs and powerful as an elephant's trunk, his arms spread on the bed looked like five-hooded snakes. They were anointed with sandal as red as hare's blood. The same arms that had been lovingly caressed by beautiful women made the gods, *gandharvas, dānavas, pannagas* and *yakṣas* cry out in pain.

As Rāvaṇa exhaled in his sleep, his breath seemed to fill the entire palace. His golden crown, slightly awry, was studded with pearls and jewels and his face was illuminated by his glittering earrings. His broad chest was smeared with sandalpaste and his exquisite necklace added to his blazing splendour. A dazzling white cloth, fine and silken, was draped carelessly across his body and his loins were covered in yellow silk. Dark as a mound of black beans, Rāvaṇa breathed like a hissing serpent and he appeared like a mighty elephant asleep on the banks of the Gangā. Lamps blazed at the four corners of his bed and illuminated him as lightning would a dark cloud.

In the king's own chamber, Hanumān saw more of his lovely wives lying at his feet, for they loved him dearly. The monkey gazed at their beautiful moon-like faces, their dazzling earrings, their unfading garlands and their rare jewels. They were all skilled musicians and dancers and Rāvaṇa would often hold them in his arms as they played their instruments. These slim-waisted women, exhausted from lovemaking, seemed to have fallen asleep during a lull in their pleasures. Some of them slept holding their musical instruments clasped to their breasts like lovers.

And then, Hanumān saw the most beautiful woman of them all. She slept alone, in a bed a little apart from the rest. Adorned with pearls and other shining jewels, she seemed to light up the entire room with her beauty. She was the golden-skinned Mandodarī, Rāvaṇa's beloved and the queen of the inner apartments.

As he stared at that lovely woman endowed with youth and beauty, Hanumān became convinced that she was Sītā. Delirious with joy, he jumped up and down and kissed his tail. He played and sang and ran from pillar to pillar, displaying his essential monkey nature.

But he banished the thought from his head and calmed himself. 'Sītā would never eat or drink or adorn herself while she is separated from Rāma,' he said to himself. 'Nor would she sit near another man, even if he were the king of the gods! This woman must be someone else,' he decided and continued his search inside the palace.

As he wandered from room to room, he saw that Rāvaṇa's palace lacked nothing in the way of any luxury that the heart might desire. In the vast dining halls, he saw heaps of venison and boar and buffalo meat, roasted peacocks, capons, pork and rhino and leftovers from a feast of partridges, game birds, fish and mutton done to a turn. He saw pickled meats and preserves that were salty, sweet and sour. The banquet halls were made even more beautiful by flowers used in ritual offerings, and there were overturned pitchers and jars and fruit scattered all over the floors.

There were plenty of couches and seats which were so lovely that they seemed to light up the room. There were wines and sherbets, sweet as nectar, made from honey and different kinds of fruits and flowers. Flowers lay in heaps all over, between jugs and casks made of gold and silver and crystal. Golden pitchers overflowed with rare and priceless wines, and liquor was stored in golden pots. Some containers were empty, others were half full, while others had not been touched at all. Everywhere he looked, he saw rare and exotic delicacies, fine wines and half-eaten foods. The halls were strewn with broken pots and overturned jugs so that water mixed with the overflowing liquors.

And again Hanumān saw scores of lovely women, lying on couches and embracing each other, for there was no male company. Their clothes and garlands rose and fell as they slept, their breathing as gentle as a whisper of breeze. The air was redolent with the fragrance of sandal, flowers, incense, bath oils and unguents, and a soft wind carried these scents through the halls of Puṣpaka.

Hanumān searched through these halls but he did not see Sītā. Suddenly, as he looked among the women, the monkey was seized with panic and became anxious about the propriety of his actions. 'I have violated *dharma* by looking at the wives of another man as they lie asleep in their private apartments,' he thought.

'But my gaze was not really directed towards them at all,' he reassured himself. 'I was looking at an adulterer, one who has taken the wife of another man.' Then another thought occurred to the monkey who was single-minded and devoted to his task. 'Granted that I looked upon Rāvaṇa's women while they were relaxed and secure. But they did not create any turbulence in my mind. It is the mind that causes the agitation of the senses. My mind is firm and unwavering, even in adverse circumstances. I could not possibly have searched for Sītā in any other place, a woman must be sought among other women! Surely I could not have found a missing woman amongst a herd of deer! I have looked for Sītā with a pure heart in the midst of all Rāvaṇa's women and I have not found her.'

# *Chapter Forty-Seven*

Eager for a glimpse of Sītā, the monkey scoured the arbours and the galleries, but he did not see her lovely face anywhere. 'Since I cannot find Sītā in any of these places, I must conclude that she is dead!' he thought. 'She has been killed by that wicked *rākṣasa* for being determined to protect herself from his assault! Or maybe she died of fright when she saw Rāvaṇa's women who are all ugly and deformed!

'I have achieved nothing and a great deal of the monkeys' time has been wasted. I cannot go back to the mighty Sugrīva like this, for his punishments are harsh. When I return, all the monkeys will ask me what I did here. How can I tell them that I saw no sign of Sītā? They will starve themselves to death! What will the elders, Jāmbavān and Angada, say about my fruitless leap over the ocean?

'But perseverance is the root of success and self-reliance is the highest goal. I shall search in all the places that I haven't yet seen. The banquet halls, the arbours, the galleries, the gymnasia, the groves, stables and coach houses, I have searched them all, but I shall do so again!' Hanumān went through cellars, temples, multi-storied buildings, up and down, to and fro, over and over again. The great monkey went everywhere, opening and closing doors, entering and exiting rooms. There was not even four fingers of space that he left unexplored in Rāvaṇa's mansion.

Hanumān searched in the streets and among the fortifications, on the platforms that surrounded the trees and at the crossroads, in the lotus pools and in the wells. He saw all kinds of deformed and ugly *rākṣasīs* but he did not see Sītā. He saw exquisite *vidyādharīs* but not the woman who delighted Rāma. He saw gorgeous *nāga* women with faces as lovely as the full moon but not the slim-waisted Sītā. The *nāgas* had also been abducted by Rāvaṇa, but Sītā was not among them. And now that he had seen all kinds of women and still not found Sītā, Hanumān became anxious. In utter despair, he climbed down from Puṣpaka.

'Sampāti said that Sītā was sure to be found in Rāvaṇa's mansions, but I have not seen her anywhere!' thought Hanumān. 'Could it be that, utterly helpless, she has succumbed to Rāvaṇa?

'Maybe Rāvaṇa, as he flew away quickly to avoid Rāma's arrows, let her fall from his arms along the way? Or did she die of fright when she saw the ocean as she was being carried through the air? Did she fall into the ocean as she struggled? Or, did Rāvaṇa devour that virtuous woman, so far from her friends and family? Could it be that Sītā, still undefiled, was eaten by Rāvaṇa's wives? Maybe she died with her thoughts fixed on Rāma's handsome face, crying "Oh Rāma! Oh Lakṣmaṇa! Ah Ayodhyā!"

'How could this delicate, noble creature have got away from Rāvaṇa? I do not have the courage to tell Rāma that his wife is either dead or lost! It would be a mistake to tell him and a mistake not to tell him. I really don't know what to do!

'If I tell Rāma that I did not see Sītā, he will end his life. And Lakṣmaṇa, who is so attached to him, will see Rāma dead and he too will die! When Bharata hears that his brothers are dead, he will die and then so will Śatrughna. And the mothers, Kausalyā, Sumitrā and Kaikeyī will die when they see their sons dead. Sugrīva, the honourable king of the monkeys, will give up his life when he sees Rāma dead. And virtuous Rūmā will die of grief for her husband and so will Tārā who is already upset about Vālī's death. How will young Angada cling to life without his parents and without Sugrīva? And then, upset over the death of their leader, all the monkeys who live in the forest will kill themselves by beating their heads with their fists. They will no longer play and frolic in the mountains and caves and forests! They will jump off cliffs with their wives and children and retainers. They will hang themselves, jump into fires, fast to death or throw themselves upon their unsheathed weapons!

'I cannot return to Kiṣkindha. I cannot see Sugrīva unless I have seen Sītā! But if I do not return, those two mighty warriors and all the monkeys will continue to live in hope.

'I shall become an ascetic eating only plants and roots and the things that come into my hands without any effort. Maybe I will find a pleasant spot by the ocean shore, one that abounds in plants and fresh water, make a huge pyre there and jump into the flames! Or wait until my body is wasted and let the vultures and birds of prey eat it. Or I may jump into the water.

'There are many disadvantages to suicide and many good things can be gained by living. I shall live! Rāma and Sītā's reunion is certain if I live!' The monkey pondered these problems and did not allow himself to succumb to despair.

'Shall I kill the ten-headed Rāvaṇa? Or shall I haul him over the ocean and offer him to Rāma as a sacrificial animal is offered to Paśupati?

'I will look for Sītā again and again until I find her. There is an *aśoka* grove here that I haven't searched yet. Let me go there! I am sure it is heavily guarded and that even my father does not blow there very much. I shall reduce my size for Rāma' sake! May the gods and the sages give me success!'

Hanumān leapt off Rāvaṇa's palace and landed on the wall that enclosed the grove. Feeling rather pleased with himself, the mighty monkey stood there, looking over the tops of the flowering trees. Like an arrow loosed from a bow, Hanumān flew into a mango grove which was covered with creepers and hidden from view. Birds sang joyfully and the trees all around seemed to be made of gold and silver. Flowering trees were visited by bees intoxicated with honey. It was now the season that delighted the hearts of men and the garden was filled with strutting peacocks and all kinds of birds.

As the monkey searched for the lovely princess, he woke the sleeping birds. As they rose from their nests, their wings brushed against the many coloured flowers, making them rain onto the ground. The flowers covered Hanumān and all the animals that saw him moving through the garden mistook him for Spring incarnate. Strewn with fallen blossoms, the earth looked like a lovely woman adorned with jewels. Hanumān rocked the trees as he leapt through them and their leaves and fruit fell to the ground. Birds flew away from the trees that had been denuded as if by storm winds, for they were no longer hospitable. Hanumān crashed through creepers and vines, scattering them as the wind scatters the rain clouds over the Vindhyas.

He wandered through courtyards paved with gold and silver and pearls. He saw pools of different shapes and sizes, filled with clear sparkling water, with jewelled steps leading into them. They had crystal bottoms and banks of coral and pearls. They were lined with golden-hued trees which made them shine pleasantly. Lotuses and lilies bloomed there and the calls of waterbirds could be heard.

In the distance, Hanumān saw a charming little hillock with a tiny stream running down it, like a beautiful woman who leaves her lover's lap and throws herself on the ground in a fit of pique. There was an artificial lake brimming with cool clear water with jewelled steps and gem-encrusted banks. It was surrounded by landscaped gardens abounding in deer and other animals and adorned with pavilions created by Viśvakarmā.

Close by, Hanumān noticed a *śiṁśapa* tree, dense with leaves and covered with creepers. He was amazed to hear the tinkling of bells as the tree swayed in the breeze. He climbed onto the tree quickly. 'I will definitely be able to see the pining Sītā from here,' he said. 'She may come here by chance, oppressed by her grief.

'I am sure this lovely pleasure garden belongs to Rāvaṇa. Sītā will come here because she loved to wander through the forest. Her grief for Rāma will bring her here. She will come to the clear waters of this pool to perform her evening ablutions, for she is particular about these things. I know that Sītā will come to this spot if she is still alive!' Hanumān settled down, hidden in the leafy tree, to wait for Sītā, keenly observing everything around him.

Not far from where he was, Hanumān noticed a lovely pavilion. White as Kailāsa, it had a thousand pillars of beaten gold and steps of coral. It dazzled the eye with its brightness and was so tall that it seemed to touch the sky.

In front of it, he saw a beautiful woman surrounded by *rākṣasīs*. She was wearing a dirty, soiled garment and was thin and pale from fasting. She sighed deeply again and again but she shone still like a moonbeam in the bright half of the lunar fortnight even though her beauty was diffused, as a flame is dimmed by smoke. Her yellow silken garment was fine but worn and without any jewellery, she was like a pool without its lotuses. Her sad face was tear-stained, her hair hung down her back in a single braid. She was emaciated from not eating, for her grief never left her. In fact, it grew all the time.

Hanumān watched her and inferred that she must be Sītā. 'She looks exactly like the woman we saw being carried away by that form-changing *rākṣasa*!' He looked again at her face which was as lovely as the full moon, her delicate eyebrows, her shapely rounded breasts, her jet black hair, berry-red lips, lotus eyes and lovely limbs. She dispelled the darkness with her beauty. But this woman who had delighted all creatures with her loveliness now laid her slender body on the ground like an ascetic who had taken firm vows and Hanumān recognized her with great difficulty.

After a closer examination, he decided that she was definitely Sītā. He saw that she was still wearing all the ornaments Rāma had described, the earrings and the other jewellery studded with pearls and gems. Though they no longer sparkled and had dimmed with constant wear, Hanumān was sure they were the very ones Rāma had described to him. 'The ornaments which fell on the Ṛṣyamūka mountain are missing, but the others are exactly as Rāma had said! Her clothes are now soiled and worn, but they seem to have the same colour as the cloth which was tossed onto the mountain. I am sure this golden-skinned woman is Rāma's beloved wife, never absent from his thoughts. Rāma can do many difficult things but he has done the impossible by continuing to live without her!' Hanumān was beside himself with joy at having found Sītā and his thoughts flew back to Rāma.

The moon rose higher into the sky, white as a pool of lotuses, bright as a white-winged swan. As Hanumān was trying to keep an eye on Sītā, his glance fell upon the fearsome *rākṣasīs* who surrounded her. There was one who had only one eye, another had a single ear, another had ears large enough to cover her whole body, another had no ears at all, another's ears were twisted like a conch shell. One of them breathed through a nose that was located on top of her head. Some had huge bodies, but one had a tiny body and a huge head. One had a single tuft of hair, another was totally bald and there was yet another with hair like wool. One had a drooping forehead and sagging ears, another had a pendulous belly and breasts. One had enormous pouting lips, another's lips touched her chin, another had protruding knees.

They were tall and short, hunch-backed and twisted like dwarves. They had yellow eyes and crumpled faces. Some were yellow and some were black, but they were all ugly, bad tempered and quarrelsome and were armed with vicious weapons. They had the faces of boar, deer, tigers, buffaloes, goats and jackals and the feet of elephants, camels and horses. These cruel *rākṣasīs* with their smoky grey hair were addicted to eating meat and they drank alcohol all the time. Hanumān looked at them with blood and gore spread all over their mouths and his hair stood on end. They all sat at the foot of an immense tree with wide-spreading branches, surrounding the flawlessly beautiful princess Sītā.

# *Chapter Forty-Eight*

Meanwhile the night had come to an end and in the hour before dawn, Hanumān heard virtuous *rākṣasas* chanting the Vedas.

Ten-headed Rāvaṇa was woken at that hour by the strains of pleasant music. As he rose, his clothes and garlands in disarray, his first thought was of Sītā. Drawn irresistibly to her by his lust, he could not hide his feelings. Adorned with all his jewels and flaunting his majesty, he made straight for the *aśoka* grove.

Hundreds of women followed Rāvaṇa, the descendant of Pulastya, as the women of the gods and the *gandharvas* follow Indra. Some carried lamps of gold, others carried fly whisks and palm-leaf fans. Some walked ahead of him with golden pitchers full of water and others walked behind him carrying a grass seat and the royal umbrella which was as white as the moon and had a golden handle. Befuddled with sleep and drink, the women accompanied Rāvaṇa as lightning flashes accompany a cloud.

Hanumān heard the tinkling of anklets and girdles. He looked up at the gate and saw Rāvaṇa, whose deeds were unrivalled and whose strength and power were unimaginable. His face was lit up by the sweet-smelling oil lamps that were carried before him. Intoxicated with drink, arrogance and lust, his red eyes gleaming, Rāvaṇa looked like the god of love without his bow. His lovely shawl, white as the froth that was produced when the ocean was churned, had slipped off his shoulders and he dragged it along behind him carelessly.

Hanumān watched in fascination as Rāvaṇa, endowed with youth and beauty, entered the garden surrounded by his women, still a little drunk from the night before. 'This must be Rāvaṇa!' thought Hanumān and climbed higher into the tree. Though Hanumān himself was immensely strong, he was absolutely stunned by the raw power exuded by Rāvaṇa and he hid himself deeper among the leaves.

And Rāvaṇa, desperate to see Sītā with her dark hair, her slim waist, her full hips and her rounded breasts, came closer and closer. The moment the innocent princess saw the king of the *rākṣasas* in all his glory, she trembled like a slender banana plant in a high wind.

'You cover your breasts and your belly when you see me, as if in fear, as if you would like to be invisible!' said Rāvaṇa gently to Sītā. 'Ah, dark-eyed lady with the perfect body! I love you! Be good to me! No one can come close to you here, neither a mortal nor even a form-changing *rākṣasa.* Do not fear me!

'Consorting with the wives of other men and carrying off women against their will is natural to *rākṣasas.* That is the way we live. Let my body be ravaged by desire, I will not touch you until you want me to! Trust me, you have nothing to fear. Be good to me and stop wallowing in your grief!

'This single braid, these dirty clothes, this sleeping on the bare ground and not eating for no reason, these things are not for you! Beautiful flowers, sandal and priceless unguents, fine clothes, celestial ornaments, the best of foods, the softest beds, music, dance! All this can be yours, Sītā, if only you would accept me! You are a jewel among women! You cannot stay like this! Adorn your body! Accept me and take the best that you deserve!

'You are young and beautiful but our youth is passing us by! The past is like a flowing river, it cannot be recaptured. Give up your delusions and become my wife. You can be my chief queen, ruling over all the women I have gathered from all over the place. The jewels and wonderful things I have collected from all the worlds shall be yours, along with my kingdom and myself. I will conquer the whole earth, garlanded with cities, and bestow it upon Janaka, just for your sake. There is no one on earth stronger than me. Look how powerful I am! Even the gods and the *asuras* cannot face me in battle, for I have trampled upon their fallen battle banners on the field of war.

'Adorn yourself with jewels that dazzle and glitter and let me gaze at your beauty enhanced by these ornaments! Do it as a favour to me and you can enjoy all the pleasures you like. Eat! Drink! Make merry! Do whatever pleases you, give away as much wealth as you desire.

'Think of my wealth, my glory, my majesty! What do you want with Rāma, who has to wear rough and simple clothes? Rāma has lost all opportunities to be successful. He has renounced his royal splendour and wanders in the forest. He has taken the vows of an ascetic and sleeps on the ground. I wonder if he is even alive! You shall not catch even a glimpse of Rāma, for you shall be hidden from view like the moonlight covered by a thick curtain of rain clouds. Nor will Rāma ever get you out of my hands.

'You have captured my heart with your lovely eyes and your charming smile. Even though you are thin and pale and clad in tattered silks, I have lost interest in all my other wives. You can rule over them all. They are the finest women in the three worlds and they shall wait on you the way *apsarases* serve the goddess Śrī.

'Rāma cannot rival me in wealth, strength, courage or the performance of austerities. I can give you the pleasures of the earth to enjoy. Be happy with me and let your family share in your happiness. Enjoy yourself with me in the flowering woods and groves at the edge of the sea! Adorn your body with the finest golden ornaments!'

Sītā thought only of her husband and as she placed a blade of grass between Rāvaṇa and herself, she answered in a small, miserable voice. 'Take your mind off me and devote yourself to your own women! You cannot have me any more than a wicked man can aspire to heaven. I was born into a noble family and married into one just as great. I cannot do anything that would be condemned by the whole world!'

The virtuous woman turned her back on Rāvaṇa and continued. 'I cannot marry you. I am the chaste and virtuous wife of another man. Respect the conduct of good men and learn to behave like them! Protect the wives of others as you would protect your own. Act as you would have others behave towards you. Enjoy your own wives, Rāvaṇa! A man who has a roving eye and lusts after others' wives will soon be disgraced.

'Are there no good men here? Do you not listen to their advice? Or do you pretend to listen to them with mock humility and then disregard their words? Kingdoms ruled by unrighteous kings will perish, no matter how prosperous they may be. Even Lankā, which abounds in wealth and luxury, will be destroyed because of you and your crimes! People rejoice when a shortsighted and wicked creature is destroyed by his own misdeeds. All the people that have suffered because of you will celebrate when you are destroyed, Rāvaṇa!

'You cannot tempt me with wealth and power. I belong to Rāma the way the rays belong to the sun. I have lain in the arms of the lord of the worlds! How can I lie in the arms of another, whoever he may be? I am Rāma's, just as the Vedas belong to the *brahmin* who has studied them and taken the right vows.

'Do the right thing and give me back to Rāma! Make friends with Rāma if you wish to keep your position and avoid a horrible death! If you don't, you shall soon hear the sound of Rāma's mighty bow that resounds like Indra's thunderbolt! Arrows that blaze like serpents and carry the insignia of Rāma and Lakṣmaṇa shall rain upon this place!

'My husband will rescue me from here! When you could not retaliate for the massacre at Janasthāna, you did this lowly thing. You abducted me from our isolated forest settlement while the princes were away. If you had even smelled the presence of Rāma and Lakṣmaṇa, you would have hidden yourself, like a dog hides from tigers! My husband and Lakṣmaṇa will kill you the way the sun sucks up moisture!'

'The more a man tries to please a woman, the more he falls into her power!' replied Rāvaṇa harshly. 'The more he speaks sweetly, the more she insults him! My love for you makes me hold back my anger, as a good charioteer reins in his horses that have gone off the road. Love is a terrible bind! A man cannot act against the wishes of the woman that he desires. That is the only reason I do not punish you Sītā, even though you deserve disgrace for being attached to a fake! You deserve a horrible death for all the harsh things you have said to me, Sītā!

'I shall respect the two-month period I gave you earlier,' he continued angrily. 'But after that, lovely woman, you shall have to share my bed! If you do not take me as a husband at the end of two months, you shall be slaughtered in my kitchens for my breakfast!'

The daughters of the gods and the *gandharvas* who had accompanied Rāvaṇa felt sorry for Sītā as Rāvaṇa bullied and threatened her. They gestured with their eyes and lips and tried to comfort her and express their sympathy, and Sītā was somewhat reassured.

'Obviously, there is no one here who cares enough about you to dissuade you from this disgraceful course of action,' she said spiritedly. 'Who in the three worlds, other than you, would dare to covet me? I am wedded to Rāma as Saci is to Indra. Now that you have spoken these terrible words to Rāma's wife, where will you run to, to hide from his power?

'Your ugly yellow eyes should fall out of your head as you stare at me so lustfully. Your tongue should rot for speaking to me, the wife of righteous Rāma and the daughter-in-law of the honourable Daśaratha, like this! The only reason I do not reduce you to ashes, Rāvaṇa, is because I want to preserve my ascetic vows and because Rāma has not ordered me to do so.'

Rāvaṇa's eyes dilated with anger when he heard Sītā's words. He was as large as a dark rain cloud and his arms and neck were enormous and strong. He walked with the gait of a lion and his eyes and tongue were a fiery red. His flower garlands and clothes were the colour of blood, his ornaments were of beaten gold and his crown added to his height. He wore a golden belt around his waist that made him appear like Mount Meru circled by the serpent when the ocean was being churned.

Staring at Sītā, he hissed like an angry snake. 'You are stuck on a man who is unrighteous, whom even fortune has deserted! I can destroy you right now.' Rāvaṇa, who made his enemies wail with fright, turned to the fearsome *rākṣasīs* and said, 'Do whatever is necessary to make Sītā submit to my will! Threaten her, cajole her, bribe her, make her suspicious of her friends, use force, do anything you like to make her think positively about me!'

The *rākṣasī* Dhanyamālinī quickly came up to Rāvaṇa. She embraced him and said, 'Come, play with me, my king! Why are you so interested in this Sītā? A man who desires a woman who does not love him burns within his body, but the one who is attracted to a woman who loves him can be fully satisfied!' Rāvaṇa was easily diverted and went back to his palace which was as bright as the sun. All the women, the daughters of the gods and the *gandharvas* and *nāgas,* followed him into his splendid mansion.

# *Chapter Forty-Nine*

Then the ugly *rākṣasīs* gathered closely around Sītā and began to torment her with their harsh words.

'Why are you so averse to living in Rāvaṇa's inner apartments, Sītā? They are so beautiful and they have fine soft beds!'

'You are only a mortal woman and yet, you think so highly of yourself! Banish Rāma from your mind. You shall never be his wife again! You yearn for that feeble mortal, but he has lost his kingdom. He is weak and vulnerable and will never achieve his ends!'

Sītā's lotus eyes filled with tears. 'This terrible thing you ask me to do is not even an option for me! No mortal can ever be the wife of a *rākṣasa*! Eat me up if that's what you want, but I will never do what you ask! So what if my husband is weak and helpless and without a kingdom! He is still my lord!'

Sitting hidden in the *śimśapa* tree, the monkey listened to the *rākṣasīs* harassing and threatening Sītā as Rāvaṇa had ordered. They licked their fiery lips as they surrounded the trembling woman and brandishing their weapons, they shouted, 'This woman does not deserve to marry the king of the *rākṣasas*!'

Terrified by the *rākṣasīs,* lovely Sītā came and sat at the foot of the *śimśapa* tree and dried her tears. But the loathsome creatures followed her even though she was overwhelmed by her grief, thin and emaciated in her soiled garment. A particularly frightening *rākṣasī,* Vinatā, with a huge protruding belly, her face distorted with anger, shouted, 'You have displayed more than enough loyalty to your husband, Sītā! An excess of anything leads only to grief! You have done all you can to abide by the rules of conduct for mortals. Now do as I tell you!

'Take Rāvaṇa, the king of the *rākṣasas*, as your husband! He is as brave and as handsome as Indra, the king of the gods! Renounce that pathetic creature Rāma and turn to Rāvaṇa for refuge. He is strong and capable and everyone loves him! Anoint your body with fine unguents! Adorn yourself with celestial ornaments and become the queen of the worlds! If you ignore our words, we shall eat you in a short while!'

Another *rākṣasī* named Vikaṭā, with huge breasts, clenched her fists and roared, 'We have borne your harsh words out of kindness and gentleness, Sītā! But you still ignore our advice which is appropriate for the situation and meant for your benefit! You have been brought here to the far shore of the ocean and you are secluded in the inner apartments of Rāvaṇa's palace, zealously guarded by us! Not even Indra can rescue you from here!

'Listen to us, Sītā! Dry your tears and stop this grieving! Laugh! Rejoice! Enjoy yourself with the king of the *rākṣasas*! You know how short-lived a woman's youth is, take your pleasures before it passes! Wander through wooded hills and pleasure gardens with Rāvaṇa. When you take Rāvaṇa as a husband, seven thousand women will be at your service! But if you don't listen, I will pull out your heart and eat it!'

The *rākṣasī* Caṇḍodarī with a horrible face, brandished an enormous spear and said, 'Ever since this lotus-eyed woman with the heaving breasts was brought here by Rāvaṇa, I have been seized with a terrible yearning to devour her liver and spleen and all her entrails!'

'Let's strangle her!' said Praghasā. 'What are we waiting for? We can tell the king she is dead and I am sure he will give us permission to eat her!'

'We can make balls of her flesh,' said Ayomukhī, 'and divide them amongst ourselves! Enough talk! Let us fetch other things to eat and drink!'

'I agree,' said Śūrpanakhā. 'Bring the drink that erases all suffering and sorrow. Today, we can eat human flesh and dance all night!'

Sītā began to weep as the *rākṣasīs* continued their threats. She trembled like a doe in the forest surrounded by lions and could see no end to her misery. She clung to a branch and, her heart breaking, she thought of Rāma as her tears bathed her breasts. Pale with fear, she shook like a slender banana plant in high wind and fell to the ground, her long black braid writhing like a serpent as she trembled.

'Oh Rāma!' she cried. 'Ah Lakṣmaṇa! Oh mother-in-law Kausalyā! Oh Sumitrā! Wise men say that death can never come before its time. This must surely be true! Otherwise, how could I live for a moment without Rāma, tormented by these *rākṣasīs*! What terrible thing did I do in my previous life that I should suffer like this now? I cannot bear this sorrow any more. I shall kill myself. There is no hope of my ever seeing Rāma again as long as I am guarded by these creatures! I curse this mortal weakness that makes us dependent on others! One cannot even die when one wants!'

The *rākṣasīs* were angry when they heard Sītā talking like this. Some of them went off to report her words to Rāvaṇa and the others gathered around and renewed their threats.

An old *rākṣasī* named Trijaṭā had just woken up and she watched as the others harassed Sītā. 'Eat your own flesh, you vile creatures!' she said. 'You cannot eat Sītā. She is Janaka's daughter and the daughter-in-law of Daśaratha. I had a terrible dream about the destruction of the *rākṣasas* and the power of her husband. It made my hair stand on end!'

The other *rākṣasīs* asked her to tell them what she had seen and Trijaṭā began to recount the dream she had had just before dawn.

'I saw Rāma decorated with flowers in an ivory chariot drawn by a thousand horses standing in the sky. In my dream, I saw Sītā dressed in white and standing on a white mountain which was surrounded by the sea on all sides. She was united with Rāma like the rays are with the sun. Then I saw Rāma with Lakṣmaṇa, mounted on a four-tusked elephant which was the size of a mountain. They were dressed in dazzling white and, blazing with their own splendour, they stood with Sītā. She climbed onto the elephant which was standing in the sky and as she rose from her husband's lap, she stroked the sun and the moon with her hands. The elephant came and stood over Lankā and then they were all in a white chariot that was yoked with eight white bulls.

'I saw Rāvaṇa fall from Puṣpaka onto the ground. Then I saw him, dressed all in black, being dragged by a woman. I saw him again with a garland of red flowers in a chariot drawn by donkeys. He was travelling through mud and going south. I saw a black-skinned woman dressed in red, smeared with mud and dirt, dragging him south by a cord around his neck. Then Rāvaṇa was riding a boar, Indrajit was on a crocodile, Kumbhakarṇa was on a camel and they were all heading south.

'I saw this beautiful city of Lankā with all its horses and chariots and all the *rākṣasas* wearing red clothes and garlands, drinking and dancing to music. I saw the city plunge into the sea, its huge gates toppled. All the *rākṣasa* women were drunk on oil. Laughing and dancing and making a huge noise, they all came to Lankā which was only a heap of ashes. Kumbhakarṇa and the other *rākṣasa* leaders jumped into a pit of dung.

'Run from here! Hide yourselves! Rāma will get Sītā back and in his rage, he will kill all the *rākṣasas* as well as all of you! He will not forgive you for tormenting his beloved wife who followed him into the forest! Stop your cruel speeches. Make friends with Sītā. I think the best thing for us to do is to plead with her. When you have a dream like this about a grieving woman it means that her sorrows are at an end. Beg for Sītā's forgiveness! There is no doubt that it is Rāma who presents the greatest danger to the *rākṣasas.* Sītā is the only one who can save us now. She will be gracious and forgive us for tormenting her!'

Meanwhile, Sītā was still considering the options before her. 'Clearly, death cannot come before its time!' she wept. 'I have been deprived of happiness and I am inundated with sorrow. My heart must be hard indeed, that it does not shatter into a thousand pieces, like a mountain struck by a thunderbolt.

'It would not be wrong to kill myself since I am going to die at the hands of this odious creature in any case. I can no more accept him than a *brahmin* can teach the Vedas to someone who is not twice-born! I feel sure Rávaṇa will cut me up into little pieces before Rāma gets here. The two months he has given me to make my decision shall pass quickly, like the night before an execution passes for a prisoner condemned to death.

'Ah Rāma! Lakṣmaṇa! Sumitrā! Mother of Rāma who is like my own! I shall be destroyed like a boat upon the stormy seas! I am sure those two valiant princes were killed by that vile creature disguised as a deer, like lions or bulls struck by lightning! Ah Rāma! You have a face like the full moon, you are true to your vows, devoted to all creatures and loved by all! But you have no idea that I am going to be killed by the *rākṣasas.*

'I have suffered much for you, even slept on the ground to uphold my ascetic vows. But all my fidelity has brought me nothing, like a favour done to an ungrateful man! My adherence to *dharma* and to my marital vows has been in vain, for I lie here pale and emaciated without you,

Rāma! And I have no hope of seeing you again. When you comply with your father's wishes and complete your forest exile, you will return to your wide-eyed women, free from fear and with your aims accomplished. I have loved you for long, Rāma, and now I am ready to give up my life. I would be happy to die quickly, by poison or with a sharp weapon. But there is no one here who will give me any of these things!'

Sītā grabbed her dark braid. 'I will hang myself by my own hair and go straight to death's abode!' she cried and trembling with fear, she went up to a huge tree that was covered with flowers.

Suddenly, Sītā noticed a flood of auspicious omens which indicated a change in her fortunes. Her beautiful left eye with its long curving lashes twitched like a lotus blossom disturbed by a fish. Her plump and rounded left arm, which was worthy of the finest ointments and had been caressed by her incomparable lover, quivered. Her left thigh, as graceful as an elephant's trunk, shook and rubbed against her right thigh, suggesting that Rāma was close by. As she stood there, her clothes of yellow silk suddenly seemed to hang loose on her body. Her fears vanished and her burden of sorrow appeared to have lightened. Fortified by her newfound joy, Sītā's face was as radiant as the moon rising during the bright lunar fortnight.

# Chapter Fifty

Meanwhile, the mighty Hanumān had heard all that Sītā and Trijaṭā had said and had listened to the derision of the *rākṣasīs.* As he watched that beautiful woman, lovely enough to have come from the garden of the gods, many thoughts ran through his mind.

'I have found the one for whom hundreds of millions of monkeys have been searching! I have also secretly found out about the strength of the enemy, the fortifications of Lankā and Rāvaṇa's power. But Rāma instructed me specifically to reassure his wife who longs to see him. I must console this lovely woman. She has no experience of suffering and now she sees no end to her woes.

'It will be a mistake to leave here without comforting her in some way. If I leave, this splendid princess will kill herself because she sees no sign of deliverance. And Rāma, too, deserves some reassurance from me.

'But how can I speak to her in front of all these *rākṣasīs*? Yet, if I do not, she will end her life before the night is over. If I do not speak to her, what will I say to Rāma when he asks me what she said? If I leave Sītā without any message, Rāma will be extremely angry and will consume me with his fiery eyes. Now that I have actually reached here, I find myself among *rākṣasas.* Despite that, I must reassure this lovely woman.

'I am very large, especially for a monkey. I shall speak to this refined and cultured woman in Sanskrit. But if I speak Sanskrit like a *brahmin*, Sītā will be terribly frightened. She will think that I am Rāvaṇa! And yet, I must speak to her meaningfully in a human language. How else could I possibly reassure this virtuous woman?

'But when she sees my shape and size and hears me speak, this poor woman who is already so terrified by the *rākṣasīs,* will be even more frightened. She will take me to be Rāvaṇa, who can change his shape at will, and she will cry out in fear. And when she does that, these fearsome *rākṣasīs* who resemble death will gather around her with their awful weapons. These deformed creatures will surround me and try to kill me or capture me. But when they see me leaping from branch to branch in my gigantic form, they, too, shall be frightened. And then they will call for the *rākṣasas* who guard Rāvaṇa's palace. They will come here armed with their weapons and rush into battle. When I have destroyed these *rākṣasas* in my anger, I will not be able to reach the far shore of the ocean again. The *rākṣasas* will fall upon me and capture me and I will become a prisoner without having accomplished my purpose.

'*Rākṣasas* are accustomed to violence and they may harm Sītā. Then Rāma and Sugrīva's plans will be fruitless. Sītā is guarded by *rākṣasas* in this secret place surrounded by the ocean which has no approach paths. Even if I am killed or captured, I can see no other way of accomplishing Rāma's purpose. Now that I think about it, I see that there is no other monkey capable of leaping over these hundred *yojanās* when I am dead. I can kill thousands of *rākṣasas,* but then I shall not have the strength to leap back over the ocean.

'The outcomes of battles are never certain and uncertainty makes me uncomfortable. Which wise man would do something of which he is unsure, as if success were guaranteed? Talking to Sītā might turn out to be a mistake, but if I do not speak, she will definitely kill herself. Obstacles of time and place as well as a confused messenger destroy goals and purposes just as surely as the sunrise destroys the darkness. Even a resolute intelligence cannot always distinguish between advantage and disadvantage. And messengers who assume themselves to be wise often destroy everything. How can the success of this enterprise be ensured? How can confusion be eliminated? How can my leap over the ocean not be in vain? How can my words not cause Sītā fear?'

Hanumān went over all these ideas in his mind and finally came to a decision. 'Sītā will not be frightened if I praise Rāma's flawless deeds! Her mind is on her beloved and so if I present Rāma's righteous and auspicious words in a sweet and gentle voice, she will have faith in me!'

'Once there was a king named Daśaratha,' said Hanumān sweetly to Sītā. 'He had chariots and elephants and horses. He was famous, righteous and had gathered great merit. He delighted in non-violence. He was compassionate and truthful. He was the scion of the Ikṣvākus and he increased their prosperity. Lord of the earth, that bull among kings was famous all over the world. He was joyous and was a giver of joy.

'His eldest son, whose face was like the full moon, was his most beloved. His name was Rāma. He was wise and the best of all archers. He was the protector of his kingdom, his peoples, all beings and *dharma.* Heroic Rāma went to live in the forest with his wife and brother to honour the word of his righteous father. While he was in the forest, he was drawn away in a chase and Sītā was carried off by Rāvaṇa in revenge for Rāma's killing of Khara and Dūṣaṇa in Janasthāna.

'I heard all about Sītā's beauty and glory from Rāma. Now I am sure I have found her,' said Hanumān and fell silent.

Sītā was astonished when she heard this, and her hair dishevelled, she looked up into the tree and saw Hanumān, the son of the Wind, bright as the rising sun, hiding among the branches.

'This must be a dream!' she cried in agitation and fainted. Slowly, she regained consciousness. She thought, 'This must be a nightmare! The traditional texts state that to dream of a monkey is a bad omen. I hope Rāma and Lakṣmaṇa are well and that everything in my father's kingdom is all right!

'This cannot be a dream since my sorrows will not allow me to sleep!' she continued. 'There can be no peace for me while I am separated from moon-faced Rāma! Today, I have been thinking of him with all my heart. That is why I am seeing and hearing things! I am sure this is an illusion, but then I tell myself that this creature who speaks to me is perfectly visible!'

Hanumān joined his palms in reverence and said, 'You stand leaning against this tree, wearing soiled and dirty clothes. Who are you, lady with the lotus eyes? Why do tears stream from your eyes like water from a broken pot? God, *asura, nāga, gandharva, rākṣasa, yakṣa,* or *kinnara,* which one are you? You seem to be divine! Or are you Rohiṇī, the brightest of the stars, endowed with all the virtues, fallen from the sky without the moon? Are you Arundhatī who angered her husband in her confusion?

'Slim-waisted lady, do you mourn the loss of a father, a husband or a brother? You have the appearance of royalty. I think you must be the consort of a king! I ask you, were you abducted from Janasthāna by Rāvaṇa? If you were, then you must be Sītā! Tell me, please!'

Sītā was pleased with Hanumān's praise of Rāma and she said, 'I am the daughter of Janaka, the great king of the Videhas. I am Sītā, the wife of Rāma! For twelve full years I lived in Rāma's palace, enjoying all the pleasures known to humans and satisfying my every desire. Then, in the thirteenth year, the king and his ministers decided to consecrate Rāma heir and when everything was ready for the ceremony, the lady Kaikeyī spoke to her husband, "I will not eat or drink the food that is brought to me every day. If Rāma is consecrated heir, I will end my life! Best of kings, remember the boons you gave and send Rāma into the forest!"

'The honourable king recalled his boons but he was bewildered by Kaikeyī's cruel and hateful words. Weeping, the king who stood so firm on the path of righteousness asked his illustrious elder son for the kingdom. Effulgent Rāma held his father's word dearer than the consecration and accepted his instructions completely, in thought and deed. Rāma would never give or receive anything unworthy, even to save his life! With great sincerity, Rāma took off his priceless clothes and renounced the kingdom. He entrusted me to his mother's care, but I, too, put on the simple clothes of an ascetic and stood beside him. I would not care to live even in heaven without him! Then, Lakṣmaṇa, the joy of his friends, also put on simple clothes so that he could follow his older brother. Firm in our vows, determined to honour the promise of our lord, we entered the dense and impenetrable forest. While we were living in the Daṇḍaka forest, I, the wife of mighty Rāma, was abducted by the vile *rākṣasa* Rāvaṇa. He has given me two months to live. After that, I will kill myself!'

'I have come to you as a messenger from Rāma!' said Hanumān. 'Rāma, best among the learned and best of all warriors, the son of Daśaratha, is well and he asks about your welfare. Mighty Lakṣmaṇa, the companion of your beloved and grieving husband, bows his head to you!'

Sītā's entire body quivered with joy when she heard that Rāma and Lakṣmaṇa were both well. An extraordinary pleasure suffused Sītā and the monkey and they began to talk to each other in good faith. But when Hanumān came closer to the emaciated woman who was racked by grief, Sītā drew back in fear. 'Oh no! This has to be Rāvaṇa in another form! He mocks me with his sweet words!' She let go of the branch she was holding and fell to the ground.

Hanumān stepped closer and bowed to her but Sītā was so frightened that she could not even look at him. She sighed and said in her sweet voice, 'If you are Rāvaṇa, master of the magic arts, and if you have taken on another form, all you do is increase my distress. That is not very nice of you! You are the same Rāvaṇa who took me from Janasthāna in the form of a mendicant! Oh cruel *rākṣasa*! You can take any form you choose. I am thin and weak from fasting. How can you torment me like this?

'If you really are Rāma's messenger, I call blessings upon you! Tell me the story of Rāma, it will make me very happy! Recite Rāma's virtues to me, monkey, and carry away my soul as the river current overwhelms its banks!

'I was abducted so long ago that I now see a monkey messenger from Rāma in pleasant dream! If only I could see Rāma and Lakṣmaṇa again, even if it is in a dream, I would not be so depressed. Even these dreams make me happy!

'But this cannot be a dream! Seeing a monkey in a dream cannot lead to happiness and I am definitely happy! Am I deluded? Can this be the result of indigestion? A hallucination sprung from my insanity? I am not mad and delusions are definitely a sign of madness. I know myself and I know that this is a real monkey!'

Sītā sorted through these thoughts in her mind. Because she knew that *rākṣasas* could change their shapes, she suspected Hanumān of being Rāvaṇa. She decided that he was, indeed, the *rākṣasa* and stopped talking to him.

Hanumān was wise and understood the source of her anxiety. He placed her mind at ease with appropriate words.

'Bright as the sun, loved by all like the moon, king of all creatures, equal to the god of wealth, handsome, prosperous and as fortunate as the god of love, never angry without reason, the best charioteer on earth, that is Rāma, whose mighty arms protect the entire world! Rāvaṇa took the form of a deer and lured Rāma away and then he abducted you from that lonely place. He will face the consequences of this! Before long, heroic Rāma will kill Rāvaṇa in battle with his arrows that blaze like fire when he releases them in his anger! He sent me as a messenger to you. That is why I am here!

'Rāma grieves desperately in his separation from you and he asks about your welfare. Mighty Lakṣmaṇa greets you and sends you good wishes! There is a monkey named Sugrīva who is Rāma's friend and ally. He is the king of the monkeys and he, too, sends you greetings and good wishes. Rāma thinks of you all the time and so do Lakṣmaṇa and Sugrīva.

'Even though you have been captured by the *rākṣasas*, at least you are still alive! It won't be long before you see Rāma and Lakṣmaṇa and Sugrīva surrounded by the monkey hordes! I am mighty Hanumān, Sugrīva's minister. I leapt over the ocean and entered Lankā! I have come to see you relying on my own strength. I shall place my foot on vile Rāvaṇa's head! I am not who you think I am, Sītā! Give up your doubts and trust me!'

'Where did you meet Rāma? How do you know Lakṣmaṇa? Why did these men make an alliance with the monkeys!' asked Sītā eagerly. 'Describe Rāma and Lakṣmaṇa to me so that my grief will be bearable! Tell me, what does Rāma look like? And Lakṣmaṇa?'

Encouraged by Sītā, Hanumān launched into an accurate description of Rāma. 'I am glad you have recognized me for who I am,' he said. 'Listen while I tell you about Rāma and Lakṣmaṇa.

'Lotus-eyed Rāma delights the minds of all creatures with his good looks and his innate virtues. Bright as the morning sun, he is as steadfast as the earth, equal to Bṛhaspati in wisdom and to Indra in valour. He protects the people of the world in the same way as he protects his own family. He upholds *dharma.* He nurtures it and establishes its limits in the world while he maintains the fourfold division of society. He knows when to help good men, he is learned in all the necessary rituals and skilled in the arts of administration. He is respectful to *brahmins* as well as humble, courteous and kind. He is a fine archer and is well-versed in the sacred texts.

'Broad-shouldered and mighty-armed, he has a strong neck and a powerful chest. With his shining face, he is well known to all. His skin glows, his limbs are well-proportioned and his voice is as resonant as a drum. His lips are full, his jaw is firm and his fingers and hands are well-shaped. He is devoted to truth and gathers good men around him. He knows what is appropriate for time and place and he speaks sweetly to everyone.

'His brother, invincible Lakṣmaṇa, was born to his second mother Sumitrā and he resembles Rāma in his looks, his virtues and his loving nature.

'As they were wandering in the forest in search of you, they came upon the king of the monkeys who had been dethroned by his brother. Handsome Sugrīva had taken refuge on the Ṛṣyamūka mountain from fear of his brother and we served him there. The two princes arrived, dressed like ascetics and armed with bows. The monkey king saw them and ran to the top of the mountain in fear and confusion. Once he was safe, he sent me to them.

'I bowed before those magnificent men, rich in looks and auspicious marks, and they were pleased when I had told them all about Sugrīva. I carried them on my back to Sugrīva and mutual confidence and pleasure was established between them. Rāma reassured Sugrīva who had been displaced by his brother and Lakṣmaṇa then told him all about the grief Rāma bore because of your abduction. Sugrīva's face dimmed as he listened to the story.

'Lovely lady, when you were being carried off by the *rākṣasa,* you dropped your jewels on the ground. The monkey leaders brought them to Rāma but they could not tell him where you were. I gave Rāma the jewels that I myself had picked up, the ones that fell with a tinkling sound. Rāma was very distressed when he saw them. He placed them on his lap and looked at them again and again, weeping as he did so. He fell to the ground in his grief and I had to raise him up with many sweet words. When Rāma and Lakṣmaṇa had gazed at the jewels for a long time, they gave them back to Sugrīva.

'Rāma is terribly depressed at being separated from you. He burns in a perpetual fire of grief, like a mountain that houses a volcano, He cannot sleep and he is deeply tormented. He finds neither peace nor joy in the beautiful woods and lakes and flowing rivers because you are not by his side. But soon he shall come to rescue you. He will kill Rāvaṇa and all his family and followers!

'Rāma and Sugrīva made a pact to destroy Vālī and to search for you. Rāma killed Vālī in combat with his strength and made Sugrīva the king of all the monkeys and bears. This was how their alliance was formed. I am their messenger!

'Once Sugrīva regained his kingdom, he summoned all the great monkeys and bears for your sake. He sent them out in the ten directions and they set out all over the earth. Angada, Vālī's heroic son, was sent out with three quarters of the monkey army. We spent many days lost in the mountains and we were very depressed. As the stipulated period for the search drew to an end, we were thoroughly disheartened and we decided to kill ourselves because we feared the king of the monkeys. We had searched everywhere in the impenetrable forests and in the lakes and rivers of the mountains, but we had found no trace of you.

'Angada had given up all hope and sat there, lamenting your loss, the death of his father and of Jatāyu, and the fact that we had decided to fast to death. The king of the vultures, Sampāti, overheard the part about the death of his brother Jaṭāyu and said angrily, "Who killed my brother and where does he live? Tell me, great monkeys!" Angada told him how Jaṭāyu was killed by the *rākṣasa* in Janasthāna for your sake. Sampāti was overcome by grief and told us that you were now in Rāvaṇa's palace.

'We were delighted with Sampāti's information and were now eager to see you. But the monkey army grew despondent again when they saw the ocean. I set aside my fear and leapt over the one hundred *yojanās.* At night, I entered Lankā which was teeming with *rākṣasas.* I saw Rāvaṇa and now I have seen you, overcome by your grief.

'Virtuous lady, I have now told you everything exactly as it happened. Speak to me, for I am Rāma's messenger! I am here because of you, to accomplish Rāma's goal. Know that I am Sugrīva's minister and the son of the Wind! I can change form at will and I can go where I please. I have travelled the southern regions in search of you! Fortunately, I can now dispel the monkeys' grief with news of you. My leap over the ocean has not been in vain and I shall be famous for having seen you. And soon, mighty Rāma will join you here after he has killed Rāvaṇa and his family and all his kin!

'Sītā, I was born to the wife of Kesarī the monkey, created by the wind god. I am known in the worlds as Hanumān and I am famous in my own right. I have said all this to you to inspire your trust!'

Sītā, even though she still grieved, was reassured by all that Hanumān had said to prove that he was a genuine messenger from Rāma. Tears of joy fell from her eyes fringed with dark lashes. Her face grew radiant like the moon released by Rahu and she believed that Hanumān truly was a monkey.

'I really am Rāma's messenger,' continued Hanumān. 'Look at this priceless ring with Rāma's name etched on it! Comfort yourself, for you do not deserve to suffer!'

Sītā took her husband's ring and felt as happy as if she had been re-united with her husband. She was rather embarrassed by the pleasure she displayed when she saw the ring and she said, 'Best of monkeys, you are brave, wise and very capable. This *rākṣasa* fortress can be assaulted by you alone! You made the mighty ocean, one hundred *yojanās* wide and teeming with sea monsters, seem like a puddle in the hoofprint of a cow by leaping over it with your amazing strength! You cannot be a real monkey! You are neither frightened nor bewildered by Rāvaṇa!

'You must be worthy of my company if you have been sent here by Rāma. Invincible Rāma would never have sent you to me without testing your capacities. I am glad that Rāma and Lakṣmaṇa are both well. But if Rāma is well, why does he not consume the entire earth, girded by oceans, with his anger, like the doomsday fire? Those two mighty princes can even subdue the gods! Is there no end to my sufferings?

'I hope Rāma, the best of men, continues with his great deeds, that he is not suffering or grieving. I hope he carries on with his duties and that he is making alliances and pacts. I hope he seeks the favour of the gods and that he receives the just fruits of his efforts as well as good fortune. O monkey! I hope Rāma has not lost affection for me through this separation and I hope that he releases me from this misery!'

'Rāma does not know that you are here,' said Hanumān with his palms joined and his head bowed. 'He will be here in an instant as soon as I give him the news. Accompanied by a huge army of monkeys and bears, Rāma will churn up the ocean with a storm of arrows and destroy Lankā with all its *rākṣasas*! He will kill anyone that stands in his way, be it the gods, the *asuras* or even Death itself.

'Rāma is plunged into an ocean of sorrow at this separation from you. He knows no peace, like an elephant attacked by a lion. He neither eats meat nor drinks honey. He consumes the produce of the forest only once a day. He is so absorbed in thoughts of you that he does not even brush away the mosquitoes and gnats and crawling insects that settle on his body! Distraught with grief, he broods all day long and thinks of nothing but you. He cannot sleep, but even if he dozes off, he starts awake and calls out your name. Whenever he sees a fruit or a flower or anything beautiful, he sighs and says, "Ah! my beloved!" Rāma is utterly tormented and calls your name all the time. The mighty prince holds to his vows and is making every effort to get you back!'

'Ah, monkey! Your words are like nectar and poison at the same time—Rāma is determined to rescue me and he is overcome with grief! Death drags mortals away with his noose, be they at the height of their success or in the depths of their suffering. Fate is inexorable. Look how Rāma, Lakṣmaṇa and I are bewildered and confused by our sorrows!

'When will Rāma reach the far shore of the ocean, like a weary boat that has been shipwrecked reaches land? When will my husband destroy Lankā and the *rākṣasas* and see me? Tell him to hurry, for I shall not survive the year! Ten months have passed and the two that are left have been stipulated by Rāvaṇa as the time left for me to live. Vibhīṣaṇa, Rāvaṇa's brother, pleaded that I be restored to Rāma but Rāvaṇa decided against that. He does not want to return me, but death follows him as he goes into battle, impelled by his own destiny.

'My heart is pure and I have been virtuous. I only hope I can be reunited with my husband soon! Rāma has many great qualities, energy, courage, loyalty, valour and graciousness. Which foe would not tremble before a man who has killed fourteen thousand *rākṣasas* in Janasthāna? His grief must be unimaginable. I know his feelings the way Saci knows Indra's. Rāma is like the sun, his arrows like the sun's rays. He will dry up this ocean of *rākṣasas* with them!'

'Rāma will come here with his army of monkeys and bears as soon as he hears my news!' said Hanumān reassuringly. 'But I could free you from the *rākṣasas* and from this misery right now. Climb onto my back and I shall carry you across the ocean. I have the strength to carry away Lankā and Rāvaṇa! I can take you to Rāma in Prasravaṇa today, as the fire brings the oblation to the king of the gods. Today itself, you can see Rāma and Lakṣmaṇa. Rāma sits and waits for you, like Indra seated on the head of the king of elephants.

'Climb onto my back, lovely one. Have no fear or suspicion! Climb onto my back and I shall carry you over the ocean! No one from here will be able to follow us as I leap over the ocean with you. I can return the same way that I arrived here!'

Sītā was thrilled with Hanumān's words, but she said, 'Why do you wish to carry me such a long distance? This idea betrays your essential monkey nature! Bull among monkeys, how can you do this with your little body? You wish to carry me over the ocean to my husband who is like the king of the gods!'

Hanumān, son of the Wind, was deeply insulted. 'This woman clearly has no idea of my strength or of my true nature,' he thought to himself. 'Let her see the form I can take whenever I choose!' And Hanumān, the best of monkeys, the subduer of his foes, showed himself to Sītā in his true form. He jumped down from the tree and began to expand himself to inspire confidence in Sītā. He became as large as the mountains Meru and Mandara and his body blazed like fire. He stood in front of Sītā with his coppery face, his nails and teeth as hard and bright as diamonds.

'I have the capacity to carry off the whole of Lankā with its king, its forests, mountains and its massive gates!' he cried. 'Do not fret! Do not hesitate! Come with me and dispel Rāma and Lakṣmaṇa's grief!'

'Great monkey, I am aware of your strength,' said Sītā gently to the gigantic son of the Wind. 'Your speed is as awesome as the wind's and your splendour is like the fire's! How could any ordinary monkey have crossed the boundless ocean and reached this place? I know you have the strength to take me away from here, but we must think carefully for the success of this enterprise.

'It is not right for me to go with you. You move with the speed of the wind, it might make me faint in terror. I might fall from your back as you cross the ocean and I would quickly become a meal for the monsters that fill the ocean!

'I cannot come with you. Carrying a woman would place you in great danger. When the vile *rākṣasas* see you taking me away, Rāvaṇa will order them to follow you. You will be surrounded by these fierce creatures armed with their weapons and you will be in danger all because of me! They will be armed and you shall have no weapons. How will you protect me in the sky?

'I might fall from your back while you fight the cruel *rākṣasas.* I might fall when they have somehow managed to defeat you. I might fall when your face is turned the other way. Then, the wicked *rākṣasas* would catch me as I fell and carry me off! They might grab me from your hands and rip me to bits! Victory and defeat are uncertain in war!

'If I were to die, abused by the *rākṣasas,* then all your efforts will have been in vain! If you were to return and kill all the *rākṣasas,* Rāma's success will be diminished because you have slaughtered them all. When the *rākṣasas* have captured me, they will throw me away and neither the monkeys nor Rāma will find me. And that, too, would make your efforts fruitless.

'The best thing is for you to come back here with Rāma. The lives of Rāma, his brothers and the royal family lie with me. The two princes, hopeless and consumed with grief because of me, might give up their lives along with all the monkeys and bears.

'I have dedicated myself to serving my husband and I cannot think about touching another man, not even with my foot! When Rāvaṇa carried me away, I was forced to touch his body even though I was a chaste wife. What could I do? I was helpless and unprotected.

'It would be worthy of Rāma to kill Rāvaṇa and all the other *rākṣasas* and take me away from here. I have seen and heard his great deeds. Not even the gods, the *gandharvas* or the *asuras* can rival him in battle! Who would challenge Rāma, who blazes like the fire fanned by the wind, when they see him in battle, armed with his bow and accompanied by Lakṣmaṇa? Who would challenge him when he appears like a rutting guardian elephant, his arrows bright as the sun's rays at the end of time?

'Ah, monkey! Bring my husband here as soon as you can! Bring Lakṣmaṇa and all the other monkey leaders! I have suffered too long for Rāma's sake. Now bring me happiness!'

'You have spoken appropriately, in keeping with your nature as a virtuous woman and a devoted wife,' said Hanumān. 'It is not right that a woman should cross the ocean on my back. Sītā, the second reason you mentioned, that you would not touch any man other than Rāma, makes you worthy of being honourable Rāma's wife. Who else but you would speak like this?

'There were many reasons why I spoke the way I did. I was compelled by my affection for Rāma and by a desire to please him. I boasted about my abilities because it is so difficult to cross the ocean and enter Lankā. I wanted to take you away because of my friendship for Rāma. It is my affection for him and my devotion to my elders and masters that made me speak thus.

'But since you cannot come with me, blameless lady, give me a token by which Rāma will know that I have met you.'

Sītā, who was like a daughter of the gods, replied softly, her voice broken by her tears. 'The best token that I can give you is this message. Say to my beloved Rāma:

'"Earlier, when we lived on the north-eastern slope of the Citrakūṭa mountain, in the region where the Mandākinī flows, near the settlements of the holy ascetics, the area was filled with flowering trees and beautiful plants. One day, when my body was still wet from my bath, you fell asleep with your head in my lap. A crow carrying a piece of meat in its beak began to attack me and I tried to ward it off with clods of earth. The bird clung to me with its vicious claws and began to tear at the flesh it carried. I was angry with the bird and drew off my girdle. But my clothes slipped off and at that very moment, you woke and saw me. You began to laugh and I was terribly embarrassed. I hid in your arms to get away from the crow and though I was still angry, I was mollified by your laughter. You wiped the tears from my eyes and my face and then, hissing like an angry serpent, you said, 'Lady with the thighs like an elephant's trunk, who has dared strike you on the breast?' You looked around and saw the crow with its bloody claws. But the bird was the best of all creatures that can fly. He was one of Indra's sons and, with the speed of the wind, he entered the earth. You made a terrible decision. You took a blade of grass and invoked Brahmā's weapon. The blazing blade flew towards the bird, following him through the air and everywhere as he tried to look for protection. The bird was renounced by his father and by all the holy sages. Finally, when he had travelled through the three worlds, the bird came to you for refuge. You protected him with compassion, even though he deserved death. But you could not recall the weapon once it had been invoked and so you injured the crow's right eye. The crow thanked you and honoured you and then flew back to its home.

'"Lord of the earth, you would use the Brahmā weapon against a lowly crow for my sake! How can you tolerate my being abducted by another creature? I have heard about your benevolence and your righteousness. Be compassionate to me and let me live in hope! I know you are brave and loyal and strong, as deep as the ocean and equanimous in all situations. You are skilled in the use of all weapons. Why do you not use them against these vile *rākṣasas*?"' said Sītā.

'No creature can match Rāma's skills and strength in battle,' she continued. 'If heroic Rāma is still interested in me, why doesn't he loose his sharp arrows against these awful *rākṣasas*? Or Lakṣmaṇa, why doesn't he rescue me on the instructions of his brother? The princes are equal to Indra and Vāyu in splendour and they are invincible even against the gods. Why are they so indifferent to me? I must have done something terribly wrong for them to disregard me like this!

'Kausalyā bore Rāma, the lord of the worlds. On my behalf, bow your head to him and ask after his welfare. And mighty Lakṣmaṇa, broad-chested, good-looking and so protective, who followed his brother into the forest. Lakṣmaṇa respects Rāma as much as he does his parents. He did not know that I was being abducted. Lakṣmaṇa is dearer to Rāma than I am. He is gentle, pure and wise and when Rāma is with him he even forgets his noble father. Honour Lakṣmaṇa for me.

'Say to my husband again and again, "Son of Daśaratha, I have but one month to live. I swear to you that I will not survive more than that! Come and rescue me from this vile creature!"' Then Sītā pulled out the jewel that she wore in her hair and gave it to Hanumān saying, 'Give this to Rāma!' Hanumān took the jewel and bowed to her, placing it on his finger. He was filled with joy at having met Sītā and his thoughts flew at once to Rāma.

'Rāma will recognize this token,' said Sītā. 'It will make him remember three people, his mother, me and King Daśaratha. Monkey, you must now make an even greater effort than you did before. But think carefully about the consequences of all that you do. You are the sole authority here. Think about what you can do to end my grief!'

Realizing that Hanumān was about to leave, Sītā spoke in a voice that was thick with tears. 'Give my best wishes to Rāma and Lakṣmaṇa and Sugrīva, his ministers, the elders and all the monkeys! Do whatever you must to enable Rāma to rescue me from this ocean of grief! Give Rāma my message and tell him to take me way from here—you will gain much merit if you do! When he hears my words, he will be doubly eager to see me again and will make preparations to attack!'

'Never fear, sweet lady! Rāma will soon be here with the army of monkeys and bears and he will put an end to your suffering,' said Hanumān with his head bowed. 'He is eager to subdue the entire earth, girded by the seas, because the victory will be for your sake!'

Sītā knew that what Hanumān said was true, and she watched as he made preparations to depart. 'If you think it's all right, will you stay here for another day? You can hide somewhere, rest and leave tomorrow,' she said. 'Your presence would lighten my burden of grief for at least a little while! If you leave and return again, my life is in danger. I could not bear the pain of not seeing you and I might die of grief!

'But the biggest doubt before me now is about your allies, the monkeys and bears. How will that army and those two mortal heroes cross the boundless ocean? There are only three creatures who can cross the ocean, you, the wind and Garuḍa! Do you see any means by which this impossible task can be accomplished? You are capable of doing all this by yourself, but then, you would gain the fruits of this success.

'But it would be appropriate if Rāma were to defeat Rāvaṇa and all his armies in war and take me back to his own city, if he were to conquer Lankā and take me away himself. That would be worthy of a hero such as Rāma! You should ensure that Rāma can do all this himself!'

Hanumān listened to Sītā's wise and sensible words and replied, 'Sugrīva leads the army of monkeys and bears. He is intelligent and devoted to your success. Sugrīva will come here with hundreds of thousands of monkeys who are courageous and determined. They are so swift that they can fly up, down and sideways, their energy is so great that they can accomplish great deeds. I am but one among many that are my equals. If I could reach here, they will do so much more easily. The best of beings are never sent as messengers, only the inferior are!

'Do not worry about this. Stop grieving. The monkeys will reach Lankā in a single bound. Rāma and Lakṣmaṇa are like the sun and the moon and soon those heroes will be before you, riding on my back. They will destroy Lankā with their arrows and Rāma will take you back to his own city after he has killed Rāvaṇa and all the *rākṣasas*! Have courage and wait for that moment! Rāma will stand before you, blazing like fire! Soon, you shall cross over this ocean of grief!'

Sītā was touched by Hanumān's comforting words. 'Seeing you and hearing you speak has cheered me up a lot, like the earth that rejoices when rain comes to almost ripened crops!' she said gratefully. 'Have pity on me and make sure that I am reunited as soon as possible with Rāma. I yearn for him so! Remind him of the blade of grass he sent after the crow that put out one of his eyes. Tell him to remember the vermillion he smeared on my cheek when the one on my forehead had been wiped off! How can he, the equal of Indra and Varuna, tolerate the abduction of his wife and her living among the *rākṣasas?*

'Tell him, "I have treasured and protected this jewel, born from the sea, that I am sending you now. I would look at it and think that I was looking at your face and it would make me happy! I cannot live like this for much longer. For your sake, I have borne the cruel taunts of the *rākṣasis* which pierced my heart. I will hold on for another month, but after that, I cannot live separated from you, great prince! The king of the *rākṣasas* is a vile creature and he looks at me with lust in his eyes. If you delay much longer after you have heard about my misery, then I am afraid that I will not survive!'

Hanumān listened to her miserable words and her weeping. 'Rāma is terribly upset about your suffering. I swear this is the truth. And Lakṣmaṇa is upset because Rāma is unhappy. I have found you! This is no time for sorrow! Your troubles will be over in no time at all! Rāma and Lakṣmaṇa will reduce Lankā to ashes in their eagerness to see you.

'Give me some other tokens that Rāma will recognize and which will increase his joy,' said Hanumān.

'But I have already given you the best of them all,' replied Sītā. 'He will believe all you say when he sees this jewel from my hair!'

Hanumān bowed to Sītā and began to expand in size in preparation to leave.

# *Chapter Fifty-One*

'Now that I have seen Sītā, there is very little left for me to do,' thought Hanumān as he left. 'There are four ways to approach the enemy. Negotiation is not possible with *rākṣasas* because of their nature, bribery does not work among the prosperous, and creating dissension among enemy forces is never used by those who take pride in their abilities. Which leaves the use of force—and that makes me very happy!

'He who is appointed to do one thing and manages to do others as well without jeopardizing the task he was sent for is worthy indeed. There is no single approach to anything and the one who understands that his goal has many aspects will definitely be successful. I have finished what I was sent to do but if I return with information about how to crush the enemy, then my master's aim will truly have been achieved. I should engineer a confrontation with the *rākṣasas* such that Rāvaṇa has to pit his powers against mine!

'I will consume this beautiful grove, this pleasure garden, as fire consumes a dried forest. That is sure to make Rāvaṇa angry. He will call up his mighty army with its enormous infantry, its chariots, elephants and heavily armed warriors and there will be a huge battle. I will destroy the army and then return to the monkeys with no trouble at all!'

Hanumān, son of the Wind, called up his terrible energy that was like the storm winds and began to uproot trees with his powerful legs. He wreaked havoc upon the lovely garden with all its trees and creepers, where the trumpeting of rutting elephants could still be heard. Its pools were destroyed, its mountain peaks crushed, its pavilions and vine-covered arbours shattered, its animals and snakes were set free and its palaces and stone huts were totally wrecked.

Now that he had achieved what he knew would cause great pain to the king of the *rākṣasas,* Hanumān stood at the gate, blazing with splendour, ready to take on the mighty *rākṣasas.*

Lankā's citizens were disturbed and confused by the shrieking of the birds and the crashing of trees. Animals and birds ran, terrified, in all directions and inauspicious signs for the *rākṣasas* began to appear.

The hideous *rākṣasīs* in the grove woke suddenly, their sleep shattered, and they saw the destruction around them. Then they noticed the enormous monkey who had taken on his gigantic form in order to frighten them.

'Who is this!' they asked Sītā when they saw Hanumān. 'Where has he come from? Why is he here? Why did he speak to you? Don't be frightened, tell us why he spoke to you?'

'How would I know who he is, since *rākṣasas* can change their form at will?' said Sītā demurely. 'You should know who or what he is and what he might do. A snake knows another snake's tracks! I don't know who he is. I am too terrified of him. He must be a *rākṣasa* that has changed his shape and come here!'

The *räksasis* scattered in all directions. Some of them stayed where they were and others went to tell Rāvaṇa about the terrifying monkey in a completely unnatural form.

'There is an enormous monkey in the grove, O king, and he is very powerful. He has had a conversation with Sītā!' they cried.

'We asked the doe-eyed Sītā about him many times but she refused to talk about him!'

'He may be a messenger from Indra or Kubera! Or maybe he has been sent by Rāma to find out about Sītā!'

'This amazing creature has utterly destroyed your lovely pleasure garden with all its animals!'

'He has destroyed everything there except the place where Sītā sat. Maybe he was tired, or maybe he wanted to protect her.

'A creature like him cannot possibly know fatigue, he must have wanted to protect her!'

'He has destroyed your garden and spoken to Sītā! You must inflict a harsh punishment upon this awful creature!'

'Who would dare speak to Sītā, who has captured your heart, and still preserve his life?'

Rāvaṇa's eyes flashed with rage when he heard all this and he blazed like a sacrificial fire. He summoned the *kinkaras,* who equalled him in their courage, and ordered them to capture Hanumān. Thousands of armed and violent *kinkaras* emerged from the palace. They were strong and hideous to look at, proud of their fighting skills and eager to capture the monkey. They ran towards the gate where Hanumān stood, like moths to flame, carrying their clubs and maces and their golden bracelets and their arrows shone like the sun.

Resplendent Hanumān, full of energy and like a mountain in size, flung his tail to the ground with a resounding crash. The *kinkaras* were filled with trepidation when they heard him roar and when they saw him, looking like a massive evening cloud. Under strict instructions from their master, the *kinkaras* began to strike Hanumān from all directions with their various weapons. Hanumān grabbed an iron bar from the gate and attacked those warriors who surrounded him on all sides. He killed them all and still willing to fight some more, he went back and stood at the gate.

The few *kinkaras* that escaped fled back to Rāvaṇa and told him how the others had been slaughtered. Rāvaṇa's eyes rolled in anger and he called the mighty son of Prahasta into battle.

Having massacred the *kinkaras,* Hanumān stood for a while in thought. 'I have destroyed the pleasure grove,' he said to himself. 'Now I should destroy the *rākṣasas* worship hall.'

Displaying his might and blazing with his own splendour, the monkey leapt to the top of the sacred hall that was as tall as Mount Meru and crushed it. He took on his gigantic form again and filled Lankā with his roars. Birds fell out of the sky when they heard that sound and all kinds of creatures were hurt.

'The mighty Rāma, Lakṣmaṇa and Sugrīva, who is Rāma's ally, will all be victorious!' he yelled. 'I am the servant of the king of Kosalā, Rāma the magnificent! I am Hanumān, the son of the Wind, the killer of enemies! A thousand Rāvaṇas cannot face me in battle when I throw trees and rocks around by the hundreds! I have honoured Sītā and I have destroyed Lankā. Now I will leave from here while all the *rākṣasas* watch!'

Hanumān's words rang through Lankā and inspired fear among the *rākṣasas.* Thousands of enormous guards appeared and hurled their weapons at him, arrows, spears, swords and axes, appearing like a whirlpool in the Gangā as they swirled around the great monkey.

Hanumān pulled up a shining, golden pillar from the hall and attacked the guards, killing one hundred of them. 'Hundreds of thousands of monkeys who are as brave and as powerful as I am have been called up under Sugrīva's command!' he shouted as he stood in the air. 'They will come here in their countless numbers and soon there will be no city of Lankā, no Rāvaṇa and none of you! All because you have chosen enmity with Rāma, the lord of the Ikṣvākus!'

Then, Jambumālī, Prahasta's invincible son, came out to do battle with Hanumān, as Rāvaṇa had instructed. He was a mighty archer and he wore a red garland and clothes of shining white. His bow was like Indra's and his arrows shone. He drew his bowstring, and the sky and all the directions were filled with its thunderous twang.

Jambumālī assailed Hanumān, who stood on top of the gate with arrows that never missed their target. Some had iron tips, others crescent heads and some were decorated with plumes. They struck the monkey all over his body. Hanumān found a huge rock and hurled it at the *rākṣasa* in anger. Jambumālī split the rock into pieces with his arrows and did the same to the *sāla* tree that Hanumān threw after it. Hanumān grabbed a club and hit Jambumālī on the chest so hard that neither his head nor his arms, nor his knees, bow, arrows, chariot or horses could be distinguished from one another.

Rāvaṇa was enraged when he heard about Jambumālī's death and sent out the seven sons of his ministers who were known for their skills in battle.

They were the vanguard of the mighty *rākṣasa* army and were renowned archers, skilled in the use of all kinds of weapons. They drove forth in their horse-drawn chariots, rumbling like the ocean. Their banners flying, they drew their bows decorated with gold and were like dark clouds touched by lightning. They egged each other on and charged towards Hanumān, releasing a flood of arrows at him. Hanumān dodged the arrows as he ducked and weaved in the air, almost as if he were playing with them, the way his father, the wind, plays with rain clouds.

Suddenly, he flew into the midst of the *rākṣasas* and attacked with his hands and feet and nails. He whirled some of them around, he crushed some of them between his thighs and still others were felled by the might of his roar. Those that survived fled in terror while horses sank to the ground and elephants trumpeted. The earth was strewn with broken chariots, seats, banners and flags.

Hanumān was still eager to fight and once he had slain these *rākṣasas,* he returned to his position at the gate.

Rāvaṇa called upon his five great generals, Virūpāksa, Yūpākṣa, Durdura, Praghāsa and Bhasakarṇa, when he heard about the death of the ministers' sons. They were all brave and skilled warriors who could move with the speed of the wind, and Rāvaṇa ordered them to attack Hanumān.

'Go forth, my generals, surrounded by your troops and accompanied by your horses, chariots and elephants. This monkey has to be subdued! Remember that you must act with restraint as you approach him. His actions lead me to believe that he is no ordinary monkey. He has taken on a wondrous form to do all the things he did. Maybe he was created by Indra because of us. All of you have defeated *nāgas*, *yakṣas,* gods, *gandharvas, asuras* and the great sages. I am sure they are plotting against us. Seize that creature!

'Do not dismiss this monkey. I have seen many monkeys who are swift and mighty, like Vālī, Sugrīva, the powerful Jāmbavān, the general Nīla, Dvivida and others. But none of them have this sort of speed, energy, power and intelligence. Nor can any of them take on this kind of form. This is some other great being that has appeared in the form of a monkey! You will need all your skills to subdue him!'

The generals went out, fully armed, blazing like fire. They were accompanied by chariots, rutting elephants, magnificent horses and mighty warriors armed with every kind of weapon. They located Hanumān and after taking stock of the situation, they positioned themselves around him and began the attack.

Durdura released a rain of sharp arrows at the monkey but Hanumān leapt high into the air and landed on the chariot like lightning striking a mountain. Durdura's chariot was shattered, his eight horses were crushed and the *rākṣasa* fell to the ground, dead. Hanumān grabbed a *sāla* tree and killed Virūpākṣa and Yūpākṣa. Praghāsa and Bhasakarṇa attacked Hanumān together, but Hanumān hurled an enormous mountain peak with all its trees and animals at them and killed them in an instant.

Then the great monkey set about destroying what was left of the army. Dead elephants and horses, smashed chariots and slain *rākṣasas* lay all over the place, blocking all the roads to the battlefield. Hanumān saw this and went back to the gateway to rest, like Time when all creatures have been destroyed at doomsday.

Rāvaṇa's messengers came back with the news that the five generals had been killed, and, while Rāvaṇa was deciding what to do next, he caught the eye of the young prince Akṣa, who was eager to fight. Akṣa understood the meaning of his father's look, and he immediately grabbed his golden bow and leapt up from his seat, like a flame leaping up from a fire when oblations are poured upon it. He climbed into his chariot made of burnished gold which shone like the sun and went out to face Hanumān.

Akṣa stared at the monkey in amazement mixed with respect and provoked him by loosing three arrows at him. When the battle between Akṣa and Hanumān began, the earth groaned, the sun dimmed and the wind died down. The mountains shook, the sea rose and the sky was filled with a huge noise. Hanumān swelled with strength and power as he burned Akṣa's horses and chariots with the fire from his eyes. Akṣa was young and inexperienced, but he was proud of his exploits in battle and filled with arrogance about his fighting abilities. He charged towards Hanumān like a tusker charging towards a well covered with grass.

Hanumān roared like thunder and rose up into the sky. He was an awesome sight, with his arms and legs spread wide. Seated in his chariot, Akṣa continued with his onslaught of arrows, battering Hanumān as a mountain would be battered by hail. Hanumān saw his opponent's skills and realized that he would have to kill his enemy at once. With a single blow of his open palm Hanumān slew Akṣa's magnificent horses and the *rākṣasa's* chariot tumbled to the ground. Akṣa leapt into the sky armed with his bow and arrows and sword, but Hanumān grabbed him by his feet and whirled him around and shook him as Garuḍa would shake a serpent. He turned him around one thousand times and flung him to the ground. Akṣa's head and limbs were smashed, his sinews, muscles and entrails were strewn everywhere and his eyes and bones mingled with the blood that flowed from his body.

The other *rākṣasas* were terrified when they saw Hanumān squeeze the life out of Akṣa, who rivalled Indra in splendour, and return to the gate like Time when all creatures have been destroyed.

Rāvaṇa had to bring his emotions under control and steady himself when he heard about Akṣa's death. He summoned his son Indrajit and said, 'You are the best among all those who control celestial weapons and you are a skilled warrior. You have tormented the gods and the *asuras* and you have earned special weapons from Brahmā. The gods and the *asuras* cannot counter the strength of your weapons and there in no one in the three worlds who can fight as tirelessly as you. You are my equal in terms of the power you have earned from your austerities as well as your strength and skills. I am confident in battle when you are by my side.

'The *kinkaras* have been killed. So have Jambumālī, the sons of our ministers and the five generals. Even your beloved younger brother Akṣa is dead. But I never had the faith in their skills that I do in yours. Match your strength against that monkey's! Use your intelligence and all your experience and attack him!

'It is not appropriate that I should send you out on this mission, but it is possible for a *kṣatriya* to do this since it is in keeping with the code of kings.'

The splendid *rākṣasa* prince with the lotus eyes went forth like the ocean at high tide. His chariot was drawn by four white horses who were as swift as Garuḍa.

Hanumān was delighted to hear the rumbling of the chariot and the twanging of Indrajit's bow. He let out a mighty yell and began to expand in size. He stood in the sky and dodged the mighty archer's arrows, skipping and jumping, making it impossible for the expert marksman to take aim. He would stand still and then leap into the air waving his arms.

Indrajit saw that his arrows were ineffective and thought about what else he could do. He realized that the monkey could not be killed and began to think of ways to capture him alive. Heroic Indrajit released Brahmā's weapon against the valiant monkey.

Hanumān was trapped by the weapon and fell unconscious to the ground, bereft of all his powers. He realized that he had been struck by Brahmā's weapon and thought, 'I cannot free myself because of Brahmā's power. It has been ordained that I should be felled by this weapon and I must endure this!' Hanumān submitted himself to the weapon's power because of the respect he had for Brahmā. 'Even though I have been bound, I am not in danger, for I am protected by Vāyu and Indra as well as by Brahmā,' he said to himself. 'The *rākṣasas* have captured me because I displayed my powers. Now I can meet the king of the *rākṣasas*!'

Hanumān stopped struggling and allowed himself to be tied up with ropes of bark and hemp. 'It is good that the king of the *rākṣasas* wants to see me,' he thought as he lay motionless. Once he had been bound with ropes, he was no longer subject to the power of Brahmā's weapon but though he was dragged along and beaten and kicked and punched, he remained quiet.

Hanumān was brought into Rāvaṇa's presence, and Indrajit displayed him to the king and his retinue. 'Who is this?' 'Whom does he belong to?' 'Where does he come from?' 'What is he doing here?' 'Whom is his master?' asked the other heroic *rākṣasas.* Talking among themselves, they said, 'Eat him!' 'Kill him!' 'Burn him!'

'I have come here as a messenger from the king of the monkeys!' shouted Hanumān in response to their questions.

Hanumān, whose deeds had excited so much amazement and wonder, stared at the king of the *rākṣasas* with his red eyes. Rāvaṇa blazed with his own splendour and with the brilliance of his golden crown which was studded with pearls. His jewels were dazzling and he wore the finest silks. His body was anointed with rare red sandalpaste. He sat upon a crystal throne inlaid with diamonds. As Hanumān gazed at him in wonder, the *rākṣasa* king reminded him of a rain cloud on the peaks of Mount Meru. Though the *rākṣasas* had beaten Hanumān badly, he could not help but be impressed by their king. He was stunned by his glory and effulgence.

'How magnificent he is!' thought Hanumān. 'What beauty, what courage, what grace! He has all the signs of a great king! Had he not been so unrighteous, he may well have been the protector of the world, of the heavens, even of Indra himself! But all the worlds, including the gods and the *dānavas,* fear him, for in his anger, he could destroy them instantly!'

Mighty Rāvaṇa looked at the yellow-eyed monkey standing in front of him and his anger grew. He said to Prahasta, 'Ask this wicked creature where he is from and why he destroyed the *aśoka* grove. Why did he frighten the *rākṣasīs* there?'

'Monkey, rest assured that you have nothing to fear!' said Prahasta to Hanumān. 'Have you been sent here to Rāvaṇa's city by Indra? Tell us the truth and you will go free! Or was it Kubera or Yama or Varuṇa that sent you here in this magnificent form? Are you a messenger from Viṣṇu? Your splendour is not like a monkey's, only your form is! If you tell us the truth, you shall be set free, but if you lie, you will not live much longer! Why are you here?'

'I am not from Indra, Varuṇa or Yama,' replied Hanumān. 'I am not allied with Kubera nor am I under instructions from Viṣṇu. I am really a monkey and I came here to see the king of the *rākṣasas*. He is not easy to see and so I destroyed the *aśoka* grove in order to be brought before him. Then I ran into these mighty *rākṣasas* who seemed eager to fight. I fought back in self-defence. I cannot be bound by any celestial weapons! That is the boon Brahmā gave me! I submitted to the Brahmā weapon and the beating by the *rākṣasas* only because I wanted to see the king.

'Know that I am a messenger from Rāma!' he said. 'Listen to the good advice I have for you!'

'I came here to your realm on Sugrīva's instructions,' continued heroic Hanumān. 'He asks after your welfare and sends you this advice which is wise and just and intended for your benefit, appropriate here on earth as well as in heaven.

'There was a great king named Daśaratha who had many chariots and horses and elephants. Equal to Indra in majesty, he was like a friend and father to the world. His oldest and most beloved son entered the Daṇḍaka forest in obedience to his father's wishes. His brother Lakṣmaṇa and his wife Sītā went with him. His name was Rāma. He is splendid and takes refuge on the path of righteousness. His wife Sītā, devoted to her husband, was the princess of Videha and she was lost in the forest.

'Searching for her, Rāma and his younger brother reached Ṛṣyamūka and formed an alliance with Sugrīva. Sugrīva agreed to search for Sītā and Rāma promised to help him regain the monkey kingdom. Sugrīva killed Vālī with Rāma's help and was established on the throne as lord of the monkeys and bears. True to his word, Sugrīva sent out monkeys in search of Sītā in all directions. Hundreds of thousands of millions of monkeys searched everywhere, above and below and in the sky. Those mighty monkeys are strong and powerful, as swift as Garuḍa and the wind, unmatched in their prowess.

'I am Hanumān, son of the Wind. For Sītā's sake, I leapt over the ocean, a leap of one hundred *yojanās*! I came here to see her!

'Wise one, you are so learned in what is right and just and have gained so much through ascetic practice. It is not right that you should carry off the wife of another man! Intelligent beings like you are not attracted to acts of unrighteousness which destroy the very roots of your existence!

'Who, even among the gods and the *asuras,* can withstand the arrows Lakṣmaṇa releases under Rāma's angry instructions! Can there be a single king in the three worlds who will gain happiness if he has insulted Rāma? Consider these words that are appropriate for all times and for all intentions. Return Sītā to god-like Rāma!

'I have done the impossible and seen Sītā in Lankā. Rāma will accomplish all that is left to be done! I saw Sītā, burning with grief. You do not realize that this woman you abducted is as dangerous as a five-headed serpent. She cannot be had even by the gods or the *asuras,* just as even strong people cannot withstand poison!

'Do not destroy all the merit you have earned through your asceticism! It is not right to destroy the substance of one's life like this! Do not take refuge in the invincibility you gained from the gods. For Sugrīva is neither a god nor an *asura.* He is neither a man nor a *rākṣasa,* neither a *yakṣa* nor a *gandharva*, nor even a *nāga.* Sugrīva is the king of the monkeys and Rāma is a mortal. How will you save your life now, king? The fruits of good and bad deeds cannot exist together. Good and bad acts deliver separate results and *dharma* destroys *adharma.* There is no doubt that you have enjoyed the fruits of your righteousness until now. But soon, you will have to face the consequences of your vile behaviour!

'Keep in mind the massacre in Janasthāna and the killing of Vālī. Think of the alliance between Sugrīva and Rāma! Consider all these things for your own sake! I alone can destroy Lankā with all its elephants, horses and chariots! And Rāma has sworn in the presence of the monkeys and bears that he will kill the enemy who took Sītā.

'The woman who is now in your power, the one whom you think of as Sītā, she is the long night of death that will destroy you and your city! Don't place your head in death's noose. Think about how you can save yourself! You will have to watch as Lankā is consumed by Sītā's effulgence and the fire of Rāma's wrath!'

Rāvaṇa listened to the unpleasant truth that Hanumān placed before him and he was incensed. His eyes rolled with anger in his ten heads and he ordered that the monkey be put to death immediately.

# *Chapter Fifty-Two*

Vibhīṣaṇa did not agree with Rāvaṇa's decision to kill the monkey who had declared himself to be messenger. He knew that the king of the *rākṣasas* was angry and that the deed was as good as done, so Vibhīṣaṇa, who was skilled in what to do when, began to worry about doing the right thing. He made up his mind to speak and the eloquent Vibhīṣaṇa addressed his brother with the best intentions.

'It not right nor is it sanctioned by the rules of conduct that this monkey be killed. It is also unworthy of you to do such a thing. There is no doubt that this creature is a mighty enemy and that he has caused enormous problems, but the wise ruler would never think of killing a messenger. There are many other punishments that can be inflicted upon him instead. You can disfigure him or whip him or shave his head or even brand him. But I have never heard of anyone killing a messenger.

'How can someone like you, whose intelligence is modulated by righteousness, who knows the past, the present and the future, who is so resolute and determined, how can you be overpowered by rage? The truly virtuous never succumb to their anger. You are the foremost among the gods and the *asuras,* you are unrivalled in your knowledge of *dharma,* in your modes of conduct and your understanding of the traditional texts.

'I see no point in killing this monkey. Death should be reserved for those who sent him here. A messenger who speaks on behalf of others does not deserve to die. Good or bad depends on his masters. Even if we were to kill him, I cannot think of any other flying creature who could cross the ocean. Do not waste your time on this creature. Put your energies into planning a battle against Indra and the gods.

'You love a fight, but if you kill this messenger, I can think of no one else who could incite those two princes to come here. They are already deterred by the long and arduous journey to Lankā. You are so powerful and cannot be defeated even by the gods and the *asuras*. You should not deprive the *rākṣasas* of another opportunity to go to war! Your hundreds of thousands of warriors are the best and you have kept them contented and happy. They are nobly born, virtuous and intelligent and they are armed with the best of weapons. Let a few of them go out and capture those foolish princes so that the enemy becomes aware of your power!'

Ten-headed Rāvaṇa listened carefully to his brother's intelligent advice. 'I agree with you,' he said. 'Killing a messenger is reprehensible. We must punish him in some other way. A monkey's tail is the most prized part of his body. Set his tail on fire and release him! His friends and well-wishers will see him, pathetic and miserable because his precious tail has been disfigured!'

Rāvaṇa ordered the *rākṣasas* to set fire to Hanumān's tail and lead him through the streets of Lankā. The *rākṣasas* wrapped the monkey's tail in strips of cotton and Hanumān grew in size like a forest fire fed with faggots. The *rākṣasas* drenched the cotton strips in oil and lit them. Hanumān's face grew as red as the rising sun with anger and impatience and he attacked the *rākṣasas* with his burning tail. The cruel *rākṣasas* bound him even more tightly, so Hanumān reconsidered his situation carefully.

'Even though I have been tied up, the *rākṣasas* cannot prevent me from breaking these bonds. I can create even more havoc if I run amongst them. I can defeat them all in battle! But I must tolerate this for Rāma's sake.

'I must spy on Lankā again at dawn. I could not examine its fortifications properly last night. Even though *rākṣasas* torture me by tying up my tail and setting fire to it, my mind is calm!'

The *rākṣasas* grabbed the shining monkey and went out with great joy. They blew conches and trumpets and boasted about their exploits as they led him through the city. Hanumān observed everything around him as he was taken through Lankā. He saw the beautiful mansions and towers and highways and streets while the *rākṣasas* declared that he was a spy.

When Hanumān's tail was set alight, the hideous *rākṣasis* ran to Sītā to give her the unpleasant news. 'Sītā, that red-faced monkey who spoke to you is being led around the city with his tail on fire!' they shouted.

Sītā thought of her own abduction when she heard their cruel words and she was distraught with grief. She wished the best for the monkey, so she collected herself and called upon the god of fire. 'If I have been a devoted and chaste, wife, if I have performed austerities and been loyal, be cool for Hanumān!' she pleaded. 'If you have any compassion for me and if I have any good fortune left, be cool for Hanumān! If noble Sugrīva is going to keep his word and rescue me from this misery, be cool for Hanumān! If righteous Rāma knows that I have been virtuous and that I yearn to be with him again, be cool for Hanumān!'

The blazing fire turned its flames to the right as if in deference to her wishes, indicating to the large-eyed woman that the monkey would not be harmed.

Even as his tail was burning, Hanumān thought, 'This fire is blazing! How come it does not consume me completely? I can see the huge flame but I do not feel the heat! It is as if winter has fallen upon my tail. It must be yet another miracle because of Rāma's power. When I was crossing the ocean, didn't a mountain rise up out of the waters? If the ocean and Mainaka could do this, so can fire! I am sure the fire does not burn me because of his friendship with my father the wind, because of Rāma's majesty and because of Sītā's virtue!'

Hanumān leapt forward and roared fiercely. He reached the gates of the city which were as high as mountain peaks. He expanded himself till he was the size of a mountain and then contracted himself as much as he could and slipped out of the bonds that held him. Once he was free, he grew again and picked up a club that he saw lying near the gate. He used it to kill the guards stationed there and then turned towards Lankā, his burning tail forming a circle around him like the aureole around the rising sun.

Fired with enthusiasm, Hanumān thought about what he could do next. 'How can I torment the *rākṣasas* even more?' he wondered. 'The *aśoka* grove has been uprooted, cruel *rākṣasas* have been killed, a part of the army has been slain. Only the fortifications remain to be destroyed! Once that has been done, the rest will be easy and my efforts will bear fruit. I should feed this kindly fire that burns my tail with an offering of these buildings!'

With his tail blazing, the monkey looked like a rain cloud streaked with lightning as he ran along the roofs of Lankā and set off a conflagration that was like the doomsday fire. Because of its intimacy with the wind, the fire grew larger and larger as it moved from house to house. Beautiful palaces with their windows of gold studded with pearls collapsed like the mansions of the *siddhas* that fall to the earth when their merit has been used up in heaven. Hanumān saw rivers of precious metals mixed with diamonds and pearls and coral and silver flowing out from the burning mansions.

As fire is not satisfied with wood and straw, so, too, Hanumān was not satisfied with the destruction he had wrought among the *rākṣasas.* Conquered by Hanumān's anger, Lankā was as if under a curse, her warriors routed, her heroes dead, surrounded by flames. Hanumān watched as the *rākṣasas* were tormented by the blaze as Brahmā watches the earth cursed by his anger.

Now that Hanumān had killed countless *rākṣasas,* destroyed the *aśoka* grove and set fire to the mansions, his thoughts turned to Rāma. He extinguished the fire on his tail by plunging it into the ocean.

As he watched the city burn, a terrible thought entered his mind and he was disgusted with himself. 'What have I done by setting fire to Lankā?' he thought fearfully. 'Those who are restrained by their intelligence are fortunate indeed, for they can repress the anger that rises within them like water can extinguish fire. If Sītā has been burned along with Lankā then I have ruined my master's plans because of my ignorance. I did not protect Sītā before I set fire to Lankā. The very person for whom this enterprise was undertaken has been destroyed! No doubt what I did was simple enough, but because I was overcome with anger, I have cut at the very root of our goal.

'The whole city is in ashes. There does not appear to be a single part that has not been burned. I am sure Sītā is dead! Now that I have ruined everything because of my perverted intelligence, I find the thought of killing myself very attractive. Should I jump into the fire? Or into water? Or offer my body as food to the creatures that live in the ocean? Now that I have wrecked everything, I cannot bear to stay alive and face the king of the monkeys and the two princes!

'I have proved my monkey nature to the three worlds because I succumbed to anger. I curse the fact that I could not restrain myself. Even though I was capable of protecting Sītā, I did not do so because of my lack of control.

'When Sītā dies, Rāma and Lakṣmaṇa will die and when they die, so will Sugrīva and his family. When Bharata and righteous Śatrughna hear about this, their love for their brother will not allow them to go on living. When the Ikṣvāku dynasty perishes, their subjects will be overcome with grief. I am the unfortunate creature who has not only destroyed his personal store of merit by this lack of control but has also led to the destruction of the world!'

Hanumān continued to worry in this fashion and then he recalled the auspicious omens he had seen earlier. 'Could it be that the beautiful woman is protected by her own merit? Fire cannot burn fire. A virtuous woman cannot be destroyed. Fire dare not touch this woman who is protected by her own virtue and who is the wife of the effulgent and righteous Rāma. In fact, it is because of Rāma's power and Sītā's virtue that the fire did not burn me either. If he did not burn my tail, how could he consume this noble woman? Sītā can burn the fire because of her devotion to her husband, her asceticism and her wisdom!'

Hanumān felt much better when he thought about Sītā's store of merit, and then he heard the *cāraṇas* speaking from the sky. 'Hanumān has done the impossible by spreading this fierce fire amongst the *rākṣasas'* mansions! Lankā burns along with its highways and gates and towers but Sītā remains unharmed! What a wondrous thing this is!'

Hanumān was relieved when he heard what they said and now, having accomplished his mission, he decided to see Sītā once again. He greeted Sītā, who was sitting under the *śimśapa* tree, and said, 'I am delighted to see that you are not injured!'

Sītā gazed up at him as he stood there and repeated the loving messages for her husband. 'I know you are capable of doing all this single-handed. But it would be more appropriate if Rāma were to wreak havoc in Lankā and take me way from here himself. You have to create the conditions for Rāma to display his prowess in conformity with the *kṣatriya* code!' she said to the monkey.

Hanumān reassured her again that Rāma and his army would soon be there and that her suffering would end. Then, eager to see his master, he climbed to the top of Mount Ariṣṭa, spurred on by the thought that he would see Rāma again soon.

The rocks on the mountain were crushed under Hanumān's feet and they broke to pieces with a crash. Hanumān grew in size as he prepared to cross over to the northern shore of the ocean which teemed with fish and sea monsters. The son of the Wind leapt into the sky and as he did so, the mountain was smashed. Its trees were uprooted, its inhabitants cried out in pain, its peaks trembled as it shattered, as if struck by Indra's thunderbolt. The roar of the mighty lions that lived in its caves pierced the sky, *vidyādharas* fled with their clothes and ornaments in disarray and enormous serpents whose tongues blazed moved away from the area. *Kinnaras, nāgas, yakṣas* and *gandharvas* left the mountain and took refuge in the sky as the mountain was smashed and entered the underworld. Ten *yojanās* wide and thirty *yojanās* high, the great mountain was entirely levelled.

# *Chapter Fifty-Three*

Hanumān flew over the ocean swiftly, like an arrow released from a bow. He saw Mount Mahendra on the northern shore, large as a cloud, and he roared with delight.

The other monkeys were anxious to see their friend again and were thrilled when they heard his roar. 'I am sure Hanumān has accomplished his mission,' said Jāmbavāṇ 'Otherwise, he would not roar like this!' The monkeys ran here and there, leaping from rock to rock and peak to peak in their eagerness to see Hanumān. They grabbed flowering branches and waved them like bright flags. They saw Hanumān looming in the distance like a huge cloud and they all stood together, their palms joined in reverence.

Hanumān landed on mighty Mount Mahendra and at once all the monkeys surrounded him, their faces shining with joy. They brought him roots and fruits and honoured him as they sang and danced and played with huge trees, making a great commotion.

Hanumān honoured the elders and teachers, Jāmbavān and Prince Angada and returned the greetings of the monkeys. 'I have seen her!' he announced briefly.

He took Angada's hand and sat down among the pleasant woods of Mount Mahendra. Then Hanumān addressed the brave monkeys. 'I saw Janaka's daughter in the *aśoka* grove!' he said. 'That blameless woman is guarded by fearsome *rākṣasīs.* She sits there, the poor child, with a single braid, longing for a sight of Rāma. Weak with fasting, she is emaciated and dirty.'

The moment the monkeys heard Hanumān say the words 'I have seen her' which were as sweet as nectar, they were overcome with emotion. Some ululated, some roared and others roared back. They shouted and cried in their delirious joy. They raised their tails and waved them, they leapt on and off the mountain peaks and they caressed Hanumān, who was as large as an elephant.

'O monkey, none can equal you in valour and purity. You have leaped over the boundless ocean and returned,' said Angada. 'It is our good fortune that you saw Sītā. Now Rāma can give up the grief he endures because he is separated from her!'

The monkeys formed a circle around Hanumān, Angada and Jāmbavān, bringing rocks to sit upon. They were anxious to hear all the details about Hanumān's leap over the ocean, about Lankā and his meeting with Sītā and Rāvaṇa. They sat facing Hanumān, their palms joined in respect. Angada sat in the centre of innumerable monkeys, as splendid as Indra in heaven and the mountain peak blazed with the glory of Hanumān and Angada.

'How did you see Sītā? What happened there?' asked Jāmbavān. 'How does cruel Rāvaṇa treat her? Tell us everything so that we can decide what to do next. What can we reasonably expect when we return and what should we conceal?'

Hanumān bowed his head to Sītā and started the tale of his adventures.

'In front of all of you, I leapt from the mountain into the sky. I concentrated all my energies on reaching the southern shore of the ocean. As I went along, I saw a huge obstacle. It was an enormous mountain with a man standing on its peak. I was sure I had to break it and I touched it with my tail so that the peak shattered into a thousand pieces. Then the mountain called me 'son' and spoke to me in a sweet voice that gladdened my heart. He told me that he was Mainaka and a good friend of my father's. He also wanted to help Rāma in his enterprise because Rāma is foremost among the righteous and equal to Indra in valour.

'He let me go onwards and I travelled a great distance. Then I saw Surasā, the mother of the snakes. She stood up in the middle of the ocean and said that I had been sent to her as food, that I had to pass through her mouth. I told her Rāma's story and that I was going as his messenger to find Sītā. But she was not convinced and so I expanded and forced her to open her mouth very wide. Then I contracted my body, became as small as a thumb, and flew through her mouth. She blessed my journey and wished me good luck with my mission and all the celestial beings praised me from the sky.

'As I went farther, I felt something grab my shadow but I could see no one. I was very disturbed and when I looked down, I saw a huge *rākṣasī* lying in the water. She laughed and said that she was going to eat me, but I expanded in size and then ripped out her heart. She collapsed into the sea like a mountain and I heard the *siddhas* praising me for killing Simhikā.

'I recalled the urgency of my mission and kept going until I saw the southern shore of the ocean, where the city of Lankā is located among the mountains. When the sun set, I entered the city of the *rākṣasas* without being seen. I spent the entire night looking for Sītā but I could not find her even in Rāvaṇa's inner apartments. I was very depressed and was wondering what to do, when I saw a beautiful grove of trees surrounded by a golden wall.

'I jumped over the wall and in the middle of the grove, I saw a *śimśapa* tree. Near it was a beautiful woman with eyes like lotus petals, emaciated and thin from not eating. She was surrounded by ugly and deformed *rākṣasīs,* eaters of flesh and blood, as a doe is surrounded by tigers. I knew she was Rāma's virtuous wife and I stayed there, watching her.

'I heard a huge commotion coming from Rāvaṇa's mansion and it was mixed with the tinkling of girdles and anklets. Apprehensive, I hid myself in the dense tree like a bird. Mighty Rāvaṇa and his women arrived and came up to Sītā. She saw the king of the *rākṣasas* and was so frightened that she pressed her thighs together and covered her breasts. Rāvaṇa told her that if she did not accept him he would drink her blood in two months' time. Sītā scolded him angrily, berating him for carrying her away while Rāma was absent. She told him that she would never accept him as her husband.

'Rāvaṇa blazed with a sudden rage, like a fire is fed with wood. He rolled his eyes and made as if to hit her with his fist but the lovely Mandodarī, his wife, stepped forward from among the women and distracted her lustful husband. He was led away to his own apartments. When he left, the ugly *rākṣasīs* began to torment Sītā, taunting her with their cruel words. But she was unmoved and finally, they were discouraged and fell asleep.

'Sītā began to cry piteously and I had to think of some way to talk to her. I began to praise the clan of the Ikṣvākus and she asked me who I was, who had sent me and how I had got there. I told her about Rāma's alliance with my master, Sugrīva, the king of the monkeys, and that I was Rāma's messenger. I gave her the signet ring Rāma had sent for her. I asked her what she wanted me to do and she replied that she wanted Rāma to take her away after he had destroyed Rāvaṇa. She told me to tell Rāma about her condition so that he would come to Lankā as soon as he could, for she had only two months to live.

'I grew angry when I saw how miserable she was and I realized what else I had to do. Eager to fight the *rākṣasas,* I made my body as large as a mountain and set about destroying the grove. The deformed *rākṣasis* woke up and saw the chaos in the grove and the agitation of the birds and animals. They were terrified when they saw me and ran off to report to Rāvaṇa. Rāvaṇa sent the mighty *kinkara* warriors after me, armed with spears and maces and clubs. I killed fifty thousand of them with an iron bar. The ones that survived went to tell Rāvaṇa that his army had been decimated and I decided to attack the palace temple.

'There, too, I killed hundreds of *rākṣasas* and shattered the building that was the jewel of Lankā. I killed Jambumālī, the son of Prahasta, and his forces with my club. And I slew the seven sons of Rāvaṇa s ministers as well as five of his mighty generals. Then Rāvaṇa sent his son Akṣa, a skilled warrior, to face me. I grabbed him by his feet when he leapt into the air. I whirled him around and flung him to the ground. Rāvaṇa was enraged and sent Indrajit, his invincible son, to do battle with me. He launched a huge attack and felled me with Brahmā's weapon. Then the *rākṣasas* bound me with ropes and led me to Rāvaṇa.

'Wicked Rāvaṇa asked me why I had come there and why I had killed the *rākṣasas.* I told him I had done everything for Sītā and that I was the son of the Wind. I also declared that I was a monkey, one of Sugrīva's ministers and a messenger from Rāma. I told Rāvaṇa that Sugrīva sent him greetings and that he had made an alliance with Rāma for 'Sītā's rescue. I said Sugrīva asked that Sītā be returned to Rāma, otherwise his army of monkeys would arrive and destroy Lankā.

'Rāvaṇa stared at me with his red eyes as if he would burn me up, and ordered that I should be killed. Then his brother, the wise Vibhīṣaṇa, pleaded with the king that I should be spared because killing a messenger was not the right thing to do. Rāvaṇa ordered that my tail be set on fire and the *rākṣasas* wrapped my tail up with strips of cotton and bark. They set it alight and pounded me with their fists. But I felt no pain and decided to set fire to the city. The *rākṣasas* bound me and dragged me, covered with flames, through the city, announcing what I had done.

'I contracted my large body and slipped through the ropes that bound me and returned to my natural form. I picked up an iron bar and killed the *rākṣasas* and then leapt to the top of the city gates in a single mighty bound. I set fire to the city with its massive gates and highways with my burning tail and everyone there mistook that conflagration for the doomsday fire. I was suddenly filled with doubt that I had burned Sītā along with Lankā but I heard the *cātaṇas* reassuring me that Sītā was safe. I went to see Sītā, again and again she sent me away.

'I have told you everything exactly as it happened. Now let us do what remains to be done!' concluded Hanumān.

'Rāma and Sugrīva's mission will be accomplished because of Sītā's powers and my leap over the ocean,' he continued. 'Sītā's ascetic power is so great that she can uphold the worlds or burn them in her anger. The only reason Rāvaṇa was not destroyed when he touched her was because of the merit from his austerities. Even a burning flame cannot do what Sītā can when she is roused to anger!

'But now, that good woman sits miserably under a tree in Rāvaṇa's grove. Surrounded by cruel *rākṣasīs,* she is emaciated and tormented by grief, lustreless as the moon hidden by clouds. She is devoted to her marital vows and stands firm in her *dharma.* She is not in the least interested in arrogant Rāvaṇa. She thinks of nothing but Rāma all the time, with her whole heart.'

Angada took permission from the elders and addressed the monkeys. 'Now that this matter has been reported to you all, it seems proper that the princes be reunited with Sītā. I can reach Lankā and kill Rāvaṇa with my own strength. How much easier, then, it would be when I am accompanied by heroic warriors like yourselves who are skilled in the use of weapons and are eager to fight!

'I will kill Rāvaṇa and his sons and his servants in battle! I will slay the *rākṣasas* and counter the infallible weapons the gods gave Indrajit! I will create a rain of rocks and stones which could destroy even the gods in battle, to say nothing of these *rākṣasas*!

'If the sea were to overflow or the mountains tremble, Jāmbavān would not be perturbed at all. A *rākṣasa* army in battle holds no fear for him!

Hanumān alone massacred the vanguard of the *rākṣasa* army. Panasa and Nīla can make Mount Mandara quake with the power of their feet, how will the *rākṣasas* face them? Dvivida and Mainda are capable of attacking the gods and the *asuras,* the *yakṣas* and the *gandharvas* and the *nāgas.* They are born from the *aśvins* and Brahmā gave them boons. They used their strength to drink the nectar of the gods and they can destroy Lankā with its horses and elephants and chariots in their anger.

'I do not think it is right for us to return to Rāma without Sītā, now that we have seen her. It is not worthy of us, famed for our courage, that we should report that we saw Sītā and did not bring her back with us. Hanumān has already killed a number of heroic *rākṣasas.* There is nothing left for us to do except rescue Sītā. Let us take her and return!'

'What you have said is true,' said Jāmbavāṇ 'But we must do what will ensure Rāma success!' Hanumān agreed and all the monkeys went to the top of Mount Mahendra and leapt off.

# *Chapter Fifty-Four*

The monkeys seemed to cover the sky with their huge bodies which were the size of mountains. They were delighted with the success of their mission and eager to see Rāma again and give him the good news. The golden monkeys flew through the sky and arrived at a beautiful little grove called Madhuvana. It was under Sugrīva's protection and was closed to all creatures. Dadhimukha, Sugrīva's uncle, took care of it.

When the monkeys got there, they were delirious with joy and began to behave wild and crazy. They begged Dadhimukha for some honey and he gave them permission to eat the honey they found. The monkeys were thrilled and they danced and sang and ran all over the place. They leapt and fell and babbled and giggled. Some of them leaned against each other for support, some leapt from tree to tree, others threw themselves to the ground from high mountains. In their excitement, they jumped from the ground to the tops of trees, they sang and laughed and yelled and shouted to each other and made a huge commotion. There was not a single one of them who was sober and they seemed utterly insatiable.

Dadhimukha watched as the grove was destroyed, its trees stripped of their leaves and flowers. He grew angry and tried to restrain the drunken monkeys, but, puffed up with pride, they were rude to him. Dadhimukha became even more determined to protect the grove and did whatever he could. He quarreled with some of the monkeys and tried to conciliate others. He yelled at some and slapped others. But the drunken monkeys could not be restrained. They knew their strength and hit back at Dadhimukha and dragged him around, not realizing their mistake. They attacked him with their nails and teeth and punched him and kicked him and in their intoxication, they laid waste the grove.

'Collect the honey calmly!' said Hanumān and Angada gave them permission to drink the honey they had collected. The monkeys honoured Angada and rushed into the grove like a river in spate. Delighted that they had found Sītā, they violently attacked the guards. They pounced on them and beat them up. They grabbed potfuls of honey, knocked over other pots, tossed away honeycombs and feasted to their hearts' content. They tore branches off trees and finally, exhausted, they spread leaves under the trees and lay down. Utterly insane and drunk with honey, they threw things at each other and stumbled around. Some whistled and others sang happily, some of them fell asleep.

The guards who had been repelled by the monkeys ran to Dadhimukha and complained that they had been kicked and beaten. 'The grove has been destroyed because of the power of Hanumān's boons. Those monkeys crushed us under their feet and nearly killed us!' they cried. Dadhimukha was angry but he rallied the guards and said, 'Come! We shall go to the grove and attack the monkeys who have eaten the honey. We will fend them off!'

The guards followed Dadhimukha back to the grove quickly, armed with trees and rocks. The drunken monkeys, led by Hanumān, charged towards the guards, eager for a fight. Angada attacked noble Dadhimukha with a tree. In his intoxication, he did not realize that Dadhimukha was his relative and threw him to the ground. Dadhimukha's arms were crushed and he was covered with blood. He lost consciousness for a moment and when he recovered his senses, he withdrew to a quiet place and said to his assistants, 'Let them be! We shall go to where Sugrīva, our master, sits with Rāma! I will tell the king all about Angada's appalling behaviour and he will punish these monkeys. This grove belongs to Sugrīva and his ancestors and he loves it very much. It is closed even to the gods. Sugrīva is sure to punish these greedy monkeys and their friends. When these wicked creatures who have ignored the king's orders have been killed, our rage will have borne fruit!'

Dadhimukha leapt into the air with the guards, and he reached Sugrīva's home in the forest in the twinkling of an eye. He saw Rāma and Sugrīva and stepped down from the sky onto the firm earth. Looking miserable, he honoured Sugrīva by placing his forehead at the monkey's feet.

'Stand up, stand up!' cried Sugrīva in agitation. 'Why have you fallen at my feet? Have no fear and tell me truthfully what the matter is!'

'The grove which has been closed to all except you, Vālī and your father has been destroyed by monkeys, great king!' said Dadhimukha. 'The guards tried to stop them but they pushed them away. Even now they eat and drink the honey there without a care in the world!' Dadhimukha told them what the monkeys had done and how they had behaved.

'Who is this forest guard, this monkey who stands before you? Why is he so unhappy and what has he just told you?' asked Lakṣmaṇa.

'Noble Dadhimukha says that a troop of monkeys led by Angada has consumed a large amount of honey,' replied Sugrīva. 'They would never have done such a thing if they had failed in their mission! Since the grove has been destroyed, I am sure they have met with success!

'I am also positive that it was Hanumān who saw Sītā. He is the only one capable of doing that! He is intelligent and strong and resolute. With Jāmbavān as the leader of the expedition and Angada as the commander of the troops and Hanumān as its moving spirit, this group of monkeys had to be successful!

'The monkeys must have arrived at the grove after searching the southern region. They attacked the guards and beat them up and then they violated the grove. Dadhimukha has come here to tell me this. Ah, Lakṣmaṇa! Understand what has really happened. The monkeys have seen Sītā and so they are celebrating by drinking honey! Otherwise, they would never have laid waste that divine grove which was given to us as a boon!'

Rāma and Lakṣmaṇa rejoiced when they heard the good news from Sugrīva. 'I am delighted that the successful monkeys have destroyed the grove,' said Sugrīva to Dadhimukha. 'They are forgiven for their behaviour. I cannot wait to see the monkeys led by Hanumān. Now that they have succeeded in their task, the princes and I want to hear all about the efforts that were made to find Sītā!'

Dadhimukha bowed to Rāma, Lakṣmaṇa and Sugrīva and leapt into the sky. He returned to the grove and saw that the monkeys were no longer drunk. But they were still excited and they were urinating honeyed water all over the place. Dadhimukha went up to Angada and with his palms joined, he said sweetly, 'Don't be angry with these guards who attacked you under my instructions. Crown prince, you are the master of this grove! Forgive us for the mistake we committed in our ignorance! Your father was the king of all the monkeys before. You and Sugrīva are no different from him.

'I went and reported everything to Sugrīva, your uncle. He told me to bring all the monkeys there as soon as possible. He was thrilled that you had arrived here and is not at all angry about the destruction of the grove. "Send them here quickly!" he said to me.'

'I am sure Rāma has heard all this, too,' said the eloquent Angada. 'We should not stay here much longer since we have been successful in our mission. You have drunk honey to your hearts' content and you have rested. There is nothing left to do except return to Sugrīva. But I will do whatever you think best. Even though I am the crown prince, I am not capable of commanding you all. You are the ones who made the mission a success and it would be improper for me to tell you what to do!'

'Which master would speak like this?' said the monkeys. 'Drunk with their sovereignty, most would think they are masters of all! No one other than you would be so humble. We are ready to leave immediately and return to Sugrīva! But we cannot take a single step without your command. Tell us what we should do!'

'Let us go!' said Angada and leapt into the sky. The monkeys followed him, filling the sky like smoke from the sacrificial fire, thundering like clouds driven by the wind.

Sugrīva saw Angada coming and said to Rāma, who was still overcome with grief, 'Have faith, Rāma! They would not have returned unless they had seen Sītā, for the stipulated time has long passed! Prince Angada, best of all the monkeys, would never have come back to me if he had not been successful! His face would be woebegone and his mind troubled if he had failed. That grove has been in my family for generations. He would never have destroyed it in celebration if he had failed.

'I am sure Hanumān is the one who has seen Sītā. No one else was equal to the task! Don't worry, Rāma!'

The sky was filled with the sound of the monkeys roaring as they came back to Kiṣkindha, as if announcing their success. Sugrīva was delighted and curled and uncurled his tail with joy. Led by Hanumān and Angada, the monkeys returned, eager to see Rāma.

Hanumān bowed his head and told Rāma that Sītā was a prisoner but that she was unharmed. Then they all went to the pleasantly wooded summit of Mount Prasravaṇa and honoured Rāma, Lakṣmaṇa and Sugrīva. They began to tell him all about Sītā's trials, her imprisonment in

Rāvaṇa's palace, the harassment by the *rākṣasīs,* her love for Rāma and the two-month period that Rāvaṇa had given her to live.

'Where is Sītā? What is happening to her? How does she feel about me? Tell me everything about her!' said Rāma anxiously as the monkeys were recounting their exploits. They pushed Hanumān forward and urged him to tell Rāma everything.

'I leapt over the ocean that was one hundred *yojanās* across because I wanted to see Sītā,' began Hanumān. 'Rāvaṇa's city is called Lankā and it is situated on the southern shore of the southern ocean. There, in Rāvaṇa's inner apartments, I saw the chaste Sītā. She lives there with her mind firmly fixed on you, Rāma!

'I saw her surrounded by hideous *rākṣasīs* in the pleasure garden. They guard her and torment her all the time. That virtuous woman, who is not used to suffering, is now overwhelmed by discomfort. Her hair in a single braid, vulnerable and terribly anxious about you, she is pale and thin and lies on the ground like a lotus in winter. She ignores Rāvaṇa and has decided to end her life, Rāma.

'I somehow managed to locate Sītā, who is so devoted to you. I gained her confidence by reciting the glories of the Ikṣvāku clan and then I told her everything. I told her about the alliance between you and Sugrīva and she was very happy. Restrained, chaste and devoted to you is how I saw Janaka's daughter. She occupies herself with the practise of austerities. She gave me a story as a token of recognition for you. She told me about the incident with the crow in Citrakūṭa, Rāma.

'She said to me, "Tell Rāma all that you have seen here in great detail. While you are speaking in front of Sugrīva, give Rāma this jewel which I have taken great pains to look after. Tell Rāma that I have preserved this jewel I wear in my hair and tell him that when I see it, even in my misery, I feel better, for I feel as if I am seeing Rāma. Tell him I can stay alive only for another month because I am a prisoner of the *rākṣasas*."

'I have told you everything, Rāma!' said Hanumān as he gave Sītā's jewel to Rāma. 'Let us prepare to cross the ocean!'

Rāma pressed the jewel to his heart and wept aloud with Lakṣmaṇa. Tears streamed from his eyes as he said to Sugrīva, 'My heart melts at the sight of this jewel, as a loving cow spills milk at the thought of her calf! Sītā's father gave her this jewel when she got married and it shone all the brighter when she fixed it in her hair. My beloved's beauty enhances the splendour of this jewel and today, when I look at it, I feel as if I am looking at her!

'What did Sītā say? Satisfy my thirst for her by telling me what she said. Tell me again what she said. Tell me again and again! What could cause me greater sadness than seeing this jewel born from the ocean and not seeing Sītā? Sītā can survive for another month, but I cannot live for another second without my dark-eyed beloved!

'Take me to where she is! I cannot live without her for another moment now that I have news of her! How does my shy and gentle darling survive among those terrifying *rākṣasa*? Her face must be as pale as the autumn moon released from darkness but covered by clouds! Tell me, Hanumān, what did Sītā say? Tell me!' begged Rāma.

Hanumān repeated what Sītā had said. He recounted the incident with the crow in Citrakūṭa that Sītā had told him about. 'Then she asked me to say to you, "Rāma, you are the best of all warriors, why do you not employ your weapons against the *rākṣasas?* No one, not the *nāgas, gandharvas, asuras* nor the troops of *māruts,* can face you in battle. If you have any feelings left for me, Rāma, kill Rāvaṇa with your arrows quickly!

'"Why does Lakṣmaṇa not protect me under the orders of his brother?" she asked me,' continued Hanumān. '"Rāma and Lakṣmaṇa equal Vāyu and Agni in splendour. Even the gods cannot defeat them. Why have they forsaken me? I must have done something terrible since they do not rescue me even though they are together!"

'I heard Sītā's sad words and said to her, "I swear to you that Rāma is overwhelmed with grief for you. And Lakṣmaṇa is also very upset. I have found you! This is not the time for sorrow! In a short while, your troubles will be over! Those magnificent princes will turn Lankā to ashes in their eagerness to see you! Rāma will kill vile Rāvaṇa and his family in battle and take you back to his own city. Give me something that Rāma will recognize and that will make him happy!"

'Sītā looked all around her and then pulled this jewel which she used to wear in her hair from her clothes and gave it to me. I took it for you, Rāma. Then I bowed and prepared to return. As I expanded my body, the lovely woman said to me with tears streaming down her face, "Hanumān, give my good wishes to the heroic princes and to Sugrīva and all his minsters! Act in such a way that Rāma helps me cross this ocean of grief!

Go to Rāma and tell him about my pitiable state and the insults of the *rākṣasīs*! May you have a safe journey, monkey!"

'This is what Sītā said to me in her grief, Rāma! Consider what I have said and have faith in her virtue!' said Hanumān.

'Before I left, she said more to me out of her love for you,' continued Hanumān. 'She said, "Tell Rāma all this so that he will come here quickly and kill Rāvaṇa. Or, if you think it's all right, rest here for the night and return in the morning. Your presence makes me feel better, even for a while. I have had so little to be happy about lately! I doubt if I will still be alive when you return! Your absence will add to the grief that already overwhelms me.

"I have some doubt about your companions, the monkeys and bears. How will the princes and the monkey army cross the boundless ocean? How do you think they will accomplish this difficult task?

"I know you can do all that needs to be done on your own. But then, the merit and fame it brings will go to you alone! If Rāma destroys Rāvaṇa and his army and takes me away from here, then the success will be his. It is not worthy of Rāma that he carry me off stealthily, as the *rākṣasa* did, out of fear. Destroying Lankā and the enemy army and taking me away would be a feat worthy of Rāma. You should act such that Rāma can display his might."

'I assured her that splendid Sugrīva was determined to rescue her and that the monkeys and bears under his command were strong and resolute. I said the monkeys were equal to me in their skills and strength and that they could reach Lankā even more easily than I did. I said, "Enough of this sadness! The monkeys will reach Lankā in a single bound. Rāma and Lakṣmaṇa, who are like the sun and moon, shall soon be here and you shall see them along with the army of monkeys who fight with their teeth and nails. Before long, you will hear the monkeys roaring like thunder on Lankā's mountains. And soon, you shall see Rāma returning from his forest exile and consecrated in Ayodhyā!"

'Sītā was comforted by my words and she felt better even though she suffered terribly at the thought of your grief.'

# WAR

# *Chapter Fifty-Five*

Rāma was delighted to hear about all that Hanumān had done. 'Hanumān has done the most difficult thing in the world. No one else could have done this, not even in their imaginations! I cannot think of anyone other than Garuḍa, Vāyu and Hanumān who could have crossed the great ocean. Hanumān entered that impregnable and inaccessible city, a city that not even celestial beings can enter! The servant who is assigned a difficult task and who fulfils it with energy is surely the best of all beings! And the servant who does not complete the task assigned to him is the worst!

'Now that the mighty Hanumān has seen Sītā, myself, Lakṣmaṇa and the entire family have been saved. But I am ashamed of the fact that there is nothing I can do in return for Hanumān that would please him as much as he has pleased me. This affectionate embrace is all I possess now and all I have to offer.

'I am terribly disheartened when I think of the ocean. How will the monkeys reach the southern shore of that boundless mass together? The news of Sītā lightens my heart but what is the solution to the monkeys crossing the ocean?' And once again, Rāma began to brood.

'How can you give in to your grief in this way, Rāma, like other ordinary mortals?' said Sugrīva. 'What is the reason for this sorrow? We now know where Sītā is, we know where our enemy lives. You are far-sighted and skilled in the arts of rulership. You are capable and able to tell right from wrong. You should not give in to such destructive doubts and fears. We shall cross the ocean, filled with sea monsters, with millions of monkeys, and destroy your enemy!

'The man who succumbs to dejection and misery never achieves his ends and the only thing he gains is more grief. All our monkey leaders are strong and brave and they would not hesitate to jump into the fire for your sake. Do whatever is necessary for me to kill Rāvaṇa and rescue Sītā.

'Ensure that we can build a bridge over the ocean, Rāma, so that we can approach Lankā, the city of the *rākṣasas*. You can rest assured that Rāvaṇa is as good as dead from the moment we set eyes on the city. Without a bridge over the ocean, even the gods led by Indra would not be able to reach Lankā. But once we have built a bridge and the monkey army has crossed over, I promise you, we shall be victorious. My troops consist of brave and skilled warriors!

'Low spirits will ruin our hopes! Stop grieving, that would diminish all our efforts. Call up your valour and the power you need for the performance of great deeds. Men like you should never succumb to sorrow, no matter how great the calamity. That could only lead to them not achieving their ends.

'You are bound to be victorious with the help of advisors like me. I can think of no one in the three worlds who can face you in battle when you are armed with your bow! You shall see Sītā again before long. Call up your anger, Rāma, for *kṣatriyas* who are calm are doomed to failure! The world fears an angry man.

'We shall cross the ocean in some fashion or other. What is the point of talking on and on like this? You will certainly be victorious for I have seen many good omens and my mind is filled with peace!'

'Tell me about Lankā's fortifications,' said Rāma to Hanumān. 'I want to know everything, as if I had seen it all with my own eyes. How strong is the army? How have the city gates been fortified? What are the ramparts like? And the houses of the *rākṣasas*? You had time enough to see every inch of Lankā and I know that you are capable of making these judgements!'

'Listen and I will tell you everything about Lankā's fortifications, her hidden defences and about the army that protects the city,' replied the eloquent Hanumān. 'I will tell you about the opulence of the city and the formidable ocean that surrounds it, about the divisions of the army and the number of their mounts and vehicles.

'Lankā is a city of joy and celebration. It is filled with elephants and chariots and teeming with *rākṣasa* clans. It has four enormous gateways that are secured with massive doors. There are huge catapults stationed there to hurl arrows and stones at an attacking enemy force. There are hundreds of vicious spiked machines and *rākṣasas* standing by, ready to operate them. There are impregnable ramparts made of gold and studded with lapis and pearl and all kinds of other gems. They are surrounded by deep moats of ice-cold water which are filled with fish and crocodiles. There are four bridges that lead to the four gates and they are raised and lowered mechanically. They prevent the invading army from entering the city for they can toss enemy soldiers into the surrounding moat.

'Rāvaṇa himself is a mighty warrior, Rāma! He is strong and alert and monitors his army. He is eager to fight. Lankā cannot be penetrated even by the gods. It has the perfect fourfold protection of water, mountains, forest and forts. It stands on the southern shore of the vast ocean. There are no sailing routes or paths or any means of communication with any other place. Lankā is situated on the top of a mountain and it is filled with horses, elephants and chariots. It is as well fortified as the city of the gods.

'Mechanical weapons and war machines adorn this city that belongs to Rāvaṇa. The western gate is manned by hordes of *rākṣasas* armed with spears. They are formidable warriors and can even go into battle with swords. The southern gate is guarded by an entire four-divisioned army of mighty warriors. The eastern gate is protected by swordsmen who are capable of using any weapon at all. The northern gate is guarded by the finest and noblest warriors who are renowned for their skills as horsemen and charioteers. And there are hundreds of smaller groups of warriors in the middle of the city and they, too, are brave and invincible.

'I have already smashed the drawbridges, filled up the moats, breached the ramparts and burned the city. If we can manage to cross the ocean somehow, you can be sure that the monkeys will destroy Lankā!'

'Hanumān, you have told me all that I need to know about Lankā and the terrible *rākṣasas*,' said Rāma. 'I swear to you that I will destroy it!

'Sugrīva, this is a good time for us to leave. The sun is in a position that is auspicious for victory. I see other good signs, too. I know I will kill Rāvaṇa and bring Sītā back. My right eye twitches which means that I shall have my dearest wish, victory!

'Let Nīla go ahead with hundreds and thousands of monkeys. Let him scout a path for us, a path that is abundant in roots and fruits and cool water and honey. It is possible that the wicked *rākṣasas* have polluted the water sources and the roots and fruits along our path. The monkeys must be constantly alert and keep their weapons at the ready. Let them search the forests and the valleys for the enemy. Let hundreds of millions of monkeys form an advance guard that is as vast as the ocean.

'I myself shall ride on Hanumān's shoulders in the middle of the army, like Indra upon Airāvata. Lakṣmaṇa shall ride upon Angada's shoulders. Jāmbavān, Suṣeṇa and Vegadarśī can bring up the rear.'

Sugrīva called the monkey troops together and they emerged from caves and from mountain peaks, leaping around in their eagerness to fight. Righteous Rāma and Lakṣmaṇa set out for the south, surrounded by thousands of millions of monkeys that were the size of elephants. The monkeys were thrilled at the prospect of battle and they laughed and roared and played and jumped around. They ate the honey and fruit they found along the way and they broke off trees and flowering shrubs. They carried each other and threw things at each other as they went, shouting, 'We shall kill Rāvaṇa and all the *rākṣasas*!'

The monkey army surged forward, rumbling like the ocean at high tide. They marched behind the sons of Daśaratha like trained horses controlled by their bits. Riding on the shoulders of the monkeys, Rāma and Lakṣmaṇa looked like the sun and the moon in conjunction with the planets. 'I see auspicious omens everywhere. I have no doubt you will kill Rāvaṇa and return to Ayodhyā with all your goals accomplished!' said Lakṣmaṇa.

The monkeys covered the earth as they marched forward as swift as the wind and the cloud of dust they raised darkened the sun and hid the world from view. Eager to perform great deeds on the battlefield for Rāma's sake, they boasted and bragged in their youthful enthusiasm about all the things they could do with their strength. Some raced ahead, others galloped. They talked and laughed, they gouged the earth with their feet and tails, they broke off rocks and uprooted trees with their mighty arms. They climbed to the tops of mountains yelling and shouting, they crushed creepers into a tangled mass with their powerful legs. They drew themselves up to their full height and played with treetops.

Driven by the desire to see Sītā, the army marched day and night and did not stop for a single moment. Soon, they reached Mount Sahya, covered with trees and frequented by deer and other animals. The monkeys ate the sweet fruit and honey they found there and continued on their way. When they came to Mount Mahendra, Rāma climbed to its summit and looked out over the roaring, swelling ocean that was filled with fish and turtles.

Rāma, Lakṣmaṇa and Sugrīva were the first to reach the pleasant forest on the shore. 'Here we are at the ocean, the abode of Varuṇa,' said Rāma. 'Now we must once again consider the matter that concerned us earlier. From here, the ocean seems endless. We cannot hope to cross it without a proper plan. Let us make camp here and consult the others about the best way for the monkeys to cross to the southern shore.'

Rāma, still tormented with grief over the separation from Sītā, gave orders for the monkey army to make camp. The huge army of monkeys seemed like a second ocean of honey-coloured water on the shore. They camped in the forest and watched the waves rise and fall with great delight. They looked out over the endless waters that teemed with fish and sea monsters and serpents with glittering bodies. The ocean was particularly terrifying at twilight and seemed to ebb and swell with the moon.

The ocean had submarine mountain ranges and its unplumbed depths were as dangerous as the realm of the *asuras*. The waves rose and fell with the wind, filled with the fish and serpents that lived in the waters. Drops of water gleamed like sparks from a fire. The waters were like the sky and the sky like the waters. You could not tell one from the other. Sky and water mingled, the only difference being that one was filled with stars, the other with precious gems. Waves filled the sea as clouds fill the sky and the waves crashed against each other, making a noise like drums on the battlefield. The monkeys watched in wonder as the waters were tossed by the wind and seemed to fill the sky.

# *Chapter Fifty-Six*

Meanwhile, Rāvaṇa had seen the terrible destruction Hanumān had wrought upon Lankā, so devastating that only a being that was Indra's equal could have done it. Somewhat disturbed, the king of the *rākṣasas* said, 'My impregnable and unassailable city was entered and attacked by a mere monkey. He even managed to see Sītā. The monkey destroyed our buildings and killed a number of *rākṣasas* and threw the entire city into a panic.

'What shall I do now? What is the appropriate course of action?' he asked his advisors. 'You must tell me what is the right thing to do as well as what we are capable of doing. Great men who are known for their courage have said that consultation and advice are the roots of victory. I would like to discuss this problem with you. You are wise and circumspect. Consider the matter carefully and decide what we should do. I will do exactly as you say. Rāma will soon be here with an army of hundreds of millions of monkeys to lay siege to our city. He will find some way of crossing the ocean. Briefly, this is the situation we find ourselves in. Think about the welfare of our city and our army.'

The heroic *rākṣasas* joined their palms in respect and said, 'Our army is vast and has all kinds of weapons. What is there to worry about? Kubera lived on Mount Kailāsa surrounded by hordes of *yakṣas*. You defeated them all and made them subordinate to you, even though Kubera had Śiva for a friend and thought very highly of himself. He was a guardian of the quarters but in your anger, you defeated him in combat. You wrought havoc among the *yakṣas* and stopped their advance from Kailāsa. You even got the wondrous Puṣpaka for yourself!

'The king of the *dānavas,* Māya, sought an alliance with you out of fear and gave you his daughter in marriage. You even brought the *dānava* Madhu, renowned for his strength and courage, under your control! You went to the underworld and conquered the *nāgas*. After a battle that lasted a whole year, you subdued many *dānavas* and learned the magic arts. You defeated Varuṇa's sons in battle even though they were backed by a massive four-divisioned army.

'Long ago, the earth was full of *kṣatriyas* who rivalled Indra in their heroism. They were as numerous as trees. And you killed them all even though they were invincible to others. Rāma has neither their skills nor their courage in battle. Do not be disturbed by this challenge from such mediocre beings. You are bound to kill Rāma!'

Various mighty *rākṣasa* warriors leapt up from their seats and began to shout. 'We shall kill Rāma and Lakṣmaṇa and Sugrīva today! And that wretched Hanumān, who caused so much trouble in Lankā!'

They grabbed their weapons, ready to fight, but Vibhīṣaṇa made them all sit down again. He placed his palms together and said, 'Wise men say that war should be sought only after the first three options have been tried and have failed. My child, force will only succeed if it is used correctly after proper deliberation, according to the rules, or if the enemy is destined to die, or if he is engaged with other enemies, or if he is unaware. How can you think of attacking someone who is vigilant, who is supported by a huge army, who is determined to win, who has conquered his temper and is invincible?

'Who would have ever imagined that Hanumān would be able to leap across the ocean and do what he did? Do not underestimate the enemy! They are brave and have limitless forces. Besides that, what has Rāma ever done to Rāvaṇa that would justify the abduction of Sītā from Janasthāna? It was Khara's behaviour that made Rāma kill him in combat. All beings are entitled to defend their lives.

'Sītā should be given back. What do we gain by incurring their enmity? It is not right to unnecessarily incur the wrath of a righteous man who holds to *dharma.* Let us give Sītā back! If we do not volunteer to return Rāma's beloved wife, this lovely city and these brave *rākṣasas* will definitely be destroyed. I beg you as a brother, listen to me! Do as I say! My advice is based on righteousness and it is for your good. Return Sītā! Give her back before Rāma shoots you dead with an endless stream of arrows that sting like the rays of the sun and never miss their mark! Renounce this anger which destroys happiness and virtue. Follow the path of righteousness that leads to fame and joy. Have pity on us! Let us live in peace with our children and our families. Give Sītā back to Rāma!'

Rāvaṇa listened to his brother's well-intentioned words, but impelled by his fate, he replied harshly, 'One can live with a rival or with a poisonous snake but one cannot live with someone who claims friendship and then serves the interests of the enemy. I know how family members feel—they rejoice in the misfortunes of their kin. If a person is the best in his family, if he is capable, learned and righteous, they do not respect him. Instead, they try to bring him down. Of all the dangers in the world, the danger from your family is the worst! We know that cows yield with abundance, that *brahmins* exercise self-control and that women are fickle. So, too, it is evident that one's family is dangerous! The fact that I am respected by the world does not sit well with you! Neither does my power and majesty. If anyone else had spoken to me like this, Vibhīṣaṇa, he would be dead! Damn you! You are a disgrace to the family!'

Honourable Vibhīṣaṇa leapt up from his seat, holding his mace, along with four other *rākṣasas*. Enraged, he stepped into the air and said to his brother, 'You are my brother, great king. You can say whatever you like. But I will not forgive you for these cruel words and for your unrighteousness! Those who are doomed to die do not listen to good advice from their well wishers. It is easy to find companions who will tell you what you want to hear. It is hard to find those who will speak the unpleasant truth. It is harder still to find those who will listen to it.

'I cannot stand by and watch you place your head in death's noose any more than I can stand and watch a house on fire. I do not want to see you killed by golden arrows that are like tongues of flame. Even men who are strong and brave and who have performed great feats in battle crumble like walls of sand when they are in death's grasp. Protect this city and all the *rākṣasas*! I wish you well! I am leaving now. I hope you will be happy without me!'

Vibhīṣaṇa left almost immediately to find Rāma and Lakṣmaṇa. The monkeys who were on the ground with Sugrīva saw Vibhīṣaṇa coming through the air. He was as large as Mount Meru and he shone like lightning. Sugrīva thought for a moment and then said to Hanumān and the others, 'Look at this *rākṣasa* fully armed! I have no doubt he has come here with his four companions to kill us!'

The monkeys armed themselves with trees and rocks and said, 'Give the word, king, and we shall kill them and drop them to ground in an instant!'

As they were talking amongst themselves, Vibhīṣaṇa reached the northern shore of the ocean and stood there calmly. He noticed Sugrīva and the others and addressed them in a loud voice. 'I am Vibhīṣaṇa, the younger brother of Rāvaṇa, the wicked king of the *rākṣasas*! He is the one who abducted Sītā from Janasthāna and killed Jaṭāyu. Sītā is constantly guarded by *rākṣasīs* and she is helpless and miserable. I have argued with Rāvaṇa again and again and given him many reasons why he should return Sītā to Rāma. But he is trapped by his fate and refuses to take my advice, as a man who wants to die refuses medication. He has insulted me and treated me like a slave. So I have renounced my wife and children and have come to Rāma for refuge. Rāma is the refuge of all creatures in the world. Tell him that Vibhīṣaṇa has come to see him!'

Sugrīva went hurriedly to Rāma, greatly agitated and, in front of Lakṣmaṇa, he said, 'Rāvaṇa's brother Vibhīṣaṇa has come here with four other *rākṣasas* to take refuge with you. I am sure he has been sent here by Rāvaṇa as a spy. We must imprison him. He will gain our confidence and then he will kill you, Rāma! I think we should be ruthless with Vibhīṣaṇa and his companions. Remember, he is vile Rāvaṇa's brother!'

Rāma understood what Sugrīva was trying to tell him, and, after he had finished speaking, Rāma addressed Hanumān and the other monkey leaders who were standing nearby. 'You have heard what the king of the monkeys has to say about Rāvaṇa's brother. He has spoken clearly and to the point. When a problem like this has to be resolved, all one's intelligent and capable companions should express their opinions.'

They all spoke eagerly but courteously. Angada was the first to speak and suggested that Vibhīṣaṇa's loyalty be tested. Vibhīṣaṇa is our enemy. It is appropriate that we be suspicious of him first. We cannot just assume that he is worthy of our trust. Deceitful people hide their intentions and move amongst the enemy and then they strike when the time is right. That would be a disaster for us. Let us test him before we take him into our confidence. If he proves to be virtuous, we shall take him and if not, we must drop him.'

Śarabha, who was very practical, said, 'Let us put a spy on him as soon as possible. Once he has been watched and investigated by someone with a keen intelligence, we can decide what to do next.'

Jāmbavan was learned in the traditional texts of kingship and he considered the matter in that context. 'Vibhīṣaṇa comes from our sworn enemy, the wicked king of the *rākṣasas.* He has not acted appropriately and we must be suspicious of him because of that.'

Mainda, who knew the difference between right and wrong and who was very eloquent, said, 'Let us question Vibhīṣaṇa gently and without hostility about Rāvaṇa's plans. We will be able to assess his real intentions and decide whether he is good or evil.'

Then Hanumān, who was the finest of all the councillors, rich in learning and wisdom and familiar with the rules of conduct, said, 'The strategies suggested by the others, that we assess Vibhīṣaṇa's merits, seem flawed to me. I cannot see how such a scheme would work. It would be all right if we could conceive of some huge test for him. At the same time, we cannot simply take a stranger into our midst like this.

'The suggestion that we have him spied upon is also faulty. The circumstances are not suitable for something like that. The idea that Vibhīṣaṇa has come to us at the wrong time and in the wrong place is also incorrect. In fact, I feel it is just the opposite. I think he has come to the right place at the right time. He saw how wicked Rāvaṇa is and how great and powerful Rāma is. He made the right choice by deciding to come here.

'The idea that we should question him is based on faulty logic. Any intelligent person who is questioned like this would become suspicious and we run the risk of alienating someone who has approached us in genuine friendship. One can never get to the real intentions of another by questioning him.

'He never showed any indications of deceit or lies when he was speaking. His face and manner were open and friendly. I am sure he is sincere. There is no hint of unrighteousness in anything he has said. He has observed your actions and seen Rāvaṇa's deeds. He has heard about the killing of Vālī and Sugrīva's coronation. I think he has come here because he wants a kingdom. Keeping all this in mind, I think it would be all right to take him as an ally!'

Rāma listened with interest and delight to Hanumān's intelligent response. 'I, too, have something to say on the subject of Vibhīṣaṇa,' he said. 'Listen to it, for you have my interests at heart. You should never turn away anyone who comes to you in friendship, even if he has evil intentions. A good person would never do that.'

Sugrīva was moved by what Rāma said and his love and respect for Rāma swelled. 'There is nothing surprising in this! You are the lord of the world and you are honourable. You know *dharma* and you do and say the right thing all the time. I know in my heart that Vibhīṣaṇa is a good man. That is the only conclusion anyone would come to if they observed him carefully. Let Vibhīṣaṇa be made equal with all of us, Rāma. Take him as an ally!'

'What difference does it make if this *rākṣasa* is good or wicked,' said Rāma. 'Nobody can hurt me in the slightest way. I could destroy all the *piśācas,* the *dānavas,* the *yakṣas* and the *rākṣasas* in the world with my little finger if I wanted to! Even at the cost of his own life, a righteous man must protect a fugitive from the enemy, no matter if he be arrogant or in abject misery. I give him my protection, whether it is Vibhīṣaṇa or Rāvaṇa himself. Bring him here, monkeys!'

Vibhīṣaṇa was relieved that Rāma had accepted him and fell at his feet along with his companions. 'I am Rāvaṇa's brother. But he has dismissed me and so I have come to you, the refuge of all creatures!' he said. 'I have renounced Lankā, my friends and all my wealth. Now my hopes for a kingdom, life and happiness lie with you. I will do all I can to help you destroy the *rākṣasas* and conquer Lankā. I will even infiltrate the enemy army!'

Rāma embraced Vibhīṣaṇa and told Lakṣmaṇa to fetch water from the ocean. 'Use this water to consecrate Vibhīṣaṇa king of the *rākṣasas* so that he knows how pleased I am with him!' he said. Lakṣmaṇa did as he was told and Vibhīṣaṇa was crowned in the presence of all the monkeys who shouted 'Well done! Excellent!' at this sign of favour from Rāma.

# *Chapter Fifty-Seven*

Then Sugrīva asked Vibhīṣaṇa, 'How shall we cross this boundless ocean? We cannot think of a way to get across with the entire monkey army.'

'Rāma should ask the ocean for help!' replied Vibhīṣaṇa. 'This ocean was dug up by Sagara and he will use all his resources to help Rāma!'

Vibhīṣaṇa's plan was simple and practical and it appealed to Rāma. 'I like this idea, Lakṣmaṇa' said Rāma. 'Tell me, do you and Sugrīva approve? You are both experienced advisors. Consider the plan and tell me what you think.'

Sugrīva and Lakṣmaṇa replied together, 'How could Vibhīṣaṇa's idea not appeal to us? It is timely and practical. We cannot cross the immense ocean without building a bridge. Even an army of the gods and *asuras* led by Indra could not reach Lankā any other way! Let us put Vibhīṣaṇa's plan into action immediately. We have wasted enough time already!'

Rāma sat down on a bed of *kuśa* grass on the ocean shore, blazing like the sacrificial fire. He sat there beside the ocean for three days and three nights in constant vigil, adhering strictly to his vows. But the ocean, the lord of the rivers, did not appear before Rāma, who was doing this to propitiate him. Rāma's eyes turned red with anger and he said to Lakṣmaṇa, who stood beside him, 'Look, Lakṣmaṇa! The ocean does not present himself despite the honour I do him! He is so arrogant that he will not show himself!

'The virtues of good men, like calmness, patience, honesty and sweet speech bear no results. They are seen as signs of weakness. The world respects only those men who are wicked and cunning, who dole out punishments in all directions and who constantly praise themselves. One cannot achieve fame and success in the world without violence, just as one cannot achieve victory in battle without it.

'Today you shall watch as the ocean overflows with fish pierced by my arrows, Lakṣmaṇa! You shall see the carcasses of sea creatures shredded by my arrows! Today I shall declare war on this mighty ocean, filled with shells and fish, and I shall dry up his waters! The ocean thinks I am weak because I have been patient. What is the use of patience with someone like this? Bring me my bow, Lakṣmaṇa, and my arrows which are like poisonous snakes. I am going to agitate this calm ocean. Even though it never transgresses its bounds, I shall cause such huge waves that the ocean will overflow!'

His eyes dilated with anger, Rāma grabbed his bow and he blazed like the doomsday fire. He held his mighty bow in the middle and made the earth tremble as he released a storm of arrows as Indra would release his thunderbolt. The arrows shone with splendour and they forced themselves into the ocean, causing great fear among the sea creatures. A huge wind arose and mighty waves crashed to the shore, carrying fish and sea serpents with them. The ocean was terribly agitated and threw up vast quantities of shells and filled the air with spray from its swiftly receding waters. The serpents and *dānavas* who lived in submarine worlds were terrified and their eyes blazed like fire. Thousands of waves as high as mountains rose from the ocean and the waters were filled with floating fish and other creatures.

Then, the ocean himself rose from the middle of the waters, like the sun rising over the peaks of Mount Meru. He made himself manifest, surrounded by sea serpents with flaming jaws. He was as smooth as emerald and was adorned with gold. He wore red clothes and a garland of red flowers and his eyes were like lotus petals.

He joined his palms in respect and said to Rāma, who was still holding his arrows, 'Rāma, the earth, the wind, sky, water and fire are all bound by their essential nature. I, too, have my own nature which makes me impossible to cross and impossible to swim. It would be completely unnatural for me to let you cross over. There is nothing, not desire, not greed nor fear, that can make these waters still. The only thing I can grant you is something that I, too, can endure; and that is that the sea monsters will not prey on you until the army has crossed the waters.

'Nala, the son of Viśvakarmā, stands right here with you. He has been given many boons by his father as a result of which, they are exactly alike. He can build a bridge across me and I will hold it up!' said the ocean and vanished.

'What the ocean said is true!' said the monkey Nala. 'I am exactly like my father. I can build a bridge across the ocean. My father, Viśvakarmā, gave my mother a boon on Mount Mandara. He said that the son born of him would be his equal. I did not mention my talents because I was not asked. But today, let the monkeys build the bridge!'

Under Rāma's instructions, hundreds of thousands of monkeys ran all over the forest to collect wood for the bridge. They uprooted trees and carried them to the water as if they were carrying Indra's banners. They broke off mountain peaks and threw them into the ocean, filling up the waters. Nala built a bridge that was ten *yojanās* wide and one hundred *yojanās* long in the middle of the ocean, the lord of rivers, and it shone like the stars in the sky.

The gods and *gandharvas,* the *siddhas* and the great sages gathered in the air to look at the wondrous bridge. The monkeys jumped in and out of the water as they yelled and screamed with delight at the miraculous bridge. Millions of monkeys used the bridge to cross the ocean. It was wide and firm, solidly built and had a shining floor. It cut through the ocean like a parting in the hair.

Once they had crossed the ocean, Vibhīṣaṇa stood ready to ward off any enemy attacks with his mace. Rāma, Lakṣmaṇa and Sugrīva stood at the head of the army. Some of the monkeys walked in the middle of the bridge, others walked on the sides, others jumped in and out of the water, others strayed off the path and still others flew around in the air like birds. The huge din made by that enormous monkey army as it crossed the bridge drowned out the rumbling of the ocean. As the gods, *siddhas* and *cāraṇas* watched the wondrous feat that had been achieved for Rāma, the monkey army reached the other side and camped on the shore which abounded in roots, fruits and water.

# *Chapter Fifty-Eight*

When Rāma had crossed the ocean with his army, Rāvaṇa summoned two of his ministers and said, 'A bridge over the ocean has never been built before but Rāma and his army have done it. They have crossed the ocean and arrived here. I still cannot believe that they actually built the bridge! More important, I have to know about the size of the army. Infiltrate the army and find out all you can about its size and strength. Find out who the commanders are, who are the advisors that Rāma and Sugrīva trust the most, who leads the army in battle and who are the most heroic monkeys. Find out how they built the bridge and where the chief monkeys have been accommodated. Find out what Rāma's strategy is going to be, how brave he is and what his weapons are. And about Lakṣmaṇa's courage and skills. Get as much information as possible and come back as soon as you can!'

The two *rākṣasas,* Śuka and Sāraṇa, took on the form of monkeys and joined Rāma's army. But they had no idea how to assess the numbers in a force that was so massive that it seemed endless and was so frightening that it made the hair stand on end. There were monkeys everywhere, on mountaintops and in the valleys and forests. Some of them were still coming over the ocean, others waited for their turn to cross to the northern shore. The army made a huge din as it settled on the shores of Lankā.

Vibhīṣaṇa saw the two *rākṣasas* and recognized them. He had them captured and brought before Rāma, saying that they were spies from Lankā. Śuka and Sāraṇa took one look at Rāma and were terrified. They lost all hopes of staying alive and they joined their palms and cried, 'We only came here on Rāvaṇa's instructions to assess the strength of the army!'

Rāma, who was devoted to the welfare of all creatures, laughed and said, 'If you have done what you were asked to do, you can return. Go back to Lankā and give Rāvaṇa this message from me: "Show me the strength you resorted to when you abducted Sītā. Show me the strength of your army and your followers. Tomorrow you will see Lankā with its ramparts and gateways and all its *rākṣasas* destroyed by my arrows! Tomorrow I shall loose my arrows in anger against the *rākṣasas* as Indra loosed his thunderbolt against the *dānavas*!"'

The *rākṣasas* returned to Rāvaṇa with Rāma's message. 'We were captured by Vibhīṣaṇa and though we deserved to die, Rāma spared our lives,' they said. 'Rāma, Lakṣmaṇa, Vibhīṣaṇa and Sugrīva are all mighty warriors, equal to Indra in strength and courage. They can destroy Lankā with its ramparts and gates, they don't even need the other monkeys for this! And Rāma can do all this single-handed with his weapons! Even an army of the gods and *asuras* led by Indra cannot conquer those monkeys who are protected by Rāma, Lakṣmaṇa and Sugrīva! All the monkeys are willing and eager to fight. Renounce your hostility with them, Rāvaṇa! Give Sītā back to Rāma!'

'Even if the gods, *gandharvas* and *dānavas* were to unite against me I would not give up Sītā!' roared Rāvaṇa. 'Not even for fear of all the worlds! You are frightened because you have just seen that enormous army. That is why you think it is appropriate for me to return Sītā! Where is the foe that can beat me in battle!'

'Do you see those huge monkeys standing there like rutting elephants, like banyan trees on the banks of the Gangā, like *sāla* trees on Mount Himavān?' said Śuka to Rāvaṇa. 'They are the sons of gods and *gandharvas*. They are immeasurably strong and heroic, they can change their form at will and they are equal to the gods in their strength and valour. There are hundreds of thousands of millions of monkeys like this!

'See those two handsome monkeys over there, as beautiful as the gods? They are Mainda and Dvivida and they are unrivalled for the skills in battle. They had Brahmā's permission to drink the nectar of immortality and they are now determined to destroy Lankā with their strength. And behind them, the two monkeys that you see are Sumukha and Vimukha. They are the sons of Yama and they are just like their father. The next one there, the one the size of an elephant, he can churn up the ocean when he is angry. He is the one who came to Lankā and saw Sītā. Look again, you have seen him before! The same monkey has returned! He is Hanumān, son of the Wind, and he is already famous for his leap over the ocean. He is the best of all the monkeys and he can take any form he likes! He is strong and powerful and goes wherever he pleases, just like the restless wind.

'That one over there always walks the path of righteousness and upholds *dharma*. He is learned in the Vedas and has the use of Brahmā's weapon. He can pierce the sky with his arrows and bring down the mountains. He is like death when he is angry and he rivals Indra in courage. He is Rāma, whose wife you took from Janasthāna. He has come to fight you, Rāvaṇa! The one who stands beside him and shines like the purest gold, broad-chested, bright-eyed and dark-haired, that is Lakṣmaṇa, Rāma's younger brother. He is dearer to Rāma than his own life. He is learned in all the traditional texts and in the arts of war. He is impatient, invincible, strong, powerful and intelligent. He fights on Rāma's right and he is like the breath outside his body. He will give up his life for Rāma and is determined to destroy the *rākṣasas*.

'To Rāma's left stands Vibhīṣaṇa whom the *rākṣasas* rejected. He is now under Rāma's protection and has been consecrated king of Lankā. He will also fight against you because he is angry and resentful. And that one who stands as tall as a mountain in the middle of the monkey hordes is the king of them all, Sugrīva. He outshines all the other monkeys with his splendour, his fame, his intelligence and courage.

'All the billions of monkeys under Sugrīva's command have come here to do battle. Consider the size of this massive army that shines like a planet and do whatever is necessary to ensure that we are victorious!'

Rāvaṇa looked out over the enormous army and its mighty leaders as they had been described by Śuka. He saw Rāma with his own brother Vibhīṣaṇa close by him, he saw the mighty Lakṣmaṇa standing to Rāma's right and Sugrīva, the king of the monkeys. He grew angry but he felt fear touch his heart. He berated Śuka and Sāraṇa soundly after they had finished speaking. They stood before him with their heads hanging down and he shouted at them in a voice that shook with anger

'It is not a good idea for advisors, who live off the patronage of a king, to say unpleasant things to him. A king can make or break them! Do you think it wise to praise the enemy who has come here to destroy your king? All the time you spent with elders and teachers has been wasted. You have learned nothing about politics! Maybe you learned it all and understood nothing. Which is why it is now a burden to you! I can't believe I've survived this long with such fools for advisors! I can make you miserable! Have you no fear of death that you speak to me like this? Trees that have been in a forest fire may survive, but not those who have offended their king! I would kill you at once, you wretched creatures who praise my enemy, but the memory of all you have done for me in the past cools my anger! Go to hell, both of you! Do not make me angrier! Your ingratitude will be enough punishment for you since you have scorned my affections!'

Deeply ashamed, Śuka and Sāraṇa slunk away after wishing Rāvaṇa success in battle.

Rāvaṇa was rather concerned after hearing reports on the size and strength of the monkey army. He summoned his ministers and said, 'Bring my advisors together! We have important business to discuss!'

The advisors arrived quickly and after Rāvaṇa had discussed the matter with them, they were dismissed and the king returned to his own apartments. He sent for Vidyujjivha, a *rākṣasa* skilled in magic and sorcery, and together they went to Sītā. 'We must bewitch Sītā with magic and illusions,' said Rāvaṇa. 'Come with me! Create an illusion of Rāma's head and his bows and arrows and hold them in your hand!' The sorcerer agreed and Rāvaṇa was so pleased, he gave him a precious jewel right there.

Rāvaṇa entered the *aśoka* grove and saw Sītā, pathetic and miserable, her head hanging low. She sat there with her mind fixed on her husband, still guarded by the fierce *rākṣasīs* who followed her wherever she went.

Gleefully, Rāvaṇa went up to her and had the cheek to address her by her first name. 'The one you cling to, the one for whose sake you have rejected all my propositions, that husband of yours who killed Khara, he is dead! He was killed in battle! I have destroyed the root of your arrogance and pride. Your misery will force you to be my wife! Your little store of merit has been exhausted, conceited woman! Listen and I will tell you all about your husband's gruesome death!

'Rāma crossed the ocean and came here, intending to kill me, with an enormous army of monkeys. The army was tired after its long march and camped for the night. While they were asleep, my spies went and had a look around. Then, my magnificent army, led by Prahasta, destroyed the monkeys at night and killed Rāma and Lakṣmaṇa. The *rākṣasas* wreaked havoc among the monkeys with their clubs, maces, spears, arrows and swords. Prahasta himself severed Rāma's head as he slept with a single stroke of his sword. Vibhīṣaṇa tried to run away but he was caught. Lakṣmaṇa and the other monkeys fled in all directions. Sugrīva, the king of the monkeys, lies dead with his neck cut off. And Hanumān, slain by the *rākṣasas,* has a broken jaw.*

'Monkeys have been pulverized and trampled into the earth by elephants and chariots and horses as swift as the wind. Others were killed from the back as they fled in terror from the *rākṣasas* who chased them, killed like lions hounded by elephants. Some of the monkeys jumped into the ocean, others tried to take refuge in the sky. Bears behaved like monkeys and climbed into trees to save themselves. *Rākṣasas* have killed thousands of monkeys in the forests, in the mountains and along the ocean shore. Your husband and his army were destroyed by my forces. And look, they have brought your husband's head here, covered with dust and blood!'

Rāvaṇa turned to the *rākṣasīs* and said loudly enough for Sītā to hear. 'Bring Vidyujjivha here, the one who carried Rāma's head off the battle-field!'

The sorcerer came forward and bowed to Rāvaṇa, holding the phantom head. 'Put Rāma's head in front of Sītā!' Rāvaṇa said to him. 'Let this wretched woman take a good look at her husband's last state!' Vidyujjivha placed that well-loved, handsome head at Sītā's feet and disappeared. Rāvaṇa picked up the shining bow that was famous in the three worlds and said to Sītā, 'This is your precious Rāma's bow, already strung! Prahasta took it away after he had killed that pathetic man at night!' Rāvaṇa placed the bow next to the head and said to the princess of Videha, 'Come! Surrender to me!'

Sītā recognized her husband's eyes and hair, his complexion and his features. The head even had his crest jewel. She was overcome with grief and wailed piteously, railing against Kaikeyī in her anger. 'Ah, Kaikeyī! Your wishes have come true! The scion of the Ikṣvākus is dead! The clan has been destroyed by you with your desire to make trouble. What did noble Rāma ever do to you that you had him banished into the forest with me, wearing the rough clothes of an ascetic!'

---

* The significance of Sugrīva's neck being broken and Hanumān's smashed jaw lies in their names. 'Sūgrīva' means 'the one with the beautiful neck' and 'Hanūmān' means 'the one with the jaw.'

Trembling, Sītā fell to the ground like a young banana plant struck with an axe. She regained consciousness in a moment and sighed as she drew that lovely head close to her. 'I am destroyed!' she wailed. 'Great hero, you clung to your vows and this is how your life ended. I have become a widow!

'When a husband dies before his wife, it is attributed to her misconduct. But I never did anything wrong and yet, you, whose conduct is exemplary, have died before me! All those who predicted a long life for you have been proved liars! How could death have taken you by surprise? You were so wise in the ways of statecraft and you knew so many ways of avoiding danger! You have abandoned me, great hero, and now you lie hugging the earth as if she were your beloved!

'Ah! this bow of yours! We used to adorn it with flowers and worship it together! Why don't you look at me! Why don't you speak to me? I am your wife, whom you married as a young girl, who has been your constant companion! Remember, when you married me, you promised that we would go everywhere together? Then why have you left me here and gone on to the next world? You have left me here alone with my grief! I was the only one who embraced your body. Now it will be dragged through the dust by carrion eaters!

'When Lakṣmaṇa is the only one of us three that returns to Ayodhyā Kausalyā will question him closely even though she will be distraught with grief. When she hears that your army was massacred at night by the *rākṣasas* and that you were killed in your sleep and that I am a prisoner of the *rākṣasas,* she will die of a broken heart. Kill me, Rāvaṇa! Throw me on top of Rāma's body! Do the only good deed of your life, reunite a wife with her husband! Let my head be with his head, my body with his body! I must follow my husband for I cannot live for a minute without him!'

Sītā mourned and wept as she gazed at her husband's head and at his bow. As she was crying, a *rākṣasa* guard came up to Rāvaṇa and announced that the army commanders and ministers were waiting to see him. Rāvaṇa left the grove quickly and went to see them to discuss what could be done to counter Rāma's army. As soon as Rāvaṇa left the grove, Rāma's head and bow disappeared into thin air.

A *rākṣasī* named Saramā, who had been placed in charge of guarding Sītā, loved her as a friend for she was compassionate and loyal. She saw that Sītā had been completely deceived by the illusory head and that she was utterly miserable and hopeless. Because she loved Sītā, she comforted her. 'Do not be upset by what Rāvaṇa just said! I hid myself because I am so fond of you and I overcame my fear of Rāvaṇa and heard everything he said to you. I would give up my life for you!

'I know why the king of the *rākṣasas* left here in such a hurry! It is not possible to kill someone as alert and vigilant as Rāma in his sleep. In fact, I feel sure that he cannot be killed at all! Nor is it possible to kill the monkey warriors who use trees and rocks as weapons. Rāma protects them as Indra protects the gods. I am sure mighty Rāma has not been killed! You were bewitched into thinking he was dead by the powers of the sorcerer who abuses his intelligence by dabbling in magic. He is the enemy of all creatures.

'Your troubles are over! Prosperity and happiness are coming your way. Listen to the good news I bring! It will make you very happy! Rāma has crossed the ocean and is camped on the southern shore. I have seen him and Lakṣmaṇa with my own eyes! He has come supported by the entire monkey army. Rāvaṇa despatched *rākṣasas* who came back with the news of Rāma's arrival and, that is why he has gone in to consult his ministers!'

As Saramā was speaking, they heard battle drums and all the commotion of the army preparing for battle. 'Those drums that roll like thunder are the call to arms, my sweet lady!' said Saramā. 'Rutting elephants are being decorated, horses are being yoked to chariots and foot soldiers are spoiling for a fight. The highways are filling up with warriors of all kinds. It is as lovely a sight as the ocean swelling at high tide! Look at the lights that glint off the armour and weapons of the warriors and the trappings of the animals and chariots, like sparks from a forest fire in summer! Listen to the bells tinkling and the horses neighing and the chariots rumbling! These are the sounds of the *rākṣasa* troops preparing for war!

'Your sorrows are ended. Good fortune awaits you and danger for the *rākṣasas* is imminent! Your husband is unimaginably strong and he has controlled his temper. He is bound to kill Rāvaṇa and rescue you! I see you seated in his lap with all your wishes fulfilled after he has killed his enemy. When you are reunited and he embraces you, you will shed tears of joy on that broad chest. It won't be long before Rāma unbinds your hair from this single braid that reaches your hips. Soon, you shall rejoice in his presence as the earth, rich with crops, rejoices in abundant rain!'

Saramā's words brought happiness to Sītā, who had been parched with grief like the dry earth. Saramā wanted to make her friend happy and she knew how to do that, so she said with a smile, 'I can easily go to Rāma and come back without being seen. I can find out how he is and give him your good wishes. Neither the wind nor the king of the birds can keep pace as I fly through the sky!'

'I know you would do anything for me,' said Sītā, her voice sweet and pleasant with no trace of grief. 'If you really want to help me, then I would like to know what Rāma is planning. Wicked Rāvaṇa keeps me confused with his magic, as if I had drunk alcohol. He threatens and intimidates me and keeps me guarded by fierce and cruel *rākṣasīs.* I am constantly fearful and suspicious and my mind is never at ease. I fear him even though I am in the *aśoka* grove. If you can find out Rāvaṇa's plans and his intentions and report them to me, you will have done me a great favour!'

Saramā wiped Sītā's tear-stained face with a gentle hand and said sweetly, 'If this is what you want, I shall leave immediately and find out about the enemy's plans!' Saramā went to where Rāvaṇa was in council with his ministers and listened to their conversations. She heard all their plans and came quickly back to the *aśoka* grove.

Sītā embraced her and made her sit down. 'Sit here comfortably and tell me all about vile Rāvaṇa's plans!' she said and Sarama reported all she had heard. 'Rāvaṇa's mother and his oldest advisor Aviddha have told him several times that he should give you up but Rāvaṇa is determined not to do so,' began Saramā. 'That wicked creature and his advisors have decided that you will not be returned until he has been killed in battle. Rāma will kill them all with his countless arrows. Then he will rescue you and take you back to Ayodhyā, dark-eyed lady!'

At that very moment there was a huge sound that seemed to shake the earth and the entire *rākṣasa* army trembled. The *rākṣasas* were thoroughly disheartened, knowing that their king's transgressions had left them little hope.

The blaring of conch shells and the beating of drums announced the arrival of Rāma, destroyer of enemy cities. Rāvaṇa heard the sound and fell to thinking. Then he said to his ministers, 'I have heard all you have to say about Rāma crossing the ocean, his courage and the strength of his army. But I also know that all of you are invincible in battle.'

'A king who is learned in statecraft can rule for years and keep his enemies at bay,' said Mālyavān, who was Rāvaṇa's grandfather and was old and wise. 'He declares war or peace according to the circumstances and through that, he increases his own power. A king should wage war only against those who are weaker. He should make alliances with his equals and with those that are superior to him. An enemy should never be underestimated. Rāvaṇa, I think we should make peace with Rāma. Sītā has become an obsession with you! Give her back! You should not oppose someone who has the gods and the celestial beings praying for his victory.

'Brahmā created only two ways of life, *dharma* for the gods and *adharma* for *asuras* and *rākṣasas*. When *dharma* vanquishes *adharma,* it is the *kṛtayuga* and when *adharma* triumphs, it is the *kaliyuga.* When you conquered the world, you allowed *adharma* to flourish and this made our enemies stronger. The *adharma* you nurtured now works against us and strengthens the gods. The smoke from the *ṛṣis'* sacrifices covers all the directions and dissipates the power of the *rākṣasas.* In all the sacred areas, good and pious men have been keeping firm vows and practising austerities; that has brought bad times upon the *rākṣasas.*

'I have seen terrifying portents of doom that signify the destruction of the *rākṣasas.* Fierce clouds rumble harshly, striking fear into the hearts of the people as they rain blood all over Lankā. Tears fall from the eyes of our horses and elephants. Our battle banners are faded and dusty, they do not shine like they used to. Jackals, vultures and beasts of prey howl hideously. They are coming into Lankā and gathering in large numbers. Women are dreaming about evil spirits who laugh and grimace and bare their white teeth. The spirits call out to the women and toss their household goods around. Dogs are eating the offerings meant for the gods. Cows give birth to asses, mongooses are producing rats. Cats mate with tigers, dogs with pigs, *kinnaras* with *rākṣasas.* White birds with red legs wander around the city foretelling the death of the *rākṣasas.*

'I am sure Viṣṇu has taken the form of a mortal and arrived here as Rāma. There simply cannot be a human being like him! Make an alliance with Rāma, Rāvaṇa!' The distinguished Mālyavān fell silent and watched Rāvaṇa as he thought the matter over.

But Rāvaṇa was impelled by his own fate and ignored Mālyavān's sound advice. He frowned, his face distorted with anger. His eyes blazed as he said, 'You may be well-meaning, but your advice favours the enemy. You have spoken harshly and against my interests. And you expect me to listen to you? How can you think so highly of Rāma's powers? He is a mere mortal, alone and unaided, backed only by forest animals! His father has renounced him and he lives in the forest!

'And how can you think so little of me? I am the king of the *rākṣasas*! Even the gods fear me. I am stronger than Rāma in every way! Sītā is like Śrī without her lotus and I was the one who carried her off from the forest. You expect me to give her back because I am frightened? Watch! In a few days I will have killed Rāma and Lakṣmaṇa and Sugrīva and all the monkeys.

'How can Rāvaṇa be afraid when no one, not even the gods, dare face me in battle? I may break, but I will never bend! This may be a flaw in my character, but it is who I am. So what if Rāma built a bridge across the ocean? Why should that frighten me? Now that Rāma has crossed over with the monkeys, I swear to you, he shall not return alive!'

Mālyavān saw that Rāvaṇa was angry and in a foul mood and so he did not press the matter further. He invoked the blessings of the gods for Rāvaṇa's victory, as was proper, and taking permission, returned to his own apartments.

Rāvaṇa went back to his consultations with his ministers about the strategy to fortify Lankā. Prahasta was placed at the eastern gate and Mahāpārśva and Mahodara were sent to the southern gate. Rāvaṇa sent his son, Indrajit the sorcerer, to the western gate with a huge armed contingent. Śuka and Sāraṇa were sent to the northern gate and Rāvaṇa told them that he himself would join them there. The mighty Virūpākṣa was placed at the centre of the city with an enormous force of fierce *rākṣasas*. Now that he had made these arrangements, the king of the *rākṣasas* deluded himself into believing that he had ensured his safety. He accepted his ministers good wishes for victory and after dismissing them, he returned to his opulent apartments.

# *Chapter Fifty-Nine*

Meanwhile, Rāma was organizing his forces and giving them last-minute instructions. 'No one will appear on the battlefield in the form of a man. This will be the distinguishing feature of the monkey army. When we see a monkey, we shall know him to be our own person. There are only seven of us who will fight in the form of men: me, Lakṣmaṇa, Vibhīṣaṇa and his four companions!'

'Let us go to the top of the Suvela mountain,' continued Rāma. 'It is very pleasant. We can spend the night there. From its summit, I will be able to see Lankā, the home of the creature who abducted my wife and brought about his own death!' Rāma and the monkey leaders went to the top of the mountain and spent the night there. They saw the magnificent city of Lankā with its mansions and ramparts and tall gateways and they also observed that it was guarded by heavily armed *rākṣasas.*

The next morning, Rāma spoke to Lakṣmaṇa. 'Let us begin the preparations for battle. We must establish control over pools of clear water and the forests filled with fruit. We must also deploy our commanders and their troops and give them their positions.

'I see ill omens that portend the deaths of thousands of *rākṣasas* and monkeys and I see signs that indicate destruction for the worlds. A mighty gale blows, the earth trembles, the mountains quake and trees fall to the ground. Clouds form in the shape of beasts of prey and carrion eaters and they rumble harshly as they rain down bloody water. The evening sky burns red as sandal and fireballs fall from the sun. These signs indicate the end of the *yuga,* Lakṣmaṇa! Let us surround Rāvaṇa's impregnable city without any further delay and lay siege to it!'

Rāma and Lakṣmaṇa quickly descended from the mountain. Rāma looked out over his own immense army that no enemy could hope to defeat. When the right moment arrived, Rāma took up his bow, placed himself at the head of the army and started to move towards Lankā. Vibhīṣaṇa, Hanumān, Nala, Jāmbavān, Nīla and Lakṣmaṇa followed behind him and after them came the huge army of monkeys and bears that covered the earth. As large as elephants, the monkeys armed themselves with mountain peaks, rocks and huge trees.

After a while, they reached the outskirts of Lankā. The monkey army settled into its positions and laid siege to the city. Rāma and Lakṣmaṇa positioned themselves at Lankā's northern gate which was as tall as a mountain and particularly well fortified. Rāma chose this gate for himself and Lakṣmaṇa because he knew that Rāvaṇa had placed himself there, and because there was no one else capable of sealing off the gate. Nīla, Mainda and Dvivida were placed at the eastern gate, the mighty warrior Angada took the southern gate with Ṛṣabha, Gavākṣa, Gaja and Gavya. The mightiest monkey of them all, Hanumān, guarded the western gate with Pramāthi, Praghasa and other valiant warriors. Sugrīva himself took the centre with a band of monkeys that were as swift as Garuḍa and as powerful as the wind.

Fierce monkeys whose teeth were like tigers' fangs picked up their weapons, eager and ready to do battle. They used their nails and teeth to fight, stood with their tails erect and twisted their faces and bodies into terrifying shapes. Some of them had the strength of ten elephants, others had the strength of a hundred and still others had the strength of a thousand. The army consisted of hundreds of millions of monkeys and it was like a swarm of locusts that covered the earth and sky. The hills that surrounded Lankā were covered with monkeys and even the wind could not get past these great warriors who were armed with trees.

The *rākṣasas* were stunned when they found themselves surrounded by monkeys who were as large as clouds and were equal to Indra in valour. Their roaring could only be compared to the ocean at high tide and the walls and gateways of Lankā as well as the hills and forests resounded with their noise.

On the advice of Vibhīṣaṇa, who was skilled in the arts of kingship, Rāma called Angada and gave him a special task. 'My child, go to the ten-headed Rāvaṇa in Lankā and give him my message. Enter Lankā without fear and tell him this:

'"O *rākṣasa*! You have been deluded and have done terrible things against the *ṛṣis,* the gods, *gandharvas, apsarases, nāgas, yakṣas* and kings. But now the time has come for the destruction of your power and majesty! The arrogance you developed because of your boon from Brahmā will soon be crushed. I have come here to punish you for your transgressions! Show me the strength you used when you carried Sītā off, after you had lured me away with your magic tricks. I shall destroy the earth with my sharp arrows unless you return Sītā and beg for mercy!

'"Righteous Vibhīṣaṇa, the best of all *rākṣasas,* has joined me. He shall inherit the glories of Lankā completely unencumbered. Summon your courage and all your resources and come and fight me, *rākṣasa*! My arrows will purify you and bring you the ultimate peace on the battlefield! You cannot escape, now that I have seen you! Even if you take the form of a bird and fly through the three worlds as swift as thought! I speak for your own good. Organize your last rites, take a good look around Lankā for the last time. Your life is now in my hands!"'

Angada rose into the air and reached Rāvaṇa's palace in an instant. He saw Rāvaṇa seated amidst his advisors and blazing like fire, golden Angada delivered Rāma's message.

Rāvaṇa was incensed with Rāma's strong words. His eyes blazed and he screamed at his ministers, 'Catch that idiot and kill him!' At once, four shining *rākṣasas* jumped up and grabbed Angada. Angada allowed himself to be caught so that he could display the strength he would use against the *rākṣasa* army. The *rākṣasas* clung to his arms like birds and Angada carried them away as he leapt to the top of the palace that was as high as a mountain. As Rāvaṇa watched, the *rākṣasas* were tossed to the ground by the speed of Angada's movements. Angada shattered the top of the palace with a single kick and it collapsed right in front of Rāvaṇa. Angada roared out his name and rose into the sky. Rāvaṇa was enraged by the destruction, but he also heaved a great sigh, knowing that his end was near.

Meanwhile, millions of monkeys had covered the area between the city and the ocean. The *rākṣasas* stared at them in amazement, some agitated, others rejoicing at the prospect of a fight. They saw that the ramparts were swarming with monkeys and that they had filled the spaces between the ramparts as well as the moats. The *rākṣasas* raised a terrible din as they set about arming themselves and they sounded like the howling winds at the end of time.

The *rākṣasas* went and told Rāvaṇa that the city was under siege by Rāma and the monkeys and Rāvaṇa immediately doubled the guard around his palace. He watched as the monkeys swarmed over Lankā for Rāma's sake. The monkeys with their coppery red faces and gleaming golden bodies were ready to die for Rāma and they began to attack with rocks and trees and with their clenched fists. They broke buildings and crushed them into the ground. They clogged the clear water moats with rocks and grass and logs of wood. Hundreds of thousands of millions of monkeys climbed into Lankā, clambering over the golden gates and over the towers that were as tall as Mount Kailāsa. They roared and jumped up and down and took any form that pleased them as they swarmed over the ramparts.

Rāvaṇa was beside himself with rage and called for his entire army to march forth at once. With great delight, the *rākṣasa* hordes surged out of the city like the ocean during a storm.

There began a terrible battle between the monkeys and the *rākṣasas* that recalled the battle between the gods and the *asuras* in the old days. The *rākṣasas* ploughed through the monkeys with their spears and clubs and maces and battle axes, boasting about their valour as they did so. But the monkeys fought back with their teeth and nails and with rocks and trees. *Rākṣasas* stationed on the ramparts attacked the invading monkeys with their weapons and the monkeys retaliated by hurling them off the walls. The indescribable battle between the monkeys and the *rākṣasas* went on and on and soon the ground under their feet was drenched with blood and smeared with bits of flesh.

As they fought on, the sun set and the night, which was to take a number of lives, came on. But the fighting continued, for the monkeys and the *rākṣasas* were sworn to enmity and both sides were equally determined to win. In that terrible darkness, they attacked their own kind, the *rākṣasas* shouting, 'You are a monkey!' and the monkeys shouting, 'You are a *rākṣasa*!'

'Kill him!' 'Cut him up!' 'Why are you running away!' were the shouts heard through the darkness above the din. As they went on a rampage and devoured the monkeys, the black *rākṣasas* with their golden armour gleamed like mountains covered with medicinal herbs that emit light. In their rage, they fell upon horses with golden trappings whose plumes were like flames and tore them apart with their sharp teeth. Elephants decorated with plumes and banners were dragged here and there and crushed along with their riders. The dust that rose from the hooves of the horses and from the chariot wheels filled the warriors' eyes and ears and a river of blood flowed as if in spate.

The blaring of conches and beating of drums rose into the air and it mingled with the groans of dying *rākṣasas* and the roars of wounded monkeys. Weapons lay in heaps like piles of flower offerings and the battlefield could not be reached or even be recognized because of the blood and gore everywhere. The night which had come to claim the lives of the monkeys and *rākṣasas* seemed determined to destroy everything, like the night at the end of time.

In the darkness, the *rākṣasas* attacked Rāma together, deluging him with their arrows. But in a split second, Rāma had killed six of them with six sharp arrows that consumed them like tongues of flame. He lit up the directions with his shining, golden arrows, and other *rākṣasas* who tried to attack Rāma were burned like moths at a flame. Thousands of arrows powered by golden feathers flew in all directions and the battlefield was like an autumn night illuminated by fireflies.

That awful night was made even more so by the roaring of the *rākṣasas* and the monkeys that echoed and reverberated through the caves of Mount Trikūṭa. Angada was determined to kill the enemy and he destroyed Indrajit's horses and chariot. Indrajit quickly got rid of his chariot and vanished. Rāvaṇa's terrifying son was invincible in battle because of a boon he had received from Brahmā. He made himself invisible and loosed a shower of arrows. In his fury, he wounded Rāma and Lakṣmaṇa all over their bodies with arrows that turned into snakes.

Rāma wanted to know where the *rākṣasa* prince had disappeared to and appointed ten monkeys to find him. The monkey warriors armed themselves with trees and leapt into the sky in search of Indrajit. But Indrajit was a skilled warrior and harried those swift monkeys with even swifter arrows. The monkeys were wounded by Indrajit's arrows despite their quick movements, but still, they could not see him in the dark, as the sun cannot be seen behind clouds.

Indrajit then attacked Rāma and Lakṣmaṇa and his arrows struck them in their vitals. In fact, there was not a single part of their bodies that was spared the onslaught of Indrajit's arrows. Indrajit, who was as black as collyrium, twanged his bow and struck them again and again. His arrows turned into snakes and bound the brothers so that they could not move. In a moment, they had fallen onto the battlefield, unable, even, to open their eyes. The arrows bit into their flesh as they lay there, like Indra's flagstaff lies when the ropes that hold it have been severed.

Their bodies were immobile and covered with arrows right down to their fingertips. Blood flowed from them like rivers from Mount Prasravaṇa. Indrajit, who had even defeated Indra, turned his arrows onto Rāma first and the great hero fell to the ground. He was still holding his mighty bow with the three bends, decorated with gold bands, but it was split right at the point where he held it. When Lakṣmaṇa saw Rāma fallen, he lost the will to live. The monkeys gathered around the two heroic warriors who lay on the ground and were plunged into grief.

Indrajit rested after accomplishing his task, as Indra rests after he has sent the rains. Vibhīṣaṇa and Sugrīva came with all the other monkeys to where the brothers lay. Rāma and Lakṣmaṇa were unconscious, barely breathing, as they lay on their bed of arrows in agony with blood pouring from their bodies. The monkeys surrounded them, their eyes dim with tears. They looked up into the sky and in all directions but they could not see the invisible Indrajit anywhere. But he continued to torment the monkeys with his arrows, laughing as he said, 'Look at those brothers, bound by my snake arrows!'

The *rākṣasas* were thrilled and awed by what Indrajit had done and they praised him profusely. 'Rāma is dead!' they shouted gleefully and the sound of their cheers swelled as they honoured Rāvaṇa's son. Indrajit saw Rāma and Lakṣmaṇa lying there, unable to move, and presumed they were dead. He went back into the city in high spirits.

Sugrīva was terribly frightened when he saw Rāma and Lakṣmaṇa covered with arrows from head to foot. 'Stem the flow of your tears!' said Vibhīṣaṇa to the dejected Sugrīva. 'This is no time for sorrow. These things happen in battle, for no one is assured of victory. We may have a little good fortune left and with that, Rāma and Lakṣmaṇa may recover from their swoon. Pull yourself together. That will cheer me up as well. The righteous are never afraid of death!'

Vibhīṣaṇa gently wiped Sugrīva's shining eyes with his hand. 'This is not the time to display our weakness, king of the monkeys! If we succumb to our affection for Rāma and Lakṣmaṇa now, we shall surely die! Let us look after Rāma until he regains consciousness. He will banish our fears when he is better. This injury is nothing to Rāma. He is not going to die! Look, death's pallor has not yet touched his bright face.

'Compose yourself and go and reassure your troops. I will do the same thing. The troops are very upset. They gaze at each other, their eyes filled with fear, and they whisper among themselves.' After comforting Sugrīva, Vibhīṣaṇa went to rally the troops who were on the verge of flight.

Meanwhile, Indrajit had returned to Lankā with his army and went to see his father. He bowed before him and with joined palms, he announced that Rāma and Lakṣmaṇa were dead. Delighted, Rāvaṇa leapt from his seat and embraced his son in front of all the *rākṣasas.* He kissed him on the forehead and questioned him eagerly. In great detail, Indrajit told his father how he killed the brothers.

Meanwhile, the monkeys kept an alert watch over Rāma, looking in all directions and imagining even a moving blade of grass to be a *rākṣasa.*

Rāvaṇa had dismissed his son and now, with great delight, he sent for the *rākṣasīs* that guarded Sītā. They came at once, led by Trijaṭā. 'Tell Sītā that Indrajit has killed Rāma and Lakṣmaṇa! Take her to the battlefield in Puṣpaka so that she can see that the husband and the brother-in-law she relied upon to protect her are dead! Now that she has no hope of being rescued, she will adorn herself with jewels and come to me!'

The *rākṣasīs* did as they were told and put Sītā in the magical chariot. Rāvaṇa had the city decorated with flags and banners and announced everywhere that Rāma and Lakṣmaṇa were dead. Sītā went to the battlefield with Trijaṭā and saw that the entire monkey army had been struck down. She saw *rākṣasas* celebrating and the monkeys gathered around Rāma and Lakṣmaṇa, distraught with grief. She saw Rāma and Lakṣmaṇa lying unconscious upon a bed of arrows, tortured by their wounds. Their armour had been torn open, their bows had fallen from their hands and every inch of their bodies were covered with arrows. Sītā's grief knew no bounds as she gazed at the brothers who rivalled the gods. Her eyes clouded with tears and she began to wail.

As she lamented her fate, Trijaṭā said to her, 'Don't cry. I am sure your husband is still alive! Listen and I will tell you why I think Rāma and Lakṣmaṇa are not dead.

'An army would not display anger and suppressed excitement if its leaders were dead. If Rāma were truly dead, this magical vehicle would not carry you. This army is calm and collected, Sītā. They watch over the brothers as if they were still alive. All these signs point to a happy conclusion of affairs. I say all this because I am fond of you!

'Look at their vital signs Sītā. They may be unconscious but death's pallor has not come to their bright faces. Curb your morbid thoughts and your grief! They cannot possibly be dead!'

Sītā joined her palms and whispered, 'May all this be true!' Trijaṭā turned Puṣpaka around and took Sītā back to Lankā. Sītā entered the beautiful *aśoka* grove but her thoughts stayed with Rāma and Lakṣmaṇa and she was still depressed.

Even as the monkey leaders stood around Daśaratha's sons miserably, Rāma recovered consciousness though he was still bound by Indrajit's snake arrows. When he saw his brother lying there, pale, bloodied and obviously suffering, he cried out in despair. 'What use to me is Sītā or my life when I see my brother lifeless like this on the battlefield? If I looked hard enough, I would find another woman like Sītā in this world. But I would never find anyone like my brother Lakṣmaṇa, my companion and advisor! If Lakṣmaṇa dies, I will kill myself in front of all the monkeys!

'How can I return to Ayodhyā without him when he followed me into the forest? How will I endure Sumitrā's reproaches? I cannot go on living, I shall kill myself! Damn me and my ignoble acts that have led to Lakṣmaṇa lying like this, covered with arrows, as if he were dead!

'Ah Lakṣmaṇa! You always comforted me and cheered me! Now I am filled with sorrow and you say not a word! I shall follow this brave hero to the world of the dead just as he followed me into the forest! The empty boast that I would make Vibhīṣaṇa the king of the *rākṣasas* will haunt me always! Sugrīva, you should return. Rāvaṇa will pursue you thinking that you have been weakened without me. Take your army and your followers across the bridge over the ocean. It is not possible for mortals to counter their destinies, Sugrīva! You have done all that a friend and ally can do without transgressing *dharma*. I give you leave to depart, monkey! Go your own way!'

The monkeys heard Rāma's lament and tears poured from their eyes.

Vibhīṣaṇa came over and when he saw the two lifeless bodies, he stroked their faces and wept. 'These heroes have been laid low by the *rākṣasas* who fight unfairly! My wicked nephew tricked and deceived them! He has brought disgrace upon his father by fighting in this unethical way!

'They lie here, covered with arrows and bathed in blood, sleeping the endless sleep. I had centred my hopes for kingship on them! I am as good as dead without a kingdom and my enemy Rāvaṇa has done what he said he would do. His wishes have been fulfilled!'

Sugrīva embraced Vibhīṣaṇa and consoled him, saying, 'I feel sure you will become the king of Lankā! Neither Rāvaṇa nor his son shall have their wishes come true. Rāma and Lakṣmaṇa are not dead! As soon as they recover consciousness, they will kill Rāvaṇa and all his followers!'

Sugrīva turned to his father-in-law, Suṣeṇa, who stood by his side and said, 'When Rāma and Lakṣmaṇa have regained consciousness, take them back to Kiṣkindha along with the monkey army. I will kill Rāvaṇa and his family and rescue Sītā!'

'During the terrible war between the gods and the *asuras,* the *asuras* defeated the gods by disappearing again and again,' said Suṣeṇa. 'Bṛhaspati revived the gods who were close to death and those that were unconscious with medicinal herbs and *mantras.* Let the monkeys go to the ocean of milk and bring those herbs here quickly!

'The herbs we need grow on the mountains Candra and Droṇa which lie in the ocean where the nectar was churned. Let Hanumān, the son of the wind, go and fetch those herbs!'

At that very moment, a huge gale arose accompanied by clouds and lightning. The waters rose, the mountains trembled and islands with their great trees tumbled into the ocean. A little later, the monkeys saw Garuḍa, the king of the birds, bright as a fire, approaching. The minute they saw him, the arrows that had become snakes and bound Rāma and Lakṣmaṇa fled.

Garuḍa honoured the princes and touched their moon-like faces with his hands. The moment he did that, their wounds were healed and the bodies shone golden. Their energy, vigour, intelligence and memory as well as their good looks and all their virtues were doubled.

Garuḍa raised the princes who were Indra's equals and embraced them. 'Because of you, we have been able to overcome this terrible thing Rāvaṇa's son did to us,' said Rāma. 'You have given us back our strength! Your presence makes me as happy as if I were with my father. Who are you, mighty one, with your good looks, your celestial garlands and ornaments and clothes and sweet perfumes?'

Garuḍa's eyes were wide with joy as he replied, 'I am your dear friend, Rāma, the breath outside your body! I am Garuḍa and I have come here to help you both. No one, not the gods nor the *gandharvas* nor any of the celestial beings could have released you from these terrible bonds wicked Indrajit created with his magical powers.

'Rāma, you and your brother are fortunate indeed that I heard what had happened and came here immediately because of my affection for you! Now that you have been freed from those terrible bonds, you must be vigilant. It is in the nature of *rākṣasas* to fight by duplicitous means, but heroes fight honourably. That is their greatest strength. Never trust a *rākṣasa* on the battlefield!' said Garuḍa as he embraced them and prepared to leave.

When the monkeys saw that Rāma and Lakṣmaṇa had been revived, they shouted and yelled and whipped their tails. They beat their drums and blew their conches and laughed and danced and went back to their monkey pranks. They slapped each other's backs and pulled up thousands of trees, ready to do battle again. They surged towards the gates of Lankā, lusting for a fight, and the din they raised made the *rākṣasas* anxious.

# Chapter Sixty

Rāvaṇa heard the sound of the monkeys that swelled like thunder and remarked to his ministers, 'This thunderous din sounds as if the monkeys are rejoicing. They are obviously very pleased about something, for the noise they are making is enough to agitate the ocean! But Rāma and Lakṣmaṇa are supposed to be bound by Indrajit's snake arrows. This uproar produces grave doubts in my mind!'

He turned to his personal guards who stood around him. 'Find out what makes the monkeys rejoice at a time when they should be in despair!'

The guards were confused and climbed to the tops of the ramparts. They saw Sugrīva in full control of the army. Then, they saw Rāma and Lakṣmaṇa standing there, freed of their bonds, and they were filled with despair. Fear clutched at their hearts as they climbed down and went back to Rāvaṇa with crestfallen faces. They reported the bad news to him in great detail.

'Indrajit felled the brothers with his arrows, binding them so that they could move neither hand nor foot. They have snapped their bonds with the strength of elephants and can now be seen on the battlefield!'

A wave of sadness washed over Rāvaṇa, and he grew somewhat worried. He kept his eyes on the ground as he said, 'Indrajit's arrows were like the sun in splendour and they were a gift from the gods. They were infallible, like poisonous snakes. If my enemies were able to free themselves from these, it does not bode well for the rest of my forces.' Hissing like an angry snake, Rāvaṇa called upon Dhūmrākṣa. 'Go out with a huge force of fierce *rākṣasas* and kill Rāma and the monkeys!'

Dhūmrākṣa lost no time in carrying out Rāvaṇa's commands and quickly organized a band of heroic *rākṣasas*. The frightful *rākṣasas* with bells on their girdles shouted with glee as they came from all directions, armed with every kind of weapon. Laughing, Dhūmrākṣa rode out of the western gate, surrounded by the *rākṣasas.* A host of bad omens appeared as he went out and Dhūmrākṣa was scared. Then he saw that enormous monkey army that was as large as the ocean, commanded by Rāma.

The monkeys were delighted to see formidable Dhūmrākṣa marching forth and, in their eagerness to fight, they sent up a huge shout. A great battle ensued between the monkeys and the *rākṣasas* as they attacked each other with trees and stones and spears and iron clubs. The *rākṣasas* attacked the monkeys with their vicious weapons, tore their limbs apart with arrows and pierced their bodies with spears. The monkeys retaliated with huge trees and rocks, tearing at the *rākṣasas* with their nails and teeth, smashing them with their fists and crushing them underfoot as they yelled and shouted. The ground was littered with fallen horses, chariots, elephants and dead *rākṣasas* as the monkeys continued to fight enthusiastically, even though they were drenched in blood from their wounds. Some had been disembowelled, others had had their chests ripped open and some lay dead on the ground.

Hanumān saw that the monkey army was having trouble and he surged towards Dhūmrākṣa with a massive rock. Hanumān was his father's equal in strength and speed, and he hurled the rock with all his might towards the *rākṣasa.* Dhūmrākṣa jumped out of his chariot as it was smashed into little pieces along with its horses. Hanumān then turned his attention to the *rākṣasa* army and wreaked havoc among them, assaulting them with trees and rocks. The *rākṣasas* fell to the ground, their heads broken, their bodies bathed in blood, tormented by their wounds.

Hanumān renewed his attack on Dhūmrākṣa, uprooting an entire mountain crest as he ran towards him. Dhūmrākṣa struck Hanumān with his spiked mace but the monkey did not even feel the blow. Hanumān threw the mountain peak at Dhūmrākṣa and it hit him on the head. Dhūmrākṣa collapsed on the ground, his body limp. When the *rākṣasas* who were still left alive saw that their commander had been slain, they ran back to Lankā in terror. Hanumān was tired, but glad that he had routed the enemy and received the praises of the monkeys with joy.

Rāvaṇa was enraged when he heard about the death of Dhūmrākṣa. He called the famed general Akampana and ordered him to go out and meet the monkey forces. A huge number of truly frightening *rākṣasas* came to join him as Akampana, black as a cloud and with a voice like thunder, rode out in his chariot of burnished gold.

There was another great battle between the *rākṣasas* and the monkeys who were ready to sacrifice their lives. The air was rent with battle cries and great shouts as they fought with speed and power. The warriors could not see each other or anything else because of the dust, white as washed silk, that rose and covered the battlefield. Horses, chariots, flags, banners, weapons and armour were all obscured by the dust and the fighters ran here and there, practically invisible. The *rākṣasas* and the monkeys attacked each other, killing friend and foe alike, and the earth was drenched in blood.

Akampana inspired the *rākṣasas* to great deeds, but the monkeys fought with equal valour and killed huge numbers of the enemy.

Akampana worked himself up into a mighty rage and brandished his bow. He ordered his charioteer to drive straight into the heart of the battle and he slaughtered monkeys all around him with his sharp arrows. The monkeys could not take a stand against him and fell back.

Hanumān saw the rout and arrived there to face Akampana. The monkeys rallied around him with great shouts of joy and stood firm against the enemy. Akampana greeted Hanumān with a rain of arrows but the mighty monkey stood there, steady as a rock, unmindful of the arrows that struck him, like a mountain in a storm. He concentrated his mind on how he was going to kill Akampana. He charged towards the *rākṣasa* with all his might and realizing that he was unarmed, he grabbed a mountain peak along the way, blazing like fire. But Akampana shattered the peak from a distance with his sharp arrows. Hanumān was enraged and uprooted a tree as tall as a mountain. He whirled it around over his head gleefully and renewed his charge, tearing up the earth with his feet. He killed and maimed *rākṣasas* as well as horses and elephants here and there and finally, the terrified *rākṣasas* fled.

Akampana roared and rushed towards Hanumān, striking him with fourteen arrows. The great monkey pulled up another tree and smashed it down on Akampana's head. The *rākṣasa* fell down in a heap and died. The other *rākṣasas* fled in terror, their hair dishevelled, sweat pouring from their bodies. The monkeys gathered around Hanumān and praised him for his prowess in battle.

Rāvaṇa was disheartened to hear about the death of Akampana. He brooded for a while and then held discussions with his ministers. He walked around the city with its flags and banners and inspected the fortifications and defences and saw that it was well-guarded at every post. He called for Prahasta, the veteran warrior, and told him to mount an attack against the monkeys.

Prahasta summoned his forces and within an hour, Lankā was swarming with mighty warriors brandishing their weapons. They poured oblations into the fire and honoured the *brahmins* as the air filled with the fragrance of *ghee.* Ready for battle, they joyfully took the wreaths and garlands over which *mantras* for their invincibility had been uttered and saluted their king before they set forth.

Drums were beaten and music from other instruments rose into the air as Prahasta's forces rumbled out of the city from the eastern gate, sounding like a mighty ocean. Prahasta resembled the god of death at doomsday. Evil omens appeared everywhere, clouds rained blood over Prahasta's chariot, a vulture perched on his flagstaff and his natural splendour dimmed as his horses stumbled on level ground.

But Prahasta, famous for his strength and prowess, continued forward and the monkeys came to meet him armed with their weapons. A huge din arose as the fighting forces met. Misguided Prahasta moved into battle against the monkey king's army as a moth rushes to a flame, hoping to destroy it.

The *rākṣasas'* weapons glittered and shone as they advanced and the monkeys armed themselves with trees and rocks and huge boulders. Hundreds of monkeys and *rākṣasas* were killed in this massive encounter. Some were impaled on spears, some felled with discuses, some hacked to death with battle axes, some crushed with mighty clubs, some pierced by arrows, others cut open with swords. *Rākṣasas* were crushed and pulverized with trees and rocks and stones, smashed by fists and feet. They vomited blood and their teeth and eyes fell out of their heads.

Meanwhile, Prahasta wreaked havoc among the monkeys with his arrows while the two armies, locked in deadly combat, swirled like a whirlpool and filled the air with thunderous roars. A river of blood flowed swiftly past. The broken weapons it carried looked like uprooted trees, it had liver and viscera for mud, fat for foam, entrails for floating vegetation, heads and bodies for fish and dismembered limbs for the grass on its banks.

The great monkey Nīla watched as Prahasta slaughtered the monkeys all around him from his chariot. Nīla charged towards him and was met with a hail of arrows that pierced him all over his body. He grabbed an enormous tree and crushed Prahasta's fine horses with a single blow. He snatched Prahasta's bow from his hand and smashed it with a huge roar. Prahasta jumped out of his chariot and prepared to face Nīla with his club. The two mighty commanders faced each other like rutting elephants, like a lion and a tiger. They rained blows upon each other, Prahasta using his club and Nīla using rocks and boulders. Blood poured from their bodies but they continued to fight. Finally, Nīla smashed an enormous rock on Prahasta's head which shattered into a thousand pieces. He fell to the earth like a tree axed at the root, blood streaming from his head like a cascade from a mountain.

The *rākṣasas* were totally demoralized with the death of Prahasta and, losing heart, they could not make a stand against the monkeys any more than water can be contained by a broken dam. They returned to Lankā, plunged into an ocean of grief, while the monkeys rejoiced and praised Nīla for his deeds.

At this point, Rāvaṇa decided that it was time for him to enter the fray. 'I cannot ignore the fact that my general, who had even defeated Indra in battle, was killed by this army of monkeys. I myself will go into battle and wrest victory from the hands of these creatures. I shall consume Rāma and Lakṣmaṇa and all these monkeys with my arrows as a forest is consumed by fire!' He climbed into his chariot that was yoked with the finest horses and blazed like a fire with its own splendour.

As Rāvaṇa, the king of the *rākṣasas,* went forth, he was honoured with the beating of drums and the blaring of conches, the shouting of battle cries and the singing of hymns. Surrounded by flesh-eating warriors with blazing eyes who were the size of mountains, he looked like Śiva surrounded by the *gaṇas.* The mighty one left the city quickly and beheld the army of fierce monkeys, armed with trees and rocks, roaring like the ocean at high tide.

Vibhīṣaṇa pointed Rāvaṇa out to Rāma, and Rāma, deeply impressed, said, 'Rāvaṇa, the king of the *rākṣasas,* blazes with his own splendour and dazzles the eye like the sun! I can see him clearly from here, lit up by his majesty. Even the bodies of the gods and the *dānavas* do not shine with this kind of brilliance. All the warriors under his command are as large as mountains and are armed with shining weapons.' Rāma stood with Lakṣmaṇa at his side, his bow at the ready, arrows chosen from his quiver.

Sugrīva, the king of the monkeys, rushed towards Rāvaṇa, armed with an immense mountain peak. He hurled it at him with all his might but Rāvaṇa shattered it with his golden arrows. Then he picked an arrow that hissed like a serpent and shot it at Sugrīva with such force that sparks flew as it travelled through the air. It pierced Sugrīva with the force of Indra's thunderbolt and split open his chest. Sugrīva fell to the ground with a cry of pain and lost consciousness.

Then the other monkey leaders joined the attack against Rāvaṇa, but he fended them off with a shower of golden arrows that tore at their bodies, making them collapse on the ground. Hanumān saw that Rāvaṇa's arrows were coming so thick and fast that nothing was visible. 'You have been granted invulnerability against gods and *gandharvas, dānavas, yakṣas* and *rākṣasas*. But you have reason to fear a monkey!' he shouted angrily as he moved towards the *rākṣasa.* 'My left arm will drive the living breath from your body!'

'Come! Strike me!' shouted Rāvaṇa, his eyes red with rage. 'What are you waiting for? I shall test your strength and then I shall kill you!'

'Have you forgotten how I killed your son Akṣa?' taunted Hanumān, Rāvaṇa dealt him such a mighty blow in the middle of his chest that the great monkey staggered and reeled. Nīla rushed in to help Hanumān, but he was met with a hail of fiery arrows that burned him all over his body. Meanwhile, Hanumān had recovered his strength, but when he saw Rāvaṇa engaged in combat with Nīla, he held back, knowing that it was wrong to attack an enemy when he was fighting another. Nīla hurled trees and rocks and stones at Rāvaṇa, but the *rākṣasa* shattered them all with his arrows while they were still in the air.

Then Nīla contracted his body and leapt to the top of Rāvaṇa's chariot. He hopped from the flagstaff to Rāvaṇa's bow and onto his crown, dodging Rāvaṇa all the time. Rāma, Lakṣmaṇa and Hanumān watched in amazement, and the other monkeys broke into shouts of laughter. Incensed, Rāvaṇa invoked the power of Agni's weapon and used it against Nīla. Struck by the flaming weapon, Nīla fell to the ground.

Rāvaṇa turned his chariot towards Lakṣmaṇa and bore down on him through the battle, shaking the earth around him and blazing like a fire. 'Come and fight with me, king of the *rākṣasas*!' shouted Lakṣmaṇa. 'Why do you fight only with monkeys?' And then began a battle of wondrous arrows with golden shafts, crescent heads and divine feathers. Lakṣmaṇa repelled everything that Rāvaṇa threw at him, and, finally, Rāvaṇa drew out the arrow that Brahmā had given him, which was as powerful as the doomsday fire. It struck Lakṣmaṇa in the middle of his forehead, and the great warrior reeled from its impact even as he managed to split Rāvaṇa's bow and strike him with three arrows.

Rāvaṇa recovered his strength and hurled a spear at Lakṣmaṇa that was as bright as a smokeless fire and struck terror into the hearts of all the monkeys. It hit Lakṣmaṇa in the middle of his broad chest and felled him. Just then, Hanumān jumped into the fray and punched Rāvaṇa in the chest with his great fist. Rāvaṇa fell to his knees and vomited, blood pouring out of his eyes and ears. He reeled and fell into a faint and even when he regained consciousness, he was unsteady on his feet. All the monkeys rejoiced when they saw Rāvaṇa laid low in battle.

Hanumān lifted Lakṣmaṇa from where he lay and carried him to Rāma. Seeing that Lakṣmaṇa was invincible, the spear left him and returned to its place in Rāvaṇa's chariot. Lakṣmaṇa's wound healed and he recovered completely. that's weird

Meanwhile, Rāvaṇa had also recovered and he harried the monkey army with his arrows. Rāma decided to go after him and Hanumān came to him and said, 'Climb onto my back and attack the *rākṣasa*!' Rāvaṇa charged towards them and struck Hanumān with his sharp arrows. Rāma was enraged and assailed Rāvaṇa with his arrows that destroyed his chariot with its fluttering banners. He struck Rāvaṇa in the middle of the chest with an arrow that hit him with the force of Indra's thunderbolt. The king of the *rākṣasas* staggered as his bow fell from his hands. Rāma chose a crescent-shaped arrow and shattered Rāvaṇa's golden crown. humiliating

Rāvaṇa was now like a serpent bereft of poison, like the sun dimmed, as he stood there, his crown in pieces, his majesty crushed. 'You have done many terrible things. You have deprived me of the valiant warriors you killed. But I know you are exhausted so I will not kill you now!' said Rāma.

Dismissed with these words, Rāvaṇa hurried back to Lankā, his pride in tatters, his horses and charioteer slain, his crown in pieces. Rāma saw to it that Lakṣmaṇa and the wounded monkeys were attended to before the next battle. The gods and the *ṛṣis,* the *asuras* and the *uragas* and all the creatures from all the directions rejoiced that the enemy of the three worlds had been humbled.

# *Chapter Sixty-One*

Rāvaṇa returned to Lankā and sat on his golden throne, his eyes cast down. 'All my austerities and penance have been in vain,' he said, 'for I, Indra's equal, have been defeated in battle by a mere mortal! Brahmā's warning that I would have to live in fear of mortals has come back to haunt me. What he says must come true! I asked for immunity from gods, *gandharvas, yakṣas, rakṣasas* and *pannagas* but I did not ask for the same protection against mortals.

'Make sure the *rākṣasas* who guard the towers and gates are fully alert. And go and wake Kumbhakarṇa who sleeps under Brahmā's curse. He can humble the pride of the gods and *dānavas*!' said Rāvaṇa as he realized the significance of his own defeat and Prahasta's. He sent a huge force to wake the giant Kumbhakarṇa. 'That *rākṣasa* sleeps for six, seven, eight and nine months at a time,' he said. 'Wake him immediately! He is the mightiest of the *rākṣasas* and he will kill the monkeys and the princes in no time at all! Kumbhakarṇa is addicted to the vulgar pleasure of sleep but once he is awake, I, who have suffered this terrible indignity, will have nothing to worry about. What use is he to me, even if he is Indra's equal, if he cannot help me in this time of trouble?'

The *rākṣasas* obeyed Rāvaṇa's command and went with great trepidation to Kumbhakarna's home. They took flowers and incense and huge quantities of food with them and entered the door of his home which itself was one *yojanā* wide. The house was filled with fragrances of all kinds but the wind from Kumbhakarṇa's breathing was so strong, it was difficult for the *rākṣasas* to stand. They managed to enter his house with a great deal of trouble. His room was paved with gold and the *rākṣasas* gazed in wonder at that creature who was terrifying even in his sleep.

Kumbhakarṇa lay sprawled, as large as a fallen mountain, and the *rākṣasas* began their efforts to wake him. His hair stood straight up and his hissing breath came out in huge blasts. His open mouth was like hell itself and even his nostrils were terrifying. The *rākṣasas* prepared a huge pile of meat, tall as a second Mount Meru, that consisted of boar and deer and buffalo in order to tempt Kumbhakarṇa. They placed pots of blood and enticing liquors before him and they anointed him with priceless unguents and covered him with rare, fragrant flowers. They lit perfumed incense and they sang his praises. They blew moon-white conches as loud as they could and shouted and raised a terrible din.

Then they lost patience and yelled and screamed and shook him and pounded on his body. When they found that even that had no effect, they beat him with trees and rocks and clubs and maces and with their fists and feet. Even though the *rākṣasas* were strong and powerful, they could barely stand under the onslaught of Kumbhakarṇa's breath.

Some of them resorted to stronger measures. With whips and goads, they drove horses and camels and elephants and asses over his body. They played drums and conches as loudly as they could and beat the giant with whips. Their noise filled the city of Lankā but they could not wake Kumbhakarṇa. He continued to sleep under a powerful curse and the *rākṣasas* began to get angry. They yelled and shouted and pulled his hair and bit his ears but Kumbhakarṇa did not even stir in his death-like sleep. They armed themselves with hammers and clubs and beat him on his chest and head. Finally, they drove one thousand elephants over his body and Kumbhakarṇa twitched, for, at last, he had felt something.

The *rākṣasas* had pounded him with trees and rocks and the giant had ignored them. But now that he was awake, he was hungry. He yawned widely, flinging up his arms that were as long and strong as snakes and as powerful as mountains. His yawning mouth was as deep as hell and as red as the sun rising over Mount Meru. He exhaled with a huge sigh that was like the wind blowing off a mountain and his flashing eyes looked like planets in a malignant configuration.

Kumbhakarṇa gorged himself on the meats and foods and liquors until he was completely sated. When the *rākṣasas* saw that he was finally satisfied, they gathered around him with bowed heads and joined palms. Surprised at being awakened, Kumbhakarṇa looked around at them all and said, 'Why have you woken me up? Is everything all right with the king? Is he in danger? There must be some trouble for you to have woken me with such urgency. I will kill whoever it is that threatens the king, even if it is Indra or Agni! My brother would never have had me woken up for something trivial! Tell me, why have I been awakened?'

Yūpākṣa, one of Rāvaṇa's ministers, said, 'We are not in danger from the gods, the *dānavas* or the *daityas*. This time, it is a mortal that threatens us. Lankā has been surrounded by monkeys that are the size of mountains and it is Rāma, who grieves for Sītā, who frightens us. A lone monkey set fire to the entire city. He also killed prince Akṣa along with his army and his elephants. And even Rāvaṇa, the thorn in the side of the gods, was granted his life by Rāma, who shines like the sun! Rāma has done what the gods, the *dānavas* and the *daityas* could not do to our king! He let him go after nearly taking his life.'

Kumbhakarṇa's eyes widened in amazement when he heard this. 'I will go right now and kill all the monkeys and Rāma and Lakṣmaṇa!' he said to Yūpākṣa. 'Then I will go and see Rāvaṇa. Let the *rākṣasas* feast on monkey flesh while I drink the blood of Rāma and Lakṣmaṇa!'

Mahodara, a veteran warrior, joined his palms and said, 'Listen to what Rāvaṇa has to say first. Weigh the pros and cons of the situation and then go out and be victorious in battle.' The *rākṣasas,* having persuaded Kumbhakarṇa to agree, ran ahead to Rāvaṇa's palace and said, 'Your brother has woken up! Should he go straight into battle or do you want to see him first?'

'Send him to me so that I can receive him with honour!' said Rāvaṇa with delight.

Kumbhakarṇa rose from his bed when he heard that his brother wanted to see him. He gargled and took a bath and adorned himself and asked for something to drink. The *rākṣasas* brought him all kinds of fine liquors and Kumbhakarṇa drank a thousand pots of wine. Pleased with himself and a little tipsy, Kumbhakarṇa set off, looking like the doomsday fire. The earth shook under his feet as he walked to his brother's palace.

When the monkeys saw Kumbhakarṇa, some of them ran to Rāma for protection, others fell down in a daze, some sank to the ground and others ran away in terror. Tall as a mountain peak with a crown that seemed to touch the sky, Kumbhakarṇa blazed with splendour and his body seemed to grow bigger and bigger.

Kumbhakarṇa touched his brother's feet. Rāvaṇa rose, embraced the giant and seated him on a magnificent throne. Kumbhakarṇa's eyes blazed as he said, 'Why did you have me woken up, king? Tell me who it is you fear and he shall be a corpse today!'

Rāvaṇa saw his brother's eyes rolling and knew that he was in a mighty rage. 'It has been a long time since you fell asleep,' said Rāvaṇa. 'Fortunately for you, you know nothing of the troubles Rāma has created. Along with Sugrīva, Daśaratha's son is destroying us! The monkeys built a bridge and crossed over the ocean to Lankā with no trouble at all. Now they run amok in its woods and forests. I do not see any monkeys being killed, but they have killed the best of *rākṣasas* in battle.

'My resources are dwindling. You must come to the aid of Lankā which is the refuge of old people and children. Mighty one, for the sake of the love we share as brothers, help me! I have confidence in you. I have never begged anyone like this before!'

Kumbhakarṇa embraced his brother and after bowing to him, he prepared to go out into battle. Rāvaṇa invoked blessings upon his head as he left. Drums boomed and conches blared as Kumbhakarṇa went forth followed by fully armed warriors on horses and elephants and in chariots. Intoxicated with alcohol and the smell of blood, the mighty Kumbhakarṇa strode out, armed with a spear. He was showered with flowers and a canopy was held over his head.

An immense band of foot soldiers, fierce *rākṣasas* with baleful eyes and prodigious strength, followed him into battle. Their huge bodies were as dark as mountains of collyrium and they made a great din as they marched along with their weapons raised. Mighty Kumbhakarṇa seemed to have taken a newer and more immense body which was so terrifying that it caused the monkeys' hair to stand on end. He was six hundred bow-lengths tall and one hundred bow-lengths wide, his eyes were like cartwheels and he glowed like a mountain.

Kumbhakarṇa ignored the evil omens which appeared as he left the city. He crossed the ramparts and gazed at the army of monkeys that was as huge as a bank of clouds. And when the monkeys saw that giant who was the size of a mountain, they scattered like clouds in the wind. Kumbhakarṇa laughed aloud when he saw the monkeys running in all directions and caused many monkeys to fall down in a swoon.

Angada and the other monkey leaders tried to stop the fleeing monkeys. 'Have you forgotten your powers and your noble lineage? How can you run away in fright like common cowards?' they shouted. 'Come back, friends! How can you care only for your own lives? This thing that terrifies you is not real. It is an illusion created by the *rākṣasas* and we can destroy it with our strength!'

Somewhat reassured, the monkeys regrouped and armed themselves with trees and rocks. They turned around and attacked Kumbhakarṇa in fury but he remained unmoved despite their repeated assaults. The rocks shattered and the trees snapped against his huge body. Meanwhile, he ploughed through the apes, crushing them and tossing them about. Some tumbled into the sea, others fled into the sky, some ran down the bridge they had built.

Angada exhorted them to return. 'Stand and fight!' he screamed. 'Women laugh at warriors who fling down their weapons and run away from the battlefield. Surely that is worse than death! Remember your ancestry and stop behaving like common creatures! Our life on earth is short in any case. If we die in battle, we shall go to Brahmā's realm. We shall earn fame and renown if we kill the enemy! Like a moth rushing into a fire, Kumbhakarṇa will not live once Rāma has set eyes on him. If we run from Kumbhakarṇa, we shall be branded cowards and will never achieve fame!'

Encouraged by Angada's words, the monkeys rallied and with renewed vigour they prepared to meet Kumbhakarṇa again. They attacked him with trees and rocks but Kumbhakarṇa flung them about, seven and eight hundred at a time, and they fell to the earth, their limbs smashed. He gathered sixteen and eighteen monkeys into his arms and threw them into his mouth, devouring them the way Garuḍa would snakes. Unable to have any effect on the giant, the monkey leaders set about destroying his forces by crushing them with mountain peaks.

Hanumān rained rocks and stones upon Kumbhakarṇa from the sky but Kumbhakarṇa shattered them all with his spear. Hanumān placed himself in Kumbhakarṇa's path and hurled a mountain peak at him with all his energy. Kumbhakarṇa whirled his shining spear above his head and struck Hanumān with it in the middle of his chest. Dazed and bewildered, Hanumān vomited blood and let out a terrible scream while the *rākṣasas* rejoiced to see him injured.

Thousands of monkeys rushed upon Kumbhakarṇa. They climbed up his body as they would climb a hill, they bit him and scratched him and pounded him with their fists and feet. But Kumbhakarṇa ignored their blows and shovelled them into his mouth. He consumed the monkeys the way fire consumes a forest, making the earth slippery with blood and gore.

Sugrīva, the heroic king of the monkeys, rose and rushed towards Kumbhakarṇa, brandishing a mountain peak. He threw an immense rock at Kumbhakarṇa with all his energy so that it struck him with the force of a thunderbolt. But the rock shattered into pieces against the giant's massive chest. Enraged, Kumbhakarṇa hurled his spear at Sugrīva but Hanumān rose up and caught the iron spear adorned with gold, breaking it in two across his knee. Kumbhakarṇa seized a peak and brought it down on Sugrīva's head, knocking him out cold.

Kumbhakarṇa lifted Sugrīva in his arms and carried him away into the air, looking like Mount Meru with a cloud. The *rākṣasas* on the battlefield rejoiced but the army of monkeys scattered in all directions. Hanumān felt sure that he could rescue Sugrīva but then decided against it. Since Sugrīva was capable of freeing himself, it would not be the right thing to do. So he set about rallying the monkey army that was in retreat.

Kumbhakarṇa entered the city of Lankā with the twitching Sugrīva in his arms. He was greeted with a rain of flowers from the people who crowded the towers and mansions. Refreshed by the cool water and the breeze that blew along the road, Sugrīva regained consciousness and found that he was in the arms of his enemy who was much stronger than himself. Quickly, he tore off Kumbhakarṇa's ears with his nails, bit off his nose, digging into his sides with his feet. Bleeding profusely, Kumbhakarṇa howled in pain and hurled Sugrīva onto the ground. *Rākṣasas* attacked Sugrīva in a group but he sprang into the air and returned to Rāma.

Without his nose and ears, Kumbhakarṇa looked like a mountain drenched in cascades of blood. Relying on his phenomenal strength, he decided to go back into battle. He realized that he had lost his weapon and so he armed himself with a mighty iron club. Hungry and hankering for flesh and blood, he devoured the monkeys like the doomsday fire. He gobbled up monkeys and *rākṣasas* indiscriminately, shoving them into his mouth twenty and thirty at a time.

Rāma invoked Śiva's weapon and pierced Kumbhakarṇa's heart with many sharp arrows. Sparks and smoke emerged from Kumbhakarṇa's cavernous mouth and his huge mace fell to the ground as the peacock-feathered-arrows lodged in his chest. Kumbhakarṇa found that he was unarmed and lashed out with his feet and fists. Weak and disoriented from loss of blood, he ran around in circles, attacking monkeys and *rākṣasas*.

Rāma picked up his great bow and bore down upon Kumbhakarṇa, followed by Lakṣmaṇa. The sight of Rāma with his magnificent bow and quiver full of deadly arrows reassured the monkey army. Rāma saw Kumbhakarṇa, his gleaming crown upon his head, covered in blood, devouring everything in sight. His eyes bloodshot, he licked the blood that poured from his face and trampled upon the monkey army like death at the end of time.

Rāma twanged his bow and the sound drove Kumbhakarṇa into a frenzy. He charged towards Rāma, who shouted, 'Come! I am ready for you, armed with my bow! Know that this is Rāma who speaks to you. You shall be dead within the hour!' Kumbhakarṇa laughed hideously and the monkeys' hearts leapt into their mouths. 'This is not Virādha or Khara or Kabandha, Vālī or Mārīca! I am Kumbhakarṇa! Look at my massive iron club with which I have destroyed gods and *dānavas* in the past! Do not look at me and think that I have neither nose nor ears. I feel no pain from those injuries. Show me your strength, tiger among men, and then I shall eat you up!'

Rāma loosed his splendid arrows against Kumbhakarṇa to no effect. The same arrows that had pierced the *sāla* trees and killed Vālī made not the slightest impression upon Kumbhakarṇa. Rāma invoked Vāyu's weapon and severed Kumbhakarṇa's right arm which was wielding the enormous club. The club fell to the ground, killing hundreds of monkeys. The ones that survived retired to a safe distance, trembling, and watched the terrible battle from there. Then Rāma invoked Indra's weapon and cut off Kumbhakarṇa's other arm which brandished a tree. That arm crushed trees and mountains and monkeys and *rākṣasas* as it fell. But still, Kumbhakarṇa lumbered towards Rāma, roaring as he came. Rāma cut off his legs with two crescent-headed arrows. Kumbhakarṇa opened his mouth wide and came forward. Rāma filled his terrifying maw with sharp, golden arrows. And then, Rāma picked his most formidable arrow, powered by Indra himself. It blazed like the sun and was as invincible as death. He loosed it against the *rākṣasa* and it sped through the air with the force of Indra's thunderbolt, lighting up the ten directions. It severed

Kumbhakarṇa's mountainous head with its bared teeth and dangling golden earrings. The head smashed towers and ramparts as it fell and his massive body collapsed into the ocean, crushing fish and mighty serpents as it buried itself in the seabed.

When Kumbhakarṇa, the enemy of the gods and the *brahmins*, was killed, the earth shook and all the heavenly beings rejoiced. The monkeys broke into shouts of joy and honoured Rāma for his incredible feat. The surviving *rākṣasas* ran to tell Rāvaṇa that Kumbhakarṇa had been slain. The king of the *rākṣasas* was overwhelmed by grief and fell into a swoon. After a while, he regained consciousness and began to lament the loss of his brother.

'Ah, heroic and mighty Kumbhakarṇa! Conqueror of the enemy! Why have you left me and gone? I am as good as dead now that you, my right arm, upon whom I depended and did not fear the gods or the *asuras,* have fallen. How could a hero like this, who has smashed the pride of the gods and the *dānavas,* who is like the doomsday fire, how could he have been killed in battle by Rāma?

'I am sure the rejoicing monkeys will seize this opportunity and swarm over the walls of Lankā. What use is the kingdom to me now? Or Sītā? I have no interest in life now that Kumbhakarṇa is dead! I would rather die than live this worthless life if I do not kill Rāma, my brother's killer, in battle! I shall follow my brother to the abode of death today! I cannot live for a moment without him! I am reaping the fruits of insulting noble Vibhīṣaṇa and ignoring his words!' Rāvaṇa mourned the loss of his brother and, overcome with grief, he swooned again.

he is willing to be killed now that he is grieving the loss of his brother

# *Chapter Sixty-Two*

Rāvaṇa's sons and nephews saw him grieving and they spoke words of encouragement, begging to be allowed to join the battle. All his sons were equal to Indra in valour. They could fly in the air, they were masters of the magical arts, they were invincible in battle and could humble the gods. Skilled in the use of all kinds of weapons, they were famous for their exploits. They were experienced warriors and had all won mighty boons for themselves.

Rāvaṇa called blessings upon his sons and embraced them and decorated them with jewels and ornaments before he sent them out. The *rākṣasa* princes rubbed themselves with medicinal herbs and sweet perfumes before they set out, impelled by fate. Bright like the sun, they wore glittering crowns and with their gleaming weapons, they shone like planets in the sky. Determined to vanquish the enemy, they thundered and roared and snatched arrows from their quivers. The earth trembled under their feet and the sky was pierced by their battle cries.

The monkey army saw them coming and roared with delight, eager to show off their strength and skills. And the *rākṣasas,* not to be outdone, yelled back as they prepared to attack. The monkeys greeted them with a hail of stones and rocks and trees. They crushed and smashed and pulverized the *rākṣasas* through their armour, even if they were riding in chariots or on horses or elephants. The *rākṣasas* fought back with arrows and other deadly weapons, tearing the monkeys' bodies apart. They even snatched rocks and trees from the monkeys and pounded them with their own weapons.

Riding on a horse that was as swift as the wind, Rāvaṇa's son Narāntaka cut through the monkey army with his spear like an enormous fish slicing through the waters. He killed seven hundred monkeys with a single blow leaving bloody corpses in his wake. He was everywhere, trampling the monkeys and attacking them before they could run to safety.

Sugrīva told Angada to confront Narāntaka and Vālī's splendid son emerged from the mass of monkeys like the sun emerging from the clouds. He had no weapons apart from his nails and teeth but he stood in front of Narāntaka and taunted him. Narāntaka whirled his spear above his head and attacked Angada, but the deadly spear shattered against the monkey's chest. Angada pounded Narāntaka's horse with his open palm and it collapsed in a heap, its eyes popping out of its head. Narāntaka attacked Angada with his fists and Angada retaliated by punching Narāntaka in the chest. It was a deadly blow, swift as a thunderbolt and with the weight of a mountain, and the *rākṣasa's* chest broke open, blood spurting from it like tongues of flame.

Rāvaṇa's other sons cried out when Narāntaka was killed and Devāntaka, Triśiras and Mahodara attacked Angada together. Angada rained trees and mountain peaks and rocks upon them but the *rākṣasas* cut them to bits with their sharp arrows. Though they all pounded him with their weapons, Angada showed no signs of fatigue or pain. He slapped Mahodara's great elephant and it fell to the ground. Then he grabbed its tusk and struck Devāntaka with it. Devāntaka dealt Angada a mighty blow with his club while Triśiras pierced the monkey's head with his arrows.

Hanumān and Nīla came to Angada's rescue and the *rākṣasas* were delighted with the prospect of new enemies to fight. Devāntaka rushed at Hanumān with his iron club raised but Hanumān killed him with a single blow to the head with his fist. Devāntaka fell to the ground, his head smashed to pulp, his teeth and eyes knocked out, his tongue lolling.

Triśiras and Mahodara attacked Nīla with a shower of arrows and Nīla succumbed. But he recovered very quickly and, uprooting an entire hill, he brought it down on Mahodara's head, killing him in an instant. Triśiras turned his attention to Hanumān, sending his magnificent spear through the air towards the monkey. Hanumān caught it as it flew like a firebrand and roaring fiercely, he snapped it in two. Triśiras then came at Hanumān with his sword but Hanumān felled him with a blow to the chest, snatching the sword that fell from his nerveless hand. Enraged, he severed the *rākṣasa's* three heads with their crowns and golden earrings. The blazing heads fell to the ground like planets dislodged from their orbits.

The monkeys shouted for joy and the earth trembled as the *rākṣasas* fled in all directions, leaving their weapons behind as they ran in terror of their lives.

Mountainous Atikāya, who was strong and powerful, was enraged when he saw his brothers being killed. He had been given a boon by Brahmā and had humbled the gods and the *dānavas* in battle. He blazed like a thousand suns in his chariot and his crown and earrings shone with splendour. He roared like a lion, declaring his name and his exploits and twanged his bow. The monkeys were terrified at the sight of his immense body and fled in all directions, seeking refuge with Rāma.

Atikāya plunged forward into the monkey army with his chariot, twanging his bow and roaring. The monkey leaders attacked him with trees and rocks but he splintered them with a shower of arrows. The monkeys could not retaliate and withdrew. 'I am seated in a chariot and armed with a bow and arrows!' he shouted arrogantly as he approached Rāma. 'I will not fight with just anyone! Let whoever dares come and confront me!'

Lakṣmaṇa drew his bow in anger and the sound filled the earth, the mountains, the sky and the ocean. Atikāya shot an arrow at Lakṣmaṇa and it sailed through the air, hissing like a serpent. Lakṣmaṇa shredded it to bits with his crescent-headed arrows and then chose another gleaming, razor-sharp arrow from his quiver. It struck Atikāya on the forehead and the *rākṣasa* reeled from the impact. Atikāya produced a rain of arrows but Lakṣmaṇa cut them to bits with his own weapons. Lakṣmaṇa loosed an arrow powered by the fire god and Atikāya retaliated with one powered by the sun god. Their tips blazing, the arrows met in the air like hissing serpents. They burnt each other out and were reduced to ashes.

The two mighty warriors assailed each other with all the celestial weapons at their command but they were perfectly matched and neither could get the better of the other. Finally, the wind god came to Lakṣmaṇa and whispered, 'Atikāya was granted a boon by Brahmā and he is protected by celestial armour. Use Brahmā's weapon, there is no other way to kill him!'

Lakṣmaṇa picked an arrow that would not miss its mark and called upon Brahmā to direct it. The universe shuddered in fear as Lakṣmaṇa fitted it into his bow and loosed it against Atikāya. Atikāya saw it blazing through the air with its golden shaft and though he tried to counter it with his own arrows and all his other weapons, it descended on him with the speed of Garuḍa. It severed his head which crashed to the ground like a Himalayan peak.

Those *rākṣasas* that still lived, weary and wretched from being routed by the enemy, wailed aloud when Atikāya fell. They fled back to Laṅkā, having lost all their leaders. But the monkeys rejoiced and praised Lakṣmaṇa, who had triumphed over a formidable enemy.

Rāvaṇa was beside himself with grief over the death of his sons and he mourned and lamented. His eyes filled with tears and he swooned in sorrow. And as he sat there grieving, his son Indrajit, the best of all the chariot warriors, came to him and said, 'Father, do not succumb to confusion and despair. I, Indrajit, am still alive. I am the enemy of Indra and no one can escape my arrows! Today you will see Rāma and Lakṣmaṇa lifeless on the battlefield, their broken bodies covered with my arrows!'

He went out of the city in his splendid chariot, surrounded by fully armed warriors who were eager to fight. The sound of drums and conches filled the air and with the white canopy held over his head, Indrajit seemed like the moon rising into the sky. When Indrajit reached the battlefield, he placed warriors all around his chariot and propitiated the fire with oblations and *mantras*. He offered flowers and perfumes and the head of a black goat as he surrounded the fire with his weapons. The fire god himself appeared, dressed in red and enveloped by flames, to receive the offerings. Indrajit invoked Brahmā's powers and muttered *mantras* over his chariot, and over his bow and other weapons. He made himself invisible in the sky with all the powers he had gathered through the ritual.

The *rākṣasa* army marched forward and slaughtered the monkeys with their arrows. Indrajit killed seven and eight monkeys at a time with a single arrow and they ran helter skelter, their bodies streaming with blood, fear lodged in their hearts. Determined to make a stand for Rāma's sake, they turned and showered Indrajit with trees and stones and boulders but the mighty warrior warded them off and deluged the monkeys with arrows.

Indrajit inflicted terrible wounds on the leading monkey warriors with his various weapons and they fell to the ground. Indrajit then attacked Rāma and Lakṣmaṇa with showers of arrows that were as bright as the rays of the sun. They did not affect Rāma, who turned to Lakṣmaṇa and said, 'The mighty *rākṣasa* is using Brahmā's power for his weapons. Now that he has felled the monkey leaders, he has turned his arrows upon us.

He has a boon from Brahmā. How can we kill him when we cannot even see him? Let us pretend to be struck by the arrows and fall to the ground as if we are unconscious. He will definitely return to the city, thinking that he has won the first round of battle!'

Rāma and Lakṣmaṇa fell to the ground and Indrajit shouted with joy at having created trouble for the monkey army as well as for Rāma and Lakṣmaṇa and returned to Rāvaṇa's city.

The monkeys were perplexed and troubled, but there was nothing Sugrīva, Nīla, Angada or Jāmbavān could do. Vibhīṣaṇa saw how disheartened the army was and reassured the monkey leaders. 'Do not be afraid. This is not the time for grief. It is true the princes have fallen, but it is only because they respect Brahmā's power that they have succumbed to Indrajit's arrows. How can this be an occasion for grief?'

'Even though much of the monkey army has been destroyed, let us console those that are still alive!' said Hanumān. Along with Vibhīṣaṇa, the best of *rākṣasas,* Hanumān walked through the battlefield at night, lighting the way with torches. They saw the earth covered with tails, arms, torsos, legs, fingers and scattered limbs. Blood flowed from the bodies of fallen monkeys who were the size of mountains and abandoned weapons glowed in the dark. Hanumān and Vibhīṣaṇa saw Sugrīva, Angada, Nīla, Śarabha, Gandhamādana, Jāmbavān, Suṣeṇa and Vegadarśī, Mainda Dvivida, Nala, Jyotimukha and Panasa, all injured on the battlefield. Seventy-six million monkeys had been slain on the fifth day of battle by Brahmā's weapon.

Hanumān and Vibhīṣaṇa looked among the bloodied bodies which resembled the ocean at high tide, for Jāmbavān. They found the old bear, pierced by hundreds of arrows, shining like a fire that was about to be extinguished. 'Can it be, noble one, that you are still alive after being pierced by all these arrows?' asked Vibhīṣaṇa.

Jāmbavān replied slowly and painfully, 'King of the *rākṣasas,* I recognize your voice, but the pain from my wounds dims my eyes and I cannot see you. Tell me, is Hanumān, the son of the Wind, still alive?'

'You ignore the princes and ask about Hanumān!' cried Vibhīṣaṇa. 'Not for king Sugrīva nor Angada, not even for Rāma do you display the kind of affection that you do for Hanumān!'

'Listen, *rākṣasa,* and I will tell you why I ask about Hanumān,' said Jāmbavān. 'If Hanumān is alive, then even though the army has been slaughtered, they are not dead. If Hanumān lives, we shall all live, even though we lie here dead. My child, Hanumān's powers are equal to his father's and his courage rivals that of Agni, so we have hope for life!'

Hanumān came up to Jāmbavān, touched his feet and greeted him with respect. Jāmbavān's senses were flickering, but he felt as if he had been reborn when he heard Hanumān's voice. 'Come here, tiger among monkeys!' he said. 'You can save us all! You are the monkeys' best friend and you are the only one who has the power to save them. This is the time to display your prowess. I can see no other who can do what you can. Heal injured Rāma and Lakṣmaṇa and bring happiness to the army of monkeys and bears!

'Hanumān, fly over the ocean and go to Himavat, the best of mountains. You will see the golden peaks of Kailāsa which are difficult to scale. Between these two mountains lies the herb mountain where all the medicinal herbs shine with unmatched splendour. There you will find four herbs, the *mṛtyasañjīvanī, viṣalyakarṇī, sauvarṇakarṇī* and *saṃdhānī.* They shine so brightly that they illuminate the directions. Collect all four and bring them back here as soon as you can! Son of the Wind, put heart into the monkeys by reviving them!'

Hanumān expanded with strength as the wind swells the waters of the ocean when he heard Jāmbavān's words. He went to the top of a mountain and, crushed under his feet, the mountain sank into the earth. Hanumān shattered its peaks and its trees caught fire as they fell. The monkeys could no longer stand on that mountain which had been shaken to its roots. Lankā seemed to dance in the night as its doors, windows and gateways were smashed and as agitated people ran here and there.

Hanumān was like a mountain himself as he made the earth and the ocean tremble. He roared as he prepared to leap and the *rākṣasas* were petrified. Hanumān honoured Rāma and steeled himself to perform another great deed for Rāma's sake. He raised his tail which looked like a serpent, he crouched and flattened his ears against his head. He opened his mouth which blazed like the submarine fire and leapt into the sky. He carried off rocks and trees and natural monkeys but they fell into the ocean because of the speed with which Hanumān flew.

He stretched out his arms and flew in the direction of Mount Meru. He travelled over the ocean, garlanded with waves and filled with moving and unmoving creatures, as he went onwards like a discus released from the hand of Viṣṇu. Flying as quickly as his father, he crossed mountains and forests, lakes and rivers, ponds, cities and flourishing peoples. He took the path of the sun and soon. He saw Himavat, its peaks like white clouds, covered with streams and waterfalls, caves and the settlements of pious sages. He saw Brahmāloka and the navel of the earth and golden-peaked Kailāsa.

Between Himavat and Kailāsa, he saw the herb mountain shining like the fire because of the plants that grew on it. He was wonderstruck as he gazed at it, but he quickly alighted and began to gather herbs. He wandered all over the rocky mountain but the herbs saw him coming and, knowing his purpose, they made themselves invisible. Hanumān became impatient and roared loudly.

'Why are you not sympathetic to Rāma's cause!' he cried to the mountain. 'I can crush you in an instant with my strong arms!' He grabbed the mountain by its peaks and uprooted it along with its trees, elephants, minerals and plateaux. He leapt into the sky with the mountain and the sky dwellers praised and honoured him as he flew along the path of the sun with the shining mountain. He passed close to the sun as he blazed along, shining in the sky like the thousand-spoked discus released by Viṣṇu.

The monkeys saw him returning and roared with joy. Hanumān roared back and Lankā's mansions echoed and resounded. He came down from the sky in the middle of the monkey army, bowed to the monkey leaders and embraced Vibhīṣaṇa. The human princes inhaled the sweet-smelling medicinal herbs and were instantly revived, their wounds healed. The other monkeys were also restored to health and vitality. Hanumān took the herb mountain back to its place near Himavat and returned quickly to Rāma.

# *Chapter Sixty-Three*

Sugrīva told Hanumān what had to be done next. 'Since Kumbhakarṇa and the *rākṣasa* princes are dead, Rāvaṇa cannot order another attack. Let the strongest monkeys jump over the ramparts into Lankā with burning firebrands!'

When night fell and a deep darkness covered everything, a band of monkeys crept towards Lankā with firebrands in their hands. The *rākṣasas* deserted their guard posts when they saw the monkeys approaching and the monkeys gleefully set fire to the towers, gates and lofty mansions.

Thousands of buildings began to burn as the homes of *rākṣasa* householders were destroyed. Some of the *rākṣasas* were wearing golden armour and were adorned with garlands and wonderful garments. Their eyes rolled back and they reeled from all the liquor they had drunk. Some of them left their clothes in the hands of their wives, others raved and ranted against the enemy. Some were armed with clubs and spears, others were eating and drinking. Some were asleep with their women on fine couches, some ran as fast as they could, trying to get away with their children.

The fire devoured them all in the thousands and burned ever more brightly. It consumed their beautiful, spacious homes which were decorated with all kinds of gems and jewels and had been filled with the sweet songs of birds. Enveloped by flames, the gates shone like clouds touched by lightning in the summer sky. Women who had been sleeping in their homes screamed as they burned, their bodies now bereft of all ornaments. From afar, the burning mansions looked like the peaks of the Himālayas lit up by medicinal herbs.

Elephants and horses who had been freed ran around in confusion and made Lankā seem like the ocean boiling over at the end of time. Torched by the monkeys, in a single hour, Lankā had become like the universe blazing with the doomsday fire. Women suffocated by smoke and burned by the flames could be heard wailing ten *yojanās* away. When the burning *rākṣasas* ran out of the city, they were attacked by the monkeys who were waiting for a fight.

Rāma and Lakṣmaṇa were perfectly recovered and healed and they stood there, ready to use their bows. Rāma twanged the string of his great bow and the sound put fear into the hearts of the *rākṣasas*. Lankā's towering gateway, which was as high as Mount Kailāsa, came crashing down under his arrows. The *rākṣasas* who were still in their homes prepared themselves for battle and struggled into their armour. Sugrīva ordered his leaders to man the gates and fight with any creature that dared to pass.

When Rāvaṇa saw the monkeys at the city gates with torches in their hands, he flew into an uncontrollable rage. He summoned Kumbha and Nikumbha, the sons of Kumbhakarṇa, and sent them out against the enemy with a huge force of *rākṣasas,* urging them to shout their battle cries and spurring them on to victory.

The warriors emerged from Lankā, their bright weapons gleaming, their elephants and horses and chariots raising a terrible din, their colourful flags waving in the wind. The monkey army surged forward to meet them and the *rākṣasas* charged on, like moths into a flame. A terrible battle ensued with the monkeys and the *rākṣasas* clashing, weapon against weapon, body against body. The *rākṣasas* demolished the monkeys seven and ten at a time and the monkeys did the same. But when the *rākṣasas* tried to flee, their hair dishevelled, their clothes and armour and battle banners in shreds, the monkeys surrounded them.

Many great warriors lost their lives in this terrible battle. Angada smashed the *rākṣasa* Prajangha's head, Śonitākṣa and Yūpākṣa were killed by Mainda and Dvivida, and Sugrīva himself killed Kumbha who had injured a number of monkey leaders. Enraged that Sugrīva had killed his brother, Nikumbha jumped into the fray with renewed vigour. After a frightful battle, Hanumān took the *rākṣasa's* life by twisting off his neck.

Then Rāvaṇa sent Khara's son, Makarākṣa, onto the battlefield with specific instructions to kill Rāma and Lakṣmaṇa. Makarākṣa was motivated by the idea of avenging his father's death and though he was a skilled and brave warrior, he was no match for Rāma. Rāma eventually killed him with a magnificent arrow powered by the fire god and once again, the other *rākṣasas* ran back to Lankā in terror.

Meanwhile, Indrajit grew angrier and angrier as he thought about the innumerable heroic *rākṣasas* who had been killed in battle. Mighty Indrajit, thorn in the side of the gods and a descendent of Pulastya, rode forth from the western gate surrounded by *rākṣasas*. When he saw that Rāma and Lakṣmaṇa were still full of energy and enthusiasm for battle, he felt he had to resort to sorcery. He decided to surround himself with a large band of *rākṣasas,* create a phantom Sītā and kill her in front of all the monkeys in order to crush their spirit.

The monkeys surged forward when they saw Indrajit emerging from the city gates and Hanumān charged towards him, armed with a huge tree. Suddenly, he noticed that a pathetic and miserable Sītā was seated in Indrajit's chariot. Emaciated and pale, her hair in a single braid, Rāma's beloved was dressed in dirty clothes and was covered with dust. Hanumān looked twice to make sure that it was really Sītā and his eyes filled with tears at the sight of her terrible state. He wondered why Indrajit was displaying the miserable woman and asked this question aloud as he approached Indrajit.

Indrajit was in a rage when he saw the monkey forces. He unsheathed his sword and grabbed Sītā by the hair. In front of everyone, he slapped her hard and she cried out, 'Oh! Rāma! Rāma!' Hanumān was outraged and berated Indrajit angrily. 'Vile wretch! Wicked creature! You have called for your own destruction by grabbing Sītā by her hair! You were born in a line of royal sages even though you emerged from the womb of a *rākṣasī*! Damn you! Your powers are rooted in unrighteousness! Who but the vilest and most dishonourable would do something like this? Sītā has neither a home, nor a kingdom, nor even Rāma! What did she ever do to you that you should want to kill her? If you kill Sītā, you will soon die, for your life will be in my hands! And you deserve death for this terrible deed! You shall die and go to the hell reserved for killers of women. Those hells are reviled even by the lowest of the low!'

Hanumān and the other monkeys rushed towards the *rākṣasa* prince. Indrajit loosed thousands of arrows at them and shouted to Hanumān, 'Sītā was the reason for you and Rāma and Sugrīva coming here! I shall kill her in front of your eyes! And after this, I shall kill Rāma, Lakṣmaṇa,

Sugrīva, you and that vile traitor Vibhīṣaṇa as well! As for your idea that women should not be killed, I think one can do anything to demoralize the enemy!'

With that, Indrajit killed the phantom Sītā, slitting her across her body from her shoulders to her hips. The lovely woman fell to the ground as Indrajit yelled, 'Look! I have killed Rāma's wife!' Standing in his chariot, Indrajit shouted for joy and the monkeys were filled with despair as they turned away.

Hanumān rallied them, for they were utterly disheartened and ready to flee. 'How can you run away like this in dismay? What has happened to your legendary courage? Follow me into battle! The noble and the brave do not run away like this!'

The monkeys' spirits revived and they armed themselves with trees and stones, roaring as they fell behind Hanumān, who led them against the enemy. Hanumān hurled a huge rock against Indrajit but the skilled warrior moved his chariot away from it. The rock fell to the ground, creating havoc among the *rākṣasas* as it smashed many of them to pulp. The monkeys continued their onslaught and more and more *rākṣasas* fell writhing to the ground. Indrajit unleashed his fury on the monkeys, attacking them with every kind of weapon and killing a great number of them. But Hanumān inflicted an equal amount of damage on the *rākṣasas,* wielding trees and hurling rocks with great skill.

But suddenly, Hanumān decided that it was futile to continue fighting. 'We have been throwing our lives away for Rāma's sake. Now that Sītā has been killed, the reason for doing this no longer exists! We must go and tell Rāma and Sugrīva that this has happened. Then we shall do as they think best.' Slowly, Hanumān and the other monkeys retreated and went back to Rāma. Indrajit saw the monkeys turning away and went quickly to a nearby temple. He fed the sacred fire with flesh and blood until it blazed like the morning sun. As his followers stood around and watched, he made offerings to the fire and conducted a special ritual for the *rākṣasas'* success in battle.

Hanumān hurried back to Rāma and sadly, he said, 'During the battle, Indrajit killed Sītā in front of our very eyes! I was overwhelmed with grief when I saw this and came immediately to tell you about it.'

Rāma fell to the ground in a faint, like a tree axed at the root. The monkeys came running from all directions and sprinkled water perfumed with lotus and lily on his face. Lakṣmaṇa embraced his grieving brother, trying his best to console him. 'All this talk of *dharma* is futile!' he said. 'Your adherence to *dharma* has not protected you from all these calamities. We cannot see *dharma* the way we can see other objects. I am beginning to believe that there is no such thing! If *dharma* really did exist, Rāvaṇa would be in hell and you would not be suffering like this! Rāvaṇa suffers nothing. Has *dharma* become *adharma*? If *dharma* did exist, nothing bad should ever happen to you!

'Or maybe *dharma* rallies around might, it supports the strong. Which means that we should never ally ourselves with the weak. If *dharma* helps only the mighty, then give up your allegiance to it and rely, instead, on your strength. Taking refuge in either *dharma* or *adharma* on principal is ultimately destructive. A man should choose which of them to follow according to circumstanes.

'You cut at the root of *dharma* when you renounced the kingdom. Purposeful action flows from the accumulation of wealth from all possible sources, like rivers from a mountain. Men who lack wealth and power can never act in any significant way. The man who renounces wealth will continue to hanker after pleasure because he is accustomed to it. That will lead him to unethical practices. A wealthy man can support his friends and well-wishers who will then proclaim his wealth, his learning, his skills and his virtues. I do not know what you were thinking about when you gave up the kingdom!

'Wealth gives access to pleasures and happiness, to the fulfilment of desires. It sustains a man's pride and allows him to cling to *dharma.* You were obedient to your father's wishes and went into exile. A *rākṣasa* abducted your wife who is dearer to you than your own life. As a consequence of all that, Indrajit has brought this disaster upon you today.

'But I shall put and end to all this! I shall release my anger and avenge the killing of Sītā. I shall raze Lankā to the ground, along with all its elephants and chariots! I shall kill the king of the *rākṣasas*!'

While Lakṣmaṇa was comforting his brother, Vibhīṣaṇa came back from an inspection of the forces. He saw Rāma overwhelmed with grief, lying with his head in Lakṣmaṇa's lap, almost senseless with sorrow, and all the monkeys with tears in their eyes. His heart sinking, Vibhīṣaṇa asked, 'What is the matter?' Lakṣmaṇa looked at Vibhīṣaṇa, Sugrīva and all the monkeys and said, 'When Hanumān told Rāma that Indrajit had killed Sītā, he fainted!'

Vibhīṣaṇa interrupted him before he could say any more. 'What Hanumān reported is as unlikely as the ocean drying up! I know what vile Rāvaṇa's intentions are towards Sītā! He would never have her killed. I told him many times for his own good that he should give Sītā back but he would not do it.

'Indrajit has done this to confuse and demoralize the monkeys. Now he has gone to the temple to perform a special sacrifice. If he can complete it, then even the gods led by Indra will not be able to defeat him in battle. He will use magic and sorcery to prevent the monkeys from using their skills in battle. Let us go there with our forces before he can complete his rituals.

'Shake off this dejection. It has no basis! The entire army suffers when they see you like this! Rāma, stay here and pull yourself together. Let Lakṣmaṇa come with us. His sharp arrows will prevent Indrajit from completing his ritual. Then it will be simple to kill him. Command Lakṣmaṇa, the mighty warrior, to destroy this *rākṣasa*!'

must interrupt Indrajit or he can defeat them

# *Chapter Sixty-Four*

'Listen and I will tell you what is the best course of action,' continued Vibhīṣaṇa. 'Let Lakṣmaṇa lead a large force to the temple where Indrajit is and then let Lakṣmaṇa kill him in battle. His snake-like arrows will fly from his bow drawn back to its fullest extent and they will take Indrajit's life! Indrajit has won his boons from Brahmā because of the austerities he performed. He has the power to use Brahmā's weapon and he has horses that can take him anywhere he pleases. Brahmā decreed that the enemy who prevents Indrajit from completing this ritual would be the one to kill him. We must kill him as soon as we can, for when he is dead, Rāvaṇa and all the others are as good as dead, too!'

Rāma replied that he knew the kind of power Indrajit commanded as a result of his knowledge of sorcery and magic. He instructed Lakṣmaṇa to go with Hanumān and the other monkey leaders and to kill Indrajit. Mighty Lakṣmaṇa picked up his great bow, girt his sword, picked his arrows and put on his armour. Full of joy, he touched Rāma's feet and said, 'The arrows released from my bow will pierce Rāvaṇa's son and then fall in Lankā as swans alight in a pool! My arrows will cut that vile creature's body to pieces!'

Lakṣmaṇa set out quickly, eager to kill Indrajit. Hanumān, Vibhīṣaṇa and many thousands of monkeys accompanied him to the temple where Indrajit was performing his ritual. From a distance, Lakṣmaṇa could see the *rākṣasa* forces, ready and waiting. He lifted his bow and prepared to kill Indrajit in the manner that Brahmā had ordained.

Vibhīṣaṇa gave Lakṣmaṇa some advice on his battle strategy. 'Force the *rākṣasa* army to break their formation. Then you will be able to see Indrajit. Shower him with arrows which will land with such impact that he will not be able to complete the ritual. Kill this unrighteous creature who has mastered the arts of magic and who torments the worlds!'

Lakṣmaṇa loosed a rain of arrows upon Indrajit and the monkeys attacked the *rakṣasa* army ferociously with trees and rocks and boulders. The *rākṣasas* used all their weapons, determined to slaughter the monkeys, and the din raised by the clashing armies could be heard all over Lankā. The sky was blotted out by the multitude of weapons and trees and rocks that were hurled in all directions.

Indrajit could hear the sounds of his army under attack and the invincible *rākṣasa* had to leave his ritual incomplete. He emerged from the dark grove of trees in a rage and mounted his chariot. Carrying his frightful bow, Indrajit looked like death, with his red eyes and skin the colour of a rain cloud. The *rākṣasa* forces rallied the moment they saw him.

At that moment, Hanumān began his assault with huge trees which were impossible to counter, consuming the *rākṣasa* army like the doomsday fire. Thousands of *rākṣasas* charged towards him and attacked him at the same time with any weapon they could find, even using their fists. Hanumān ploughed through them with ease but Indrajit saw what was happening and told his charioteer to take him into the middle of the battle.

Indrajit hurled spears, swords, clubs and battle axes at Hanumān but the monkey ignored the weapons and taunted the *rākṣasa*. 'Fight me if you dare, son of Rāvaṇa!' he shouted. 'I am the son of the Wind! You shall not return alive! Fight me in single combat with your bare hands! Then you really will be the best of the *rākṣasas*!'

Vibhīṣaṇa pointed Indrajit out to Lakṣmaṇa as he was fighting with Hanumān. 'There he is, the one who defeated Indra in battle! Kill him with your unrivalled arrows that never spare the enemy's life, Lakṣmaṇa!' Lakṣmaṇa looked carefully at his powerful foe who was as large as a mountain and was yelling on the battlefield in order to intimidate the monkeys.

Lakṣmaṇa twanged his great bow and shouted to Indrajit, who was seated in his shining chariot, clad in armour and wielding a huge bow. 'I summon you to battle! Come and fight with me!'

Indrajit looked over at Lakṣmaṇa from his chariot. The mighty archer raised his enormous bow and chose the finest of his arrows, the ones that had wrought the most destruction among the enemy. He saw that Lakṣmaṇa shone with his own splendour as he sat on the shoulders of

Hanumān, like the sun on a mountain. 'You shall see my powers today! My arrows shall consume you the way fire consumes bales of cotton! Who can oppose me when I shower arrows like a thundering cloud showers rain!' shouted Indrajit.

Lakṣmaṇa was not in the least bit intimidated by Indrajit's ranting and he replied, 'You are promising the impossible, *rākṣasa*! An intelligent person backs up his boasts with action! Making yourself invisible in battle the last time was not the act of a heroic warrior but of a coward!'

Indrajit drew his bow to its fullest extent and loosed a series of arrows which were sharp and swift and as vicious as snake poison. But they fell to the earth, hissing like snakes before they reached Lakṣmaṇa. Then he showered more arrows on Lakṣmaṇa, covering the warrior's entire body. Wounded and drenched with blood, Lakṣmaṇa blazed like a smokeless flame. Indrajit shouted with joy. 'My deadly arrows will take your life today, Lakṣmaṇa! Packs of jackals and vultures shall devour your body when I have killed you!'

'Why don't you do something instead of talking?' roared Lakṣmaṇa. 'Do something to prove that we should respect your skills as a warrior!' and he fitted five arrows into his bow. He drew it back right to his ear and loosed the gleaming arrows which struck Indrajit in the chest and shone there like the rays of the sun. Lakṣmaṇa and Indrajit continued to assault each other with arrows which were sharp and swift. They were well matched as opponents, for both were determined to win and both were known for their strength and skill and their mastery over all kinds of weapons, even celestial ones. The invincible warriors fought like lions as they deluged each other with arrows, delighting when they found their mark.

Lakṣmaṇa kept shooting, hissing like an angry snake. But suddenly, Indrajit heard the bowstring snap against Lakṣmaṇa's palm. He turned pale and appeared distracted. Immediately, Vibhīṣaṇa said to Lakṣmaṇa, 'The signs indicate that Indrajit is done for! Finish him off quickly!'

Lakṣmaṇa hit Indrajit with arrows which burned like flames and the *rākṣasa* was stunned for a while. But he recovered and shot ten arrows at Lakṣmaṇa and another seven at Hanumān, wounding the monkey. Lakṣmaṇa loosed such a formidable rain of arrows that Indrajit's golden armour was shattered and fell to the floor of the chariot like a cluster of stars. Bereft of his armour, Indrajit's body was covered with arrow wounds and seemed like a mountain with trees growing out of it. Indrajit used a thousand arrows to destroy Lakṣmaṇa's armour and the warriors pursued each other relentlessly, their bodies a mass of bloody wounds.

They fought for hours, neither gaining the upper hand. They used every weapon at their command and sometimes their arrows would lock in combat in midair while thousands of others splintered each other before they reached the ground. Bent on destroying one another, Indrajit and Lakṣmaṇa went on and on with their fight, showing no signs of fatigue. Their bodies were drenched with blood and covered with arrows, making them resemble tongues of flame.

Indrajit's charioteer and horses had been killed by enthusiastic monkeys who jumped into the fray to help Lakṣmaṇa. The other monkeys and the *rākṣasas* continued their own battle, inflicting as much damage as they could upon each other, but they took care to see that they were never too far from their commanders.

Displaying his skill, Indrajit struck Lakṣmaṇa on the forehead with three splendid arrows with feathered shafts and Lakṣmaṇa shone on the battlefield like a mountain with three peaks. He retaliated by sending five arrows against Indrajit. They fought close to one another, wounding each other in every limb. Indrajit hurled his golden spear but Lakṣmaṇa destroyed it in the air with a hail of arrows. Indrajit then pulled out the incomparable arrow that had been given to him by Yama, but Lakṣmaṇa recognized it and took out one that matched it. It had been given to him by Kubera in a dream and was utterly invincible; not even the gods or the *asuras* could withstand it. Both warriors pulled back their bowstrings till they sang and loosed the arrows which blazed through the air. They lit up the sky as they headed for a midair collision. They clashed against each other like mighty planets and split into a hundred pieces as they fell to the ground. Indrajit and Lakṣmaṇa were ashamed and angry that their precious weapons had been used in vain and they resorted to the other celestial weapons at their command. Lakṣmaṇa loosed Varuṇa's weapon and Indrajit countered it with Śiva's.

The battle between Indrajit and Lakṣmaṇa raised a terrible din and the sky was filled with beings who watched the encounter in amazement. Gods and *gandharvas, ṛṣis,* the ancestors, Garuḍa and *uragas,* even Indra himself, allied themselves with Lakṣmaṇa and hoped for his victory.

Picking an arrow which burned to the touch like fire, Lakṣmaṇa chose it for Indrajit's death. Its shaft was perfectly rounded, it was well-proportioned and smooth-jointed, fitted with splendid feathers and adorned with gold. It was incapable of missing its mark and it struck fear into the hearts of the *rākṣasas.* As deadly as venom, it was respected even by the gods. Lakṣmaṇa invoked the power of Indra for this incomparable arrow as he fitted it into his magnificent bow. As he drew the bow back as far as his ear, auspicious Lakṣmaṇa whispered, 'If Rāma, the son of Daśaratha, is righteous and devoted to truth, if he is unrivalled in valour, then may this arrow slay the son of Rāvaṇa!'

The arrow severed Indrajit's head with its helmet and golden earrings and flung it to the ground. That mighty head gleamed like beaten gold as it lay there and Rāvaṇa's son, still in his armour, tumbled to the ground, holding his bow. At once, Vibhīṣaṇa and all the monkeys began to shout with delight, rejoicing at the death of Indrajit. Their shouts of joy were echoed from the skies where the celestial beings and the gods joined in the celebration. The *rākṣasas* realized that Indrajit had been killed and they abandoned their weapons and fled towards Lanka chased by the victorious monkeys. Some jumped into the ocean, others took refuge in the mountains. Thousands of *rākṣasas* disappeared as the sun's rays disappear when it has set. Indrajit lay sprawled on the ground like the sun that has been quenched, like a fire that has died down.

The worlds shone brightly, freed from their torment and anguish now that Rāvaṇa's son was dead. The gods, *dānavas* and the *gandharvas* gathered and said, 'May the *brahmins* go about their business free from anxiety and torment!' The monkeys praised the victorious Lakṣmaṇa. They surrounded him, laughing and shouting. They slapped their arms and whipped their tails and hugged each other, telling tales of Lakṣmaṇa's exploits on the battlefield.

Even though his own body was covered with blood, Lakṣmaṇa rejoiced at having killed Indrajit. He went as quickly as he could to see Rāma and Sugrīva along with Hanumān, Jāmbavān and the other monkey leaders. He greeted Rāma and honoured him. Then, he stood to one side as Bṛhaspati would stand with Indra, and told Rāma that Indrajit was dead. Vibhīṣaṇa told Rāma how Lakṣmaṇa had severed Indrajit's head and Rāma was filled with delight.

Rāma embraced Lakṣmaṇa and drew him onto his lap. He caressed him gently and said, 'You have done an incredible thing by killing that wicked creature. Rāvaṇa depended heavily on Indrajit and now he will soon be destroyed. I am sure the king of the *rākṣasas* will soon come forth surrounded by a huge army. The recovery of Sītā and my kingdom seem simple now that you have killed Indrajit in battle!'

Rāma held his brother close as he turned to Suṣeṇa and said, 'Lakṣmaṇa, who is loved by all his friends, is in agony from his wounds. You must restore him to health. And you must also heal the wounds of the other monkeys who fought so valiantly with trees and rocks.' Suṣeṇa gave Lakṣmaṇa a fragrant herb to inhale and did the same for Vibhīṣaṇa and the injured monkeys. In a moment, Lakṣmaṇa's wound healed and his pain vanished. The monkey army was delighted to see Lakṣmaṇa back to normal and rejoiced with Rāma at the death of Indrajit.

Rāvaṇa's retainers heard about Indrajit's death and, filled with sorrow, they went to tell Rāvaṇa. 'Your heroic son was killed in battle by Lakṣmaṇa while we were all present, great king! He was felled by Lakṣmaṇa's arrows in an encounter between two majestic warriors.'

Rāvaṇa heard the terrible news and fell into a dead faint. He recovered consciousness after a long time and overcome with grief, he mourned the death of his son. 'Ah, my son! Best of all the chariot warriors! Finest of the *rākṣasas*! You even defeated Indra, how could you have fallen to Lakṣmaṇa? When you were angry, you could pierce the peaks of Mount Mandara, vanquish even time and death! What was Lakṣmaṇa in battle compared to that! The man who dies in the service of his king goes straight to heaven. This is the path taken by great warriors, even among the gods.

'Now that Indrajit has been killed, the gods, immortals and the guardians of the earth shall sleep without fear! But the three worlds and the earth with all its forests seem empty to me without Indrajit! I shall hear *rākṣasa* women in the inner apartments weeping piteously over his death. Where have you gone, my son, leaving your mother and me and your wife? Why have you left us when Rāma, Lakṣmaṇa and Sugrīva are still alive, when the thorn in my side remains?'

Rāvaṇa's grief turned into a bitter, all-consuming rage as he mourned. His face, already fearsome, became truly terrifying and he seemed as unapproachable as Śiva. Angry tears fell from his eyes like scalding oil from burning lamps. He ground his teeth and the sound filled the air like thunder. He blazed like the doomsday fire and as he looked around, *rākṣasas* ran from him in terror. No one dared come near him as he stood there, looking like death.

Hoping to inspire the *rākṣasas* to fight again, Rāvaṇa roared, 'I have practised fierce austerities for thousands of years and I have propitiated Brahmā! And because he was pleased with me, I have never had to fear the gods or the *asuras*. Brahmā gave me armour that shines like the sun, which cannot be pierced by the weapons of the gods. I stand here in my chariot, who would dare oppose me now? Brahmā also gave me a magnificent bow and arrows to use in the wars with the gods. Bring them to me and I shall use them to kill Rāma and Lakṣmaṇa!'

Thousands upon thousands of *rākṣasas* with their horses and chariots which blazed like fire and were decorated with colourful banners had been destroyed. Heroic *rākṣasas* who could change their shapes at will had been killed by Rāma's arrows which were swift and sharp and adorned with gold.

Utterly demoralized, the surviving *rākṣasas* gathered along with the widows and wives and mothers and sisters and children of those that had been killed. Overcome with grief, they came together to mourn, weeping and wailing. 'Why did that ugly Śūrpanakhā, that potbellied hag, attach herself to Rāma in the forest? He is as beautiful as the god of love, young and strong and intent on the welfare of all creatures. How could that deformed creature with no virtues at all throw herself at that honourable, handsome man?

'Unfortunately, her actions led to the killing of the *rākṣasas* as well as Khara and Dūṣaṇa which led to the deadly enmity with Rāvaṇa. He abducted Sītā and that will be the cause of his death. Sītā will never accept Rāvaṇa! Now he has an invincible foe in Rāma. We need no further displays of Rāma's strength and valour!

'It is Śiva or Viṣṇu or Indra, perhaps death itself, that has come to claim us in the form of Rāma! Rāma has killed all our mighty warriors and we have lost all hopes of living! We see no end to our fears and so we wail together!

'Rāvaṇa has been given boons for battle and he remains oblivious to the threat that Rāma poses. Not the gods nor the *gandharvas,* not the *piśācas* nor the *rākṣasas* can save a man whom Rāma has targeted. Portents of doom have appeared in battle after battle and they surely mean that Rāma will kill Rāvaṇa! Brahmā gave Rāvaṇa immunity from gods, *dānavas* and *rākṣasas,* but he is not protected from mortals! The end for Rāvaṇa and the *rākṣasas* has arrived in the form of a man!

'When the gods were being harassed by the *rākṣasas,* they appealed to Brahmā and he promised them that a woman would be born to destroy the *rākṣasas.* Urged by the gods, Sītā is bound to cause the annihilation of the *rākṣasas.* Rāvaṇa's terrible deeds and unrighteous behaviour have brought this catastrophe upon us. Where can we take refuge? No one can protect us from Rāma, just as there is no protection from the deluge at the end of time.'

The *rākṣasīs* clung to each other and wept, their hearts filled with fear. Rāvaṇa could hear the sad sounds of *rākṣasīs* wailing and weeping from all over Lankā. He sighed heavily and remained lost in thought for a while but then his anger returned and he was terrifying to behold. He bit his lips and his eyes blazed red. He seemed like the doomsday fire and even the *rākṣasas* were afraid to look at him. 'Tell Mahāpārśva, Mahodara and Virūpākṣa to get the forces ready for battle immediately!' he roared.

The three mighty *rākṣasas* did as they had been instructed and presented themselves to Rāvaṇa. 'Today I shall kill Rāma and Lakṣmaṇa with my arrows which blaze like the doomsday fire!' he said, laughing maniacally. 'I shall avenge the deaths of Khara, Kumbhakarṇa, Prahasta and Indrajit. Nothing, not the skies nor the directions, not the rivers nor the seas will be visible because the shower of my arrows will blot them out. I shall kill all the monkeys with my arrows adorned with feathers. I shall crush the monkeys as an elephant tramples upon a pool of lotuses. With arrows sticking out of their bodies, the monkeys will cover the earth like long-stemmed flowers. With every arrow I shall kill hundreds of monkeys who are armed with trees. I shall kill them and wipe the tears of all those whose husbands, sons and brothers have been killed. I shall feed the jackals and vultures with enemy flesh until they cannot eat another thing. Prepare my chariot! Fetch my bow! And tell all the surviving *rākṣasas* to follow me at once!'

# *Chapter Sixty-Five*

The army commanders went from house to house to summon the *rākṣasa* warriors. In no time at all, the heroic *rākṣasas* gathered, armed with all their weapons, shouting for a fight. A magnificent chariot yoked with eight horses was prepared for Rāvaṇa. Rāvaṇa mounted the chariot which was illuminated by his splendour and as he moved forward, the earth trembled beneath his feet. Mahodara, Mahāpārśva and Virūpākṣa followed him in their own chariots, roaring with delight in their eagerness for battle. Surrounded by heroic warriors, Rāvaṇa set forth like Death.

He departed through the gate and went to where Rāma and Lakṣmaṇa waited for him. The sun dimmed, the four quarters were covered in darkness, the earth trembled and birds cried out in pain. The gods rained blood, Rāvaṇa's horses stumbled and a vulture settled on his flagstaff as jackals howled hideously. Rāvaṇa's left eye twitched and his right arm quivered. His face lost colour and his voice trembled, but he continued onwards despite these portents of defeat. A firebrand thundered out of the sky, vultures cried and crows called back to them. Rāvaṇa ignored these signs and went towards his own destruction, impelled by his fate.

The monkeys heard the sound of the approaching *rākṣasas* and prepared themselves for battle. A noisy fight ensued as they challenged each other in anger, determined to win. Rāvaṇa sent his gold-decorated arrows out among the monkeys. Some of them had their heads cut off, others had their chests split open, others stopped breathing in their tracks and fell dead. Still others had their heads broken and some had their eyes fall out. Everywhere Rāvaṇa went on the battlefield, the monkeys could not withstand the power of his arrows.

The earth was littered with the mangled bodies of monkeys that Rāvaṇa had killed. They ran from there, screaming like elephants fleeing from a forest fire. Rāvaṇa scattered them with his arrows as the wind scatters the clouds. And having wrought terrible destruction among the forces, Rāvaṇa sought out Rāma.

Sugrīva advanced towards Rāvaṇa holding an immense tree and all the monkey leaders arranged themselves behind and around him, armed with rocks and stones. Sugrīva shouted as he showered stones and rocks upon the enemy as a cloud might shower hail on birds in the forest. As Sugrīva was tormenting the *rākṣasa* forces who were falling down all over the place and screaming, Virūpākṣa grabbed his bow, leapt out of his chariot and climbed onto the back of an elephant. Releasing a stream of arrows, he chased after Sugrīva and rallied the *rākṣasas* who were losing heart.

Sugrīva struck the elephant with a huge tree and the animal collapsed, trumpeting in pain. Virūpākṣa came towards Sugrīva with his sword and dodged the rock the monkey flung at him. The *rākṣasa* sliced at the monkey and Sugrīva staggered. But he soon recovered and pounded Virūpākṣa with his fist. Virūpākṣa cut off Sugrīva's armour with his sword and then went for him with his fists. Enraged, Sugrīva slapped Virūpākṣa with his open palm on his forehead and the blow resounded like thunder. Drenched with blood, Virūpākṣa fell to the ground, appearing even more cross-eyed than he actually was. The monkeys watched as the *rākṣasa* writhed in pain and cried out and then they plunged into battle again with their enemies. The battle between the forces raged on, thundering like an ocean that had transgressed its bounds.

As the battle went on, the armies diminished in size like lakes which dry up in the summer. Rāvaṇa called upon Mahodara to stem the destruction of his forces and Mahodara went into battle eagerly, like a moth towards a flame. Sugrīva saw that Mahodara was troubling the monkey forces and he picked up a rock that was large as a mountain. He hurled it at the *rākṣasa* but Mahodara splintered it with his arrows. It fell to the earth like a flock of frightened vultures. Sugrīva uprooted a tree, but Mahodara treated it in the same way. Enraged, Sugrīva grabbed an iron club lying nearby and pounded Mahodara's horses to death with it.

Mahodara advanced with his mace and the two warriors began to fight like bulls, roaring like thunder clouds. They clashed so mightily that their weapons destroyed each other. Then they attacked each other with their fists, blazing like twin fires. Quick as lightning, Mahodara picked up a sword and Sugrīva did the same. They bellowed with delight as they came at one another, each an expert at handling weapons. They circled each other, determined to wrest victory. As Mahodara was trying to retrieve his sword from the shield in which it was stuck, Sugrīva struck his head a mighty blow. The head with its helmet and earrings fell to the ground and the *rākṣasa* forces did not wait to see any more. The monkeys cried out with delight and while Rāvaṇa raged, Rāma rejoiced.

Mahāpārśva stepped in immediately and harried the monkeys with his arrows. He caused heads to roll like the fruit from palm trees, he sliced off arms and shoulders and ripped into the sides of the monkeys. Angada saw that the monkeys were in trouble and he summoned all his energies together and hurled a sun-bright iron club at Mahāpārśva. Mahāpārśva fell senseless but soon recovered and stormed Angada with a hail of arrows. Angada hurled the same shining club at the *rākṣasa* and it ripped the bow and arrows from Mahāpārśva's hand and the helmet from his head. Mahāpārśva struck Angada with a magnificent battle axe and Angada retaliated by hitting him with his fist. From his father, Angada had learned about the most vulnerable parts in the body and he struck Mahāpārśva just below the heart. His blow landed like a thunderbolt. Mahāpārśva's heart burst open and he fell dead.

Rāvaṇa was incensed when he heard the monkeys rejoicing and was doubly determined to make a firm stand on the battlefield. As Rāvaṇa drove his chariot towards Rāma, the earth with its mountains, rivers and forests was filled with the rumbling of its wheels. He loosed a terrible weapon, powered by darkness, upon the monkeys and they fell all over the battlefield, burnt to death. Rāvaṇa saw Rāma with Lakṣmaṇa standing by his side, like Indra with Viṣṇu, preparing to join the fray. Leaning on his bow, Rāma watched as the monkeys were routed and Rāvaṇa continued to advance. He twanged the string of his magnificent bow and the sound seemed to rend the earth. Thousands of monkeys and *rākṣasas* fell to the ground.

Now within range of the princes' arrows, Rāvaṇa was like Rāhu approaching the sun or the moon. Lakṣmaṇa was keen to loose the first weapon and so he shot a stream of arrows at Rāvaṇa that burned like tongues of flame. Rāvaṇa intercepted them while they were still in the air and turned his attentions to Rāma, who stood there steady as a rock.

Rāma and Rāvaṇa assaulted each other with showers of splendid arrows that rivalled each other in their powers. The arrows circled each other in the air and eventually destroyed one another. The air was so thick with missiles that it seemed as if the sky was filled with rain clouds. Arrows flashed like lightning through the dark sky as the battle between the two mighty warriors raged on.

Rāma invoked the power of Śiva for his arrows and shot a stream of them at Rāvaṇa. They fell all over Rāvaṇa's impenetrable armour which was as dark as a cloud and the *rākṣasa* felt no pain at all. Rāma, skilled in the use of all kinds of weapons, struck Rāvaṇa on the forehead with a powerful missile that split his arrows down the middle and entered the earth, hissing like a snake. Unable to use his arrows any more, Rāvaṇa invoked the power of the *asuras* in his anger and Rāma was assaulted by weapons with the heads of lions, tigers, crows, vultures, jackals, and wolves, their terrifying mouths wide open. Rāma was unmoved by the illusions created by the weapons of the *asuras* and calmly released the weapon powered by the god of fire. Sharp, blazing arrows that shone like the sun, the moon and the planets poured out of it and stopped Rāvaṇa's fierce arrows in the air. Rāma was delighted and the monkeys shouted for joy.

Rāma and Rāvaṇa fought on and on with all the magical and celestial weapons at their command. Lakṣmaṇa joined the battle and with his well-chosen arrows he ripped apart Rāvaṇa's battle banner, splintered his bow and arrows and cut off the head of his charioteer. Vibhīṣaṇa used his mace to pulverize Rāvaṇa's splendid horses which were as dark as rain clouds.

Enraged, Rāvaṇa hurled a spear which blazed like lightning at his brother, but before it could reach him, Lakṣmaṇa destroyed it with three arrows. The monkeys whooped with joy when the spear fell to the ground, leaving a trail of sparks like a meteor. Rāvaṇa yelled, 'Since you rescued my brother with your admirable strength, Lakṣmaṇa, I shall leave him alone and attack you instead! I shall hurl this spear at you and it will split your heart in two!'

Rāvaṇa chose a spear that had been created by the sorcerer Māya, so bright that it dazzled the eye. As he hurled it at Lakṣmaṇa, Rāma muttered, 'May you stay well, Lakṣmaṇa! And may the spear fail in its purpose and fall, useless, to the ground!' The spear blazed through the air and lodged itself in Lakṣmaṇa's chest and he fell to the ground. Rāma's eyes filled with tears and for a few moments, he stood still. Then, anger welled within him, like the fire that rages at the end of the *yuga.* He realized that this was not the time for grief and decided to fight Rāvaṇa even more ferociously than before.

The monkeys gathered around Lakṣmaṇa and tried to pull out the spear that was stuck in his chest but they were scattered by Rāvaṇa's arrows which fell upon them like rain. The spear had passed through Lakṣmaṇa's body and pinned him to the earth. Rāma exerted his enormous strength and pulled out the spear, breaking it in two. Rāvaṇa took the opportunity to pierce Rāma all over his body with arrows. Rāma ignored them and, embracing his brother, he said to Hanumān and Sugrīva, 'Look after my brother, great monkeys!

'The time for which I have waited has finally come, like the rain clouds at the end of summer. I shall kill wicked Rāvaṇa! I promise you, before long, you will see the world deprived either of Rāvaṇa or of Rāma! By killing Rāvaṇa today, I will avenge myself for all that I have suffered: the loss of my kingdom, the exile in the forest, the abduction of Sītā and all the encounters with the *rākṣasas.* Rāvaṇa will not live, now that I have set eyes on him!

'Go and sit on the top of that mountain, mighty monkeys, and watch as I battle Rāvaṇa! I shall accomplish something that the three worlds, the gods, *gandharvas, ṛṣis, cāraṇas* and all living creatures shall talk about forever!'

Rāma calmed his mind and released a hail of arrows against Rāvaṇa, who was so terrified that he ran away like a cloud chased by the wind.

'My brother has been struck down by Rāvaṇa's mighty arrows and he lies here writhing in pain!' said Rāma. 'My heart is filled with sorrow. How can I fight when he lies here drenched in blood? What use is life and happiness to me if my beloved brother dies? My courage withers within me in shame, my bow slips from my hands, my arrows fail and my eyes are blinded by tears. My mind is filled with anxiety and I would almost welcome death! I have no interest in fighting, or in my life or even in Sītā when my brother lies dead in battle!'

'Heroic Lakṣmaṇa is not dead!' said Suṣeṇa, comforting Rāma. 'His face is still bright and he has a peaceful look. His palms are as red as lotus petals and his eyes are clear. This is not the look of a dead man! Do not grieve, hero, for Lakṣmaṇa is alive! He lies asleep on the earth, his heart beating, breathing steadily.'

Suṣeṇa turned to Hanumān, who stood by his side. 'Go quickly to the mountain that Jāmbavān told you about earlier, the one with all the medicinal herbs. Bring me the *viṣalyakarṇī*, the *sauvarṇakarṇī* and the *sanjīvanī* that grow on its southern peak. I shall need them all to revive Lakṣmaṇa!'

Hanuman left immediately for the mountain, but when he got there, he could not recognize the herbs. 'I will take the entire mountain back with me,' he decided. 'If I go back without the herbs, the delay may be fatal and my reputation will suffer.' Hanumān lifted the entire mountain and carried it back to the battlefield. 'I could not recognize the herb,' he said to Suṣeṇa. 'So I brought back the whole mountain!'

Suṣeṇa praised Hanumān and crushed the herbs. He placed them under Lakṣmaṇa's nose and in an instant, Lakṣmaṇa, the mighty slayer of his enemies, revived, his wounds healed. He rose from the ground and the monkeys praised Suṣeṇa as Rāma embraced his brother with tears in his eyes.

# *Chapter Sixty-Six*

Rāma returned to the battle with Rāvaṇa, deluging him with arrows. Rāvaṇa leapt into another chariot and attacked Rāma with arrows that fell with the force of a thunderbolt.

The gods and the *gandharvas* felt that with Rāvaṇa in a chariot and Rāma on the ground, the fight was no longer equal. Indra summoned Mātali, his charioteer, and called for his own chariot which shone like the sun. It was made of gold and covered with tinkling bells and jewels. It was drawn by green horses, adorned with golden ornaments and they, too, shone like the rising sun. It was crowned with a dazzling white battle banner.

Mātali took the chariot to Rāma on earth and said to him with his palms joined, 'Indra has sent you this chariot so that you can be victorious. He has also sent you this shining armour, his mighty bow and arrows and this bright spear! Climb into the chariot, hero. I shall be your charioteer. Kill the *rākṣasa* the way Indra killed the *dānavas*!'

Rāma climbed into the chariot and the battle that ensued was so terrifying that it made the hair stand on end. Once again, Rāma and Rāvaṇa called upon all the celestial weapons. When Rāvaṇa employed arrows that turned into hissing snakes, Rāma invoked the powers of Garuḍa, the king of the birds. His arrows, which could take any form they chose, turned into eagles and destroyed Rāvaṇa's snake arrows.

Enraged, Rāvaṇa loosed a flood of arrows and struck Mātali. He cut down the battle banner on the chariot with a single arrow and even struck Indra's horses. The gods, *gandharvas, dānavas* and *cāraṇas* were very upset and the monkeys and Vibhīṣaṇa were terribly disheartened. The sea blazed with anger and soared up as if to touch the sky, its waves covered in smoke. The sun turned blue but was hot to the touch. A headless corpse with a comet for a tail was seen. With his ten heads and his twenty arms, Rāvaṇa looked like Mount Mainaka. Rāma found that he could not fit his arrows into his bow. He frowned and in his anger, he seemed to consume his enemies with the fire of his eyes. The earth trembled when it saw Rāma's wrath. The mountains and trees and animals quaked and the sea was in turmoil. Terror filled the hearts of all creatures and even Rāvaṇa was afraid.

Rāvaṇa thought for a while, considering which weapon he should use. He chose a spear which was as hard as a diamond. It terrified all that saw it for it was sharp and flew through the air covered with smoke like the doomsday fire. Even the god of death could do nothing to counter it. Rāvaṇa grasped it in the middle, his eyes red with anger, roaring as he did so to encourage the forces that surrounded him. His cry shook the earth and the sky and the four quarters as he hurled the spear at Rāma.

Rāma greeted the spear with a shower of arrows, but the spear consumed them in midair. Rāma was beside himself with anger when he saw his arrows reduced to ashes. He grabbed Indra's spear that Mātali had brought for him and whirled it around his head. It lit up the sky as it confronted Rāvaṇa's spear, shattering it to pieces. Then Rāma attacked Rāvaṇa's horses, piercing them with his arrows. He struck Rāvaṇa on the chest and on the forehead. Wounded in every limb and drenched with blood, Rāvaṇa was in trouble, but his anger continued to burn.

The two great warriors attacked one another relentlessly with arrows that blotted out the sun. They could barely see each other on the battlefield. Because Rāma was determined to kill his enemy, his courage surged and doubled and he felt sure of all the weapons under his command. The weapons seemed to jump into his hands when he needed them and his confidence added to his skill. Seeing these auspicious signs, Rāma intensified his assault on Rāvaṇa. He loosed arrows upon him and the monkeys showered the *rākṣasa* with stones. Rāvaṇa was confused and could not find his weapons. He was filled with despair and even the arrows that he managed to use failed him. Death hovered over him and when his charioteer realized his plight, he slowly moved the chariot out of the range of attack.

But Rāvaṇa, deluded and impelled by his fate, berated the charioteer, his eyes red with anger. 'You idiot! You are doing exactly what you want, as if I were defeated or helpless, a coward who has lost his nerve, as if I had forgotten all my magic powers and the use of celestial weapons! Why did you not consult me before you drew the chariot away? You have destroyed my reputation for courage and skill in battle that I built up over long years in a single instant!

'What you just did was not the act of a friend or a well-wisher. I am tempted to believe that you are working for the enemy! If you have any regard for our long relationship and for my prowess, you will turn the chariot around and return to the battlefield!'

The charioteer obeyed Rāvaṇa's command and the king of men saw the king of the *rākṣasas* approaching. Drawn by black horses, terrifying in its splendour, its flags flashing like lightning, producing a storm of arrows like a rain cloud, Rāvaṇa's chariot rumbled along like thunder. 'Look, Mātali,' said Rāma, 'Rāvaṇa's chariot comes towards us in an anti-clockwise direction. He is bound to die in battle. I want to destroy this creature. Drive forward without fear. Hold your head high!'

Mātali took Rāma's chariot forward, moving clockwise, and covered Rāvaṇa in the cloud of dust that rose from the chariot wheels. Rāma raised Indra's bow for the attack and the celestial beings gathered to watch the fierce battle between these warriors who were like lions.

The gods rained blood upon Rāvaṇa's chariot and it was tossed about by mighty whirlwinds. A huge group of vultures hovered in the air, following his chariot wherever it went. The sky over Lankā turned bright red and the earth under it seemed to be burning. Blazing meteors thundered down from the sky, creating panic among the *rākṣasas* for they seemed to bode ill for Rāvaṇa. The earth shook wherever Rāvaṇa went and as he reached for his weapons, his fingers seemed to be pulled away by an invisible force. The wind lifted dust into his eyes, blinding him, and lightning struck his forces even though there were no rain clouds in the sky.

The omens indicating Rāvaṇa's destruction multiplied even as signs of good fortune for Rāma appeared. Rāma was skilled in the reading of these signs and he was filled with joy to see auspicious signs for his victory. He threw himself into battle with even greater vigour.

A vicious chariot duel began between Rāma and Rāvaṇa which filled the worlds with fear. The monkeys and the *rākṣasas* stood absolutely still, holding on to their weapons, and marvelled at the awesome combat between man and *rākṣasa*. Even though they were armed, they were too engrossed in the encounter to do anything other than watch, the *rākṣasas* fixing their eyes on Rāvaṇa and the monkeys on Rāma.

The two warriors read the omens and knew what the outcome would be, that Rāvaṇa would die and Rāma would live—but they fought on relentlessly, summoning up all their energy and courage. Rāvaṇa loosed his arrows at the flag on Rāma's chariot. They never reached the flag, for the moment they touched the chariot, they fell to the ground. Rāma attacked Rāvaṇa's flag fiercely, with sharp arrows that blazed with their own splendour and were as hard to endure as a snakebite. They pierced Rāvaṇa's flag and entered the earth as the flag fell to the ground.

Rāvaṇa was incensed when he saw his flag crushed and crumpled and he loosed a volley of arrows at Rāma's shining horses. Though they were hit, the horses did not stumble and were not more affected than if they had been assaulted with lotus stalks. Rāvaṇa grew angrier and, using his magic powers, he made thousands of arrows and clubs and spears, maces, discuses, mountains, trees and rocks rain down upon his enemy. The shower of weapons created a terrible din as they flew past Rāma and fell upon the monkey army.

The battle of the arrows went on and they locked together in the air so that is seemed as if a new, bright sky had been formed. Not a single arrow missed its mark as they struck each other and fell to the ground.

Monkeys and *rākṣasas* and other beings continued to watch as the chariots pursued each other, each determined to destroy the other. They executed complex manouevres as each tried to gain the upper hand. Rāma and Rāvaṇa were equally skilled and swift as they advanced and retreated and circled each other. They even faced each other head-on, their yokes touching, their horses nose to nose, their flags fluttering against each other. Rāma shot four sharp arrows from his bow and pushed Rāvaṇa's horses back. Rāvaṇa retaliated with a storm of arrows that struck Rāma. But Rāma felt no pain and did not lose heart.

Then, Rāvaṇa struck Indra's charioteer Mātali all over his body but Mātali did not falter. Rāma was more enraged by the attack on Mātali than he was at being hit himself and he loosed hundreds and thousands of arrows against Rāvaṇa. The seven seas erupted with the hail of weapons that followed, their turbulence making the submarine creatures suffer terribly. The earth with its forests and mountains trembled, the sun dimmed and the wind died down. The gods, *gandharvas, siddhas,* great *ṛṣis*, the *kinnaras* and the *uragas* grew worried. 'May all be well with the cows and the *brahmins* and may the worlds last for ever. May Rāma be victorious!' they muttered.

Then Rāma, the augmenter of his family's fame, fitted his sharpest arrow, deadly as a poisonous snake, into his bow and cut off Rāvaṇa's head with its glittering earrings. The three worlds watched as the head fell to the ground. But immediately, another one exactly like it grew in its place. Rāma's swift hands quickly severed that head as well but another grew to replace it. One hundred magnificent heads were cut off in this fashion but there seemed to be no end to Rāvaṇa's life.

Rama still had many arrows left but he wondered, 'These arrows killed Mārīca, Khara, Dūṣaṇa, Virādha and Kabandha. They have never failed me in combat before. Why are they so ineffective against Rāvaṇa?' He continued to shower Rāvaṇa with arrows and Rāvaṇa fought back from his chariot with all his weapons. The gods and celestial beings watched this encounter that went on and on. Not for day or night, nor even for an hour or a moment did Rāma and Rāvaṇa stop fighting.

'Why do you counter Rāvaṇa's attack as if you don't know what to do?' asked Mātali. 'Use Brahmā's weapon against him. His hour of death has arrived!' he prompted.

Rāma chose a gleaming arrow that hissed like a snake. The arrow was a gift from Brahmā and had been given to Rāma by the great sage Agastya. Long ago, Brahmā had created it for Indra, for the conquest of the three worlds. The wind god was in its feathers, the sun and fire in its head. Its shaft had the essence of the skies and it was as heavy as the mountains Meru and Mandara. It was decorated with gold and shone with splendour. Bright as the sun, it contained the combined energies of all beings. Dark as the smoke from the doomsday fire and as deadly as a serpent, the arrow could destroy all the elephants, horses and chariots of the enemy. It had pierced gates and towers and walls, even mountains. Covered with the blood of all kinds of creatures, the arrow was truly terrifying to behold. Hard as diamond, it ripped through entire armies with a hiss, terrifying all those that heard it. The arrow was death incarnate and provided food for vultures, jackals, ghouls and other carrion eaters on the battlefield with unfailing certainty. Decorated with Garuḍa's multi-coloured feathers, the arrow brought joy to the monkeys and death to the *rākṣasas*.

Mighty Rāma fitted that incomparable arrow, which was about to destroy the menace to the Ikṣvākus, into his magnificent bow. He muttered the prescribed *mantras* over the arrow, drew his bow to the fullest and aimed the arrow at Rāvaṇa's vitals. The arrow, which could not be opposed any more than death, was loosed with as much force as Indra might loose his thunderbolt. It struck Rāvaṇa in the chest and pierced his heart. It took Rāvaṇa's life as it plunged into the earth and then, still drenched in blood, it came quickly back into its quiver.

Rāvaṇa's bow and arrow slipped from his hands and the king of the *rākṣasas*, who had befuddled the world with his strength and speed, tumbled out of his chariot and fell to the ground. The *rākṣasas* saw him fall and scattered in all directions. And the monkeys, who fought with trees for Rāma's sake, chased them, laughing with joy. The *rākṣasas* ran back to Lankā with tears streaming down their faces. The monkeys proclaimed Rāvaṇa's death and Rāma's victory with glee. The sky resounded with the beating of drums and a perfumed breeze wafted through, soothing everyone.

Rare and beautiful flowers rained down on Rāma's chariot and the gods shouted 'Marvellous!' 'Wonderful!' from the skies. The gods and celestial beings were delighted with Rāvaṇa's death, for he had tormented the worlds for a long time. The sky and the four quarters cleared, the earth stood still, the sun shone bright and steady and the gods were at peace. Sugrīva, Vibhīṣaṇa, Lakṣmaṇa and other well-wishers gathered around Rāma and they praised and honoured him with joy in their hearts. Now that Rāma had kept his promise and killed the enemy, he shone on the battlefield, surrounded by his own people as Indra is surrounded by the gods.

As the *rākṣasī* women wept for Rāvaṇa, Mandodarī, his senior wife and most beloved queen, gazed sadly at her dead husband, the mighty *rākṣasa* whose feats surpassed the imagination, who had been killed by Rāma.

'Ah, my heroic husband! Even Indra could not face you when you were angry! The *ṛṣis, cāraṇas* and *gandharvas* fled from you in terror! How could you let a mere mortal kill you in battle? You were covered in glory and had conquered the three worlds with your prowess, how could this man who wanders in the forest kill you? You could take any form you liked, you went where you pleased, how could you have fallen to the mortal Rāma? You were fully armed and fighting at the head of an enormous army. I cannot believe that Rāma was able to do this!

'When your brother was killed in Janasthāna along with the other *rākṣasas,* I knew this was no ordinary man! And when Hanumān entered

Lankā, the city that is impregnable even to the gods, we were all very worried. You would not listen when I told you not to seek enmity with Rāma. Now you reap its consequences!

'How can you justify your obsession with Sītā when it has cost you your majesty, your family and your life? Misguided creature! You did wrong when you abducted Sītā, who is more steadfast than Arundhatī and Rohiṇī! In your delusion, you did not see that Sītā was not superior to me, nor even equal to me in birth, in beauty and in skills! Death comes to everyone through some agent or the other. Your death came through Sītā.

'Sītā will now be happy with Rāma. But I shall be alone, plunged into an ocean of grief! I have wandered through the pleasant woods of Kailāsa, Meru, Mandara and Caitraratha and the gardens of the gods with you! I have travelled with you to beautiful places and worn the finest clothes and jewels. Now I am bereft of all these pleasures.

'What Vibhiṣaṇa foretold has come true. The *rākṣasas* have been destroyed. Your lust and anger made you do these terrible things and now the entire race of rākṣasas is without a protector. You were famed for your strength and courage and though I may not mourn for you, I feel compassion because I am a woman! You have reaped the fruits of your good and bad deeds and you have gone your own way. I weep for myself now, for I am nothing without you!

'Why do you lie there as if you are asleep? Why do you not answer me when I am desolate with grief? Your iron battle club decorated with gold filigree, with which you killed so many enemies, which you prized as much as Indra prizes his thunderbolt, it lies smashed into a thousand pieces by Rāma's arrows! Damn my heart that does not break now that you are dead!'

'Send the women away,' said Rāma to Vibhīṣaṇa, 'and perform the last rites for your brother!'

Vibhīṣaṇa knew *dharma* and was devoted to it. He also wished to please Rāma and so he thought over the matter and said, 'I cannot perform the last rites for a creature who was so cruel, so ruthless and unrighteous, who coveted the wives of others! He may have been my brother but he was an enemy, intent on causing harm to all creatures. Even though he was older than me, Rāvaṇa does not deserve this honour! The world will say that I am heartless because of this, but when they hear about Rāvaṇa's behaviour, they will know that I did the right thing!'

Rāma, the best of all those who uphold *dharma,* was very pleased with Vibhīṣaṇa's words and he replied, 'I should do what makes you happy since I was victorious because of your courage. But I must also tell you what is the right thing to do. It is true that this *rākṣasa's* life was full of lies and deceit and cruelty and unrighteousness. But he was also splendid, brave and strong and he had never been defeated in battle. Death ends all hostilities. We have won. Now perform the funeral rites for him. I am as interested in his welfare as I am in yours. It is fitting that you perform the last rites for Rāvaṇa. An act like this will only add to your fame.'

Vibhīṣaṇa performed the prescribed rites for Rāvaṇa and when they were completed, he joined Rāma and the monkeys in their victory celebrations.

The gods, *gandharvas* and *dānavas* went away, talking among themselves about the wondrous things they had seen: Rāvaṇa's brutal death, Rāma's skills in battle, the splendid fight put up by the monkeys, Sugrīva's wise advice and Lakṣmaṇa's affection and courage. Rāma honoured Mātali and dismissed the brilliant charioteer sent to him by Indra. Mātali bade Rāma farewell and took the shining chariot back to the heavens.

Then Rāma embraced Sugrīva with great joy and after accepting honours and congratulations from the other monkeys, he went back to where the army had camped.

'Vibhīṣaṇa has been devoted and loyal,' said Rāma to the effulgent Lakṣmaṇa, who stood beside him. 'We must crown him king of Lankā without any further delay. It is my greatest wish to see Rāvaṇa's younger brother crowned king.' Lakṣmaṇa fetched two golden pots filled with water and anointed Vibhīṣaṇa king by Rāma's decree in the presence of all the *rākṣasas.* His four *rākṣasa* companions were appointed ministers.

Vibhiṣaṇa established peace within his realm and then presented himself to Rāma. The citizens brought him offerings of food, water and flowers and Vibhīṣaṇa gave them all to Rāma and Lakṣmaṇa. Rāma accepted them with a deep satisfaction because he knew that Vibhīṣaṇa had achieved his ends.

Rāma turned to the mighty monkey Hanumān, who was as large as a mountain, and said, 'Take King Vibhīṣaṇa's permission and go with all courtesy to Rāvaṇa's palace. Give Sītā greetings from Lakṣmaṇa, Sugrīva and myself. Tell her about my victory and Rāvaṇa's death. Give her all the good news and bring back any message she may have for me!'

# *Chapter Sixty-Seven*

Hanumān entered the city of Lankā and was honoured by all the *rākṣasas*. He went to Rāvaṇa's palace and saw Sītā, pale and uncomfortable, like Rohiṇī without the moon. He bowed to her humbly and gently began to tell her all that had happened.

'Rāma, the hero of the Ikṣvākus, sends you his greetings, princess, and asks about your welfare. I have good news for you. Rāma says to tell you, "It is our good fortune that you are alive and I have won the war. Calm yourself and grieve no more! Rāvaṇa has been killed and Lankā is now in my power."

'Rāma has killed his enemies and achieved his goals. Rāma has killed Rāvaṇa with Lakṣmaṇa's advice and the help of Vibhīṣaṇa and the monkey army! Do not be confused. It is now all right for you to be in Rāvaṇa's palace, for Vibhīṣaṇa has been made king of Lankā.'

Sītā rose in confusion. Overwhelmed with joy, she could not say a word. 'What are you thinking?' asked Hanumān gently. 'Why don't you say something?'

In a voice that trembled with happiness, Sītā, who always trod the path of righteousness, said, 'The news of my husband's victory left me speechless for a moment! I cannot see anything to give you as a reward for the good news you have brought me! I cannot think of anything in the world that will equal the news you bring, not gold, not jewels, nor even lordship over the three worlds!'

'Gentle lady, your sweet words are worth more to me than a heap of jewels and the kingdom of the gods!' said Hanumān. 'I have achieved all I wanted when I saw Rāma victorious over his enemies. But I would like to kill all these cruel and ugly *rākṣasīs* who used to torment you and make you unhappy! With my fists and feet and teeth, I shall bite off their ears and pull out their hair. I shall kill them by jumping up and down on their ugly, dried-up faces!'

'How can you be angry with women who are slaves?' said Sītā. 'They are under the control of the king, they do his bidding and are utterly dependent on him! All that happened to me earlier was because of things I must have done in the past. It was obviously ordained that I would have to suffer these circumstances. I want to forgive Rāvaṇa's helpless slaves! They only harassed me because he told them to. They will not bother me now that he is dead.

'The truly noble are compassionate and forgive both good and wicked people, criminals as well as those that deserve death. There is no one who has never done anything wrong! You should not even harm those who enjoy hurting others!'

'You are indeed worthy of Rāma!' said Hanumān when Sītā had finished speaking. 'You are noble and righteous! Now, command me to return to Rāma!'

'I want to see my husband, monkey!' said Sītā quietly.

'You will soon see Rāma, whose face is like the full moon, as well as his friends and well-wishers!' cried Hanumān and returned to Rāma.

'You must see Sītā!' he said to Rāma, the best of all archers. 'It was for her that we undertook this enterprise which has ended in success. She has been consumed by grief and her eyes have been filled with tears. She rejoiced when she heard about your victory. She knew me from before and so she trusted me and said, "I want to see my husband who has achieved his ends and Lakṣmaṇa as well!"'

Rāma was silent for a moment and his eyes filled with tears. He sighed and looked down at the ground and then said to Hanumān, 'Let Sītā bathe and wash her hair. Let her adorn herself with jewels and anoint her body with rare unguents. Then bring her here as soon as you can!'

Vibhiṣaṇa went into the inner apartments and told the women to help Sītā and to tell her that her husband wished to see her after she had bathed and adorned herself. But Sītā insisted that she wanted to see her husband before she bathed. 'You should do as your husband says,' replied Vibhīṣaṇa. Sītā did as she was told because she was devoted to her husband who was like a god to her. She bathed and washed her hair and the young women adorned her with fine clothes and rare jewels. Vibhīṣaṇa placed Sītā in an exquisite palanquin and guarded by several *rākṣasas,* he took her to Rāma.

With great delight, he honoured Rāma and announced Sītā's arrival. Rāma seemed preoccupied and deep in thought, even though he knew that Sītā, who had spent so many months in the home of the *rākṣasa* had come. Joy, depression and anger flooded over him.

Vibhiṣaṇa tried to organize and control the surging crowds that had gathered there. Men in turbans and coats, their hands rough from wielding whips, moved among the people, getting them to disperse. Monkeys, bears and *rākṣasas* were driven away and they retreated to a safe distance. Rāma saw that they were disappointed at being pushed along and thinking of their hurt feelings, he put a stop to Vibhīṣaṇa's actions. His eyes blazed with anger as he said to Vibhiṣaṇa, 'Why are you going against my wishes and treating these people so harshly? Stop it immediately! These are my people! A woman's behaviour is what protects her modesty—not a home, nor fine clothes, nor high walls or honours such as these! Women can be seen in public in times of calamities and emergencies, in times of war, at their own weddings and at religious rituals. A war has just been fought on Sītā's account. She faces a crisis in her life. There is nothing wrong if she is seen in public, especially in my presence! Bring Sītā here quickly, Vibhīṣaṇa! Let her see me surrounded by all my friends!'

Vibhīṣaṇa wondered what Rāma had in mind but he quietly did as he was told. Lakṣmaṇa, Sugrīva and Hanumān were all very disturbed when they heard Rāma's sharp words. They felt sure that he was angry with Sītā because of what he had said and because he showed no desire to see his wife.

Deeply embarrassed and shrinking into herself, Sītā approached her husband, followed by Vibhīṣaṇa. When she found herself in the presence of such a huge crowd, she covered her face in shame and whispered, 'Noble one!' She gazed at her beloved husband who was like a god to her and her face lit up with love, pleasure and wonder. Her weariness and sorrow fell away the moment she saw her husband's moon-bright face which she had not seen for so long.

Rāma looked at Sītā standing meekly by his side and gave vent to the anger in his heart.

'I have killed the enemy, my dear, and I have won you back. In doing so, I have displayed the courage expected of me. I have avenged the insult and it no longer bothers me. I have destroyed the enemy and the disgrace together. I have displayed my prowess and achieved my goals. I have kept my promises. Now I am free.

'You were carried off by a restless *rākṣasa* while you were alone with no one to protect you. I, a mere mortal, have redressed that wrong decreed by fate. If a man cannot avenge the insults heaped upon him he is a weakling and of no use to anyone. Hanumān's spectacular feats of leaping over the ocean and causing havoc in Lankā have not been in vain. Sugrīva's excellent advice and the efforts of his army in battle have all borne fruit. Vibhīṣaṇa, who abandoned a worthless brother and chose to attach himself to me, has also achieved his ends.'

Sītā's doe-like eyes filled with tears as Rāma spoke. But the more he looked at her, the angrier Rāma became, blazing like a fire when *ghee* is poured upon it. He frowned and glared at Sītā, speaking to her cruelly in front of all the *rākṣasas* and monkeys.

'I have done my duty by rescuing you from the enemy and avenging the insult to myself. You should know that this war, which was won by the heroic efforts of my friends, was not fought for your sake. I did it to vindicate my honour and to save my noble family from disgrace. I have terrible suspicions about your character and conduct. The sight of you is as painful to me as a lamp to a man with diseased eyes!

'You are free to go wherever you want. The world is open to you. I have no more use for you, Sītā! How can a man born into a noble family lovingly take back a woman who has lived in the house of a strange man? I am proud of my noble lineage. How can I take you back when Rāvaṇa has touched you and when you have lived under his lustful gaze? I have regained my reputation. That was the sole motivation for rescuing you! I do not want you any more! You can go where you like!

'I am saying this to you after a great deal of deliberation. Go to Lakṣmaṇa or Bharata or to anyone else who pleases you! To Sugrīva, the king of the monkeys. Or to Vibhīṣaṇa, the king of the *rākṣasas*! Go wherever you want! Rāvaṇa was aware of your beauty and your good looks. He cannot have kept you in his house for so long without touching you!'

Sītā could not believe the cruel words her husband had spoken after their long separation. She, who deserved kindness and sweet words, began to weep, like a tender vine crushed by an elephant. She hung her head in shame at being spoken to like that in public. She seemed to shrink into herself, weeping at the arrow-sharp words that had pierced her heart. She wiped the tears that streamed down her face and said, choking, 'How could you say such things to me, the kind of things a low, common man would say to his woman? I am not what you think I am, hero! I swear to this on my virtue! You judge all women by the conduct of a few. You should know better than to reject me like this!

'If my body was touched by another man, it was not because I wanted it! Destiny must bear the responsibility for that. My heart, the only thing I could control, was always with you. What could I do about the other parts of my body that were subject to the will of others? What hope can there be if you do not know me even now, after we have lived together so intimately for so many years?

'When you sent Hanumān to Lankā to find me, why didn't you tell me then that you were not going to take me back? If you had told me then that you had abandoned me, I would have killed myself at that very moment, before the very eyes of that great monkey. Then you would not have had to make this tremendous effort, risking your life and causing hardship to your friends, for nothing!

'But you have surrendered to your anger and acted like a common man and you have treated me like a low and vulgar woman! You have not considered that I am the daughter of Janaka, that I was born from the earth. Nor did you consider the fact that my conduct has always been impeccable! The fact that we are married and that I am devoted to you is of no consequence to you at all!'

Weeping, Sītā turned to Lakṣmaṇa, who stood there silent and miserable. 'Build a funeral pyre for me, Lakṣmaṇa! That is the only solution I see to this terrible calamity that has befallen me! I cannot bear to live under these false accusations! Despite my virtues, my husband has rejected me in front of all these people. He holds the past against me and I cannot vindicate myself in his eyes. The only thing I can do now is walk into the fire!'

Lakṣmaṇa looked over at Rāma with pain in his eyes. He understood what Rāma wanted and so heroic Lakṣmaṇa built the pyre. Sītā honoured her husband with a bowed head and approached the flames. She honoured the gods and the *brahmins* and stood in front of the fire with her palms together. She said, 'If my heart has never strayed from Rāma, let the god of fire, eternal witness to all that happens in the world, protect me!' She walked around the fire and then, her mind calm and serene, she stepped into it.

The massive crowd of young and old that had gathered watched with trepidation as Sītā entered the flames. And when they enveloped her, a huge wail arose from the monkeys and *rākṣasas.*

Suddenly, Kubera, Yama, Indra, Varuṇa, Śiva and Brahmā, creator of the worlds and the knower of the Vedas, arrived in Lankā in their chariots which were as bright as the sun. They raised their strong arms that were adorned with jewels and addressed Rāma, who stood in front of them with his palms joined.

'You are the creator of the worlds and the foremost of the wise! How could you let Sītā walk into the fire? Don't you know that you are the greatest among the gods?

'Long ago, you were Ṛtadhāmā, the best of the *vasus.* Then you were the self-born Prajāpati, the creator of the three worlds. You were the eighth *rudra* and the fifth *pancama.* The *aśvins* are your ears, the sun and the moon are your eyes. You are visible in the time between the end and the beginning of the worlds. And yet, you have humiliated Sītā as if you were an ordinary man!'

Rāma, the lord of the worlds, the best among those who practise *dharma,* said, 'I always thought I was human, that I was Rāma, the son of Daśaratha. Tell me who I am. Where did I come from? Why am I here?'

'You are Narāyaṇa, the wielder of the discus,' replied wise Brahmā. 'You are the single-tusked Varaha, victorious over past and future enemies! You are the eternal *brahman,* the truth, the middle and the end. You are the supreme *dharma,* the four-armed commander of the world's forces. You are the holder of the Śārnga bow. As Puruṣa, you are the first of men. You have conquered your senses, you are mighty and undefeated. You are Kṛṣṇa and Viṣṇu. You are the leader of the celestial army. You are restrained and self-controlled. The worlds arise from you and are absorbed into you. You killed the *asura* Madhu as Indra's younger brother. You are Indra. The lotus emerges from your navel. You are Death in battle. Celestial sages come to you for protection because you are the refuge of the oppressed. You are the hundred-fold Veda and its thousand recensions emerge from you. You are the sacrifice, the *mantra* and the sacred syllable. Your origins and end are unknown. No one knows who you are. Wise men see you in everything: in *brahmins,* in cows, in the directions, in the sky, the mountains and the forests. You have a thousand feet, a thousand eyes and a thousand heads. You are the upholder of the worlds, of the mountains and of all creatures. Rāma, at the dissolution of the worlds, you are visible lying on the waters like a huge serpent and holding the worlds, the gods, *gandharvas* and *dānavas* within you. I am your heart, Rāma, and Sarasvatī is your tongue. The gods are as insepa-rable from you, *brahman,* as the hairs on the body. The night is the blink of your eye, the day is your eye unblinking. The Vedas are your rules for the world. Nothing can exist without you. The world is your body, you are the endurance of the earth. Fire is your anger, your grace is the moon. You carry the mark of Viṣṇu. Long ago, you covered the worlds with your three strides. You made Indra king after you had captured the *asura* Bali. Sītā is Lakṣmī, you are Viṣṇu, the dark one, the creator.

'You took human form for the destruction of Rāvaṇa. You are the best among those that uphold *dharma.* You have done what was necessary. Rāvaṇa has been killed. Now return to heaven! Your strength and heroism are infallible and the man who is devoted to you shall always be success-ful. Those who are firm in their devotion to you, those who recite your glorious deeds shall always be successful.'

The fire god rose, carrying Sītā in his arms. Sītā shone like the morning sun. She wore ornaments of beaten gold and red clothes, Her hair was dark and curly and her garlands were unwithered. Seated in Fire's lap, she was exactly as she had been before. The Fire handed her over to Rāma. 'Here is your Sītā, Rāma,' said the eternal witness. 'She is pure. She never wavered in her loyalty to you, not in word or thought or even by looking at someone else. She was abducted from the forest by mighty Rāvaṇa when she was alone and unprotected. She was imprisoned in his palace and was guarded by fierce *rākṣasīs.* But she was always faithful to you. She was threatened and humiliated and tempted with all kinds of things. But she never gave Rāvaṇa a single thought because her heart was with you. She is pure and chaste, Rāma! Take her back! I will not tolerate any criticism of her!'

Effulgent and resolute, Rāma, the greatest among the upholders of *dharma,* said to the great gods, 'Sītā had to be vindicated in the eyes of the world because this lovely woman had lived inside Rāvaṇa's palace for such a long time. If I had not subjected her to this test, good people would have said that Rāma, the son of Daśaratha, is blinded by his love for a woman.

'I know Sītā, the daughter of Janaka, loves me dearly. She is devoted to me and lives by my wishes. I take refuge in the truth and so I had to remain detached as she entered the fire. I wanted everyone in the three worlds to believe in her. Wide-eyed Sītā is protected by the power of her own chastity. Rāvaṇa could no more have violated her than the ocean can exceed its bounds. She is as unapproachable as the blazing fire. He could not possibly have touched her. She would never had enjoyed Rāvaṇa's opulence and splendour because she is as integral to me as the rays are to the sun. Sītā has now been proved innocent in front of the three worlds. She is as inseparable from me as fame is from a renowned man.

'Besides that, I must respect the advice you have given me for my welfare, for you are honoured and loved by all the worlds!'

The gods praised Rāma for his words because they understood the significance of what he had said. Rāma was reunited with his beloved and was happy, as he deserved to be.

Śiva now said something that was truly worthy. 'Mighty Rāma, lotus-eyed, broad-chested enemy burner, best of all warriors, you have done a great thing! You have dispelled the darkness that covered the worlds by killing Rāvaṇa, who terrified all creatures!

'Comfort Bharata and virtuous Kausalyā. Go and see Kaikeyī and Sumitrā. Reclaim the kingship of Ayodhyā and make your friends and well-wishers happy. Have children and establish the line of the Ikṣvākus in the world. Earn the highest honour by performing the horse sacrifice. Give generous gifts to the *brahmins* and then come back to heaven.

'Here is your father Daśaratha in this celestial chariot. In the world of men, this great man was your teacher and mentor. Because of all that you did, Daśaratha went to Indra's realm after he died. Now you and Lakṣmaṇa must honour him!'

Rāma and Lakṣmaṇa honoured their father who was standing in his chariot. He wore dazzling clothes and shone with his own splendour and majesty. When Daśaratha, the king of the earth, saw his son who was dearer to him than his own life, he was filled with joy. He lifted him onto his lap, embraced him and said, 'All the pleasures of heaven and the respect of the gods were nothing to me without you, Rāma! I swear this is the truth! Kaikeyī's words which caused your exile still rankle in my heart. But now that I see you and Lakṣmaṇa well and happy, now that I have embraced you, my sorrow has lifted, like a mist dissolves in the sun.

Your deeds saved me, my child. Only now have I learned that all this was planned by the gods for the killing of Rāvaṇa.

'Kausalyā shall have her heart's desire fulfilled! She shall rejoice when you return from, the forest. And those who see you anointed king, dripping with water as you return from your ritual bath, they shall also have their wishes fulfilled. I wish I could see you reunited with righteous Bharata. He is strong and pure and has always been devoted to you.

'You have lived in the forest with Sītā and wise Lakṣmaṇa for fourteen long years! You fulfilled your vow and you made the gods happy by killing Rāvaṇa! You have performed incredible deeds and won fame and affection. Establish your kingdom firmly along with your brothers. I wish you a long and happy life!'

'Forgive Kaikeyī and Bharata, righteous king!' said Rāma with his palms joined. 'You declared that you had renounced Kaikeyī and her son! Take those words back!'

'It shall be so!' said Daśaratha. He embraced Lakṣmaṇa and said to him, 'You have been devoted to Rāma and Sītā and you have made me very happy. You have been righteous. If Rāma is pleased with you, you shall earn the fruits of righteousness here on earth as well as in heaven and glory in the afterlife. Serve Rāma well, for he is devoted to the welfare of all creatures in the world. You have seen that Indra and the three worlds, the *siddhas, cāraṇas,* the great souls and the *ṛṣis* honour Rāma as the best of men. They have declared he is the eternal *brahman* and the essence of all the gods. You shall earn limitless fame when you serve Rāma and Sītā!'

'It shall be so!' said Lakṣmaṇa as the righteous king turned to Sītā. 'Do not be angry with Rāma because he renounced you,' Daśaratha said to her. 'He did this in your best interests and so that you would be purified. You need no instruction in devotion to your husband. But it is my duty to tell you that he should be like a god to you.'

Shining with splendour, Daśaratha returned to heaven in his celestial chariot after he had given this advice to his sons and daughter-in-law.

Indra was very pleased and said to Rāma, who stood in front of him with his palms joined, 'Your encounter with us should not be fruitless, Rāma! We are very pleased with you. Tell us what you want!'

'If you really are pleased with me, king of the gods,' replied Rāma, 'then be gracious and grant what I ask. Let all the monkeys who fought so bravely and died for my sake be brought back to life! I would like to see all the heroic monkeys and bears alive again, restored to full health, strength and vigour! May there be an abundance of fresh water, roots and fruits in all seasons wherever they choose to live!'

'This is no small thing you ask, Rāma!' said Indra affectionately. 'Let the dead rise as if they were waking from a long, deep sleep! Let them happily be reunited with their families and their own people! Trees shall give them fruit and flowers all year round and their rivers shall always be full!'

All the monkeys whose bodies had been covered with wounds rose up, their injuries healed. 'What can this be?' they said to each other in amazement.

Now that all Rāma's wishes had been fulfilled, the gods praised him, for he was worthy of praise. 'Dismiss the monkeys and return to Ayodhyā!' they said to Rāma and Lakṣmaṇa. 'Console Sītā and cherish her. She loves you and has been devoted to you. Go and see your brother who has been firm in his vows. Crown yourself king and bring joy to your citizens!' They bade the princes farewell and returned to heaven in their celestial chariots which shone like the sun.

Rāma and Lakṣmaṇa honoured the gods and then Rāma gave instructions for everyone to return to their camps. The army, now that it had won fame, was filled with joy and shone like the night lit up by the moon.

Rāma spent the night pleasantly. When he woke in the morning, Vibhīṣaṇa greeted him as a conquering hero with his palms joined above his head. 'Your bath water is ready and so are fine new clothes, unguents, sandal paste, jewels and garlands,' he said. 'These lovely women are waiting to help you bathe and adorn yourself.'

'Call Sugrīva and the other monkey leaders to bathe,' said Rāma.

'Bharata, that brave and righteous prince who takes refuge in truth and who deserves all happiness and comfort, he suffers because of me. I cannot bathe and adorn myself unless I am with Bharata! I want to return as soon as I can to Ayodhyā. The journey is long and arduous and I shall take the path along which I came.'

'I will send you back to Ayodhyā in a single day!' said Vibhīṣaṇa. 'I have the wondrous chariot Puṣpaka that shines like the sun. It used to belong to Kubera but my brother Rāvaṇa took it away from him by force.

Puṣpaka is as large as a cloud. It will take you to Ayodhyā. There is nothing to worry about.

'But if you have any regard for my virtues, if you consider me a friend and if I am at all worthy of you, stay here for a while with your wife and your brother. Let me honour you and give you all that your hearts desire! Give me the pleasure of accepting my hospitality along with your army and your friends. I ask this favour out of friendship and affection but I cannot demand that you comply with my wishes!

In front of all the monkeys and the *rākṣasas,* Rāma replied, 'I am honoured Vibhīṣaṇa and I am grateful for all that you have done, your good advice, your deeds and your friendship. It is not as if I do not want to do as you have suggested, but I long for my brother Bharata. He followed me to Citrakūṭa and with his head bowed, he begged me to return. But I could not do as he asked. I long to see virtuous Kausalyā, Sumitrā, Kaikeyī and all the elders, my teachers, all the citizens and their children.

'King of the *rākṣasas,* send for your magical chariot quickly. My work is done, there is no reason for me to linger here. Let me go, dear friend! You have honoured me enough. Do not be angry with me, let me leave as soon as possible!'

Vibhīṣaṇa announced the arrival of the Puṣpaka, adorned with flowers. It could move as swiftly as thought and could not be restrained by anything. He stood beside it, waiting for Rāma.

With his palms joined, he said humbly, 'What shall I do now?'

Rāma thought for a moment and said, 'Vibhīṣaṇa, the monkeys have made a heroic effort. Honour them all with gifts and jewels and ornaments. Unconquerable Lankā was taken with their help. They all fought with enthusiasm, ready to sacrifice their lives in battle. We must be grateful to these mighty monkeys. Honour them well! Give them gifts that will make them happy!' Vibhīṣaṇa honoured them all and gave them gifts according to their rank and status.

Rāma and Lakṣmaṇa climbed into the wondrous vehicle. Rāma placed Sītā on his lap and she blushed with embarrassment. Rāma addressed Sugrīva, Vibhīṣaṇa and all the monkeys.

'You have all done great things because of your affection for me. You have my permission to leave now. Go wherever you please. Sugrīva, you have proved that you are a friend and a well wisher and that you will not tolerate unrighteousness. Return to Kiṣkindha with your army! Vibhīṣaṇa, you shall stay in Lankā and rule the kingdom I have given you. Even the gods led by Indra will not dare attack you!

'Let me say goodbye. With your permission, I shall return to Ayodhyā, my father's capital city.'

The great monkeys and the *rākṣasa* Vibhīṣaṇa joined their palms and said, 'We want to go to Ayodhyā! Take us with you! We shall watch as you are crowned king, pay our respects to Kausalyā and return to our homes soon after that!'

'I would be delighted to return to Ayodhyā with all of you, my beloved friends!' said Rāma. 'Come and enjoy all that Ayodhyā has to offer. Come! Sugrīva, climb quickly into Puṣpaka with your army. Come, Vibhīṣaṇa, with all your ministers!'

They all climbed into the wondrous vehicle, and, with Rāma's permission, Puṣpaka rose into the sky.

# *Chapter Sixty-Eight*

Rāma's glance fell upon Hanumān, the best of all monkeys, who was so dear to him. 'Go ahead to Ayodhyā and find out if all is well with the people in the royal palace!' he said to him. 'Go to Śṛnagavera and give my good wishes to my friend Guha, the king of the Niṣādas. He will be glad to know that I am well and he will show you the road that leads to Ayodhyā and Bharata.

'Ask after Bharata's welfare on my behalf. Tell him about my success and about Sītā's abduction by Rāvaṇa and my alliance with Sugrīva and the killing of Vālī in battle. Tell him about the search for Sītā and how you found her when you leapt over the boundless ocean. Tell him how we built the bridge and how Rāvaṇa was killed. Tell him how we saw our father again because of the grace of the great gods.

'Tell him, "Mighty Rāma has achieved his goals. He has killed his enemy and earned fame. Now he is coming here with his friends." When Bharata hears all this, he will reveal his emotions through his gestures. Observe them carefully, especially any sign that indicates he is not favourably disposed towards me. Note everything he says and does. Whose mind would not turn towards the kingdom of his forefathers which is filled with elephants and horses and chariots? Monkey, find out Bharata's state of mind and his intentions and return to us before we have gone too far!'

Hanumān took the form of a man and went quickly towards Ayodhyā. He leapt into the sky and took the path of his father the wind. He flew over the confluence of the Gangā and Yamunā and arrived in Śṛngaverapura. He gave Guha the news of Rāma's success and his imminent arrival and swiftly flew onwards to Nandigrāma.

When he was about one *yojanā* away from Ayodhyā, he saw Bharata, pale and emaciated, wearing the skin of the black antelope and living the life of an ascetic. Bharata was tormented over his brother's misfortune. His hair was matted and his body was covered with dust. He lived righteously, performing severe penances and eating only roots and fruits. He had restrained his senses and shone like a great *ṛṣi*.

Hanumān went up to him and with his palms joined, he spoke to him respectfully. 'Rāma, the one you mourn, the man who lived in the Daṇḍaka forest with his hair matted, asks after your welfare. I bring you good news! Renounce your grief, for soon you will be reunited with Rāma. He has killed Rāvaṇa and rescued Sītā. He has accomplished his mission and is coming here with all his friends. And so are Lakṣmaṇa and Sītā!'

Bharata swooned with joy, but after a moment, he rose and took a deep breath. He embraced the monkey and anointed him with tears of happiness. 'I don't know if you are a man or a god that has come here out of compassion for me. But I would like to give you something valuable for the good news you have brought. Hundreds and thousands of cows or a hundred villages, or sixteen virtuous virgins with curly hair, golden skins, firm thighs and faces like the moon, wealthy and well-born!'

'After all these many years in the forest, I finally have some good news about Rāma!' continued Bharata. 'The old saying, that happiness comes to a man even if after a hundred years, is true! Tell me everything! How did Rāma come to make an alliance with the monkeys? Where did it happen and for what purpose?'

Hanumān sat down and began to tell Bharata all that had happened to Rāma in the forest. 'Rāma was banished by the boons given to your mother and then, King Daśaratha died of grief for his son. You were brought back quickly from Rājagṛha but you did not want the kingdom. You went to Citrakūṭa and, acting righteously, you invited our brother back. He renounced the kingdom but you did also and returned with his sandals. You know all this already, mighty one! Now let me tell you all that happened after you left Citrakūṭa.

'Rāma, Lakṣmaṇa and Sītā went deeper into the desolate forest after you left. Virādha appeared in front of them, roaring loudly. But they killed him and threw him into a pit. Then they arrived in Janasthāna and Rāma killed the fourteen thousand wicked *rākṣasas* who lived there. Then Śūrpanakhā arrived and instructed by Rāma, Lakṣmaṇa grabbed a sword and cut off her nose and ears. Tormented, she went to Rāvaṇa. Then, one of Rāvaṇa's people, a *rākṣasa* named Mārīca became a jewelled deer and excited Sītā's greed. She wanted to have it and Rāma went after the deer, killing it with an arrow in its back.

'Lakṣmaṇa, too, had left the settlement and Rāvaṇa came there, the way a malignant planet approaches Rohiṇi in the sky, and quickly took Sītā. Rāvaṇa killed the vulture Jaṭāyu who tried to stop him from taking Sītā away. A group of wondrous monkeys, large as elephants, stood on top of a mountain and watched in amazement as they saw Rāvaṇa, the king of the *rākṣasas,* carrying Sītā away. He took her to Lankā and tried to win her over with sweet words.

'Then, Rāma returned and when he saw the dying bird who was his father's friend, he was very distressed. As he wandered in the region of the Godāvarī, he came to a forest full of flowers. The brothers were approached by Kabandha. On his advice, they went to Ṛṣyamūka where Rāma made an alliance with Sugrīva. Rāma killed the mighty Vālī in battle and gave Sugrīva a kingdom of his own. Sugrīva promised Rāma that he and the other monkeys would search for the princess.

'Sugrīva sent thousands of millions of monkeys in all directions. A long time passed and we were all depressed and overcome with grief in the Vindhyas. Sampāti, Jaṭāyu's brother, told us that Sītā was in Lankā, in Rāvaṇa's palace. I resorted to my innate strength and leapt one hundred *yojanās* over the ocean. I found Sītā alone and miserable in the *aśoka* grove. She was wearing a single soiled garment and though she was very unhappy, she had remained firm in her vows.

'She gave me a token of recognition and I returned to Rāma. Once he heard that Sītā was alive, Rāma felt better and renewed his interest in life. He decided to destroy Rāvaṇa and called up all his resources. When we reached the ocean, Nala built a bridge that allowed the army of monkeys to cross over to Lankā. Rāma killed Kumbhakarṇa and Nīla killed Prahasta and Lakṣmaṇa killed Rāvaṇa's son. Then Rāma himself killed Rāvaṇa.

'Rāma received many boons from Indra, Yama, Varuṇa and from the other gods and sages. He was very happy and along with the monkeys, he is coming back in the magical chariot Puṣpaka. He has reached the Gangā and is spending the night there with the sages. Tomorrow, during the auspicious hour of Pūṣa, you will see Rāma again!'

Bharata was delighted. He joined his palms and said, 'At last! My dearest wish has been fulfilled!' He went over to Śatrughna and said, 'Let all the people who have purified themselves honour the gods in all the temples. Decorate the public places in the city with flowers and let music fill the air! Let the courtiers and bards and commanders of the army get ready to welcome moon-faced Rāma!'

Śatrughna sent out labour forces by the thousands to level the roads between Nandigrāma and the city. They filled the holes, moved away the rocks and stones and made the roads smooth and firm. 'Sprinkle the area with cold water and let the road be strewn with flowers and puffed rice. Hoist flags and banners on the highways and make sure that the city's mansions have been decorated before sunrise! Adorn them with wreaths and garlands and cover the main thoroughfare with hundreds of flowers!'

Chariot warriors went out in their magnificent chariots and rutting elephants adorned with gold were led out of the city. Daśratha's women climbed into lovely vehicles and went out behind Kausalyā. The earth shook with the sound of horses and mules neighing, chariots rumbling, drums beating and conches blaring as the entire city moved to Nandigrāma.

Bharata went out to meet Rāma along with the prominent *brahmins*, the leaders of the trade guilds and his ministers who were carrying flowers and water. They were accompanied by the music of drums and conches. Righteous Bharata carried his brother's sandals on his head. He also took with him the white umbrella of state that was adorned with white flowers as well as fly whisks decorated with gold that were worthy of a king. Bharata was thin from fasting and he still wore the skin of the black antelope, but now he was filled with joy at the prospect of his brother's return.

He scanned the directions and looked all around. 'Are you sure you were not indulging in the fickleness of your monkey nature?' he asked Hanumān. 'I do not see Rāma anywhere!'

'I am sure the monkeys are enjoying the perennial fruit and flowers and the plentiful honey at Bharadvāja's hermitage,' replied Hanumān. 'This was the boon Indra gave the monkeys and Bharadvāja has been able to entertain them and offer them hospitality. I can hear the huge din the monkeys are making. From that, I can conclude that they must be crossing the Gomatī.

'Look at that cloud of dust! The monkeys must be playing with the trees in the *sāla* forest. And look! There in the distance you can see the wondrous Puṣpaka that was created for Brahmā, bright as the moon! It travels faster than thought and in it are your heroic brothers and Sītā, splendid Sugrīva and Vibhīṣaṇa, the king of the *rākṣasas*!'

A roar of delight that seemed to pierce the sky rose from the crowds of women, children and old people gathered there. 'Rāma is here!' they shouted. The men dismounted from their chariots, horses and elephants and watched Rāma approaching as the moon rises in the sky. Bharata stood with his palms joined, ready to welcome his brother and to honour him.

Rāma shone like Indra as he stood in that fabulous chariot. He looked like the sun on Mount Meru and Bharata prostrated himself on the ground. The vehicle landed and Bharata went and threw himself at Rāma's feet. Rāma raised his brother whom he had not seen for so long and embraced him joyfully. Bharata greeted Lakṣmaṇa and Sītā with delight. All the great monkeys appeared in human form, for they could change their shapes at will, and they asked after Bharata's welfare as he embraced them all. 'It was only because of your help that they were able to accomplish this marvellous deed!' said Bharata sweetly to Vibhīṣaṇa. Śatrughna greeted Rāma and Lakṣmaṇa and humbly touched Sītā's feet.

Rāma went up to his mother who had been so full of sorrow. He touched her feet, making her heart overflow with happiness. Then he greeted Sumitrā and Kaikeyī, all his other mothers and the family priest who had come with them. 'Welcome back, son of Kausalyā!' said the citizens with their palms joined in respect. Rāma gazed at those thousands of joined palms that were like lotuses about to bloom.

Bharata took the sandals and placed them on his brother's feet himself. 'With these, I return to you the kingdom I have looked after for so long!' he said with his palms joined. 'Now that you are back in Ayodhyā as king, my life and all my wishes have been fulfilled. Inspect the treasury, the granary and the army. By the authority you gave me, I have been able to multiply everything ten-fold.'

The monkeys and Vibhīṣaṇa wept when they saw the love and devotion Bharata had for his brother. Rāma drew Bharata into Puṣpaka and they all went together with the army to Bharata's settlement. When they reached there, Rāma dismounted and gave Puṣpaka permission to depart. The vehicle rose into the air and went back to Kubera.

Rāma fell at the feet of the family priest who had been his teacher and whom he loved as much as he loved his own life. They sat down next to each other, like Indra and Bṛhaspati.

Bharata joined his palms above his head and said to Rāma, 'The kingdom was given to me to please my mother. And just as it was given to me, I now give it to you! I can no longer carry the burden of the kingdom any more than a calf can bear a load that a mighty ox struggles with. Just as you cannot control a flood until you dam the river, so, too, a kingdom can only be held together by a strong ruler. I can no more step into your shoes than a donkey can imitate a horse, or a crow a swan.

'If a man were to plant a tree that grew tall and strong with many branches difficult to climb, and if it produced only flowers and no fruit, all the hopes the man had for the tree would be in vain. We would be in a similar position if you, the best of men, were not to rule over us. Let the world see you crowned king today, blazing like the midday sun. Let yourself be woken every morning to the sweet sounds of music and the tinkling of anklets and bells. As long as the planets move in their orbits and the earth exists, so long shall you be our lord!'

Rāma acquiesced to Bharata's request and sat upon a magnificent seat. On Śatrughna's instructions, hair dressers with swift and gentle hands attended to Rāma. After Bharata, Lakṣmaṇa, mighty Sugrīva and the king of the *rākṣasas* had bathed, Rāma took his ritual bath. He cut off his matted locks and anointed himself with sweet ointments. Blazing with glory, he put on garlands and fine clothes. Meanwhile, Daśaratha's women lovingly prepared Sītā for the necessary rituals.

Sumantra brought a dazzling chariot yoked with magnificent horses and Rāma, always devoted to the truth, climbed into it. Daśaratha's ministers, led by the family priest, had made all the arrangements for the coronation in Ayodhyā. Rāma approached the city in his shining chariot like Indra. Bharata held the reins, Śatrughna held the royal umbrella and Lakṣmaṇa waved the plumed whisk over Rāma's head. Sugrīva, king of the monkeys, and Vibhīṣaṇa, king of the *rākṣasas,* held the other whisks. The sweet sounds of the *ṛṣis* and the gods praising Rāma could be heard from the sky. The monkeys took human form and resplendent in their jewels, rode upon nine thousand elephants.

The city with all its beautiful mansions was alerted by the beating of drums and the blaring of conches. The citizens watched as Rāma came closer, his body shining with splendour. They praised him and honoured him and received his thanks as they followed behind him. With his ministers, *brahmins* and the common people around him, Rāma seemed like the moon surrounded by stars. Musicians and singers made sweet music and sang auspicious songs as they walked in front with young women, cows and *brahmins* carrying saffron rice. Rāma told his ministers all about the alliance with Sugrīva, about Hanumān's skills and powers and the wonderful exploits of the monkeys. The citizens listened to all these tales with amazement. Surrounded by the monkeys as he told these stories, Rāma entered Ayodhyā, which was teeming with happy, prosperous people. The citizens had placed flags on every house and Rāma went past them on his way to his father's palace.

Rāma entered the palace and was greeted by his mothers. He turned to Bharata and said these righteous words. 'Take Sugrīva to my own palace which is decorated with gold and lapis and has a beautiful pleasure garden.' Bharata took the king of the monkeys there himself and retainers hurried in with oil lamps and fine fabrics for the couches and seats.

Śatrughna asked Sugrīva to send out his people to make the necessary arrangements for the coronation. Immediately, Sugrīva gave four golden pots studded with jewels to four monkeys saying, 'Come back before dawn tomorrow with water from the four oceans!' At once, the monkeys leapt into the sky with the speed of Garuḍa. Jāmbavān, Hanumān, Vegadarśī and Ṛṣabha came back with water from the four oceans while the others collected water from five hundred rivers. Śatrughna and the ministers courteously told the family priest that everything was ready for the ceremonies.

Vasiṣṭha and the *brahmins* seated Rāma and Sītā upon a jewelled couch and began the rituals. The *brahmins* joyfully anointed Rāma with cool, fragrant water and then the ministers, young women, the warriors and merchants did the same. The gods and the guardians of the four quarters sprinkled Rāma with the essences of medicinal and celestial herbs. Śatrughna held the royal umbrella over his head, Sugrīva held one whisk and Vibhīṣaṇa the other, which was as bright as the moon. Indra instructed Vāyu to give Rāma a brilliant necklace made of one hundred golden lotuses and a string of pearls that contained all kinds of other gems and jewels as well.

The gods and the *gandharvas* sang and the *apsarases* danced at Rāma's coronation since he fully deserved that honour. The earth yielded her bounty, trees produced fruit and flowers released their perfumes for Rāma. Rāma distributed one hundred thousand horses, bulls and cows with calves to *brahmins* along with gold and jewels and clothes. He gave Sugrīva a golden garland studded with jewels that shone like the sun, lapis armbands studded with diamonds to resolute Angada and a necklace of incomparable pearls as white as the moon to Sītā. Sītā watched as Rāma gave clothes and jewels to Hanumān. She unhooked the pearl necklace and said softly to her husband, 'Give this to Hanumān for all he did to make you happy. He is brave and strong and intelligent at all times!' Sītā gave the pearls to the son of the Wind and with them around his neck, he shone like a white cloud on top of a mountain when it is lit up by the rays of the moon. All the other monkeys received gifts that were worthy of them. They were all thrilled and they honoured Rāma before they returned to the place from where they had come.

Righteous Rāma, who was known for his generosity, began to rule his kingdom now that he had defeated his enemies and won fame. 'Stay by me to rule this kingdom that was established by the strength of our forefathers, honourable Lakṣmaṇa!' he said. 'You are my equal in every way. You must rule along with me as my regent!' Even though Rāma asked him again and again, Lakṣmaṇa refused and finally, Rāma had to consecrate Bharata his heir.

Thus, Rāma reclaimed his incomparable kingdom along with his ministers, friends and family. He propitiated the gods with many magnificent sacrifices. He ruled for ten thousand years and performed one hundred horse sacrifices with the finest horses and extravagant gifts.

Under Rāma's rule, no one ever heard the wailing of widows, nor was there any fear of disease or poisonous snakes. There was no cruelty or injustice and the old never had to do the work of the young. There was happiness everywhere and *dharma* flourished. People took their example from Rāma and were never violent towards each other. Everybody lived for a thousand years and had a thousand sons. They knew neither disease nor unhappiness. Trees yielded fruit and flowers all year, the rains always came at the right time and the touch of the wind was always pleasant. Everybody did their own work and happily lived the lives prescribed for them. Everyone abided by *dharma* and there was no unrighteousness. Rāma ruled his honourable and prosperous people for ten thousand years.

# EPILOGUE

# *Chapter Sixty-Nine*

Rāma was pleased to see that his wife was beginning to show signs of being pregnant. 'I see that we shall soon have much to celebrate!' he said to her. 'What can I do for you? Tell me, which wish of yours can I fulfil?'

'I want to see the peaceful places for meditation in the forest,' she replied with a smile. 'I would like to sit at the feet of the powerful sages who live on the banks of the Gangā and eat only roots and fruits. It is my dearest wish to spend at least one night with them!'

'You can go there tomorrow,' promised Rāma as they went into the middle enclosure of the palace, surrounded by their friends.

When Rāma had seated himself, a number of storytellers and jesters gathered around. All kinds of stories were told, some of which were very funny, and Rāma was pleased. 'What do the common people in the city talk about?' he asked. 'What do they say about me and Sītā, about Lakṣmaṇa and Bharata? About Śatrughna, Kaikeyī and my mother? New kings are often the subject of discussion amongst the people.'

'The people speak very highly of you,' said Bhadra with his palms joined. 'They talk particularly about your victory over Rāvaṇa.'

'Tell me everything the people say, without leaving anything out,' urged Rāma. 'Tell me the good and the bad. By listening to this, I can act for their welfare and avoid things that are not good for them. Speak freely and without fear. Tell me, what are the people saying?'

'Listen, and I shall tell you everything the people are saying,' said Bhadra calmly. 'I shall tell you the good and the bad that is discussed in the public squares, the forests and the gardens.

'"Rāma did the impossible by building a bridge over the ocean. Such a thing had never been done before, not even by the gods and the *dānavas* together! He killed an invincible enemy and slaughtered his army. And then he brought the monkeys, bears and *rākṣasas* under his control. He killed Rāvaṇa and rescued Sītā. He placed the intolerable past behind him and took her back into his own home. How could he take Sītā back into his heart? How could he live with her again so happily when she had been abducted and had even sat upon Rāvaṇa's lap?

How can he not be repelled by her? She was in the *aśoka* grove for so long and was under the control of the *rākṣasas*! Now we shall have to do the same thing with our wives in a similar situation, for subjects must do as their king does!"

'These are the things that people are saying all over the city!' said Bhadra.

Rāma was extremely upset and asked his friends, 'What do you think of this?' They all bowed their heads and admitted that what Bhadra had said was true.

Rāma dismissed all his friends so that he could think things over. He considered the matter carefully and came to a decision. He called the doorkeeper who stood close at hand and said, 'Bring my brothers, Lakṣmaṇa, Bharata and Śatrughna, here immediately!' The doorkeeper bowed and went to Lakṣmaṇa's house where he was allowed to enter without any trouble. 'The king wishes to see you,' he said to Lakṣmaṇa. 'You must go to him without delay!' Lakṣmaṇa climbed into his chariot and went at once to Rāma's palace. Then the doorkeeper went to Bharata and with his palms joined, he said, 'The king wishes to see you!' Bharata leapt up from his seat and went on foot to see Rāma as quickly as he could. The doorkeeper watched Bharata leave hurriedly and went to Śatrughna. 'The king wishes to see you. Lakṣmaṇa and Bharata have already gone to him.' Śatrughna bowed his head, acknowledging the command, and went to Rāma's palace at once.

Rāma was told that the princes had arrived. Sadly, he hung his head and instructed the doorkeeper to let them in. The princes entered wearing white clothes, their minds calm and composed. They saw that Rāma's face was pale, like a moon in eclipse, or the sun dimmed at twilight. His eyes were filled with tears and his sad face was like a lotus shorn of all its glory. The princes touched his feet and waited for him to speak. Rāma embraced them all in his strong arms and led them to their seats.

'You are my life. You are everything to me!' he said. 'I rule this kingdom that all of you obtained for me. You are all learned in the traditional texts and you are wise and experienced counsellors. Advise me on a matter that is very close to my heart!' The princes grew somewhat apprehensive as Rāma continued. 'Listen to me carefully and do not argue with the decision I have made.

'Let me tell you what ordinary people are saying about Sītā. Commoners as well as prominent citizens hold me in contempt. I find that very painful. I was born into the great and noble family of the Ikṣvākus! How can they speak so poorly of Sītā?

'You know how Sītā was abducted from the deserted forest by Rāvaṇa and how I killed him for that. And in front of you, Lakṣmaṇa, the gods declared Sītā innocent when she walked into the fire. In the presence of the gods and *gandharvas* in Lankā, she was given back to me after she had been declared pure. I knew in my heart that the virtuous woman was innocent and so I accepted her and brought her back to Ayodhyā.

'But now, the terrible things people are saying make me unhappy. An infamous man who is the subject of common discourse goes to the hells of the unrighteous and stays there as long as the story of his disgrace is told. The gods do not love the notorious and even the world loves a man who is well spoken of. Good men's deeds are motivated by a desire for fame. I would give up my life, even renounce all of you, for fear of a scandal. How can I hesitate or do anything less in Sītā's case? So you see why I am so upset. I cannot imagine a greater sorrow than this!

'Tomorrow morning, Lakṣmaṇa, tell Sumantra to have the chariot ready. Take Sītā and leave her just outside the borders of the kingdom! The sage Vālmīki's hermitage lies on the banks of the Tamasā, on the far shores of the Gangā. Leave her in that desolate place and come back quickly.

'Do as I say, Lakṣmaṇa! Do not say anything that will contradict my decision about Sītā. I will be very upset if you oppose me on this! Swear to me that you will say nothing about my decision, that you will not criticize it in any way. Those who speak against my wishes are not my friends because they want to see my desires frustrated. If you are obedient to me, you will respect my instructions and take Sītā away from here! She has already said she would like to visit the sages who live by the Gangā. Let her wishes be fulfilled.'

His face wet with tears, Rāma sent his brothers away.

When the night had passed, Lakṣmaṇa miserably called for Sumantra. His face pale, he said, 'Yoke swift horses to our finest chariot and place a comfortable seat in it for Sītā. Bring it to the palace at once! I have to take Sītā to the sages' settlements.'

Sumantra prepared a chariot with fine, soft cushions in it and brought it around. 'The chariot is ready for you to do whatever you need,' he said to Lakṣmaṇa.

Lakṣmaṇa went into the palace and said to Sītā, 'The king has asked me to take you to the banks of the Gangā, to the sages' settlements there.' Sītā was delighted and was eager to leave. She prepared for her departure by taking all her lovely clothes and jewels. 'I will give these to the wives of the sages,' she said to Lakṣmaṇa as he helped her into the chariot.

'I see bad omens, Lakṣmaṇa!' said Sītā. 'My eye twitches, my limbs tremble and my heart is uneasy. My enthusiasm wanes, my courage falters and the whole world seems devoid of happiness. I hope everything is all right with your eldest brother and all your other brothers as well as with all my mothers-in-law. May all be well with the citizens and all creatures!' Sītā joined her palms and invoked the blessings of the gods. Lakṣmaṇa bowed his head and echoed, 'May all go well!' even though his heart was heavy.

They reached the banks of the Gomatī and rested for the night. In the morning, Lakṣmaṇa said to Sumantra, 'Yoke the horses quickly! I want to bathe in the Gangā!' He asked Sītā to climb into the chariot and with horses that travelled as swiftly as thought, they had reached the banks of the Gangā by mid-day.

Lakṣmaṇa saw the clear waters of the river and burst into tears. Sītā was keen to bathe in the river but when she saw Lakṣmaṇa in such distress, she stopped and asked him what the matter was. 'Why are you weeping, mighty one? I have waited so long to return to the banks of the Gangā. This is an occasion for happiness. Why are you crying, Lakṣmaṇa? Why do you make me unhappy?

'I know you are used to being with Rāma all the time. Are you upset because you have been separated from him for two nights? Rāma is dearer to me than my own life, Lakṣmaṇa, but I do not weep like this! Stop this childish behaviour!

'Take me across the river so that I can visit the sages. I want to give them the clothes, money and jewels I have brought with me. We can spend one night there and return to the city after we have honoured the sages.'

Lakṣmaṇa wiped his eyes and called for a boat to take them across the river. He placed Sītā in the boat the Niṣādas had brought and climbed in after her. Filled with sorrow, he told Sumantra to wait on the shore and asked the boatmen to push the boat off.

When they reached the further shore of the Gangā, Lakṣmaṇa joined his palms and in a voice choked with tears, he said to Sītā, 'My heart is filled with grief when I think of how the world will condemn me for this, but I am acting on the orders of a wise and noble man. I would prefer death to what I have to do today, this thing which will bring me disgrace in the world! Forgive me! Do not hold this against me, good lady!' cried Lakṣmaṇa and sank to the ground.

Sītā was alarmed when she saw Lakṣmaṇa weeping and praying for death. 'I don't understand what is going on,' she whispered. 'Tell me the truth, Lakṣmaṇa! I can see that something is bothering you. Is everything all right with the king? Obviously, the king has made you promise to do something that causes you pain. I command you to tell me, Lakṣmaṇa!'

Urged by Sītā, Lakṣmaṇa hung his head and said pathetically, 'Rāma has heard the harsh and unfair things people say about you in public. I cannot repeat those words in your presence, my lady, but Rāma was very upset when he heard them.

'Even though you were declared innocent in my presence, the king has renounced you for fear of gossip and scandal. That's all there is to it! I have been asked to leave you in the sages' settlements, for that is what you wanted. These are the king's orders.

'The woods along the banks of the Gangā are pleasant and they are filled with pious sages. You have nothing to worry about. The great sage Vālmīki was a good friend of my father, Daśaratha. You can live comfortably by his feet, fasting and meditating. You can keep Rāma in your heart all the time. You shall earn fame and renown from this conduct as a pure and devoted wife!'

Sītā was overwhelmed with grief when she heard Lakṣmaṇa's cruel words and she fell to the ground in a swoon. When she recovered, her eyes filled with tears and she said to Lakṣmaṇa in a sad voice, 'This body of mine must have been created for grief, Lakṣmaṇa! You can see that I am overcome with sorrow today, that I am the very embodiment of pain! I must have done something really terrible in my last life. I must have caused the separation of husbands and wives.

'How could the king have renounced me when I have always been so good and virtuous? I even lived in the forest and bore all kinds of hardships because I have always served at Rāma's feet. How can I live in a hermitage now, separated from all the people I love? Who can I talk to about this terrible grief that I must bear? What shall I say to the sages when they ask me what I did wrong? What reason can I give for the king forsaking me? I would kill myself by jumping into the river right now, except that the king's royal lineage would be destroyed along with me.

'Do as you were told, Lakṣmaṇa! Abandon me, a poor, wretched woman! You must obey the king. But listen to what I have to say. Bow to all my mothers-in-law and touch their feet. Give them my greetings. Give them and the king my best wishes for their welfare. Tell the king, "Always treat your subjects as you would your own brothers. That is the highest *dharma* and it will earn you incomparable fame and glory. I care nothing for this corporeal body of mine! You should do whatever it takes to prevent the people from gossiping!"'

Lakṣmaṇa was too upset to speak and he kept his eyes fixed on the ground. Weeping aloud, he honoured Sītā and climbed back into the boat. When he reached the other shore, he quickly got into the chariot, unable to bear the burden of his grief. He kept turning around to look at Sītā as she stood there, alone and vulnerable, but he had to go onwards. Sītā watched as Lakṣmaṇa's chariot went further and further away and she grew sadder and sadder.

The children from the sage's hermitage saw Sītā crying and ran to where the pious Vālmīki was practising austerities. They honoured him and told him about the weeping woman. 'There is a woman here we have never seen before. She is as lovely as a goddess and does not appear to be a mortal. She seems to be married but she is weeping uncontrollably. We must offer her hospitality!'

The righteous sage, who had earned the power of second sight through his austerities, knew that this was Sītā. He went to her immediately with the *arghya* offering. When he reached the shores of the Gangā, he saw Sītā, Rāma's wife, alone and helpless. Blazing with splendour, the sage spoke to her kindly, gladdening her heart with his gentle words.

'I know you are Daśaratha's daughter-in-law, the wife of Rāma and the daughter of Janaka. You are welcome here, good wife! Even as you were coming here, I learned everything about you in the course of my meditation. In my heart I know the reason for your arrival. My divine eye shows me that you are innocent. Have no fear, you can live with me. There are some women ascetics not far from here, engaged in the practise of austerities. They will look after you as one would look after a child. Accept this *arghya* water! You can live here without any anxiety, as if you were in your own home!'

Sītā bowed her head and touched Vālmīki's feet and then she followed him as he went onwards. The women ascetics, who had controlled their senses and who were very virtuous, saw the sage approaching with Sītā and went forward to receive them. 'Welcome, great sage! You have come here after a long time! Tell us what we can do for you!'

'This woman I have brought here is Sītā, the wife of wise Rāma. She is Daśaratha's daughter-in-law and Janaka's daughter. She has been renounced by her husband even though she is virtuous and innocent. She is now under my protection. You must treat her well, not just because of my words, but also because of her status and majesty!'

Making sure that Sītā would be cared for, the great sage went back to his own hermitage surrounded by his disciples.

Some months later, Sītā gave birth to twin boys. In the middle of the night, the women and children of Vālmīki's hermitage came and gave him the good news. 'Come and protect the children from evil spirits and calamities!' they said. The sage was delighted with the news and uttered the appropriate *mantras* for the infants. He named the twin boys Lava and Kuśa.

# *Chapter Seventy*

One day, Rāma said to Lakṣmaṇa, 'Call Vasiṣṭha, Vāmadeva, Jābali and all the other important *brahmins* together for the performance of a horse sacrifice. I will talk to them and then, after meditating, I shall set free a horse that has all the auspicious marks.' Lakṣmaṇa summoned the *brahmins* and presented them to Rāma. They blessed invincible, god-like Rāma, who had prostrated himself at their feet. With joined palms, Rāma told them of his decision to perform the horse sacrifice and they were very pleased.

'Send for honourable Sugrīva,' said Rāma to Lakṣmaṇa. 'Let him come here with the mighty monkeys and let them all share in these wonderful celebrations. And tell heroic Vibhīṣaṇa to come here with the *rākṣasas* who can go where they please. Call the kings who are my allies along with their retinues to witness this magnificent sacrifice. Call the righteous *brahmins* from other kingdoms. And the great sages who are rich in austerities as well as their wives. Set up the sacrificial pavilion in the sacred Naimiṣa woods along the Gomatī.

'Have all the materials required for the sacrifice sent there. Tell Bharata to go ahead with heaps of gold and silver. Let him go there with traders, cooks, actors, dancers, *brahmins*, young and old people, and with carpenters and skilled workers and mothers and sons and all the residents of the inner apartments as well as men skilled in the performance of these rites. Let him also take a golden statue of my wife.'

Rāma ensured that all the preparations for the sacrifice had been made and then he released a jet black horse which had all the auspicious marks. He told Lakṣmaṇa and the sacrificial priests to accompany the horse so that all the rituals could be correctly observed and he himself went to the

Naimiṣa forest. He saw the splendid enclosure that had been constructed for the sacrifice and exclaimed, 'How magnificent!'

A great many kings came to Rāma while he was installed in the Naimiṣa forest and he honoured them with gifts of food and clothes. He gave gifts even to their relatives while Bharata and Śatrughna took care of the hospitality and entertainment. Sugrīva and the mighty monkeys who had accompanied him attended to the needs of the *brahmins* while Vibhīṣaṇa and his *rākṣasas,* who were adorned with garlands, looked after the righteous sages. And so the magnificent and well-organized sacrifice began while Lakṣmaṇa guarded the wandering horse.

At the sacrifice, you could hear nothing other than the litany, 'Give freely and as much as you can, until those who want and ask are satisfied!' There was no one there who was dirty or unhappy, no one who was oppressed. The splendid sacrifice conducted by the great king was filled with happy and prosperous people. Even the long-lived sages could not remember another sacrifice quite like this one, with such an abundance of gifts and giving. Though gold and silver and clothes were constantly being distributed, their store never seemed to diminish. 'Never before, not even with Indra, Soma, Varuṇa or Yama, have we ever seen a sacrifice like this!' said the sages who were rich in austerities. The monkeys and *rākṣasas* gave away huge quantities of wealth and clothes, as much as people wanted. The sacrifice conducted by the best of kings went on for a whole year, never diminishing in its enthusiasm and zeal.

As the sacrifice continued, the sage Vālmīki came there with his students. He saw the opulence of the sacrifice which rivalled anything performed by the gods and set up camp near the settlements of the great sages. He built a few pleasant little huts there and then he said to Kuśa and Lava, 'Go and sing the Rāmāyaṇa in its entirety. Sing with emotion and sincerity. Sing among the sages and the *brahmins*, on the roads and the highways. Sing in the camps of the kings. Sing at Rāma's door, at the site of the rituals. Sing especially in front of the priests performing the sacrifice.

'Sustain yourself with the sweet fruits that grow on mountains and your voices will remain melodious. You shall not grow tired if you eat those fruits. If Rāma asks you to sing among the sages, do so, keeping in mind all the finer points of the art. Observe all the rules of music and song I have taught you. Sing only twenty cantos a day and sing them sweetly. Do not hanker after wealth and gifts. What use are such things to those who live in forest settlements and eat only roots and fruit?

'If the king should ask you whose sons you are, tell him only that you are Vālmīki's students. Tune your instruments as I have taught you. Sing with all your heart, sing sweetly and without concern for anything else. Start at the very beginning. Be sure not to show any disrespect to the king, for this righteous ruler is the father of all creatures.

'In the morning, collect your thoughts, calm your minds and after you have tuned your instruments, sing this poem that deserves to be sung,' said the sage, giving his students detailed instructions.

The twins woke in the morning and after they had bathed and performed the morning worship, they began to sing as the sage had instructed them to do.

Rāma listened to the poem composed by the great teacher. It was melodiously set to music and was quite unique, the first of its kind. As he heard more and more of the wonderful poem which was bound by the rules of metre and was set in time to music, he became extremely curious.

When the rituals for the day were done, Rāma would make the boys sing in front of the sages, kings and respected scholars. He made them sing before those who knew the legends of the past and in the presence of venerable old *brahmins*. The sages and powerful kings were all delighted with the poem and they gazed at the young boys as if to drink them in with their eyes. 'These boys look so much like Rāma that they could well be mirror images of him!' they said to each other. 'But for their matted hair and their simple clothes, we cannot tell which is Rāma and which are the singers!'

The boys from the hermitage continued to sing so sweetly that the audience went into raptures. Their music was so lovely that it seemed divine rather than human and the listeners simply could not get enough of it. The boys began their song with the first canto, with the arrival of Nārada, and they went on to sing twenty cantos a day on a regular basis.

When Rāma heard the first twenty cantos, he said to his brother Bharata, 'Give eighteen thousand gold pieces to these boys immediately!' But Kuśa and Lava would not accept the shining gold. 'What can we do with this?' they asked with surprise. 'We live in the forest and eat only roots and fruit. What do we need this gold for?' Rāma and the others were amazed at their response.

Eager to hear the rest of the poem, Rāma asked the boys who shone with splendour, 'What is this poem about? Who composed it? Where does that great sage live?'

'It was composed by the blessed Vālmīki who has come to attend your sacrifice. The poem tells the story of your life in great detail in five hundred cantos. If you like, you and your brothers can hear the entire poem in the intervals between the rituals.'

'Excellent!' said Rāma. The boys took his permission to leave and returned to the sage's hut. And Rāma went back to the sacrificial enclosure with the kings and the sages.

Rāma listened to that lovely poem for many days in the company of the kings, sages and monkeys. He learned from the poem that Kuśa and Lava were the sons of Sītā. In the midst of the assembly, Rāma said, 'Go to the sage with this message. Tell him, "If Sītā is really innocent and virtuous, let her come here with your permission and clear her name!" I would like to hear what the sage has to say on the matter and I am also curious about whether Sītā would be inclined to prove her innocence. Find out all this and come back quickly! Let Sītā prove her innocence tomorrow morning in front of this entire assembly. I can establish the sincerity of my intentions at the same time.'

The messengers went at once to the sage and told him what Rāma had said. Vālmīki immediately understood what Rāma wanted to do and said, 'Bless you! Sītā will do as Rāma says because for a woman, her husband is like a god!' The messengers returned and Rāma was delighted with their news. 'Blessed sages, you and your disciples and the kings and their retinues shall watch as Sītā proves herself!' he said to the assembly. 'Anyone else who is interested can also come along!' The sages praised Rāma when they heard his words and the kings said, 'No one other than you would be so magnanimous!'

I don't think this is magnanimous

Now that he had decided what was to be done the next day, Rāma, the slayer of his enemies, dismissed the gathering.

When the night had passed, the king went to the sacrificial enclosure and sent for the effulgent sages. All the heroic *rākṣasas* and the mighty monkeys gathered there out of curiosity. Thousands of *kṣatriyas*, *vaiśyas* and *śūdras* also assembled, eager to see Sītā take her oath of purity.

When Vālmīki heard that everyone had arrived and that the crowd was as still as a mountain, he hurried there with Sītā. Sītā walked behind the sage with her head bowed. Her palms were joined, her mind was fixed on Rāma and her eyes were filled with tears. A roar of approval went up from the people, who grieved deeply in their hearts when they saw Sītā following Vālmīki as Śrī follows Brahmā. Some shouted Rāma's praises, others praised Sītā and still others praised them both.

Vālmīki made his way through the throng with Sītā and went up to Rāma. 'This is the virtuous and righteous woman you abandoned in the forest near my hermitage even though she is innocent,' he said. 'You renounced her because you feared people's gossip. She has now come to prove her innocence. You should let her do so.

'Her two sons, these wonderful bards, are your sons, Rāma. I swear this is the truth! I am the tenth son of Pracetas, Rāma, and I have never told a lie. These are your sons! I have practised austerities for thousands of years. May I lose all the merit I have gained if Sītā is not innocent! This blameless woman has never behaved inappropriately and thinks of her husband as a god. You were so scared of a little gossip! Now she will prove herself in front of you!'

Rāma looked at Sītā, who was as lovely as a goddess. He joined his palms and said to Vālmīki, 'It shall be as you say, for you know *dharma*! But your words have been proof enough for me. Sītā has already declared her innocence before the gods. And I abandoned her, even though I knew she was innocent, because I feared a scandal. You must forgive me for that. I also know that these twin boys are my sons. When Sītā proves her innocence before the world, I shall be able to love her again!'

Realizing that Rāma wanted Sītā to prove herself, all the gods arrived there, led by Brahmā. The heavenly and celestial beings came with them. Just then, Vāyu released a gentle breeze, redolent with divine perfumes. As it wafted through the assembly, it made everyone calm and happy. The people who had come from other countries marvelled at this, thinking that such a wondrous thing could only have happened long ago, in the *kṛtayuga*.

Everyone watched as Sītā, wearing an ochre robe, joined her palms. Her head was bowed and she kept her eyes on the ground. 'If I have never thought about any other man but Rāma, let the goddess Mādhavī create a chasm for me!'

As soon as she had finished speaking, a truly wondrous event occured. A splendid celestial throne appeared from within the earth. It was borne on the heads of immeasurably strong *nāgas* who had taken on celestial bodies and were adorned with jewels. Then, the goddess of earth lifted Sītā in her arms and with all due honour, she placed her on the throne. Heavenly beings showered Sītā with blossoms as they watched her descending into the earth. 'Well done!' cried the gods with delight as they stood in the air. 'Such a thing is worthy only of someone like you, Sītā!'

The kings and sages at the site of the sacrifice expressed their amazement and all the moving and unmoving creatures of earth and sky, the large-bodied *dānavas* and the *pannaga* kings of the underworld, were deeply moved. Some shouted for joy, others slipped into meditative trances, some gazed at Rāma and others at Sītā in a state of utter bewilderment. They were awed by Sītā's entry into the earth, and for a whole hour, it seemed as if the entire universe was spellbound.

Brahmā consoled Rāma, who was terribly distraught, and then he went back to his own realm. But the effulgent sages who lived there with him took his permission and stayed behind on earth because they wanted to hear the rest of the poem.

'The sages from Brahmā's realm are eager to hear what happens to me in the future,' said Rāma to Vālmīki. 'Start reciting that part from tomorrow.'

Rāma dismissed the gathering, and, taking Kuśa and Lava with him, he retired into the sacrificial enclosure.

When the sacrifice was over, Rāma was very depressed that Sītā was no longer with him. The entire world seemed empty to him and overcome by his grief he knew no peace of mind. He rewarded the *brahmins* suitably and sent them away along with the kings, the *rākṣasas* and the monkeys. When they had all left, he went back to Ayodhyā, carrying Sītā in his heart.

He did not marry again and for every sacrifice after that, he placed a golden statue of Sītā by his side. For the next one thousand years, he performed all kinds of sacrifices and distributed huge amounts of wealth. A long time went by as mighty Rāma actively pursued *dharma* and ruled his kingdom wisely and well.

The bears, monkeys and *rākṣasas* lived under his control and every day, the vassal kings did what would please Rāma. The rain god sent the rains on time and the people in the cities and in the countryside were happy and prosperous. Under Rāma's rule, no one died an untimely death, no calamities occurred and no one acted unrighteously.

After many years, Rāma's illustrious mother died, surrounded by her sons and grandsons. Soon after, Sumitrā and Kaikeyī followed her. They were all reunited with Daśaratha in heaven where, together, they enjoyed the fruits of *dharma.* Rāma distributed gifts to *brahmins* and ascetics at the appropriate times to ensure the welfare of his mothers equally. He also performed many difficult sacrifices which entailed the donation of wealth for the benefit of his paternal ancestors.

# *Chapter Seventy-One*

Years later, as Rāma was pursuing the path of *dharma,* Time arrived at his door in the form of an ascetic. 'Tell Rāma I have come to see him on an urgent matter, 'he said to resolute Lakṣmaṇa. 'I am the messenger of an effulgent and splendid sage and I have important business with Rāma.'

Lakṣmaṇa went quickly to Rāma and said that an ascetic had come to see him. Rāma instructed that he be admitted at once and Lakṣmaṇa led in the ascetic who blazed like fire. Rāma shone with his own splendour and the ascetic greeted him sweetly, saying, 'May you prosper, Rāma!' Rāma honoured him with the *arghya* water and made the customary enquiries. He led the ascetic to a splendid throne and seated him. 'Welcome, splendid one! Give me the message from the sage who has sent you!' said Rāma.

'I can only tell you what he said where no one else can see or hear us,' said the ascetic. 'If you care for the message the sage has sent you, then whoever sees or hears us must be put to death, Rāma!'

'Send away the doorkeeper and stand there in his place,' said Rāma to Lakṣmaṇa. 'I shall have to kill anyone who sees or hears our private conversation!'

Then Rāma turned to the ascetic and said, 'Tell me, what is the message? Deep in my heart, I already know what it is, but tell me anyway!'

'Listen, mighty Rāma, and I will tell you why I am here,' began the ascetic. 'Brahmā, the grandfather of the gods, has sent me. I am Time, the destroyer of all! Blessed Brahmā, the ruler of the worlds, asks that you come back and protect your own realm.

'He says, "Long ago, you took upon yourself the protection of all creatures. You became Viṣṇu and then, when all creatures were being tormented, you became a mortal in order to kill Rāvaṇa. You decided that you would live in the world of men for eleven thousand years. You were born on earth of your own free will. Now your human life has ended and you must come back to me! But if you still want to protect your subjects, you are free to do so!'

'If you do return to the realm of the gods, they will be relieved of their anxiety because you, Viṣṇu, are there to protect them!'

Rāma smiled and said to Time, the destroyer of all things, 'I am glad you came here with this message from Brahmā. May all go well with you! I shall return to where I came from. You arrived even as I was thinking about you. There is nothing left for me to consider. But I still have a few duties to discharge towards those that depend on me. When I have completed those, I shall do as Brahmā says!'

While the two of them were talking, the blessed sage Durvāsā arrived at the door, eager to see Rāma. 'I want to see Rāma at once, before my purpose in coming here is defeated!' he said to Lakṣmaṇa.

Lakṣmaṇa honoured him and said, 'What do you need? Tell me, what have you come for? What can I do for you? Rāma is very busy right now. Can you wait for a little while?'

Durvāsā flew into a rage and looked at Lakṣmaṇa as if he would consume him with the fire from his eyes. 'Go at once and tell Rāma that I am here! Or I shall curse you, Rāma, the city and the entire kingdom as well as Bharata and all your children! I cannot control my anger!'

Lakṣmaṇa considered the matter and said to himself, 'It is better that one man, I, myself, die, than all creatures be destroyed!' He made up his mind and went in to see Rāma. Rāma dismissed Time and quickly came out with Lakṣmaṇa.

He honoured the sage who shone with splendour and with his palms joined, he said, 'What can I do for you?'

'Listen, lover of *dharma*!' said the sage. 'Today I have completed one hundred years of practising austerities and I am very hungry. Fulfil my desire to eat!'

Rāma ordered a delicious meal for the sage and Durvāsā ate his fill of the food that was as fine and sweet as nectar. He thanked Rāma and praised him and went back to his hermitage. Rāma was very happy until he remembered Time's words. He recalled their frightful implications and burning with grief, he hung his head and did not say a word. 'This cannot be true!' he thought to himself.

Lakṣmaṇa noticed that Rāma was depressed and dull, like an eclipsed moon. 'Do not grieve for me, Rāma,' he said gently. 'Do as Time said, for it has been ordained. Kill me without any hesitation and fulfil your promise. The man who breaks his word goes to hell! If you love me and want to make me happy, then kill me without any second thoughts or misgivings! You must nourish *dharma,* Rāma!'

Rāma's senses were in a whirl when he heard what Lakṣmaṇa said. He sent for his ministers and the family priest and told them what had happened. They were silent when they heard the story and then, Vasiṣṭha said, 'Mighty one, I knew long ago that this calamity, this separation from Lakṣmaṇa, was going to happen! Time is all powerful. You must abandon Lakṣmaṇa and keep your word. *Dharma* is destroyed when a man breaks his promise. And when *dharma* is destroyed, you can be sure that the three worlds with all their moving and unmoving creatures, with the gods and the sages, will also perish! You are responsible for protecting the three worlds. If you kill Lakṣmaṇa today, you will have established the universe firmly!'

'I must renounce you, Lakṣmaṇa, or else *dharma* will be violated!' said Rāma when he heard Vasiṣṭha's words which were filled with purpose and meaning. 'Whether I kill you or abandon you or am separated from you, it will all be the same to good men!

Lakṣmaṇa's eyes filled with tears and he left hurriedly, but he did not go to his own home. He went straight to the banks of the Sarayū where he stopped the activities of his senses and ceased to exhale. When his breathing stopped, the gods, *apsarases* and groups of *ṛṣis* rained flowers from the sky. Unseen by the others, Indra lifted Lakṣmaṇa's body and took him into heaven. Thus, Lakṣmaṇa reverted to his original state as one quarter of Viṣṇu and the gods and sages rejoiced and celebrated and honoured him.

When Lakṣmaṇa left, Rāma was filled with grief. He called together his ministers and the family priest and said to them, 'Today, I want to anoint righteous Bharata king of Ayodhyā, He can rule the kingdom and I shall retire to the forest. Collect the materials for the consecration as quickly as you can. I want to go the way Lakṣmaṇa has gone.'

The citizens were terribly upset when they heard this and threw themselves on the ground at Rāma's feet as if they were dead. Bharata fainted when he heard Rāma's words and immediately, he rejected the kingdom. 'I swear on truth and on my place in heaven that I do not want the kingdom. What use is it to me without you, Rāma? Divide the kingdom between Kuśa and Lava and consecrate them kings! Send messengers to Śatrughna at once and tell him about your imminent departure for heaven!'

Vasiṣṭha saw how upset the people were and he had heard Bharata's words. 'Rāma, my child, look how the citizens have thrown themselves on the ground! You must find out what they want and fulfil their wishes,' he said.

Rāma raised the people up and asked, 'What do you want me to do?' and they replied, 'We shall go with you wherever you go! That would give us the greatest happiness and would also fulfil our highest duty. We want to follow you!' Rāma saw that the people were truly devoted to him and he agreed to their plans.

That very day, Rāma anointed Kuśa and Lava kings of Kosalā. He gave them three thousand chariots each, ten thousand horses and elephants and huge quantities of money and jewels. Once he had established them in their own separate cities, he sent messengers to Śatrughna. Śatrughna heard the news and after organizing the affairs of his kingdom he came to Rāma as quickly as he could. 'I have crowned my sons and given them all my wealth. I have made a firm decision to follow you,' he said to Rāma. 'You must not oppose me on this or try and argue with me. I would prefer not to disobey your commands!' Rāma saw how determined Śatrughna was and agreed.

Just as he had finished speaking, the monkeys who could change their shapes at will came there with the bears and the *rākṣasas*. All of them were sons of gods and *gandharvas* and they had arrived because they had heard about Rāma's departure. They honoured him and said, 'We have gathered here because we want to go with you! If you leave without us, you will have destroyed us as certainly as if you had struck us with the rod of death!'

Rāma said gently to Vibhīṣaṇa, 'You have to rule for as long as there are citizens in Lankā! Protect your subjects honourably. I will not hear any arguments about this!'

Then Rāma turned to Hanumān. 'You had decided to live on earth. Do not break that vow now! As long as my story prevails on earth, best of monkeys, so long shall you live and keep your promise!'

'The rest of you can come with me as you wished!' he said to the other bears and monkeys.

Early the next morning, mighty Rāma with the broad chest and the lotus eyes called for the family priest and said, 'Let the sacred fires be lit. Make sure they are carried ahead of us on the highway!' Vasiṣṭha ensured that all the prescribed rites and rituals for setting out on a great journey were performed correctly.

Rāma went forth, wearing dazzling white clothes, carrying a bunch of *kuśa* grass in his hand and uttering *mantras* to invoke Brahmā. He left his home and walked down the road shining like the sun. He did not speak to anyone or look at anything, Śrī walked on his left holding a lotus, the Earth walked on his right and his own majesty walked in front of him. His great bow and all his arrows took human form and followed him. The Vedas appeared in the form of *brahmins* and Saviṭr, the protector of all, and the sacred syllables were also there.

The great sages and *brahmins* followed Rāma because the doors of heaven had been opened wide. All the women and children, the young and the old, the servants and retainers from the inner apartments came, too. Bharata and Śatrughna went along with their retinue and attendants. The sacred fires were carried in front and the *brahmins* followed along with their wives and children. The ministers and their families also came and the happy and prosperous citizens of Ayodhyā followed their king, enthralled by his many virtues.

With immense delight, the people bathed and chattered and enjoyed themselves. No one was unhappy or wretched or miserable and it was a miracle that everyone was so happy. Even the people of the countryside who had only come there to watch, decided to follow Rāma to heaven. The monkeys, bears and *rākṣasas,* the townspeople and the country folk walked behind Rāma with calm and collected minds.

After going one and half *yojanās,* Rāma came to the clear, pure waters of the Sarayū that lay to the west. At that moment, Brahmā, the grandfather of the worlds, arrived, surrounded by all the gods and great sages in their wondrous vehicles. Flowers rained from the sky and a gentle breeze blew. Thousands of *gandharvas* and *apsarases* came there as Rāma approached the Sarayū on foot.

'Welcome, Viṣṇu!' Brahmā's voice rang out from the sky. 'It is our good fortune that you have returned to us, Rāma! Enter your own body along with your god-like brothers!'

Rāma did as Brahmā said and entered Viṣṇu's effulgent and splendid body with his brothers. The gods and heavenly creatures and celestial beings all worshipped him, praising him and saying that the heavens had been purified by his arrival.

Effulgent Viṣṇu then said to Brahmā, 'We must provide for all these virtuous people who have followed me out of love. They are devoted to me and are willing to give up their lives for my sake.'

'They can all go to the realm known as Santānika,' said Brahmā. 'Any creature that gives up his life thinking of you and is devoted to Rāma can live there. It is a wonderful place, second only to the realm of Brahmā. Since the monkeys and bears were born of the gods, they can revert to their original forms.'

The monkeys were reunited with the gods they were born from and the bears returned to the *nāgas* and *yakṣas* who had created them. The crowd moved to Gopratāra on the banks of the Sarayu, their eyes filled with tears of joy. Creatures that entered the waters happily were freed from their earthly bodies and climbed into fabulous chariots. Even the lower orders of being that entered the waters obtained celestial bodies and shone like the gods. Moving and unmoving creatures that got wet entered heaven and when the monkeys and bears who had been born from the gods entered the river, they renounced their bodies immediately. Now that he had taken them all to heaven, Brahmā was very happy and along with the other gods he returned to the sky.

This story, along with its supplement, the *Uttara,* is honoured by Brahmā. It was created by Vālmīki and is known as the *Rāmāyaṇa.*

# *Glossary*

Agni god of Fire

*apsaras(es)* celestial woman of Indra's court; known for her dancing skills and beauty

*arghya* water offered as a sign of respect and welcome to a guest; the word means 'valuable' and sometimes, rice, *druva* grass and flowers are also offered

Āṣāḍha the month of June–July according to the Hindu calendar

*asura(s)* enemy of the gods

*aśvins* divine twins

Brahmā part of the triumvirate of the great Hindu gods; commonly called the 'grandfather' of the gods

*brahmarākṣasa(s)* ghost of a *brahmin* who was guilty of misconduct during his previous life; often a flesh eater

*brahmin* priestly caste at the top of the fourfold division of Hindu society

Bṛhaspati advisor to the gods

Caitraratha Kubera's gardens

*caṇḍāla(s)* lowest and most despised of all mixed castes, born from a *śūdra* father and a *brahmin* mother

*cāraṇa(s)* celestial singer

*daitya(s)* demonic son of Diti; enemy of the gods

*dānava(s)* demonic son of Danu, enemy of the gods; sometimes identified with the *daityas* and *asuras*

Dhatṛ Vedic deity associated with ordering, arranging and upholding

*gaṇa(s)* inferior deity in the service of Śiva; often depicted as ugly, deformed or frightening *gandharva/ī* attendant in Indra's court; known for their skills as musicians and dancers as well as for their good looks

Garuḍa king of the birds; Viṣṇu's vehicle, deadly enemy of snakes and serpents

*ghee* clarified butter used for cooking as well as ritually in sacrifices and worship

Indra king of the gods

*Kāma* desire; also the god of Love

Kārtik month of October-November in the Hindu calendar

*kinkara(s)* generally a servant or slave, but in this text, also a type of *rākṣasa* in the service of Rāvaṇa

*kinnara(s)* semi-divine being with the body of a man and the head of a horse

Kubera god of wealth; Rāvaṇa's brother

*kṣatriya* warrior and ruling caste; second only to the *brahmins* in the fourfold division of Hindu society

Lakṣmī goddess of prosperity; Viṣṇu's wife

*mantra(s)* spell, incantation, verses used in rituals and ceremonies

Manu progenitor of mortals

*mārut(s)* winds, aerial spirit associated with Indra

*mokṣa* final liberation through union with the Absolute, the ultimate goal of Hindu life

*nāga(s)* semi-divine being with a human face and the hood and tail of a cobra; dwells in the underworld

Nandana Indra's paradise

Niṣāda tribe of the Vindhya region

*pannaga(s)* serpent

*pāyasa* sweet rice in milk

*piśāca(s)* vilest of all malevolent beings

Prajāpati progenitor; one of the creators

*puṣya* auspicious lunar conjunction

*rākṣasa/ī* malevolent being; often thought to be divided into three classes: semi-divine and sometimes benevolent in nature, or enemies of the gods, or beings that flourish at night and haunt cremation grounds as well as disturb sacrifices

*ṛkṣa(s)* bear

*ṛṣi(s)* divinely inspired seer-sage

Sarasvatī goddess of learning

Savitṛ Vedic deity of the sun

Sāvitrī wife of Satyavān; regarded as the epitome of wifely devotion and conjugal duty

Satyavān mythological figure known for the fact that his wife bargained with the god of Death for his life

*siddha(s)* semi-divine being who is a 'perfected' individual; pure and virtuous person who lives in the sky because of the merit earned in his earthly life

Śiva part of the triumvirate of great Hindu gods

*śrāddha* ceremonies performed after the funeral for the soul of the dead person

Śrī another name for the goddess of prosperity, Lakṣmī

*śūdra* serving caste at the bottom of the fourfold division of Hindu society

Sūrya Sun god

Ucchaiḥśravas celestial horse

*uraga(s)* serpent, sometimes identified with *nāga*

*vaiśya* merchant and cultivator class; third in the fourfold division of Hindu society

*vānara/ī(s)* female monkey

Vāyu god of the Wind; Hanumān's father

Vidhātṛ Vedic deity associated with giving and boons

*vidyādhara/ī* magical being who can fly as well as change shape and form; generally lives in the sky

Viṣṇu part of the triumvirate of great gods of Hinduism

Viśvakarmā architect and builder for the gods; also their weapon maker

*yakṣa/ī* benevolent semi-divine being; often the attendant of Kubera; rarely malevolent as in the case of Tāṭakā, though she is also referred to as a *rākṣasī*

Yama god of Death

*yojanā* unit of distance approximating about nine miles

*yuga* age; aeon. There are four ages in Hinduism: *kṛta, treṭa, dvāpara* and *kali. Dharma* declines as the ages progress.

# Index